SHIRTALOON

HE WHO FIGHTS

WITH

MONSTERS

BOOK ELEVEN

www.aethonbooks.com

HE WHO FIGHTS WITH MONSTERS ELEVEN
©2024 SHIRTALOON

ALSO IN SERIES

HE WHO FIGHTS WITH MONSTERS

BOOK ONE

BOOK TWO

BOOK THREE

BOOK FOUR

BOOK FIVE

BOOK SIX

BOOK SEVEN

BOOK EIGHT

BOOK NINE

BOOK TEN

BOOK ELEVEN

BOOK TWELVE

Check out the entire series! (tap or scan)

Want to discuss our books with other readers and even the authors like Shirtaloon, Zogarth, Cale Plamann, Noret Flood (Puddles4263) and so many more?

Join our Discord server today and be a part of the Aethon community.

AUTHOR'S NOTE

As with books three and six in this series, book eleven represents the culmination of the books leading up to it. Also like books three and six, this one ends with a series of chapters that bridge what came before with what comes after. Where those books had the chapters listed as epilogue chapters, the bridge in this one is too long to really count as an epilogue.

This book is divided into two parts. Part one makes up the most of book eleven, continuing the story of the series. Part two is the bridge between the series so far and what is to come. It takes a broader approach to narrative than the normal story, and I wanted to put this note here to explain the shift in approach for part two.

That having been said, please enjoy the book.

BOOK 10 SUMMARY

THE BATTLE OF YARESH SAW THE CITY LARGELY RAZED TO THE GROUND by the messengers. In the aftermath, it is discovered that the messengers have been seeking power deep underground, only to unleash a potential cataclysm.

Jason Asano leads an expedition underground, and encounters the brightheart people, a subterranean civilisation on the brink of collapse. Magically warped messengers are being produced by a corrupted tree, leaving most of the brighthearts dead. Jason is forced to ally with not only the brighthearts but his old enemy, the Builder cult, in order to stop the cataclysm.

In the heat of battle, it is revealed that things are even worse than they seem. With most of the brightheart civilisation left dead and rotting, the god of Undeath has sent his priests to raise an undead army. Jason, his companions and his allies have to race against time to stop the cataclysm, holding off the undead in a pitched battle.

Against an ever-growing army of undead, defeat seems inevitable. Even more so with the rise of Undeath's avatar, a giant filled with divine power. Jason's friend Gary makes a sacrifice, taking on power that will buy them much-needed time, but ultimately kills him.

In a desperate move, Jason and his allies stall the cataclysm by dragging the entire battlefield into a pocket reality. Known as a transformation zone, they have little idea how the battle there will play out, but the only alternative is death. With the grand magic enacted, both sides wait in the final moments before the transformation zone takes them all.

PART I

1
WHAT MAKES THEM OUR ENEMIES

JASON STOOD NEXT TO GARY, CHATTING IN AN ODDLY CALM FASHION given their presence in an underground necropolis. They both felt the surging disruption in the fabric of reality and Jason gave him a smile.

"See you on the other side, brother," he said.

"Is this going to hurt?" Gary asked.

"I don't know," Jason told him. "You're the first person I know to pick up a temp job as a god. Are you prone to exploding under dimensional duress?"

"I'm not a god, Jason, even a temporary one. That's blasphemy."

"That's—"

"Kind of your thing, I know. I'm only a demigod, Jason, and the power is not mine."

"So, you're more like an intern?"

"What's an intern?"

Then Gary was gone and the world fell apart. Jason could still feel his own body but nothing else. The absence of even gravity's familiar pull left him feeling untethered. Most of Jason's mundane senses were blanked, with nothing to see, smell or hear. His magical perception suffered the opposite, however, bombarded with what once would have been an incomprehensible deluge of sensory input.

Jason had been through a lot since the last transformation zone back on Earth. While his essence abilities had barely shifted, his knowledge and power in other metrics had advanced by orders of magnitude. Half-transcendents stood at the peak of diamond rank, be they essence-users, messengers or some other magical entity. The other half of transcendence was something many spent millennia trying and failing to achieve, yet Jason was already striding down that path.

Between his gestalt body and his astral throne and gate, Jason was unharmed and unbothered by the dimensional maelstrom, reforging the reality around him. He observed the forces at play with detachment, seeing patterns in the seemingly random chaos. He only comprehended a fraction of what was going on, but it was a valuable education in the nature of both reality and the astral realm beyond it. It was a perspective normally reserved for gods and their ilk.

It was not the first time Jason had felt the universe break around him. This was his third transformation zone, and each time, the experience was different. In the first, he had broken into a zone already in place, with little power to manipulate the forces involved. The zone itself had transformed him, taking one of his outworlder powers and forcibly evolving it into the Spiritual Domain ability. This gave him the power to imprint himself on physical reality, reshaping it to his own will. It had been an early and critical step on the path to becoming an astral king.

In the second transformation zone, Jason possessed the power to reshape it from the beginning. In doing so, he had caused a fundamental change on Earth. The base level of magic had risen; magic no longer manifested in proto-astral spaces before spilling into the world. He had begun a new age of magic, where monsters and essences manifested directly in the world.

The third time was set to be different again. Transformation zones on Earth were the result of the World-Phoenix intervening in eons past, to prevent Earth from breaking under the influence of magic. Pallimustus had no such need, not being as fragile. As a result, the dimensional rupture that had now appeared required another hand to trigger the transformation zone. Jason was the only one available.

An unmoving stone in a whirlpool of cosmic power, Jason could feel the fundamental design of the universe. The original Builder had taken imprints from countless realities that had come before and melded them into a blueprint for two linked universes. This cosmic experiment in recycling was the very act that had gotten the first Builder sanctioned.

As Jason sought out every scrap of power and knowledge within himself, he found a tenuous thread of power, something he was barely conscious of. Shade had called it destiny magic, a power to sense the most powerful and fundamental aspects of the cosmos.

Shade suggested that Jason had been using that power instinctively from his first introduction to magic, but they had also seen it used more actively. Gordon was a young familiar where Shade was ancient, but he had demonstrated a connection to that same power, something even great astral beings were wary of. Jason suspected his own connection to it was the very reason the familiar had chosen him.

Jason now called on that power, crudely and instinctively. He felt Gordon offer guidance and support from within Jason's soul realm, pushing him in the right direction. Jason followed that thread, feeling some distant thing at the far end. It was a whisper in the hurricane of power raging around him, but he put all that aside, reaching out with his soul.

He could barely sense what was tethered at the end of that thread. Stretching his senses to the limit, he could feel that it was broken, yet it was so much more vast than he was. Even sundered, it rivalled the might of the great astral beings.

Jason could barely touch it, unnoticed like kelp brushing past a whale. Even so, just the echo of it helped Jason understand how to tame the power storming around him. The distant power was a thing of boundaries and that was what he needed. He could not control the power so much greater than himself, but he didn't need to. The right nudge, in the right way, would cause the power to bind itself, setting in motion the forces that would resolve into a transformation zone.

Jason drew on his soul realm, tapping into his astral throne and gate, along with his power to create spiritual domains. He took a delicate hand with making changes, aware of his shallow understanding of the forces at play. Calling on the knowledge and intuition he had painstakingly built up about cosmic forces and physical reality, he did what he could to reshape the reality still in flux.

His meagre power was far from enough, like trying to redirect a river with a bucket. For the first time, he actively called on his connection to that distant cosmic power, letting it guide and strengthen his efforts. He strove to be the butterfly, flapping its wings and waiting for the hurricane.

Jason felt it when the storm of dimensional forces took the first step towards a transformation zone. It was a tiny thing as the patterns within the chaos became slightly more ordered. The crux of a transformation zone coming into being was the imprints of older universes used by the old Builder. Broken shards of reality coalesced, taking shape in accordance with those imprints, forming the territories that would make up the zone.

The physical area containing the underground realm of the bright-hearts stopped existing by most metrics. The astral space inside it ruptured and the whole area was encapsulated in a dimensional boundary. From there, the transformation zone began forming in earnest.

Jason wasn't familiar with lesser transformation zones, the most common type that had appeared on Earth. Those were self-resolving, leaving a scar on the universe but repairing the damage without intervention. He had stepped in when they were too unstable, repairing them from the inside before they blew a hole in the side of the universe. Those zones were comprised of territories, far larger on the inside than the space outside. Only by unifying those territories could the transformation zone be repaired.

Jason had plenty of experience claiming and unifying transformation zone territories, and as he watched territories form in this new zone, he decided to get a jump on the competition. Given his access to the already forming zone, he was confident that he could not just pre-emptively claim a territory for himself but establish a solid foundation from which to expand and unify the entire zone.

Experience let Jason know that, in the early stages, claiming territories was easy. The more that were claimed, however, the more difficult it would become. The baseline was also set by the most powerful people within a zone. In this case, that meant gold rank or even something more powerful given the presence of Gary and the avatar of Undeath. If the zone reacted to their divine power, things would become more dangerous than anything Jason had faced before.

These thoughts galvanised his resolve to establish himself quickly and strongly. He picked a single territory as it formed, something that had a familiar feel so he could better work with it. The territory was something close to Earth-like, which made it easier for him to shape.

He exerted his will, shaping its formation and imprinting himself upon it. There were limits and restrictions, elements he didn't fully understand, but this was something he was comfortable with, both in scale and scope. Claiming transformation zone territories was something he'd done many times, and he was just getting in early. He couldn't define the specifics, but the territory would be a reflection of him as his will imprinted upon it.

The wild forces calmed as the transformation zone developed. Territories formed and linked together to establish the geography of the zone. The space was highly manipulated, like others he had seen, with the dimensional barrier containing it smaller than the space inside.

Everyone in the underground realm had been dragged in and would be scattered around the territories at random. Jason suspected that only he and Gary, who was filled with divine power, had managed to retain consciousness throughout the process. The Undeath avatar was an open question, as it was a direct conduit of Undeath's power and the god was now cut off. Ideally, they would eventually find the avatar standing around doing nothing. The messengers were another question, with their gestalt bodies, but that alone was unlikely enough to let them keep their senses.

Jason had sensed presences floating through the dimensional chaos but had not dared reach out to them. Not only could he not identify them, but he did not want to risk affecting them adversely. Essence-users were highly resistant to change, but not everyone here was an essence-user. What effect the zone would have on the elemental messengers, the Builder cultists and the brighthearts, Jason could only wait and see.

On Earth, many normal-rankers had been transformed into other races, in accordance with the transformation zones in which they found themselves. He'd seen humans become leonids, celestines and other races native to neither Earth nor Pallimustus. Some managed to resist the change, but most were affected, their souls accepting the transformation. As best Jason understood, the process was a more gentle version of what the Builder had attempted on him when trying to implant a star seed: applying pressure until the soul willingly accepted the change.

The various transformation zones settled into their final form. Jason pushed himself into the territory he had shaped for himself. It had taken the form of his hometown, the sleepy tourist destination of Casselton Beach, with one major change. There was a mountain behind the town that did not exist on Earth and had been carved into the shape of Jason's head. He manifested inside the reality, high in the air. His cloak formed around him, although it was his aura he used to hold himself aloft.

- This area of the local physical reality has been in a state of dimensional flux and has been isolated by [Nascent ??? Intervention]. The influence of a broken astral space on the area has prevented the natural resolution of the transformation zone. This special transformation zone must be unified to restore stability, reintegrate it with physical reality and re-establish an astral space.

- The transformation zone can be unified by claiming all non-central territories.
- Territories can be claimed by eliminating a final anomaly that will appear in each territory when all other anomalies are eliminated. If multiple people are present in a territory when the conditions for claiming it are met, it must be ceded to one individual through conflict or forfeit.
- Claiming additional territories after the first will unify them with already claimed territories.
- The central territory cannot be claimed until all other territories are unified. The central territory is in an incomplete state. The final state of the central territory shall be defined when it is unified with the other territories.
- Final unification requires the ability to reshape the transformation zone to reintegrate it with physical reality. Final reunification without this ability will cause a dimensional rupture as the transformation zone attempts to reintegrate with physical reality.
- Some inhabitants of the transformation surge have been affected by elements isolated in the central territory and cannot effectively function without replacing that influence. Those inhabitants have been placed into stasis in the territories in which they arrived. They will be imparted with the influence of whomsoever claims the territories in which they are held. The inhabitants in stasis may or may not survive this process, depending on the nature of the influence.
- The influence of the [Nascent ??? Intervention] on the special transformation zone has established an interface available to all inhabitants.

Jason read over the system box, although some of this information was already imparted by his senses. He could feel his influence finalising his control over the territory below. His efforts had created it without anomalies, thus making it his own. He could feel the last vestiges of his influence still taking hold and he looked over the terrain while he waited for the power to settle.

Below him was the town, the small mountain behind it not much more than a very large hill. Even so, having a mountain fortress in the shape of his own head ticked one of the big-ticket items off his bucket list. He looked at it proudly as his familiars manifested around him. Shade emerged from his void cloak while Gordon just appeared. Blood spilled from Jason's hand, collecting into a blob that became a replica of Jason himself. The blood clone conjured a starlight cloak to keep himself in the air.

"It would seem that you have much more control here," blood clone Colin said in Jason's voice. "No need to unlock powers and it appears everyone will have your system interface."

Shade was looking at the mountain fortress.

"You couldn't help yourself, could you, Mr Asano?"

"Hey, that just happened on its own," Jason said. "I only got to shape this place vaguely, not set all the details. It just turned out this way."

"Of course it did, Mr Asano."

Jason turned his gaze to the distance, far beyond the reach of his own territory. Although the air was hazy, the shape of an impossibly large tree loomed over the horizon.

"I'm pretty sure the messenger tree, soul forge or whatever it is got sealed away in that central territory," Jason said. "Now it's winner take all."

"We knew that going in," Colin said. "Learning the specifics doesn't change that."

"You're right," Jason agreed, "and we've even got a head start. I think we should use it to get a handle on things. Can you sense those people in the air, way above us?"

Shade and Colin looked up while Gordon flashed his orbs in the blue and orange flickering patterns he used to communicate. He was the familiar most closely tied to Jason's aura and his perception was boosted accordingly, so he had also sensed them.

"They're messengers," Jason said. "Held in stasis, which apparently means just hanging way up in the air. I think they were the elemental messengers, but with the tree sealed away, they're just regular messengers now. But without the imprinting of an astral king, or even the corrupted imprint from the tree that left them all messed up, they're incomplete."

"The inhabitants that cannot effectively function," Shade said. "The ones mentioned in the system box. This means that when a territory is claimed, any messengers in it will be claimed as well."

"They could be trouble," Colin said. "I should go up there and eat them before they wake up."

The others all turned to look at him.

"It was just a suggestion," he said defensively.

"Not all the messengers were spawned by the tree," Jason pointed out. "Some were sent down by Jes Fin Kaal and already have an astral king. They're probably free of the tree's influence now and will be competitors."

"They were sent to create the soul forge from the natural array," Shade said. "They likely have the magical knowledge to unify the transformation zone properly."

"Yeah," Jason agreed grimly. "If they don't know how already, they can probably figure it out."

"Still doesn't change what we have to do," Colin said. "We fight, we win, we eat what's left. Oh, don't look at me like that; there aren't any vegans here."

"I think Shade and Gordon are technically vegan," Jason said. "They only eat raw magic. Mostly. I did keep catching Gordon disintegrating candy and trying to inhale the fumes, but only while we were in America. I think he likes high-fructose corn syrup."

Jason felt a shift as his influence finished permeating every corner of the territory.

- Conditions to claim this territory have been met.
- Due to your influence already having been established, other individuals in the territory cannot contest your claim.
- You have claimed a territory.
- You may extend your influence into another territory in order to claim it.
- Your influence is being imposed on the inhabitants in stasis.

Jason felt a connection to the space around him as if the land, air and sea were all extensions of himself. It felt like his spirit domains back on Earth. He could sense two people on the ground and hundreds of messengers in the air. His power, invested in the territory, was already reaching out to influence the messengers.

After helping the messengers in his soul space shrug off the influence of their astral king, Jason wasn't about to create an angelic slave army. Using his experience, he altered the influence of his power as it seeped into the messengers. He guided the power as they awakened, leading them to not bear his brand on their souls but to each make one of their own, setting them free. It was the work of a few moments; soon the messengers were descending from on high.

"I assume you've set them free," Shade said.

"Of course," Jason said.

"Our enemies won't do the same," Colin pointed out. "They'll use them as weapons."

"Which is what makes them our enemies," Jason said. "Also, how is setting them free worse than eating them? That is what you suggested, right?"

"It would make for better planning," Colin said.

"How do you figure that?" Jason asked.

"I think better on a full stomach."

Gordon's orbs flashed a sequence that pointed out that Colin belonged to a species that devoured every living thing on entire planets, suggesting he was incapable of having a full stomach.

"That's a good point," Jason said as Colin glared at Gordon. "Do you even have a stomach?"

"Do you not remember when I ate that world-taker worm queen?" Colin complained. "It took me weeks to sleep that meal off."

"Ooh, you're right," Jason conceded. "He's got you there, Gordon."

Gordon flashed more lights in response and Colin jabbed a finger in his direction.

"I do not look fat!"

2

SHARE THE RESPONSIBILITY

BOTH IN THE UNDERGROUND REALM OF THE BRIGHTHEARTS AND PREVIOUS transformation zones, dimensional powers had been tricky. Still floating in the air with his familiars, Jason tried opening a gate to his soul realm and was pleasantly surprised to find that it worked. A circle of milky white stone appeared in the air and was filled with rainbow light as the portal opened.

At least in the territory he had claimed, Jason had access to his soul realm and the resources within. What he needed right now were the messengers he had stashed away at the end of the messenger invasion of Yaresh. Jali Corrik Fen and Marek Nior Vargas emerged from the portal.

Marek was a gold-ranker who had led his personal followers to Jason in hope of escaping the oppression of the messenger astral kings. His obsession was joining the Unorthodoxy, the messenger resistance movement. Before that could happen, however, he needed to convince Jason to set them free.

Jali was only silver rank. Despite a life of misgivings about messenger doctrine, she had carefully avoided becoming entangled with the Unorthodoxy out of fear. Used as a pawn by her masters, she had been liberated by Jason.

Messengers were far from aerodynamically sound, but the magic that allowed them to fly was primarily seated in their wings. Marek and Jali both spread their wings to hold themselves aloft, situating themselves in front of Jason and his familiars. They turned their gazes upward, sensing hundreds of messengers released from stasis, purged of the corrupted messenger tree's influence. They had stopped descending and were having some kind of discussion.

"Where are we?" Marek asked. "Some kind of dimensional space? A spirit domain? I can feel your power everywhere. Who are those messengers?"

"It's complicated," Jason said. "For now, just stand behind me and don't say anything unless I tell you to."

"I am your prisoner, Jason Asano, not your servant."

"Then go back through the portal; there's too much to explain right this second."

Marek looked at Jason, then the sky above them and then the still-open portal.

"This is not the moment to test me, Marek," Jason warned.

"Those are my people up there."

"You don't know what they are. And I just realised that having you here was a mistake. Go back in."

Marek stared Jason down for a long moment before turning and vanishing through the portal.

"He'll want them for the Unorthodoxy," Jason explained. "I can't let that happen."

"Why not?" Jali asked. "Are you concerned that the other astral kings will actively pursue you if you start freeing messengers in large numbers?"

"I am now," he said, giving her a pointed look. "But my concern is about something more important than that. These messengers are young. None are more than a year old, and until moments ago, their minds had been corrupted for their entire lives."

"I can sense their confusion," Jali said. "Their uncertainty. They're worried about coming down to face us. Where did they come from?"

"They were elementally corrupted messengers."

Jali had been one of the few messengers to see the underground realm and get out alive and uncorrupted, so she knew what he referred to.

"The corruption was removed when they were brought into this space, but it left them in a condition I suspect your kind are in directly after being created. They are, practically speaking, newborns."

"That would mean they needed to be imprinted."

"Because I'm already imprinted on this territory, it tried to spread my imprint to them. I intervened and had them form their own marks. Like you, but without the need to access your soul."

"That's normal for new messengers, but I've never heard of messengers being born without an astral king to obey. Not surprising, given that they'd probably purge entire collectives to cover something like that up. Where did they come from, though? There are more messengers up there now than were corrupted when we went down there."

"A corrupted birthing tree."

Jason pointed and Jali followed his gaze to the massive tree on the horizon. Her jaw dropped.

"That's perverse," Jali said. "A birthing tree outside of a birthing world? The messengers it produces would be—"

"Twisted monstrosities?" Jason finished. "Yes. But this place seems to have rectified the corruption."

"It doesn't matter. There's no way they would ever be accepted. There's a reason we worked with the Purity church to summon our forces into this world. Our doctrines fall into alignment in areas such as on excising the tainted."

"Will you be able to accept them?"

"I don't know. My whole life, I've been forcing myself to follow the line, even inside my mind. I need to re-examine everything I believed."

"And Marek?"

"I'm not sure. He rejects the astral kings so absolutely, yet his thinking remains extremely traditional. But if he thinks he can use them as a weapon, he will."

"So much of what I've learned about your kind has profoundly disturbing implications. The need to brand newborns? I won't let Marek have these children."

"They're not children," Jali said. "We come into being with ancestral knowledge. Language; an understanding of the cosmos. The ways of conquest and war."

"Knowledge is not wisdom. It's not experience. You, of all people, understand the harm that can be done from an insulated upbringing built around a single, extreme point of view. I support the Unorthodoxy in principle, but Marek would turn them into child soldiers. I won't let him have them any more than I would an astral king."

"And if they want to go with Marek?"

"Then they'll have a chance to make that choice—once they're ready to make an informed one."

"And who decides when that is? You?"

"Us. You and me."

Her eyes went wide.

"I'm not ready to take responsibility for that. I've barely broken away from my own subjugation."

Jason laughed out loud.

"You think being ready has anything to do with it? I would love the chance to be ready for things. It would have made the last half-dozen years a lot easier. I'm sorry, but if you only want to do things you're ready for, you need to get very far away from me. And, if I'm being honest, I think you're too late for that to be an option."

"Where would I go anyway? I don't want anything to do with the astral kings or the Unorthodoxy."

"You don't?"

"Marek Nior Vargas is passionate, but he's also driven to the point of rigidity. Whether serving or fighting the astral kings, he is entirely defined by his relationship to them. I want to figure out what I am apart from all that. The people that enslaved me as well as the ones fighting them. I don't know what to do or where to go, even assuming you allow me to go anywhere. I don't even know where I am now."

"I know that feeling. Lost, directionless. Suddenly aware of just how wrong you were about everything. Don't let it show. It's going to take some time to figure out, but until you do, don't let the world see it."

"Is that what you did?"

"Yeah."

"How did that work out?"

"Mixed results, if I'm being honest. But these messengers up there? Deciding if they're going to come down here and face us? They're more lost than you or I will ever be. We should at least give them the illusion that someone knows what they're doing."

"I don't know what's going on," Jali said. "What you've brought me into. But it's obviously complex and ongoing. It would have been more practical if you'd let your brand imprint on these and change it once things have calmed down."

"Even assuming the next crisis would be kind enough to wait for this one to pass," Jason said, "that's not acceptable. Yes, it would be more practical, but the thing about good and evil is that no one ever chooses evil. They choose selfishness or prejudice or easy answers over hard truths. They choose the expedient path, even if it means getting their hands a little dirty because they can make up for it later, right? Sometimes getting your hands dirty is what it takes. The ends justify the means."

Jason looked down at his own hands.

"I've told myself those things. Sometimes I've been right, and sometimes it was just an excuse. It would be easier to let those children become slaves. To pretend they're adults because they look like it, despite only having been truly conscious for a matter of minutes. If they do what they're told, at least for now, we wouldn't have to deal with their confusion. Instead of a liability, they would be an asset, and a much-needed one for what lies ahead. And I could always erase my brand when it's over. Of course, that would be cutting them loose to face everything serving me pushed aside, plus the trauma they'd just been through. And there will be another threat they would be so useful for. I can set them free when there's time to stop and help them properly. I'll just leave the brand for now."

Jason's face was filled with disgust.

"We like to think we're better than we are," Jason said. "I've had to confront the fact that I'm not, but I've also seen that I can be. It takes discipline. Diligence. Determination. Recognising that while sometimes you do have to compromise, other times, you don't. The temptation doesn't come with a choice between right and wrong. It comes with a choice between right and easy."

He ran his hands over his face and took a deep breath.

"I have a habit of going off on moralistic rants," he explained. "It's one of the ways I work through my insecurities about my own moral worth, and my friends tend to get caught up in it. And my enemies, sometimes. My dad. I have a lot of family issues, but I have trouble imagining a life like yours where the concept of family is so alien. We think so differently, yet I find myself searching for common ground. I never found it with Marek."

Jason and Jali were floating in the air. Their heads were at the same level, which left the much shorter Jason's feet somewhere around her thighs. He looked at her, his nebulous eyes searching for something within her own.

"Does anything I've said make sense to you?" he asked. "I've been trying to find some empathy in Marek for a while now, but you were right: his first concern is taking the fight to the astral kings. Even his companionship is more camaraderie than friendship. That's not inherently bad, but it's a more mercenary sensibility than I'd like. I have higher hopes for you."

"Why does any of this matter?"

"The way we treat people always matters. If you want something grander, then I'm still deciding how to interact with your people. I suspect that, in the millennia to come, how I deal with the messengers will affect a lot of people."

"And what? You're going to decide that based on me?"

"Not just that, of course, and not just now. But you have the chance to make me see something I don't in Marek or Tera Jun Casta. What you and I learn from each other could end up being very important."

"That's too much responsibility."

Jason grinned. "I know, right? You get used to it. With a good support system and enough therapy."

"You're joking, but this isn't a small thing you're putting on me."

"Yeah. Joking helps, trust me. I tried being super-serious and I turned into an angry prick."

Jali turned her back to Jason, rotating in the air.

"This is too much to put on me."

"Yes," he agreed. "But you're the person on the spot, and you're stronger than you think. I saw you stand up to your astral king. The reality is, I don't know how many free messengers are out there, but I'm guessing not a lot. That makes you important, and being important sucks. I'm hoping you can help me find a way forward with the messengers beyond the options I already have. The astral kings and their Nazi angel army obviously can't be worked with. Marek's Unorthodoxy has some real 'victory or death' energy, which is less bad but definitely not good. I'm starting to get a Project Mayhem vibe that I don't like."

She turned back to face him.

"How much of what you say do people understand?"

"You're a smart woman, Jali. Are you telling me that you're not getting the gist from context clues?"

"No. But why would you talk to people like this?"

Jason held out his hand and squeezed as if holding an invisible ball. Jali's magical senses felt the fabric of reality around her bend alarmingly. He opened his hand and the sensation was gone as if it had never been.

"I have to remember who I am, Jali. I change, but if I ever let go of who I am without all this power, the power becomes who I am. That's not good for anyone. Except the god of dominion, maybe."

"You're sharing a lot with me."

"I'm hoping it will help you. You're not on the path I walked, but I think you'll see a lot of the same landmarks."

"Should you be thinking about things like this when you have more immediate issues to deal with?"

"Yes, I should. I've always had this idea in my head that I didn't choose the responsibilities that now rest on me, but that hasn't been true for a long time. I did choose, many times. Now, I have to live up to those responsibilities because they affect a lot more than just me. You've sensed the brighthearts in my soul realm. I've kept them underground, away from the rest of you, but you've felt their presence."

"Yes."

"They represent what's left of an entire civilisation. An entire species. I'm responsible for them now because I chose to be. Just like you and I are about to be responsible for these messengers above us. And a lot more before we're done. This is just one territory of many."

He drifted closer and put his hands on her shoulders.

"If you don't want to be part of that, I get it. My asking you isn't fair, I know that. Not when there is so much I haven't told you and you're still coming to terms with the massive changes you've gone through. The portal is right there. If you go through it, I won't ask you to do anything like this again. But I'm certain that you and I, together, can do better for these people than I can alone. I hope you'll choose to share this responsibility with me."

"I... you're asking a lot that I wasn't ready for."

"Yes. And I haven't given you a lot of time to choose."

They both looked up at the messengers gathered in the air. While Jason and Jali had been talking, so had they.

"I think they're picking someone to come and talk to us," Jason said. Proving him right, two of the messengers broke off and started floating downwards.

"Alright, team," Jason said. "Let's not spook the hopefully nice baby angels."

Shade disappeared into the void of Jason's cloak, Colin dissolved into a blood mist that Jason absorbed and Gordon just vanished, Jason's aura pulsing as he did. Jason looked at Jali.

"I'll stay," she told him.

"Good. Now just try and look like you know what you're doing."

"I don't know what I'm doing."

"Which is when looking like you do is most important."

Jali floated to Jason's right and they hovered side by side to meet the pair of descending messengers. Jason pushed his hood back to show his face.

The messengers hovered in front of them, wings extended like Jali's. Jason's cloak floated out to his sides like the celestial wings of a star phoenix. The messenger pair showed no trace of elemental taint and wore diaphanous robes apparently conjured up by the transformation zone. One was female, with long dark hair, while the other was a sandy-haired male. Both had the statuesque proportions and exquisite features common to messengers. They glanced at Jali before locking their gazes on Jason.

"You are the ruler of this place," the female messenger said.

"I am. My name is Jason Asano."

"I... I should have a name," the female messenger said, her expression breaking into confusion and fear. "I can feel that I should have a name, but something is wrong."

"There is much you don't know," Jason said. "Yes, something has gone wrong and I know you have many questions. We have the answers you need."

The two messengers looked at him with a mixture of wariness and hope.

"You are right that you should have a name," Jali said.

"Then why don't we?" the male messenger asked.

"We'll go through everything," Jason told them. "Some of it will be hard to hear, but we can answer your questions, and we will. But I think we should tell all of you together."

He glanced up then back at the main messenger group, far above them, then back to the two in front of him. They shrank back, their nervousness almost startling coming from messengers.

"If you were hostile," the female messenger said, "is there any place we could hide from you?"

"Perhaps," Jason said. "There are many territories in this realm and, for now, I only possess this one."

"We were going to belong to it," she said. "To you. We could feel your influence being imprinted upon us, but then it stopped."

"I apologise for that experience," Jason said. "It is an unfortunate interaction between the nature of this place, the nature of your kind and the circumstances that brought all this about. I will explain it all. For now, just know that I intervened because I do not own people. I made sure that I have no intrinsic hold on you."

"He has helped me in a similar way," Jali said. "I was slave to another and he freed me, as he has freed you."

"Yet you serve him?" the man asked.

"I... stand by him," Jali said, prompting a sideways glance from Jason. "That is my choice."

The woman continued staring at Jason.

"You are not of our kind," she told him. "Yet, I feel something from you. When we awoke, there was an instinct to kneel. To acknowledge ourselves as less than you. But what you did, what you changed, it altered that instinct as well. I sense your power, but I'm no longer driven to obey it."

"Good," Jason said. "As I already told you, I don't own people. It's a personal policy that's caused me more problems than it really should."

He gestured to Jali.

"This is Jali Corrik Fen. I hope you will collect your people and wait with her while I go deal with some of the others who share this space with us. Then we can have a nice long talk."

3

CONTRITION BORN AT THE POINT
OF A SWORD

RICK GELLER WAS NOT HAPPY. HE HAD NO COMPUNCTION ABOUT PUTTING his life on the line to protect people; he was an adventurer and that was the job. He'd known that when he signed up and he'd lived that life ever since. But every time he was in the same city as Jason Asano, that job got extravagantly out of hand.

He knew Jason wasn't causing these things, or even involved all of the time. Jason hadn't participated in the disastrous expedition out of Greenstone or the fortress city battles in the Storm Kingdom. But there was no escaping that when Rick and his team were nowhere near Jason, they lived a regular adventuring life. Leisurely roaming from place to place, protecting normal people from ordinary monsters.

The moment they were anywhere near Jason, though, a monster surge felt relaxing by comparison. Suddenly, it was kings and princesses, diamond-rankers, secret cultist armies and interdimensional invasions. The only time they got to live normal lives was when he got himself killed, sent to another universe or both.

Rick found it increasingly hard to not resent Jason, despite it being mostly undeserved. It seemed like every time the Adventure Society had a Jason problem, they pulled in Rick to be the reluctant ambassador to their most troublesome silver-rank member. As often as not, he arrived to discover the problem had resolved itself already, leaving Rick and his team idle. And since they weren't doing anything else, why not bring them along on the latest insanity?

In this case, it was an underground expedition culminating in an unexpected undead army and being yanked into some bizarre unreality that, of course, only Jason understood. Now Rick was separated from his team in unfamiliar surroundings that were soaked in Jason's aura like a biscuit dipped in tea. If that wasn't enough, there was a mountain looming over the town, carved into the shape of Jason's head.

He had read through the long message that Jason's interface had shown him, but he partially understood what it had to say at best. Something about fighting something and claiming territory. It fit Jason's earlier warnings of how things would work, but Rick didn't care. None of it helped him find his team, and getting them out alive was all that mattered. The rest was Jason business, and he could be the one to deal with it.

Step one was getting his bearings and finding anyone else nearby. He was in a town, on a street sealed with some manner of seamless black stone. That wasn't the only material he didn't recognise in the buildings pressed together, many with glass front walls. He suspected it was a shopping district but couldn't read the language on the signs. There was writing everywhere, as if they weren't concerned that most people couldn't read.

His aura senses were tamped down, either a natural effect of the transformation zone or from Jason's aura interfering, he wasn't sure. That meant he was startlingly close to the other person when he sensed them. It was the aura of an essence-user, not a Builder cultist, brightheart or messenger. He didn't recognise the aura, which meant it wasn't a member of the expedition. That meant one of the Undeath priests, which suited Rick just fine. He was really in the mood to kill something.

Whoever it was clearly sensed him as well. They started moving in the other direction at speed, and a silver-ranker's speed was very fast. Rick conjured a spear and used a leap power, hurtling through the air in the next best thing to flight. He landed on another black street and leapt again immediately, rapidly closing the gap. A third leap put him in sight of the person, who had stopped and was standing in front of a portal.

Rick landed on the street, some way behind the person he'd been chasing. He was backing away from the portal, his body language afraid. Rick looked closer at the portal, realising that it wasn't a portal at all but Jason, wrapped in a void cloak that looked like a hole in the universe.

It truly appeared less like an article of clothing than a window into some deep, distant void where stars sparkled and colourful nebulas shone over impossible distances. That Jason didn't register to Rick's senses, despite his aura pervading everything else, added to the uncanny sense that his friend was not a person but a dimensional phenomenon.

As he walked forward at a measured pace, spear still in hand, Rick watched Jason and the other man. The stranger was a silver-ranker in grey scholar's robes, bulkier than the sleek combat robes used by some adventurers. Jason showed off such robes, the colour of dried blood, when he pushed back the cloak wrapped around him. It also revealed the sword at his hip, which he drew unhurriedly. The stranger fell to his knees and started begging.

"You don't have to do this."

"You belong to Undeath," Jason said, his tone cold as the rime on a frozen corpse.

"I never wanted any of this," the man pleaded. "I had no choice! My family all worship the dark gods."

"You think that helps your case?" Jason asked.

"My name is Jeffrey Colling-Setton. My family have served the dark churches for generations. If I ever went against them, ever tried to run, they'd have killed me. And you know that wouldn't be the end of my torment, not with what they do. You can help me! And I can help you! You can save me from them and I can tell you their plans! We can…"

The man trailed off as Jason raised the tip of his sword to the man's face.

"I try to be merciful when I can," Jason said, his voice still cold but also faintly apologetic. "Unfortunately, these are not circumstances where I have the luxury of giving you a chance. There is too little time and too much at stake. Contrition born at the point of a sword is not to be trusted."

The man scrambled into a run, sprinting away from Jason to find Rick in his path. Rick didn't waste time, dashing forward with a charge special attack to impale the man. Another power then shot barbs out of the spear, further digging into the man from the inside. Jason followed up and they made short work of him; he wasn't much of a fighter.

Jason flung off his cloak. The blood spattered on it, falling to the ground as it vanished. He took out a vial of crystal wash and handed it silently to Rick. Rick's barbed spear powers were messy, leaving him covered in gore, so he tipped the vial over his head. The liquid flowed over him, spreading to coat his entire body and wash off all the filth.

"Jason, I'm going to be honest and tell you that I don't care what nonsense you've got going on this time. I just want to make sure my team comes through it alive."

Jason nodded.

"I can respect that. There's a good chance that most of the people in this transformation zone are still unconscious, scattered around the territories," he explained. "You and this guy probably came through awake because I modified this territory as we entered it. It's more stable than the unclaimed ones. I need to expand it methodically, claiming one territory at a time. You're more free to leave this territory and search than I am. You can go looking for more of our allies, your team included."

"I'm all for that, but there are gold-rank threats out there. If I go alone, with no plan and no precautions, I'll get myself killed before I find anyone."

"Agreed," Jason said. "I might have a solution for that, but you're not going to like it."

"Not to sound unkind, Jason, but I've gotten used to not liking what's happening when I'm around you."

Rick looked down at the remains of Jeffrey.

"I think he was telling the truth about his family," he said. "Maybe not about wanting to leave, but I've heard of the Colling-Setton line. They crop up in every forbidden power group you can think of. Dark temples, necromancer covens, the Red Table, experiment programs into restricted list essences. In a lot of ways, they're an evil counterpart to my family, and we've been clashing for centuries."

"Should we have kept him alive for questioning?"

"No, we couldn't trust anything he said. So, what's this plan I'm not going to like?"

"Well, you know those messengers I have prisoner?"

"The ones the Adventure Society wants you to hand over? The ones they want me to convince you to hand over?"

Jason's expression grew awkward.

"Those are the ones, yeah. They have some gold-rankers amongst them. I want to put them under your command, to roam the territories, collect anyone on our side and bring them back."

"You're right; I don't like it. You want to send me off with some messengers—including gold-rank messengers—under the assumption that they won't turn on me the moment they're clear of whatever hold you have on them?"

"I do assume that, yes. They don't care enough to kill you because we're not their enemies. The astral kings they used to serve are. Also, they know I'm a good ally and a bad enemy, especially here. I've got an avatar in my soul space explaining things to them already, so they understand that making an enemy of me before they're free of the transformation zone is suicide."

"Jason, your word is all well and good, but what if you're wrong? Or only partly right? They may not kill me, but they could easily stop listening to me. Drag me around, doing whatever they like, or leave me behind entirely."

"If you don't want to do it, I won't force you, but at least let me talk you through it. The leader of the messengers we're talking about is named Marek Nior Vargas. For all his faults, he does care about his people, much like you care about yours. That's going to be important."

"That doesn't sound like a messenger."

"Not the messengers you know. Just sit down with me and him. We can talk it out and then you can make a decision."

"Alright," Rick said. "It's not like I'm looking to go out there alone."

Jason's head-shaped mountain fortress was no less villainous on the inside than the exterior. Imposing stone walkways looked out over massive chambers where magma flowed in narrow, glass-sealed channels along the floor. More magma flowed through glass pipes that poked out from the dark stone of the walls and ceiling, providing the facility with ominous illumination. The air throughout the fortress was hot and heavy.

In a massive conference room, Jason gathered with Rick and a panoply of messengers. He sat at the head of the table with a window wall behind him through which a lava waterfall could be seen spilling past. Rick sat in the first seat to his right and Jali to his left. Tera Jun Casta sat next to Jali while Marek Nior Vargas sat next to Rick, leaving the adventurer uncomfortable.

What came next was a lot of talking. Explanations of what was happening and why. Much of the time was spent giving the newborn messengers insight into their own kind and the unconventional circumstances of how they came into being. They introduced them to the messenger factions and the motivations of Marek Nior Vargas and his people.

The discussion process was extremely long, running into a third, fourth and fifth hour, but proved far more civil than Jason had anticipated. Rick took a mouth-closed, ears-open approach that Jason could never quite master. Or even get close to, if he was honest with himself.

Marek behaved after a warning from Jason about not attempting to recruit the new messengers to the Unorthodoxy. Jason's verbal rebuke was mild, but the pinpoint spike of aura he sent Marek's way was a much sharper message.

Jason's largest concern had been Tera Jun Casta, who continued to hate him with a passion. She was the only member present who still venerated traditional messenger authority, even if that authority would have killed her on sight. Like Rick, she sat and listened, contributing neither questions nor answers to the discussion. Jason quietly hoped that everything she heard would help open her narrow mind, even if by just a crack.

All the discussion ultimately led to the next step for each person at the table. Tera Jun Casta would be returned to Jason's soul realm and left there. She had no interest in contributing and couldn't be trusted if she did. Most of Marek's people would go with her. Marek agreed to aid Rick with his gold-rankers and some of his silver-rankers. Rick reluctantly went along because most of Marek's group would be left with Jason, who wished Rick hadn't used the word 'hostages,' but took the win.

The new messengers would, for the moment, reside in Jason's mountain fortress. They were the most adrift and he had no doubt they would spend yet more hours talking amongst themselves about everything they had heard. He made Jali his liaison to them and could do little more than hope they didn't found a new messenger empire or something equally unfortunate.

When the discussion was finally done, the various participants departed. Rick left with Marek and his people while the still-nameless messengers stayed in the conference room to talk amongst themselves. Tera and the rest of Marek's people returned to Jason's soul realm. Jason moved outside, sitting atop his massive stone head and soon found Jali joining him.

"At some point, they're going to want names," she said and sat down next to him. Her wings vanished as she shrank down to human size.

"Any idea on how that will go?"

"No. Normally, they come into being with a name. I think the lack of a proper and situated birthing tree stopped that."

"Then they'll have to name themselves?"

"Perhaps. Or perhaps their names will come after you decide what to do with that." She pointed to the vast tree looming over the horizon.

"Even if this does all go right, I don't know that I'll get to choose. It may be that whatever happens is going to happen and I don't get a say."

"Either way, we can decide then."

"What about until then? Are they just going to refer to each other by numbers?"

"Messengers communicate through auras as much as other people do body language. They will differentiate themselves through that."

"That doesn't help me, so I might have to number them. I could make them all shirts."

"You'll be fine. You already communicate with your aura as we do. It's one of the many reasons you unsettle us."

"Wait, I do?"

"You didn't notice? Haven't you seen the extreme way people tend to react to you? That's your aura at work."

Jason tilted his head in thought.

"I guess I do," he said. "I must have been doing it unconsciously. For years, maybe. I think it started when I started learning aura tricks to affect others more subtly, from a vampire I know. Huh."

"It certainly helped you control that meeting we just had," she told him. "I've never seen messengers interact like that before."

"It seemed pretty normal to me," Jason said. "What made it strange to you?"

"That we spoke as equals. For the most part. Your rebuke of Marek was the only interaction I saw that felt familiar. Messengers only enter discussion because a leader wants options or is playing her subordinates against one another. There's always a hierarchy."

"I don't like hierarchies."

"Which is odd coming from the one person who stood above all others in that room."

Jason went to deny it but stopped, admitting to himself that it would have been a lie.

"I'm mentally exhausted after that," he said instead. "I came up here to clear my head, but I don't have time. I need to set things in motion. Start expanding. As soon as I do, anomalies will pour in from the territory I'm invading and we'll have to deal with them."

"I've watched messengers push the people they enslave to their limits and beyond. Most of my kind care more about wielding power than doing so efficiently. If you rush because you think you should—or someone else thinks you should—then not only will you work slowly, but you'll work badly. If you rest, you'll work better and make fewer mistakes."

"Yeah," he said, giving her a smiling side glance. "I know, yet I always seem to need someone to remind me in the moment."

———

At the edge of the territory, Rick stood in front of a shadowy wall that marked the border between Jason's domain and the unclaimed one beyond. Before he stepped through, he turned and looked back, his silver-rank vision picking out Jason on top of his fortress. He was sitting next to the messenger girl he'd been running around with, Jali. Without her wings and shrunken down, she was indistinguishable from a fair-skinned, brown-haired human.

"Even with messengers?" he muttered.

"What was that?" Marek asked.

"Nothing," Rick said. "Let's go."

4

OVERESTIMATING THE LENGTH

THE MAIN ENTRANCE TO THE MOUNTAIN FORTRESS WAS THE MOUTH OF Jason's giant stone head. Inside was the central transport hub where three elevating platform shafts were set out in a triangle, giving access to the upper and lower reaches of the complex. Archways were set into the walls all around, one of which held an active portal. Filled with blue, silver and gold light, it led to Jason's soul realm and had been left open continuously.

Jason emerged from the portal with a sandwich and a yawn. He frowned as he expanded his senses over his claimed territory. He shoved the sandwich into his inventory and moved towards the open entrance, quickly building up to a sprint. Reaching the entrance, he leapt out with silver-rank strength that propelled him through the air. He used his aura to make adjustments in his trajectory but carefully, so as not to steal his momentum. He finally landed on the street in the replica of his hometown.

Jali had sensed his movement and followed, soaring on eagle-like wings of brown and white. When she landed beside Jason, she found him leaning over the corpse of the priest of Undeath, peering curiously.

"What is this still doing here?" she asked.

"I was just wondering the same thing," he said. "It should have turned to rainbow smoke long ago, but it's just withered. It looks like it's been dead for more than just a few hours."

"This man was a priest of the undeath god, yes? Perhaps he's going to reanimate."

"Which makes me wonder why he hasn't yet. Maybe it's just an enchantment to prevent his body from decaying so his friends can reanimate it when they find him? Necromancers are big into organics recycling."

"Either way, we should destroy the body."

"Agreed."

"What about other undead?" Jali asked. "You said there were tens of thousands of them left and they would be scattered amongst the territories. Why was this guy here but none of his undead?"

"That's another good question. Probably because my aura is anathema to undead and this territory is infused with it. Any undead being placed here may have been ejected or destroyed outright. This guy would have gotten a pass due to being alive."

Jason poked the body with his shoe. He skittered back as the corpse spasmed on the ground.

"You may have been on the money with reanimating," Jason said. "Are you feeling a draining sensation from it?"

"No, should I be? Do we need to get away from it?"

"I think we're good. It's not after life force or mana. It feels like it's trying to drain something that isn't there to drain. I think that's why it's not getting up."

The body continued to thrash on the ground as if it were having a seizure. After a short time, it dissolved into rainbow smoke, slowly at first but accelerating until all that remained was an empty set of robes.

"That didn't seem dangerous," Jali said.

"No," Jason said. "I could take some guesses as to what just happened, but that's all they'd be. I hope we find Clive soon."

The battle with the Undeath priests was extremely short. On one side was a trio of silver-rank priests commanding around a thousand assorted undead. On the other side were three gold-rank adventurers—Emir, Constance and the Healer high priestess, Hana Shavar. There were also two gold-rank non-adventurers in the commander of the Builder cult, Beaufort, and the brightheart commander, Marla. They commanded a large group of silver-rankers, including Kalif from team Storm Shredder, along with brighthearts and Builder cultists. Clive was also present, but attempts to command him weren't working. He had been constantly researching their new environment and he got snippy when people bothered him during his work.

The environment caused significant trouble for the brighthearts who had never seen the sky before. Their reactions ranged from excitement and awe to existential crisis. The space around them was filled with thick, towering trees into which a large town comprised of tree houses and rope bridges had been built. There were discrete buildings constructed around and into the trunks, as well as sprawling complexes held aloft by multiple massive trees.

The group was on the ground below where they had dealt with the undead and the priests. The forest floor had been devastated by the battle and a few toppled trees had left the township above damaged as well, pulling down bridges and buildings.

The forest calm that followed the battle with the undead gave the group the chance to rest and for the brighthearts to acclimatise to such an alien environment. The pause did not last, however, as anomalies spawned by the transformation zone moved to the attack.

Humanoids with chihuahua-like heads streamed from the undergrowth and dropped from the heights above. They registered as gold rank to aura senses, but their physical prowess was more like high-end silver-rankers and they had no special powers. They posed a challenge for the silver-rankers, and the gold-rankers weren't moving to defend. Beaufort and Marla had been about to, but the adventurers stopped them, giving the lower-rankers the chance for growth.

Clive did not participate in the battle. He could sense the unusual nature of the attackers and understood that they were the anomalies Jason had warned them about. He'd made a point of their value in ranking up, early in the transformation zone, but there would be plenty more to come. Other opportunities took precedence.

One of the dead Undeath priests lay where he fell, amongst shin-high grass on the forest floor. The other two were less viable for examination. One was in pieces, scattered liberally over a kilometre of forest, while the other had gone into spasms when touched and then dissolved into rainbow smoke.

Clive had a suspicion as to the cause of the seizure and subsequent disintegration of the corpse. This came courtesy of the Healer priestess, Hana Shavar. She had reported an odd sense from the twitching undead before it dissolved, as if it were trying to draw in something when there was nothing to drain.

Hana stood back, observing as Clive pulled out a variety of objects, carefully setting them up around the corpse without touching it. She occasionally tossed a casual bolt of healing energy at the silver-rankers fighting the anomalies, but most of her attention was on Clive's work. Most of his devices were magical analysis tools, running the gamut from crystal lenses to more elaborate devices with elements that spanned or floated separately, slowly shifting colours.

A scream drew her attention to the fight, and she noticed a heavily injured adventurer. Clive glanced over before turning back to his work.

"His name's Kalif," Clive said. "He's one of the key damage dealers in one of those specialised Rimaros teams. He doesn't know how to watch his own back without a dedicated team to protect him. Go save him, and maybe tell him to stand at the back."

"I'm a gold-ranker and you're a silver-ranker. I'm meant to be the one giving orders."

"That's normally how it works, yes."

"If I tell you to do something, will you?"

"Probably not. I'm busy with this."

"Is your entire team like this?"

"No, we have one guy who does what he's told. By his mother."

Hana let out a grumbling sigh.

"I'm going to go heal that man."

"What's this?" Hana asked, looking at the quivering rod Clive had pulled out immediately on her return.

"Grab it, please," he said. "I can't leave it just flopping around in the grass."

"Then perhaps you shouldn't have taken it out."

"I need it to be ready when I go to use it. So, would you please just grab it for me?"

She frowned but put her fingers around Clive's throbbing shaft.

"I don't like this sensation," she said.

"You'll get used to it," Clive assured her. "I've found that most people come to enjoy how it feels. I think it's the girth that puts them off at first."

"I can handle the girth. I'm just not comfortable with it throbbing in my hand like this."

"Even so, you should just use your hand until you know what you're doing. Use both hands if you prefer."

"I think you may be overestimating the length. What even is it?"

"It's a threshold resonator. I can't have it too close to the other devices until I'm ready or it'll ruin their calibration."

The last thing Clive withdrew from his inventory was not another magical measuring device but a small lidded pot. It was made of a lacquered ceramic, with the symbol of the church of Purity emblazoned upon it.

"Is that a god's grace relic?" Hana asked.

"Yes," Clive said as he dropped it casually into some soft grass, showing none of the care he had for his other equipment. He made minor adjustments to the positioning of his devices and tossed a recording crystal into the air.

"How did you get that?" Hana asked.

"It's a recording crystal. I bought it at a shop."

"No, the relic."

"While we thought Jason was dead—I don't know how familiar you are with Jason, but he dies a lot. There were a few years where we thought he was dead, but he was just in his home universe. I spent a lot of that time mapping a dimensional travel network the church of Purity and the Builder cult were using. This was after the Ecumenical Council declared Purity a fallen god. Me and a couple of friends spent a lot of time chasing that up until we finally got our full team together for a big operation. Oh, but Jason was still dead, so we had a duck guy instead."

"A duck guy?"

"Yeah, you know. Quack, ponds, being quite comfortable in the rain. Ducks."

"I know what ducks are."

"Then it's odd you asked for clarification. Anyway, this operation led to us stumbling right into one of their big summoning plans and accidentally setting it off early. This was one of the messenger mass-summons that ended up happening all over."

"Are you talking about the first one? The one near Cyrion?"

"Yes."

"That was you?"

"Yes. Anyway, through that time chasing after the Purity loyalists, I picked up some holy relics here and there. It was a good chance to have a poke around and see how they work."

"The relics?"

"Kind of. The gods, more accurately."

"That's blasphemy."

"Is it? I was never clear on the difference between blasphemy and heresy. The people who yell stuff like that at me always wind up being terrible, so it never seemed worth finding out. And that's saying something because I love finding things out."

"And if the gods take issue and send their servants after you?"

"You say that like I've never killed a priest before. The first priest I ever killed was the archbishop of the local Purity church in my hometown. That was *before* the Ecumenical Council declared Purity a fallen god, but he had it coming. Plus, we'd just dropped a building on him, so it was going to be a fight either way."

"You dropped a building on him?"

"Yes, but he had a solid shield power. Hard to kill, especially being silver rank to our bronze. We took a proper beating, but Humphrey's hard to kill as well. Jason not so much, but the trick with him is in getting the death to stick. It was a year or so after that when I started collecting relics, seeing if I can't figure out how divine power works."

"I still say it's blasphemy."

"Go ahead. After being on my team, I could run a lecture series on the praxis of blasphemy. Or heresy, whichever one it is. I'd have to look that up before the first lecture."

"Your team cannot be entirely heretical. Your healer is a priest in my church."

"He doesn't blaspheme," Clive admitted, then tilted his head in thought. "Which is odd, now that I think about it. Neil seems the type. Also, Jason hangs out with gods and I'm pretty sure he convinced Death to use a miracle. I'm not sure he's a heretic so much as a rude acquaintance."

Clive picked up the small pot he'd dropped earlier.

"These are fun," he said. "I never made much headway on the rules of divine influence on magic, but these little pots store a tiny bit of holy power. More an echo of it, really, but even third hand, divine power's not to be dismissed."

"Yet you dismiss the danger of angering the gods."

"My friend Rufus backhanded a priest of Knowledge right across the face once. Now, the way these little pots work is—"

"I know how god's grace relics work, Mr Standish. Even if Purity is fallen, I do not like the way you are treating such objects."

"Are you going to do something about it?"

"Not right now."

"Then I don't care. Now, the great thing about Purity's holy power is that it does all manner of interesting things when you taint it. I had no idea why that worked rather than dispelling the purity power, until it turned out that Purity was the god of disguise this whole time. That way, it makes more sense that the holy power adapts when altered rather than dispersing—"

"Is there a point you're trying to make, Mr Standish?"

"No. I was trying to work while the priestess watching me kept asking questions in an increasingly judgemental tone."

"What are you using the holy relic for?"

"I suspect that the Undeath priests have had enchantments placed into them. Possibly engraved onto their bones."

"That's used for punishing criminals by... hold on."

She extended her arm and chanted a spell.

"*Knit the flesh and salve the wound.*"

A surge of healing magic washed out of her and off towards the ongoing combat. The other gold-rankers were still letting the silver-rankers take care of it and injuries were accumulating.

"As I was saying," Hana continued. "Engraving skeleton enchantments is for permanently suppressing the powers of criminals."

"There's a lot more potential to the practice than that," Clive said. "It's just incredibly wrong to use it. The process is excruciating and very risky. Did you know that one in four criminals sentenced to it doesn't survive? I don't even think it should be used on criminals. If you're going to kill someone, do it clean and quick. Unless your whole power set is slowly rotting people's flesh off. But do you expect the church of Undeath to share my misgivings?"

"No," Hana said. "I do not."

"Exactly. I think the Undeath priests have been enchanted to rise as some form of undead if they get killed. Maybe just garden-variety zombies for the weaker ones, but probably revenants for silvers and golds running around in this place."

"But they didn't rise as undead. That one corpse we disturbed…"

They wrinkled their noses as patches of rainbow smoke rose from all around.

"…did that," Hana finished.

"Someone must have stepped on a finger or something of that third priest," Clive said. "I'm surprised it took this long. And yes, the Undeath priest corpses are breaking down when disturbed, but what you said sparked an idea."

"What I said?"

"That they were trying to drain some power that only you could sense. I think what they need is divine power. The god of Undeath's energy is required to animate them, which normally isn't a problem. But if it is, and that power isn't available, they break down instead. These territories are dimensionally locked; we can physically pass through the boundaries, but magic can't. Not even that of the gods."

"None of that explains what you're doing with that relic."

"I'm seeing if I can get this corpse to react to divine power. As I said, it's just an echo of the real thing, but that's good. I don't want to go animating this priest by accident."

"That relic is from Purity. You've got the wrong god to try animating the dead."

"Yes, but I'll tweak it a bit."

"Tweak it?"

"I told you I didn't make much headway on how divine magic works. I never told you I didn't make any."

"That's—"

"Yes, blasphemy, I know. I'm starting to see where Jason is coming from."

Clive finished placing his devices around the corpse lying in the grass and picked up the pot. He held a hand out to Hana.

"Threshold resonator, please."

She handed him the rod. He then held the pot over the corpse and waved the rod around it twice before letting the pot go. It floated in the air over the corpse by itself. Clive reached out and removed the lid. White light shone from within the small pot and the corpse sat up, identical white light shining from its eyes. Then its head caught on fire and it rapidly dissolved into rainbow smoke.

"Yeah, I'm fairly certain they need the power of their god to reanimate. Otherwise, they'll lie dormant until something disturbs them and they forcibly attempt to animate. That's when they break down."

"We need to make sure we destroy the bodies when we kill the Undeath priests," Hana said. "If a live priest finds them, they could be animated into something powerful."

"No," Clive said. "We don't destroy the bodies. We don't even kill them. We need to start taking them alive."

5

GOOD FRIENDS

JASON SLOWLY MEANDERED ALONG AN EMPTY STREET WITH SHOPS TO HIS left and the beach to his right. The ghost town wasn't a true replica of his hometown but a nostalgic version of it from his youth. There was an Aussie rules football memorabilia store, several of which had cropped up, failed and closed as he grew up. He stopped in front of Mrs Kim's Take-away, a favourite before she sold up and moved to Coffs Harbour.

He stared at the glass storefront, plastered in the usual stickers advertising ice creams and soft drinks. He went inside, the bell on the door jingling. There were no people, but the bain-marie was filled with artery-clogging delights, steam teasing at the bottom of the glass case. Jason opened the flip-top counter and moved behind it, then slid open its glass door. The smell of deep-fried oil wafted out, the scent of his childhood summers. He smiled sadly.

"I wish the territory hadn't taken this form," he said.

"Why is that?" Shade asked, emerging from Jason's shadow.

"Because it's time to expand my territory. As soon as that boundary thins, living anomalies will come swarming in. Even if they don't trash everything, I'm going to paint this town with their bodies. I don't want to see that. There aren't many memories of Earth I have left that aren't tainted in some way."

Jason grabbed a metal scoop and a paper bag, half-filling it with hot chips. He gave it a liberal sprinkle of chicken salt from a shaker before filling the bag and doing it again. He let the bag drop lightly to the bench a couple of times to shake down the salt.

"You look like you've done that before," Shade observed.

"I worked here for the summer when I was sixteen. The last summer before Mrs Kim sold the place. The new owner wasn't as good, but he didn't have to be. If you sell chips so close to the beach in this town, you can make enough money in the summer to coast through the rest of the year."

Jason plucked a chip from the bag and bit off half its length.

"Just as good as I remember," he said. "Which is probably better than they actually were. Memory is funny like that. For me, anyway. I imagine yours is a lot better than mine, you being immortal and all."

"Yes, Mr Asano, but that doesn't always mean better. I will never get to experience the kind of nostalgia you are feeling right now. Becoming a familiar allows astral entities like myself to slowly accumulate authority, but that was never my motivation. I want to experience the cosmos in ways that I, as a shadow creature of the astral, otherwise could not."

Jason looked at Shade with a speculative expression.

"You know, Shade, I use your senses all the time. See and hear what you see."

"Yes, Mr Asano."

"Do you think we could do it the other way?"

"We cannot, Mr Asano."

"Something to work on when I summon your next vessel, then."

Jason let out a cleansing sigh and put the other half of the chip in his mouth. He wandered outside and used his aura to float up into the air, Shade rising beside him. He looked over the town while snacking on his chips.

"Enough putting it off," he said.

He closed his eyes, spreading his senses out through his territory. Each of the transformation zones Jason had experienced was a little different from the others. A quirk of this one was that expansion wasn't a matter of spreading out in every direction but choosing a neighbouring territory and expanding into that one specifically. He had no information on the neighbouring territories, so he chose one on the opposite side of the mountain from the town. He would spare it for as long as he could.

Jason conjured his cloak and flew around the mountain. He soared over green bushland that ran up to the shadowy veil that marked the territorial boundary. When he expanded his power to try and claim the territory, the veil would thin and living anomalies would spill through. The bushland was good terrain for him, hard for large numbers to group up and filled with shadows.

Jason closed his eyes, letting his senses blend into the space around him. He felt the earth, the trees and the air; the people inside the fortress and even the dim sims in Mrs Kim's bain-marie. He pushed out, the territorial boundary resisting for a moment before starting to shimmer.

- You have chosen to expand the territory of your established spirit domain into an adjacent genesis space. Expanding your spirit domain into a territory of unstable genesis space will define and stabilise it but trigger anomalous reactions from the territory expanded into.

He sensed the living anomalies spilling in through the veil and let himself drop from the sky. He fell through the canopy below, letting the bush swallow him.

The territory Rick was in looked like a city where architect and alchemist was the same job, one carried out with extreme enthusiasm. It was a cross between a dirty industrial centre and a giant's alchemy set, with glass vats sticking out of walls and massive pipes running under steel catwalks that ran between buildings.

Rick jabbed his spear into the cobbled street vertically, like tapping a ceremonial staff. Dozens of spears pierced back up in a wide area around him, each one impaling a gelatinous creature. The spears then immediately sprouted barbs that riddled their bodies, visible through their semi-translucent flesh.

The creatures were vaguely humanoid, in a 'getting craned out of your house on the news' kind of way. Their bodies looked like someone had put something they shouldn't in a jelly mould when the mould itself was already dubious. They were naked and fully, although not generously, anatomically equipped. They didn't have a mouth or nose, but they did have large eyeballs floating in their jelly heads.

More unpleasant than the appearance of the creatures was their smell. This was made significantly worse when they tore themselves off Rick's barbed spears, shredding their bodies in the process. This left them a splattered mess on the ground, crawling slowly in his direction. Marek descended from the sky to land next to Rick and immediately winced at the stench.

"I do not care for your approach to combat against these particular foes," Marek told him. "From a tactical perspective, it is a sound path to victory. From an olfactory one, it feels like defeat."

"We're not here to win," Rick told him. "We're here to scout the territory, find any allies and move on."

"Then move on we shall," Marek said, his voice choked off as he tried to not use his nose. "I envy your ability to shut off your sense of smell."

"I thought envying the 'lesser races' was against your religion."

"It's indoctrination, not religion, as much as Jason Asano is disinclined to recognise the difference. But if it were, my companions and I would be in apostasy. As has been explained to you at length."

"A couple of months ago, you were cutting down adventurers for the people you claim to hate now."

"Our actions could not have been different. I will not lie and claim to feel great remorse for what I have done as a slave of the astral kings, but know that the alternative for us was death."

"Some things are worth dying for. Like not killing a city's worth of innocent people."

"I do not expect you to understand, Rick Geller. I hope you never do. Having your very soul enslaved is not something I would wish on another. But we took our chance to escape that fate. We did not turn against our old masters at the point of Jason Asano's sword; we sought him out. To go against him at this point would obviate the purpose of everything we have done while soiling a relationship I expect to benefit us for centuries. Furthermore, attempting to escape him now would be suicide. As would trying to escape later once he unites the transformation zone. All of which means that you put us in an awkward position. I can only hope that you can see how our interests are aligned."

The sloppy, stinking blob creatures were crawling closer, and the pair left, Rick leaping to the rooftop of a three-storey building and Marek flying after him.

"My people found only undead and these living anomalies in this territory," Marek said. "No allies or intelligent enemies, so we should head for the next."

"Agreed," Rick said.

Marek sent out aura pulses that served as simple commands for his scattered allies. They had access to Jason's interface, but only as it pertained to the territories. They couldn't use functions like group chat. He and Rick stood waiting for them to regroup before setting out.

"What did you mean by me putting you in an awkward position?" Rick asked.

"If anything happens to you, whether I could have prevented it or not, Jason Asano will hold me responsible. That makes your life more valuable than mine, or that of any of my people individually. Asano did not put that dynamic in place by accident. You are more valuable to him than any of us."

"That doesn't change the fact that you and your band of murder angels could kill me any time you feel like. Telling me that you promise not to when we were fighting each other not that long ago doesn't fill me with confidence."

"Trust is built over time and this is the beginning of that time. We have mutual interests."

"Oh, mutual interests, great. I'm starting to understand Jason's approach of making friends rather than allies."

"I suspect that we would not make good friends, Rickard Geller."

The living anomalies that swarmed into Jason's territory took the form of bone feasters. His early days in Rimaros included a supply delivery to a fortress town besieged by this type of monster, although the living anomaly version was not quite the same.

The appearance was a match, being emaciated purple humanoids with giant mouths for faces. They had the power to grow and reshape bone, creating blades, projectiles and armour they wielded with surprising skill for frenzied monsters. That and their impressive agility served to compensate for a lack of raw power. They were monsters that could easily punish unskilled adventurers.

The normal version was silver rank and relatively weak, manifesting in massive numbers. During the monster surge, Jason had fought what amounted to an army of them to lift the siege on the town. He swiftly found that these living anomaly replicas were different, courtesy of their higher rank.

While the anomaly bone feasters were ostensibly gold rank, their power level was not. By the later stages of the transformation zone, when the last territories were being claimed, the anomalies would be a match for most monsters of their rank. In this early stage, they were relatively pitiful. This meant that Jason could handle them, although not easily. They still had gold-rank damage reduction and resistances against lower ranks, but many elite adventurers could ignore the rank disparity, Jason included. Capable silver-rank adventurers could handle anomalies at this stage, to the point that they made good training.

While the anomaly feasters were even weaker for their rank than the real thing, weak for gold rank was still a large power spike over weak for silver. Their strength and speed were closer to that of a high-end silver-rank monster, and their bone powers were also enhanced. They couldn't do anything new with them, but the resilience and growth of their bones were much higher.

The anomaly feasters also grew the bones with more refined shaping than the real monsters could manage. This made for weapons that were sharper yet stronger, and armour that was less restrictive. This meant superior coverage with less impedance to their agility.

The difference between these bone feasters and the ones Jason knew meant that he needed to make the most of his advantages. His most prominent asset was the environment they were fighting in. His battle with the real feasters had been in a wide-open gulch with countless enemies and nowhere to hide. Fighting the anomaly feasters in the same environment would force him to quickly flee at best, and quickly die at worst.

In this replica of the Australian bush, it was a different story. It wasn't the thick rainforest of the far north, but the feasters were still forced to break up to navigate the terrain. Jason, on the other hand, could move undetected and untouched, a wraith in the darkness. He was weakest at the start of fights when he had yet to harvest the life force of the defeated. Even two or three of the bone feasters were dangerous in the beginning, being faster and stronger than he was. Their agility also allowed them to fight relatively well despite the uneven ground, mixed surfaces and obstacle-filled environment.

That was not enough to compensate for Jason's hit-and-run tactics as he flickered through shadows like a staccato ghost, landing hits and vanishing. They made the most of his moments of exposure, however, landing hits with arm blades or bone darts. It put his regenerative powers through a workout.

The armour of the bone feasters made it hard for Jason to score early kills. Their armour not only had superior coverage to regular bone feasters, but also blocked many forms of magic attack. Jason's afflictions were largely ineffective, and Colin's leeches couldn't find gaps to dig through before being scraped off or squished between armour segments.

Jason had a solution to this, another advantage he'd lacked when fighting the real feasters. His sword, Hegemon's Will, could not only absorb the power of Jason's conjured dagger but added a corrosion affliction when it did so. This proved effective not just at melting holes in the armour, but also in preventing it from growing back.

This offered Jason weak points to target and land afflictions, although the whole process was laborious. He tried using Gordon's butterflies to spread afflictions faster, but it proved futile. The projectile attacks and incredible reflexes of the feasters meant that the butterflies were taken out before they could spread. The scant few that did slip through proved incapable of sinking through the bone armour to be absorbed and were quickly scraped off. Jason discarded that strategy and resolved to finish things the hard way, which ultimately he did not mind. Fights like this would push his sluggish essence abilities towards faster advancement.

As the long and gruelling fight dragged on, Jason finally began making headway. Bone feasters were falling to his afflictions and he was diligent in draining their remnant life force. This boosted his speed until it overtook that of his enemies, allowing him to fight more safely, even as he fought more boldly. Even so, there was still a long fight ahead of him. He knew that painstakingly whittling the feasters down would be a lengthy process unless something changed.

That change came with two silver-rank auras that shot out of the territorial boundary at speeds that would satisfy gold-rankers. Immediately after they arrived, a column of lava smashed down like a satellite weapon, incinerating bushland and bone feaster alike. The column swept back and forth, carving a fiery swath of destruction.

Jason rose through the canopy to where he could see Farrah, in obsidian armour and held aloft by fiery wings. She was blasting down with her lava cannon power, setting fire to the bushland. Sophie, floating next to her, moved next to Jason in a blur of motion he could barely track.

"We thought we'd help," Sophie told him. "From what I'm sensing down there, it looks like you're kind of slow. Well, not kind of slow as much as just slow. Really, really slow."

"You think you would be faster?"

"Than you? Yes. Than Farrah? Well, she's going to run out of mana pretty quick like that."

"She's starting a huge bushfire in my territory."

"She uses fire to replenish her mana."

"And I use my territory to not be burned to the ground!"

Sophie turned slowly in the air, taking a look at Jason's territory.

"Why does that mountain look like the back of your head?"

6

LACKEYS

Farrah wore obsidian armour, covering everything but her head. She flew down to join Jason and Sophie just over the bush canopy, rubbing her temples. All around them, the bush was aflame.

"There's still plenty of them left," Farrah said. "I'll go again once I get some mana back. The lava cannon is fun, but not especially precise, and these monsters seem quite springy. I don't remember bone feasters being this quick on their feet while armoured up."

"They're not really monsters," Jason explained. "They're fakes. Also, maybe we could try an approach other than a massive lava cannon that most of them just dodge. One that doesn't involve burning my territory to the ground."

"What's the big deal?" Farrah asked. "I bet that mountain has whatever passes for a central base in it. No fire's getting in there. Did you carve it into the shape of your own head?"

"The big deal," Jason said, "is that on the other side of this mountain is a replica of Casselton Beach, which a bushfire will rip through. Including the ice cream shop."

"What?" Farrah yelped. "Okay, hold on. There's a fire and we need to stop it. This is fine, it's all going to be fine. Right, I can absorb fire to get mana back. I just have to absorb all the fire and everything will be okay. You two can deal with the monsters."

She shot off towards the nearest batch of flames.

Jason shook his head and turned to Sophie.

"Shall we?" he asked, pointing down into the bushland and the anomalies within.

"Let's," she said and let herself fall.

Korinne Pescos frantically scrambled between massive rocks in the bottom of the vast desert canyon. She stopped, pressing her back against the stone left scorching hot by the unyielding sun. She glanced up at the massive crystal jutting from the rock she hid behind. The powerful alien aura it pulsed out was masking her presence from her gold-rank pursuer.

The crystal was one of many, blanketing the canyon that was kilometres across and dozens of kilometres long. The clashing auras they produced left her with a splitting headache, but she was grateful for them nonetheless. The Undeath priest hunting her could not sense her any more than she could him, and there were plenty of rocks, gullies and overhangs to hide her.

She'd been so happy in the beginning. Of all the places she could have been dropped in the transformation zone, she ran into two of her team members almost immediately. Then they had met the priest, and now the animated bodies of Jetta and Polix were chasing her through the canyon. They were trying to flush her out like hunting hounds while she had to flee, even as she mourned them.

The priest was in no rush, loudly and gleefully taunting her. He had the power and was making a game of it. He could track her down and make short work of her if he tried but, instead, teased her like a cat with a mouse. Korinne knew it was only a matter of time until he got bored or she made a lethal mistake. She could feel the despair clawing at her like an animal, stalking around in the shattered remains of her hope.

Suddenly, she felt a surge of power that somehow cut through the pervasive aura of the crystals. Almost the moment she felt it, there was a massive crash that thundered in her ears and shook the ground. Dust flooded the canyon like a tidal wave, washing past her and cutting off her vision.

She came out from her hiding place, navigating carefully with her hands held out in front of her. All she could see was dust and an occasional golden flash in the distance. A ringing sound of hammering metal rang out like a blacksmith working a piece of iron.

Korinne flinched back when she almost stumbled into Jetta. Her friend, now a slack-jawed corpse, showed no reaction to Korinne and stood still as a mannequin. She continued towards the sound, barely caring if the commotion was made by enemy or ally. Finally, she encountered two figures walking through the dust cloud, their blurry shapes resolving into people she recognised.

One was the leonid, Gareth Xandier, but larger than she remembered by some two feet. His eyes blazed with golden light and she could sense his aura when she concentrated on it, even through the interference of the crystals. He was gold rank despite having been silver when she had seen him just hours previous. The man walking alongside him was Rufus Remore, looking unchanged. Korinne quickly approached them, looking up at the leonid.

"The priest?" she asked. Dust crawled into her mouth, leaving it dry and chalky.

"Dealt with," Gary told her.

"What happened to you?"

"Cup of Heroes."

"Oh. Oh, I'm sorry. How long do you have?"

"In this place? As long as we're here. Perhaps another three hours after we leave."

"You get to keep the power that long?" she asked.

"The gods cannot reach us here. There is nowhere for the power to return to, so it does not try."

Rufus, who had remained silent, walked past her to look at Jetta's unmoving body. The dust was beginning to settle, increasing visibility distance. Rufus' expression turned dark as he asked Korinne a question.

"Isn't this—"

"My team member, yes," Korinne told him. "There's another one out there somewhere. I suppose the dust will have to clear before we find him."

"Would you like me to put them to rest?" Rufus asked.

"No," Korinne said. "I couldn't save them, but at least I can do this."

Tears cut through the dust caking her face as she marched grimly towards Jetta. Rufus glanced at Gary but said nothing.

In a jungle-filled territory, far from Jason, the messengers there were in a state of confusion. Their last clear memories were of initiating the ritual that would convert the natural array into a soul forge. After that was an incoherent mess of images and sensations that could only be called memories by the most generous definition.

Now that the external influence of the corrupted messenger tree had been purged, the messengers were trying to put together the pieces of what had happened. They needed to know where they were, what their circumstances were and what to do about it. They had some information from the system message, Jason's power having imprinted elements of his system interface on the entire zone. The messengers, however, lacked critical elements of context.

There were two gold-ranked and what they believed were five silver-ranked messengers. The fifth was a disguised Belinda. She wasn't sure how many of the messengers had been overtaken by the elemental tree, rather than spawned from it, but she guessed this was a good percentage of those that survived. The gold-rankers seemed well-versed in magical theory, which made sense. These were the ones sent to transform the natural array into a soul forge. Given that they had failed spectacularly, their competence in employing that theory was up in the air.

The messengers were gathered atop the ruins of a stone ziggurat, one of many ruins poking out from the canopy of a sprawling jungle. Belinda wasn't sure about the size of most territories in the transformation zone, but this one was enormous. There were plateaued mountains in one direction, some hundred kilometres away. In the opposite direction, that land was mostly flat to the horizon, blanketed in lush green jungle. The air was hot and wet, the sun scathing in a clear sky. Insects buzzed around but were not fool enough to approach such powerful auras.

They had all been dumped in the transformation zone separately, wiping out undead and living anomalies until they found one another. The anomalies took the form of jungle beasts, from lizards and cats to clouds of insects and lurking bog monsters. Belinda had been doubly lucky, first in finding an isolated silver-rank messenger. The others were too distant to sense Belinda killing her and sinking her to the bottom of a swamp. A concealment and preservation ritual kept the corpse from turning to rainbow smoke too quickly, and make it hard to find. It would take a gold-ranker making a concerted search from relatively close to find it.

Belinda's second lucky break was that the messengers were isolated from their astral king. This meant that they could not rely on that connection to identify an outsider in their midst. She hadn't been certain of that point until she'd already infiltrated the group, but their conversation quickly confirmed it.

Infiltrating the messenger group had been a gamble, but several key things had gone her way. Being isolated from their astral king was one, and their confusion another. She had no idea of the personality of the messenger she had replaced, but generic arrogant prick seemed a safe bet. With all of the messengers out of sorts from their ordeal, being somewhat out of character let her fit right in.

The gold-rankers had managed to scavenge enough materials for a basic ritual to assess their environment. Messenger bodies were highly magical and their feathers could stand in for various materials. Their blood likewise made good material to draw out the lines and sigils. Naturally, one of the silver-rankers was 'volunteered' to supply them, the gold-rankers unwilling to pluck their own feathers.

Belinda got lucky that they didn't pick her; her shape-shifting power would not imbue her body with the intrinsic magic of the messengers. Just maintaining a messenger-like aura was tricky enough; the strength and nature her aura seemed to have would easily crack under scrutiny.

They spread out to gather material from the jungle around them, in addition to the messenger body parts. Plants and rocks with high concentrations of magic weren't too hard to find and they gathered the required material in a few hours. Belinda's knowledge would have allowed her to go faster, but she had quickly realised that the silver-rankers were not meant to have a lot of magical knowledge. That was for the gold-rankers, while the rest of them were merely lackeys.

Belinda hadn't figured out the name of her identity yet. Unless someone else used it, she might have to take a risk to get it. If someone used it and she didn't answer, not realising they were speaking to her, that could be the end. It was a dangerous contradiction that could help or ruin her, depending on how it went. Her best bet was to try and get someone to use it, but that held risks.

The gold-rank messengers proved that they were quite good at not just using magic but interpreting the results, despite their failure with the natural array. As an enthusiast of improvised magic herself, Belinda learned a lot from the process of the messengers cobbling together their ritual. She hoped that studying the messengers and their magic would give her a critical chance down the line.

The ritual itself was not much to look at, just the gold-rankers floating in the air above the ritual circle. Afterwards, they discussed what the ritual had shown them, along with their physical exploration of the zone and the scattered memories from their time under the messenger tree's control.

Messenger arrogance helped Belinda out; they did not bother with the silver-rankers at all during this process. The gold-rankers decided that only their insights and recollections were valuable, saving Belinda from the need to invent any.

The messengers demonstrated some impressive deductive reasoning, grasping the main points of their circumstances. They didn't have everything, but put together more than she expected, relative to what she and the other expedition members had been told by Jason.

Galis Jay Vahal was one of the gold-rankers, the other named Kol Kelis Vel.

"In short," Galis said, "we need to claim and unify these territories before anyone else in here. If that means eliminating any opposition we encounter, then all the better. We do not know everything yet, so we can extract answers from them before we let them die."

"Should we?" one of the silver-rankers asked. "Haven't we been tainted by what happened to us? Removed from the pure messenger ideal? Perhaps we should destroy ourselves, rather than return to Vesta Carmis Zell corrupted."

"Don't be an idiot," Belinda snapped, hoping this was her moment. "If the gold-rankers thought that, they would have destroyed us already. We need to listen to their words and obey their commands. Thinking for yourself will get you nowhere. Obviously."

Galis looked to Belinda with approval, then at the other messenger.

"Relia Vin Vala is correct," he said. "Do not presume that your understanding of anything is greater than ours, Cas Vin Baral. You should thank Relia Vin Vala, as her wisdom has saved you from a more violent education at my hands."

The look Cas Vin Baral gave Belinda was not one of gratitude. She had made an enemy, but getting her name and ingratiating herself with the gold-rankers had been worth it. It was a good beginning.

Neil's early days as an adventurer had been a mixed bag. Assigned as a lackey to Thadwick Mercer through family obligation, dealing with a fool whose arrogance and incompetence only escalated over time had been a miserable experience. Outside of Thadwick himself, however, things had been good.

The Mercer family seemed to understand exactly what they had piled onto Neil and went out of their way to compensate. From the day his training began, years before absorbing his essences, the Mercer family had given him training, facilities and resources that only the Gellers could match.

Whether all that was from guilt or a desire to give Thadwick the best companions, Neil still didn't know. If it came down to Thadwick's mother, he would put faith in her good intentions. But the Mercer family was large and Thadwick was raised primarily by his father. In that man's good intentions, Neil had no faith at all.

Other aspects of Neil's early years made life with Thadwick bearable. He was another face in the crowd as an admirer of Thadwick's sister, Cassandra, but had more proximity than most. His early hostility to Jason had not come from any loyalty to Thadwick but outrage that Cassandra had chosen Jason, of all people. He would eventually—and grudgingly—come to recognise that Jason wasn't without virtue, but remained convinced that Jason had unscrupulously seduced her through other-worldly culinary delights.

More than any of that, what had gotten Neil through working with Thadwick was the third member of their team, Dustin Kettering. Dustin was in the same position as Neil, forced to train and work with Thadwick through the obligation of his family to the Mercers. Neil and Dustin, two people in the same circumstance, with the same problems, unsurprisingly built up a camaraderie.

Dustin had joined Rick's team, not long after Neil had joined Jason and Humphrey. Like Neil and Dustin, Rick's group were struggling with the repercussions of the disastrous expedition out of Greenstone. Thadwick and Rick's party member, Jonas, had been captured by the Builder cult and implanted with star seeds, leading to unpleasant ends for both. Dustin might not have cared for Thadwick, but there was an understanding that allowed him to find a place with Rick and his teammates.

Both Neil and Dustin had been lost after Thadwick had gone completely off the rails. Neil had been lured into Jason's team, mostly by the assurances of Humphrey's mother. He still might have refused because of Jason himself if Jason hadn't paid Neil a visit. Jason's approach of honesty had made Neil realise that Jason would be an annoyance, but one he could live with. Respect had taken quite a bit longer and a large number of sandwiches, reaffirming Neil's suspicions about Jason and Cassandra.

When Neil and Dustin found themselves dropped in the same territory, it made for a welcome reunion. It also gave them a frontline and healer combination. They discussed this as they walked beside a canal in a city with looming gothic architecture.

"We need some damage dealers," Dustin said.

"Sure, but that can be anyone," Neil said dismissively. "Damage dealers get all the glory, but it's people like you and me that determine victory and defeat. We just need to recruit the first idiot we encounter who can lob a firebolt or shoot an arrow. I'd even be willing to accept an affliction specialist, so long as he brings snacks."

7

YELLOW BELL

THE THREE-HEADED DOG HADN'T BEEN HARD TO TAKE DOWN WITH THE gold-rankers Clive's group had on hand. The creature dissolved into rainbow smoke almost immediately, leaving behind a basketball-sized crystal orb. Inside, motes of blue and orange light swirled through inky darkness. Clive took it to examine.

Item: [Stable Genesis Core] (unranked, common)

A refined vessel of transformative potential energy (consumable, magic core).

- Effect: Use to set up or expand spiritual domains.
- You lack the ability to establish a spirit domain. You may use this core to establish or expand territory within a genesis space, but additional requirements must be met to establish a spirit domain.

"What are we looking at?" Constance asked.

"It says you can establish a spirit domain," Clive said. "Like the sanctified ground within a temple. There's some requirement I don't meet, but I can still use this thing to claim the territory. Are you sure it shouldn't be a gold-ranker doing this?"

"Jason is on your team," Emir said. "Since the territories will all need to be handed over to him eventually, it's best if we let the person most loyal to him claim them. I don't think there would be a problem, but we should still do our best to avoid one."

"I guess I'll just use it, then?" Clive said, his voice not hiding his uncertainty.

"If you're not going to use it then give it to me," said Beaufort.

"Uh, no," Clive said to the Builder cult leader. "I'll use it."

The two gold-rank messengers had finished preparing the ritual that would let them not just claim a territory but establish the basis for a spirit domain. The orb they had taken from the final anomaly sat in the middle of a ritual circle drawn in messenger blood. Rather than spread out the duty of supplying blood and feathers, they used Cas Vin Baral for all of it, due to his 'complaining in a fashion unbecoming of the most advanced species in the cosmos.'

The reason they had yet to conduct the ritual was the unanswered question of who would use the orb. The two gold-rankers had to decide between them, and the discussion did not go well.

"I am the senior," Galis Jay Vahal said.

"Age is an irrelevant factor," Kol Kelis Vel shot back. "I was the expedition leader's direct subordinate, so I should be leader in her absence."

Belinda stood with the silver-rank messengers, still disguised as one of them. They watched in silence, all knowing better than to interject. She certainly wasn't going to bring up any of the things she'd off-handedly mentioned to the individual gold-rankers in private. As it turned out, prodding the ambitions of high-ranking messengers was startlingly easy.

Jason, Farrah and Sophie ate ice cream as they watched messengers fly around in the air over the mountain fortress.

"I think you're trusting her too easily," Farrah said, not for the first time.

"I've literally walked through her soul," Jason said. "It's nowhere near as sketchy as mine."

"She's a messenger," Farrah pointed out. "Whether you've traipsed through her soul or not, it's a risk."

"Sometimes you just take a risk on someone," Sophie said, glancing at Jason. "Even if they don't make it easy on you. You never know what helping someone just because they need it might lead to."

"But sometimes you don't have time for that," Farrah said. "You're making this harder on yourself than you have to, Jason."

"Yep," Jason agreed. "I don't know if you've noticed, but making things harder than I have to is kind of my thing. Sophie's right. Helping people isn't about getting benefits, but it does seem to have a lot of them. I had no idea that I would need Jali's help keeping a bunch of confused messengers calm after setting them free, yet here we are."

Jason finished his ice cream, happily crunching through the waffle cone. He then pulled the glowing orb from his inventory.

"Every transformation zone is a little different," he said. "Time to see what consolidating territory looks like this time."

"When are you going to start?" Emir asked.

"I've already done it," Clive said, nodding at the orb in his hands. "Look."

The orb dissolved, slowly at first but sped up quickly. The dark energy, speckled with blue and orange, seeped into Clive's body. The others looked around for any change but saw nothing different.

"That's it?" asked Marla, the gold-rank brightheart commander.

- You have claimed a territory.
- You may initiate territorial conflict in order to annex hostile territory.
- Another territory holder may annex your territory should you surrender it to them or if you are killed while in territorial conflict.
- You may voluntarily allow another territory holder to annex your territory without conflict.
- You have the right to imprint upon the inhabitants of this territory kept in stasis. You lack any inherent power that would allow you to imprint on the inhabitants held in stasis. They will be removed from stasis but will remain in a comatose state

until imprinted or they die. Remaining in this state will eventually lead to their deaths.

The gold-rankers looked to the sky.

"Those messengers just became a lot easier to sense," Emir said. "They came out of stasis. What's going on?"

"We need to catch them," Clive said. "They're all comatose."

"Comatose?" Emir asked. "We could let them hit the ground, and then make sure they're dead."

"You're the one who said I should claim this place," Clive told him. "I say we keep them alive."

"I'm with Bahadir," Marla said. "The only messenger I would come close to trusting is the one I'm certain is dead."

"Jason already has a messenger collection," Emir said. "He doesn't need any more."

"I don't think that's how he'd see it," Clive said.

"Why do we care about what someone who isn't here thinks?" Marla asked.

"Because," Clive said, "all of these territories ultimately have to be handed over to him, at which point he'll do some rewriting of reality. Jason can be rather extreme when he feels like something has gone the way it should not have, and this process is going to be unreliable as is. I think it's best if we don't prompt him to do something even more outlandish than necessary."

"I'm not sure this sounds like someone we want rewriting reality," Marla said.

"Then you shouldn't have let me claim this territory," Clive said. "I trust him over every person here."

"Clive is right to trust Jason," Emir said. "He has experience with what's going on here that none of us share. I shouldn't have suggested killing the messengers. The fall is unlikely to kill silver-rankers, but we should make sure."

"No need," Clive said curtly. "I'll deal with it, but please refrain from interfering."

Clive pointed upwards and drew with his finger. A few meters above him, golden lines appeared where he pointed as he drew a massive ritual circle. When he had finished drawing out the lines and sigils of the ritual circle, he opened his storage space, a small circle of runes ringing a portal.

He pulled objects from the portal one by one, tossing them into the air.

Instead of falling back down, they floated up to different areas in the ritual diagram. There were several fistfuls of spirit coins, feathers of different colours and a blob of pale blue slime in a glass jar. Once each item reached their designated position, they hovered in place.

Clive had worked swiftly and with confidence, the entire process taking less than half a minute. Even so, the messengers had almost reached the end of their monumental fall from well over a dozen kilometres in the air.

As the unconscious messengers reached the final half kilometre, they slowed slightly, their trajectories curving towards the ritual circle. The first messenger was still plummeting when it reached just a few metres from the ritual circle and struck a sheet of magic that became visible on impact.

The sheet reacted to the impact like a trampoline made of fly paper. The magical sheet flexed down as the messenger hammered into it before springing back, but the messenger wasn't bounced off. She adhered to the sheet like glue as it shook back and forth several times. The second messenger hit the sheet and the first was suddenly loose, drifting slowly down. She passed through the ritual diagram without impacting it and came to rest in the long grass.

More messengers fell like rain, although none crashed into one another on the magical sheet. While that was happening, Clive pulled out a notebook and started scrawling in it with a pencil.

"You didn't pull out any notes before drawing out the magic diagram," Emir observed.

"No," Clive confirmed.

"It's a rather niche ritual to have memorised."

"I didn't have it memorised," Clive told him. "I just made it up."

"You just invented a complex, wide-area ritual, off the top of your head?"

Clive snorted a laugh.

"Sure, complex."

"Clive, I'd try and poach you for my treasure-hunting operation again. I'm just not sure I can afford to pay you what you're worth."

———

The shadowy veil between Jason's territory and the one he had expanded his influence into was barely visible after dealing with the living anomalies. After the bone feasters had been dealt with, a massive monstrosity had come lumbering through. It had some physiological similarities to the bone feasters, being bone exoskeleton over leathery flesh, but that was the extent of it. Where they were human-sized, the final anomaly was the size of a cottage and looked like a cross between a beetle and a mantis, walking on six legs but with two arms sporting serrated bone blades.

The boss anomaly had been relatively easy to deal with, being too big to share the agility of the bone feasters. Jason had loaded it with afflictions and let it stomp around the blackened remains of the bushland until it dropped. He knew it would be the easiest fight he experienced in the transformation zone.

Through what was now the nearly translucent veil to the next zone, what they could see was a massive gorge running through a mountain range. Mist shrouded the space below, giving them no sense of how high up it was, although it would have been deep underground in Jason's territory. The border between the territories was both extreme and abrupt.

Natural stone spires jutted up all along the gorge, intermingled with islands that floated in the air through some magical effect. The mountains framing the gorge were a mixture of sheer stone cliffs and terraced areas large enough for trees and grass to grow. They even sported the occasional wooden building in what Jason found reminiscent of a traditional Japanese style. The floating islands and a couple of the spires with flattened tops had the same greenery.

They could see multiple waterfalls, mostly from the mountains to the side. One spilled out from the top of a natural spire while another spilled from the edge of a floating island, despite no apparent source.

There was a path running a meandering passage through the gorge. It was comprised of rope bridges between the spires, the islands and the mountainsides, switching back and forth more than it moved forward. Some parts of the path passed by the greenery and the buildings. Other sections went up or down stairs hewn into the mountains or around the circumference of the spires. Natural trails were mingled with carved ones, all of them precarious.

Jason, Farrah and Sophie looked out, through the veil. Jason's eyes panned up and down, the upper and lower reaches of the territory reaching much further than his own.

"That is picturesque," Jason said.

"This is what adventuring is meant to be like," Farrah said.

"It does look like we're going to fall off ledges a lot, though," Jason said.

"We can all fly," Sophie pointed out.

"Oh yeah," Jason said. "Why couldn't I see those mountains before? They're definitely taller than the veil, and I can see the magic tree that's much further away."

"We started on the other side and couldn't see your giant head mountain," Sophie said. "The veil must block all vision other than the big tree in the middle."

"At least until you push your influence through the veil and take out all the anomalies that come out to object," Jason said.

He held the orb out in front of him.

- You have expanded your influence into an adjacent territory and expunged all anomalies. You may use a [Stable Genesis Core] to finalise the expansion and unify the two territories into one.
- Will you consume the [Stable Genesis Core]?

"This all feels too easy," Jason said. "The genesis core is already stable, and it looks like we just need the one per territory, from the boss drop. Well-defined territories mean expansion is only on one front. We know where the anomalies will come from instead of having them stream in from every direction."

"Are you complaining because things are good?" Sophie asked. "Are you an idiot?"

"I'm hoping all this is because I was able to shape this transformation zone as it formed," Jason explained. "Since my last transformation zone, I've picked up an astral throne and an astral gate, and a lot of experience with quasi-real dimensional spaces. Plus, I've also built up a tolerance for dimensional forces."

"There you go, then," Farrah said. "You've just countered your own concern."

"But what if I'm wrong? What if it all goes to—"

"What if you're wrong?" Farrah cut him off. "Then we do what we always do and figure it out. You'll come up with some lunatic idea and save the damn day. It'll probably annoy Neil and be so ridiculous that Rufus tries to talk you out of it. Maybe you'll convince Clive to turn Gary into a giant hairy arrow or something, I don't know. Then you'll get a weird power and make a king or someone angry in the process. You know how this goes, and yet, after all we've been through, not only are you whinging about it, but you're doing so because it's too easy?"

She ran her fingers through her hair in frustration before continuing her rant.

"I've been putting up with this staring-into-the-middle-distance sad boy routine for a long while now because, yeah, some crappy stuff happened. But now it's time to put on your big girl pants, fight the bad guy and save the day. There's even a princess out there to rescue, so get off your butt, make some reference we don't understand and get moving."

"Um…?" Jason voiced hesitantly.

"What?" Farrah snarled.

"I'm not on my butt?"

Farrah's eyes went maniac wide and Jason flinched.

"Right, uh, obscure pop culture reference. Did you ever see *Ferris Bueller's Day Off*?"

"I did," Farrah said impatiently. "And Ferris Bueller was a little prick. You can't do better than that?"

"Uh… everybody Wang Chung tonight?"

"It'll do," Farrah said. "Now, shut up and go fight some evil."

8
ROCK CLIMBING

Farrah glowered as she reached for another handhold on the icy cliff face. The steam produced by the ice carried on the powerful winds blasting her was immediately carried off by those same winds.

"Oh yeah, let's all just jump off this cliff," she said bitterly in voice chat. "We can all fly."

"How was I meant to know?" Sophie asked from the top of the cliff. Her flight power involved wind manipulation, and while not working as normal, had at least allowed her to return to the clifftop instead of being smashed into it like Jason and Farrah.

- You have entered a zone of wind infused with abnormal magic.
- Flight powers are impeded or disabled, depending on their nature.

The flight powers of Jason's shadowy void cloak and Farrah's fiery wings had both been entirely negated, turning their attempt to fly into a swift plummet. They were both smashed into the cliff face by the wind, tumbling down until they managed to grab handholds on the rock. After Sophie returned to the top, Jason shadow-jumped to a Shade body hidden in her shadow, leaving Farrah to climb alone. Rock climbing, even in extreme conditions, wasn't a challenge for anyone with silver-rank strength and coordination. That fact did not improve Farrah's mood.

"I blame you," Sophie told Jason as they waited side by side. The cliff edge was a narrow ledge just beyond the veil beyond which lay Jason's territory.

"How is this my fault?"

"You're the one who wanted to explore the new territory before unifying it with the one you've already got. If you'd used the magic ball first, you could probably control those winds."

"I should," Jason said. "But don't you have the spirit of adventure? Don't you want to cross rickety rope bridges over bottomless chasms? Traverse windswept mountain trails as the vast panorama spans out before you?"

"That does appeal," Sophie said. "It's nice when adventuring means something other than going places just to kill things. I don't know how open to it Farrah will be."

They both looked to the edge as an arm came up like a zombie bursting from the grave. Farrah clambered up, not bothering to stand. She rolled onto the ledge and just lay there.

"You're not wrong," she told them. "We promised you fun adventures back in the day, and this is the kind of thing we were talking about. We didn't think it would be in some fragmented reality fissure, but that's just how it goes sometimes. Or most of the time when you're around, Jason."

"So you're up for following this trail through the gorge?" Jason asked.

"I would be," Farrah said, "but we've wasted enough time already, and you know that. We can't spend days making our highly inefficient way through an entire mountain range while the Undeath priests are out there claiming territories."

Jason's shoulders slumped.

"Yeah," he begrudgingly acknowledged. "I'll go get Jali so she can first-contact the messengers when they come out of stasis."

The leader of the priests of Undeath was Garth. The drape of the robes over his skeletal body showed that it did not have the shape of a human, while masking exactly what form it did take. Most of those who knew had been slain and turned into Garth's undead puppets or new elements of the body whose secrets they had died for.

Having claimed the territory, a strange land of glass buildings and steel automatons, the messengers now free of stasis were descending from the sky. They looked nearly identical to one another with corpse-white skin, grey hair and glowing purple eyes. In perfect unison, they alighted on the ground and dropped to one knee in supplication, heads bowed.

"This," Garth said, "will do very nicely."

———

Neil and Dustin found that claiming their first territory had been easy enough, their defender-healer combination being very hard to eliminate. The only problem was that it had taken too long to clear out the undead and living anomalies without specialised damage dealers. The final boss monster had been an especially exhausting slog. In the aftermath of taking it down, the pair were engaged in an argument as to its nature.

"I'm telling you, it's a radish," Dustin said.

"Turnip," Neil said. "Look at the pink and white skin. Radishes don't have that."

"And turnips aren't ten metres across with six legs and a mouth full of teeth the length of my hand."

"You're suggesting that radishes are?"

"They might be," Dustin said unconvincingly. "Radishes can be quite varied."

"That would be quite the exotic varietal."

He used his loot power on the boss, so along with the genesis orb that would have come out anyway, there was a pile of spirit coins and a large basket full of vegetables.

"Hey, check that," Neil said. They ignored the magic sphere to look over the basket.

"There are radishes *and* turnips in here," Dustin complained. "That doesn't resolve anything."

Neil eventually absorbed the orb, claiming the territory. Once he did, his senses expanded over the whole space and he looked up.

"Uh oh."

"What is it?" Dustin asked.

- You have claimed a territory.
- You may initiate territorial conflict to annex hostile territory.
- Another territory holder may annex your territory should you surrender it to them or if you are killed while in territorial conflict.

- You may voluntarily allow another territory holder to annex your territory without conflict.
- You have the right to imprint upon the inhabitants of this territory kept in stasis.
- You are currently separated from your deity and none of your personal powers were sourced from your god to provide an imprint template.
- You lack any inherent power that would allow you to imprint on the inhabitants held in stasis. They will be removed from stasis but will remain in a comatose state until imprinted or they die. Remaining in this state will eventually lead to their deaths.

"Silver-rankers can survive a fall from just about any height, right?" Neil asked.

"Yeah," Dustin said warily. "Why do you ask?"

———

Neil pulled the last comatose messenger from the divot it had made upon landing and carried it to where he and Dustin had put the others. They were set out in rows along the gentle slope of a hill with short grass and just enough tree coverage to let sunlight dapple through a loose canopy. Neil's new territory was a pastoral region and Dustin had picked out the pleasant spot. The pair looked at their work with satisfaction.

"Of all the places you could wake up confused and oblivious as to who you are and what's going on," Dustin said, "this is probably where I'd pick."

"Assuming they don't wake up in murder mode," Neil said. "We don't know what state they'll be in. These are the messengers that were created by the tree. They've spent their entire lives in a state of violent madness. Who knows what they'll be like with that influence removed."

"Maybe they'll be nice," Dustin suggested.

"That would be great, but I'll be happy if they stay unconscious and we never find out."

———

Neil pushed his influence into a neighbouring territory, anticipating a flood of living anomalies. Instead, there was more of a light drizzle. After dispatching them, he and Dustin moved to the veil between territories, looking through. The veil was almost completely translucent, compared to the shadowy boundary to other neighbouring territories.

- Each [Living Anomaly] in this territory has been eliminated.
- Multiple territory owners have extended their influence into this territory.
- All other territory owners must abandon or cede this territory or die before it can be claimed.
- Body of final [Living Anomaly] is currently sealed. It will not produce a [Stable Genesis Core] until a single claimant remains in the territory.

The new territory was darkened by the black clouds choking the sky. Rain was pouring down hard, and the darkness was lit up every few seconds by a flash of lightning. Most of the bolts were quite distant, yet a few struck close every minute, throwing up dirt and mud.

The landscape was black earth and dust that pounding rain had turned to a mud slurry. The wet, heavy air smelled of ozone and charcoal. The terrain was dotted with mesas, cracked and blackened by lightning. The flashes shone blindingly from black stone rendered glossy and slick by the rain washing over it. There was no visible plant life, not even charred remains in the inhospitable landscape.

In place of trees, a forest of rough iron poles jutted from the earth, rocks and even the tops of the mesas. Anywhere from five to ten metres tall, the poles grounded any lightning strike that came close, crackling with energy as they grounded the electricity.

Both men had pulled rain-deflecting items from their dimensional bags before stepping through the veil. The devices were brooches that shrouded them in magical fields that caused water to slide right off. They were usually more convenient than the floating umbrella Jason had left back on Earth, but not when the rain ignored the magic. The water passed right through, soaking their clothes immediately, and they turned to look at each other.

"Iron-rank rain deflector?" Neil asked, yelling over the sound of rain. Dustin nodded with a laugh.

The lightning rods didn't stop the bolts of electricity from flaring magic, not just blinding but bombarding their magic and aura senses. Like a constant chain of flash-bang grenades, the thunder and lightning assaulted their spiritual senses as savagely as their physical ones. Trudging through the rain, soaked to the bone in seconds, Neil and Dustin soon had pounding headaches.

The pair moved forward by dashing from pole to pole between lightning strikes. They went close enough to be shielded from the strikes but not so close the energy channelled by a struck rod arced into them. Fortunately, while the poles didn't stop the sensory bombardment, they did make it less overwhelming. It was enough that Neil and Dustin could talk between peals of thunder, although they didn't chat as they made their way through the zone.

Silver-rank speed allowed them to cover a lot of ground, yet as one hour led into two, the territory was feeling both endless and empty. Finding a rocky overhang for a break, the pair discussed their situation.

"That system message said multiple people were claiming this territory," Dustin said. "Where are they?"

Neil looked at the space around them. The overhang rested over a slight slope and the ground under them was wet dirt instead of ankle-deep mud. They were both dripping onto it as they leaned against the stone wall.

"Best guess?" Neil said. "Huddling under rocky overhangs."

"Are we wasting time here?" Dustin asked. "We've already sunk a couple of hours into this and found nothing. It feels like that could continue indefinitely. We might have passed right by someone and not even noticed."

"You're suggesting an alternative?"

"We could go back and try another territory. There were more bordering yours, right? We picked this one at random."

"It's an option," Neil said. "I can sense the direction of my territory, so I'm not worried about finding it. I'd like to keep going, though, at least for now. With multiple people looking to claim this territory, odds are high that one of them is an ally."

"Like the Builder cult," Dustin grumbled.

"That wouldn't be an ideal pick, but we lack some damage options if we're going to progress at any real pace. Not to mention that we need to find a gold-ranker from our side before we find one from the other. They're likely almost as blind as we are here, so it offers us a better chance of escape if we get unlucky."

"Alright," Dustin agreed. "But how long do we keep at it?"

"It's been about two hours," Neil said. "If the next two are the same, we'll cut our losses."

Jason watched Jali fly off with the new batch of messengers towards the fortress.

"Sandwich?" he offered.

"That'd be nice," Farrah said.

Jason opened his inventory and frowned at the window.

"What is it? Farrah asked.

"I just noticed that something the Healer gave me isn't in my inventory anymore. How did it get taken out of my soul?"

"Could the Healer have taken it back?"

"I'm pretty sure he couldn't. Where did it go?"

More than an hour after their rest stop, Neil and Dustin finally stumbled upon signs of other people. Flashes of magic, not just white lightning but the smouldering red of fiery elemental magic, lit up in the distance. They stopped, huddled near a lightning rod.

"It must be quite the battle," Dustin yelled over the sound of rain. "That's a lot of flashing."

Neil pointed at the top of a tall mesa, closer to the battle than they were. Dustin followed his gaze, seeing a lightning bolt strike the top. It hit across not just one lightning rod but a ring of them, dancing around before being dissipated.

"We might actually see something from up there," Neil yelled.

"Looks like there might be something special up there," Dustin shouted back. "Worth checking out?"

Neil nodded and they moved in that direction, finding the mesa to be made up of smooth wet stone. Despite the realm only having existed for hours, it felt like the rain had been polishing the rock for centuries. Despite this, the climb was without mishap. Both Neil and Dustin were strong, even for their rank, and could push their fingers into the rock like pitons.

Reaching the top, they found the first signs of civilisation outside of the lightning rods. The rods themselves were much taller than normal, some twenty metres high. The lightning that struck them was not grounded, instead playing around the circle of rods, diminishing with each leap.

Underneath the rods, around three metres high, was a series of glass panels like slanted rooftops, sloping into funnels to direct the water flow. The rain was being collected in pipes that ran into the stone top of the mesa which itself was artificially flattened. That dry stone was red rather than charred black like everything else in the territory. The final feature was an elevating platform in the middle of the mesa top.

Under the cover of the glass roof, the constant hammering of thunder was muffled to almost nothing. Even with nothing but rain in the way, the lightning flashes were less blinding, as if seen through smoked glass. Both men let out sighs of relief.

"Is there a tiny man with a chisel in your head too?" Dustin asked with a wince. He grinned at not needing to shout.

"Yeah," Neil croaked, grinning back. "I never thought flat stone would look so luxurious. And I once spent six months in an astral space that was a broken city overgrown with jungle."

"What do you think this is?" Dustin asked, waving an arm at the elevating platform. "Do you think it works? If not, we could probably pry it up. This place must be at least partially hollowed out, right?"

"So it would seem," Neil said. "We should probably check out the battle before we take a look. I get the feeling it won't be a quick glance when we do."

"Yeah," Dustin said. "But just throwing an idea out there, how about we have a nice nap first? Pull out some bedrolls and sleep for… not that long. Two or three days, tops."

Neil chuckled and started peeling off the drenched clothing plastered to his body.

"That might be a bit much," Neil said, "but I will take a change of clothes first. Remind me to buy a better water shield when we get out of here. That's what I get for buying a rain deflector in the desert, I guess. I've had this one since Greenstone."

"Same," Dustin said. "This weather's heavier than anything the delta threw at us."

They stripped down, shared a vial of crystal wash and put on dry clothes. Only then did they move closer to the edge and look out at the battle. Despite the improved view, they couldn't see much more than flashes of magic through the dark and the rain.

"Well, that's not very helpful," Neil said.

"What did you expect, looking that far through the driving rain?" a voice said from behind them. They both spun around to see an unusual, but non-threatening, figure.

"What, you've never seen a four-foot humanoid rabbit in a top hat and tuxedo before? [Bleep]ing rubes. Wait, what the [bleep] was that? [Bleep]. [Bleep]. What the [bleep]? This is some grade-A bull[bleep]."

"You don't have four feet," Dustin pointed out. "You've got hands."

"It's a unit of measurement," Neil said. "I've heard Jason using it but he gets angry at himself when he does. He always blames dungeons for some reason. And also dragons somehow."

"What do dragons have to do with units of measurement?" Dustin asked.

"I don't know who your friend is," the rabbit said, "but it's not an actual dragon, you chuckleheads. It's a [bleep]ing game. Ah, [bleep] this [bleep] for a bag of [bleep]s. What [bleep]ing [bleep]hole installed a [bleep]ing bleeper in me?"

9

GRUNTS AND SIZZLING NOISES

NEIL AND DUSTIN SHARED A LOOK AS THE ANTHROPOMORPHISED RABBIT paced back and forth over the elevating platform, its low muttering punctuated by regular bleeping sounds.

"This is strange, right?" Dustin asked. "I know that we're adventurers roaming through a strange unreality after battling an undead army deep underground to win a tree by breaking the universe, but…"

Dustin trailed off and Neil gave him a curious look.

"But what?" Neil asked.

"It's fine," Dustin told him. "When I say it all out loud, suddenly, the rabbit-man who makes weird noises when he swears and the giant carnivorous radish aren't that outlandish."

"It was a turnip."

"Look, I love you, man, but I need to get back to my own team. Things around you get weird. And it was definitely a radish."

"It's not me, it's bloody Jason!" Neil complained loudly.

"Oh, so you can [bleep]ing well say [bleep]," the rabbit shouted in their direction. "That's not even a proper swear word. [Bleep] you, Neil!"

"How does it know your name?" Dustin asked.

"I'm a *he*, not an *it*, Kettering, you [bleep]. I identify as the guy that will beat the [bleep] out of you if you don't show me some [bleep]ing respect. Which will make you the guy who got beaten to death by an adorable mother[bleep]ing rabbit."

"Have you ever considered not swearing?" Dustin asked. "It seems to be making you quite angry."

"[Bleep] you."

"Do you know who we are?" Dustin asked him. "Also, what's your name?"

"How would I know who you are?" the rabbit asked. "I've only existed for about a day and the first people I had the misfortune to meet were you two chumps. And no, I don't have a name."

"He's very hostile," Neil said. "I think I know this rabbit."

"He just said he'd never met anyone before."

"But he knows us. I think I've seen this rabbit fishing inside Jason's soul."

"You do realise that you just said those words with a completely straight face, right?"

"It wasn't a joke. I really saw—"

"That's my entire point. I'm starting to understand why Rick always wants to go home."

"Can we get back on topic?"

"You mean the question of whether the angry rabbit-man popped into being with a bunch of knowledge or if he just has rabbit amnesia?"

"Is rabbit amnesia different from regular amnesia?"

"I don't know, Neil. This is my first talking rabbit."

"I don't know what's going on," Neil said. "It's probably memory loss from the transition from whatever he was to whatever he is now. I think he was some kind of spirit construct that couldn't leave Jason's soul realm, which is clearly not the case anymore."

Dustin glanced over at the humanoid bunny. It had stopped pacing and was looking out from the edge of the mesa while absently munching on a sandwich it didn't have earlier.

"But you believe it's the same rabbit?"

"I think so," Neil said. "There is a way to test it, though. Hey, rabbit. *Airwolf* is terrible."

"Yeah, no [bleep]," the rabbit said without turning around. "If you put Jan Michael Vincent in a magic room that could only be escaped with a display of nuanced thespianism, he'd starve to death in there."

"Yeah, that's Jason's rabbit," Neil said. "Rabbit, why do you remember things like our names when you're less than a day old?"

Expecting another tirade, they instead saw the rabbit turn around.

There was a look of unease in his expression, oddly easy to recognise despite his rabbit facial features. He took off his top hat, running the rim through his fingers as he looked at the ground.

"I don't know," he said, his voice subdued from its previous aggressive bluster. "I don't know where I come from, or who this Jason you're talking about is. I know things I have no reason to know. Your name, Dustin, or that Neil has trouble getting to sleep without his taxidermied piglet. I don't remember things from before I was here, but it's like I have the memory of having memories, if that makes any sense."

"We'll help you," Dustin said. "We think we know where you come from."

"Yeah, I got that much," the rabbit said, looking up to glare at them. "I've got giant [bleep]ing ears, remember?"

The rabbit's expression turned sullen with self-recrimination and his head dipped, not meeting their eyes.

"Sorry," he said, his voice soft again. "And thank you. I've kind of been at a loss up here. All alone, no idea where I am or…"

He cleared his throat in exaggerated masculine fashion as he jammed the hat back on his head.

"What are you two [bleep]s doing up here, anyway?" he asked, his voice back to normal. "You're trying to get a look at that battle over there?"

"We are," Neil confirmed.

"You'd best come with me, then."

The rabbit marched over to the elevating platform. It was an ordinary example of the type, a three-metre circle of metal set into the floor. Like most magic items, it was operated by simply reaching out with mana, control being instinctive. The rabbit sent it descending into the mesa through a shaft of smooth red stone.

Dustin turned to look at Neil as the platform carried them down. "I'd like to hear more about the taxidermy piglet."

"No, you wouldn't," Neil said.

"I'd say you're no fun, but I've heard about your taxidermy piglet."

"There is no taxidermy piglet."

"Are you accusing this sweet, innocent creature of being a liar?" Dustin asked.

"Given that he's neither sweet nor innocent, and knowing where he comes from, then yes. I'm saying he's a liar."

The rabbit held his hat in front of him, trembling as he looked up at Neil from his four-foot height with big rabbit eyes.

"Looking adorable doesn't get you a pass, rabbit," Neil said, although he turned his gaze to the wall instead of meeting the rabbit's.

The platform arrived in a wider room and stopped on reaching the floor.

"There are more rooms below," the rabbit said, "but this is the one you want."

The room was circular and large, although noticeably smaller than the mesa itself. This left a lot of supporting stone to prevent the upper reaches from collapsing in, and several support pillars around the room were engraved with magical reinforcement sigils. Around the edges of the room were several stations consisting of a seat in front of a metal box set into the wall and floor. Each box was solid and desk high, with numerous glowing runes on the top and drawers on the side. Set into the wall behind each station was a dark crystal panel.

"They look like the control panels for mirage chambers," Dustin said.

"Yeah," Neil agreed, looking them over. There looked to be several different panel layouts, each one repeated at least once. There were eleven stations in total, one of which stood out from the others. This panel was wider yet had fewer control runes. The screen set into the wall was also bigger than the others, the size of a large window.

The larger panel was the only one active, showing live images of the battle that Neil and Dustin had been looking for a vantage on. The screen showed a much closer perspective than looking off the side of the mesa, offering a clear view of what was going on. There was no sound to go with it, though, the moving image playing out in silence.

"This is what you were looking for, right?" the rabbit asked.

"Yes, thank you," Neil said as he and Dustin moved closer to the screen.

"I can turn the sound on if you like," the rabbit offered. "I wouldn't bother, though. It's mostly grunts and sizzling noises, like a porn movie set in a steakhouse."

"What's a—"

"Don't," Neil said, cutting Dustin off. He stood in front of the station, panning his eyes over the battle taking place.

"Where is the image coming from?" he asked. "Some kind of scrying device on the mesa?"

"No, it's a series of little drones," the rabbit said. "Basically just overblown recording crystals."

"My team uses ones like that," Dustin said. "They're expensive. Stealth magic, precision control, extended range. I'm guessing these ones are even more impressive, given the fancy control panels. And the lightning. Even small, they'd get hit by it sooner or later."

"They're actually powered by the lightning," the rabbit said. "It's an impressive setup."

"How do you know about all this?" Neil asked.

"I don't know," the rabbit said with a shrug. "I just woke up downstairs knowing how most of it works. I've been playing with it all day."

As they talked, they watched the battle playing out on the screen in front of them. The battlefield of thousands covered the same lightning-blasted landscape they had spent hours traversing themselves. The scale of the conflict meant there was no careful use of the rods to shield the combatants and lightning bolts regularly struck down into them.

The rough iron poles were scattered across the battlefield, just like everywhere else, but in the thick of the fighting, people got too close. More than once, the trio of observers watched lightning strike a rod only to arc off the pole and hit someone nearby. Unlike non-magical lightning, it seemed more interested in hitting people than obeying the laws of physics.

The lightning wasn't lethal if it hit a healthy silver-ranker, but it was debilitating enough to affect the same. Between the severe damage and paralysis it inflicted, anyone struck was soon killed by vindictive enemies or trampled by allies either oblivious or uncaring.

Most of the combatants were messengers, a thousand or more to each of three factions. There were also hundreds of undead amongst them. They clashed on the ground, feet churning up the mud. Any that took flight soon found the lightning more interested in them than the iron poles.

Each of the three messenger factions were visually distinctive. The largest group looked closest to normal messengers, but seemed to have been bleached, their skin pallid and hair a washed-out grey. Their glowing purple eyes were the only pop of colour; even their bland clothing was grey and blank. This faction was led by a trio of Undeath priests who were also controlling the undead.

Another faction was comprised of elemental messengers, much like those the expedition had fought through to reach the underground realm.

They had less of a maniacal frenzy to them and were commanded by brighthearts. The final and smallest group were led by Builder cultists and their messengers had been bizarrely modified with metal additions to their bodies.

"Are those pasty ones undead or just very unhealthy?" Neil asked.

"Let's check," the rabbit said. He moved to one of the other stations, hopping into a chair so he could access the control panel with his short height. He ran his adorable paw hands over the controls and the wall panel for that station lit up. It showed an example of each of the three messengers with lines of text underneath that neither Neil nor Dustin could read. The two men moved to look.

"I don't know that language," Neil said.

"Neither do I," Dustin added.

The rabbit shook his head with disapproval, hopped off the chair and moved around the metal siding of the control panel. He opened a drawer, took out a rod with a crystal on the end and pointed it at the two men. Light shone from the crystal, washing over the two men for less than a second.

"What is that?" Neil asked suspiciously.

The rabbit ignored him, hopping back on the chair and inserting the rod into a hole on the control panel. The text on the screen blurred and reformed, this time in the trade language common to merchants and adventurers the world over. In port cities like Greenstone and Rimaros, it was just as common with the populace as the local tongues.

The text gave facts on each of the three messenger types, the details written out in the same style as Jason's interface windows. Neil glanced over the first.

- Entity: Messenger slave.
- Affinity: Undeath.
- Recoverable: Yes. Undeath energy has not created a state of actual undeath. Removing that affinity is survivable but likely to have mental and physical side effects.

The elemental messengers had a similar entry.

- Entity: Messenger slave.
- Affinity: Elemental.

- Recoverable: Yes. Brightheart association has caused a stable elemental affinity. That affinity could be left intact or excised with minimal side effects.

The final example was different. While the first two messenger types could pass for normal messengers in very good cosplay, the final type could not. Their bodies had been segmented and were linked together by metal struts and joints, creating macabre figures that moved unnaturally and towered over the other messengers.

- Entity: Messenger slave.
- Affinity: Converted (Builder).
- Recoverable: No. Extreme body modification is reliant on Builder mechanisms to sustain life. Removing Builder control would trigger an automatic shut-down response from life support functions.

"This is why my messengers all stayed comatose," Neil said. "I don't have anything that can imprint on them like the Builder cult or the Undeath priests. Not while I'm cut off from the Healer."

"You should have taken a divine awakening stone or two," Dustin told him.

"I didn't need them. My family has more money than most, so those are best left to those who can't afford regular awakening stones."

"I didn't realise the gods had a limited supply," Dustin said.

"It's more like a quota they get to use. Like everything with the gods, the limit isn't about how much power they have but how much they can leverage. Using too much disrupts the balance between them and things get dangerous. I'm happy to leave the holy wars in the ancient past."

"An undead army led by priests of Undeath doesn't count as a holy war?" Dustin asked.

"Not compared to the fallen age," Neil said. "The historical records from that period are so scant because whole civilisations were wiped out. The world never saw that scale of global conflict again. Not until the Builder and messenger invasions, anyway."

"That would never happen," the rabbit said. "Religion is super harmless. It never leads to anything bad as contemporary values clash with those of the archaic belief systems people cling to without truly examining them."

"Definitely Jason's rabbit," Neil muttered.

"If we're going to fight a religious war," Dustin said, "we should lump the Builder cult right in with the undead." He pointed to the body-horror image of the magic cyborg messenger on screen. "I hate that we allied with those monsters."

"I think everyone involved agrees," Neil said. "Even the cultists. But sometimes every choice is bad. The brighthearts had to ally with them or they wouldn't have survived as long as they did."

"I know," Dustin said with a sigh. "We can't kill them to make ourselves feel better if it means holes in the universe or some kind of undead cataclysm. I'm not sure anyone told this lot, though. They can't get enough of killing each other."

They moved back to the large screen where the battle raged on, remaining a three-way conflict. The ostensible alliance between the brighthearts and the Builder cult was not being demonstrated, their messenger slaves fighting each other as much as those of the Undeath priesthood.

It wasn't just messengers on the field, although they were the vast majority. Each faction had Builder cultists, Undeath priests or brighthearts leading them, issuing commands and participating in the battle.

"That's a lot of messengers," Dustin said. "How many do you think?"

The rabbit hopped onto a chair and touched a couple of runes on the control panel. They went from dark to glowing green. On the large panel, each of the figures was outlined, mostly in silver. Some of the undead were marked in bronze, their weakness making it clear that the outlines were an indication of rank.

"That's useful," Dustin said. "How accurate is this?"

"Don't know," the rabbit said.

"No gold-rankers on any side," Neil pointed out. "We didn't get lucky or unlucky."

"We ended up here instead of in the middle of that fight," Dustin said. "I think we got plenty lucky."

Along with the outlines, text had appeared at the bottom of the screen.

- Total combatants: 5065.
- Undeath faction: 2461 (3 priests, 1828 messenger slaves, 630 undead)
- Brightheart faction: 1487 (19 brighthearts, 1468 messenger slaves)

- Builder faction: 1117 (9 cultists, 1108 messenger slaves)

The undead had the numbers, and while they only had three priests, each one was a powerful essence-user. Their individual impact on the battle outstripped any of their brightheart or cultist counterparts, and while their messengers were proving the least powerful of the three types, they were also the most numerous.

The undead were the weakest combatants on the field, especially the bronze-rankers, who were often mowed down incidentally. They were far from useless, however, even if only as shields or distractions. More important was their relation to the three priests whose abilities were tied to the undead. They boosted the weak undead to be more powerful, turned them into ambulatory bombs or sacrificed them for power.

Despite both being on the losing end of the battle, the brighthearts and Builder cultists fought each other as much as the undead.

"What are they thinking?" Dustin muttered. "I get that they hate each other, but even if they weren't allies, they clearly need to be."

"They aren't thinking," Neil said. "Not clearly. You and I were trained in everything from personal combat to command strategy from when we were children. The brighthearts lived in peace and isolation for generations before the Builder cult arrived. They never had the training in large-scale conflict. They weren't introduced to carefully chosen battles like we were, objectivity in combat drilled into us. These are people who have seen most of their population slain and turned into fertiliser or undead mockeries. They also don't seem to have any of their key leaders with them. It's not hard to imagine them stumbling into a fight like this, where the sky is dark and trying to kill them as much as their enemies are. Who wouldn't lash out in blind rage?"

"We can't leave it like this, though," Dustin said. "If the undead win, not only do we then have to deal with them ourselves, but we lose a lot of potential allies."

They looked at the numbers on the screen, declining as combatants fell.

"I just don't see how," Dustin continued. "We're just a pair of silver-rankers. As good or better than anyone down there, sure, but the two of us can't turn the tide in a battle of a thousand people."

"We have to convince the cultists and the brighthearts to stop fighting one another," Neil said.

"In the middle of a pitched battle where they have been and continue to slaughter each other?" Dustin asked.

"It won't be easy," Neil acknowledged. "If you have a better idea, I'm open to it."

"Maybe there's something in this place we can use," Dustin said.

They turned to look at the rabbit.

"Is there?" Neil asked.

"Sure," the rabbit said. "Did I not mention we can control the lightning from here?"

10

THE MAN WHO COMMANDS THE LIGHTNING

Rain hammered from a dark sky, the light choked off by black clouds that turned day into night. The erratic flashes of illumination were unwelcome, coming as they did from the deadly strikes of lightning. Each stroke of lightning passed, leaving fresh victims and thunder rumbling in the dark. The flashes meant that no one adapted to the lighting conditions.

In this battle, the powers possessed by the combatants were not those usually valued in open combat. In a pitched battle, the power to soar over the battlefield and drop large-area attacks was the ideal. In this case, humble perception powers were key. Anyone able to understand what was going on through the darkness, mud and chaos was a precious treasure.

Fearful of the lightning, no one took to the sky. The muddy ground had been turned to slurry by thousands of feet slamming down with the strength to smash rocks. Enemies were hard to tell from allies, especially when alliances were reluctant. The grace and power of silver-rankers had devolved into a slogging muddy brawl. Sodden clothes were plastered to bodies caked in mud. The icy chill of the rain crawled under armour and into every wound and body crevice.

The largest of the battle's three sides belonged to a trio of Undeath priests. The priests were elite essence-users, making them the strongest individuals on the field. Their pallid messengers and the undead they commanded were weaker than the opposing forces but compensated with sheer numbers. Two out of every three combatants belonged to their side.

The second-largest faction belonged to the brighthearts. They had more than twenty brighthearts before casualties, but only two had claimed territories and imprinted on messengers. One of these was Lorus, a fire-aspect brightheart whose messengers were likewise possessed of flame powers. Each was shrouded in steam as they evaporated the rain around them and flung out streams, bolts and exploding balls of fire.

Shielding the fire messengers were earth-affinity messengers. They had inherited the toughness of the massive brightheart Durrum, who led them from the front. Lorus was pushing aggressively, in spite of casualties, while Durrum was more conservative. He could feel the enemy numbers through the ground and knew that victory meant every life on their own side had to be traded for three or more of the enemy. He had no interest in being the last man standing in a field of death.

Both Lorus and Durrum had arrived in the territory after claiming another and looking to expand. While their standoff never came to blows, it lasted so long that the choice was taken from them. The Undeath priests and the Builder cult showed up almost simultaneously, each staking a claim.

The brighthearts naturally joined up to fight the interlopers, but Lorus had surprised Durrum by also attacking the Builder cult. Durrum hated the Builder cult as much as every other brightheart, yet had been willing to abide by their alliance. The Undeath faction's numerical advantage showed exactly why it was needed.

The Builder cultists had apparently thought the same and were surprised by the attack of the fire messengers. This swiftly devolved into a three-way battle, all to the benefit of the undead whose enemies fought amongst each other.

Durrum attempted to reconcile the Builder cult and the brighthearts, to little success. The cult was wary after the sneak attack and Lorus had no intention of stopping his offensive, even without the earth-element messengers. Durrum ordered his forces, brightheart followers and messengers, to do nothing but defend themselves and disengage from the cultists. Unfortunately for his efforts, the concept of orders was optimistic in the face of pounding rain, crashing thunder and brutal, chaotic battle.

Durrum was determined to unify the cultists and the brighthearts. He knew the attempt was almost certainly doomed, but almost certain was not absolutely certain. If things stayed as they were, he had no doubt they would all die, so he decided to make one last attempt to get Lorus to stop attacking the cult. If it failed, he would withdraw his forces in the hope that abandoning the field would prompt Lorus and the cult to do the same. They would lose the battle but at least some would survive. Not all would become meat for the necromancy of the priests.

Durrum fought his way close to Lorus. His earth powers left him unobstructed by mud and strong enough to hurl any obstacle aside, meaning enemy messengers or undead who got in his way. He tossed into the backline or straight up with his massive strength where lightning would strike them out of the air.

He came close to where Lorus was surrounded by his followers. The brighthearts other than Durrum and Lorus had split themselves into three groups, following one, the other or neither of the territory holders. Lorus was surrounded by his followers while Durrum had only one beside him, the rest still manning the frontline.

"LORUS!" Durrum roared. "Are you betraying us?"

"I'm not the one trying to make nice with Builder cult filth!" Lorus shouted back. "You think I don't see you backing off from every fight?"

"They're our allies! We need them and they need us, or the undead will kill everyone. Even with them, it's going to be a hard battle. Without them, we all die!"

"Help me kill the cultists and then we can focus on the undead."

"That won't work, Lorus. Every second we spend arguing or fighting the cultists takes us closer to defeat. You're killing us."

"I will burn out the cultists and I'll burn out the undead."

"Can you not count? We don't have the numbers. Even if we unify right now, we might get overrun anyway."

"We don't need numbers when we have the power!"

"What power? I don't know what you're talking about, but we don't have that!"

"Of course you don't think so, you earthen clot. Those of us who carry the fire know better."

"You're just talking about fire powers?" Durrum asked incredulously. "Then see how your fire messengers do without my earth messengers shielding them. I'm withdrawing and saving everyone I can. I suggest you do the same."

"Traitor!"

"Traitor? You attacked our allies! I'm not a traitor, Lorus. I just have my eyes open to see the completely gods-damned obvious."

"Durrum," the earth brightheart's companion said, grabbing the big man by the shoulder. "Something's happening."

Someone was saying the same to Lorus and they all turned to look at the frontline of the battle, as much as there was one in the chaos. The lightning that had plagued the battlefield was no longer coming down on everyone, but only the Undeath faction. Not only was the lightning suddenly target selecting, but it was also behaving abnormally.

After striking one target, the bolts arced to another, jumping from one target to the next like links in a chain. Each arc was weaker than the one that came before, diminishing until the power was expended. Even the lesser damage was still impressive and the bolts came down thick and fast. Some arcs even met, exploding in a discharge that was fairly weak but covered a wide area. Every arc brought a fresh peal of thunder, assaulting the air with a constant, violent crash.

"What is going on?" Durrum muttered, inaudible over the staccato rumbling.

Lorus proved more focused and opportunistic. While Durrum was distracted, he ordered his messengers to rise into the air and make a sweeping strike on the Builder cult. Realising what was happening at the last moment, Durrum dropped to his knees and plunged his hands through the elbow-deep mud and unto the earth below. The fire messengers, having risen into the air, unleashed a barrage of fire powers, from bolts and spears of flame to explosive fireballs and burning wheels, spinning through the air like fireworks.

Durrum dumped almost every scrap of mana he had, retaining just enough to stay conscious. A wall of stone erupted from the ground in front of the Builder cult's gathered forces, disappearing in a cloud of dust as the fire attacks landed on it. Blasting and sizzling sounds emerged from the dust, orange, yellow and white light flaring within.

Durrum knew that even expending all of his power was not enough to stop a barrage like that alone. Even so, he knew the cultists were not easy to kill and hoped they would withdraw. If they were alive, he at least had a chance to mend fences later.

The observers didn't wait long to see the results, the rain setting the dust within seconds. It was followed by a cloud of steam that lingered a little longer before also clearing.

The stone wall was all but gone, only a few shattered remnants left behind. Some sections had been detonated by the attack magic while others had melted through, leaving pools of lava throwing up more steam as the rain cooled it. The source of the larger steam cloud was a second wall behind the first, this one made of ice.

The ice wall was in better shape than the stone one, but not by much. Most of it had melted away, the resulting water disappearing in the rain and mud. Large chunks of ice were scattered around, but some slender sections of wall remained standing. They were chipped and cracked, often with shards of stone embedded in them.

Not many paid attention as an exhausted Dustin poked his head out from behind one. Most eyes were on the startled Builder cultists that had been shielded by the twin walls. Even with that protection, no small number of them looked frazzled by fire magic, but there had been no life-threatening injuries. The cultist messengers, body parts held together by metal joints and beams, were the most powerful of the messenger slaves. The cultists themselves were looking wary, watching for attacks from all sides. They were the only ones paying real attention to Dustin, who was just as spent as Durrum.

"THAT'S ENOUGH!" a voice bellowed from above. It carried past the rain and even cut through the thunder, clearly through the aid of magical enhancement. Neil descended through the air in a personal flight device in the shape of a cage with a curved iron top and bottom, connected by vertical bars. Electricity arced around it, over the cap, down the bars to the base and back up again. The fire messengers moved to surround him and Neil looked to Lorus.

"Have your forces descend," Neil ordered him. He spoke softly yet his voice carried.

"You're in no position to make demands, outsider," Lorus shouted.

Lightning struck Neil's cage, shrouding it in a storm of electricity before it subdued to the previous level.

"I won't ask again," Neil said, his voice filled with calm promise.

The air calmed with him, the lightning abating. The last peals of thunder finished rumbling, leaving only the sound of the rain. Even the battle had stopped as all eyes were on Neil.

"Don't be even more the fool, Lorus," Durrum said. "He's looking for someone to make a demonstration on. Don't give him a reason to make it you."

Lorus glared up at Neil but made an angry downward gesture and the messengers floated to the ground. Neil turned from Lorus to address the distant priests of Undeath, his voice flooding out from the cage.

"Priests. I command the lightning and you have tasted what that means. You have numbers enough that if you fight to the death it will cost us, but the death will be yours. If you yield your claim to this territory and leave, we will not chase. You can live to fight another day, in another place. One where the sky itself is not against you."

One of the brighthearts around Lorus yelled at Neil that they would never let the undead go. Neil didn't look, only casually pointed. The bolt of lightning didn't kill the man and Neil cast a spell, still without looking. Life Bolt was a healing spell faster than it was powerful, but it would keep the man alive. Neil turned to look at Lorus who glowered back but stayed silent. A small smile crossed Neil's face and he turned his gaze back across the battlefield to look at the distant priests.

"Well?" he demanded, but he already had his answer. The undead and the pale messengers were already pulling back. None gave chase; no one was foolish enough to cross the man who commands the lightning.

11

STYLE OVER SUBSTANCE

THE BRIGHTHEARTS AND THE CULTISTS HAD GATHERED UNDER A humungous stone arch not far from the battlefield. It was the best shelter they had found while roaming the territory before the battle. There wasn't enough room for all the messengers who had been left scattered around various lightning rod poles.

The space was large enough to fit all of the cultists and brighthearts comfortably. Comfortable was relative in the lightning fields, but hard earth instead of knee-deep mud was a welcome change. It was sufficiently sheltered that the stone over their heads and the dirt under their feet was red instead of scorched black. It didn't keep the thunder from rolling in, though, the lightning having resumed its normal behaviour.

Neil had left the cage, diplomatically putting himself on the same level as the other faction leaders. Lower, given his lack of messenger slaves. He did not miss the avaricious looks that the brightheart and cultist leaders, Lorus and Higgins, were giving the cage. The other brightheart leader, Durrum, had shown little interest. Neil hoped that was out of honourable intentions and not just the massive brightheart being too big to fit inside.

The two brightheart factions and the cult were arrayed in a contentious triangle with the leaders, Neil and Dustin in the middle. Neil's threats and the protective wall used by Durrum and Dustin had at least kept the cultists from attacking the brighthearts on sight, enough that all sides agreed to talk it out.

The question was what to do with not just the territory they were in, but the territories already claimed. Would they unify them into a whole or leave them as separate entities? On realising that Neil had a territory but no messengers, and seeing him out of the cage, Lorus had started loudly grandstanding.

"What makes you think you can come here and start giving orders?" Lorus demanded. "Your intervention was welcome, of course, but it does not…"

Thunder crashed, muffling his words and forcing him to repeat himself.

"…it does not put you in a position to claim the territory. If you can't build a messenger army, then you don't meet the qualifications to lead us through what lies ahead."

That struck a chord with the others, and not just with Lorus' group. Durrum's followers were less performative about it but showed clear agreement with the point.

"We don't want a slave army," Neil said.

"Speak for yourself," Lorus said. "I definitely want a slave army, and I don't see you convincing anyone else to give up theirs. Not only do we get to use our enemies as weapons but without the messengers, we wouldn't have had the forces to defeat the undead priests."

"Strictly speaking, they were Undeath priests, not undead priests," one of the brighthearts behind Durrum said. "They were alive."

All eyes turned to her and her dark brown skin kindly hid her blush.

"Which is not important enough that it was worth the interruption," she said. "I see that now."

The leaders turned their gazes back on one another and Dustin spoke up.

"You seem to have forgotten that your messengers weren't enough to defeat the Undeath priests. You were on the losing end of that battle until we came along, and we didn't have any."

"You found a way to command the lightning," the cultist Higgins pointed out.

"Yes," Dustin said. "We were moving in a small group. All but impossible to find in this place. Faster to move than an army, especially one wading through mud and dodging lightning. How much time did relaying all your messengers from storm rod to storm rod cost you? In the meantime, we didn't stumble into battle and instead investigated the thing that won it."

Neil knew exactly how much of what Dustin described was dumb luck, but he wasn't going to say anything.

"If you weren't hauling around an army of messengers," Dustin continued, "you wouldn't have needed the battle. Do you have any idea how hard it is to spot anyone out there? A small group could have used the environment to strike from hiding and take down the priests in one fell swoop. Instead, you waded into a losing fight."

"A battle where not only were you outmatched, but you then made things worse by fighting one another," Neil pointed out.

"We approached in good faith and were ambushed," the cultist Higgins said.

"Is that true?" Neil asked, looking at Durrum, but it was Lorus that answered.

"We should never have—" Lorus began, only for Neil to cut his tirade off before it got going.

"It's clear what happened here, then," Neil said. "And who is responsible."

He turned to Higgins.

"We'll never get along well," he told the cultist. "Not you and us or you and the brighthearts. But I do believe we can get along well enough to get out of this alive. We all know that the outcomes here won't be great for anyone, and worse for some than others. But getting out alive is better than dying in reality's butt-crack. I'm asking you, all of you, to put aside what just happened and look forward."

"We can," Higgins said. "So long as the fire brightheart gives up his territory to someone else. We cannot work with him while he still commands messengers. He won't give it up to us, I know, but we would accept his giving it up to you, or even the other brightheart. The earth one."

"I will not hand over my power on their say-so," Lorus said. "Those cultist abominations invaded our city. They were the beginning of the end for our entire people!"

"Yes," Neil agreed calmly.

"Believe us that we have no love for their kind," Dustin added. "With the things they've done, I'd love to execute them out of hand. But we allied with them for a reason, as distasteful as it is for them and us. There's a larger picture."

"Fine," Lorus said. "If they want to work with us, they can cede this territory and surrender their existing territory to us. And since I represent the larger portion of the brightheart forces—"

"Because you hid yours behind mine and let them do the dying," Durrum interrupted.

The two brightheart leaders started arguing over one another until Neil's voice rang out.

"STOP!"

The brighthearts were silenced less by Neil's voice than the two lightning bolts that struck the ground to either side of the arch, sending thunder crashing through like a sonic weapon.

"No," Neil said in the aftermath, his calm voice contrasting with the bluster of the two brighthearts. "You're not getting the territory, Lorus, and you know that. You're just trying to establish a negotiating position you can argue from to keep your own territory. But we've seen your leadership and it will bury us all."

"You don't have any messengers," Lorus said. "You can't control them, can you?"

"I can't imprint on them," Neil admitted, "and I don't think I should. I don't want a slave army."

"We don't have a choice," Durrum said. He had calmed down, but the earth brightheart's voice still carried a deep, arresting rumble. "I don't like using these things, but our enemies will. We have to match them."

"You already tried that, and what did it get you?" Dustin asked. "Two brighthearts and a cultist, all with messengers, and you still would have died without the people who had none."

"Because you found a way to control the lightning," Durrum pointed out. "If you can bring that power into each new territory, I will agree to your leadership. If we could expand this territory from here on all sides and use the lightning to wipe out the anomalies, that would be one thing. But almost all the border territories here have been claimed already. By you, me, Lorus and Higgins. By the Undeath priests as well, and they won't come back. They'll make us come to them."

"He is right," Higgins said. "They are probably still one or two territories bordering this one, but that is not enough to justify handing all our territories and their messengers over to you. I think the earth brightheart will make the better leader than either of you adventurers. If nothing else, who is to say if the messengers would even survive passing into your control?"

"Yours would not," Neil told him flatly. "Outside of Builder cult control, your messengers will die, be that under my command or Durrum's. The elemental messengers will not, but that doesn't matter. We shouldn't be using them at all."

"If there was time to indulge in ideals," Higgins said. "You would all be fighting me like the fire one wants to."

"It's not just a matter of ideals," Neil said. "We can't play a numbers game with the Undeath priests. With every territory they claim, their numbers grow more than ours. Not only do they pick up the undead we have to fight, but when we win a fight, our numbers drop. They turn the fallen into undead servants, allies and enemies alike. It's what makes the church of Undeath so dangerous. Why they are so thoroughly stamped out whenever and wherever they are found."

"If we had lost," Dustin said, "everyone here would have joined their army. We can't fight them on their terms because we'll lose. That's the undeniable weight of numbers and everyone here just felt it. You're all talking like the messengers are the only way, but you've just seen what that will get you. We have to fight them on our terms, not theirs. Find other ways. In this place, the lightning was the key. Other territories will have other quirks we can use. It might be as simple as territory well-suited to hit-and-run attacks, or some strange magic like the lightning."

"We need to move as a lean, efficient, elite force," Neil said. "While they are lugging around their ponderous army, we fight smarter, not harder. The adventurer way."

"This is all just you trying to make the messengers not matter," Loris said. "If we need the messengers, then you're off the table as the one to unify the territories."

"It doesn't matter who unifies it," Neil said, "so long as they don't lead the rest of us to oblivion. In the end, the territories will all go to Jason Asano. That's the only way we get out of this place instead of dying along with everyone and everything you've ever known, Lorus."

"Then give the territories to me," Lorus said. "Once everyone actually obeys, I will make us stronger as we go. I'll show you that we can fight the undead. Our messengers are stronger than theirs."

"And ours are stronger than yours," Higgins said. "By that standard, I should be the one to unify the territories. If you take ours, the strongest messengers we have will die. The adventurers admitted that."

"How do they even know?" Lorus asked.

"The same way I command the lightning," Neil lied. It was the rabbit watching through surreptitious drones who was commanding the lightning from the mesa. Neil appreciated the dramatic flair with which the rabbit used it, not that he'd ever admit it. Jason's stance on style over substance was not something Neil would allow to propagate, even if adventuring was *occasionally* about how good you look doing it.

"How do you control the lightning?" Durrum asked. "I think that is something that should be shared."

"And I will," Neil said. "With the person that ends up unifying the territories. All of them. Higgins, you know we won't let it be you. Any more than we will Lorus."

"Don't think you can speak for everyone, outsider," Lorus said. "Yes, the cult messengers are strong, but we won't allow the cult to lead us. The earth messengers are tough, but you are right about the undead's numbers. What you failed to mention was that those numbers are weak individually. Their messengers are weak and their undead weaker. My fire messengers have the offensive power to wipe them out fast and make those numbers irrelevant. Giving the territories to me is the only responsible choice. You're painting me as ambitious, but the truth is, I'm the only one who can lead us to success. I only want the power to lead us all out of here."

"So you say," Neil told him, "but talk is easy. Actions tell the real story, and what have your actions told us about your intentions, Lorus? What do they say about your reason for wanting all the power? If the benefit of all was your objective, the way you claim, you would have put aside your distaste and allied with the Builder cult. I don't think leading everyone to safety is what your actions tell us."

"You—" Lorus was cut off by Durrum.

"You spoke your piece, Lorus," the earth brightheart rumbled. "Let the aboveworlder finish."

"Thank you," Neil said with a nod to Durrum. He turned back to Lorus and continued.

"Your actions, Lorus, tell us that you like the power. Having command of all these messengers. Your leaders aren't here to tell you what to do and you've been revelling in the authority. Indulging in something it feels like you've wanted for a long time. Even if we gave you all the territories here and let you lead us, it would only last so long. Sooner or later, you will have to hand over the power that you've built. That you've earned. Whether to one of your gold-rankers or to Jason Asano."

"Of course," Lorus said.

"Are you genuinely willing to do that, though?" Neil asked. "Or do you have some idea in your head of accruing so much power for yourself that you can decide how this ends? Strike down the Builders, do as you will? Force Jason to show you how to unify the territory yourself and come out of this as ruler of the brighthearts? You know that you all have to capitulate to him, right? Your kind has no recourse but to obey him. He may be a stranger to your realm, but it's his to rule now."

Neil was gambling that he understood Lorus, despite having just met him. He was confident the fire brightheart was a volatile mix of ambition, impatience and pride, with an unearned sense of entitlement. He and Dustin understood the type better than most. He remembered how easily Jason had provoked Thadwick in those early meetings, prodding him until he erupted. The fire brightheart did the same when Neil kept poking.

"THIS IS NOT SOME OUTSIDER'S PLACE TO TAKE!" Lorus roared. "You have come here and torn our home asunder, but it is still our land! Our land to fight for and our land to rule!"

"And you're the one to rule it?" Neil asked calmly. "With an army of brainwashed slaves? Your people have been fighting the elemental messengers for how long? And now you're going to use them to seize power?"

"These messengers obey. And so will everyone else, so long as I have them!"

Lorus realised he had gone too far and looked around at the faces of his fellow brighthearts.

"We have leaders," Durrum said, his voice as soft as the sound of grinding gravel could be. "They are wise leaders, who have led us through greater tragedy than any of us thought we could endure. They have earned our trust with sacrifice and sage guidance. Look around you, Lorus. None here will follow you and your ambition. Not anymore."

Lorus looked around again, seeing that Durrum was right. Even his own followers failed to meet his eyes, their faces showing disgust, disdain or disappointment.

"Lorus cannot lead," Durrum announced to the group. "But the cultist was right that we should not give up the power of the messengers. Ideals are all well and good, but they avail you nothing if you're dead. The Undeath priests are not shy about taking control of the messengers, and neither should we be. These messengers were grown in pods, using our people as fertiliser. We will use them in turn and, when we're done, put them down like the twisted creations they are."

"Then you will lose," Dustin said. "You may not be Lorus, but you don't know how to lead an army. That much was clear from the battle we just saw. Neil and I have been taught strategy and large group tactics, and you know what we've learned? Just enough to realise that neither of us should command an army either. We don't have the experience to make it work, especially when the Undeath priests will be growing their forces faster than we can."

"We've already said it," Neil added. "We need to be fast and effective, not ponderous and unwieldy. Armies are hard to move and harder to feed. I suspect that even these messengers need to eat, but the undead ones maybe not. They're weaker than yours, but I bet that's a trade-off. Do you have a spirit coin supply? A food supply? My territory is lush and replete with food, and I imagine some of you can say the same. But this place has nothing, and marching a hungry army through more barren territories will turn them from a weapon into an anchor."

"If we move as a small group," Dustin said, "without messenger slaves, we can carry enough food that we only have to resupply so often. Fast and effective. Hitting the Undeath priests and taking out their territory leaders while they are still trying to establish and consolidate. They have the numbers, so instead of trying to match them and falling short, we should use those numbers against them. Leave them with the weaknesses of an army while we gain the advantages of an elite strike force."

"You talk a lot," Lorus said. "But all I hear are reasons that we should hand over what brighthearts have won to you."

"Then don't," Neil said. "The cult has already said they will follow Durrum. I will accept that as well, under the condition that he is at least willing to explore small-group tactics. To see for himself whether motivated champions or enslaved armies are the way forward."

"Durrum," Lorus said. "Don't let this outsider lead you to disaster. Without enough messengers—"

"I am willing to trust in our people," Durrum said. "In the strength *we* have, not that of the monsters we've shackled. You have never been content with what you have, Lorus, long before today. Always wanting more. Coveting that which was not yours. If these aboveworlders are wrong, then I will use the messengers. But first, I will see for myself what we can accomplish by relying on each other."

"And if I refuse to hand over my territory?" Lorus asked, pulling himself up to his full height. It didn't have the effect he hoped, given that the earth brightheart, Durrum, stood head and shoulders above him.

"Then you will die," Durrum said. "If you use your messengers to fight under this arch, you will have no range and die quickly. If you fight under open sky, you will face the lightning in the air. On the ground, my earth messengers will make short work of you. Give up your ambitions, Lorus. They have cost us already, but we will forgive and accept if you're willing to come back to the fold now. This is your last chance."

"It's a shame," Durrum said as one of the brighthearts carried away Lorus' body. "He was a fool, but a strong fool."

"We need strength," Neil said. "But even the greatest strength can be sapped away by poison, and that man was poison."

Durrum nodded his acknowledgement. "I don't like how that went, but perhaps it was for the best. Now, I will accept your territory and you can show me how to command the lightning."

1 2

PRECISE CONTROL

NEIL, DUSTIN AND DURRUM RODE A FLAT STONE THROUGH THE MUD LIKE a barge, courtesy of Durrum's earth powers. Neil looked up at the sky, guessing it might be sundown, but it was hard to tell when he blanket of black clouds made for perpetual night. At least the lightning bolts were avoiding them, courtesy of the rabbit controlling them from the mesa.

"It was weird seeing a bunch of messengers eating root vegetables, right?" Dustin asked.

"Definitely," Neil agreed.

The area that had once been his territory now belonged to Durrum, and he was surprisingly happy about that. After claiming the territory, he'd experienced a growing sense of power, but in its absence, he now felt relief. He didn't realise it until the power was gone, but something about it hadn't quite fit. Like an octagonal peg forced into a round hole, it worked but didn't belong. That the power had blinded him to that made him reassess the behaviour of Lorus.

The stone they rode ploughed through the mud, no small amount flying up to spatter them. Given that mud was unavoidable in this territory, they hadn't bothered to clean themselves again. The stone arrived at the base of the mesa and stopped.

"This is it?" Durrum asked in his rumbling voice.

"This is it," Dustin confirmed.

At the base of the mesa, just above the mud line, a section of stone drew back into the surrounding rock and then slid aside, revealing a passage. Neil hopped off the stone they stood on and went inside, the others following.

"This was here the whole time?" Durrum mused.

"There are advantages to not having to wrangle an army," Neil said. "Yes, you'll stumble into more things out in the open, but you're too busy to dig around and find the hidden treasures."

The tunnel ended in an elevating platform that carried them up, passing several floors along the way. The rooms were round and largely empty, although one had sleeping alcoves cut into the wall.

"We'll need to sort out some furnishings," Neil said. "But this will make a nice, secure home base."

"It's nice that we can access storage bags and storage spaces again," Dustin said, "but I don't know how many people brought furniture in them. But even natural materials in those alcoves could make them a pleasant enough place to sleep."

"I like sleeping on hard rock," Durrum said. "Beds are too soft. I don't know how much time we'll spend sleeping, though."

"Some, at least," Neil said. "According to Jason, his previous transformation zone experiences each lasted more than a month."

The replica of Jason's hometown was looking a little worse for wear after a sequence of territory captures. Each neighbouring territory into which he'd expanded his influence caused a stream of living anomalies to spill out of it, across the boundary and into his previously claimed land. The volcanic territory had gone as well as could be hoped, the town not getting much more than singed around the edges. Farrah had done most of the work of keeping the anomalies modelled after fire, earth and magma elementals in check.

Jason's claimed land was not entirely land, with the boundary to a couple of territories cutting through the water offshore. One ran along the beach while another fronted the marina where Jason had once lived in a cloud houseboat on Earth. This was the one he had expanded into most recently, unleashing living anomalies in the form of aquatic and amphibious creatures. Octopi that walked awkwardly on land, lobster centaurs and an army of shabs, the crab-shark hybrids that left Jason nostalgic.

By the time the living anomalies had stopped emerging, the marina was an ugly black soup with dead monster croutons. Jason stood on the roof of the harbourmaster's office with Sophie and Farrah, all three were wincing at the smell.

"That is genuinely foul," Sophie said with watering eyes. "Even reducing my sense of smell right down, that is piercing."

"It's not quite as bad as rainbow smoke," Farrah said, "but it's close, and there's just so much of it."

"My first monster was a shab," Jason reminisced. "I stabbed it from underneath a few times and got some stinky goo on me. Never had much time to think about it, though. I was investigating a magic waterfall inside a mountain that had turned off and it turned back on again, blasting me right off the side of the mountain."

"I remember that," Farrah said. "I missed it because... what was I doing again?"

"Looking for the person that set you up with the cannibals," Jason said. "But Anisa killed him before he could talk."

"And then Rufus kicked her out of the group, yeah," Farrah said.

"Why does all the fun stuff happen to you two?" Sophie asked.

"I'm not the one who put all my character points into appearance instead of luck," Jason muttered.

"Don't go including me," Farrah said. "I wasn't even there for the waterfall thing. I'm not the one who gets all the exciting adventures."

"You came back from the dead in another universe," Sophie pointed out.

"Only because Jason was doing it already and they gave him a plus one."

"Yeah, but you were there," Sophie said. "When will I get to go to another universe? Or find a mountain in the shape of my head?"

"I think yours would be more popular than Jason's," Farrah said, turning to look at the fortress. Sophie did the same.

"What's in the chin?" Sophie wondered. "Extra storage? A theatre maybe?"

"It's not that big," Jason said.

"It's not small," Farrah said. "Have you ever noticed that now the inside of Jason's hood isn't completely dark, his chin kind of sticks out?"

"I have," Sophie said. "I thought it had gotten a lot smaller as he ranked up, but that beard is doing a lot of work. Seeing it in silhouette really shows off the size."

"As does carving an enormous version of it out of stone," Farrah observed.

"Now that I think about it," Jason said in a shameless attempt to change the subject, "the shab wasn't my first monster, just my first iron-rank one."

"Lesser monsters don't count," Farrah said.

"You say that," Jason told her, "but you didn't see the potent hamster. They like to jump and bite, two very unwelcome things when you don't have pants."

"We don't need to hear about you not having pants again," Farrah said.

"Not even a pair of boxer shorts," Jason said with a winsome shake of the head.

"How about we get away from this smell?" Sophie asked. "Why are we even expanding from this territory? Didn't you want to protect your town from damage?"

"That's why we're doing these first," Jason said. "All through the transformation zone, our allies and enemies are claiming territories as well. With each one, the remaining territories grow more dangerous."

"So, we're taking these neighbouring ones while we have the best chance to reduce the damage?" Sophie asked.

"Exactly."

"And you're saving the mountain range for later," Farrah said. "Now that you can control the winds, there it will be a big advantage."

"Yeah," Jason said. "This ability to use the environment as a control-lable weapon is new to me. It wasn't a feature of the previous zones I've been in. And if there's one territory where that can be done, I have to assume there's more."

"We'll have to be careful about entering occupied zones," Sophie pointed out. "We don't want some Undeath priest setting off earthquakes under our feet or something."

"Maybe," Jason said. "I'm not sure how much precise control they'll have over their territories. I'm built for claiming territories. If Undeath showed his priests how to claim and unify territories properly, then maybe. I can control the wind there, but I don't think most people claiming that territory could. Anyone that can is a threat, so you're right, Sophie. We need to be careful about pushing into occupied zones."

"Should I start giving them a thorough scout before we decide to make a move?" Sophie asked.

"Yeah," Jason said. "I think that's a good idea."

"Well, pick which one you want to go for next," Sophie said. "I'll check it out while you go pick up your next set of messengers from the water territory."

The gold-rank messengers in Belinda's group had been unable to agree on which of the two would lead their group, claiming and unifying the territories. Resolving that difference of opinion had left the survivor, Kol Kelis Vel, with a supply of gold-rank messenger body parts for use in rituals.

The group now consisted of the now-singular gold-rank leader and most of a second gold-ranker being carried in a trio of sacks by one of the five silver-rankers. That duty fell to Cas Vin Baral, who had drawn the ire of the gold-rankers and himself been used as a source of ritual materials.

Another of the five was Belinda, who had not missed the glee of Cas at the gold-ranker's death. Since the gold-ranker had been tormenting Cas and using him for ritual parts, she found his attitude to be fair.

She'd been observing the others as she continued formulating a plan, deciding who would be an asset, a liability or an obstacle. Cas was a complainer, an idiot and too caught up in his sense of persecution to be a problem. The occasional nudge from Belinda kept that persecution coming, just to make sure.

Two of the remaining silver-rankers were sheep, going wherever they were shepherded. They would get in her way, given the chance, but lacked the imagination to be a real hindrance. They could always get lucky, though, so Belinda didn't dismiss them entirely.

The real problem was the final silver-ranker. He was quiet, but not like the two sheepengers. When they went quiet, it was like they turned their brains off to avoid wasting magic charge until they were given their next instruction. This last messenger was quiet because he kept his mouth shut and ears open, a dangerous trait in an enemy. He was always watching but rarely spoke, to the point that she hadn't even gotten his name yet. She'd caught him watching her more than once.

If she knew what his motivation was, she'd be a lot happier. Did he see her as a threat to the upper position amongst the silver-rankers? The other three certainly weren't. Did he suspect her? Had he known the messenger whose identity she stole well, or notice that she floated around a little differently from the others?

Any silver-ranker could levitate unless their training was either non-existent or utterly shambolic. Doing so with the effortless finesse of a messenger was another thing entirely, as she could fake the feel of their auras, but not the abilities. That was why, before infiltrating the group, she'd installed floating devices in her clothes. Into the toga-like outfit with sandals, she'd incorporated spots where the devices could be slipped in without being noticed.

The devices were designed for moving heavy cargo that couldn't be placed in dimensional bags. She'd been using them for years, although rarely for their intended purpose. An innovative adventurer found almost as much use for them as an innovative thief. It wasn't even the first time she'd made a levitation suit out of them, so it didn't take too much practise before she was ready. As long as she wasn't under close observation during heavy action, she was confident she had enough precise control to pass for a messenger using their aura to float.

Or so she had been. Perhaps the final silver-ranker was onto her, either waiting to take advantage or looking for proof before making a play. Whatever shape her final plan ended up taking, it would involve dealing with him.

Durrum made a sound like gravel being crushed as he looked at the panel inside the mesa's lightning control room. Neil, Dustin and the rabbit were watching from the far side of the room.

"Is he angry or getting ready to poop?" the rabbit asked.

The other two gave him a reprimanding look.

"What?" the rabbit asked. "All he does is make different rock sounds. Can you tell the difference?"

"He can hear us," Dustin said. "Even if you whisper."

"Yeah, but he needs me," the rabbit told him. "And he won't go [bleep]ing off the healer either, but you're expendable."

"What does he need you for?" Dustin asked.

"Because I cannot understand these controls!" Durrum said angrily from across the room. "This is my territory. Why will it not obey me?"

"Because you aren't built to rule it," Neil said. "It has to be someone like Jason Asano. Who you agreed to hand everything over to, remember? The way Lorus wouldn't."

Durrum marched across the room to loom over the rabbit.

"You know how this place works," he said, more accusation than question.

"Yep," the rabbit said, not bothering to look up at him. "Also, can you back off? You're twice my height, which leaves me looking at a bag of rocks. Congratulations on what you've got going on there, by the way, but not what I want hanging in front of my face."

"You will tell me how to control this place," Durrum said.

"Not going to move, okay. I'm just going to pop around you and get some space on my own there."

The rabbit ducked around him and into the middle of the room. Neil observed that this put the rabbit atop the elevating platform, although the rabbit didn't activate it. Durrum turned to face the rabbit.

"You must obey me, creature."

"Is that so?" the rabbit asked. "As you've just pointed out, I'm the only one who can run this place. Where I came from, that's what we call leverage."

"You don't come from this territory?" Durrum asked. "Where do you come from, then?"

"How the [bleep] would I know?"

"You just said they do something a certain way where you're from," Durrum pointed out. "How would you know that if you don't know where you come from?"

"I know, right? I'm a man of mystery. Or a rabbit of mystery. Rabbit-man of mystery? No, that sucks. I'm going to stick with man of mystery."

"STOP BABBLING NONSENSE!" Durrum roared. Though his voice did not literally shake the room, it felt like it did.

"Say it, don't spray it, mate."

Durrum lumbered in the rabbit's direction only for Neil to duck between them.

"It's fine," he assured the brightheart, whose rage made the large room feel small.

Neil then turned to the rabbit.

"You need to show him some respect," Neil said.

"I'm open to that," the rabbit said, "but respect is a two-way street. Which part of the phrase 'you must obey me, creature' has the respect in it? The part where I'm his slave or the part where I'm his pet?"

Neil took a calming breath.

"Sometimes in life, rabbit, you have to be the bigger man. Especially when you're the smaller one."

"Sure. But once I've taught that guy how to run this place, he's going to snap my neck in as little time as it takes him to grab it. Tell me I'm wrong with a straight face and I'll start teaching him right now."

Neil's lips pressed together unhappily.

"Rabbit, can you go downstairs and give us all a chance to cool down?"

"My [bleep]ing pleasure," the rabbit said, the elevating platform descending before he'd finished the sentence. A metal plate slid out and up to fill the hole in the floor and Neil turned back to Durrum.

"Durrum, I know the rabbit is annoying. Dear gods, do I know, because I have a better idea where he came from than he does. Which is why what I know and the rabbit does not is that if you kill him, what comes for you will be worse than anything this transformation zone can throw at you."

"Is that a threat?"

"It's a warning, Durrum. Honestly, we can probably stop him from killing you, but he'll be angry enough at you that Lorenn and Marla will be angry at you too, for putting him in that mode."

Durrum frowned at the mention of the brightheart leaders.

"You're talking about Jason Asano."

"I am," Neil said.

Durrum nodded and his body language settled until he no longer looked like a carnivorous mountain.

"Asano took what was left of my people and gave them a haven," Durrum said. "My family. I would never do anything to offend him."

"Then let me make a suggestion. Some people don't get along with Jason, and there's a lot of him in that rabbit. The best thing in those situations is to have a go-between. This place is complicated to control. You don't want to learn how anyway because you're not going to stay in here and use it. You're going to be out there, leading and fighting."

Durrum nodded.

"Pick out some of your people," Dustin said, moving to join the conversation. "Some of the ones who are a bit smarter than the rest but won't be missed as much on the battlefield."

"Smart fighters are good fighters," Durrum said.

"True," Dustin said, "but pick some smart ones anyway. Let the rabbit teach them, since this place will work better with more people at all these control panels."

"There are more panels than we have people to spare," Durrum said.

"I'll bring some messengers to control it. Unless you are against using them for even that, healer."

"That seems fine," Neil said. "I just don't like the idea of sending people to their death when they don't get a choice in the matter."

"We don't get a choice in the matter," Durrum said.

"Yes, we do, and you know it," Neil said. "We could hole up in here, use the lightning to protect us and wait for allies to come. But if you tell those messengers to go die, they will. Even if, inside their heads, they're screaming in fear and despair."

"I think you give them too much credit," Durrum said. "They are unfeeling monsters."

"Maybe," Neil said. "But I think you know how it feels when the only thing between you and death is misery and a complete inability to control your own fate. I want to see if we can check before feeding them into the meat grinder."

"You let the cultist messengers die."

"Some are beyond saving," Neil said. "As a healer, it's the hardest thing to accept, but we have to. We can't do what we do otherwise, and it makes us fight all the harder to save the rest."

"So you say, but how many have you participated in killing?"

"Too many," Neil admitted. "I'm not perfect. All we can do is our best. And when we get it wrong, when we make bad choices, the best we can do is learn from them and make better ones."

Durrum shook his head.

"Those are the words of a man who has not watched his civilisation die. Who has not seen nineteen out of every twenty get massacred. I don't want to be better. I want victory. I want vengeance. I want to scour the world of everyone who came to my home and killed in search of plunder. Who used the bodies of the people I love as fertiliser to grow more killers. As meat to build deathless abominations. If I have my way, I will drive every messenger to the most painful death I can manage, the moment we're done with them. I will hunt every cultist, yank the metal from their bodies and beat them to death with it. I will burn every priest and stamp their ashes into the mud until I'm sure that they're dead. I will kill and kill and kill until all that is left is the knowledge in every place and every people that this is what happens when you come for the brighthearts."

Neil looked at Durrum, the big man's eyes wet with tears. He said nothing.

13

IMPOSTOR SYNDROME

With each territory Belinda's group claimed, the number of messengers in their group expanded. The messengers brought from stasis weren't abnormal like the elemental messengers of the soul forge tree; they were instead ordinary, if rather confused. The gold-ranker, Kol Kelis Vel, no longer had a peer to discuss the situation with and had taken to using a silver-ranker instead.

Of the silver-rankers, Relia Vin Vala had proven the pick of the bunch. Most of them knew when to keep their mouths shut, but only Relia had both the boldness to open hers occasionally and have something worth saying when she did.

They based their operations out of the territory where Kol could use concentrated sunlight as a weapon. Kol and Relia stood side by side on a jutting cliff, looking out over the flatlands from the solitary mountain.

"The messengers coming out of stasis," Kol said. "Each territory hands them over as rewards for its conquest and I am concerned about their provenance."

"I would imagine they are the elemental messengers the tree created when we were tainted," Relia said. "We were purged of the tree's influence on reaching this place, so it stands to reason that they were as well. But they are not imprinted until someone claims the territory."

"I agree with that assessment," Kol said. "My concern is with the nature of the imprinting. Are they copying the imprint on our souls, that of Vesta Carmis Zell?"

"You wonder if, being cut off from the astral king, they are being imprinted by you?"

"I do wonder that, yes. These new messengers obey, but they seem confused and uncertain."

"This is the first time they have existed with clear heads," Relia pointed out. "They have not been shown our ways. They are yours to shape."

"But they are also a danger. If they have been imprinted by me, I have intruded on the domain of astral kings. Once we leave this place and Vesta Carmis Zell can reach us again, she might destroy me for the temerity."

"Then use them for now, and kill them when we reach the end. Destroy the power in your hands and show your loyalty."

Kol turned to give Relia an assessing look.

"I did not know you before we were sent below," Kol said. "Was your leader with us?"

"Yes," Relia said. "He was not turned by the tree; he fell."

"Would you like to serve under me once we return?"

Belinda smiled.

"I would like that very much."

"Good. Now, it is time for another territory."

"May I make a suggestion?"

"Please do."

"When you expand your influence into a territory, these living anomalies come out. It seems to me that the anomalies are growing stronger with each new territory. It could be they get stronger over time, when you claim a territory or when anyone in the transformation zone claims one."

"We have handled them well enough so far."

"Yes, but we've also made use of the power in this realm. Being able to focus the sunlight into destructive beams has made short work of the anomalies, but we haven't needed that power. We should be saving it for when we do."

"You're suggesting I expand from another territory I've claimed instead? Leave the remaining one adjacent to us until later?"

"Yes. That power saves us a little time and that is all. I recommend holding off until the anomalies are more of a threat and it will save us from wasting the lives of the new messengers you command."

"Then we shall expand from one of the other territories. I have claimed several; which would you advise we use?"

"While the anomalies are at their weakest, we should expand from the hardest to defend against."

Kol nodded her agreement.

"The elemental forest, then. We'll need to get it ready if that's our choice. Clear out the undead and map it as best we can."

The elemental forest was a place where all manner of elemental forces were in play, their strength waxing and waning in pulses. This made elemental powers unreliable, either overcharged or underpowered. It also had a detrimental effect on magical perception.

The geography was a series of gorges laid out like spokes on a wheel. A river ran through each one, converging at the heart of the territory in a massive sunken basin. They spilled off the sharp edge of the basin, creating a spectacular ring of waterfalls.

The gorges were thickly forested, from the ground above them to the floors where the trees framed the riverbanks. Even the steep sides had trees and bushes growing right out of the rock. Cave systems riddled the gorge walls, linking them up in a complex network of caverns and tunnels.

In the outer reaches of the territory, the gorges were at their most spaced out. There were several cenotes, massive holes in the ground with flooded bottoms. The rivers moved from underground to above ground in these outer reaches, each one gushing from a cave at the head of its gorge.

Belinda's plan was falling into place. Making a move against a gold-ranker was always going to be a sketchy proposition and the open plains where Kol could harness death beams from the sky was not the right pick. Convincing her to move their base of operations was the win that Belinda needed to move forward.

While her plan had a basic shape, there was a plethora of potential problems in the aftermath. Would Kol Kelis Vel survive? Probably, given how hard to kill gold-rankers were. Even if Kol died, what about her growing army of messengers? Would they mill about in confusion or methodically hunt her down? What about the other messengers that weren't just confused, docile recruits?

The various possibilities meant that she needed contingencies, and the elemental forest gave her everything she needed. The nodes of elemental power, seated in rocks and trees, even carried on gusts of wind, made a great resource. For an improvised magic specialist like Belinda, it was clay to be moulded in her hands. Often literally.

Once she made her move, she needed to get away. Whether from gold-rank senses or a horde of messengers hunting her, being able to hide was essential and the forest provided again. The fluctuating energy of the forest messed with magical perception; she would be out of prying eyes while setting up and have a better chance to escape in the aftermath.

Most of the magic she needed to set up was well within her capabilities. It was the main element that was a gamble, messing with Kol Kelis Vel's ritual. When assimilating a new territory, the messenger used a ritual to do it properly. Kol asserted that simply claiming and uniting the territories using the orbs dropped by the final anomalies was flawed. It introduced instabilities that would affect the person doing it and ultimately doom a final unification. The ritual seemed to accomplish much the same thing as what Jason said his power could do. That made the messenger a threat that needed to be dealt with.

After watching the ritual carried out several times, Belinda had come to understand how much more advanced her magic was. Messenger magic was leaps and bounds ahead of what they had on Pallimustus, at least when it came to astral magic and the kind of dimensional manipulation at play here.

What she needed was Clive and his freakish mind for magic, especially astral magic. He'd probably started putting together aspects of the underlying theory already. She was not Clive, however, and the theory was beyond her. She didn't even try to figure it out and instead focused on her own specialty.

The key to improvised magic was not in grasping the higher-order elements of magical workings. It was about the foundational elements; the nails and bolts that held a magic framework together. Crucially, these operated by rules that were the same for magic everywhere, be it messenger magic, Pallimustan magic, or whatever crude dabbling they did on Jason's planet.

She didn't count the bizarre magic Jason's familiar pulled out now and again. Once gods and cosmic beings got involved, it was best to ignore whatever Jason had going on. It wasn't relevant, as the messenger's magic didn't use any such strangeness. For all its advancements, it was built on a foundation that fell within Belinda's understanding.

She might not know exactly what the messenger was doing with her ritual, but she did grasp the basic underpinnings of how. The ritual followed fundamental principles of magic that Belinda not only knew, but knew how to sabotage.

The lack of communication and muddled perception of the elemental forest gave Belinda time to work. She had a lot of quick and dirty magic to set up and only so long to do it. As she moved around the territory, she encountered elements that seemed natural but highlighted the artificiality when examined more closely.

The geography looked like ordinary wilderness from up close, but the wheel and spoke shape visible from the air did not appear natural. The rivers were sourced underground, close to the borders of the territory. Having seen the abrupt geographical shifts where territories met, she was willing to bet they weren't flowing in from outside. There was probably some hidden magical source for each of the rivers.

There was also the question of where all that water went after emptying into the huge basin. The water level wasn't rising, which meant there was five rivers worth of draining going on. Exactly five rivers worth, since the water level wasn't dropping either. This wasn't idle speculation; the rivers were part of some of her various contingencies.

She worked for hours, drawing ritual diagrams on rocks and trees, hiding them as best she could. She was filthy after carving diagrams into clays banks and the inside of hollow logs, jamming spirit coins and other ritual materials into key points.

She washed herself in a river since appearing crystal-wash clean would be too suspicious. She took a rest, leaning against a warm tree that radiated fire element magic. The light dappled pleasantly through the leaves above, making her think about the sun producing it. It was, perhaps, the largest incongruity in the strange dimensional realm. The burning orb in the sky had to be a facsimile, given the magnitude of the real thing. It had to be astoundingly scaled down, relying on the reduced distance to produce the same result with reduced size and power. If it had the scope of the real thing, this dimensional space would be countless times larger than her entire planet.

She thought of Clive again, who would definitely want to explore the truth if he had the chance. She could imagine him hassling her to assemble some kind of flying research vessel for them to do just that together. For all their differences, they shared an incredible passion for magical knowledge.

Belinda and Clive's disparate approaches to magic were born from very different educations. Clive had been plucked from obscurity, raised by a mentor and given dedicated, personalised training. Belinda had the opposite. She had grown up either on the street or one step from it, depending on how sober her father had been in any given month.

Belinda's mother was long dead or long gone before she had any memory of her. Her father spoke of her rarely, and only while in his cups. Sometimes he said she was dead, other times run off. Belinda had never gotten the truth and didn't much care either way. She'd never shared Sophie's curiosity on that front.

Belinda didn't hate her father. He'd been a good enough one by Old City standards, especially in the early days. While a regular drunk, he was never a mean one. Even though they had trouble enough getting by, he'd taken in Sophie after her own father had died, without so much as a word of pushback. However bad things may have gotten by the end, Belinda would love her father forever for that.

He'd done the best he could for a daughter he knew was far smarter than he. Teaching her to read was as much education as he could provide, but he tried. He was always scrounging, scraping and bargaining for books, even when they barely had enough to eat. They were tattered, mouldy or water-stained, often with the cover missing. A couple had been loose pages he'd crudely bound back together with string himself. She remembered the pride on his face every time he produced a new one.

After he passed, Belinda and Sophie made their own way. They were decent thieves at the beginning, and much of her proceeds went to buying books of actual magic. They hadn't been good enough to steal them until they were a little older and a lot better.

The Magic Society had always been the treasure trove for magical knowledge. The pair had been careful about going after the Magic Society directly, and wisely so. It was in doing so out of desperation that had allowed Clive and Jason to finally catch them, after all. Instead, she'd gone after Magic Society members individually. Most were sloppy about security, especially with the kind of magic basics that they didn't even consider valuable. To Belinda, they had been precious. She took great pleasure in giving the books a home where they were more appreciated.

Clive had been taught magic with every resource at his fingertips. She'd stolen from so many who squandered such opportunities, but in Clive, she found someone who understood the value of even the most basic magic. Instead of mocking her hodgepodge, self-taught knowledge, he'd praised her resourcefulness. He'd taken her as an assistant, filling the gaps in her knowledge as if their existence was a personal affront.

Clive's earnest enthusiasm for magic—any magic—was like nothing she'd ever encountered. She grew up where everyone was guarded, trying to get ahead or even just get by. She was long past caring about the people she stole from, and Clive's openness and joy were everything she'd been told to look for in a mark. Even so, she never even considered taking advantage. Just the thought of it felt like kicking a puppy.

What Clive gave her most of all was someone she didn't feel like she had to slow down around. Her whole life, she'd been constantly slowing herself down. She didn't understand why the people around her seemed so slow to figure things out or miss the completely obvious.

Jory had come closest to keeping up, and he was a lot like Clive in a lot of ways. He lit up when talking about his alchemy, and his passion for helping people was wildly appealing to someone who had spent a lifetime around the self-serving. But while Jory was smart, Clive was on another level. Even now, Belinda knew the people around him didn't understand how brilliant he was.

Despite his brilliance, Clive was never too proud to learn from her in turn. He was fascinated by the unorthodox methodology she'd developed to work around the gaps in her knowledge. Rather than pushing her into a more straightforward path, he'd encouraged her to build on what she already had, pushing her to innovate. She came to realise that, like her, he was excited to have someone he didn't have to slow down around.

Working as Clive's research assistant had been a life she'd never imagined possible. There was more magical knowledge to delve into than she had hours of the day to do it, with no one to tell her not to. She continued to serve as his assistant on and off through her adventuring career. With every passing year, she became less of a student and more of a peer.

For all of that, even years later, there was a part of her waiting for the truth to drop. A voice inside, telling her that she didn't deserve any of it. That deep down, her friends knew that she was still nothing but a jumped-up street thief. She took things she didn't have to; did things that hurt the team as if subconsciously testing them. Waiting for the day they realised she didn't belong and sent her packing.

She leaned her head back against the tree, her hair getting mussed as it rubbed on the bark. Tears trickled down her face, the mocking expression on it directed at herself. She only realised her uncharacteristic inattention when she heard footsteps in the leaves behind her.

She sprang up on alert, turning to find a messenger standing in front of her. It was the quiet one whose name she still didn't know. The one she wanted to get rid of before enacting her plan. He wasn't floating in the air the way messengers did, but that was not the change from his normal appearance that left her startled and disarmed. She didn't react as he moved forward and gathered her in a hug, his bushy moustache tickling her ear.

14

GAUNTLET

BELINDA WAS HUDDLED INSIDE A HOLLOW LOG AS IT FLOATED DOWNRIVER, banging off rocks. She'd conjured a plug at the open end to keep out the water and was back in her human form. Messengers were just too big. Her arms were curled around puppy Stash. Light came from the now-active ritual circle carved into the inside.

There was little chance of the gold-ranker sensing them through the interference of the elemental forest, but Belinda's ritual meant that he would need to be both extremely close and extremely focused to find them. It was the first kind of ritual magic she'd learned and the one she'd used the most.

She'd set many such rituals in place around the elemental forest. They fell mostly within the path she expected to take after kicking the hornet's nest, although there were outlying places as contingencies. They would help her hide or sneak if her expected pursuers drew a little too close. Compared to the other preparations she'd made, though, the concealment rituals were quite modest in number.

A roar of fury and pain filled the sky, clearly audible even through their wooden haven and the sound of rushing water.

"What does it take to kill that thing?" Belinda wondered.

Belinda's plan had seen some positive modifications with the revelation that her biggest obstacle, the quiet messenger always watching her, was actually an ally. The critical part had been sabotaging the ritual Kol

Kelis Vel had been performing, and that had gone without a hitch. Belinda had 'found' the perfect spot for the ritual, a flat rocky surface that she'd conjured herself.

After years of diligent practise and a few rank-ups, Belinda could conjure material that seemed natural and didn't radiate any aura. It wasn't very strong, being normal-rank material, but the strength of ordinary stone was enough. It held up to Kol magically abrading a flat surface for her ritual, reacting like normal stone.

Kol Kelis Vel had conducted her ritual, unaware of the other ritual circle under the layer of what she thought was solid stone. Belinda's ritual circle had been undetectable, having no magic of its own. Instead, it lay dormant until a second ritual provided the magic for it.

This trick was something Belinda had developed herself and required clever improvisation to implement. The self-developed technique had most impressed Clive, who had gushed over the innovation. There were very few people who added something genuinely new to magic and he considered it her signature technique. Belinda disagreed, finding the niche magic less a signature than her well-practised concealment rituals. They might be common as dirt, but so was Belinda herself and they were both extremely practical.

The technique of using a hidden second ritual to drain a first did have its uses, though, as she had demonstrated. Kol Kelis Vel's ritual drew in an astounding amount of power, tapping into all the territories she had claimed and linking them to herself. This was the moment Belinda had been targeting: when the messenger was both exposed to a vast power and making herself vulnerable to it.

The hidden ritual circle interfered with the main one by blocking the most fundamental magical channels. Charged mana accumulated dangerously, neither moving on to the parts of the ritual that needed it nor dispersing safely. Combined with the complex messenger magic Belinda didn't understand, the result was a lot of pent-up magic in a very unstable construct.

The messenger noticed once things had started going awry, but it all happened in moments. By the time she realised what was happening, it was too far along. She had bound herself to the ritual and a moment's hesitation was all it took.

The detonation threw up a mushroom cloud of dirt and dust, flaring rainbow colours as the elemental power of the territory reacted. The blast would have annihilated a silver-ranker in an instant, leaving not so much as a scrap of flesh behind. Gold-rankers, however, were not so easy to kill.

The other messengers, aside from the ones unlocked through territory control, had been standing around as witnesses. This included Belinda and Stash, who had acted before the others. They knew what to expect and had moved first and fast before the others realised what was happening.

The pair even had time to sneak attack some of their fellow messengers, the two gormless sycophants, before ducking into a hidden bunker to endure the explosion. The attacks weren't much, but they made sure the genuine messengers were right in the path of the blast wave. The last messenger was the complainer, Cas Vin Baral, but he was a marginal threat. She suspected that he would survive, having a strong self-preservation streak and no loyalty to his gold-rank master. Belinda didn't entirely dismiss him as a threat, but he was one far down their list of current problems. With a little bit of luck, she could even use him, should she run into him again.

Belinda and Stash fled their bunker the moment the blast wave had passed, charging into their pre-planned route. They could barely see through what would have been choking dust if they'd needed to breathe. Their initial escape path and the first few traps along it had been flattened by a blast much bigger than they anticipated. They kept their messenger forms but did not fly, knowing escape in the air was impossible. Escape from what, they were unsure of at first, not knowing if Kol had survived and what the territorial messengers would do. They fled anyway, assuming the worst.

The pair had found their path when the gold-ranker's survival was confirmed in intimidating fashion. A wounded bellow of pain and rage rang out, aura-amplified noise shaking the sky. Her aura even cut through the interference of the zone's elemental power for a brief moment, pinging against Belinda's senses. She could feel that Kol Kelis Vel was wounded, and badly, but that was subsumed by rage.

Kol Kelis Vel may have survived, but she was considerably worse for wear. At one point, Belinda had almost been caught, hiding in one of her concealment spots as the gold-ranker stormed past. She looked almost undead, covered in blood and draped in the scant rags that were what remained of her clothes.

Her body was covered in massive wounds, chunks of flesh missing and holes punched in her wings. Any one of those injuries would have killed a bronze-ranker and severely slowed down a silver. The left side of her torso was stripped down the ribs and her right arm stopped at the elbow. Her hair was gone entirely, along with one eye and a third of the flesh on her head, her grisly skull visible underneath.

Belinda had hoped the gold-ranker would die while betting she wouldn't, devising the rest of her plan accordingly. Their escape route was not just about getting away but about drawing an angry messenger through a gauntlet of traps.

The time it had taken Kol to start hunting them was a testament to how badly she'd been hurt. Kol had begun by ordering the messengers she gained from the territory to sweep the forest. Belinda had discovered this quickly as they fanned out, scanning their senses over the terrain. This was within her calculations as the nature of the territory made that kind of search fruitless.

Messengers were imperious by nature. They stood above their lessers, and using their magical perception to search the elemental forest from above fit that mentality perfectly. Belinda couldn't be sure about the new messengers, but they were following the commands of Kol Kelis Vel, who was a very traditional messenger. She started them sweeping but quickly realised it was useless, given the situation. Their perception was so compromised by the environment that they couldn't detect what was happening in the gorges and under the canopy. Instead, she sent them into the trees, beating the bushes in an expanding circle from the blast zone.

Kol herself was forced to hunt, going down to ground level and following Belinda and Stash's trail. They weren't hard to track, the pair having barrelled through the forest with no attempt to hide their passage.

Being deceived for days and then almost killed by a silver-ranker mixed with general messenger arrogance to form a heady cocktail of obsessive frenzy. Kol smashed her way through the forest in pursuit of Belinda with no fear of the silver-rankers, despite her massively damaged condition. The messenger knew the trap that left her in that condition could only have been set through patience, circumstance and opportunity. It would take another of the same magnitude to finish her, and that was something they had neither the time nor the chance to accomplish.

Belinda had come to the same conclusion. Assuming the gold-ranker survived, she had planned on Kol's single-minded quest for revenge. She'd been drastically outplayed by a silver-ranker and, like a person startled by a harmless insect, her humiliation turned to anger. The messenger would not stop until the source of that humiliation had been swatted to death, even when the smart choice was to let it go.

Unable to produce another trap so destructive as the first, Belinda had used all the preparation time she'd wrangled to produce many lesser ones. The elemental nodes that littered the territory made the perfect basis for a gauntlet of quick and dirty traps along their escape path. Not only were they easy to tap into, but the prevalence of such nodes left any pursuers with an unpleasant choice.

The nodes themselves weren't hard to sense, but it was difficult to tell which were normal and which were traps without stopping to study each one. With so many nodes, that meant slowing to a crawl or accepting that some would be traps and walking into them. The territorial messengers quickly learned to slow down and make a careful path forward while Kol Kelis Vel took the opposite approach.

The gold-ranker ploughed through one trap after another. Explosions of fire and rocks, water jets that were sharper than swords—Kol shrugged it all off. Even in her current state, the accumulated damage wasn't crippling, but it was slowly stacking up.

What frustrated her, though, were the non-damaging traps. Earth nodes were used to create false trails while air magic masked scents and hid the real ones behind illusions. None of them slowed her for long, the slapped-together illusion rituals quickly falling under magical scrutiny.

At close range, Kol's senses were still effective, making each delay only slight. But even a slight delay added wood to the bonfire of her rage, while being deceived again was pouring on oil. Every fresh wound and annoying misstep drove her more and more into a blind rage as she wildly thrashed through the forest in her pursuit. Her rage at being diverted became an obsession with moving in a straight line, beyond the point of reason. She even started smashing through trees when it would have cost no more time to walk around them.

After the initial escape, the next stage of the plan was to buy time. Belinda and Stash dropped their large and obvious messenger forms, making their passage less eye-catching. They still moved swiftly, but their pursuer would need to slow down at least a little to keep following the trail.

Stash became nigh untrackable by turning into a small bird and flitting through the air. Belinda used her Instant Adept ability, causing her speed and agility to soar. She wasn't a match for Sophie, but she still became much harder to track. Not only did it give her advanced mobility skills and powers, but also additional abilities based on her gear.

Belinda's abilities made her the biggest prepper on her team, and she had equipment for all manner of terrain. She switched to woodland gear that allowed her to blend into the environment, a mix of the design and the magic on the silver-rank clothes.

- Your ability [Instant Adept] has produced a special ability from [Forest Hunter's Garb]. You will lose this ability on removing the garb. Silver-rank gear has produced the ability at a rank of [Silver 0].

Ability: [Woodland Walker]

- Effect (iron): You are much harder to track through forest terrain, including leaving a diminished scent trail. This extends to most abnormal forest conditions due to weather and limited magical influence.
- Effect (bronze): Makeshift shelter you assemble has basic camouflage magic incorporated into it.
- Effect (silver): You are immune to natural poisons of up to bronze rank. Your resistance to natural poisons of silver rank is increased and the duration of such poison is reduced.

Taking the log downriver was critical to the second stage of the plan. So long as it was effective, it would cause a massive delay in the messenger's efforts to track them. Belinda had no illusions of losing Kol entirely; gold-rank senses were too sharp, even mundane ones. Despite all her precautions and all her magic, it was still silver rank versus gold. The now-obsessive messenger could be slowed, but not stopped. But with enough time, she could set up the final stage of the plan and the final confrontation with Kol Kelis Vel.

15

CREEPY STUFF

Cas Vin Baral signalled that he'd found the infiltrators by firing a magical projectile in the air. When Kol Kelis Vel arrived, however, he was in a far from triumphant position. He was in an area with powerful ice energy, leading to trees white with snow and a large frozen pond. On that pond were two Cas Vin Barals, both of whom started babbling that they'd been captured and they were the real one. One of them was shrouded in an air node illusion.

Kol wasn't even floating like a messenger anymore as she emerged from the trees and stomped over to the pond. Her muddy feet struck the ground like she was attacking it. She looked more like an animated corpse than ever, burned, stabbed and impaled by countless traps. Yet, she kept coming like a revenant, stopping only when she reached the edge of the pond. She stared, with her remaining eye looking over the two identical messengers.

"This is the best you can do after all that running around?" Kol asked, her voice low and rough. She wheezed from the missing side of her neck. "After making me chase you through this whole forest, you think I'll fall for shape-changing now? That illusion is a crude play. You expect me to believe, after all this time tricking me perfectly, that you'd bet everything on that?"

Kol looked from one Cas Vin Baral to the other.

"You knew I would see through it, of course," Kol continued. "That is why you've cast an illusion of Cas Vin Baral over the man himself, to make me think he's you. At the same time, you pretend to be him with the same skills that have fooled me all this time. Or perhaps you've thought that far ahead, realising I would not fall for such a ruse and placing yourself under the illusion after all. But you have made two critical errors."

"And what are they?" Belinda asked, her voice coming from both versions of Cas Vin Baral.

"One is that you let yourself get anywhere near me. Now that you are this close, there is no more escape. You have some play here, probably messing with my mind. You think I am oblivious to the rage you are trying to instil in me with your schemes?"

"It doesn't matter if you know about the plan, so long as it works."

"I am filled with fury, yes, but my rage will not rule me. You, however, will feel it all. My wrath will not be satisfied with a quick death for you."

"If you say so," Belinda told her. "Actions speak the truth, not words, and I don't think you're as objective as you believe. But tell yourself what you like."

"You will see the truth for yourself. You want me to kill the last ally I have, as pathetic as he is, and think that will drive my mentality over the edge?"

"Something like that. You see, I know this guy. You won't have heard of him because you turned yourself into the slave of a tree…"

Both versions of Cas paused as Belinda's mocking laughter escaped their mouths.

"I've never said that out loud before," Belinda said. "Anyway, where was I? Right, you were a tree's slave, so you didn't hear about this man I know, but he's become famous amongst your lot. And he talks about a power that sounds stupid when you hear about it, but I've seen it work. I've seen it defeat far more powerful beings than you."

"You think you can bluff me?"

"I do. This is the kind of trick my friend likes to pull. He calls it villain banter, and I'm starting to see the appeal. I mean, yeah, I'm riding the knife edge of death here, but I've taken drugs that didn't make me feel this alive. But you're not worried about what I can do, right? You're an almighty messenger; you've seen through all my schemes. What could I possibly do to you? You know which one of us is the real me, don't you? You've figured it all out."

Kol gave a bloody grin that revealed multiple missing teeth.

"Traps within traps within traps. But I told you, you made two mistakes. I won't even count the fact that I could just kill both of you because that's another trap. Your mistake was talking. You think you're buying yourself time, wrapping me up in mind games that will give you the edge in escaping, perhaps even killing me. But in the time you think you've been playing me, I've had time to properly make use of my magical perception."

Kol gestured at the space around them. The frozen pond was ringed with frosted grass and trees heavy with snow.

"Choosing this ice node was a smart move," she said. "It's probably the most powerful of the elemental forces in this territory. Even this close, it interferes with my magical perception, and you've even amplified it with a ritual. But I am gold-rank. More than that, I am a messenger. You have brought me low and I don't even know your name, but now you will know what you have chosen to confront. While we have been talking, I have been piercing the veils of your illusions."

Kol gestured and the illusion over Cas Vin Baral vanished. It revealed him, not standing on his feet but lying on the ice in magical shackles. The much harder-to-detect illusion over the other Cas vanished as well, revealing a mannequin with a powerful trap rune glowing on the chest.

"While you have been prattling on and playing games," Kol said, "I have found your true hiding place."

With another gesture, the ice in the middle of the pond exploded up, spraying water that froze in the air, raining droplets of ice. Belinda was yanked out as if by a winch. Water spilled from the force bubble keeping her dry.

"Your concealment magic is exquisite," Kol said. "Given the limits of your world's magic, even I find myself impressed. But the cold and wet were your undoing. I did not sense you, but the magic you used to keep yourself dry and warm."

Kol finally stepped onto the pond, spiderweb cracks forming with every footfall. She stopped in front of the dangling Belinda, held high to match the messenger's nine-foot height.

"It's disappointing," Kol said. "Your true self could have been so much more useful than the identity you took on. If only you had known your place and served."

"Oh, I'm about to serve," Belinda said.

"You think I would be willing to take you in at this stage? After all you've done, after all your defiance? You overestimate your value if you think I will let you serve me still."

"Oh, I'm going to serve you," Belinda said defiantly. "Serve you up on a goddamn plate."

Ice magic poured up out of the pond like a geyser, not in the form of icy water but icy mist. Belinda, Kol Kelis Vel and Cas Vin Baral were all frozen in place, an icy patina coating their bodies.

Compared to the ritual trap that damaged the gold-ranker so badly, the ice trap had the merest fraction of that power. Even so, Belinda had leveraged the potent ice node, masking the ritual as one to interfere with perception. It would hold Belinda and the silver-rank messenger indefinitely, but Kol immediately started breaking free.

The frosty mist quickly thinned and drifted away, leaving only the three frozen people. Belinda, who had been hung in the air, was dropped. The broken ice had already frozen over and she landed on it like a hard fruit falling from a tree. The ice coating Kol was being shaken off as she moved, slowly but inexorably, like pushing through molasses.

The gold-rank messenger was moving, but not close to fast enough to intercept her attackers. Taika and Humphrey were both high-mobility brawlers, coming in hard and fast.

Humphrey's massive blade swung in and struck the existing wound on the side of the messenger's neck. His sword, shaped like a dragon's wing and wreathed in flames, buried itself deep enough to strike her spine, but there it stopped dead. Taika crashed into her torso from the other direction, his fist landing with a force that sent ripples through her flesh.

Neither blow was lethal, the near-limitless tenacity of gold-rankers proving itself again. The messenger was still moving slowly but shrugged off more of the ice magic with each passing moment. By the time Humphrey landed a second blow, she was moving with the speed of a bronze-ranker, and the third strike missed as she ducked out of the way.

Humphrey and Taika moved fast while she was still in the realm of silver-rank speed. Humphrey seized her left arm while Taika grabbed what remained of her right.

Stash didn't have the swiftness of the two adventurers, arriving from his hiding spot later than they did. What he did have was a gorilla body twice the height of Humphrey, along with six arms that each held an icicle like a spear.

Both adventurers had abilities that enhanced their physical strength to levels approaching gold rank. This made them hard to shake off for the severely injured gold-ranker, but shake them off she did. Not in time to stop Stash, however, who brought all six icicles down to impale her.

One of the icicles shattered on her ribs, but the other five dug into her body, lighting up with runes as they did. The messenger was once again frozen, the patina of frost returning to shroud her body. Humphrey didn't waste time, hacking away at her body like a lumberjack. Taika's arms worked like pistons as his fists hammered the messenger, the tattoos on his skin lighting up and shining through his clothes.

The messenger struggled but found the ice magic harder to resist when it was inside her body. Even so, she once again started to move, breaking out of the frost like a chicken from an egg. Her molasses speed was still too slow for anything but endurance until she could expel more of the magic.

She managed to get back to silver-rank speed again, but was too late. She wasn't dead yet, but Humphrey and Taika had done their work; her body was too far gone. Her head and wings were gone, as was what had been her remaining arm. She still had her legs and tried to flee, only to be tripped up by tentacles. Stash had turned into a horrific blob monster with tentacles emerging from his mouth.

Even with the gold-ranker in that condition, it took minutes to finish the job. They started with the legs and then worked on the torso until nothing was left but chunks. The grass was painted in silver-gold messenger blood, dotted with chunks of flesh no larger than a fist.

"Is that it?" Taika asked. "That has to be it, right?"

He was panting, having burned through his mana and stamina. He was spattered with silver-gold liquid and drenched to the elbows in it.

"Use your aura senses to find what's left of her life force," Humphrey said. "That will give you the answer."

"There's no way she could be faking it, is there? You should hit her a few more times to—"

- You have slain gold-rank messenger [Kol Kelis Vel].
- Kol Kelis Vel had claimed and properly unified six territories. Those territories may not be claimed without an ability or method to claim them in their properly unified state.

The blood and body parts dissolved into rainbow smoke, from the ground as well as from the two men and the familiar. Taika waved it away ineffectually.

"Do you ever get used to it?" he choked out.

"No," Humphrey said. "There are advantages to fighting from range."

Left in the wake of the messenger's disappearance was an orb with rainbow colours that shifted like oil on water.

"You park that in your storage space," Taika said. "I'll see about thawing out Belinda. Give me the magic-awayer."

"The magic-awayer?"

"Yeah. That enchanted stone she gave us to take the ice magic away."

"You already have it."

"No, bro. You've got it."

"I definitely don't have it."

They both turned to look at Belinda, still frozen out on the ice.

"Uh, she'll be fine, right, bro?"

"I think we'd better find that rock."

———

Belinda rubbed her temples, still feeling the splitting headache. She had moved the group from the site of the battle to another nearby area. A water and fire node had balanced each other out, resulting in the production of a hot spring. After finding it during her preparation for the plan, she'd promised herself a return when the job was done. She now kept that promise, lying against the bank and letting out a sigh as a puppy swam in merry circles.

The two men were on the other side of a large rock. She'd conjured them chairs, but not comfortable ones.

"You lost it in a bush?" Belinda called out in disbelief. It wasn't the first time she'd asked the question, but none of their answers had been satisfactory.

"We found it eventually," Taika called back.

"If I'd been a normal person or even an iron-ranker, I'd be dead," Belinda scolded. "Even a bronze-ranker would need some serious healing after being frozen like that."

"We appreciate your sacrifice," Humphrey said. "You were right that she would be fixated on you."

"And the other messengers haven't done anything?" Belinda asked.

"Not that we've seen," Taika said. "We've seen some flying around, but they're all pretty aimless. They saw us too, but they ignored us."

"I can't believe you made a speech about the power of friendship," Humphrey said.

"Don't tell Jason," Belinda said. "He's insufferable enough as it is."

"We need to decide where to head next," Humphrey said. "My only plan was to follow the familiar bond until I found Stash. I picked up Taika along the way, but we didn't see anyone else, friend or foe."

"Except for the undead and the living anomalies," Taika added. "I guess they're more like murdery terrain."

"Neither of us have claimed any territories," Humphrey said.

"I don't think you should start now," Belinda said. "Those anomalies are getting tougher. Taking territories is a slow enough way to progress when it's easy, but now it will be a crawl. Instead of unifying territories, we should unify people. I advocate moving fast and finding groups to join up with. Or avoid, if it's the other team."

"That's a sound approach," Humphrey said.

"We also need to decide what to do with the last messenger," Taika said. "The one with the bags of body parts. That's creepy stuff."

"Taika," Belinda said, "you just tore a lady to pieces with your bare hands."

"It was more like tenderising," Taika said. "Humphrey did the actual chopping. Plus, I saw worse stuff working in a slaughterhouse when I was a kid. That messenger blood looks like it came from a craft shop."

"You killed animals for a living?" Humphrey asked.

"No, I just sold drugs."

16

GROUP DYNAMICS

"I don't like leaving it here," Taika said.

"We can't use it and we can't take it with us," Humphrey told him. "Our best move is to leave before it brings trouble down on us."

Belinda and the two men were standing over a shimmering orb that had refused to enter either Humphrey or Belinda's storage spaces.

Item: [Stable Genesis Core Amalgam] (unranked, legendary)

An amalgamation of refined vessels of transformative potential energy (consumable, magic core).

- Effect: Use to set up or expand spiritual domains. This is a refined amalgam linked to multiple stably unified territories.
- This core cannot be used without the proper ability or method. This core cannot be subject to dimensional stasis or removed from the territories to which it is linked. This core is radiating energy that can be sensed by those who have claimed a properly stabilised territory. The energy will increase over time, extending the range at which it can be sensed.

"This thing is going to draw the most dangerous people here like feliculars to a bostirion," Belinda said.

"I agree," Humphrey said.

"I don't know what either of those things are," Taika said.

"You don't have bostirions on your world?" Humphrey asked. "You're missing out."

"On the other hand, not having to deal with feliculars would be great," Belinda said.

"That's true," Humphrey said, nodding his agreement.

"Are bostirions food?" Taika asked. The other two immediately erupted into laughter.

"He thinks you eat bostirions," Belinda said.

"You should never, ever eat a bostirion," Humphrey said. "My great-uncle got one near his mouth once. He didn't even eat it and still suffered something I'm not sure you can even call diarrhoea. The house was uninhabitable, and we have a big house. We had to call in a priest of the Healer to make it stop and a priest of Purity to make the building liveable again."

"Bro, your great-uncle is normal rank?"

"No, he's a gold-ranker," Humphrey said. "He hadn't used a toilet in twenty years."

"Okay," Taika said. "I still don't know what this thing you're talking about is, but you have to point it out if you see one. I haven't pooped in three years and I don't want to catch up all at once."

"That's not how it works," Belinda said. "You're not saving it up."

"That's what you say," Taika said, "but Humphrey just told us a twenty-year poo story."

"Which I'm now coming to regret," Humphrey said. "Let's get out of here."

He walked towards the nearby territorial boundary and Belinda joined him.

"I'm not kidding about this," Taika called after them. "You have to tell me if you see one of those things."

Belinda and Humphrey shared an amused look and kept walking. Taika shook his head and followed.

"I want to go home and see my mum," he muttered.

Jason floated in the air over flat savannah that sprawled out to the horizon. His silver-rank eyesight picked out the dinosaurs roaming around, some he recognised, some he didn't. They were easy to pick out, massive herbivores that chomped on trees or lounged in waterholes.

His gaze turned to the distance and the shadowy veil at the bounds of his territory. He was still staring when Farrah flew up to join him. They hovered in the air, side by side.

"What is it?" she asked.

"There's something out there. A large territory, waiting to be claimed by the first one who can get there and take it."

"Are you going to go?"

"No. It's going to attract the undead avatar, and we haven't found Gary to fight it yet. Anything that drives it in a direction that's not here is a good thing."

"And if the avatar does find us before Gary?"

"Then I'll have to try something drastic."

Farrah sighed. "You have something in mind?"

"Yeah."

"Will it work?"

"Probably, but I'm hoping to not find out."

"The consequences are uncertain but maybe worse than the problem they fix?"

"Yeah," Jason said. "Vast cosmic power isn't everything it's cracked up to be."

"Yes, it is."

Jason gave her a side glance, then snorted a laugh.

"Yeah, I guess it is."

He turned his gaze back down to the territory below.

"I just wish I had more time to stop and enjoy places like this."

"It won't always be like this, Jason."

"So people keep telling me. At this rate, I'll have to conquer the cosmos and make everyone knock off their crap."

"Jason?"

"Yes, Farrah?"

"Don't conquer the cosmos."

"No promises."

He turned to look in the direction of his core territory and grinned.

"Rick just got back, and he brought friends."

Jason sat at the head of the conference table. His backdrop was a wall of glass behind which a lava waterfall spilled down out of sight. Sitting around the table were members representing every faction of their alliance —adventurers, brighthearts and cultists. Not everyone was happy about Jason adding messengers to the alliance by fiat, but he informed them that if they didn't like it, they could challenge him for his territory and see how that went. Not everyone was happy about that either.

The relative positions around the table told a story of the group dynamics between the factions, and the individuals within those factions. Jason sat at the head of the table with Sophie and Farrah to his left. The other adventurers ran down that side of the table in a line, ending in Rick Geller.

The gold-rank adventurers Rick had managed to find were Arabelle Remore and Miriam Vance, the tactical commander for the underground expedition sent by the Adventure Society. He'd also rounded up Gabriel Remore and Amos Pensinata, but they were sleeping off the after-effects of handing their territories to Jason. They had accumulated eleven territories between them and the result of handing them over was hangover-like symptoms that were resistant to healing magic.

The silver-rankers he'd found were Zara Nareen, Orin Pensinata and Rick's sister Phoebe.

"…only found one of my team members," Rick said, continuing his report. "I would have liked to continue, but, given all the people we'd found, consolidating our forces seemed like the right move."

Past Rick was the messenger Marek Nior Vargas and his gold-rank right-hand man. Jason didn't anticipate friendship anytime soon, but gauged Rick and Marek to have formed a functional working relationship. There was one more messenger in the room, Jali Corrik Fen, seated to Jason's right. Jason had not missed the disapproving glances from close friends and reluctant allies alike.

The largest group Rick had brought back were the brighthearts, including their leader, Lorenn. She was seated opposite Jason at the foot of the table. Many of her brighthearts were in the territory, but only two were with her in the meeting. Lorenn had also handed multiple territories to Jason but had not wanted to miss the conference. Her complexion was pale and sickly, but she otherwise showed no sign of her discomfort.

There was a large gap between Jali, on Jason's right, and the row of Builder cultists further down that side of the table. One gold-ranker was flanked by silvers; they had other gold-rankers in the territory but only one had come to the conference, to proxy for their still-missing leader.

From his interactions with the cultist, Jason knew he was less amenable to the alliance than their leader, Beaufort. Rather than causing trouble, he chose to listen in silence unless directly addressed, at which point he followed the group consensus. Jason didn't care for the cult any more than they did him, but was grateful that the man was smart and loyal enough to not cause problems.

The meeting continued going through the experiences of Rick and those he had brought back. Of major concern was the effect that claiming multiple territories had on people without the correct means to do so. Arabelle had the most to say, as not only did she get to watch the process closely with her husband but she was an expert in mental health.

"Gabriel's behaviour became increasingly erratic the more territories he claimed," Arabelle told the group. "It seems that those who cannot claim the territories properly are subjected to increased anger and paranoia with each one they accumulate. After collecting six territories it had reached the point of becoming dangerous. He was lashing out and becoming overprotective of his power. It took us some time to calm him down and convince him to hand it over peacefully. Fortunately, the symptoms immediately vanished on handing over the territories, although the aftermath is apparently unpleasant."

"I can confirm that," Lorenn said.

"Six seems to be the threshold at which it becomes a real problem," Arabelle continued. "Both Amos Pensinata and Councilwoman Lorenn showed similar effects, but both maintained self-control with their five and four territories respectively. Also, there do seem to be ways to ameliorate this. From speaking with our cultist ally, he experienced these effects but handled them readily, with diminished after-effects. My guess would be that the star seeds in their souls have helped them adapt to external influence."

Discussion moved on to the messengers claimed from each territory. The cultist messengers had died immediately upon leaving cultist control. Their segmented bodies, held together with Builder magic, were unable to live on without Builder influence. That had almost been enough to drive Jason to do something he'd regret to the cultists, but he held his temper.

The elemental messengers of the brighthearts had suffered no ill effects from being placed under Jason's control. On the contrary, their minds had cleared, taking them from simpletons to intelligent communicators. Jason had felt his brand replacing that of Lorenn when she handed over her territories and immediately stopped it. As he had with the others, he guided them to place their own marks on their souls, setting them free.

From there, he had handed them over to Jali, now used to inducting fresh messengers to their existing population. Those claimed by Lorenn retained their elemental nature, even after being handed over to Jason. It didn't seem to impede them or draw any ire from the others. These messengers had never gone through messenger indoctrination to build up prejudices.

"The biggest problem we have with the messengers," Jason said to the conference group, "is that many of them were left abandoned. We have eleven territories worth of messengers left comatose and they've all just woken up."

"You're sure?" Arabelle asked.

"I felt it," Jason said. "I felt them wake and I set them free."

"Are you certain that was wise?" Phoebe Geller asked.

"I'm tired of explaining that I don't own slaves," Jason said. "I don't want to hear anyone bring it up again."

"That's it?" Lorenn asked. "We have to accept what is arguably the most powerful weapon at our disposal being set aside because you say so, and we don't even get to talk about it?"

"Yes," Jason told her.

"And if we don't accept that?"

"I've already told you all once, Councilwoman. If you don't like the way I do things, challenge me. Take this territory and do it better."

"You know that's not practical."

"Then when I say something is done, it's done."

"If you're just going to issue decrees, then what is the point of even having us here?"

"Because I'm well aware that a group will come up with better ideas than I will alone. But the final decisions are mine."

Lorenn scowled. "You never struck me as a tyrant before."

"You don't know me that well. But let me be clear, Councilwoman: I will never hold your people in my soul realm over you. They are not hostages and never will be. Regarding their disposition, I am at your command. If you want them out here instead of in my domain, I will bring them out. I imagine we can keep them safe and fed here."

"Telling me I have to do what you say but you won't use my people as hostages doesn't comfort me, Asano. And even if you bring them out, this is still your domain."

"That's true," Jason said. "This situation is not built for equanimity. There needs to be a chain of command, and I need you all to understand that I am at the top of it. I don't want to be a despot, but if that's what it takes to get us to the other side of this, I will. Anyone who can't accept that should leave now."

Silence reigned.

"Good," Jason said. "Now—"

"Jason," Phoebe Geller said. "I think we should discuss the possibility that claiming all these territories is affecting your mind as well. Less than the others, but I think it might be influencing your behaviour."

"It's not," Farrah and Arabelle said simultaneously.

The two women shared a glance and Farrah continued.

"I can tell you that the only thing affecting Jason's mindset is the circumstance. I've seen him like this before. It's not always pleasant to be around, but when the world is breaking apart, this is how he gets."

"You know I'm right here," Jason said. "You're talking about me like I'm not in the room."

Jason and Farrah stared at one another until they both broke into grins.

"Okay," Jason said. "Now that you've all met Edgelord Jason, let's move on to what comes next. It's good that we've managed to unify this many territories, but having them scattered and separate poses logistical issues. Rick, if you would?"

Rick took a small, glass half-orb from his pocket and leaned over the table to place it flat-side down in the middle. He leaned back and gestured at it, causing an illusion to be projected. It showed a map with clearly delimitated sections, marking out territories.

"We took a cartography crystal with us," Rick said. "It's a recording crystal designed specifically for mapping terrain. Despite this being a dimensional space and the territorial boundaries being very odd, the geography seems to be fixed. I'll take you through what we've found and what we've guessed about the transformation zone."

1 7

AS MANY AS WE CAN GET

RICK GESTURED TO THE ILLUSIONARY MAP FLOATING OVER THE TABLE LIKE a hologram. It showed the bottom fragment of a circle, divided into territories.

"This is everything we know about the layout of the transformation zone," he said. "We can make some guesses based on this, but what you're seeing here is what we've confirmed."

He gestured again and five territories at the bottom edge lit up green and joined together.

"This is Jason's unified territory," he continued. "As you can see, it's quite close to the edge of the transformation zone. We bumped into that edge when we first set out and ended up skirting around. It slowed down our penetration of the wider zone but did give us some sense of scope. A lot of our estimations are based on this."

"What kind of estimations?" Arabelle asked.

"The overall size of the transformation zone," Rick explained. "Assuming the zone continues the roughly circular shape we've observed, it contains dozens of territories. Potentially hundreds. Of course, if the rest of the zone does not conform to the proportions we've observed, the estimations will be way off."

Another gesture filled in the guesswork boundary for the entire transformation zone. It was a rough circle, with the top two-thirds greyed out.

"Each territory we saw was a hundred kilometres across at a minimum, some quite a bit more. Depending on how accurate we are about the overall shape of the transformation zone, that puts its size somewhere between a continent and a planet. A flat planet, given there seems to be no curvature."

"Those sizes are extremely vague," Miriam pointed out. "A continent is a terrible unit of measurement."

"Yes," Rick said, "but the information I have is the information I have. Until we do more scouting, vague is what we've got."

He gestured once more and the bottom third of the map lit up in different colours. He walked the group through what they represented.

"We have five green zones. Each one is a unified territory cluster that respectively belonged to Lord Pensinata, Gabriel Remore, Councilwoman Lorenn and our cultist representative. Sorry, I didn't get your name."

"I know," the cultist said.

Rick waited for more from the cultist but got only a return stare.

"Uh, alright, then," Rick said. "If our choice is between not knowing your name and you going on a bloody rampage of betrayal, I'm comfortable with the way you decided to go on that one. Anyway, those four territories have been handed over to the owner of our fifth green map section, Jason Asano. For the other colours, we'll start with red, representing confirmed hostile territories."

"You saw messengers claiming territories?" asked Jali, the messenger at Jason's right hand.

"Yes," Marek Nior Vargas said. The messenger had accompanied Rick and was currently seated just down from him at the table.

"I recognised some of those messengers," Marek continued. "These were messengers sent down to turn the natural array into a soul forge, only to be corrupted. It seems that this transformation zone has purged their corruption and they are working to take it over."

"We have to assume that they have the magic to effectively claim territories, much as I do with my Spiritual Domain power," Jason said. "They would be a greater threat than the Undeath priests if not for the avatar."

"Which we saw no sign of," Rick said. "We did see priests, but no avatar. Moving on to grey spaces on the map, these are either unexplored or unclaimed, as of when we were there. Light grey for unclaimed, dark grey for unexplored. That only leaves the territories marked in white. You'll note that these territories form mostly direct chains that link the green ones."

"Which I assume is the point," Jason said. "I do spot a few detours, most of which look to be avoiding red zones. Not all, though."

"Some territories will be harder to clear than others," Rick said. "Some have strange environmental challenges that may become controllable once dealt with, but that would be a slow process. The white territories represent the ones we can turn green the fastest."

"Is speed that important?" Phoebe asked. "Shouldn't we go slow and steady to unify the territories?"

"No, for several reasons," Jason said.

"Yes," Lorenn agreed, the brightheart leader leaning forward in her chair. "Those of us who have held territories understand the rules instinctively. When you challenge another for a territory they have claimed, they have a certain amount of time to defend it. If no one is there to do that when the time runs out, the territory is taken without effort."

"How short a time do defenders have to arrive?" Arabelle asked.

"One hundred and seventeen minutes," Jason said. "Just under two hours."

"Reaching a challenged area in that time is possible," Arabelle said. "Gold-rankers can go hundreds of kilometres in that time if they aren't too slowed down by enemies and obstacles."

"The other key reason for a less consolidated approach," Jason said, "is that we have travel options. I've already tested portalling to other territories and my connection to them is enough to make a portal work sight unseen. I'm silver rank, so I can send through other silver-rankers, but not gold."

"Can't you let gold-rankers into your soul realm, portal yourself and then let them out on the other side?" Arabelle asked.

"Maybe," Jason said. "I've found that using my soul realm portal too often has a destabilising effect, both on the portal and the area around it. It makes the magic wonky and shuts down portals, storage spaces and dimensional bags. It also takes a while before it settles and I can use the portal again safely, even if I go somewhere else. I've been using something in my soul to influence this space more than other people claiming territories and keeping a soul portal open all the time makes the process more effective. It's interrupting that flow that causes problems. Keeping it open is fine; it's opening and closing the portal that causes trouble."

"When we were preparing for the underground expedition," Miriam said, "the idea of using your soul realm to shuttle gold-rankers through silver-rank portals was brought up. You claimed that doing so would interfere with the functionality of your regular portal. That it would treat you as if you were the rank of the people in your soul."

"That was a restriction that I once had," Jason said. "I continue to claim it exists to avoid people trying to exploit what I can do. This situation is more important than keeping the secret, however, which is why Arabelle brought it up."

"So, transporting a group of gold-rankers is a viable option?" Miriam asked.

"Yes," Jason said, "but one to be held in reserve until absolutely needed. The portal is open right now and the feedback I'm getting from it tells me that pushing too hard would be a very bad idea. That being said, I believe it will work. So long as we don't use it more than every couple of days at most, moving gold-rankers through my soul realm should work."

"Then we have an emergency response option," Miriam said. "That alleviates the immediate pressure, but it seems that unifying the territories will put us in a better position in the long term."

"Yes," Lorenn said. "If it's all one territory, defending it will be easier."

"Not to mention a better base from which to find the rest of our respective groups," Rick added.

"We need to decide what order to tackle them in," Miriam said. "As we've already established, the priorities are the two territories where unconscious messengers were left behind. If we have the power to portal people, I suggest jumping silver-rank teams into both areas. Using those areas as a base, the teams start moving towards each other and meeting in the middle, claiming white territories as they go."

She looked at Jason.

"You will need to stay on the move, Operations Commander, claiming each territory as it's cleared. While the silver-rankers link those two territories to each other, the gold-rankers can link this territory to them. They need to go the long way anyway, so we should split them into two groups as well. One moves slowly, clearing territories for you to claim. The other moves fast, joining the silver-rankers in the least amount of time."

"Aside from how much running around I'll have to do claiming territories," Jason said, "that seems efficient. We start by connecting this territory with those where the confused messengers have just woken up. Then we move on to the remaining two territory clusters."

"The territories originally unified by Councilwoman Lorenn should be the next priority," Miriam said.

"Why is that?" Jason asked.

"Operations Commander, you've stated that the welfare of the messengers released in these regions is paramount."

"Yes," Jason confirmed.

"I happen to agree," Miriam said, "although I will admit my concerns are more practical than ethical. The messengers are an asset. Even if we don't use them ourselves, we cannot expect our enemies to have the same restraint."

"And until the territories are a contiguous whole," Jason added, "they can't be defended as one. Outsiders can come along and take areas piecemeal."

"Precisely," Miriam said. "We prioritise the areas with freshly woken messengers to keep them from the hands of the Undeath priests or someone else. If they can pluck these zones from your hands with minimal fight, they gain a lot of messenger slaves with minimal effort. We need to secure these isolated territories as a unified whole."

"And then we can defend them accordingly," Jason agreed. "I'm still unclear why that means prioritising the councilwoman's former territory, though. She already released the messengers from the territories she unified and brought them here. They are the elemental ones."

"My understanding," Miriam said, "is that they are still linked to the territories the councilwoman claimed. You gained control of the messengers when Councilwoman Lorenn handed those territories over, did you not?"

"I did," Jason said, realisation dawning in his expression. "I've set them free, so maybe they're clear of the territory's influence now. But maybe not. That was a cluster of four territories before she unified them, meaning four territories worth of elemental messengers. They're amongst us now, so the idea of someone flipping a switch and turning them into enemies is a problem. I'd been thinking only Gabriel and Amos left exposed territories. but there's a third."

Jason cast his eyes over the map.

"Miriam, what you just described makes the councilwoman's territory cluster as much or more of a priority than the others. Yet, the plan you laid out doesn't involve taking that territory in the first stage."

"We don't have the forces," Miriam said. "It's the most distant and the most isolated of the four territories. Until the gold-rankers going the long way rejoin the silvers we portal ahead, we would have to spread ourselves too thin. In the meantime, I recommend reserving your ability to shuttle gold-rankers through your soul space. If that zone is targeted before we are ready, we can respond accordingly."

"The elemental messengers aren't the only ones of concern in this plan," Jali pointed out.

Attention moved back to the messenger at Jason's right hand. She hesitated for just a moment under a full table of unfriendly looks.

"The territory clusters unified by Lord Pensinata and Gabriel Remore," she continued, "each have messengers outnumbering the elemental ones. And these are the territories we'll be portalling the silver-rank teams into first. The messengers in both places have just woken up, now that Jason controls those territory clusters. The messengers won't know who they are, where they are or what's happening to them. If we have a group of warriors appear from a portal without warning, we could end up fighting before we have a chance to talk."

"A valid concern," Miriam said. "What do you suggest?"

"Jason and I should go first," Jali said. "I am a messenger, like them, and Jason rules their territories, even if he no longer rules them. He gave them their freedom and they will recognise that."

"I see no problem with this approach," Miriam said. "We want the silver-rank teams in those zones and active as soon as possible."

"I don't like this plan," Lorenn said. "It splits our forces. Not only does it divide the silver- and gold-rankers, but it further divides the ranks themselves. Refusing to use the messengers as an army means we're already outnumbered. This just makes it worse."

"I'm open to different ideas," Jason said. "What alternative do you propose, Councilwoman?"

"I know you want to spare the messengers we command, Asano, so spare the ones you have freed. The elemental messengers I commanded have already been blooded in combat. You wouldn't be putting them through anything they haven't already seen. Your arguments against their numbers being unwieldy is true, but your portal tricks could solve many of the problems of deploying such a large force."

"We've been over this, Councilwoman," Jason said, the tone of his voice a warning.

"As I've said before," Miriam said, "my perspective in devising this approach is based in practicality, not ethics. Like it or not, Operations Commander, using the messengers may well prove unavoidable in the long run. There may be no other way. But from a tactical perspective, I would prefer to keep our forces agile at this stage. Lord Geller showed us the distances we have to cover and portalling that many people isn't practical. We could use the Operation Commander's soul realm to do it, but that would leave us without the ability to rapidly deploy our gold-rankers. If we can't do that, those same elemental messengers could go from asset to enemy without our having a chance to respond."

Lorenn's nod was reluctant but definite.

"That's settled, then," Jason said. "Let's nail down the specific disposition of forces and we'll get going."

Clive was indelicate as he ran the knife along the Undeath priest's back. The crude ritual diagram he had sliced from the priest's skin was not healing, despite a gold-rank recovery attribute. Clive tossed the knife aside and slapped a hand to the priest's back, ignoring the blood soaking over his fingers. He chanted the ritual's incantation and the diagram lit up dark red for a moment before fading to nothing. He then removed his hand and tipped some crystal wash over it.

"It's done," he said roughly. "It won't stop his powers outright, but they'll be diminished and his blood will burn."

The Adventure Society largely overlooked the propagation of iron and bronze suppression collars, but at least paid lip service to controlling the silver ones. The golds were truly restricted, however, and no one present had one. As far as Clive was aware, the only gold collars they had were the ones Jason and Lord Amos used for aura training.

The ritual Clive used instead was cruel, not actually restricted but certainly iffy. Normally, he wouldn't use such a ritual, but he was not in his right mind. He could feel the power of his territories stoking his rage and ambition. His imperfect control over them was making him paranoid as well, his thoughts questioning people he should have trusted.

Clive was self-analytical enough to recognise these effects. Recognising them did not mean his judgement was unaffected, though, which he also recognised. It had been easy to keep an objective mind at first, compartmentalising useless thoughts the way he always had. But it grew harder with each new territory, more and more gunk accumulating in the cogs of his clockwork mind.

The rest of the leadership group had watched him perform the ritual, Clive ignoring their wary expressions as he moved to join them.

"We have to stop claiming territories," he growled. "If I take a sixth,

I'm certain my judgement will be dangerously compromised. A seventh would probably have me lose control altogether."

"I agree that we should stop," Emir said, looking at his wife with concern. Constance had also been claiming territories and was currently sitting alone, looking off into the distance with a thousand-yard stare.

Having Constance claim territories had been Clive's idea. Once he realised the territories were compromising his mind, he had suggested spreading the load.

"Could we just have another person start taking territories?" asked Marla, the brightheart commander.

"We've already claimed a lot," Emir said. "It's time to find Jason and hand it all over. We should switch to moving fast through territories instead of clearing them out. We move fast and only fight as much as we need to."

"Alright," Marla said. "Does that mean we leave the prisoners behind?"

Emir turned to look at the freshly sealed Undeath priest being led off to join the others. The cultist leader, Beaufort, had taken charge of him. Thus far, they had eleven silver-rank priests alive, or at least animate. They all wore suppression collars, with only the new gold-rank addition different.

"We take them with us," Clive said. "We won't have time to come back if we need them."

"I never realised how many priests they had," Marla said. "We've taken this many alive, killed others and that's just us. How many are out there?"

"Undeath hoards his forces and then uses them all at once," Emir said. "Hundred-thousand-strong undead armies don't come from nowhere. It took a lot of hands to set that up."

"Good," Clive growled. "We're going to need as many as we can get."

18

ALIENNESS AND FAMILIARITY

THE AIR WAS HOT AND HEAVY, DESPITE THE DELUGE OF RAIN. A GOLD-rank messenger, Mahk Den Kahla, floated in the air, his aura pushing aside the downpour. That didn't help visibility; the sky filled with a grey haze. He could only make out a handful of the countless massive stone spires that rose from the rainforest below like arms grasping at the sky. At the top of each spire was an ancient ruin, castles, temples and palaces brought low by the weather seemingly long ago.

Mahk knew that wasn't possible, of course; the territory had existed for less than two weeks. This strange zone was full of strange things, and rules that changed with each new territory. Annoyingly, many of the territories muted his perception significantly, this one included. Any magical sense he pushed out was soaked up by the rain, leaving only his mundane perception.

His ordinary senses fared not much better, despite their gold-rank strength. The rain and the humid haze it failed to put down cut off his vision, making only the closest few spires visible at a time. His ears fared little better, hearing nothing but the rain as it fell around him. He could taste the air, heavy but fresh, clean and not entirely unpleasant. That made it unique in the wet, hot murk of this wretched territory.

Mahk had arrived in this latest territory with his retinue of silver-rank messengers. Some had been corrupted like himself, only to wake up in this place. Some had woken beside him, while others he'd picked up along the way.

Then there were the new messengers, more released from stasis with every territory he claimed. They were blank slates, recognising none of the values that should be intrinsic to their kind. That absence in them left Mahk unsettled. He would protect the true messengers, within reason, but not these uncanny replicas of the real thing. They were weapons to be used, resources to be expended.

There were more than messengers in the territories, however. Every territory boasted different living anomalies and the same undead. The anomalies were varied and seemed tied to the zones in which they originated. The undead were a different story and perhaps held clues to the situation Mahk found himself in.

The undead were mostly brighthearts. Mahk had paid little attention to the occupants of the underground realm he and the other messengers had invaded, but clearly, something had happened to them. Not only had so many died, but they had been brought back as deathless monsters. The presence of some stitched-together abominations spoke to the involvement of necromancers, confirmed when Mahk had met one himself. Unfortunately, the fight had been hard enough that Mahk had been forced to kill him, leaving his questions unanswered.

Most disturbing were the elemental messengers turned undead. Mahk's memories were little more than hazy flashes, but he was sure he had been one of them, but the living version, not the undead. At first, he had thought some of the others were corrupted, killed and then raised, but soon realised that wasn't it. He saw more of these animated messengers than should have been possible. Between that and all the blank slate messengers, someone or something was producing new messengers.

Between the living anomalies and the undead, neither threatened a gold-rank messenger, even the gold-rank abominations. The living anomalies had been a joke, boasting gold-rank auras but strength that lingered at the lesser stages of silver. Some were barely stronger than bronze.

Two weeks later, that was no longer the case. His silver-rank minions had gone from cutting them down like servant races harvesting crops to moving in groups with readiness and caution. Mahk mostly employed the blank messengers to deal with them now, throwing away their lives because it was too slow otherwise. Claiming the territory replenished their number and more anyway.

Mahk was unsure of where he was or what was happening, but he knew enough. It was a dimensional space and it could be conquered, so conquer it he would. He was not the only one with this objective, as the Undeath priest proved, so perhaps there were allies to be found. The only issue would be conflict with other gold-rank messengers over who would claim final dominance.

After seeing the state of the territory, Mahk had almost left and sought another. The reason he didn't was that it had already been claimed; the anomalies had already been cleared out. The more he considered a future battle for dominance with other messengers, the more he reconsidered spending the lives of his messenger army. Once he eliminated the territory owner, he would get their land and forces at no cost.

He had sent his forces to scout for the owner. The odd message windows told him that his challenge was active, so they were here somewhere. His silver-rankers each had a group of blank messengers they could sacrifice if they needed to escape. The more time he spent in this territory, however, the more unease crept into his mind. The Undeath priest's territory had a feel about it, an echo of the Undeath god. This place had a feel to it as well, a mix of alienness and familiarity.

That unease was making Mahk worry about his silver-rankers. Communication was always an issue, their speaking stones lost during their corruption. Normally, they compensated with flight, visibility being clear in the sky. In the blinding rain, that didn't work.

Pushing aside his concerns, Mahk continued his own search. As hours passed and he failed to find any of his people, those worries came back, gnawing at him with uncharacteristic doubt. Finally, he spotted a splash of colour against the bleak grey of the rain, a plume of rainbow smoke rising from the rainforest canopy.

Mahk's gold-rank speed had him crashing through the trees in a flash. What he found was a group of messenger bodies scattered through the dense undergrowth. Little remained of them, as they were actively dissolving when he arrived, but he'd moved fast enough to catch a few details. Their bodies all showed signs of burn wounds, suggesting fire powers or some variant. Most of the corpses were blank messengers, an acceptable loss, but the woman leading them was not. Losing a true messenger was an unacceptable stain on Mahk Den Kahla's own dignity.

He looked around, his senses slightly less muted under the partial shelter of the rainforest canopy. He noticed the bodies were all dissolving simultaneously, not staggered at all, meaning they were not breaking down naturally with time. Someone had used a loot power to plunder the magic from them, triggering their dissolution all at once. This meant that it had only just happened, putting whoever or whatever was responsible close by.

He didn't even get a chance to start looking before he heard a voice behind him. It was a male voice with a heavy accent.

"I did not hit her, I did not."

He spun around to find a messenger floating between the trees in his direction, his shoes brushing the undergrowth. He had strange clothes, more fitted than most messengers preferred, along with shoes instead of sandals or bare feet. His face showed amusement instead of proper messenger stoicism and he nodded a too-casual greeting at Mahk.

"Oh, hi, Mark."

"How did you know my name is Mahk?"

The messenger stopped, surprise on his face. When he spoke again, his accent was suddenly gone.

"Wait, that's really your name? Wow, it's all coming up Boris today."

The Undeath avatar struggled against the golden chains that had burst from the ground to bind it like spring grass. More chains kept emerging, wrapping around the avatar until it was all but mummified.

Gary looked around to see the others had already crossed the shadowy veil of the territorial boundary. He wasted no time and followed, joining the group of silver-rank adventurers. Rufus was there and had taken charge of the group. Korinne Pescos was also present, but was not doing well after losing two members of her team. She'd put their undead bodies down herself.

Korinne had been all but catatonic until they stumbled across Rosa, another member of her team. It had brought some spark back to Korinne's dead eyes, but she remained distracted and morose.

The last members of the main group were Claire and Hannah, the elven Adeah twins from Rick's team. Other than them, Gary's army of golden-eyed messengers floated in the sky above them.

"That won't hold it long," Gary said.

He lifted his hammer to point along the shadowy boundary line.

"We need to cross into the first adjacent territory that way. It's close enough that the avatar might not chase us here before we cross over. If it does, that territory is a lightning field that muffles perception. We may be able to lose it there."

"What's a lightning field?" Claire asked.

"You'll see soon enough," Gary told her. "We have to go."

"You're sure you don't want to stay and fight?" Rufus asked.

"It's pointless," Gary said. "Me and the avatar are each too tough for the other to kill. We need to gather enough gold-rankers to tip the scales, and we won't do it standing here. Now, no more questions. Get moving, all of you."

The silver-rankers started moving at pace, Gary keeping easy pace with them. Behind them, pale messengers came pouring through the boundary. An equal army of messengers swept down from the sky to meet them, their eyes shining with golden light.

As they ran, Claire moved close to her sister and activated a privacy screen.

"Is it just me, or is that demigod extremely sexy?"

"It's just you," Hannah told her.

"I don't think it is."

"He's covered in fur!"

"I can live with that."

"He's twice as tall as you."

"I can *definitely* live with that."

<hr />

Pallid messengers flew up the mountainside while undead scrambled up the slope beneath them. At the base of the mountain, several Undeath priests looked up, watching their forces ascend.

"What power do you think is up there?" one of them wondered.

"It doesn't matter," another of them said. "Whether it helps us or we merely keep it from the brighthearts, it advantages us."

"How many brighthearts were spotted?"

"Around a dozen, and three times that in elemental messengers."

Neil and Dustin erupted from their hiding place along with Durrum and three other elite brighthearts. They had been hidden underground by Durrum and Kurik, another earth-type brightheart. The ground exploded up, showering the priests in a dirt cloud and blasting them with force. The adventurers and brighthearts struck hard and fast, going for the kill as fast as could be managed with silver-rankers.

The forces the priests had sent up the mountain had turned around, beckoned back at the moment of the attack, but they failed to return in time. With the priests dead and the territory claimed, the pallid messengers went from enemies to neutral, flying upwards aimlessly. Without control, the undead went from a focused weapon to a mindless, leaderless mob.

This left the undead ripe for a pincer attack. Although the brighthearts and adventurers lacked numbers, they had the tactical advantage. The brighthearts at the top of the mountain swept down while the ones at the bottom moved up, grinding the mindless, aimless undead between them.

None of the messengers involved themselves; the ones at the top of the mountain stayed where they were. The pale messengers, previously under priest control, hovered in the air, confused. They didn't turn into elemental messengers under Durrum's command, but they regained some of their colour as Undeath's influence diminished.

"I admit that I was wrong about the messengers," Neil said. "I was against using them even as a distraction, but it has been working out. My concern is that Durrum will command them into battle."

They watched as Durrum went on a rampage, at one point using the severed leg of one undead to beat another apart. Even when the enemy were done, their animating force dispersed, Durrum didn't stop. He stood over them, venting his berserker rage with conjured stone spears, a stone hammer and even his bare hands. He pounded already crushed skulls into the rocky ground and tore inert bodies limb from limb. The adventurers looked to Kurik, Durrum's best friend. He looked between them and Durrum with concern and nodded.

"You know that Pebbles is a few bricks short of a wall, right?" the rabbit asked. He, Neil and Dustin were standing in one of the sleep chambers below the control room of the lightning mesa.

"Am I meant to know what that means?" Dustin asked.

"He's worried that Durrum is unstable," Neil said. "Which is an appreciable concern, but it won't help anyone if he hears you talking like that."

"You've got bigger issues than what I have to say," the rabbit told him. "Or did you not see the fist-shaped hole in the wall there?"

Neil and Dustin looked to the dent in the wall surrounded by spiderweb cracks.

"And what did you say to inspire that?" Neil asked.

"Nothing," the rabbit said. "He was in here alone. I was in the control room with his mate Kurik when we heard the thump and came down to check. Kurik took him up top to cool off. Thanks for assuming that it was me, though. Real sense of camaraderie you've got going on."

Neil frowned.

"You're right," he said. "I apologise."

"Yeah, well, no worries. We're all pretty [bleep] stressed. If that guy loses it, we're all knee-deep in brown, you know that. I can control the lightning from in here, but it won't shoot at the bloke who owns the place."

"How did you find that out without testing it?" Dustin asked.

"It pops up on the monitors when you point a drone at him. Of course, I wouldn't try to shoot him with lightning. What I did try to do was tell you before the last territory that Pebbles was ready to flip his lid. Now he's not just ready; he's halfway gone. You're the ones that put him in charge, so you're the ones that have to fix this."

"Happy to dump this all on us rather than take part, then?" Neil asked.

"I already tried shooting him with lightning and that didn't work at all. It's time for you fellas to have a crack."

Neil's hands balled into fists. He closed his eyes, took a calming breath and unclenched his white-knuckled hands.

"Just stay out of his way," Neil told the rabbit. "We'll figure this out."

"No worries there, mate. I'm not going anywhere near that nut bag."

"Durrum, we need to stop," Neil said, atop the lightning mesa. He and Dustin stood with Kurik as Durrum paced back and forth. He was more a bundle of energy than the lightning hitting the circle of rods above their heads.

"You fear my power," Durrum snarled.

"Yes," Neil admitted freely. "That power is affecting your mind and you're too smart not to realise that. I know you feel it, Durrum. You're a good man. A sensible man. That's why we agreed to follow you in the first place. Just stop for a moment and consider what's happening."

"He's right, Durry," Kurik said. "You've always been the smart one. The thoughtful one. Just be who you are."

Durrum scowled, then gave a reluctant nod.

"I'm... it's hard to think. My head is so loud."

Neil and Kurik shared a look.

"Durrum," Kurik said. "It's time we found the other groups. We need to consolidate what you have won for us with someone who can control it all safely. We need to get your head cleared."

"You rest here," Neil said. "If someone comes for this place, your power is what will stop them. We'll start scouting for..."

He trailed off as Durrum went still, looking out from the mesa. The others followed his gaze but saw nothing under the cloud-blackened sky.

"Someone has come for this place," Durrum said. "Tell the rabbit and the other controllers to send out a drone and get ready to fight."

"Have they challenged your territory?" Dustin asked.

"No," Durrum said. "And gods help them if they try."

"Gary!" Neil yelled angrily. "Get that off him now!"

Lightning was attracted to the hammer the size of a large house with Durrum somewhere under it. Gary, a fraction of the hammer's size, lifted it into the air and tossed it aside. A lightning bolt passed through the hammer and into him in the process, to no discernible effect. Everyone looked into the hammer-shaped crater to see no Durrum.

"Where did he go?" Neil wondered aloud.

"We forgot something," Dustin said, drawing all eyes. "He's an earth guy."

Gary vanished under a pyramid of rock as stone spears shot from the ground, smashing into and burying him. His hammer smashed a hole from the inside, and he pushed his way out as if through thick spider webs in an old house.

"This is getting annoying," Gary grumbled. "Calm your man down."

"You did drop a giant hammer on him," Rufus pointed out.

"He attacked me first," Gary said.

"He's claimed too many territories," Neil said. "It's affecting his mind, but we can talk him around. He has to come out of the ground eventually."

"Unless he tries something else," Rufus said, pointing. Everyone turned in that direction to see a horde of elemental messengers descending upon them through the sky.

"How are they flying without the lightning striking them down?" Gary asked.

"We have a rabbit living inside a big rock," Dustin said.

"What?" Rufus asked.

"We think he belongs to Jason," Neil said.

"Oh," Rufus said, neither needing nor wanting further explanation.

"I'm not sure we can get Durrum to stand down his messengers," Neil said as he turned to look at Gary's messengers behind them. "I don't want this to be a bloodbath between allies."

"It won't be," Gary growled.

He crouched down and plunged his hands into the muddy ground. He yanked them up again, holding on to a golden chain that he pulled hand-over-hand like he was raising an anchor. At the end of the chain was Durrum, struggling futilely as Gary pulled him from the earth and lifted him into the air by the neck.

Durrum dangled from one of Gary's hands. The big brightheart suddenly looked small, thrashing ineffectually while the leonid stood still as a mountain. Durrum's eyes burned with fury while Gary's anger was tempered steel.

"I challenge for this territory," Gary growled.

19

THE REASON WE HAVE TO

MAHK DEN KAHLA FOUND THE MESSENGER IN FRONT OF HIM A WORRYING oddity. His mannerisms were bizarre, with none of the dignity expected of a messenger, especially a gold-rank one. Even his clothes were strange. Mahk had woken up in clothes not his own, but very much in the typical messenger style. This Boris Ket Lundi, as he introduced himself, wore clothes reminiscent of the servant races.

"I think it is clear which of us is the superior messenger," Mahk said. "Surrender your territories to me."

"I can't do that."

"You can and you will."

"Vesta Carmis Zell sent me here. Me and several others. To finish what you started."

"My astral king would never tolerate the likes of you."

"I don't belong to her. She bargained us from other astral kings because we have what she needed: Elemental powers that can resist the influence of the natural array. You do realise that is what corrupted you?"

Mahk frowned.

"Yes," he admitted.

Boris turned to look at the great tree jutting up somewhere past the horizon, so vast and distant that there was no guessing the true size. Mahk followed his gaze, feeling the distant echo of the tree's power.

"Did you know the natural array is a part of this place?" Boris asked.

"I can feel the power coming from the tree, but I sense no elemental energy."

"You won't at this distance. But someone has to get a lot closer before all this is done, Mahk. It will only end when someone confronts that power. Someone who hasn't already fallen to its corruption."

Mahk continued staring at the distant tree. Although many territories held mountains and other features that rose higher than the boundary veils, no such terrain was visible. Only the tree could be seen, the tree that filled Mahk with uncharacteristic doubt. Normally, the eternal presence of his astral king steeled Mahk's resolve in moments of uncertainty. Vesta Carmis Zell's touch still lay upon him, but he could feel the divide between them. In this place, he was alone.

"It cannot be me, can it?" Mahk asked softly.

"No," Boris answered gently.

The plan was to link Jason's five disconnected territory clusters. It would consolidate his area of control, make it easier to defend, and secure the messengers belonging to those territories. It would also establish a dominant position in the lower third of the transformation zone's map, giving them a base from which to expand upward.

The first step was connecting Jason's territory with those originally claimed by Amos and Gabriel. This would secure the now-free messengers in those territories from being taken over by an enemy. Jason and Jali successfully contacted the newly awakened messengers in the first target regions, convincing them not to attack the silver-rank teams he portalled in on sight.

Those teams went to work expanding the two territories towards one another, Jason swooping in at the last moment to claim each one. At the same time, gold-rankers expanded out from Jason's original domain, ultimately unifying the three territories into one.

This left two territories under Jason's control still isolated. One had belonged to the Builder cult and held minimal strategic value. The messengers that awakened there were already dead. The last territory became the new priority. Originally claimed by Councilwoman Lorenn of the brighthearts, control of the messengers she had awakened there was up for grabs if an enemy challenged for the territory and won.

That challenge came sooner than Jason and his allies would have liked, but not as soon as they feared. Having consolidated the first three territories, they were ready to move on to the next. Jason loaded up those willing to travel through his soul realm, which was not everyone.

The Builder cultists balked, refusing to submit themselves to that much of Jason's power and control. Amos Pensinata also held back, but they needed to leave the core area with defenders in any case. Marek Nior Vargas also stayed, despite his familiarity with the soul realm. He would not risk his people like that unless Jason forced him, which he did not. Marek was willing to at least stay behind and defend their main territory with the cultists and Amos.

The group had been confident in meeting any challenge, having a large force of gold- and silver-rankers at their command. Even without using messenger slaves, they were confident. The challenge came from Undeath priests, the most likely candidates, but in greater numbers than anticipated. Not only did they have more essence-users, but they led an army of pallid messengers and undead.

Numbers alone were not enough to deter adventurers. It deterred their allies a little, but they didn't worry about that. The silver-rankers focused on the minions while the gold-rankers went for the priests. Jason's new affliction, Ghost Fire, ravaged any undead it touched. His weren't the divine flames of the goddess of Death, but they still devastated the unliving elements of the enemy forces. It didn't harm the pallid messengers, but they were touched with undeath energy. Jason's aura suppressed such energy, diminishing their strength considerably. Once Gordon's butterflies got going, they fell in droves as well.

The battle was not a one-sided affair, however. The Undeath priests were experts in wielding a less powerful but more numerous force against their enemies. The strongest weapon the priests had was an understanding of their opposition. The priests had a completely expendable army while the adventurers would be maimed with every loss. Messengers and undead were sent in suicide rushes, willing to trade five, ten or even twenty of their own if it meant a kill. The priests had less personal power, but they could use the undead as weapons, detonating them in explosions of bone or poison gas.

The adventurers and their allies understood the mathematics of attrition. If they were willing to take the losses, they would certainly win, but at a price. The priests bet on them not being willing to accept the sacrifice, and they bet right. While Jason and his companions devastated the minion army, they quickly learned not to push too hard. Anyone who advanced too boldly found themselves swarmed by enemies willing to trade deaths twenty to one.

The adventurers were elites amongst elites, learning fast and reacting effectively. They switched to a more conservative approach, watching each other's backs and pulling allies out of danger. They suffered casualties but managed to escape any deaths, although there were many near misses.

Adding to the danger were the priests. Their malignant powers made healing less effective or even harmful, something Jason could also accomplish. It could be dealt with by healers with the right expertise and power, which they did have. It couldn't be dealt with swiftly, however, diminishing the power of the adventurers.

In the end, neither side was willing to push hard enough for total victory. This was not the underground death city where the priests could replenish their undead forces all but infinitely. While they were willing to sacrifice their minions there was a limit, especially with adventurers devastating those forces. Building them up again would take time and they could not afford to lose them all here.

On the adventurer side, they weren't willing to spend the lives it would take to secure a complete victory. They already held the territory, so their priority was keeping people alive. Even if the priests managed to slink away with much of their army still intact, the territory was retained.

In the aftermath, Jason worked on removing the malignant power of the Undeath priests on their wounded. Different powers excelled at removing different afflictions, and Jason's was perfect for this situation. His ability, Feast of Absolution, specialised in eliminating curses, diseases and unholy power, the exact kinds wielded by the priests. He'd been using it in the battle, but now he was joining the healers for a more dedicated approach.

The power even circumvented some of the traps such afflictions held for ordinary cleansing, as that was not what his ability did. Rather than cleanse, it consumed, devouring the malignant magic to fuel Jason's power. The result left the patients grateful to Jason, but also wary.

As Jason worked, Miriam Vance approached him.

"Did we manage to save everyone?" he asked.

"Almost," she told him, looking weary. "We lost a cultist and a couple of brighthearts, all silver rank. That's damn near a miracle for a fight like that. We brought the best down that hole with us, and it's paying off now. And those brighthearts might not have the best training, but they're seasoned. I couldn't have asked for better forces to command."

"The priests can't say the same," Jason said. "They're all about expendability."

"They'll most likely seek out unclaimed territory. Rebuild their forces by collecting more messengers and undead, animating anomalies as they go."

"Agreed," Jason said. "I have my shadow familiar tracking them, so he'll confirm it or alert us if they do something unexpected."

"We don't have time to wait for them to rebuild and come back," Miriam said. "We left minimal defenders in the larger territory we just unified and we need to reinforce them before someone else comes knocking at our door."

"You want to follow the priests. Finish the job."

"We'll recover to full strength faster than they will. Our people were hurt and shaken, but giving up the victory kept everyone alive. Even slow, painstaking healing is faster than animating a new army. A second round will have us at the advantage, especially if we're the aggressors."

Miriam followed Jason as he moved to the next group of afflicted. His power made their life force visible, vibrant red tainted with sickly colours. The taint streamed out of them, moving through the air in twisted tendrils for Jason to devour, absorbing them into his outstretched hands. It cast his face in shifting, corrupted light, his nebulous eyes shining.

"If we chase, it's into an unstable situation," Jason said, resuming their conversation.

Miriam blinked, his casual tone at odds with his villainous appearance. "I'm sorry, what?"

"I'm saying that pursuing them into unclaimed territories is a bad idea," he said. "The living anomalies are strong now, and those priests aren't fools. If we have to fight them and the anomalies at the same time, they'll bleed us in a three-way fight. Even with their diminished forces, they can afford to soak losses we can't. They've just shown us that a battle of attrition is fighting on their terms, not ours."

"But if we could afford losses…"

She left the sentence hanging, but he didn't respond, focusing on healing the next group. Seeing he would keep ignoring her, she finished her thought.

"Jason, if you lift your moratorium on using our own messengers—"

"We don't have messengers. I've set them free, Miriam. They're not anyone's to command but their own."

"If you and Jali Corrik Fen asked, I think they would fight."

"You're probably right."

Jason and Miriam stared each other down until she sighed.

"Jason, principles—"

"Are not how we win, I know. They're the reason we have to. Don't give me the hard choices speech, Miriam; I've walked that road and left a trail of bodies behind me."

"Then what do you suggest, Operations Commander?"

"I want to take a multi-faceted approach. You agree that the priority is linking this territory with the main one we've unified already?"

"Yes. Once we can defend them as a collective whole, things will get a lot easier. We can afford to ignore the remaining territory for now. With no surviving messengers attached to it, it's strategically all but worthless."

"Agreed. I suggest we balance our forces between this territory and the main one. We don't do any expanding other than to unify what we already have. Rick and Sophie are both out scouting for others, and finding more allies before taking the priests on again could tip the scales. More allies will play to our strengths while throwing messenger slaves at them will not. That's how they fight, and they'll be a lot better at it."

Miriam nodded.

"That's the best argument for not using the messengers I've heard."

"More than not using enslaved child soldiers?"

"You're the Operations Commander, Jason. Ethics is your area. I'm the tactical Commander, and my area is how to win."

"I don't believe you're that callous, Miriam."

"I have to be, with this much at stake. You seem determined to be soft, so I have to be hard."

"And we meet somewhere in the middle?"

"Ideally. If we're not going to recruit messengers to fight them, what will we do about the priests? I don't think leaving them be and hoping more of our allies show up is a good approach."

Jason let out a chuckle. As he was in the middle of devouring the dark power out of people, it came out as more than a little sinister.

"Miriam, you said yourself that they'll take longer than we will to recover. I'd like to see if we can't extend that timeframe. Not a direct attack but a harassment campaign. Attacks of opportunity, nibbling at their weak points. Striking from safety, shaving their numbers and getting out. Not enough to stop them rebuilding, just slow them down and frustrate their leadership. Exhaustion by a thousand cuts."

"You want to do it yourself," Miriam realised.

"I can hide from gold-rankers. Move alone and undetected. Since we all joined up, my role has been little more than showing up in freshly cleared territories to claim them. Since I'm jumping all over the place anyway, ducking in to annoy some priests isn't out of my way."

"Unless you make a mistake, get caught, and everything comes apart. Our leader and our territories gone. Yes, you have the skills and the power to evade and escape, but there are no guarantees. When the odds of failure are small but the price of failure is everything, it's not worth the risk unless the risk is absolutely necessary. Which it isn't."

"You're saying the captain shouldn't go on the away mission."

"I have no idea if that's what I'm saying."

"Would it help if I put on a red shirt?"

"I hope you talking nonsense means you've decided not to go risking your neck."

"It does. You've talked me around, Tactical Commander, but I at least want to participate in clearing the territories some more. The anomalies are getting feisty and I haven't had the chance to fight enemies like this for a while."

"So long as you don't do it alone."

"Deal. I still think my strategy of harassing the priests is sound, though. See if you can't assemble a small group that can handle that. Keep it small; we don't want to divert too many resources, and stealth matters more than power."

"I believe Lorenn has some brighthearts that may fit the task. They have ash and earth affinities, with powers more suited to stealth than fighting. Drifting on the breeze, moving through the ground, their auras blending into the elements around them such that even gold-rankers have trouble sensing them. Not as strong in a stand-up fight, but they're the best scouts and assassins the brighthearts have, according to Lorenn."

"That sounds perfect. We have them here?"

"Lorenn was lucky enough to assemble a good number of them on the way to finding us."

"See what she thinks about using them, then. They're her people, so let's not just deploy them on her out of hand."

A BITTER CUP

Undeath's avatar moved through the lightning field in massive strides. As tall as the iron towers dotting the landscape, lightning peppered the field to no effect. The magical electricity was more attracted to the avatar than the lightning rods. The undead behemoth reached the mesa in which the controls for the lightning were hidden. It was abandoned now, but electricity arced around the ring of towers on the top.

The giant undead avatar let out a roar that was not angry or pained but a mindless expression of power. It pulled back an arm and then unleashed it in a punch that staved in a massive section of the hollow mesa.

Several territories away, Neil and Gary's group were pushing through an unclaimed territory made up of wetlands and mud flats. Gary was annihilating anything and everything that got in their way, at that moment living anomaly mud monsters. He paused briefly before resuming battle.

Trailing behind the unstoppable demigod were adventurers, bright-hearts and cultists. Amongst them was an anthropomorphic rabbit who paused at the exact same moment as Gary. Beside him, Dustin also stopped.

"Is there a problem?" Dustin asked.

"I'm a four-foot rabbit wading through mud that's knee-deep on a tree-trunk prick like you. Of course, there's a problem."

"You're not very likeable," Dustin told him and resumed his path forward.

Belinda, Taika, Humphrey and Stash had been rushing through territories, fighting when they had to and running when they could. The living anomalies had grown more dangerous with every region they passed through, leaving them increasingly happy to not have any territories of their own. Trying to hold them would have either pinned them down or forced them to leave their claimed territory undefended.

Unencumbered by land they couldn't leave or defend, they crossed hundreds of kilometres per day, moving through multiple territories. Their mode of travel varied from territory to territory, depending on the terrain. Sometimes, Stash turned into a swift steed that could carry them all. Other times, they went on foot, relying on silver-rank speed and endurance. One territory had featured floating rocks and Belinda had built them an improvised vehicle. She never had time to figure out why it exploded.

Moving fast proved critical, as they realised both how large the transformation zone was and how far they were from their allies. They had encountered the edge of the zone in multiple territories, getting a sense of the geography. The edge was a silvery haze where the landscape broke down like pieces of biscuit dropped in a cup of tea.

They had run-ins with messengers and priests, but the living anomalies had steadily overtaken both as the greater threat. They had always been numerous, making them hard to avoid, but that hadn't been a problem until their power started approaching the strength of their auras.

In one territory, the group hid in a rocky crevice, a concealment ritual from Belinda making it seem like a flat wall. A massive herd of animals was going by, far too many to fight at their current strength. The creatures were vaguely like heidels but with strange features. They were stockier, with fur instead of scales and horns on their single head.

"Are these the horses Jason keeps talking about?" Belinda wondered.

"Nah, those are some kind of cow," Taika said. "Like aurochs or something."

"It doesn't matter what they are," Humphrey said. "It matters how strong they are. If this is their power now, we silver-rankers will end up as little more than prey once more territories have been claimed."

Onslow the rune tortoise had the power to change his size. Right now, he was the size of a small car with the neck poking out from his shell the width of a pony. A boy who looked around twelve was riding him and cheering, a leg slung over each side of that neck. The youth looked like a young Humphrey but with darker skin, along with silver hair and eyes.

"Faster!" boy Stash demanded, which Onslow was fully capable of if he flew. Instead, Onslow plodded over the grass on his thick legs, to Stash's ongoing complaint.

A group of adventurers looked on from the top of a large cloud vehicle, under the shade of an awning. After running into one another, Belinda and Clive's groups had stopped for a much-needed rest. They were in another unclaimed territory, a grassy savannah where the living anomalies were large and powerful, but easy to see coming.

Humphrey, Belinda, Taika and Stash had been increasingly desperate by the time they encountered Clive's group. They had still been able to fight small groups of anomalies, but the need to move with care had drastically slowed their pace. More than once they had been fighting one group only to flee as another joined the fray. Now they had greater numbers, gold-rankers and, most importantly, friends.

"You don't look so good, Boss," Belinda told Clive.

Clive's group's journey had been slower. They had left the territories held by himself and Constance, an anchor that had not weighed down Humphrey's group. Those territories were undefended now, but they hoped to cede them to Jason before an enemy snatched them up. Their group's subsequent movement had not been as fast as Belinda's; their numbers forced them to fight where the smaller group could hide and sneak.

The advantage had switched with the growing power of the anomalies. The smaller group were forced to slow down while the larger could still fight. Their numbers and gold-rankers had proven the match of anything they had encountered thus far.

"We can still punch a straight line through territories now that we aren't looking to claim them," Emir explained. "There's no dodging the fights, though, and no question they're growing harder."

He nodded at the bus-shaped cloud vehicle resting on the grass nearby.

"Since we were drawing anomalies like flies anyway, we've started barrelling through in my cloud vehicle. We usually stay close to the ground, though, as the sky has proven dangerous even to my vehicle.

There was a swarm of storm locust anomalies that did some real damage, and one territory had clouds that tried to eat us. We fought them off easily enough, but that one made me nervous."

"We need to find Jason," Clive said, his voice shaky. As Belinda had observed, he did not look good. Silver-rankers didn't normally perspire, regardless of the temperature.

Emir looked at his wife, who fared a little better than Clive by virtue of her higher rank.

"Yes," Emir said. "We need to find Jason. All the times he leaves his familiar in our shadows and, now we could use it, nothing. I think. Shade?"

He looked around suspiciously.

"He better not be here," Emir grumbled.

In a territory of wetlands, mud flats and mangrove swamps, they couldn't find a hard, flat surface to draw out a ritual circle. In the end, Neil had one of the earth brighthearts turn river clay into a flat plate and one of the fire brighthearts bake it dry. It wasn't ideal, but it was serviceable. They had tried calling up stone from beneath the mud, but the earth brighthearts couldn't find any.

The entire zone was clay and mud, all infused with elemental water energy that left the fire brighthearts uncomfortable. They had lived their lives with a constant background of fire energy from the natural array around which their society was built. Only the growing chambers that fed them were different, and most of the fire and magma types were kept away.

Once the platform was finished, Neil went to work. Grand Renewal was the name of Neil's most powerful healing ability, an essence ability that required a ritual to use. One of its features, common to essence ability rituals, was that he could draw it out in lines of pale blue magic. This saved him the need to pour out lines of powder or draw them with chalk. Being an essence ability ritual also reduced the materials required, just a few judiciously placed piles of spirit coins.

Once the ritual diagram was complete, the brighthearts carefully placed a delirious Durrum in the middle. Durrum had been going through withdrawal-like symptoms, worsening as the group pushed itself to move fast. Neil had been putting him through the healing ritual each time they stopped to rest, getting him back into shape enough that he could move on his own instead of being carried.

Neil had become the de facto leader of the group after Durrum's territories were claimed by Gary. Gary might have been the most powerful member of the group, but he didn't have the same trust with the brighthearts. Gary's power, and his role holding the wall against undead besiegement, were unquestionable. But to the brighthearts, he was more a phenomenon than a person.

Neil, by contrast, was approachable. They had seen him willing to work not just with but under their own kind, yet still prove not just an important but effective leader. He had been critical to their successful fights against the Undeath priests, both in developing tactics and his using his powers, both on the battlefield and in the aftermath. Everyone loved a healer. Having proven himself without elevating himself, the majority brightheart group accepted his leadership given Durrum's incapacity.

Gary was isolated within the group. Where Neil and Dustin had made a place for themselves amongst the brighthearts, Gary was a walking miracle. He was venerated, but not incorporated. The fact that he was the singular force propelling them through the territories only highlighted this, widening both the group's admiration of him and the gap between them.

He wasn't completely alone, of course. The adventurers had known him before drinking from the Cup of Heroes and offered both commiseration and companionship. It was just a very small group compared to the large collection of brighthearts and cultists.

They had picked up even more as they roamed around, mostly brighthearts but also a couple of cultists and even some essence-users. The brighthearts included a gold-ranker, Jindella, who tried to take command of the group. After words failed, the support for Neil surprising her, she foolishly tried force. On that front, Gary's support was all Neil needed.

Also amongst the essence-users were some non-adventurers: a pair of researchers from the Magic Society. They told the group about how almost half of the research contingent arrived in the transformation zone together, but now only two survived. The fate of the researchers they didn't arrive with they had no idea.

While on the move, Gary was their key to fast movement through territories. With Undeath's avatar the only thing able to challenge him, nothing was able to divert their path as they searched for others. The addition of the gold-rank Jindella gave them a strong presence to watch their backs, making progress even more stable.

No matter how strong the living anomalies grew, Gary ploughed through them. No matter how many Undeath priests appeared before him, they were driven back. The largest group they had seen was led by numerous gold-rankers, yet they turned around and fled on sight, not even attempting a battle with the demigod.

The rabbit had been moving with them but did not enjoy the mud and water of the swamps and wetlands dominating their current territory. He was able to hop across the surface while on the move, but anytime they stopped, he found himself chest deep. After waiting for Durrum's healing ritual to finish, the rabbit approached Neil and took him aside.

"What is it?" Neil asked.

"Turn on your privacy bubble thing," the rabbit said quietly.

Neil took a brooch from his pocket and pressed on the amber gem. A shimmering privacy field snapped into place around them. The rabbit looked over at Gary, who was standing alone, radiating golden light as he watched for threats.

"You need to have a talk with your hairy golden god," the rabbit said.

"Why?"

"You know how I woke up just knowing how to use the controls in the lightning mesa?"

"Yeah."

"Well, now I've forgotten it all. Whatever link I had to that place is gone."

"You think someone else claimed the territory?"

"Someone claimed the territory twice already. First Pebbles, and then great gold merkin took it from him. Neither time I lost the connection."

"Then what are you thinking?"

"Well, shiny boy and the adventurers he had with him were talking about a size-changing undead super-monster with a penchant for random destruction. I think it claimed the territory and smashed the mesa to rubble in the process. Or because it was angry, lightning kept hitting it. Or just because. And given that he owned the territory at the time, there's no way the leader of the Thundercats over there failed to notice. You might want to enquire about that before Lion-O starts falling over on us too."

"I'll speak with him," Neil said. "But, before that, there's something you and I need to discuss while we're under this privacy screen."

"What's that?"

"You call Durrum Pebbles, and Gary a lot of things."

"So what?"

"So, they both have names and you're going to start using them," Neil said. "They've both made incredible sacrifices while you were sitting in a bunker, playing with lightning. As of the moment I drop this privacy screen, you are going to treat them with the dignity they have more than earned."

"Or what?"

"Or when we leave this place, you go one way and everyone else goes another."

"You'll kick me out over some nicknames?"

"I'll kick you out over disrespecting the people that have earned our respect the most."

The rabbit stared at Neil from where he was half-submerged in the muddy water of the flats.

"Fine," he said, then started pushing through the water and out of the screen.

Neil dropped the screen, walked over to Gary and put it up again.

"That damn rabbit," he grumbled.

"You really think Jason made him somehow?"

"He keeps spouting off nonsense that no one has ever heard of and doesn't seem to care."

"That's Jason alright."

"It's like Jason was saving up every bad personality trait he's gotten rid of or toned down since we knew him, and he put them all in this rabbit."

"We'll see what happens when we put him in a room with Jason. But you didn't come over here to talk about the rabbit."

"No."

"You want to talk about the territory," Gary said.

"Yeah."

Gary's unified territory had become very large. Certainly larger than what had driven Durrum to the edge as Gary had added that to his existing territory and remained fine. Neil had initially worried about the effect of that on Gary's mind after what happened to Durrum, but it turned out he was unaffected. He'd just been grumpy about people asking questions when they should have been running away from the avatar of the evil god.

"Your territory is gone?" Neil asked.

"We left it undefended and it now it belongs to the avatar."

"We knew it was the most likely outcome when we set out."

"I could have commanded the messengers we left behind to hold it off."

"They'd have died without stopping it."

"They'd have died slowing it down."

"It's slow enough. You're the one who said it's too mindless to chase us efficiently. Has that changed?"

"Maybe. Once the Undeath high priest gets a hold of it, the avatar will stop roaming around, chasing after anything that wanders into view. You know all the messengers we left behind belong to the avatar now. The time will come when we have to fight them, and we could have avoided that. Made sure they died before they were turned against us."

"While they're alive, there's still a chance to save them."

"Messengers don't deserve saving. They deserve to die."

"I don't believe that. And I don't think you do either. I know you're angry, Gary. You were served a bitter cup, and you have every right to be furious. But I also know you're too smart and too good to let yourself take it out on victims."

"You sound like Jason."

"Whatever Jason might think, Gary, our world had morals long before Jason arrived to bequeath us his otherworldly wisdom. You know when something is right or wrong just as well as I do. Yes, we kill the Undeath priests on sight. They've made their choices, but the messengers are slaves. Slaves with shackles on their hearts and minds, and those are the adult messengers. The ones we've been waking up in these territories are children. It might not seem that way, but that's what they are. Yes, we kill the ones we have to, but we save the ones we can."

Gary nodded. It was slight and reluctant, but he nodded.

"Now," Neil said. "You lost the territory. When?"

"A few hours ago. While we were on the move."

"Any symptoms? Anything like what Durrum is going through."

"No."

"Are you sure? Don't hide it from me, Gary. We're relying on you, and we can make arrangements if you need rest. If you collapse on us at the wrong moment, though, we're in real trouble."

"I'm fine. Compared to the power inside me, what owning territories did was nothing."

Neil looked him up and down. "Alright. But if anything changes, let me know. I'm going to check on Durrum and then we can move out again."

"How is he?"

"Getting stronger, but slower than I'd like. He needs proper rest."

"Maybe he'll get it soon. While we've been talking, a group crossed over into this territory."

"Who?"

"Some adventurers and messengers. It looks like they're moving together."

Rick barrelled through the mud, splashing it aside like the prow of a boat until he reached Hannah and threw his arms around her. Behind him, Marek floated awkwardly over the mud under Gary's suspicious glare. Next to him, Phoebe Geller stood on the surface of the wet mud as if it were solid ground. She gave Gary a friendly wave before going after Rick at a more sedate pace.

"Thank the gods," Rick sobbed, holding on to his fiancée as if he was trying to cocoon her.

"Rick, you got mud all over me," she said, her words hard but her tone soft. She didn't hide the relief flooding her aura.

The rest of their team, Phoebe, Dustin and Hannah's twin, Claire, all came together.

"Thank the gods," Rick said again, his voice bursting with joy at having his full team reunited.

"Now we need to find everyone else," Dustin said. "We were just about to head off in the direction you came from,"

"Good," Phoebe said. "We're scouting from a large group. Everyone is finally coming together."

GOOD LEADER

BARELY SECONDS PASSED BETWEEN THE AURA APPEARING AT THE EDGE OF the territory and reaching the group. Only the gold-rankers had a chance to intercept it, but it avoided them with blink teleports to slam into Humphrey, bowling him over in the long savannah grass. Gold-rankers swarmed them, only for Humphrey to hold out a forestalling hand from where he lay under Sophie.

"It's fine," he said. "Not a mphflm…"

His words were muffled by pressing her lips onto his.

"SUCCUBUS!" Belinda screamed as she arrived with the silver-rankers. "Kill it!"

Sophie rose to a mounting position over Humphrey, then turned to give her friend a flat look and a rude gesture.

Emir's magical cloud bus was skimming over the savannah grass. The interior had three levels, the bottom two set out with either row seating, like a bus, or booth seating where pairs of seats faced each other. The top floor and the roof were utility and lounge spaces, more open and with amenities like food tables. Emir didn't let the cultists go up there.

On the second level, Sophie sat next to Humphrey, facing Clive and Belinda.

"You need to get off this bus and leave," a scowling Clive told Sophie. "Now."

"Clive!" Humphrey said as Belinda patted Clive on the arm.

"Okay," Belinda said in the voice of a mother trying to coax a tired, cranky child. "Maybe we should tell Sophie *why* she should go instead of just telling her to do it."

Clive turned a petulant gaze onto her.

"She's not stupid," Belinda said. "You just haven't told her what's happening yet. She can't read your mind."

Clive looked like he wanted to retort, but nodded.

"Would you like me to do it?" Belinda asked gently. "Maybe while you go have an apple?"

Clive nodded again, got up and headed for the stairs at the back of the bus.

"He's not doing well," Belinda told the others. "Holding on to those territories is messing with his head."

"What is it he didn't tell me?" Sophie asked.

"What you would have heard him tell me if you weren't busy…"

She gave a pointed look at Humphrey.

"…catching up."

Humphrey looked sheepish while Sophie grinned.

"It's about the Undeath priests," Belinda said. "You said there's a large group building around Jason. We'll find our way with your directions, but Clive's right that you should use your speed to range ahead. You have to tell them that we need to take the priests alive if possible. Or what passes for alive, with some of them. They do worship Undeath."

"Why?" Humphrey asked.

"Because they're power mad? I bet a lot of them are lonely guys, angry at the world because girls won't talk to them. They convince themselves that worshipping the god of zombies will somehow make women fall for them because we all like bad boys. But it's never their fault, no. It's the world that's unfair, not their inability to take a shower, comb their hair and talk about anything but how much better they'd be than actual adventurers if only they were given the essences. It's not like there aren't women with low standards out there, but they can't even make a modicum of effort. I bet they think they're so great now, swanning around with their evil powers and swishy black cloaks as if… why are you looking at me like that?"

Humphrey gave her a flat look while Sophie was laughing behind her hand, jabbing Belinda's leg with her foot.

"I meant," Humphrey said, "why do we need to take the priests alive, not why do they worship Undeath."

"Oh," Belinda said. "Well, have you seen what happens when you kill them?"

"Yes," Humphrey said. "You were there."

"Oh, right."

Sophie snorted another laugh.

"So," Belinda continued. "Clive's thinking is…"

Jason's office in the mountain lair was mostly open space. It was all dark stone and dark wood, washed in red light from the lava waterfall on the other side of the glass wall. On the opposite side of the room was a large pair of sliding double doors. They were made of distorted glass that showed a blurry view of the lobby beyond and were the only visible way out. There were nine secret exits.

There were bookshelves, a drinks cabinet and paintings on the wall. The art was replicas of Dawn's work, many examples of which were stored in Jason's cloud flask. A large couch was upholstered in luxurious dark velvet. Against one wall was a small table with an image projector showing the most up-to-date map they had of the transformation zone.

Jason leaned against the wall near the small table. He looked over the map, comparing it to his internal sense of the territories under his command. He was having trouble concentrating, his mind slipping off anything he tried to focus on like grabbing at wet ice.

The map showed that things were going about as well as could be expected, although not perfectly. They had unified all the key territories from the original plan, but the final territory had been lost to a force of Undeath priests. Due to its lack of value, they had chosen to consolidate rather than extend themselves and try to defend it. Now Jason was suffering the after-effects of losing territory.

Abandoning the territory was a choice that had paid off. The unified territory they kept had looked patchy at that stage, a handful of key zones hastily linked together. All their key locations were held and united, however, and they then went to work filling the gaps. Now they held most of what they believed to be the bottom third of the transformation zone. Only some edge zones and a few gaps remained in Jason's otherwise unified territory.

At first, Jason had participated in the clearing of territories. His skirmishing combat style held up against the increasingly dangerous anomalies, although Farrah never let him out without gold-rank supervision. That had come to an end when the priests took the isolated territory from him. He was affected by losing territory, like those who had ceded territory to him, but the results were rather different.

Gabriel, Amos and Lorenn had experienced symptoms somewhere between bad food poisoning and a worse hangover. They suffered skull-piercing migraines and their magical bodies underwent very unwelcome changes. Luckily, Jason's replica town included fully plumbed bathrooms, although several were no longer fit for use.

The after-effects of losing territory were a result of spiritual damage, something healing magic could not fix, alleviating symptoms at best. Jason had tapped into his astral throne and astral gate enough that he had harmed himself in this manner over and again. The tolerance he had built up left him not savagely hungover, but in a state of disorientation akin to being drunk.

He made his way unsteadily to the couch and collapsed on it. He took a glass of iced juice from his inventory and, using his aura, floated globs of liquid into his mouth like an astronaut in zero gravity. He made loud slurping noises as he sucked each one down, giggling to himself in between.

Jason fell asleep fairly quickly, Shade emerging to catch the juice glass as it fell out of the air. He stashed it in his personal storage space before returning to Jason's shadow. Jason didn't stir until the double doors slid open to permit Farrah access before closing behind her. She held a waffle cone with two scoops of white chocolate raspberry ice cream in one hand. In the other was a cone with one and a half scoops of coconut chocolate ripple.

"Another territory cleared," she said. "Are you alright to come claim it?"

"Yep," he declared with giddy confidence and swung his legs off the couch to sit up. He shifted in place dizzily, his expression confused. He got up with a grunt and stumbled slightly on his way across the room to Farrah. He accepted the white chocolate raspberry cone with a goofy grin.

"How is your magic phone going?" he asked.

"This isn't the time."

"How are you doing two-factor authentication? Is it with auras?"

"We've claimed another territory," she repeated patiently, leading him to the map by the arm.

"Another gap filled?" he asked.

"Yes."

Miriam Vance was directing their forces in as safe a manner as they could proceed in the face of growing anomaly strength. She was no longer letting any silver-rankers out into the field without gold-rank support. This made territorial expansion slower, but no one who had seen the fighting questioned her approach.

Farrah moved to the projector on the table and placed a hand on it. The map started updating with new information. One of the gap territories lit up blue, marking it as cleared but unclaimed.

"I can portal anywhere in my territory," Jason light-headedly pointed out.

"I know."

"I'm a very good wizard."

"Do think you can portal here?" she asked, reaching out to tap an area right next to the blue marker.

Jason peered at the map.

"Are we playing *Spirit Island*? I'm not good at that game. I want to be the shadowy fear spirit. I'm very scary."

"We're not playing *Spirit Island*, Jason."

"Are we playing *Risk*? I've heard the legacy version is okay. Should I conquer the Earth?"

"No."

"Are you sure?" Jason whined. "Everyone there sucks."

"Lick your ice cream before it drips."

"Oh, hey. Ice cream."

Farrah pointed to the map, trying again.

"Can you open a portal to here?"

"I can. A shadowy portal. I'm very mysterious."

"Then can you please... where are you going?"

She turned to look at Jason, who had wandered to the middle of the room and was looking around as if lost.

"I wanted to look outside," he said. "Where are the windows?"

"To the outside? There aren't any. Just the big one showing your indoor lava waterfall. Why do you want to look outside?"

"Sophie's back."

"You're sure?"

"Yep," he said and licked his ice cream. "Her aura tastes like apples."

"That was fast," Farrah said. "She must have found something."

"She's still fast," Jason said. "She'll be here in—"

There was a loud thump from the door. Jason and Farrah turned to look as the doors slid open, revealing Sophie sprawled on the floor outside, holding her nose and moaning. Farrah took Jason's arm and led him in that direction. Sophie stared up at him with an accusatory expression.

"Why does your door block teleports?" she asked from the floor.

"It does?" Jason asked.

"I tried to blink through and slammed face-first into it instead."

"Are you sure the glass on the doors isn't just too blurry to get a line of sight for your ability?" Farrah asked.

"Yes. No. Shut up."

Farrah chuckled as Sophie kicked at the air, flipping onto her feet.

"You know the doors will just open if you stand in front of them for a second, right?" Jason asked. "Like at a supermarket."

"I was in a rush," Sophie said.

"You found something?" Farrah asked.

"Yeah," Sophie said with a grin. "A big group. Humpy, Lindy. Clive, who was the one who got me running back here. He wants us to start taking the Undeath priests alive instead of killing them. As many as we can get."

Jason went to scratch his head and almost poked himself in the eye with his ice cream. He stared at it, as if surprised to find it there, then grinned and licked it.

"Is he alright?" Sophie asked.

"He's fine," Farrah said. "He's got Shade to stop him from falling into the lava waterfall."

"Please tell me he's not in charge right now," Sophie said.

"I'll take you to see Miriam Vance," Farrah said. "Shade, don't let him go through any portals on his own."

"Of course, Miss Farrah."

Farrah led Sophie back through the office doors.

"It must have been nice seeing Humphrey and Lindy again."

"Such a relief," Sophie said. "I was so happy to see they were—"

The doors slid shut behind them, leaving Jason mostly alone.

"I should get some ice cream," he said.

"You're holding an ice cream, Mr Asano."

Jason looked down at his hand.

"Oh, nice."

Gary dropped from the roof of Emir's cloud bus into the marina car park of Jason's town. Serving as a marshalling yard, it was teeming with adventurers and brighthearts. As Gary was now almost twice her height, Farrah leapt through the air to grab him in a hug.

Reunions abounded as Rick and Sophie brought the two large groups to Jason's territory. This brought most of the surviving expedition together, although each group had extant members presumed either still isolated or dead.

There was little time to celebrate as Clive and Constance handed their territories over to Jason. They both immediately started suffering the after-effects and Jason was again left with territories distant from his original one and in need of defending. Another operation was planned and launched to secure them.

Jason had largely recovered, his condition improving much faster than those more heavily stricken. Clive and Constance had passed through the bathroom-destroying phase and Constance was on bed rest. Clive was still unconscious for most of each day, coming out long enough to be fed a fistful of spirit coins.

Jason's mind was clear, but he still endured physical symptoms, mostly vertigo and headaches that came and went. He was able to use his powers well enough but didn't even try to argue he should be fighting. He was able to take half of their forces into his soul realm, portal to his new territory and let everyone back out.

The new plan to unite the territories was less aggressive than the last. The living anomalies were even stronger, meaning any group without gold-rank support was at risk. The territory clusters were further apart this time and would take longer to link, so both needed solid defences. The biggest threat was the avatar, but it had been last seen close to Durrum's former territory. That was far from the land Jason inherited from Constance and Clive.

With their forces evenly split, they would slowly work towards linking them up. Miriam Vance was in charge of the strategy. Jason deferred to her expertise and tried to stay out of her way. He felt like a worthless princeling as everyone else worked on establishing more territories for him while he just lounged around.

He was standing in one of two observation lounges in his mountain fortress. Each one was situated behind an enormous window that, from the outside, was the iris of a massive stone eye. Jason looked down on the car park of his replica small town's marina where adventurers, brighthearts and cultists were marshalling.

"You'll need to join them," Jason said. "There's never enough healers."

"Yeah," Neil said, stepping up beside him.

"I'm told you made a good leader out there."

"I could have done better."

Jason let out a tired, good-natured laugh.

"Yeah," he said. "I know that feeling."

"I think maybe I understand you a little better now," Neil said. "Getting tossed into deep water. Little to no allies, forced to rise to the challenge or die. It's harsh, but there's also something compelling about it. Like you're really alive."

Jason glanced at Neil before turning back to the window.

"I think you do understand me a little better."

"I'm not going to complain about it as much as you do, though."

Jason let out a chuckle.

"Probably for the best. Neil, I know that everyone else on our team is flashier than you. Fiery swords and flying tortoises and clouds of magic butterflies. But we see how good you are. We can only step forward the way we do because we know you're standing behind us. Covering our mistakes. We're an odd bunch, and we need a steady dose of reliable to make it all work. You just proved in a whole new way how reliable you are, and I don't say it enough, Neil, but thank you. For being amazing."

Neil looked at Jason, wary for signs of mockery. Jason didn't look at him at all, staring out the window with a weary gaze.

"Thanks," Neil said, his voice uncertain.

"Now," Jason said. "I've been sensing an odd aura that arrived with you. I felt it come here with you and stop outside the door. I assume you're here to make an introduction."

"I'm sure you two will figure it out," Neil said while shuffling towards a side door.

By the time he reached it, he was half-running. Jason watched him go with a frown, then turned to the double doors that were the main entrance to the observation lounge. He walked over and they opened to reveal an anthropomorphic rabbit in a tuxedo. He stood across the hall, nervously turning the brim of his top hat in his hands.

"Dad?" the rabbit asked.

2 2

I WANT THOSE THINGS FOR YOU

JASON LOOKED AT THE RABBIT STANDING NERVOUSLY IN THE HALL. HIS brow furrowed in thought as his mind put pieces together. The transformation zone, Healer's missing gift, the rabbit construct he created in his soul space. Now, this rabbit. This was no construct; there was a soul in there.

It was only normal rank. It must have been terrifying, crossing all those territories when everyone else was so much more powerful than it. It had been looking for him, whether it understood that or not, and now Jason could see why. Its aura had stood out from the moment it arrived, and there was familiarity to it, despite him never having seen it before. He understood it, like an architect looking at plans he had drawn up himself. More than that, the rabbit was family.

Jason instantly understood that he had created this living being, even if he didn't remember doing it. But, however thrown he was by having created a fully realised being, he knew it was nothing compared to what the rabbit was going through. It had just met its maker.

"I can't imagine what you're feeling," Jason said. "Come into my office and sit down. We can try and sort some of it out."

There was a small town atop the shaft that had carried Jason and his companions deep into the planet. The town had sprung into being quickly, most of the development coming after the expedition had departed. It was a product of the Magic Society, ostensibly built for research, but there was only so much to be learned from a massive hole in the ground. In truth, the town was little more than a luxury resort—a place for the upper echelons of the Magic Society to escape the bleak ruins of Yaresh.

There was a large tea house, a square building composed of mezzanine levels around a central courtyard. There were basement levels catering to appetites beyond those for teas, but the legitimate upper levels did a brisk trade themselves. It was popular with adventurers, merchants and the many other goods suppliers that served the town and its Magic Society patrons.

Two people sat in a room on one of the higher floors, a gauzy curtain screening them from others looking out from their rooms. One was a celestine with dark skin, silver eyes and a huge silver afro. The other was an elf whose green-flecked hair was a lighter shade of brown than her skin.

Despite their distinctive looks, none of the staff remembered them the moment they looked away. Jason had a similar aura trick to what they were using, but their mastery of it put anything he could do to shame.

"I don't understand the continuing interest in him," the celestine man, Velius, said. "The Builder is done with this world and things are on track to reach stability once again. Yes, the link between worlds needs to be stabilised, but that is just a matter of time now Asano has the messenger magic. He even has that boy the Celestial Book likes so much to help him learn it all. And that's the World-Phoenix's affair anyway. Why isn't her vessel the one languishing on this tedious rock? Why are we here instead of Helsveth?"

"You don't know?" Raythe asked. "The Reaper didn't tell you?"

"He's not exactly chatty. I'm his vessel, not his friend. Were you told by the… what is your great astral being calling itself these days?"

"It is given many names, yet claims none."

Velius groaned, shaking his head.

"That's pretentious on a scale only a great astral being can accomplish. It should pick a damn name, if only to avoid a conversation like this every time someone talks about it."

"My master does not want to be talked about."

"Tough. What do you call it?"

"Master."

Velius rolled his eyes. "Surely you have a preference."

"I will confess a soft spot for the name 'Keeper of the Sands.' I like the hourglass imagery."

"See? That wasn't hard. And that's a great name. If it doesn't pick a name, people will just call it what they like. I once heard someone call your master 'the Underclock.' That's just terrible."

"Agreed."

"So, you'll suggest to your 'Keeper of the Sands' that it picks a name? It doesn't have to be that one."

"I will not."

"Worth a try. Putting that aside, though, you know why we're here? And why the World-Phoenix's new prime vessel is not?"

"You know the astral beings are factionalising, do you not?"

"They're always factionalising. I've seen signs, but that's nothing new. These linked planets are a flashpoint, but that should be settling down."

"It's not about the planets anymore. As you said, that is the World-Phoenix's affair. The concern is Asano. He is a seed that the World-Phoenix planted, but he has grown in ways only the All-Devouring Eye anticipated. Asano's position at the nexus of various events has seen both our masters take an interest, along with gods and the messengers."

"Is that what it's about? Stirring up trouble with the messengers? What do we care if he becomes another original? There are more of them around than most of the astral kings realise And they rarely cause any trouble."

"It's not that," Raythe said.

"Then what is it? What was worth sending you here? The Reaper sending me makes sense. He's already involved himself with Asano multiple times, with one of his shadows as Asano's familiar. But what interest does the Keeper of the Sands have in this? Why did it send you here instead of the World-Phoenix sending Helsveth? Is your master going to make one of his oh-so-rare interventions?"

"The World-Phoenix has no representative here because she will be at odds with us in what comes next."

"Which is what?"

"Asano has started to touch intrinsic-mandate magic."

"So? Also, how? He's still mortal."

"One of his familiars is an avatar of doom. He has already taken steps towards it becoming a Voice of the Will, forging a bond beyond summoner and familiar."

"Alright. That's unusual, but he's not the first. It's even normal by the standards of original astral kings. That's not enough to get the Keeper of the Sands moving. Your master has always stood apart, even by the measure of great astral beings. You're the least active of us all, so what changed? Your master and the All-Devouring Eye haven't intervened in cosmic events since…"

Raythe smiled as her counterpart's eyes went wide.

"He's turning an avatar of doom into a Voice of the Will," Velius said, his voice flat.

"Yes."

"So, he's linked to the avatar through that bond. Are you saying that links him, through the avatar, to—"

"Yes."

"Oh," Velius said and drained his cup of tea. "Do our astral beings want him to—"

"Yes."

"And you think my master wants this? Yours was always against the sundering, but mine supported it."

"It seems that the Reaper has changed its mind. You are in a better position than me to ask."

Velius let out a long-suffering laugh.

"You'd think so, wouldn't you?" he said. "That's because your great astral being actually tells you things. I only ever find them out when mine's possessing me and the words are coming out of my mouth. When the intent is blistering through my mind like lightning."

Velius went to pour another cup, found the teapot empty and sighed.

"I need something stronger," he said. "You've been here a while, right?"

"We arrived at this teahouse together."

"No, I mean on this planet. Have you found anything strong enough to get us drunk?"

"No."

Velius groaned.

"How much longer is this transformation zone thing going to take?"

———

Jason and the child-sized rabbit were in the villain office of Jason's mountain fortress. The rabbit was on the couch sitting opposite Jason in a cloud chair.

"…was when I realised that the gift Healer gave me was missing," Jason continued.

"This gift that was meant to let you create a life," the rabbit said.

"Yes. I was involved in the inception of this transformation zone. All the things inside of this zone, myself included, were in a state of flux. Anything with a soul remained intact, but everything else was up for being remade. That includes the giant tree out on the horizon that was, as best I can tell, intended to be a soul forge. Somewhere in all that, surrounded by the power of creation, I think I subconsciously tapped into that power and used the gift."

"To create me."

"Yes."

"So, I was some magic puppet you made and then you brought it to life."

"No. You're not a puppet. That construct still exists; it's not you and you're not it. You are your own entity, complete with a soul. A true being, in your own right. I think I just modelled you after the construct. It wasn't a conscious act."

"Why give me the shape of some toy you made?" the rabbit asked.

"Again, I wasn't making conscious decisions in this. That means I can only try to figure out what was going on in my head when I performed this… act of creation. I like the rabbit construct. It's fun and happy. If I'm going to create a living thing, I want it to have a life of fun and happiness. I want those things for you."

"What about the rest?"

"The rest?"

"Why was I in that lightning tower."

"I don't know. My best guess would be because I have no idea of what I'm doing."

"Oh, great. That's what everyone wants to hear from their creator. As gods go, you're pretty [bleep] at this."

"I'm not a god."

"Exactly. You're so bad at being a god that you aren't one. This is a total [bleep] show."

"What was that?" Jason asked.

"What is what?"

"The bleeping."

"You don't know?" the rabbit exclaimed, hopping to its feet on the couch. "Oh, great. You did this to me and you don't even know what it is or why?"

Jason winced. "I might know."

"Then [bleep]ing well tell me, for [bleep]'s sake."

"I can be kind of a prick sometimes."

The rabbit looked at him in disbelief.

"That's it? That's all you've got?"

"It's not what you wanted to hear, I know."

"Not what I wanted to hear? NOT WHAT I WANTED TO HEAR? You [bleep]ing…"

Jason waited through the rabbit's tirade, an indecipherable series of bleeps interspersed with anatomically implausible threats. Despite the comical nature of it, he didn't find it funny at all. While he was coming to grips with having created a living thing like some deity of old, the entity he created was much worse off. Coming face to face with his creator should have answered all his questions. Instead, he discovered that his creator was weak, petty and flawed.

After waiting for the rabbit to wind down and collapse back on the couch, emotionally exhausted, Jason spoke.

"I can't make any promises," Jason said, "but I recognise that I have a responsibility to you. I don't know how much I can help, but I'm willing to try."

Jason got up from his chair.

"Come with me," he told the rabbit.

———

The marina parking lot was mostly empty, a fresh team having just set out to claim another territory. There were still a few people about, mostly lost-looking silver-rankers. Miriam had started excluding people from the teams as the threat grew too great for them to handle. That mostly meant brighthearts, but also the Magic Society researchers. Some were resting in the empty houses, but others hovered around, unsure of what to do. They had no tasks but didn't feel right to sit around, doing nothing. As the danger grew, more and more silver-rankers would face the same idle dilemma.

Jason led the rabbit to the soul realm portal currently open near the railing by the water. They stopped in front of it, looking at the rainbow sheet of energy contained in the white stone arch.

"What does it feel like?" Jason asked, his voice carefully neutral.

The rabbit took a long time to answer, staring at the archway.

"Home," he said finally, his voice barely a whisper.

"Do you want to go inside?"

The rabbit nodded and Jason made an inviting gesture. After a glance at Jason, it moved to the arch, hesitating only a moment before stepping through. The rabbit stepped out the other side, wobbling dizzily for a moment. He was unused to portal travel, but the soul realm portal was gentler than a normal one. Otherwise, the rabbit would have been throwing up on the grass.

He looked around, first noticing that Jason had already been waiting when he arrived. He looked between Jason and the portal in confusion.

"An avatar," Jason explained. "I am everywhere in this place."

The rabbit looked around. They were in a glade with a small pond, the sun shining down from a sky pleasantly, but not oppressively, warm. Around the glade was forest, with several inviting pathways leading through the trees. The forested areas not on the path looked ordinary but felt ominous.

"The construct," the rabbit said. "The one that—"

"Gone," Jason said. "I can recreate it, if you want to see, but it's an empty thing. You are real."

The rabbit's gaze turned sharply to look at Jason.

"You're real," Jason repeated. "I know that you feel lost. Uncertain of who you are and what your role in the universe is."

"Is that why you brought me here? To tell me?"

"That is for you to choose," Jason said. "I know I disappoint you."

"It would be nice if the being that created me wasn't just some guy."

The avatar looked pointedly at the arch, then vanished. The rabbit looked at the space it had occupied, then back at the portal. The real Jason stepped through, and the rabbit felt it, like being caught in a riptide. Jason was connected to this place, far more than simply a person. It felt as if the tide would rise and fall with his breath; that he could bring the night by closing his eyes. His power was unfathomable, the world itself made flesh. This was the Creator he'd been looking for.

The rabbit swallowed hard, and suddenly, the sensation was gone. Once again, Jason was just a man. Jason smiled, reached out and patted him on the head.

"You're very short," Jason said.

"Kiss my arse."

The rabbit's eyes went wide. He started reeling off profanities, interspersed with joyous laughter. Jason waited patiently for him to settle down, the rabbit standing in front of him with a huge grin.

"Is it...?"

"Permanent? Yes. You are my creation. I can change anything about you not shielded by your soul, and that too, if you want and you let me. I could turn you into a human. An elf, or a stag. A chainsaw cyborg leonid."

The rabbit looked down at his hands.

"Could you make me powerful?"

"Silver-rank is as high as I take it and have you walk out of here safe and whole."

"Can you make me an essence-user?"

"Not at silver-rank. Essences are between you and your soul. Neither gods nor great astral beings can elevate you as an essence-user. Not without breaking you. Some things belong to the cosmos."

"Why am I just a normal-ranker? I did not like having to leave that tower when everyone and everything could have killed me by accident. One sleepy silver-ranker whacks me with a careless arm while yawning and I'm dead. I only left the tower because the one thing worse than leaving was staying there alone."

"I suspect you are normal rank because being at the beginning gives you more potential than I can imbue. I can give you power, if that is what you want, but not essence abilities. What I can do is give you essences and let you take them for yourself."

"How long do I have to choose?"

"As long as you like. If you go back through that portal, you will resume ageing. In here, nothing can harm you. Not even time."

"Unless you want it to."

"Yes. But there's nothing you can do about what I want. The question is, what do *you* want?"

The rabbit frowned, contemplating, before looking back up at Jason.

"A name."

23

SMALL, EASY OR
INCONSEQUENTIAL

JASON WALKED DOWN A WIDE FOREST PATH WITH THE UNNAMED RABBIT BY
his side. Sunlight passed through the thin canopy, leaving their way well-
lit, yet also private and secluded.

"Names are important," Jason said. "I have a familiar. His name is
Colin and people love him."

"You're saying that 'Colin' is some magic name that makes people
like you?" the rabbit asked.

"A little bit. Not by itself, of course. Context is important. I'm a man
of two worlds. I come from a world where magic was hidden until very
recently. It was only seven or eight years ago that I didn't even believe in
it. Then I travelled to a world full of magic, right out in the open."

"I assume you're going to be rounding up on a point at some stage."

Jason chuckled.

"Yes, but like I said: context is important. Something I've discovered
about the magical world is that with all the big magic, people overlook the
little magic. The subtle stuff that my world has always used without ever
realising it. Music is an excellent example. Crowds are another, and
combining them is very powerful. A concert is something to behold using
aura senses. Am I confusing you with what I'm talking about?"

"I know what a concert is. Which is weird, by the way, because I've
never heard music. For a guy who talks about context a lot, you shoved
some crazy stuff in my head with no context at all. Like, what's a

turducken about? Is it a weird animal sex thing that went horribly, horribly wrong?"

Jason let out a laugh.

"No," he said. "Let's not get too distracted, though; I was talking about music."

"I'm not sure why."

"Let me get there. There's no rush."

"Aren't you fighting to stop an undead army from claiming a subterranean staging ground from which they can spill an endless flood of unliving monstrosities onto the surface world?"

"That's up to the powerful people now."

"We're walking through the universe that you're the god of."

"It's not a proper universe. Not yet. And I'm not a god."

"You created me. You're not going to make a lady rabbit from one of my rib bones, are you?"

Jason laughed again.

"No. My plans on that... I just found out about you. Give me some time to consider my next move on that front. In the meantime, I was talking about music. People didn't know about auras in the world I come from. Real auras, I mean, not the stuff your aunt with the crystals talks about."

"I'm the first member of my species; I don't have an aunt."

"The universal aunt. She's an archetype. But real auras can be manipulated without any detectable magic. The collective aura of an AC/DC concert is something to behold. There's real power there, even if there isn't real magic."

"You do remember you're meant to be talking about names, right?"

"Names are a part of it," Jason said. "A song can move hearts, the right words can move nations and a name can make an identity. Shape not just how people see us but who we are. I told you about my familiar, Colin."

"Yeah. Apparently, people love Colin."

"They do. Do you know what kind of familiar he is?"

"Let me guess: something scary? Two-headed fire crocodile?"

"He's a sanguine horror. An apocalypse beast known for scouring entire worlds of life, leaving them nothing but barren rock. He has a constant hunger for blood and flesh and he's not always discriminate about where it comes from."

"Uh, okay."

"But he is discriminate. That, to my understanding, is extremely out of the ordinary. Sanguine horrors are nothing but unrelenting hunger that you eradicate down to the last scrap or it keeps growing, keeps feeding and never, ever stops. But not Colin."

"He's a familiar, right? Obviously, you influence him."

"Yes, and that begins with his name. It sets a tone. A starting point for how the world sees him and how he sees his place in it. Names are important. Our first link to everything outside ourselves. The right name empowers us, while the wrong one has power *over* us. Either way, it shapes who we are. If your name is Mr Hoppityhop, all anyone will see you as is a rabbit. If your name is Doombringer, Lord of Carnage, all anyone will see you as is lonely."

"Is this all a massive stall while you try to think up a name for me?"

"You can choose your own if you like. Many do."

"No," the rabbit said. "It should be you. It just… feels right."

Jason nodded.

"I have been thinking about it as we talk, you're right. I could name you after someone. Kai, after my brother who died protecting his world. But I don't think you should be named after anyone. You aren't from someone else. Except me. You can carry my surname, if you want it, but we're talking about given names. You're something new, so the name I give you should be new as well."

"You have something in mind?"

"Nik."

"Nick? How is that new?"

"It's Nik. NIK, no C. It comes from the word Lehenik. In a language from the world where I was born, it roughly translates first or firstly. The first instance. That's what I want to call your people, once you're a species and not a unique being: Lehenik. The first people to belong in this place."

He gestured at the soul realm around them. They were still walking through the forest path, sunlight passing through the thin canopy.

"Everything else here," Jason continued, "either doesn't belong or is an extension of me. Except for you. You came from me, but you belong to no one but yourself, with your own fate to shape. But you said that this place feels like home and you were right. It is your home, and you will always have a place here."

"You're going to make more like me?"

"Yes. I believe I know how, and the opportunity is startlingly close. I don't want you to go through life with nowhere and no one to belong to. That would be cruel."

"I don't know how to feel about that."

"Me either. Someday, there's probably going to be a bible with you and me featuring heavily in the early chapters."

Jason stopped in front of a tree, plucked off a red fruit and offered it to the rabbit.

"Apple?"

The rabbit gave Jason a flat look but took the fruit. Jason picked another for himself and they continued on.

"Nik," the rabbit said, contemplating the sound. "Nik. Nik. Nik Asano?"

Jason gave the rabbit a side glance but did not interrupt. He bit into his apple instead.

Deep under his mountain fortress was a huge magma chamber. The molten rock of the chamber's floor washed the cavern in red light, painting the cages hanging from the ceiling on chains. Jason and the newly monikered Nik emerged from a tunnel set into the wall and ending in a stone balcony.

"Oh, great," Nik said. "You're keeping an army of Undeath priests in an overly elaborate and easily escapable trap. I'm sure that's going to work out fine."

"The suppression collars they're wearing are the real cages," Jason said. "As for the actual cages, we have to keep them somewhere."

Brisk footsteps echoed in the stone tunnel behind them until Miriam Vance joined them. She looked at Nik and then at the dangling cages before demonstrating that she had learned a lesson and asked no questions. Jason glanced at her before looking back out at the cages.

"Operations Commander," Miriam said. "I want to officially pull all silver-rankers from territory clearing. Our best estimate is that around half of the territories have been claimed and the anomalies have gotten too dangerous."

"That's going to annoy some people," Jason said. "Silver-rankers chafe at how slowly we advance, which is as true for me as anyone else. This place has been better for advancement than a monster surge."

"Silver-rankers are hard to kill by most standards, Operations

Commander, but nothing here is standard. We're getting close calls in every territory we claim now, even with gold-rankers watching over the rest. I don't want it to take a death before people accept that it's time to stop."

Jason nodded.

"I've been leaving all that to you, so I won't gainsay you now," he told her. "We'll consolidate the gold-rankers and press on?"

"We can," Miriam said. "That will slow our progress, however, even with Gareth Xandier and his demigod strength. I believe it is time to change strategies."

"You want to make a move on the Undeath priests."

"Ideally, we would find and kill the avatar before the Undeath high priest takes control of it."

"Garth," Jason said. "The high priest's name is Garth."

"I don't care what his name is," Miriam said. "I only care that we take him from undead to full dead. I think he's likely found his god's avatar by now, but I still think the time to hunt it down is now. The undead build their ranks with every enemy they face while we've collected everyone with major power in our group. We aren't going to get stronger."

Jason nodded again.

"Alright," he said. "Let's gather everyone together and explain the plan. How is Clive?"

"Not what I'd call well, but ready to brief everyone at the very least."

"The problem with—"

Clive slapped a hand over his mouth and drew a sharp breath in through his nose. He gestured at Jason who refilled Clive's glass of water from a pitcher. Clive gulped it down and slammed the empty glass on the table as he winced at his ongoing headache. Jason refilled it again.

They were in the conference room with the various leaders of the alliance factions, adventurers, brighthearts and Builder cultists. The messengers were also represented, with Marek Nior Vargas next to Rick and Jali Corrik Fen next to Jason.

"I apologise," Clive said to the assemblage. "As I was saying, the problem with dealing with the Undeath priests is their avatar. We have to assume they have control over it now, as all finding it first changes is our lives getting a lot easier. As everyone here has seen during the claiming of the latest territories, our own divine representative, Gary, is extremely powerful."

Gary was a large and shiny presence in the room but looked uncomfortable at being pointed out.

"Many of you witnessed Gary clashing with the avatar already," Clive continued. "Those who did will have noticed that these two forces are evenly matched. No one can take them down, including each other. We need to resolve that to overcome the priests, their undead and their messengers."

"And to save time here," Jason cut in, "we will not be relitigating the idea of using messengers ourselves."

"So you keep insisting," the cult leader Beaufort said. "But perhaps this should be a group decision and not one for you alone."

"No," Jason told him.

"No?" Beaufort asked. "That's it? Just 'no,' without further reason or explanation?"

"Yes."

"And if we insist?"

"Then that would be unfortunate."

"You are not making this feel like an equal alliance, Asano."

"It isn't."

Everyone at the table was aware that Jason's aura permeated the room. That the mountain fortress they were in, absurd as it was, took the shape of Jason's head.

"There will be no more talk of taking the messengers to battle," Jason said. "I won't go over the value of a chain of command again, but if anyone else has a problem with their or my place in this one, speak up now."

Jason panned the room, his gaze meeting only silence.

"Good," he said. "Now, Clive will explain the actual method we will use to deal with the avatar."

Clive nodded his agreement and immediately winced at the rapid head movement.

"I was going to make a lengthy explanation that fully encapsulated the plan," Clive said. "But since I need to go lie down, you get the quick version. The Undeath priests attempt to reanimate when they are killed. I'm sure you've all seen it. It doesn't work, though, because they're cut off from their power source, meaning the divine power of their god. The avatar is another source of that power and, unlike the god itself, limited. It too is cut off from the god, so any power drained out of it will weaken it. The plan is to kill as many priests as we can get our hands on in the presence of the avatar. Each reanimation will siphon off some of its divine power. If we can siphon off enough, it will tip the scale enough that Gary can destroy it."

"Won't that leave us with an army of animated priests to kill?" Gabriel asked.

"Yes," Miriam answered for Clive. "This will be a hard fight, which is where everyone except Gareth comes in. We will attempt to kill off the risen dead immediately, of course, and expect some success given that we will choose the conditions they animate in. It is foolish to assume that will go exactly as planned, however. We need to anticipate combating the Undeath priests with the avatar, as well as the prisoners we kill off as they reanimate. This battle will not be small, easy or inconsequential."

ANOTHER ASTRAL KING

MAHK DEN KAHLA WAS AN UNHAPPY MESSENGER. EVER SINCE MEETING Boris Ket Lundi, things had been spiralling out of control. Boris was dominant force, his arguments for Mahk handing over his territory compelling. And Mahk was not the last to be swayed, with other messengers they encountered falling into line as well. Not every gold-ranker was convinced by words, but those who survived challenging Boris ultimately accepted their subordination. Boris was not just an outstanding combatant but one well-versed in fighting other messengers.

Each individual step that brought them to their current situation had made sense. The options weren't always desirable, but they were acceptable, and Boris had a way of presenting them not just as the right choice, but as the only real choice. That was how they ended up where they were, every step the right one, yet leading down a path Mahk would never have chosen himself.

Seeking an alliance, Boris had led them right into the hands of the Undeath priests. Their massive army of undead blanketed the ground and the messengers they had awoken with their territories dotted the sky. Standing out most of all was the towering figure of Undeath's avatar, holding claim over the unliving's unified territories that the high priest of Undeath could not himself.

The messengers they had on hand were too few to handle the Undeath priests, at least until they spent themselves against the adventurers and their allies. But false alliances with the filthy unliving was not the messenger way. Power and dominance was their way and, through words or weapons, how Boris had managed to keep the other messengers in check. But having watched him closely, Mahk saw far too much that was odd about the man. Too much that was unlike a messenger.

Boris was off alone, negotiating with the Undeath high priest. Mahk and the rest of the messengers were settled high on a mountain, some way from the plateau holding the Undeath forces. Most of the territory was an endless span of red rock, sand and dust. The upper reaches of the mountain held the only greenery, the cooler air of altitude allowing the growth of some sparse woodland. The desert heat was not harmful to them, but that did not make it pleasant.

The messengers had no real place for themselves, with no lesser races to construct abodes for them. They rested on the lightly wooded mountainside, finding what limited comfort they could. Mahk hovered in the air above the trees, waiting for Boris to return from negotiating with the Undeath high priest. He could see the plateau in the distance where the unliving forces were gathered. The undead blanketed the ground while messengers taken by claiming territory dotted the sky. What held his attention most was the avatar—a beacon of power, radiating corruption.

It left Mahk unsettled, his own corruption behind him but not forgotten. He only remembered his time serving the strange tree as dream-like scraps of memory, lurking in his mind like hidden traitors.

When Boris came flying through the air, Mahk flew out to meet him. Boris slowed and stopped, unhurried in his movements.

"We need to speak, Boris," Mahk demanded. Boris didn't react to the challenge in his tone, his amused smile irking Mahk.

"Yes, Mahk, we do. Are we going to talk floating here in the air, or can we find somewhere to sit down?"

"This is exactly what I want to talk about. Sit down? We are superior beings, Boris. We float above the ground to show our lessers that we don't just stand taller than them but stand above them entirely. We are their sky, and when we choose sit, we sit on thrones."

"You think I lack the dignity of a messenger," Boris said.

"You walk on the ground. You slouch. You lounge."

"Then stop me," Boris said, the suspect lightness of his tone a promise of danger. "If you want to stand above me, Mahk, then cut me down. Take my place."

Mahk scowled. "We both know I cannot."

"Then perhaps you need to revise what your concept of standing above is, Mahk. You can talk about dignity all you like, but what does prattling on about honour or principle sound like when you lack the power to enforce it?"

Mahk pressed his lips together tightly, as if to trap his next words, but they escaped nonetheless.

"A servant race," he said through gritted teeth. "It sounds like a servant race."

"Yes," Boris said. "Now, let's go find somewhere to sit down."

———————

High Priest Garth stood on a hill atop a rocky desert plateau. A bloody red sunset pooled across the sky, blue fading into darkness as if the day had been stabbed to death. Garth's grin was permanent, as his head was a skull with only pinpricks of red light for eyes. His robe draped over a body clearly not human in shape, a sharp hump and various odd protrusions tenting the fabric in odd places.

Garth looked over his forces, gathered on the plateau. The ground was almost impossible to see, blanketed by the undead. The sky was dotted with messengers, not as thick as the undead but still a considerable force. Less pleasing was the lack of priests, the few dozen remaining representing less than half the original number.

Some had doubtless fallen victim to the transformation zone itself, or had a run-in with messengers or adventurers. The forces of the living had shifted from claiming territory to hunting them, and Garth wanted to know why. They weren't trying to snatch territory but priests, taking prisoners in a series of hit-and-run attacks. Given that he was unlikely to get an answer otherwise, Garth had decided he would wring it from their throats himself. Building up new undead was getting hard now that the anomalies were so strong, so the time to remove their enemies had come.

The biggest piece of the puzzle was now in place, the avatar of Undeath looming over their forces. It held control over their territories now, Garth himself having been pushed to the limit. His unusual nature had allowed him to hold more territories than most, and recover faster from their loss. The avatar controlled them now and Garth controlled the avatar, until such time as he could return it to Undeath.

When the battle came, the avatar would tie up the demigod while their massive horde handled the rest. Once that was done, the horde would turn on the demigod as well, breaking the stalemate between the two divine entities.

Aside from the empowered leonid, only one of their foes was a concern: whoever had the power to weaken their undead forces as a whole. The ghost fire they spread wasn't as powerful as that of Death's miracle, but clearly they were of a kind. There was also this issue of their aura suppressing the magic of undeath. That would have to be dealt with or their numerical advantage would have little impact.

Jameela strode up the hill towards Garth, graceful on her long legs. She was wearing an elegant combat robe and heavy boots, red with dust. Garth was again struck by the longing she engendered in him, despite his unliving body. The little living tissue he possessed should not be enough for such feelings. He would never act upon them, of course, not allowing himself such a lack of discipline. There was also the issue of his body being as ill-equipped to slake such urges as it should have been to feel them at all.

"You have answers?" he demanded as she crested the hill.

"It's Jason Asano," she said, moving to stand beside him.

"The same one claiming their territories?"

"Yes."

"Interesting; you are not the first to bring his name up today. You're sure?"

"I captured some of the brighthearts who were around him when he enacted Death's miracle, as well as a pair of essence-users. Asano is the one."

"Essence-users? Adventurers?"

"Magic Society researchers. I now have answers on what adventurers were doing underground. I brought them all in alive, in case you want to question them yourself before I kill and animate them."

"No, I trust your ability to make them speak the truth."

"Then we need to target Asano during the battle. Once we eliminate him, not only will they lose their power to weaken our undead, but they will lose their territories. It won't cost them power immediately, but it will hurt their morale."

Garth nodded.

"He's silver rank, which makes him vulnerable, but we need to be careful in our approach. There is a reason that Death granted him a miracle. That he's the one claiming territories when they have the demigod. Undeath himself saw fit to warn me about Asano, which says enough.

He is not to be underestimated, and the enemy will protect him with care."

"Perhaps," Jameela said. "My information is that he involves himself in battles more than the people around him would like. His aura will diminish the power of our undead, but he needs to use his powers directly to spread the ghost fire."

"Perhaps we dilute the battlefield. Strike from multiple points; spread our forces over a wider area than a silver-rank aura can cover."

"Relying on such a strategy might not be best," Jameela suggested. "I extracted as much information I could about Asano from the prisoners. They claim that his aura is like a gold-ranker's, both in strength and coverage."

"That sounds unlikely. How hard did you press them on this topic?"

"Hard. The Magic Society researchers were highly convinced of this information's authenticity. They claim Asano has been training under Amos Pensinata."

Garth jerked his head, turning his gaze from the forces arrayed below them to his subordinate priestess.

"Pensinata? Is he here, in this place?"

"Yes. I have a full list of names, but Pensinata aside, the highlights are Gabriel and Arabelle Remore, along with their old team member, Emir Bahadir."

"The treasure hunter? Those are Vitesse adventurers. What are they doing here?"

"They are allies of Asano. The son of the Remores is on his team."

A dissatisfied sound passed through Garth's skeletal mouth.

"No wonder they did so much damage with so few gold-rankers if that is the calibre of them."

"The high priestess of the Healer from Yaresh is also amongst them."

"Who is this Asano that he can rally such people around him? Adventurers from the other side of the world. Even the god of Death is paying him attention?"

"According to the researchers, Asano is the reason the Builder left this world before the monster surge was over."

Garth didn't have the eyelids to make his eyes go wide, but the red lights in the sockets of his skull shone a little brighter for a moment.

"The more I learn," Garth said, "the more this man troubles me."

"How will you deal with him?" Jameela asked.

"While you were off finding the name of our enemy," Garth said, "I was making new allies."

"The messengers?"

"Yes. They know that they lack the power to overcome either us or the adventurers and their allies. And they claim Asano is an existing enemy to them. They have offered their assistance so long as they are allowed to leave the transformation zone alive and Asano is not."

"They will attempt to play us off against the forces of the living and swoop in at the end."

"Yes. Tell me what you got from the researchers about what the messengers are doing here."

Boris sat on a mossy rock, under a tree that shaded him from the glaring sun above. He used his aura to create a privacy screen, a shimmering dome covering himself and Mahk. The other messenger had consented to sit, but was floating in the air, cross-legged.

"You are a strange messenger, Boris."

"Of course I am. To be ordinary violates the core philosophy of our culture. Being like every other messenger is to be mundane."

"We are taught to obey."

"Yeah. Funny, that. Lots of 'you are the greatest beings in the cosmos, now shut up and do what you're told.' You can't have reached gold rank without spotting the contradictions."

"I've seen you do this enough times to recognise it, Boris Ket Lundi. You are moving the discussion from you to me, but this is about you. Your eccentricities are more than just some attempt to stand out amongst our kind. Your strength does that enough that you have no need for such foolishness. You aren't one of us, are you? You're part of the Unorthodoxy."

"Yes," Boris admitted casually.

Mahk uncrossed his legs and floated higher into the air.

"You lied to me," Mahk said.

"I've never lied to you, Mahk. I haven't always told the truth, but you've never heard me tell a lie."

"That doesn't matter. What matters is that you are the enemy. The ultimate enemy."

"Do you really believe that? Mahk? You're gold-rank. Surely you've seen through at least some of the indoctrination they put you. I never lied to you, but will you lie to me and say you've never had doubts about what was drilled into your mind?"

"Don't try that with me, Boris Ket Lundi. We quash doubts because they will cost us everything. The astral king—"

"Can't get you here!" Boris cut him off. "For your entire life, Mahk Den Kahla, there has been a sword dangling over your head. It's been waiting to strike should you even think the wrong way. But, for now, the sword is gone. For the first time in your life, you are genuinely free. Use this time to think—to really think—the way you've never been allowed."

"You won't corrupt me."

"You've already been corrupted. You think Vesta Carmis Zell will take you back? After not only failing, but failing so spectacularly that the prize you were meant to deliver to her turned you into a mindless slave? One tainted by base power?"

"I am cleansed."

"By the actions of Jason Asano, which is enough by itself that she will never trust you again, soul brand or not. If you go back, you won't be welcomed into the fold. You'll be made an example of."

"You don't know that."

Boris let out a sigh.

"I do, Mahk," he said softly. "And so do you. It's just a matter of whether you'll admit it to yourself before the ignorance kills you."

"You said you didn't lie to me, but Vesta Carmis Zell would never accept a member of the Unorthodoxy."

"She didn't. She bargained for the services of messengers with elemental powers and didn't much care where they came from. Do you have any idea how many astral kings are outside the Council of Kings? The council doesn't. Astral kings are older than universes and never die. She has no idea that I'm Unorthodoxy."

"But if I tell her about you, it will lead back to a major nest of enemies."

"Yes," Boris said. Mahk narrowed his eyes.

"You're not trusting me. You're telling me to switch sides or you'll kill me for my silence."

"Yes. The reality is, you won't get to tell her about me, Mahk. You still have her brand on your soul, and she'll use it to scour your mind the moment you are back in her grasp. She'll know everything and credit you with nothing. She'll kill you for having had this conversation."

"Then you might as well kill me now. There is no escaping the brand."

"No," Boris agreed. "Not without another astral king."

25

UNORTHODOXY

THE SHIMMERING DOME OF AURA WAS IMPENETRABLE TO MAGICAL SENSES, even those of a gold-rank messenger like Fiola Min Kath. She was sitting in one of the trees, having shaped a throne in the branches with her plant manipulation powers. It was an uncommon power amongst messengers, but that rarity did not translate to respect. Messengers admired powers that worked in the sky.

Fiola had watched Mahk Den Kahla lead the other gold-rankers into the dome one after another, none of whom had returned. Created by Boris Ket Lundi's aura, the dome blocked sight and sound but not physical passage. Whatever was happening in there, Mahk and Boris did not want the rest of them to know until it was their turn. She was the fifth and final gold-ranker, so her turn was next.

She considered running. She would get a head start if she picked her moment while they were inside the dome. Boris Ket Lundi was strong, but no faster than others of their kind. She could escape if she could reach another territory, one that had more life than a desert with few scraggly trees clinging to a mountaintop. Perhaps they wouldn't chase her at all.

She could have been imagining the grim fate waiting for her in the dome, but Boris Ket Lundi had not been shy about killing their own kind. Strength might have been the way of the messengers, but it still did not sit well with her. She did not like her fellow messengers, as a rule, but that was not the same as feeling nothing when they died. Not that she showed any reaction, of course. Empathy was a dangerous sign of weakness.

If she fled, where would she go? Escaping the immediate danger was all well and good, but was it a true escape? She lacked the strength and knowledge to leave this strange place alone. Death would find her, sooner or later.

Indecision made the choice for her when Mahk Den Kahla once again emerged from the dome. He looked in her direction and spoke her name. She floated from her throne, the leaves and branches untwisting to resume their natural shape. She floated down to stop in front of Mahk, just outside the dome.

"Am I going to die in there?"

"That depends on the choice you make, Fiola Min Kath. It won't be an easy one."

"What kind of choice?"

Mahk stepped back through the shimmering dome, leaving Fiola floating alone. She turned her head, looking to the distant horizon. Then she turned back and followed into the dome. Her body tingled as she passed through the barrier. Inside, Mahk was floating towards Boris, who was painted in the shining gold-silver wetness of messenger blood. The four gold-rankers that came before were now a pile of corpses, their blood trickling down the slope. A hole had been dug to collect it, so it didn't run out of the dome.

Fiola didn't move far from the edge of the dome, primed to flee.

"They didn't choose well, then," she said, looking at the dead messengers.

"No," Boris said. There was usually a playful un-messenger-like lilt in his tone, but it was wholly absent now. "It's time to see behind the curtain, Fiola Min Kath. You have to choose between everything you've ever known and everything you've been taught to despise."

"Which one gets me killed?"

"You tell me," Boris challenged.

She looked at him for a long time. His oddly well-fitted clothes, his choice to stand on the ground instead of float.

"You're Unorthodoxy," she said.

"Yes."

"It seems obvious in hindsight."

"So much does," Boris said with a hint of the usual playfulness.

Fiola turned her gaze to Mahk Den Kahla.

"You too?"

"I was offered the choice first," Mahk said.

"Then you are a traitor," she accused.

"Yes," Mahk said. "I am not surprised at the others choosing the way they did. You were the only one we suspected might go the other way. That is why I brought you in last."

"You should have brought me in first. A pile of messengers is not a good look from someone trying to recruit."

"I said the same," Mahk told her as he tilted his head to indicate Boris. "He insisted."

"Whichever path you ultimately take," Boris said, "making this choice has consequences. It's important that you can make it honestly."

"Why do you think I am the one who will turn traitor?"

"Every gold-rank messenger has seen the cracks in the façade," Boris told her. "Some do so long before rising to gold. Most don't care and keep climbing the ladder. They keep chasing power on the road laid out before them, not seeing the invisible gates. But there are those who chart their own course. Some see the traps and realise they can never earn power, only be given it. Others realise they are slaves and long to be free. A precious few even manage to develop empathy."

Boris looked at the dead messengers and sighed.

"Most of them die," he continued. "Be they ambitious, empathetic or yearning to be free, it represents the same thing to an astral king: a threat. The vast majority of these rebellious thinkers are put down by their astral kings before they can cause trouble. But a few manage to modulate their thinking. Hide their divergent thoughts, even from themselves. Eventually, they meet one of three fates."

Boris glanced at Mahk before continuing.

"One, they suppress those thoughts so long, they stop having them and become good little messengers again. Two, those errant thoughts and feelings grow until they draw the attention of the astral king. They die. Three, they meet someone like me. Someone who can offer them a way forward that doesn't force them to choose between being a slave and a corpse."

"You're forcing me to choose between being a traitor and a corpse. A fugitive and a corpse."

"Yes."

Fiola looked at the dead messengers again.

"I can see why they refused you. Your pitch is not very compelling."

"I'm not trying to entice you. I'm going to give you the truth and then let you choose."

"Between joining you or joining this pile of the dead?"

"Yes."

"Then I have two choices. Be loyal to Vesta Carmis Zell, who will kill me if I don't, or be loyal to you, who will also kill me if I don't."

"Yes," Boris said. "But you are choosing between getting killed now and getting killed later, and loyalty to me has a clock on it. Once we are free of this place, you will be free of me."

"To do what? Be killed by my astral king the moment I leave this place? To somehow escape that fate and roam the cosmos until I'm hunted down as a traitor?"

"Very little of what you know about the Unorthodoxy is accurate. You've been taught that we are a scant few, existing in the hidden crevices of messenger society. But where are those crevices, exactly? How can we exist at all? Messengers can't exist without astral kings, and the astral kings keep our kind in line."

"You're saying that's all a lie?"

"Not all. Messengers need astral kings when we come into being, like a child needs a parent. Where now there is the brand, they once guided us in marking ourselves. No obedience, no alien eye inside our souls. Freedom instead of servitude. That is how the original astral kings did it. Those who were not messengers themselves."

"Not messengers?" Fiola asked. Her expression of shock was mirrored on Mahk's face.

"Yes," Boris said. "Our genesis came from the original astral kings, who were not messengers at all. Back then, there were no limits on rank because that is a function of the brand, which didn't exist. When messengers transcended to become astral kings themselves, they were the first to institute the brand, enslaving their own kind. At first, there was war and rebellion. Slave armies against the free. The free lost. We cared about our people; refused to sacrifice them the way our enemy did. The defeated went into hiding and the victorious began the indoctrination programs. In victory, they didn't just kill freedom but the very dream of it. In time, the leaders of the enemy became the Council of Kings. We became the Unorthodoxy."

"You speak as if you saw it for yourself," Mahk said.

"I was there. I keep myself from progressing to diamond because we need agents who can move without the attention. A gold-ranker is powerful enough to be an asset without being the potential threat a diamond-ranker is. Only at diamond-rank can we even begin to resist the brand, which would have drawn scrutiny I could not afford. My rank allowed me to deceive Vesta Carmis Zell and reach this place."

"How did you deceive her?"

"Vesta Carmis Zell would have known if I wasn't branded. She was desperate for powerful messengers with elemental powers, so I had one of our astral kings brand me. She then obtained some rather hilarious concessions for placing me at Vesta Carmis Zell's temporary service. I was hoping to have the brand removed by now, but things haven't gone my way."

"You're saying the Unorthodoxy has astral kings?" Mahk asked.

"Yes," Boris said. "I know this is all a shock, Mahk, but do try to keep up. Astral kings are rare, but they are also immortal, which complicates war. You can ravage their resources, but you cannot kill them. They exist as universes forged from souls, which remain inviolable. They may only be a fraction of the size of universes created by the Builder, but they cannot be destroyed and they do not fall to entropy, however long you wait. There are too many astral kings for anyone to keep track of. Over time, as the number of astral kings rises, the Unorthodoxy astral kings have been slipping back into the general population."

Fiola looked at Boris searchingly. What he was telling her was outrageous, flying in the face of everything she had ever been taught. But just because he admitted as much didn't mean he wasn't lying.

"Population," Mahk said, echoing Boris' word. "A *population* of astral kings."

"Transcendents are all immortal," Boris said. "Not just ageless, like us, but truly unkillable. They have their own level of interaction, as above us as our cosmic community is above those living their entire lives on some rock, hurtling around an ember. Diamond-rank is the threshold. The borderland between them and us."

Mahk looked shell-shocked, not even noticing when he drifted down to placing his feet on the ground. Fiola looked hurt and angry.

"Everything you're saying makes us seem so small," she said.

"Yes," Boris agreed. "The concept of messengers as the ultimate beings of creation, the messengers of the cosmic will, is laughable. A truth that all diamond-rank messengers realise eventually. That's the greatest danger they represent to the astral kings. And when they realise that the brand on their souls means they can never become astral kings, that danger becomes unacceptable. The astral kings either have to accept them and remove the brand, or put them down. Of course, removing the brand doesn't mean a diamond-ranker will just leap into transcendence. Most diamond-rankers set free to become astral kings fail, just like essence-users or any of the other half-transcendents floating around the cosmos."

Fiola shook her head. "You haven't given me any reason to believe any of this."

"I don't expect you to," Boris said. "I'm offering you the chance to see the truth for yourself."

"And if I turn you down, you'll kill me."

"I've told you far too much to let you go."

"You didn't tell the others. Otherwise, Mahk Den Kahla wouldn't be so shocked."

They both turned to look at Mahk, who stood on the ground, staring at nothing. He snapped out of it and looked at Boris.

"You didn't tell me any of this," he said. "You didn't tell any of us."

"I mentioned at the start that some messengers find the cracks in the indoctrination. Fiola Min Kath was already on the path of a free thinker. You were not. You didn't see until your rank let you, and even then, you ignored it. I had to open the cracks in your mind with a hammer and chisel. You were still programmed to respond to authority, so I pushed you through by force of will. But it wasn't that hard, which is good. At least you responded to it, unlike…"

Their gazes went to the pile of bodies once more. A few wisps of rainbow smoke rose from the bodies as the bottom messenger was breaking down into raw magic.

"Fiola," Mahk said. "Boris Ket Lundi took a different approach with me. He pointed out that Vesta Carmis Zell was not going to let us live, however this went. Not after the way we failed and were corrupted."

Fiola nodded absently, eyes still on the thickening plume of rainbow smoke.

"We should use a ritual to preserve them," she said. "It's a waste of resources."

"I took their lives," Boris said. "I can at least leave them their dignity."

"You sound like one of the lesser races," Fiola said.

"Now that we've come this far," Boris said, "that is the last time you say 'lesser races' in my presence."

2 6

MESSENGERS DON'T HAVE HEARTS

GARTH AND JAMEELA STOOD ATOP A HILL OF RED DESERT ROCK. THEIR vast forces spread out on the plateau they overlooked.

"So, the messengers want this soul forge, whatever that is," Garth said.

"According to the Magic Society researchers, yes," Jameela said. "And it seems that Asano is the biggest threat to that objective. He also has the ability to claim it."

"Do we?"

"I don't believe so. We could only acquire it with the help of the messengers, and they will not hand it over. To return to their leadership without it is likely worse than dying down here. I don't believe we could use it anyway. The transformation zone itself, once reunited with reality, remains the prize."

"Then we can let them have it, so long as the zone itself still goes to us."

"I would counsel caution. We are unlikely to understand any magic they use to that end."

"Yes. And promises don't always need to be kept."

Garth turned to look at the distant mountain where the messengers were lairing. Three of them flew in their direction. The two priests waited and watched until the messengers were floating in the air in front of them.

The one Garth had spoken with before, Boris Ket Lundi, was flanked by the other two.

"I sensed the death of the rest of your other gold-rankers," Garth said. More accurately, he'd sensed the aura dome into which they'd been led one by one, and then their dead bodies when the dome dropped.

"Neither of us are fools," Boris said. "We can make a deal to stay out of your fight with the adventurers, but you would doubtless expect us to turn on you when you were weakened. Now we lack the strength. However many silver-rankers we have, and whatever the cost of bringing low your enemy, we no longer have the strength to turn on you."

"You expect me to believe you gutted most of your gold-rank strength as a show of trust?" Garth asked.

"Naturally not," Boris said. "I chose the way that served my own ends as well. But the affairs of my people are not your business. How the results affect you are your business."

"Handing over your territories, and the messengers that come with them, would make for a better show of trust."

"Trust goes both ways, High Priest. If we slaughter our strongest warriors and hand over the territories, that leaves you with no incentive to accede to our modest requests. Jason Asano must not survive the battle."

"Killing Asano falls within our interests as well, I can assure you."

"I want more than assurances, High Priest. I want details."

"You are not in a position to negotiate," Jameela said.

Boris did not shift his blank expression but he glanced at Jameela briefly before turning back to Garth. The priest nodded his acknowledgement.

"You are not in a position to be a threat," Garth said, "but you could be a bother."

"We could be more than a bother," Boris said. "I am confident that we can escape your camp."

"Is that so?"

"Your avatar is powerful, but it is neither close nor fast. Not enough to stop the three of us, or our forces, if they start fleeing now. We chose you because our desire for Asano's death makes for the less uneasy alliance. If you prove that assessment wrong, you will find us on the other side of the upcoming battle."

"You're bluffing," Jameela said. "You want Asano dead and he knows it."

"And I know Asano. The last time he was in a transformation zone, he allied with the man who killed his brother and lover. He is not afraid to work with his foes."

"And what fate befell this foe of Asano in that space?" Garth asked.

"Jason Asano, silver rank at the time, was pulled into that transformation zone along with a slate of his gold-rank enemies. When the space returned to reality, two people escaped intact. One was Asano, the zone now in his possession. The other was a gold-rank vampire that went on to lead the vampires of that world in a war for domination. But despite that seeming fearlessness, she hid after leaving the transformation zone. She did not dare show her face again until Asano had left that universe entirely."

"You didn't answer my question," Garth said. "You could have just said that Asano's enemy died inside. Instead, you told me that story. Why?"

"I said that two people escaped that transformation zone intact. There was another, but I would not call him intact nor his departure an escape. Asano's enemy did die, yes, but the vampire trapped his soul in a blood clone that now serves her as a slave."

"It doesn't sound like allying with Asano while still being his enemy is likely to turn out well for you."

"Thus, I came to you first. But if you truly think we have no position to negotiate from…"

"You do," Garth said, "but walking away from us complicates things for you more than you are suggesting, messenger."

Boris snorted a smirking laugh.

"And how is that, priest?"

"Asano wants the soul forge, but we are willing to let you have it."

The smirk dropped from Boris' face. "How did… do you even understand what it is you're talking about?"

"There is a way for you to still take it while we keep the territory?"

"What? Oh, yes, that's not an issue," Boris said. His expression made plain that he was hastily reorganising things in his mind. "That's just a matter of the right ritual as you consolidate the transformation zone with reality. The only challenge there is convincing you to let us set off some magic I guarantee you won't understand while the transformation zone goes through the transition."

"Our god's avatar is the seat of our territorial power," Garth said. "Undeath instilled it with the ability to claim the zone. You don't have close to the power to interfere with that. You will need to excise this soul forge of yours while being very careful not to interfere with the god's work. If your imprecision costs you because our god puts a halt to your magic, we will consider that your failure, not a violation of our deal."

Boris looked troubled as he considered Garth's words.

"Allow me to discuss this before giving you an answer," he said.

"Be quick," Garth said. "Your leverage is as lacking as my patience."

Boris scowled but held his tongue. The three messengers floated away and a shimmering dome appeared around them. Inside the dome, Boris grinned.

"This is going great!"

"How so?" Fiola asked.

"He must have found out about the soul forge from someone they captured and interrogated."

"I share Fiola Min Kath's confusion," Mahk said. "A ritual to extract the soul forge while this dimensional realm is being reinserted into reality would take immense research by astral magic experts."

"That doesn't matter," Boris said. "The priest is lying about letting it happen anyway. He definitely doesn't believe it's as easy as I made it out to be. We're in the same position we were in the first place, making bets on who can betray the other one more effectively. He just thinks he's found some extra leverage."

"I'm not sure I understand the plan," Fiola said.

"Of course you don't," Boris said. "I didn't tell you all of it. Now, it's about time we went back out there. Remember to look stern."

The dome dropped and the three messengers floated back to Garth.

"We can accept your terms," Boris said, "so long as you make absolutely certain that Asano is dead. If he interferes in the ritual and causes your god to foul it, that *will* be a violation of our deal."

"Asano will die," Garth said.

"How?" Boris asked.

"That is our concern."

"Not good enough. I'll give you one of my silver-rank messengers. You can take for yourself their power to isolate themself with an enemy in a dimensional space. Isolate Asano from his allies and kill him yourself."

"Take their power?" Garth asked.

"I have neither the time nor the interest for playing games with you, priest. I know what you can do because I know what you are."

The red lights in the eye sockets of Garth's skull face flared brightly.

"Oh, calm down," Boris said. "I'm an ancient wanderer of the cosmos; you think you're my first zemravore?"

Garth's eyes dimmed, Jameela's gaze panning between Boris and Garth. The two stared at one another in silence for a long moment.

"Very well," Garth said. "I have heard of the duelling powers possessed by many messengers. Just make sure the messenger you bring me has one. This plan will suffice."

"No," Boris said. "It won't. You don't know Asano. Don't underestimate him because he's silver rank. He's elusive, dwelling in shadows and hiding his aura even from gold-rankers. And he's died before. You have to kill him, then keep killing him until it sticks. Take your undead with you. The ones you animated personally are linked to you like familiars."

"Don't lecture a high priest of Undeath on how raising the dead works, messenger."

Boris bowed his head in acknowledgment.

"Foolish of me, in hindsight," he said. "My point is that your undead are connected to you, and will therefore be able to join you into the sealed space. Take an army of them and don't give Asano anywhere to hide. Dig out every crevice and cut into every shadow. He will only have so much area to work with in a sealed space. Deprive him of every place he might go to ground and drag him into the light. Only then can you make the difference in rank come into play."

"You believe he can hide from my senses?"

"I know he can," Boris said. "He's hard to pin down; even catching him in an isolation power will be a trick, but that is the beginning of the fight, not the end. Victory will only come when he's dead for good. Do not dismiss what I said about his resurrections. He's been killed by the Builder's first servant and even the Builder inhabiting a mortal vessel. It will take more than—"

"I've heard you," Garth said. "Stop belabouring the point. Leave us now before you try my patience further. Go, and return only with your messenger sacrifice."

Boris' expression said he didn't want to leave it at just that, but he turned and flew off. The other messengers followed and the two priests watched. When he was confident they were out of even gold-rank earshot, Garth spoke to Jameela.

"What do you think?"

"There is unquestionably something strange between the messengers and Asano,"

Jameela said. "How close it adheres to what these messengers have presented is the question."

"You interrogated the essence-users about this adventurer and the messengers. Did you learn anything relevant to this question?"

"When the messengers invaded the elf city, they became obsessed with killing Asano. The researchers weren't certain why."

"That holds with what I know of messengers. They rarely care about any but their own kind as individuals. When they do care about someone, it is with an obsession to destroy them. Usually for having affronted their dignity in some way, besmirching their precious sense of superiority."

"Related to the fact that Asano can claim this soul forge of theirs?"

"That seems likely. I think we can at least believe that their desire for his death is true. They simply want us to do their work for them, and let the adventurers soften us up in the process."

"Then they will wait for Asano's death before betraying us."

"Yes. I suspect their weakness is feigned. The group we have seen may just be a fraction of their true strength, with their true force gathered in the territory they still hold. The ones they killed here were probably political opponents of Boris Ket Lundi. He consolidated his strength while passing it off as a show of humility and trust. But there is no humility in a messenger."

"How will you deal with them?"

"I won't. However great they have deluded themselves into believing they are, our god has sent his power into this place. Whatever their schemes, the avatar is a wall no winged beast can fly over."

Garth stared at the shadowy figure, standing alone before the full might of the undead army.

"We both have areas within our territories with environmental weapons," Jason's voice came from Shade's body. "We'll fight on neutral ground. A cleared but unclaimed territory."

"Where?"

"There's a forest made of stone adjacent to both of our territories. It hasn't been cleared yet. I suggest that our demigod and your avatar do so. Supervised by a selection of gold-rankers on each side so we can be sure that neither of us attempts to ambush the other's divine combatant."

Garth's skeletal face didn't react, despite his surprise that the enemy had gotten that close. The territory in question had been scouted. The more complex the terrain, the greater the advantage of thinking fighters over the mindless undead that made up the bulk of Garth's forces. The stone forest was acceptable. It was more difficult for the undead to navigate than empty desert, but some cover made it harder to wipe them out in swathes with wide-area magic. He suspected the enemy had chosen it knowing they would reject anything too disadvantageous to the undead.

"I am aware of the territory," Garth said. "Our avatar will clear it alone."

The response was a moment coming, Garth assuming Asano was consulting with his allies.

"That is acceptable," Jason's voice finally came. "Under the condition that it is observed from our side. If there is some hidden weapon in the territory, we cannot allow you to claim it."

"Acceptable," Garth echoed. "I will send the avatar in an hour. If your observers are not in place, that is your failing."

Mahk carried the unconscious silver-rank messenger. They were trained to be obedient, but also trained for loyalty to the astral kings. These motivations had come into conflict upon discovering that their leaders were all now Unorthodoxy. The combination of being indoctrinated to obey and seeing what happened to those who didn't made the bloodbath short. This was one of the rebellious ones, left alive for a grimmer purpose.

He delivered the messenger to the high priest of Undeath, uncertain of what would happen. The priest marched down the hill he always seemed to dwell on, going down the side opposite his own forces. Mahk didn't care if Garth wanted to keep his nature hidden from his priests and followed along, still carrying the silver-ranker.

Garth threw off the robes draped around his bizarre body, revealing a skeletal, hunchback form. Two extra legs and four extra arms, all wrapped around its body, had been bulking it out under the robes. The limbs unfurled, uncovering a rib cage containing four stony sockets held in place by bone struts, all where internal organs would be on a living thing. Inside each socket was a living, beating heart, held in place by bone spikes stabbed into them. Each side of the rib cage swung open like a door and the spikes retracted from one of the hearts. Garth reached in, plucked it out and tossed it aside like the crust of a stale sandwich.

At a gesture from Garth, Mahk approached with the unconscious messenger in his arms. Garth directed him to hold it up and Mahk did so, his hands slung under its arms. One of Garth's hands shot out, burying itself in the messenger's chest. A moment later, the messenger erupted into rainbow smoke, her body gone but for a beating heart, gripped in Garth's hand. Garth placed the heart in the empty socket and bone spikes stabbed into it.

"You can go," Garth told Mahk as his ribs closed and the limbs started curling around his body once more.

Mahk floated in place with a confused expression, staring at Garth.

"What is it?" Garth asked, irritated.

"Messengers don't have hearts," Mahk said.

"I don't care."

2 7

WILL HE BE BROKEN

TWO CLOUD VEHICLES SHOT THROUGH AN UNCLAIMED TERRITORY, hovering a few metres over the ground. The territory was an icy expanse, but far from a barren waste. In the distance, castles made of ice sparkled in the sun. Plant life was abundant, in shades of white, blue and grey over the traditional browns and greens.

Of the two vehicles, one was larger and more colourful. Painted in vibrant sunset hues, it ranged from warm shades of orange, gold and red through to cool purples, blues and teals. The other vehicle was encased in hexagonal panels of slick dark red, like blood under glass. Between the panels, the white cloud the panels were set into was visible.

The driving spaces for the two vehicles were as different as the exteriors. While they were both situated at the front of their respective vehicles, with large viewing windows, the similarities ended there. In Emir's cloud vehicle, the design was extremely minimal and made entirely of clouds. There was a chair, to either side of which was a ball of mist, hovering in the air. These balls were the only control mechanism, Emir having one hand in each as he piloted the vehicle himself.

The cockpit of Jason's cloud vehicle showed no trace of its cloud vehicle nature. It looked like someone who understood nothing about complex vehicles but was very enthusiastic about buttons had gone mad with power. There were two seats, each of which contained a Shade body that was acting rapidly to work the vehicle's numerous control mechanisms. There were buttons, switches, toggles, levers and lights, all in a hodgepodge mix of anime mecha, seventies aeroplane and mad science lab.

On the rooftop lounge of Jason's cloud vehicle, Miriam Vance was wondering why it had a rooftop lounge. Jason sat next to her, watching the terrain rush by with a mixed juice drink and a huge grin. The drink had a little umbrella and a bendy straw. Their chairs were comfortable cloud recliners, side-by-side so they could look ahead as the vehicle moved forward. They each had a side table for drinks, with another table between them.

"We should be getting blasted by air much more at this speed," he said. "I have an invisible mist shield redirecting it. I let a little in, though, because I want that sense of motion. The mist covers the whole roof, in fact."

"I figured that might be the case when our high-speed, open-air passage through a snow field was pleasantly warm."

"Yeah, that makes sense," Jason said, then took a long sip of his drink. "Ooh, that's some good stuff."

"You don't seem especially worried about what we're heading into," Miriam observed.

"Well, you can't go getting excited every time something like this happens."

"I rather believe you can."

"Don't think I'm not taking this seriously. I know the stakes are more than just life or death. If we lose here, we'll all die and a disaster of massive proportions will hit the world. But in my last transformation zone, the world would end if I didn't win and my only allies were all my gold-rank enemies. This time, I've got resources, allies, power and a plan that someone other than me came up with. I've even got a mountain fortress in the shape of my own head. The only other thing I could ask for might even be on the cards. I've been talking with Clive and… well, that's for after. Assuming we win this fight, we still need to clean up the rest of the territories while the anomalies keep growing stronger. It's going to get dangerous even for the gold-rankers by the time we're done."

"We have Xandier."

"Yeah, but I don't think you like putting all your eggs in one basket any more than I do."

"No, I do not. But, as you said, that is for another day."

"Exactly. Today, we have a climactic battle for the fate of see article one. I'm not saying that this is old hat, but I've been through it enough times that I know the best thing I can do is be rested and centred. I'm sure I don't need to tell you that anxiety, anger and grim determination make you feel powerful, yet make you weaker."

"You do not," Miriam agreed. "Being calm and mindful, without becoming placid and passive is easier said than done. Especially given what we face today."

"You get used to it. Would you like a scone? I'm going to have a scone."

True to his word, Jason was soon biting into a scone slathered generously with jam and cream, letting out a moan of pleasure.

"Shimmer berry jam," he mumbled happily, spraying crumbs. "I made it myself while I was convalescing in Rimaros."

He swallowed his mouthful and grinned.

"The greatest triumph of my time there," he said.

"Your greatest triumph?"

"Yep."

"Did you forget that you convinced the Builder to end his invasion and leave this world?"

"Nope. I stand by my statement."

Miriam looked from Jason to the tray on the table between them.

"I guess I'd better have one of these scones, then."

"How confident are you in this plan?" Jason asked.

"That sounds like a nervous question," Miriam said. The scones had proven oddly effective at diminishing her nervousness. "What happened to moving past anxiety?"

"There's a lot of people asking that question in this vehicle," Jason said. "Out loud or not."

"Well," Miriam said, "let's start with the fact that you can portal between disparate territories you control, sight unseen. That, as far as I'm aware, is an aspect of the unique connection you have with territories. Perhaps messengers could match it, connecting to the territories through their ritual magic, but we don't have any with portal magic to test. Then, we add the ability to pack up almost all our forces in your soul realm and jump them from one territory to another. Also, as far as I'm aware, unique."

"You think the Undeath priests won't know about it?"

"They might. We've clashed with them enough times to have had losses. It's possible they kept some alive and interrogated them. More likely, though, any information they had is from those they captured who hadn't joined up yet."

"Meaning they would know about much of what we can do, but nothing revealed after entering the transformation zone."

"Yes. This includes the ability to transport a large and relatively weak silver-rank force through unclaimed territory using cloud vehicles. Since we suggested the territory agreed upon for the battle, they will likely be looking for traps and plots we've put in place. Having our demigod and some of our key gold-rankers there to observe, they hopefully won't anticipate us smuggling most of our forces across dangerous territory to hit them in their own backyard."

"Letting us challenge the main force while Clive sets his plan in motion."

"Yes. The high priest will call back the avatar immediately, I'm certain, but Xandier can stall it while Standish's plan weakens it. We want to clear out as many of the undead and messengers as we can in that time, leaving the priests until the avatar regroups. Your power will be critical during that stage."

"I know."

"Be that as it may, I find drilling the plan into people's heads over and over leaves at least a small chance they'll actually follow it. Once the avatar rejoins the main force, both hopefully weakened already, we take down their priests and weaken the avatar further, teaming up with Xandier to kill it. That is about as far as we can optimistically anticipate having some control of how this battle goes."

"Assuming the inevitable chaos factors haven't already sent it careening off the rails by that point."

"Yes. We're planning to come as close to killing a god as it's possible to get, today, so chaos is inherent. Far more than I like could go wrong. If they guess what we're up to, or the messenger forces floating around choose to participate in unanticipated ways, things will get very messy, very fast. That will happen eventually, though, whatever we do. Sooner or later, we'll all have to improvise. The strength of this plan is that we have broad objectives that everyone knows and can fight for, even if things go splound-shaped. Eliminate priests and—"

"Splound-shaped?"

"A splound is a fruit," Miriam said. "It grows in lumpy, unpredictable shapes."

"Is it tasty?"

"No," Miriam said. "It's very bitter."

On the upper slopes of their mountain, Boris, Mahk and Fiola looked to the distant undead.

"Are you sure we shouldn't have reached out to Asano?" Mahk asked.

"There are too many ways it could go wrong," Boris said. "Our contact could be discovered. Even if it wasn't, Garth is no fool. If he got a sense Asano was trying to let himself be caught, he'd almost certainly back off from that plan."

"If Asano doesn't know the plan," Fiola said, "what makes you confident in him?"

"Jason Asano has been walking through fire from the moment he stepped beyond his own little life on his own little world. At some point, you just have to accept that he's not going to burn."

"I'm not sure I like hinging victory on a metaphor," Mahk said.

"I have been around for a very long time, Mahk Den Kahla," Boris said. "In all of that time, I've seen only a handful of people that can truly shake the cosmos. Bethlin the Reaver. Zithis Carrow Vayel. They're rare, but you come to recognise the signs. I doubt the World-Phoenix knew what it was getting when it stepped in to alter Asano's course, but it knows now. They all see the signs, just as I do. It's why he's gotten their attention, and why his next battle will be the one that marks his place in the cosmos. Will he stand tall or will he be broken, like the Builder?"

Floating slightly behind and to either side of Boris, Mahk and Fiola shared a look. They both had a sudden sense of being caught up in something much larger than them, which was something a messenger was never meant to feel.

Atop his hill, Garth contemplated the battle ahead. The avatar and a retinue had been dispatched to the battle site, crossing the territorial boundary. His link to the avatar, through the power Undeath bestowed to them both, did not cross the boundary. Garth had considered going himself, but he wanted to stay with the main force. There was nothing the enemy could do to the avatar, and if they somehow attempted some trickery, he needed to command the larger forces. He'd left one of his subordinate priests to control the avatar.

His faction held a massive, unified territory now, but it was not under Garth's control. Only the avatar was able to handle the strain and had been imbued with the knowledge and power to unify the entire zone. So long as they could destroy their rivals, this bizarre dimensional detour in their plan would turn out better than they could have hoped.

Not being connected to the territory, however, meant that Garth would not be immediately warned when things went wrong.

To address the communication issue, Garth had set up a relay. Next to him, a skull was resting atop a short spear stabbed into the ground. The skull could relay voices between itself and another skull set next to the territorial boundary. That way, a messenger could come through and report quickly. One did just that, crossing the border and rushing to the skull.

"High Priest, the adventurers and their allies are doing something. Their demigod has attacked the avatar."

"And the rest of their forces?"

"We have still only seen a fraction of them, but we've observed them doing something strange. They're bringing out our priests they've captured alive and started executing them."

"Why? They have to know that won't impact our morale."

"I don't understand either, High Priest. The priests are rising into revenants and immediately attacking the adventurers who are forced to fight them. Even with the enemy prepared, revenants are hard to kill—"

"—because they're infused with the power of the Undeath god," Garth said.

His mind raced over the possibilities. What did the enemy hope to achieve? Garth had lost people, and until he had found the avatar, they had not arisen as revenants the way they normally would. Once they had found it, their power to rise again had been restored by tapping into the power of—

"They're trying to drain the avatar!" Garth managed to snarl, despite not having a throat or even really a mouth. "We have to—"

"High Priest!" Jameela called out as she rushed up the hill. He turned to look and saw her pointing in the opposite direction to the dimensional boundary. Two strange vehicles were speeding across the desert, floating yet kicking up plumes of dust and sand from their sheer speed.

"Recall the avatar!" Garth yelled at the communication skull. "We have to consolidate our forces before they can!"

He started loping down the hill faster than his awkward body seemed like it would be capable of. The battle was about to begin.

28

RISKING EVERYTHING

IN THE BATTLE THAT TOOK PLACE IN THE UNDERGROUND CITY OF THE brighthearts, the priests of Undeath had largely held back. They had what amounted to an infinite supply of the unliving to throw at the enemy until the enemy crumbled. This was not the case when the two cloud vehicles came barrelling over the rocks and sand of the desert, trails of dust thrown up in their wake.

Undeath priests came in different varieties, from somewhat ordinary essence-users to bizarre undead mockeries. This included higher-order undead, like vampires commanding armies of deathless ghouls. There were liches—highly intelligent undead with powerful tricks to escape final destruction. Liches all wielded potent magic, be that the essences they had in life or more eldritch and alien powers. Others were less common forms of undead, such as the zemravore, Garth. There was a being that looked to be made of solidified shadow, in the shape of a human but twice as tall. It used magic to turn the zombies and skeletons around it into shadowy, ethereal entities that were harder to cut down.

Although there was no shortage of undead oddities amongst the priests, most were still amongst the living. Employing necromantic essence combinations banned by the Adventure Society, their powers were not focused on direct combat but on creating, commanding, and enhancing the undead. The overall undead minions under their command were fewer than they had access to in the last massive battle, but their direct participation made each undead much stronger.

The Undeath forces were situated on a plateau, looking down on the desert where the two vehicles were approaching. The priests stirred their minions into action, bolstering them with magic and sending them into the attack.

They descended the plateau, the edge of which led to a mix of steep slopes and outright cliffs. This was not a challenge to navigate as the weakest of the undead were silver-rank. Most of the army in the bright-heart city had been bronze, but anything that weak had been annihilated by the transformation zone's living anomalies.

Some undead simply leapt off, unfussed about the landing. Others were empowered in various ways, helping them to manage the terrain. Simple skeletons were turned into skeleton mages through the necromancy of their masters. Runes carved themselves into the bones of the skeletons, lighting up with different coloured magic. Dark smoke shrouded their feet and carried them into the air, at which point they flung simple projectiles of fire, electricity or shimmering force. These weren't potent attacks, taken individually, but their raw number made for a storm of magic landing on the two vehicles, still kilometres distant.

Vampire priests drained the life out of brightheart and messenger prisoners they had claimed for the purpose, using that life force to make their ghouls faster and stronger. The emaciated figures scrambled down the steep mountainside off the plateau's edge.

Zombies and other macabre creations of the undead priests were given a variety of enhancements. Some grew wings of rotting flesh and took to the skies, or claws that dug into stone, letting them climb down vertical cliffs at speed.

Alongside the undead, the messengers claimed by the undeath priests were on the move. The pallid messengers claimed by the priests had proven amongst the weakest variety, compared to those claimed by other messengers or the brighthearts. That changed when those messengers were handed over to the avatar of Undeath. The meagre undeath they had been given by the priests had been bolstered with divine might, making them both more corpse-like and more powerful. Even in the avatar's absence their new strength remained, shown off as they soared through the air, leaving trails of purple sparks in their wake.

Another factor of the messengers gaining more power from the avatar was that they now enjoyed enhancements from the auras of the Undeath priests. Although the messengers were still technically alive, the potent undeath energy inside them responded to the aura powers the same way as true undead.

Necromancers whose powers came from essence abilities—most of the priests—almost always had aura powers that bolstered the undead. This wasn't the specific transformations and extra powers from their other abilities but baseline enhancement of the undeath energy animating them. This was a massive force multiplier for the undead minions, and the reason Garth needed to hunt Jason down.

The rooftop lounge of Jason's vehicle had closed over, armour panels emerging from the cloud-stuff to shield it from the rain of magic projectiles. Jason and Miriam had gone inside, joining the Shades in the piloting room that Jason was still deciding between calling a cockpit or a bridge. He thought cockpit was more accurate, but he really wanted the spaceship vibes.

Rather than look out the windscreen, Jason closed his eyes and connected his senses to his cloud vehicle. The vehicle was a spirit domain, giving Jason near total power within it. That did not extend to outside the vehicle, but he was able to use it like a signal booster for his aura, affecting the aura itself and the magical perception that used it as a basis. It wasn't a raw strength upgrade but something that impacted specific aspects. For his perception, he was able to multitask better inside his mind, actively observing more at once. For his aura, it made it harder for the Undeath priests to push back against with their own auras.

Jason's aura carried with it not just his aura power, but also all the aspects of his aura he had developed. This included the power he had learned from the goddess of death to diminish undeath energy, which made his aura anathema to the Undeath priests.

Jason's power to affect the undead bordered on divine. Death had shown him how to reshape his aura with an effectiveness that mortals could normally not touch upon. It was the kind of gift that gods offered their followers temporarily before taking the power back. Death had shown Jason how to effectively bestow that gift upon himself. Added to the god-adjacent power of his spirit domain that he was using to bolster his aura and Jason wasn't confronting the undead like a mortal but in the manner of a god.

Jason was not a god, however. Using their tools in their way made it possible for an aura face-off against all those priests, gold-rankers included. The problem was that Jason lacked the one thing that truly made gods what they were: infinite power. His aura was still the basis for everything he was doing, and while it was implausibly strong for his rank, that rank was still silver. That he could effectively pit himself against the priests at all was a borderline miracle, complete with the divine tools to make it happen.

Jason's limits meant that he was unable to dominate the undead forces the way Death had with her miracle. He reached a spiritual stalemate with his foes, where they couldn't suppress his aura but could shield their undead from it. In turn, Jason couldn't weaken the undead beyond their normal baseline, but he could stop the priestly auras from making them stronger.

He couldn't shut down the specific enhancements of the undead from various priest powers, be it transformations or the blood-fuelled enhancements to vampire ghouls. But the aura powers enhancing the basic undead energy flowing through them was shut down, negating the force-multiplier of raising their baseline power.

While Jason was flooding the battlefield with his aura, Miriam had been using his communication power to issue last-minute commands to their forces. Most of them were on the larger vehicle belonging to Emir.

"How are you doing?" she asked Jason.

"Not as well as I'd like," Jason said as he opened his eyes. "I've put a dent in the priests' ability to give blanket strength upgrades to their minions, but that's about it."

"I'll take it," Miriam said. "It's a miracle you can do even that much, given how many gold-rankers have to be pushing back on you."

"Miracle adjacent," Jason corrected. "The goddess of Death provided me with a trick built for purpose and she didn't muck about. My team were pretty cranky when they heard what I traded for it, but they don't understand the magnitude of what she showed me. And it's not even the loss they think it is. Assuming we win."

"And if we don't win?"

"Then it won't matter either way."

"True enough," Miriam said and then moved to peer out the windscreen. "I'm not seeing a good spot to establish a beachhead. It's all just open ground leading to that plateau the undead are pouring down."

Something solid hit the vehicle, rocking it heavily. The vehicle was moving smoothly forward again a moment later, the hover bus having what amounted to perfect air suspension.

"Damage?" Miriam asked.

"We're good," Jason said. "The armour panels offer resilience and the cloud material disperses force. The extra features I picked up from that noble house in Rimaros have worked out much better than expected. We're holding up almost as well as Emir's vehicle, so I'm expecting him to ask about them once we're done."

Miriam nodded and turned back to the view through the windscreen. Magic projectiles fell like hail and undead waterfalled off the plateau in the distance, moving down to the flatlands.

"We need to start setting up before the enemy brings their full power to bear," Miriam said. "Since nowhere in this barren dust flat is better than any other, we may as well stop here."

Adventurers, brighthearts and cultists spilled out of the two vehicles after they pulled to a stop. They were on an unremarkable flat of barren red rock, the dust they kicked up dry and chalky on the tongue. The sun beat down hard, blinding glints flashing off any glossy surface, from lacquered armour to polished blades.

Under Miriam's direction, they formed a defensive perimeter. It was manned on all sides but focused on defending from the front and above where the enemy was attacking. The battle was yet to reach an earnest clash, still consisting of ranged attacks pouring in from the Undeath side. The wave of minions heading their way would arrive soon enough.

For now, the undead were harassing with projectile attacks from the enhanced undead and the pallid messengers. The messengers had picked up new abilities after being claimed by the avatar; they could now fling purple energy projectiles. The ubiquitous assault was endurable, thanks to Jason preventing the power scale of the enemy from ramping up under the auras of the priests.

The adventurers and their allies only made token counterattacks, saving their strength for the battle to come. With a tsunami of undead heading their way, it would come soon. In the meantime, they defended the space where the two vehicles were breaking down, returning to their cloud flasks. It would take time to turn the vehicles into strongholds.

Miriam barked out orders as combatants rushed around them. The brighthearts lacked the strength of the adventurers, but they were using their elemental powers to set up defensive emplacements. Trenches with walls of stone spikes waiting for anyone who leapt over. Shelters where ranged attackers could duck in and about between heavy and total cover. Tunnels allowing safe traversal between different areas of the defensive line.

Emir and Shade stood by the cloud flasks still sucking in the cloud stuff of the vehicles. Jason stood next to Miriam, looking like a human-shaped void portal with his cloak wrapped around him. The inside of his hood was dark, indicating his eyes were closed as he concentrated on challenging the priests with his aura.

"With the possible exception of when the avatar arrives," Miriam told Jason, "this will be the most precarious part of the battle. We have to hold this position long enough for our twin fortresses to set up."

"Then it's time to see if I can't go slow them down some more," Jason said.

"I still don't like letting you go out there."

"I know. But until I have a spirit domain up and running again, they're pushing me back in the aura battle. I'm holding on, but I'm slipping and the enemy is getting stronger by the moment. My ghost fire will be more impactful than my aura, but I can't just sploosh it out like the goddess of Death. Mine is a pale imitation of her miracle. I need to get out there if I'm going to use it, and you know that. It's not like I'll be the only one you're sending out there to make trouble."

"Risking them is risking a soldier. Risking you is risking everything."

"And so is keeping me in a box when letting me out could be the difference between victory and defeat."

Miriam let out a resigned sigh.

"I know. Get moving. Just make sure you come back, and that it was worth letting you go."

2 9

A DANGEROUS POWER

GARTH HAD A DANGEROUS POWER. IT DIDN'T COME FROM HIS STOLEN hearts but was inherent to his nature as a zemravore. He could kill his aura, eliminating it entirely. This made him utterly invisible to aura senses, even those of a diamond-ranker. There simply was no aura to sense. This left him exposed, however, in ways that an aura that was only hidden did not.

Auras formed a natural shield against many powers. Sometimes it was something relatively ordinary, such as telekinesis not affecting enemies unless their auras were suppressed. Other powers were far more sinister and did not work at all unless the aura could be bypassed. Those were the most dangerous, but usually found in the hands of those as insidious as the powers themselves. The adventurers and brighthearts were unlikely to pose such a threat. It was the Builder cultists and potentially the messengers he had to watch out for.

Garth was still angry about the messenger seeing through him. Like every form of undead, a zemravore had both strengths and weaknesses. Garth had taken pains to hide that such a thing as a zemravore existed at all, even from his own people. But messengers lived forever and saw countless worlds. There was no telling the scope of any messenger's knowledge. Garth himself had proven many times that the knowledge accumulated over an ageless existence was not to be underestimated. He did not enjoy being on the receiving end of that truth, but in his long unlife, it was far from the first time.

The messenger's knowledge made using his aura-killing power a greater risk than normal. Garth could sense him for now; the messenger did not hide his presence while observing from his mountaintop. But once Garth's aura was gone, his magical senses and ability to track the messenger would go with it. Magical perception was tied to aura projection, so no aura meant no magical senses. He would be reliant on his mundane ones, which would at least retain their outstanding gold-rank levels.

He would not be able to track Asano through aura senses either, but that had already been proven futile. Asano's aura covered everything from the adventurer's defensive point to the plateau, along with the soon-be-a-meat-grinder battleground in between. Any well-trained gold-ranker could hide their presence within a strongly projected aura, and Asano could demonstrably do the same. Whatever Boris Ket Lundi may have lied about, he told the truth about Asano's strength and aptitude for aura use.

Garth moved with the ground army of undead minions, surrounded by those he had animated personally. They were, on average, stronger than the rank-and-file undead. This came from crafting them with care and taking his pick of the superior base meat. There were few basic undead amongst them, mostly messenger zombies that he had gotten his hands on satisfyingly intact. Most were custom creations, fusions in which he attempted to get more out of the weaker brightheart bodies by blending them with messengers or monsters.

Garth fit in amongst them, his normal robe replaced with layers of tattered and dirty cloth crudely wrapped around him. With only his skull face showing, he easily blended in amongst his creations. Only if someone realised that there was one undead with no aura and looked closer would he stand out.

The minion army moved like a tsunami, crashing into the seawall of the adventurer's defensive line. They had put up surprisingly strong defensive emplacements, probably the work of the brighthearts and their damnable earth-shaping. If they hadn't reinforced the wall to their citadel chamber so well, they would have been overrun before the transformation zone had ever been triggered.

Powers were being flung both ways. Even though Asano's aura had weakened, the adventurers still had the power advantage, all the casualties coming from the undead side. That was nothing new, however. The

Undeath priests knew how to use their expendable numbers to bleed an enemy, burning through their mana pools and health potions to leave them exhausted. That was when the mistakes would come. If they were lucky, the enemies would get overconfident at their early advantage and one or two could be baited into overextending for an early kill.

The broader strategy was not Garth's to command, however. Only once Asano was handled and the avatar had returned would he resume control of his forces. He had designated one of his priests to control the avatar for the moment, although the man did not have true control. Only Garth himself had been given that privilege by his god, but he had directed the avatar to follow the other priest's directions for now. It should be enough to prevent the avatar from mindlessly rampaging if it returned while Garth was absent, still dealing with Asano.

To do so, Garth was on the hunt. The hope was that Asano would join the battle to make use of his anti-undeath powers, and he did not disappoint. The ghost fire, reminiscent of the damnable white flame of the Death god, had started appearing amongst the undead even before they reached the defensive line. How Asano convinced Death to share even an echo of that power didn't matter for now, and once he was dead, it wouldn't matter at all. For now, the ethereal flame was a signal flare by which Asano marked his position.

It would take more than just that to pin him down, of course. The flames lighting up across the battlefield showed that Asano was jumping around, never staying long enough for danger to find him. Garth was a patient hunter and did not rush; he would need to learn the ways of his quarry before he could make the kill.

In the many years Garth had been killing his own aura, the perception loss that came with it had led him to see things that most people missed. Relying on mundane perception alone, he had realised that aura-based stealth techniques left dead spots, not in the wider aura but in how the people around them behaved. There were certain tell-tale signs in the behaviour of someone whose aura was being manipulated to make them overlook someone nearby. Quirks of body language and odd little movements. It was harder to spot when people were spread out, but in a crowd or a thick melee, it became much easier.

With the flames and watching for reactions, Garth had two references for pinpointing Asano. The ghost fire that he could see across the battlefield and the behaviour he could observe up close. His next step was to start plotting out Asano's pattern and he quickly identified the two chief factors guiding Asano's movement. The first factor was where the defenders needed assistance. When the defence was pressured, ghost fire would frequently start spreading through the attackers, weakening the assault.

The second factor was Asano acting randomly to be unpredictable. The problem with this was that attempting to be random often accomplished just the opposite. Actual randomness did not match the idea of what was random in people's minds. Even those who knew about this still fell into less-than-random patterns when their minds were occupied with things like sneaking through an army of undead.

As the flames continued to dot the battlefield, Garth observed that the distribution was more even than truly random. Rather than leaving odd gaps or the occasional concentrated clump, the flames were spread fairly evenly. That gave Garth what he needed to start making predictions. By moving into the larger gaps, he would, hopefully, sooner or later, find himself waiting when Asano appeared.

It was a plan that still had long odds, but Garth was willing to play them. He had no doubt that Asano was both sharp and wary, so any more active approach brought more chance of being noticed. Rather than risk Asano retreating to safety, Garth would be patient.

The battle raged on, the undead pushing past the defences one after another. Undead bodies didn't pile high because the priests detonated them like bombs, pressuring the defences all the harder. The infrastructure like bunkers, trenches and spike walls were excellent for having been put up so hastily, but they were still improvised. One point of weakened defence could easily spread to an entire section.

The pressure on the defence mounted until the tide of unliving seemed on the brink of breaching the defensive line. So long as the line held, the adventurers and their allies had effective defensive formations and could efficiently shuttle the injured to the healers. Once the line broke, the battle would become an ugly mess and the defenders would see casualties.

Everything changed as the two growing mounds of cloud-substance the defenders were protecting solidified into a pair of massive fortresses. The significantly larger of the two was a set of five towers set amongst an area of walls, bunkers and attack platforms that the defenders withdrew into as soon as they appeared. The improvised defences were abandoned in favour of something more structured.

The brighthearts once again proved their worth. Those with earth powers had built the infrastructure in the first place, but it was the fire and magma types that destroyed it. As undead overran the abandoned shelters, those shelters melted or glowed with such heat that the undead storming through them combusted on the spot.

The massive multi-tower fortress did not stop at defensive measures. Atop each tower was a dome that grew brighter and brighter until it discharged a massive ball of energy. The spheres shot into the approaching horde and exploded in a massive area. Dimming after each shot, the domes immediately started charging for another.

The other fortress was a cloud pyramid, covered in dark-red hexagonal plates. Some of the plates retracted into the cloud stuff, replaced with massive, stylised eyes. The eyes shot out beams in two varieties. One was thick and shot out with a deep, resonant hum. It cut lines through the undead horde, gouging out trenches and annihilating the unliving. The other beam was much thinner, accompanied by a high-pitched buzz. It struck one undead, and then immediately started chaining through the enemy forces. Each struck undead exploded on the spot, turning the beam into a violent game of connect the dots.

Most of the beams shot from the pyramid were orange, and effective even against the most heavily armoured abominations. It would occasionally shoot out blue beams that proved more effective against the less common ethereal undead. These were mostly the minions of the priest who himself was a shadowy giant.

The appearance of the fortresses also saw Asano's aura restored to full strength, further blunting the undead wave. The timing was perfect for saving the defenders from a costly collapse and the turn in the battle was immediate and clear.

Garth knew that Asano had to be taken off the board *now*. He was beginning to have doubts about his strategy when he got his own lucky timing. Not only was his latest guess at Asano's next destination right, but it was exactly right. Asano rose from the shadow of an undead, almost within arm's reach. Asano, being this close, noticed the aura gap that Garth occupied and turned his attention towards the priest.

Asano wasn't a match for Garth's gold-rank reflexes, although he was startlingly close. Garth was surprised at how fast Asano reacted, but it wasn't fast enough. He reached out, placed a hand on Asano's shoulder and activated the power bestowed by his newest heart.

Miriam said a rude word.

- Party leader [Jason Asano] has been dimensionally isolated.
- Party interface and communication functions will continue due to access to the spiritual domain of [Jason Asano].
- [Jason Asano] cannot be contacted via party chat due to dimensional isolation.

Miriam had been ducking in and out of the front lines, alternating between commanding the defenders and adding her gold-rank power to the fight. She returned to a bunker made out of cloud-stuff, the defensive structure oddly beautiful with its swirl of sunset colours.

The worst case was Jason dying, making everything else pointless. Dimensional isolation was definitely better than that, but it still wasn't great. She felt Jason's aura vanish from everywhere but his cloud pyramid and the strength of the undead shot up immediately.

Miriam started spitting out orders in response, mobilising assets she'd been holding in reserve. The initial defensive infrastructure was abandoned in places where it had already been compromised, allowing a smoother withdrawal than if the defenders waited for collapse. The sprawling complex of Emir's massive cloud fortress became the new front line when other places had been pushed back. She directed Amos Pensinata to focus on aura attacks, doing his best to disrupt the priests now that Jason was not holding them back.

After putting out the worst fires, she concentrated on what had happened to Jason. Dimensional isolation sounded like the duelling powers used by messengers. The pallid messengers hadn't had that power before, but that wouldn't be the first new ability they'd demonstrated today. But, as they were all silver rank, challenging Jason was pointless. Even at their full strength, he could easily handle one, and their new power had come with an attendant weakness to Jason's undead suppression powers.

It wasn't hard to detect where Jason had been. The was a near-empty space in the battlefield where most of the undead in it had vanished at the same moment the notification appeared. Only a handful of skeletons and zombies were left standing around before they resumed their charge forward. Pulling back from the front line of fighting, Miriam opened a voice channel to Hana Shavar, the High Priestess of Healer, and Clive Standish.

"Commander?" Clive asked, sounding distracted.

"I don't have time to be deployed elsewhere," Hana said. "The undead just got a lot stronger and the injured are coming in thick and fast."

"High Priestess," Miriam said. "You've campaigned against the messengers more than most. Are you familiar with their challenge powers?"

"Yes. Why? We aren't fighting messengers. These pasty-looking ones the Undeath priests claimed can't use that power. Or can they now?"

"I don't know," Miriam said. "Is it possible the Undeath priests found a way to awaken that power in their messenger slaves? Then modified it so that a large group of them could challenge one person?"

"Questionable," Clive said. "Very little is impossible when you really get down to it, but I would count it unlikely. To the best of my understanding, the duel powers are predicated very heavily on the concept of balance."

"He's right," Hana said. "I've never seen a challenge power that could affect anyone of a different rank, let alone multiple combatants versus one."

"Maybe if they found a way to have the ability gauge balance on actual power and not on rank?" Clive postulated. "Perhaps a group of their silver-rank messengers could challenge a gold-ranker together."

- [Neil Davone] has requested access to the private chat channel.
- [Clive Standish] has given [Neil Davone] access to the private chat channel.

"Who is distracting the high priestess when we're already scrambling to heal everyone?" Neil demanded.

"I had a question," Miriam said.

"Is this about Jason and whatever ridiculous thing he's gotten into now?" Neil asked.

"Yes," Miriam said. "I'm deciding how to respond to—"

"You leave him alone, that's what you do," Neil scolded. "It's Jason; he's always going to get locked in an astral space or an underground chamber that's slowly flooding. Or he'll get killed and resurrected in a different universe; it doesn't matter. We don't have time to worry about whatever fool came looking for trouble and is about to get a melodramatic sack full. Jason will do what Jason does, and we need to do what we do. You, Priestess, get back to healing. You, Commander, get back to commanding and leaving the healers alone."

- [Neil Davone] has left the private chat channel.

"He knows we're both higher than him in the chain of command, right?" Miriam asked Hana. "He's lower than you in the church hierarchy as well."

"He's a journeyman priest, so a lot lower," Hana said. "It didn't seem like he especially cared. Also, he's not wrong. If you'll excuse me, Commander, I need to return to healing."

- [Hana Shavar] has left the private chat channel.

"We're not exactly one of those teams who does what they're told," Clive said, his tone not particularly apologetic. "And Neil is right. We have neither the time nor resources to mount some kind of investigation and rescue of Jason. All we can do now is trust him. If you're that worried, see if Shade is around. He'll know more than anyone else."

- [Clive Standish] has left the private chat channel.
- Private chat channel has been closed due to lack of participants.

"Shade?" Miriam asked.

"What can I do for you, Tactical Commander?" Shade's voice came from her own shadow.

"What is happening with the Operations Commander?"

"I am now cut off from communication with Mr Asano and my bodies that are with him, so I can only speak for up until the moment he was sealed away. He was abducted into a dimensional space by an unusual undead. It had no discernible aura, so I cannot confirm its rank. Based on its ability to eliminate its own aura and use a power rarely seen outside of messengers, I suspect it may have been the Undeath high priest, Garth. Whom I now suspect of being a zemravore."

"A what?"

"A rare form of undead that can eliminate its own aura and steal powers by claiming the hearts of the living."

"Claim the hearts of the living?"

"Yes."

"Is that a metaphor?"

"No, Tactical Commander. It is a gruesomely literal statement."

"And they use these hearts to use the powers of whoever they belong to?"

"Just the one power per heart, as far as I am aware."

"But that power could be the duelling power of a messenger?"

"Indeed, it could."

"But the high priest should be gold rank. How could he use a challenge power on a silver?"

"Zemravores can use the powers they have stolen at their actual rank or a lower one. They mostly use it for schemes that involve leaving deceptive power traces. It's an interesting loophole, and what convinced me that a zemravore is most likely what we're dealing with."

"Interesting? It means that Asano is locked in a dimensional bubble with a gold-ranker!"

"Yes, but I believe that this situation may have been engineered by someone antagonistic to the high priest. My guess would be the messenger Boris Ket Lundi."

"What makes you think that?"

"He is the only one who plausibly knows enough about Mr Asano, messengers and zemravores. He also has access to the Undeath priests, given that he and his messengers appear to be residing on that mountain over there. Someone had to convince the high priest to claim the heart of a gestalt physical-spiritual being."

"Why does that matter?"

"Because the high priest has now used that heart, which means he is about to experience something exceedingly rare for an undead: indigestion."

30

BIT OF AN ODD BLOKE

As soon as the bony hand landed on Jason's shoulder, the world around him swirled into incomprehensible nonsense, like a stick of dynamite going off in a drum of paint. Jason was both familiar with and inured to dimensional displacement, so was already moving when the world reformed an instant later. He kicked out behind him, hitting something solid enough that he moved rather than it. He spun, spotting an undead creature draped in ragged cloth, only his skull face and skeletal feet showing.

"Garth?"

"Hello, Asano. We meet in person."

The monstrous high priest wasn't moving, seemingly happy to talk, so Jason stopped as well. It gave them both a chance to look around and take in their surroundings. They were standing on a walkway of black and white marble, inside a building straight out of an M.C. Escher drawing. It was the size of a castle but filled with open space, crossed with walkways, stairwells and arching bridges to nowhere. It was a place of impossible geometry, optical illusions made manifest. None of it had any discernible purpose and shouldn't have been physically possible. Jason could feel the dimensional anomalies that turned illusion into reality.

Jason's void cloak was never affected by the wind and there was none in this space. The air was dead still, chalky on the tongue and dry with the scent of age and abandonment. Yet his cloak whipped around him as if he stood in a gale, impacted by the dimensional anomalies whose proximity to one another stirred up astral winds beyond the touch of mundane senses.

Jason had developed an instinct for understanding astral phenomena and suspected he could perceive enough about the dimensional anomalies to use them in the fight ahead. All he needed was enough time to explore and examine them with his magical senses, which meant stalling for time. He hoped the Undeath priest was a talker; he seemed to be from the one time they had spoken previously. This time, he would not have the safety of using Shade as an intermediary, however.

The dimensional castle was crawling with Garth's undead, for now wandering mindlessly on stairwells and over bridges. Only the walkway they stood on was clear, other than for Jason and his foe. Jason couldn't sense any aura, but that was unsurprising. Any gold-ranker with stealth powers should be able to elude him.

For the moment, the priest seemed happy to join Jason in taking in their battleground. When he saw the priest look his way, he faced his enemy in turn. Jason's nebulous eyes of blue and orange met the red glow in the eye sockets of Garth's skull.

"You know," Jason said, "I've been accused of looking sinister from time to time, but I think you've got me beat."

"I'm standing right in front of you," Garth said. "Even so, you're still full of cocksure bravado. You are not hiding behind a familiar this time, Asano. You are mine to deal with."

"You should be careful with statements like that," Jason said. "My friend Clive's wife said the same thing, and that turned into a *whole* mess. I mean, worth it, but still."

"What gives you that confidence?" Garth asked. "I must confess curiosity about what makes you so special. Everyone from my god to my rivals have warned me about you. Not to underestimate you. The importance of killing you. The fact that you, of all our enemies, are the one that can claim this realm and threaten our actual objective."

"I can tell you that, but let's make it a show-and-tell. I'm curious as to how you pulled us in here. This is a messenger duelling power, right? Or something very close. How did you get that power, and how did you get it to work on someone of lower rank than you?"

"Stealing power is a part of my nature," Garth said. "Normally, that is something I take great care to hide."

"But not from someone you're about to kill?"

"But not from someone I'm about to kill," Garth confirmed.

The rags wrapped around Garth's body were torn apart as he unfurled all six arms and four legs.

"Strewth. You were playing Skeletor when you were secretly General Grievous the whole time. Not sure that's an upgrade, to be honest. Are you packing lightsabers? I think that'd clinch it."

"I answered your questions. You have yet to answer mine."

"That's fair; my bad, bloke. It was what makes me special, right? It's not just one thing, really. It's more of a situation where I've been in the wrong place at the wrong time so often that now I *am* the wrong place and time, for whatever poor sod trundles into my path. Which, today, happens to be you."

"Clearly, you have something to rely on in this fight. Something significant, based on what I keep hearing about you."

"Would you believe rakish charm?"

"I've spoken to you for some time now, so… no."

Jason laughed.

"That stings a little, I'm not going to lie. Is it weird that I kind of like you? I'm still going to kill you with the great plan I'm definitely not lying about having, but I think we've got a good rapport going here."

"You still haven't told me the source of your confidence. Is it the power to rise from the dead? I have been warned to kill you until you stop coming back to life. Are you expecting to die, have that fulfil the release condition of the power trapping us here and then flee when you resurrect?"

"No, although now that you say it, that's pretty good. Wow, thank you. That's a good plan. I might…"

Jason felt an aura start to rise from Garth, but it wasn't a simple aura projection. It came in fits and starts, like an engine trying to turn over in the cold before finally erupting into life. Jason's jaw dropped, although Garth couldn't see it, shrouded in the dark of Jason's hood.

"You were stalling," Jason said. "You weren't just suppressing your aura. You completely turned it off somehow. You were letting me talk so I wouldn't hit you with a soul attack."

"You can make soul attacks? The Adventure Society lets you get away with that?"

"It's not a matter of 'lets' as much as—"

Garth became a blur and one of his bony hands passed through Jason's head.

Garth met no resistance when he reached through Asano's head, his claw-like hand jutting out the other side. Asano leapt from the side of the walkway they were on, his head unharmed as if Garth's arm didn't exist. Garth held out all six hands and a chunk of bone shot from each, going only a short distance before exploding into razor shards. The tiny blades peppered both combatants but injured neither. Garth's skeletal frame was unaffected by his own power and Asano's cloak absorbed them harmlessly.

That exchange had taken place in less than a second, both men blindingly fast. Garth shot larger bone spikes from his hands to intercept Asano, but the strange environment proved tricky. Rather than falling down, Asano fell up, throwing off Garth's prediction. Most of his attacks missed Asano, only one spike impaling his leg. Asano rose out of sight, moving behind a solid set of stairs.

Garth was not going to underestimate Asano. He had the rank-advantage, but he was more of a general than warrior. His body had been built to serve as a vessel for his god's power, and it was usually only when filled with it that he waded into battle himself. By contrast, Asano was clearly experienced at facing more powerful opponents. Whatever the magical boon to his speed was, it allowed him to face a gold-ranker without being entirely outclassed.

Garth was going to take his time. He would catalogue Asano's defences one by one before taking them, and Asano, apart. He already had an amount of information to go by. The cloak intercepted weak projectiles, which was not too burdensome. It ruled out less powerful blanket attacks; precise strikes would be called for.

To hit Asano with precision, he would need to get past whatever trick Asano had used to avoid his initial strike. Intangibility was the obvious answer, but Garth dismissed the possibility. There would have been some feedback, if only to Garth's newly restored magical senses. It was more likely space manipulation, which didn't bode well. If Asano was versed in using dimensional forces, their battlefield would be to his advantage.

He already knew that Asano could jump between shadows, and they were not in short supply. There was no clear source of light, but the arches and walkways cast shadows onto one another in ways that never quite made sense.

The final question Garth had about the powers he had seen from

Asano was his speed. If Asano lost that, he would lose the fight. It was a powerful enhancement, allowing him to almost rival a gold-ranker. That suggested a power that traded off limits or conditions for power, which Garth could potentially exploit. There might be conditional triggers for the power, a lengthy break between uses or a mana cost so high it could only be used in short bursts.

Garth ran the possibilities through his mind, planning out how to test his ideas in future exchanges with Asano. There would be many, as silver-rankers were hard to put down. Some gold-rankers could put one down quickly, mostly assassin types, but that was not Garth. He would dig out Asano's secrets and counter his abilities until, in the end, Asano would die. How quickly was a matter of how annoying he was to bring down.

Inside Jason's soul realm, Marek Nior Vargas slowed his descent through the air until he floated in front of a portal. With him were two other gold-rank messengers. They all looked at the avatar of Jason standing by the portal, which was situated in an English-style country estate garden.

"I've been trapped in a challenge power by a gold-rank undead who stole it from some messenger," Jason said. "I'd appreciate it if you could jump out and help me."

"Appreciate it enough to let us finally leave?" Marek asked.

"Honestly?" Jason said. "I've been working on that for a while. I have a diamond-rank friend who is approaching the goddess Liberty about smoothing things over so I can let you go without my own people dragging me over the coals. That's been happening while we're on this little expedition."

"Then we will aid you, Jason Asano."

Marek flew through the portal, which started making crackling, hissing and fizzing noises. He was flung back out, a tree exploding as he passed through it, barely slowing down. He did finally come to a stop, at the end of a hundred-metre gouge his passage had dug in the ground.

In the strange dimensional space, Jason closed the portal that was still making strange sounds like electrified popcorn.

"Well, that didn't work."

With his aura back, Garth could spread his senses through the pocket dimension. His ability to sense magic was thrown off by the ubiquitous dimensional energy, but he could feel a clear link to all of his undead. This proved disorienting as his eyes and his magical perception pointed in different directions to the same undead. When one of his undead was destroyed, it took him several seconds to look around and find it.

Asano was on a walkway that, to Garth, was at a ninety-degree angle. The priest tossed an experimental bone spear, and it went nowhere near Asano, shifting direction several times in the air. Asano looked to be draining life force from the destroyed undead, despite the fact that it shouldn't have any. He guessed it to be an affliction specialist trick, given their propensity for making things vulnerable to their powers, however implausible.

Asano was being guarded by familiars. One was a swarm type, some kind of lamprey-leech hybrid accomplishing the unlikely task of drinking blood from Garth's lifeless minions. Even though they shouldn't have any. The other was a strange floating creature surrounded by orbs that alternated shooting beams and transforming into shields.

As a zemravore and not an essence-user, most of Garth's necromantic abilities came from ritual magic. He did not have the power to easily boost his minions, something he relied on subordinate priests for. On the contrary, Asano's aura was suppressing them and setting them alight with his damnable ghost fire.

Slow, Garth decided. He didn't know how Asano had even an echo of Death's flame, but he would find out over the course of Asano's slow and excruciating demise. Then he would animate him, taking little care in the ritual. Asano's body would be a weak undead, quickly torn apart by his own friends.

Unable to bolster his undead, the best Garth could do was order them to swarm Asano. Unfortunately, the mindless creatures could not parse the dimensional geography any better than Garth himself could. They chased after Asano but ended up roaming helplessly throughout the bizarre building.

Garth watched as Asano handled the undead that found him in an almost leisurely fashion. The silver-rank undead were no challenge, only the rare golds prompting a real fight. The undead were no match for an essence-user like Asano, but the battles did reveal more of Asano's power. Each new data point refined the model in Garth's mind of how to kill him.

Garth was at least grateful that his personally animated gold-rank undead had been pulled in through the link. He had been uncertain whether his zemravore abilities could deceive the parameters of the stolen ability to that degree, but they had come through. Losing the gold-rank undead to Asano was costly, but worth it for drawing out his abilities.

While Asano fought his minions, Garth attempted to navigate the building himself. He saw Asano transitioning smoothly from one area to the next, completely confident in his direction. If Garth didn't get at least some sense of how to navigate, Asano would always be the one choosing when and where to clash.

Moving from one area to another was disorienting. Subjectively, it felt like everything was oriented normally, but it was just the opposite as Garth's vision told him one thing and his magical senses another.

While he moved, Garth kept an eye on Asano, watching as he revealed his various powers. He was convinced now that Asano's speed was maintained by draining life force from the fallen undead, even though they shouldn't have had life force to steal. The solution was to cut off the supply.

Garth decided to get rid of his minions, although he did not do so immediately. His gold-rankers could still tease out more of Asano's powers and, if he chose the right moment, he had a heart power that might well be able to end the fight on its own. If his undead hadn't been so scattered and disoriented, he'd have used it already.

It was now clear to Garth that Boris Ket Lundi had gone to elaborate lengths to set the odds in Asano's favour. The minions he had insisted on were proving more liability than asset. As for the duelling ability power he had taken from the messenger Boris fed him, it was clear it had been chosen with care. Asano's knack for navigating the strange space was his biggest asset.

When Asano finally brought the attack to Garth, it was far from unexpected. He chose his moment well, though, with Garth distracted in contemplation of a dimensional anomaly. Asano appeared from a shadow behind him, swinging a black-bladed sword. Garth managed to deflect the attack with a thick plate of bone on one of his many arms, negating whatever afflictions the attack had been intended to inflict. He was not quick enough to counterattack before Asano was gone again, disappearing back into a shadow.

It was not the last attack Asano made, but the combatants fell into a détente, neither pushing for a conclusive exchange. Asano was struggling to land inflictions or inflict decisive damage while Garth could never pin Asano down. Between shadow jumping and moving through dimensional anomalies, Asano was a ghost. When he tried to follow Asano through an anomaly, Garth simply found himself alone with his undead, Asano somehow in another space entirely.

Garth was not idle in the face of Asano's hit-and-run tactics. His attempts to learn the nature of the anomalies were slowly starting to pay off and he was sometimes able to direct his undead accurately. He did so with care and subtlety, the instances of his directions going wrong helping hide his purpose. Asano, for his part, was paying less attention to the undead in his attempts to strike at Garth directly. Finally, the priest's patient efforts paid off.

It wasn't as many undead gathered into one area as Garth would have liked, but it was enough to surprise Asano when he stepped onto the walkway and saw them all. He only paused for a moment before weaving through them, manipulating space to dodge between them on the way to his next destination. The leeches, currently looking like a blood-red clone of Asano himself, followed along as Asano's nebulous familiar flew overhead.

Watching as his enemy ran along what was, to him, a ceiling, Garth waited until Asano was fully surrounded by undead before activating his heart power.

Becoming a zemravore was something that happened in stages. It culminated in the claiming of a first heart power, with a ceremony marking the transition from the last vestiges of living to a true place amongst the undead. Garth had been proud of the heart chosen for him by the Undeath high priest he served. It came from a creature not native to Pallimustus, a celestial hound that had come to their world looking to smite the undead.

It had failed, falling to the very beings it had arrogantly sought to destroy. The Undeath priests ate its flesh, carved from the beast while it was still alive, a ceremonial final meal for Garth. Then he had taken its heart, the last of his skin, flesh and organs sloughing from his body as he took the final step from living to unliving. The final step from simply serving his god to embodying him as one of the undead.

Heart powers had come and gone over the years. It became harder to find replacements as he curated powers that suited him well. The stealth power was a perfect fit and other exceptional powers had come and gone. That first heart, though, the moonlight hound, had always remained. It was not just a nostalgic choice, either. As someone who commanded more than fought himself, who used forces that could be freely expended, he needed a power that made use of the undead at his command. Coming from a creature whose very nature was to destroy the undead, it gave Garth something that perfectly met his needs while offering something very unusual in the hands of a necromancer.

Garth activated that heart power, letting out a howl in a voice quite unlike his own. It had a pure and fierce quality that did not belong to the undead. The undead, in fact, could not tolerate it at all. Every one of Garth's undead minions exploded, in every area of the dimensional space. The undeath energy did not just detonate but was changed as it did, transformed by the stolen celestial power of the howl.

In the very instant the undead energy detonated, it changed from purple to a transcendent light of blue, silver and gold. All through the strange dimensional castle, undead exploded, flooding the space with blinding, transcendent light. Nowhere was brighter than the walkway where Asano and his familiars had been surrounded by undead.

If his skull face wasn't perpetually doing so, Garth would have grinned.

Jason felt like he'd been hit by a train that knocked him into the path of a larger, faster train. The blast had not just annihilated his conjured clothes but also the near-indestructible boxer shorts he had spent so much money on. His only remaining possessions were his sword, dropped to the marble floor, and the necklace holding his protective amulet and the shrunken cloud flask.

Even the floor had not gone unscathed. Transcendent damage had scoured the once smooth marble to leave a coarse, pumice-stone finish. Jason grimaced as his nethers scraped against it when he pushed himself onto his hands and knees. He had Colin conjure fresh robes from the biomass within his body, everything outside it having been annihilated.

That included Gordon whom Jason could barely sense a connection to. A look over the messages waiting for him confirmed that Gordon had been killed.

- You have been struck by transcendent damage. Ability [Hegemony] has degraded the damage to disruptive-force damage.
- All instances of [Guardian's Blessing] from [Amulet of the Dark Guardian] have been converted to instances of [Blessing's Bounty].
- [Blessing's Bounty] is providing an ongoing heal and mana gain effect when your life force and mana are already above the normal maximum. Ability [Sin Eater] allows your life force and mana pool to exceed normal values.
- An instance of [Blood of the Immortal] has been consumed.
- [Blood of the Immortal] is providing an ongoing heal effect when your life force is above the normal maximum. Ability [Sin Eater] allows your life force to exceed normal values.
- Vessel of familiar [Gordon] has been annihilated. Familiar [Gordon] is a lesser avatar and is guaranteed to resume the role of familiar when you summon a new vessel with ability [Avatar of Doom].

Jason grabbed his sword and pushed himself woozily to his feet. He had to be ready in case Garth had gotten his head around the dimensional maze and was en route to attack him. He looked around as the transcendent glow faded, rubbing his sore head in relief as he spotted Garth watching from, in Jason's perspective, the distant ceiling.

The red light in Garth's skull sockets flared, his equivalent of goggling wide-eyed. Asano's cloak was gone, but he was standing without apparent injury, looking no more than groggy as he rubbed his messy hair. The transcendent damage hadn't even burned his scalp clean.

Garth's rage was pushed aside by a sudden sickening pulse from his chest. It was a sensation he knew: heart incompatibility. Some hearts, because of the power they held or the creature they came from, did not play well with others.

The solution was simple enough: get rid of the offending heart. It was another trap of the messenger Garth was increasingly determined to take revenge against. Garth opened the sides of his rib cage like doors and reached in to pluck out the heart. His hand snapped back, flung off the heart with a hiss and crackle of energy.

The heart power was still active. It was the nature of messenger challenge powers that they couldn't be interfered with until the power had run its course. Having never claimed a messenger heart before, Garth had no idea, until that moment, that this meant they couldn't be discarded while the power was active. He was certain, however, that Boris Ket Lundi had known exactly that.

That was the moment Garth realised that he wasn't fighting Jason Asano, and hadn't been from the beginning. Asano was an instrument, deftly played by Boris as a distraction while he quietly slipped in the knife. The messenger had been fighting Garth long before Garth realised there was even a fight going on. The cuts had been invisible, the wounds unnoticed. Asano wasn't even the death blow. Boris Ket Lundi had convinced Garth to deliver that to himself.

Garth had been warned long ago to never keep an incompatible heart. It was both poison and bomb, weakening him as it ticked down to the final, explosive destruction. But this heart could not be eliminated while both he and Asano were alive. Until the power ran its course, Garth was stuck with this traitorous heart. Boris Ket Lundi had destroyed him, all while relaxing on his distant mountaintop.

Garth looked at Asano who looked back with confusion. There was still a chance. He could force the fight with Asano; put him down before he was killed by his own poisonous heart. It wasn't much of a chance, but it was the only one he had. He started moving, heading for the nearest stairs.

Jason's aura flooded out of the pyramid fortress and over the battlefield, cutting off the power enhancements coming from the Undeath priests.

- Party leader [Jason Asano] has joined the [Team Biscuit] voice channel.

"Sorry about popping off like that. I had a thing."

"Are you alright?" Humphrey asked.

"Yeah, no worries," Jason said. "I just need to grab some fresh underwear and I'll come help you fight some evil."

"Underwear?" Belinda asked.

"I didn't poo myself, just to be clear. It was an underwear mishap related to something else entirely. On an unrelated note, the topic of your wife did come up, Clive. Bit of an odd bloke, that high priest."

"You killed him?" Humphrey asked.

"Actually, he just kind of got lost and then blew up. It was weird."

3 1

ASKING FOR A LOT OF TRUST

IN THE DIMENSION-WARPED M.C. ESCHER CASTLE GARTH HAD TRAPPED them in, Jason watched Garth move across a bridge that was, from his perspective, upside down. The undead priest glared at him with the burning light from the eyes of his skull sockets, but could do nothing more. Although they could look at one another, they could not fling attacks across the dimensional boundaries that invisibly segmented the space. Jason watched as Garth kept hunting him, growing visibly weaker by the minute.

"And you think this messenger set all this up?" Jason asked.

"I do not know anyone else who would have the information and access to put all this into play," Shade said. "He knows a great deal about you, by means we have yet to determine."

"You could have told me what a zemravore was when Garth did his big reveal."

"And interrupt your villain banter?"

"Yeah, that's fair."

They continued to watch, Jason's superior grasp of the dimensional properties of the space allowing them to easily avoid the undead. Garth's movements grew more sluggish and awkward with each passing moment, slowing to a crawl as shimmering energy emanated from inside his bare ribcage. That energy kept growing, shuddering in instability before finally exploding, scattering shards of bone from Garth's shattered body.

Jason closed his eyes as he felt the realm collapse. He was hurled through a realm of twisted astral forces, his senses bombarded with a vortex of colour and howling wind. It lasted only a moment and Jason opened his eyes when everything went still. He was back in the transformation zone, deep in the enemy battle line. The undead around him saw his sudden appearance and moved to the attack.

Jason expanded his aura, suppressing theirs and diminishing the undeath energy animating them. He picked up the nearby undead with his aura and flung them away, clearing a space around him. He looked to his feet where the shattered remains of Garth lay in a pile.

More undead were moving in on him but Jason wasn't taking a stealth approach for the moment. A long shadow arm emerged from his back and drew his sword. It whipped and flailed in a blur of motion while Jason himself stood still. The sword delivered afflictions, including the ghost fire that was so devastating to the undead. Jason wasn't going for the kill for the moment, only warding off those who disturbed his cleared space.

Jason looked over at his pyramidal cloud fortress, jutting above the fray. He extended his will and the fortress became a beacon for his aura, once more spreading it across the battlefield. He then joined the voice chat for his team, reassuring them of his safe return and the demise of Garth.

"You killed him?" Humphrey asked.

"Actually," Jason said, "he just kind of got lost and then blew up. It was weird."

"How?" Rufus asked.

"I suspect that's something we need to ask Boris Ket Lundi," Jason said. "Conveniently enough, he's heading this way."

"Who?" Sophie asked.

"A messenger," Jason said. "One who never seems to meet a faction he won't pit against another, for reasons that are still unclear. He knows a suspicious amount about me, though."

Jason had knelt to loot the body at his feet when purple runes started carving themselves into the broken bones as Garth's skeletal body reformed. Shattered splinters united to become whole, bones mending as if they'd never been broken. At the same time, an aura flooded across the battlefield, washing Jason's away like a sandcastle before the rising tide.

The avatar of Undeath came stomping through the boundary veil of the territory. It was too far away to see, but the aura was unmistakeable. This territory was claimed by it and claimed thoroughly, the way Jason did it. This was an entity that could create spirit domains. The avatar's aura infused everything as it returned, pressing down on the battlefield and everyone in it. Only the inside of Jason's pyramid was spared, his spiritual domain impenetrable to spiritual pressure.

The suppression of the undead by Jason's aura beaming out from his pyramid proved short-lived. Quashed by the avatar, the undead it had weakened were returned to full strength. The aura radiating from Jason himself wasn't suppressed, the avatar's influence more of a broad brush, but it was diminished. The undead hovering around his cleared space went from a few pushing in to all of them shambling in his direction.

In front of Jason, Garth's body reassembled itself. Jason looked at the skull where the intelligent red light in his eyes had been replaced with mindless purple. Jason had seen the same on countless undead. Everything from body language to aura told Jason that the true essence of Garth was in the Reaper's hands now. What remained was another undead drone, more powerful than those around him but without the spark that made him a person and not just a thing.

"The plan looks to be working," Jason said through voice chat as he vanished into the shadows, escaping the encroaching undead. "Garth just got back up as a mindless drone. His original aura is gone and the new one is chock full of divine undeath energy. That definitely came from the avatar."

Similar reports came in from other adventurers. They had been avoiding killing the priests until the avatar arrived, but it didn't seem to matter. Even those who died before the avatar's arrival were reanimating, drawing power from the avatar to become powerful but mindless revenants. Even the ones that had been undead in the first place were rising once more, although as echoes of their former selves.

Jason could sense the avatar moving closer to the battle at speed as another divine aura followed it into the territory.

- Contact [Gareth Xandier] has entered voice chat range.

Miriam was using the command channel to direct forces in the wake of the two divine beings' arrival. Jason pulled Gary into the team channel to take his report.

"You have a sense of how effective Clive's plan was, right?" Jason asked Gary. "We just confirmed on our side that any dead priest will take energy from the avatar, freshly killed or not. The question is, does killing these pricks off weaken the avatar?"

"It does," Gary confirmed.

"By how much?"

"By more than we'd feared and less than we'd hoped. We need to kill a lot more priests."

"Gary," Jason said. "You just gave me a little atheist chubby."

"Little, huh?" Neil said. "I hope you didn't disappoint—"

"Neil," Clive said, "I swear to your god, if you say a damn thing about my imaginary wife, your life will become a plague of tiny, hard-to-find ritual magic. Why is Neil's cloud bed so itchy? Turns out there's a tiny ritual circle. Why does Neil keep sneezing? Turns out there's a tiny ritual circle. Why do Neil's clothes never quite fit? No ritual circle; he just keeps wearing the clothes his aunt sends him."

"What do you expect me to do?" Neil asked. "She just keeps sending them. I'm not going to snub her good intentions and throw them away. She just sends so many; I don't even know how she always knows where I am. I've been roaming all over for years now. It's as if…"

The team channel fell silent for a long moment.

"Has someone," Neil asked, his tone suggesting through clenched teeth, "been sending messages to my aunt, telling her where I am? Maybe that I go through a lot of clothes while adventuring? Maybe suggesting that they should be robust, as well as nice and loose to move around in. Padded for cold weather and brightly coloured so the team can spot me if I get in danger."

"No," Belinda said. "Although I definitely would have, if I'd thought of it."

"I know one of you did it," Neil said. "Just confess. I won't be angry."

"He's definitely going to be angry," Sophie said.

Clive let a groan out over voice chat.

"In case you haven't noticed," Clive said, "we're in the middle of a battle."

"Thank you, Clive," Humphrey said.

"That's why," Clive continued, "I'll tell you who's been doing it, Neil, on the condition that you don't make a stink about it until after the battle."

"Fine," Neil said.

"That was a little too quick," Belinda said. "He's definitely going to make a stink."

"Okay, I get it," Neil said. "I won't seek revenge until after the fighting is done. Just tell me who it is."

"I don't know if I should now," Clive said.

"Just tell me!" Neil snarled.

"Fine," Clive said, his tone reluctant. "It was my wife."

"Oh, you son of a—"

Miriam was keeping a sharp eye on the approaching messengers. They'd been happy to observe from their mountain perch thus far, but either the arrival of the avatar or the death of the Undeath high priest had stirred them to action. The concern was what that action would be.

"Operations Commander," Miriam said. "You're our designated messenger liaison. Can you go and get a sense of what those messengers are after?"

"What if they kill me?" Jason asked.

"Then we'll have a pretty good idea of what they're after."

"What?" Jason exclaimed.

"What?" Miriam asked.

"You want me to go out and see if they kill me?"

"Sure," Miriam said. "Or, you know, maybe use the voice chat we're using right now so you don't have to go near him."

"Oh," Jason said. "Yeah, that makes sense."

- [Jason Asano] has invited you to a voice chat.

Boris looked at the floating window in front of him. It wasn't the first such screen he'd seen, with everyone in the transformation zone encountering a few. Jason had imprinted on the zone, causing such windows to pop up periodically, usually related to events in the zone.

Having the windows explain the rules had been a large part of letting enemies and allies alike understand what was happening, how and why. That was especially true for the messengers that weren't Boris himself. They had been the most ignorant going in, but the messages had filled in a large piece of the puzzle.

"So, this is the Asano communication power," Boris said. "Basing it on video game chat has made it very organised and efficient by the standards of communication powers. Are there emojis?"

"Don't try to bunny-ears-lawyer a bunny ears lawyer," Jason warned him. "State your intentions, Boris, or we're coming for you."

"I think you have bigger issues than me," Boris said. "That avatar is moving fast. It'll be here any moment now."

"It's just power with no intellect behind it, now that Garth's dead," Jason told him. "You're good at playing sly, but you showed your hand a little killing him like that. You played us like duelling banjos and I don't want to end up like Ned Beatty with you telling me to squeal like a pig."

"Really? You're going with *Deliverance*? That scene? Not a classy reference. I thought *Battle of the Planets* or *A-Team* would be more your speed. Oh, you're checking if I really have been on Earth. Well, I have. For a lot longer than you."

"Good to know, but that's something to get into later. What are you and your friends up to?"

"I've been watching your people avoid the priests. That's smart. If they come back right after they die, they'll draw more power out of the avatar than if they've been dead for a while."

"You seem to know a lot about everything."

"A lot of experience and a very good memory."

"Something that makes you exceedingly dangerous."

"A lot of people say the same thing about you."

"Yeah. Then they try and kill me."

"Are you going to kill me as a precaution, then?"

"No," Jason said. "Like I said, people try that on me all the time. It hardly ever works and turns a potential threat into a guaranteed one."

"What now, then?"

"Now you answer the question you dodged. What are you and your messengers doing?"

"Coming to help."

"You, I can believe. Maybe. But that many messengers?"

"There were more. I've turned these two golds to the Unorthodoxy and killed the ones who refused. The silvers obey because they're silvers."

"You played Garth and me off against one another. If he'd won, would you be flying to help his side?"

"You're not so dense as to believe that. You and Garth were both smart enough to realise that I set him all the way up. The only good outcome for me was you being the one to come out of that. If you were so incompetent that you couldn't win with everything I put in place, you weren't worth coming down here for in the first place."

"You came here for me?"

"I'm from Earth, Asano. What do you think I came here for?"

"After the way you treated Marla? The lax sexual harassment laws."

Boris let out a laugh.

"Boris, as far as I'm concerned, you're the biggest potential threat on this battlefield. I don't think trying to kill you is a good idea, but I've been stuck with plenty of bad ones in my short but exciting career. If I think for a second that your people are going to turn on us, we'll prioritise putting you down over the avatar."

"And here I thought we were getting along."

"I think you know what not-getting-along-with-me looks like, Boris, and this isn't it. And I think that you're smarter, older and more cunning than I am. So, I'm going to be very careful."

"I thought you'd appreciate a little scheming."

"I do. I respect it too, which is why I'm going to be so careful."

"Well, I guess I can accept that. I'll follow your lead, Asano. Where do you want me to attack from?"

"The Wangaratta Performing Arts & Convention Centre."

Boris laughed again.

"That may be a little further than is strictly practical," he pointed out.

"Come at them from the opposite side to where my people are," Jason said. "Stay clear of my people and focus on the priests. If we all come through this, we'll talk again. While you and yours are standing on the ground, right next to my friend Gary."

"That's asking for a lot of trust from me."

"You're messengers."

"That's racial profiling."

"Tough. Your entire species is an Iranian wearing a 'death to America' t-shirt through airport security. You don't like those terms, you can sod off back to your mountain."

IT USED TO BE COMPLETELY
DARK

THE TWO DIVINE COMBATANTS WERE THE UNQUESTIONABLE FOCUS OF THE battlefield. Looming as tall as houses, they flung powers back and forth. Gary wielded hammers and conjured chains, all wreathed in golden fire. He called up his foundry golem summon, far larger than normal and filled with metal melted by divine fire. The avatar plucked undead from the ground and pallid messengers from the air, melding them into grotesque whips of dead flesh. It grabbed fistfuls of undead and flung them like grenades that exploded with purple fire.

Overall, Gary had a slight edge, but it was not enough to be definitive. Both entities were simply too hard to kill, recovering from any damage instantaneously. The adventurers and their allies fought to shift this balance, hunting down the priests of Undeath. Each one that fell absorbed a little of the avatar's power to rise again as a revenant. They were mindless and lacked the magical powers of their previous selves, but were stronger, fearless and extremely hard to kill.

Jason watched Boris as the messenger carved a path through the undead. The weapons in his hands shifted every few blows; a greatsword burst into a cloud of embers that blinded and scorched the undead before reforming into a rapier and sword-catcher. Next was a spear, then a sword-staff, then a pair of flails.

As he fought, he employed other powers, all variations of burning embers. Feathers shot out, burying themselves in enemies and burning them from the inside. Clouds of sparks and ash exploded like cluster bombs, Boris vanishing into one and emerging from another.

There was a grace and flow to the way Boris moved. It wasn't flashy, just profoundly efficient in a way that seemed almost prescient. Enemies moved to the attack just as he moved out of the way; not a dodge but a natural motion, as if they had been swinging to miss. There was no haste in his actions. Boris moved little faster than a silver-ranker, yet was always doing the exact right thing at the exact right time.

Jason had never seen anything like it. Not from Sophie, not from Rufus and not even from Dawn. He didn't know what to make of fighting that treated the world as a partner in a dance to which only he knew the steps. Jason knew that gold-rankers had what amounted to perfect memories, but how many battles did Boris remember? How much cumulative combat experience did it take to reach that level? Centuries? Millennia? Had Boris spent more time on the battlefield than Jason's home world had been recording history?

Not to say that Boris was invincible. He was a messenger, without the vast array of powers an essence-user held. He was also a specific kind of fighter. He fought in close, using fire powers to complement his fighting and extend his reach into the mid-range. That put him in a similar role to Farrah, but was a deft needle to her crude hammer.

If it came to a fight, they could take Boris down, but it would be a hard, ugly battle. Jason could face off against a gold-ranker with enough buffs, but not a gold-ranker like Boris. That was a place for gold-rankers only, and even outnumbering him, they would pay a price. Jason was very much hoping it didn't come to that.

While keeping an eye on Boris, Jason was not idle. He made his way through the battle, spreading ghost fire and his other afflictions to the undead masses. His role was to thin out the mindless undead and the pallid messengers, who weren't brainless but were far from imaginative.

Given the horde blanketing the ground, Jason was going to need Gordon's butterflies to spread his afflictions. Gordon had been taken out by Garth but was more than just a familiar now. Gordon's vessel had been reconstituted in Jason's soul space and was again available for battle.

Getting the butterflies to spread in sufficient numbers was easier said than done. Even ignoring all their minions, the Undeath priests outnumbered both the adventurers and Boris' messengers combined. They were also very aware of Jason and the various threats he posed. They understood the weaknesses of the butterflies and his ghost fire and put no small effort into hampering them.

The key to the butterflies was to turn enough foes into factories producing more butterflies. Everywhere that Jason popped up, there were priests ready to wipe out any butterflies they saw, along with any undead or pallid messengers producing them. They had minions enough to spare so long as they could shut Jason down.

Jason remembered back to the messenger invasion of Yaresh. For the vast majority of that battle, he'd been running around in a futile attempt to get a butterfly engine up and running. The messengers hadn't allowed that to happen and the Undeath priests were doing the same here. During the invasion, he'd tried to avoid the team of messengers tasked with shutting him down. This time, he wouldn't make the same mistake.

Emerging from a shadow amongst a cluster of priests, Jason's swordplay was clumsy compared to Boris. The messenger somehow gave a master class in elegance with what, from anyone else, would have been a frenzied onslaught. While he was dwelling on the unflattering comparison, the priests were having a very different experience. To them, Jason was anything but clumsy and inelegant.

The priests diligently crushed the easily spotted glowing butterflies, along with destroying any undead producing more of them. The retaliation began when they found themselves surrounded by what looked like void portals, but they moved around like people. These were Shade bodies, draped in the same cloak Jason wore.

Jason had Shade spread his many bodies amongst the priests while conjuring his starry cloak over each one. With all of them moving swiftly, and Jason shadow-jumping between them, it was all but impossible to pick out the real Jason.

The priests attacked the Shades and Jason alike. Their direct attack magic was quite similar to Jason's, with curses and necrotic magic featuring heavily. This affected Shade not at all, while each attack came with a price for the priests.

- [Undeath Priest] has attacked your familiar [Shade].
- Ability [Hegemony] has inflicted [Undeath Priest] with an instance of [Sin].

The priests weren't completely helpless against Shade. They were masters of the undead, including deathly shadows and ethereal ghosts. Shade wasn't an undead, so not vulnerable to their control, but many of the priests had attacks that could harm him. Once they realised what they were dealing with, the priests started to attack his bodies. Shade focused on staying elusive and avoiding their powers, but they did successfully cut some of his bodies down.

It cost Jason a lot of mana to restore one of Shade's bodies. Early in his adventuring career, doing so had taken a lot of downtime, draining most of his mana to replace just one. It was still prohibitively expensive in most cases, but not always. Jason had mana to spare, in vast excess of his normal maximum. He'd drained mana from countless undead throughout the battle, taking him well above his usual limit. He couldn't keep replacing Shade's bodies indefinitely, but in the short term, he could spit them out as fast as they were destroyed.

As for Jason himself, the priests realised that trying to pin him down was useless. They turned to powers that blanketed the area, less powerful but much harder to avoid. A purple miasma flooded the area, covering Jason and Shade, although it had no effect on the familiar.

The necrotic damage ulcerated Jason's skin, but the unfocused attack power was too weak to impede him. It would have gotten worse over time if not for Jason's formidable regeneration, although the hard-to-heal necrosis did prove persistent. The miasma also carried more insidious effects, but insidious was the wrong move against Jason Asano.

- You have suffered necrotic damage.
- Ability [Hegemony] has inflicted [Undeath Priest] with an instance of [Sin].
- You have been affected by [Creeping Death].
- You have resisted [Creeping Death].
- You have gained an instance of [Resistant] from ability [Sin Eater].
- You have gained an instance of [Integrity] from ability [Sin Eater].
- [Undeath Priest] has attacked multiple instances of your familiar [Shade].
- Ability [Hegemony] has inflicted [Undeath Priest] with an instance of [Sin] for each affected instance.

Jason noted the affliction with amusement, as it was one he could deliver himself. It wouldn't affect undead, being a disease, but he wouldn't let something like that stop him. The same power he used to inflict it, his shadow hands, also inflicted Weakness of the Flesh. That affliction made even the unliving subject to necrosis and disease. Jason could turn the power of the Undeath priests back onto them and their unliving minions as well.

Jason did exactly that, loading the priests up with those afflictions and more, consuming any sent his way and turning them into boons that boosted his healing and mana supplies. More afflictions were levied against the priests by the simple act of attacking Jason and Shade.

Jason's aura power left everyone who attacked him or an ally with the Sin affliction, which increased his necrotic damage. With enough Sin, even a small amount of such damage would melt flesh like it was month-old meat left out in the tropics. And, as it happened, Jason had a special attack with no cooldown that dealt a small amount of necrotic damage.

There was a pause in the battle as Jason and the Shades stopped moving. Jason stood, surrounded by a half-dozen silver-rank priests. Wet blood dripped from his sword's black blade onto the red sand of the desert. He looked around at the wary faces of the priests. Signs of necrosis blackened their flesh, even that of the undead one whose flesh was not alive. They variously wore combat robes like Jason or more tight-fitting outfits, suited for combat. They held staves, swords and maces; one even had a scythe that looked impressive but wasn't practical for combat.

"You could run," Jason told them.

"We have faith," one of them said.

"Good," Jason said. "I have some specific opinions on faith."

A staff with a glowing purple crystal at the end was swung at Jason. He smoothly dodged around it and counterattacked, resuming the fight. He became a dancing shadow and his sword a black blur. The priests used their full bag of tricks, from dark magic to exploding minions, to little avail. He consumed their afflictions and avoided their blasts, the priests unable to differentiate him from his familiar.

While he felt awkward comparing himself to Boris, Jason was a shadowy demon to the priests. Every strike he landed split to reveal rotting flesh underneath. Normally the masters of dark powers, the priests had their resistances suppressed by Jason. With every instance of Sin, his aura diminished their protection against his powers a little more. Jason moved through the priests and their undead minions like a ghost—untouchable, unavoidable and unstoppable.

Some held their faith and fell to Jason's blade. Others fled and he let them go, as killing priests was ultimately not his role. There were plenty of adventurers doing that, but he was the only affliction specialist on the field.

For all that he had ramped up, loaded with boons that increased his speed, bolstered his healing and left him flush with mana, Jason was not swift at killing. The priests he killed rose as revenants; mindless but swift, fearless and extremely hard to put down. By the time he had dealt with them, more priests were moving in to harass him.

"Miriam," he said in the command channel. "I'm getting more pressure than I'd like from the priests. I'm practically bait. Can you free up my team to run blocker for me?"

"I need their versatility to handle some of the stranger priest powers," Miriam said. "If the priests are chasing you that hard, how about we use you as bait? Pull in some priests, start a big clash and let you slip free in the chaos?"

"That'll do."

"We'll start small to try and lure them in by stages. I'm sending Rick Geller's team your way."

There weren't a lot of terrain features in the red desert. A few scraggly plants, some rare patches of yellow grass. Mostly, it was the occasional rock casting long shadows in the blazing sun. Jason hid in the shadow of one such rock, in a relatively sparse area of the battlefield that kept spreading over the flat landscape. He found himself again watching Boris and his almost hypnotic skill.

"Garth," he said to himself.

"Mr Asano?" Shade asked.

"Garth was the key. We're going to win because Garth isn't here to direct the avatar intelligently. For all its power, it's mindless. It has no plan to fight back with, or even the ability to recognise how our plan is weakening it. It's not a matter of win or lose now, but how much it costs us. Boris saw that. He knew it from the start and planned the excision of the problem area like a surgeon. We're all dancing in his palm."

"What do you intend to do about that?"

"That's the problem. The best course of action is to go along with what he's doing. My concern is over what happens when what he wants and what we want stops being the same. Will we have gone too far to do anything about it? Will we even see it coming? Based on what we've seen so far, my guess would be no."

"I believe that you're overthinking it, Mr Asano. The answer is to do what you always do."

Jason let out a sigh.

"The best I can with what I've got, I know."

He stepped out of the shadow, getting the attention of a pallid messenger overhead. Jason used his aura to crush the messenger's and then yank it out of the sky, smashing it into the ground. He conjured his black and red dagger and held it over the fallen messenger. He then jerked the messenger up onto the dagger and then back to the ground, each stab delivering a special attack. At the same time, he chanted a series of spells, delivering even more afflictions.

More undead and pallid messengers swarmed in on him, having noticed his actions. Jason didn't bother to move, allowing Rick and his team to intercept. They'd been rushing in his direction already and flung out powers at the approaching enemy. A wall of ice, incongruous in the scalding desert, appeared to block some of the enemy. Others were struck with spears or arrows.

One of Gordon's orbs emerged from Jason's body and entered that of the messenger bouncing up and down under his dagger. It immediately started shedding butterflies that carried each of the afflictions the messenger was suffering.

"There's a group of priests heading from over there," Jason said as Rick's team arrived beside him.

They looked at the beleaguered messenger and then at Jason.

"What?" he asked.

"Your cloak is different," said Claire Adeah, the archer. "From when we fought you in Greenstone."

"And it used to be completely dark in your hood," her twin Hannah said. "I can see the shape of your face a little bit now. Your chin really sticks out."

"Would you please go fight those priests?" Jason said. "I need to get these butterflies going."

"They're pretty," said Dustin, Neil's friend and Rick's frontliner.

"They're also plague-bearing harbingers of doom," Jason said.

"Adorable harbingers of doom," Claire said.

"You know," Jason said, "I liked it better when I could freak you all out."

"We're not iron-rankers anymore," Rick said. "Now, we'll go tie up these priests and then you can show us why you're worth getting dragged across the continent every six months for."

The battle, in the end, was an inexorable but heavily drawn-out affair. The battle that decided everything was always going to be that between Gary and the avatar, and the avatar lacked the conscious mind to fight it. All it did was attack, driven by the remnant arrogance of the god who spawned it. Even as the battle around it slowly sapped its power, the avatar did nothing but continue the attack. Garth had designated a priest to direct the avatar, but that priest's authority to do so had died with Garth.

The field saw many epic battles played out. Team Storm Shredder had lost two of their members while regrouping after first entering the transformation zone. They went on a rampage of revenge, cutting down many of the enemy before overextending and being caught out. Half of the team held the line for the rest to escape.

Zara Nareen, the former Hurricane Princess, was reluctantly forced back by Orin, the only member of the team with the strength to make her. They were guided back to friendly lines by the team scout, Rosa. She found a way through the enemy throng that had them arriving battered but alive, quickly taken away by the healers. The rest of the team, including the leader, Korinne, fell covering their retreat.

Miriam's team, Moon's Edge, was the most powerful force on the battlefield other than the cloud buildings and the two divine entities. Boris was stronger individually, but the teamwork of the gold-rank adventurers outstripped Boris and his subordinate messengers, who were not up to his standard.

Jason's team also acted with distinction, handling the more exotic silver-rank threats. They even took on a few of the weaker, isolated gold-rank enemies. Mostly, this meant the mindless undead, but not always. The team had plenty of experience and the right powers when it came to ethereal enemies, so they took down a shadow-giant priest and his army of undead wraiths.

Team Biscuit also brought about the final demise of Garth, whose revenant Jason had left behind after seeing it was mindless. The gold-rank revenant had none of Garth's powers but was incredibly hard to kill. Jason even rejoined his team briefly, just so his escalating affliction damage could carve through all the corrupted, undead vitality.

As more and more priests fell, it became easier for Jason's butterflies to become a swarm that covered the battlefield like a cloud. Rick's team helped him get started but the pallid messengers proved a large impediment. Swift and alert, more and more of them joined the fight to suppress the butterflies. Like the Undeath side as a whole, however, they fought a slow but losing battle. The more priests fell, the more Miriam devoted forces to covering Gordon's butterflies until they reached a critical mass.

The priesthood as an organised force disintegrated, falling into clusters that fought in increasing isolation. Some fled, seeking to escape the battle and find some way to live on. Most realised that there was nothing but more death out there and fought to the bitter end. One of the final priests to die was Jameela, Garth's most trusted subordinate. She refused to go down easy, fighting to the bitter end. Finally, she died, her beauty destroyed by Taika's fists and her unwillingness to accept that her cause was lost.

By the time even the most stubborn enemy accepted that it was over, the sky was hidden under the cloud of butterflies, blazing sunlight replaced with a blue and orange glow. The pallid messengers had no place left in the sky and were all but wiped out. The undead horde fared little better, the numbers that had seemed so endless were scattered and bedevilled with afflictions.

Only the avatar was still fighting. In death, the priests drained the avatar of power, turning them into revenants. That power was then snuffed out as the revenants were destroyed. Everything that could be taken from the avatar had been taken. Its battle with Gary had become one-sided, the avatar's counterattacks weaker and less frequent. The adventurers and their allies were freed to pile on ranged attacks and massive blasts of power came from the two cloud buildings.

The avatar showed no signs of collapsing under the weight of the attacks. The power that had not been siphoned away was stubbornly refusing to be annihilated. Gold-rankers were extremely hard to kill while diamond-rankers were touching on immortality. Gods weren't killable at all, and though the avatar was little more than an echo, it simply refused to die.

The sky was painted blue and orange with butterflies. At Jason's behest, Gordon directed the millions of butterflies to swarm on the avatar. As if the sky itself were moving, they flooded the avatar, disappearing into it and delivering all the accumulated afflictions they carried. The sheer number of afflictions was unlike anything Jason had ever delivered to an enemy. It was unlikely he would ever match the number again. Once delivered, all those afflictions kept multiplying, over and over, ravaging the avatar until even a diamond-ranker would have melted.

The avatar did as well, its flesh reduced to necrotic soup, yet it still did not fall. Its undead flesh melted and regenerated so swiftly that it looked less like a zombie than some corrupted water elemental. It became a roiling humanoid mass of black liquid, lit from within by swirling purple light.

The avatar became the sole foe remaining from the army of Undeath. A few priests had fled to other territories, taking some scattered minions with them, but most had been eliminated. The red desert was painted with black ichor and decorated in shattered, stained, white bones. The adventurers and their allies had startlingly few casualties, their healers proving their worth. Most of the fallen were brighthearts and Builder cultists.

Miriam and Jason, the tactical and operations commanders, stood watching Gary and the strange liquid avatar. The pair clashed over and again in a stalemate the adventurers had failed to break, despite how much of Undeath's power they had managed to siphon away.

Adventurers and brighthearts continued to pour out ranged attacks in support. The massive buildings struck it with attacks that had savaged entire battle lines, yet the avatar would not collapse. Jason even turned the countless afflictions into transcendent damage before firing off execute after execute. He wasn't the only one using transcendent damage either, yet the avatar would not fall.

"What do we do?" Miriam asked. "It holds the territories, so it has to die, but it won't. It just won't. How do you kill a god?"

Jason turned to look at her.

"What?" she asked, looking at his expression. "You've thought of something."

"You don't kill gods," Jason told her. "You sanction them."

33

HE LIKES TO NAME-DROP

THE BATTLEFIELD WAS ODDLY STALLED OUT. UNDEATH'S ARMY WAS A spent force, the priests dead or fleeing while the remnant undead were mopped up by the adventurers and their allies. Few of the enemy messengers with their pallid, corpse-like skin remained. Most had been killed by the butterflies that had blanketed the sky until they were sent to attack the avatar. Those that remained were being captured alive. Miriam had ordered their forces to do so if possible and safe, out of respect for Jason's sensibilities. The potentially allied messenger forces, led by Boris Ket Lundi, had been trying to take them alive from the beginning.

Most of Gordon's butterflies had been absorbed into the avatar, although it and the few remaining undead were shedding more. Gordon sent them high into the sky before detonating them in a chain of blue lights. They flashed like fireworks signalling victory, but victory could not be claimed until the avatar of Undeath finally fell. Riddled with a literally flesh-melting number of afflictions, it countered with a regenerative strength that only divine power could manage. Under the cycle of liquefaction, it looked like a befouled water elemental.

Jason and Miriam watched Gary and the avatar clash from afar. At this stage, the giant lion man, wreathed in golden fire, was beating down the avatar in a one-sided affair. Even so, the abomination rose over and over, putting up enough resistance that Gary had to maintain at least a little caution.

Scattered across the red desert, the allied forces looked on as well, at something of a loss. Few still had enemies to hunt down; they had ostensibly won and yet the battle was not over. It couldn't end until the avatar fell and Jason claimed the territories it held.

"Sanction," Miriam said. She was echoing what Jason had told her they needed to do to the avatar to finish it.

"That's right," Jason said.

"Isn't sanction some unusual affliction? It impedes healing, right? But it's holy when that sort of thing is usually a curse, wounding or unholy power."

"You're quite knowledgeable for such a niche power outside of your own power set."

"Lady Allayeth trained us well. There are times when knowledge makes a better weapon than sword or spell."

Jason nodded, acknowledging the point.

"You're right about the sanction affliction," he told her. "What I'm talking about is a different kind of sanctioning. It's how entities like gods and great astral beings punish their own kind."

"We aren't gods. How are we meant to do what gods do to one another?"

"I have a familiar," Jason said. "The incantation to summon him is more than a little chuuni, and I never really thought about it that much."

"Chuuni?"

"Don't worry about that. The point is, there's a part of that incantation that I never paid much attention to. I don't even need it anymore, since I can just call him back up when his vessel is destroyed now. But given the kind of things I get up to these days, maybe it's time I took another look."

"I think you'd better just tell me the incantation so I have an idea of what you're talking about."

Jason nodded as a cloud of nebulous blue and orange light shot across the battlefield. It arrived next to them and manifested into Jason's familiar.

"This is Gordon," Jason introduced. "You'll have seen each other roaming about, but I might as well give you a formal introduction. Gordon, this is Tactical Commander Miriam Vance, gold-rank leader of team Moon's Edge. Miriam, this is Gordon, avatar of doom. Also, avatar of me, but let's not get caught up on the details. What do you say, Gordon? Want to hear the old summoning incantation?"

The orbs floating around Gordon turned blue.

"That means yes," Jason explained. "Okay, here we go with the incantation: '*When worlds end, you are the arbiter. When gods fall, you are the instrument. Herald of annihilation, come forth and be my harbinger. I have doom to bring.*'"

"*That's* the incantation you used to summon a familiar?"

"Awesome, right?"

"Awesome? It sounds like you're trying to destroy the world."

"Ironic, I know. Given that saving the world is kind of my thing. And he isn't even my apocalypse beast familiar."

"What?"

"Getting back to the incantation—"

"Apocalypse beast?"

"Don't worry about that."

"The messengers have been using apocalypse beasts as weapons and you're walking around with one?"

"See, this is why I asked the Adventure Society to redact that bit from my file. I knew people would get worked up."

"Worked up? You have a worm swarm apocalypse beast, exactly like the one that just wiped out entire towns."

The joviality fell from Jason's face as he and his aura became unreadable. When he spoke, his voice was quiet and forcibly measured.

"You should be careful with your accusations, Tactical Commander. My familiar is not like those things, and was responsible for annihilating no small number of them."

"You were there? In the towns?"

"My team was included on the scouting expedition. I was the first into one of the villages. I saw the dead being marched around like puppets. I found the growth chamber and the messenger operating it. She died. Her worms died and then the queen producing them died. All at the hands of my familiar. Before you choose to question the integrity of my familiar, Tactical Commander, you should choose your words carefully."

Miriam looked at Jason. She'd always had trouble knowing what to make of the man and his mix of strange power and stranger behaviour. So often, he was overly casual and distractingly absurd. At other times, he showed a terrifying and unhesitant aptitude for violence. Here she'd scratched the surface and found something new, something she suspected to be very dangerous.

Suddenly, the moment passed as if it had never been and he flashed her a grin, the façade back in place.

"His name is Colin, by the way. Worm swarm apocalypse beast is bit of a mouthful, and not quite accurate. He's more of a leech-lamprey hybrid. Look, I'll introduce you."

Miriam watched as Jason held out his hand and blood seeped from his skin, coating his palm red. A moment later, the thin sheen of blood became a torrent spilling out, coagulating in the air as it formed a pile of creatures on the ground.

Miriam didn't watch it, her eyes staying on Jason's face. How much of his behaviour was a mask? It seemed like she'd scratched the surface and seen the reality beneath, but was his seeming struggle for control another layer of artifice?

While she contemplated Asano, his familiar was turning from a pile of creatures into a blood clone, melding together to copy Asano's shape. The clone went from slick, glossy red to matching the colours and textures of Asano. After a moment, only the eyes were different, the clone's not changing from glistening red orbs.

"I don't want to eat any of these dead things," the familiar said. "Can I eat some of those messengers real quick?"

"No," Jason said.

"Just a couple?"

"No."

"What if I promise not to devour every living thing in this pocket universe?"

"You are not helping my situation right now."

"You mean the god?" Colin asked, looking over at Gary clashing with Undeath's beleaguered avatar in the distance. "I'm definitely not going to eat that. Next time, you should fight the god of blood or flesh. I'll tuck right in there."

"That's not what I was talking about. And you probably shouldn't go trying to eat gods."

Colin took on a childish, sullen expression, kicking at the red desert dirt.

"I bet if we fought the god of sandwiches, you'd eat it," he grumbled under his breath.

"Colin..."

"What?" the familiar asked, lifting his head with a challenging glare. "What did I do wrong? I haven't eaten any babies, even though they're really easy to catch."

Jason sighed.

"I'm sorry, Colin. I know you're always a good boy."

Colin looked mollified and Jason reached out to touch his arm. Colin dissolved back into blood and was drawn back into Jason's hand in a single moment, like water sucked into the vacuum of space.

"Well," Jason said. "That didn't go how I hoped. Anyway, we were talking about the summoning incantation for Gordon, my other familiar."

"What's the summoning ritual for the blood monster like?"

"Probably best I don't say. And I told you to call him Colin. He really is a good boy."

"You realise most people don't need to point out that they don't eat babies."

"Well, in fairness, he didn't say he *doesn't* eat babies. He said he hasn't eaten any babies."

"Isn't that the same thing?"

"Not exactly. It's like me never having gone to Vitesse. It's not that I'm a person who doesn't go to Vitesse, just that I haven't gone to Vitesse. Yet."

"You're saying he's going to eat a baby."

"No, I don't think he's going to eat *a* baby. Once he starts, he'll probably be eating them in job lots."

"Now I'm going to need you to tell me what's in that summoning incantation."

"I don't even remember it properly. I don't use summoning rituals for my familiars anymore. I have these magic archways in my soul that…"

He sighed again as he looked at Miriam's expression. She clearly wasn't going to let it go and allow him to move on.

"Fine," he grumbled, sounding a lot like his familiar had earlier. "It's along the lines of '*something something, all-devouring power of the final threshold, something something, avatar of life's annihilation.*'"

She wanted to say something, but she remembered his warning about disparaging his familiar. However much his mannerisms might be layers of performance, she had believed that threat.

"Alright," she said. "Tell me about your other familiar. Why is its incantation relevant?"

"You heard the second line, right?"

"I did, but we've been rather side-tracked."

"The second line of Gordon's incantation is '*when gods fall, you are the instrument.*'"

"You think your familiar can kill the avatar?"

"Not alone. I have the beginnings of an ill-advised plan."

Clive and Farrah approached Jason and Miriam, still watching Gary fight the avatar to a goopy standstill.

"Thank you for coming," Miriam said to them.

"Even if it's completely unnecessary," Jason muttered.

"What exactly is the issue?" Clive asked.

"Jason was explaining—"

"Ah," Clive and Farrah both said, nodding.

"I'm not that bad at explaining things," Jason said defensively.

"Let me guess," Farrah said. "He starts not entirely on-topic, heading in the rough direction of a point as he tries to give context. But in the middle, he offhandedly mentions something ridiculous like getting into a knife fight with the Builder—"

"I was the only one with a knife," Jason interrupted.

"—or killing blood cultists by making them argue about gender roles in the workplace," Farrah continued, ignoring him.

"I don't know what that means," Miriam said, "but that does sound like the pattern I was encountering. Did you both know he has an apocalypse beast?"

"Colin?" Farrah asked. "Yeah, he's a good boy. You can't let Jason distract you with that stuff. He's way too excitable over running down every conversational tangent. And he loves talking about himself."

"I do not," Jason said.

"Jason," Farrah said. "How many times have you died now?"

"That's actually an increasingly tricky topic. I was talking with the goddess of Death recently, and I—"

"Also, he likes to name-drop," Clive said. "What was he trying to explain in the first place?"

Jason called a cloud chair out of the shrunken cloud flask hanging on his necklace and dropped into it with a sulky expression.

"He was trying to tell me his plan to deal with the avatar," Miriam said. "It had to do with his familiar—not the apocalypse beast one—and something called sanctioning."

Farrah looked to Clive, raising her eyebrows inquisitively. Clive frowned in thought for a moment before his eyes went slightly wide.

"You think you can do that?" he asked Jason.

"Yeah," Jason said. "It's all about will, and the god of Undeath's will is locked out of this place. The avatar is just power and the echo of intent. No active will to contend with."

"There's more to it than will, Jason."

"Yeah, but that's what would shut it down. The rest I have covered."

"Are you sure?"

"Sure enough that I'll try. You have an alternative?"

Clive looked once more at the avatar.

"No," he said. "When it comes to the practicalities of handling transcendent enemies, you're the closest thing we have to an expert since everyone that tries it dies. You just have that habit of coming back."

"Would someone care to explain?" Farrah asked. "And by someone, I mean Clive."

Clive looked at Miriam.

"Alright, I'll try and give the quick and simple version. Be aware that much of what we're discussing here is a mix of Jason's personal experience, my studies into cosmically sourced astral magic theory and no small amount of hypothesis. Essentially, guesswork. Confident guesswork, but I'm not willing to make a definitive—"

"We get it, Clive," Farrah said. "Just start, please."

"Right," he said. "Entities like gods and other cosmic beings are essentially made up of magic. This is something you've heard of?"

"Yes," Miriam said. "I won't claim to understand it, but I've heard people say that."

"Well," Clive continued, "the highest order of magic is called authority. This is the magic gods use to perform miracles and great astral beings use to regulate the mechanics of the cosmos. Birthing universes, governing the rules of life and death. You'll remember that resurrection magic became more difficult a few years ago but healing magic got stronger. This was a large working of authority that would have involved the Reaper, the Celestial Book, the gods of healing and death and probably a few others."

"Some of us also occasionally use it for home renovation," Jason chipped in.

"Quiet, you," Farrah scolded.

"In short," Clive resumed, "authority is the magic of the gods. And god-adjacent entities. We believe it is called authority because it is, in effect, the power with the highest authority. It has the power to remake everything that is, from the nature of reality to the laws of life and death. The only thing it can't do is interfere with a soul."

"Wouldn't that make it not the highest authority?" Miriam asked.

"I don't know," Clive said. "I suspect that a soul is, in itself, a form of authority. One that's sealed or frozen somehow. Whether through essences or some other magic, we ascend in rank by learning to thaw out or unseal that power."

"And diamond rank is when we tap into it fully?" Miriam asked.

"Not even close," Jason said. "I won't go into specifics of what I've seen and experienced…"

He paused to give Farrah a put-upon look.

"…but diamond rank is the point where you can truly start to unlock what the soul is capable of."

Miriam turned her gaze to the avatar again.

"This authority you're describing. You're saying that this monstrosity is made of it?"

"Yes," Clive said.

"The thing about authority," Jason said, "is that the most powerful beings who wield it do so as naturally as a human breathes. They can do so in a deliberate way if they think about it, but mostly, it just happens. They direct it through their will. For most people, will is just a metaphor for determination, mental fortitude and the like. For gods and great astral beings, will is an actual force. But you understand that, don't you, Miriam?"

Clive and Farrah looked confused, but Miriam nodded.

"It's something gold-rankers develop as part of aura training," she explained to Clive and Farrah. "It's not something shared with lower-rankers because it's possible to awaken at lower ranks through spiritual trauma."

Clive and Farrah looked at Jason, but he remained unreadable in both expression and aura.

"I didn't realise that mortals could develop will as an active force," Clive said. "I barely understand the concept."

"It gets easier once you start tapping into it," Miriam said. "To understand, anyway. Using it effectively is difficult. It's a strange thing. It feels like you can impose your will on the world around you, but you can't. It's like there's something missing. You can only really affect other people and their auras, and even that much is tricky. It's possible to make spiritual attacks if you train it enough, but it's hard to learn and I've heard it feels... wrong."

"It does," Jason said matter-of-factly.

Farrah turned an accusing gaze on Jason.

"How long have you been able to use will like that?" she asked him.

"You know since when."

"You didn't tell us," Clive said. "You didn't tell me, in all the discussions we've had about intrinsic-mandate magic."

Jason stood up from his chair like a king rising from his throne. The air around them turned still and silent as Jason's aura froze it in place.

"No, Clive," Jason said, his voice soft and dangerous. "I didn't tell you. Some things are not for you to research."

"He's right," Miriam said. "The Adventure Society has shut down wildly unethical experiments exploring it. That's why the information is restricted."

The air started moving again, the sounds of Gary and the avatar's battle once more reaching them. Jason's expression softened as he turned to Miriam.

"Will is critical to the use of authority," he explained. "Overcoming someone else's will to interfere with their authority is extremely difficult, but unlike interfering with a soul, not impossible. It's why gods have to team up on one of their number to punish them. Same for great astral beings. It takes an overwhelming amount of will to overcome someone else's sufficiently to use their own authority against them. It can be done, though, and when their authority is used against them, it's called sanctioning."

"And you want to sanction the avatar?" Miriam asked.

"Yes," Jason confirmed. "As I said earlier, it's all about will. I may be able to use will, probably better than you can, but using it against Undeath would be like trying to snuff out the sun with a glass of water. Not only would it be painfully inadequate, but I'd be dead long before I got close."

"But the god isn't here," Clive said. "His will is locked out of this place."

"There is a remnant of his will, though," Jason said. "An echo that drives the avatar's basic intentions. Even fighting just that echo will not be an easy thing."

"Before we get to that, though," Clive said, "there is the question of how we even set that fight in motion. That's your part, Jason, because I have only the most basic idea of how it works."

"What do you mean?" Miriam asked.

"We talked about authority being driven by will," Clive said. "That's fine if you're a god, but we aren't. Jason, with his domains, is more god than the rest of us, but not god enough."

"He's *what?*" Miriam asked.

"Ignore that," Farrah said.

"Sorry," Clive said. "The point is, using authority, even if we have any, is hard for us. We can't just manipulate it using will."

Miriam noticed Jason's eyes narrow as if he were about to disagree, but his expression went blank again and he said nothing.

"We have to use a special form of magic," Clive continued. "It's called intrinsic-mandate magic and Jason can access it through his familiar, Gordon. We aren't sure how, but that doesn't matter right now. The point is that he can do it."

"I can," Jason confirmed. "I've had Gordon working with an avatar in my soul realm for months to try and understand this kind of magic better. It's still early days, but I believe I can do this with Gordon executing the actual magic. My job will be employing will to guide the authority."

"There's more to it than just using a special ritual, though," Clive said.

"Yes," Jason agreed. "Authority has affinities. Authority is flavoured by the nature of the one that holds it. The Builder's, for example, is about forging reality, while that of the World-Phoenix is about dimensional forces."

"Why does that matter?" Farrah asked. "Isn't the point of this sanctioning that the authority changes?"

"We can only change it so much," Jason said. "When I stole some of the Builder's authority, I used it to modify the cloud flask and create my astral throne, which is all about modifying reality. The authority I stole from the World-Phoenix I turned into the astral gate, which is about using dimensional and cosmic forces. I think. I'm still getting a handle on it, if I'm being completely honest."

Miriam was looking at Jason wide-eyed.

"What do we do with the avatar's power, then?" Farrah asked. "I'm guessing that Undeath's authority is quite specific and unpleasant."

"Yeah," Jason said. "I do have a solution for that."

"Which is?" Clive asked.

"Well, I was talking with the goddess of Death recently, and..."

3 4

HE ISN'T ALWAYS EVIL AND HE IS NOT ALWAYS WRONG

JASON FLOATED IN THE SCORCHING DESERT AIR, STANDING ON A SMALL cloud platform. In his hand was his cloud flask, spewing out fog that was adding to the half-complete sky fortress forming in the air. It was all thin lines and sharp angles, more decorative than practical. As sections were completed, the white material turned the dark shade of a storm cloud.

He turned his gaze to the ground far below where Gary continued to beat on the avatar. It mounted token resistance but was well past the point of having any real defence beyond a refusal to be destroyed. Farrah rose to meet Jason, bright wings of fire driving her ascent. He shuffled aside on his small platform, making room for her to join him and she let her wings vanish on landing. She looked at him and he looked back with sad eyes.

"You know what I'm going to ask," she said.

"I can guess. I try to avoid reading people's emotions if I don't need to, but your aura isn't exactly hiding them."

"It's not possible, then?"

"No," he said, his voice tired. "It is."

"Then why don't you sound hopeful?"

He plucked an oval object from his inventory, holding it in his hand.

"Hero gave me this before the transformation zone took us. To save Gary."

"What is it?"

"Sort of like a skill book for intrinsic-mandate magic."

"God stuff."

"God stuff," Jason confirmed, returning the item to his inventory. "It shows me how to work with extremely higher-tier magic, like authority. To tweak it in specific ways, like taking something that is fuelled by one high-tier magic and switching that source with a different high-tier magic."

"Like swapping out Hero's authority, which will go back to Hero once we're out of here, for the authority in that avatar."

Jason nodded. "We'd still need to refine Undeath's authority into something else first," he explained. "Otherwise, that authority would do the same thing as Hero's and return to the god the moment we're out of this place."

"Then, why don't we do that?"

"Refining authority into something else isn't a simple matter, Farrah. You need something to refine it, to work with the affinity it already has. Meeting those conditions is hard and the affinity can only be changed so much. Given that I have almost no idea what I'm doing, the fact that I have the right combination of knowledge and tools is a miracle."

"You're saying we got lucky."

"No, I'm saying it's a miracle. I think Death knew what was coming when I brokered a deal with her and made sure I'd have the right tools for the job. Telling me in advance would have been nice. I have to stop hanging out with gods."

Farrah gave him one of her signature flat looks and he chuckled. Then his expression saddened again.

"I'm sorry, Farrah. Swapping out Hero's authority for Undeath's would have the same result in the end. Worse, because we'd be turning Gary into some manner of undead demigod for however long we remain here."

"What about giving him the refined power?"

"It'll be too different. Right now, Gary and the avatar are mostly clumps of raw authority. Something too processed won't work. What I'm going to refine Undeath's authority into isn't something we could use to keep Gary alive."

"Is there some way we can stop the power from leaving Gary? Prevent it from going back to Hero?"

"Yes," Jason said. "If he stayed in my soul realm forever, I could keep the power trapped. But that would only delay Gary's death. He would still die."

"Why?"

"Gary was silver rank, and now he's got divine energy flowing through him. Transcendent rank. Not contained and manageable, like my astral gate and astral throne. This is the raw stuff, blazing with power. It's slowly killing him from the inside out."

"But it changed him. Altered his body to contain it."

"Yes. He's now a gold-ranker, filled with not just diamond-rank but transcendent-rank power. Beyond anything a mortal body is meant to hold. His body was modified on the premise that he would only need to hold that power for hours. Luckily, it did the work above spec and Gary's been fine, but it won't last. We've been here what, two months?"

"How long does he have?"

"My experience and senses make me better than most at gauging what that kind of power does to a body. Best guess, I'd say he has another four to eight months before it starts turning his body into a worn rag. How long before it finally gives out, I don't know. It could be fast once the degradation begins or he could hang on."

"It doesn't matter, though," Farrah said. "We'll be out of this place before then."

"Most likely. Many territories are yet to be claimed, maybe a third of the total, and they're going to get more dangerous with time. By the end, Gary may be the only one strong enough to fight the anomalies."

"And then we leave and he dies."

"Yes," Jason said. "We leave and he dies."

"If stealing Undeath's power isn't the reason Hero gave you that oval thing, why did he? How did he expect you to save Gary? Or did he leave that for you to figure it out?"

"He did. And I have."

"You still don't sound hopeful."

"Gary has a choice to make, once we're done with this place."

"What is it?"

Jason looked down at Gary bringing his hammer down on the avatar again, gooey flesh spattering across the red sand.

"Gary should hear it first," he said. "If he wants help making that choice, he can ask us."

After being completed, Jason's cloud palace looked like a monstrous spider, dangling on an invisible thread as it eyed-off the unsuspecting prey below. There were too many legs and too much chitin, armour panels of dark glossy red covering sections of the stormy cloud structure. At the base was a gaping maw filled with dark mist, like a mouth waiting to devour. Inside the mist, blue and orange light flashed rapidly, leaving behind a glow that grew brighter over time.

Watching from below was a group comprised of most of the leadership from the expedition, the adventuring teams that made it up, and their allies. Conspicuously absent were Jason and Boris Ket Lundi. Jason was somewhere up in his fortress while the messenger was keeping his forces well clear of the spell-happy adventurers.

The messengers might have fought on their side, but that didn't make them allies. Given that the members of the Builder cult had managed to become allies, it spoke volumes of the trust any in the group had for the messengers.

"I'm surprised the avatar isn't getting out from under that thing," Humphrey said. "I know it belongs to Jason and even I don't want to stand there."

"Knowing it belongs to Jason is *why* I don't want to stand there," Rick told him. Humphrey snorted a laugh at his cousin's comment.

When they saw Boris fly in that direction alone, the group stirred.

"Don't worry," Farrah said. "If that guy makes trouble in Jason's cloud palace, he's not coming back out."

Miriam glanced at her, uncertain, but saw nothing but ease and confidence in her expression. Taking a rude peek at her aura, she saw the emotion was genuine. The underscore of worry in her aura was directed at Gary, not Jason.

Inside what the observers below had dubbed the 'smoky maw' of his cloud palace, Jason stood at the side, on a platform jutting from the wall. The open-bottomed chamber was the size of a large house, filled with dark mist. Inside the mist, Gordon was filling the space with an elaborate ritual diagram in three dimensions. The dark mist did not obscure Jason's vision, as it was all a part of his domain, a part of Jason himself.

He sensed the approach of the gold-rank messenger, moving alone.

Boris rose into the space, pausing as he crossed into the area of Jason's domain. He floated at the entrance to the maw, wings gently undulating as their magic held him in place.

"Interesting," he said. "I knew from Earth that you'd learned to imprint on physical space. Being able to carry around and reshape that space is unexpected. I'll bet the gods started quietly attempting to replicate it the moment you showed back up in this world."

"They don't have mobile temples?" Jason asked.

"They do, but they're massive temple boats and sky fortresses. Slow. Cumbersome. Certainly nothing you can carry around in a jar. Cloud flasks are hard to make, and modifying one to the extent that it can do this would be quite the feat. How did you?"

"The same way I do most things: it just happened when I was busy trying to save the world without dying in the process."

"It seems to work for you."

"It half works. I've gotten pretty good at saving the world. It's the not dying part that has always been the trick."

Boris flew up to hover in front of Jason on his platform.

"Once you're done with this place, dying won't be a concern anymore."

"No," Jason said. "It won't. Did you come up here for anything other than implying you have vast knowledge you'd be willing to share if maybe I'm more open-minded about you and your people?"

"No. I do have a lot of knowledge, though, and there are things I need."

"You've dropped the quirky Earth mannerisms."

"They served their purpose. I'll pick them up again. It's the version of myself I like being the most. I've seen your personas, Jason. I know you understand playing to the mask until you're not quite sure what's underneath anymore. If even the parts of ourselves we hide away are real. People like you and I might take it further than most, but everyone wears different masks. Like in that Billy Joel song."

"I love that song."

"Me too."

"Right now, I'm looking at you and thinking of the line about getting kicked right between the eyes. You and I are going to have a nice long talk sometime soon, but I'm kind of in the middle of something here."

"Yes," Boris said, turning to look at the growing blue and orange glow in the dark cloud. As he turned, he tucked his wing to avoid hitting his host.

Jason looked at his back. "The implication was that you should leave."

"I'm curious why you're taking this approach," Boris said, ignoring his statement as he continued to watch the glowing cloud. "Intrinsic-mandate magic is tricky at the best of times, and you can't be very good at it yet. We both know you have the power to breach transformation zones. It's how you claimed your first domain on Earth. Surely it would be easier to crack a hole in this one and toss the avatar out."

"Unreliable. Too much to go wrong."

"As opposed to using god magic you aren't even close to ready for?"

"Using power I'm not ready for is kind of my thing."

Boris let out a laugh.

"I can't argue with that," he said. "Still, I can't help but wonder."

"If we kicked the avatar out, I don't know how much control it would retain over the territories it claimed. Maybe it retains control and we'd have to go bring it back so we can destroy it properly. Even if kicking it out severed its connection to its territory, that territory would likely become unclaimed space. Maybe even divide back into separate territories, meaning weeks or even months to claim them all ourselves. Worst case, removing that much power, tied to so much of the transformation zone, could have some unintended side effects. Maybe disrupt the zone and cause it to collapse."

"All valid points," Boris said. "Did Farrah remember you could breach the zone, forcing you to explain why you shouldn't when you were explaining the plan?"

"Yes."

"So. The real reason is that you want the authority."

Jason didn't answer.

"I get it," Boris said. "You've been behind the power curve from the moment you learned there was one. Now you're on the road to playing with the big boys and you need to stop falling short. I can respect that. I've been thinking that it might be time to rank-up myself, with what's coming."

"And what's that?"

"A fight that isn't yours. I can't help but think you'll involve yourself sooner or later, though. That destiny magic really does drop you into one hole after another, doesn't it?"

"Yep."

"You know there are a lot of forces paying attention to you, right? The World-Phoenix set something in motion by nudging you onto a certain path. Now the Reaper, the Keeper of the Sands, even the All-Devouring Eye. You're a popular piece in a game that's coming to a head."

"I'm a pawn."

"Yes, but pawns can be promoted. Once we're done with this little misadventure, you might just find yourself reaching the other side of the board."

"What does that mean?"

"That once you're done here, there are already people waiting to reward you. And you know the reward for a job well done."

"Another job."

Boris glanced back with an amused smile before returning his gaze to the cloud.

"You said the All-Devouring Eye," Jason said. "I've heard of that great astral being, but I don't know its area of influence."

"No one does," Boris said. "Not for certain. The prevailing theory is that it's the end of all things, somehow. Or some cosmic, magical force of entropy, which amounts to the same thing. But your familiar, there, is a genuine avatar of doom."

"As opposed to a knock-off one I bought from a shady guy at a street market?"

"Not exactly. Avatars of doom are the exclusive domain of the All-Devouring Eye. I have never heard of the eye ever employing his reality assassins for any task. Instead, they were loaned to the Sundered Throne. Why, and what relationship the eye has with the throne, I don't know. Some say they are representations of order and chaos, not oppositional but symbiotic."

"Do you believe that?"

"It's clean, simple explanation."

"So, no."

"No," Boris confirmed. "It has been my experience that most things involve far more nuance than I am aware of. I don't trust clean, simple explanations. The cosmos is a messy place, whether you're dealing with mortals on a planet with almost no magic or contending with great astral beings."

"So, who is selling these fake avatars of doom in a side alley?"

"It's not quite like that. It's the avatars themselves. There are a few that have remained attached to the throne since the sundering. The real avatars bolster their numbers by creating constructs that are, to almost every test, identical to the genuine article. There is only one practical difference."

"Which is?"

Boris lifted an arm to point at the glowing cloud.

"Only the real ones can do that."

Jason let out a groan.

"Bloody hell," he muttered.

"I've got you intrigued about the chance to ask me a lot more questions, haven't I?" Boris asked.

"Yeah," Jason admitted.

"Well, there's a price. I have an astral king's brand in my soul. I needed it to fool Vesta Carmis Zell, and while the astral king is a friendly, I still want it gone."

"I get that. You know what that means in terms of trusting one another."

"I have to trust you because I'm giving you access to the most vulnerable parts of myself. What do you need to trust?"

"That you aren't some kind of living, soul-engineered trap."

Boris turned to stare at Jason.

"Wow," he said. "That's actually a kind of brilliant idea. I wish I'd thought of it. I mean, setting the whole thing up would be a massively elaborate pain in the ass, but yeah, that would be a great way to deal with you. I'm kind of disappointed that I'm not trying to kill you now. That would have totally worked."

"Except that I was the one suspicious of that being what you're doing," Jason pointed out. "I'm also suspicious of your reaction being a disarming way to convince me that you're not some kind of living trap."

"You're a suspicious guy. You know that messenger plans usually come down to deciding they're the best and throwing power at things until they break, right?"

"I met an outworlder who turned out to be a naga genesis egg that was transformed through soul engineering and sent to Pallimustus twenty years before the messenger invasion began."

"Really?"

"Yeah."

"I may have been on Earth too long. These messengers are getting sneaky."

Both men turned to look at the cloud that was now pulsing with blue and orange light.

"Time to go, Boris," Jason said. "We can pick this up when I don't have a god to kill."

"I know that's technically inaccurate on a number of levels," Boris said, "but that is a great line. Which I kind of ruined by talking about it instead of just leaving, I guess. I'm just going to go."

35

NEW POWER AND A FRESHLY
COOKED BATCH OF SMUGNESS

JASON PLUNGED FROM HIS CLOUD PALACE HEAD FIRST. HIS CLOAK TRAILED behind him, a black scar against the clear blue sky. His cloak was not a graceful tool of flight, but he had learned from the messengers how to compensate. They flew using the magic of their wings, enhanced by their ability to use physical force with their auras. Jason did the same, descending in a spiral to approach the ground with poise.

Close to Gary, currently four times his height, Jason floated in the air, producing a cloud disc to stand on. His cloak stopped mimicking wings and was whipped wildly as if by a gale, despite the hot, still air. The forces Jason was mustering far above caused ripples in the unstable fabric of the transformation zone.

Gary was continuing his endless but one-sided beating of the avatar. With Jason's arrival, he kicked the avatar in the chest, sending it tumbling away across the ground. Every bounce left a wet stain in the sand; the same dark, thick oil now coated Gary's armoured boot. He frowned at it standing on one leg and the golden flames wreathing his body flared. The black and purple goo was burned away and he set his foot down with satisfaction.

"This isn't the place to be, Jason," he said, not taking his gaze from the avatar as it finally rolled to a stop.

"This is the place I need the avatar to be. I need you to stop it from running."

"Easily done," Gary said, pointing with his hammer.

The avatar was rushing at him and he pulled back his hammer arm. The avatar accelerated into a blur that Jason couldn't follow, Gary moving just as fast. From Gary's pose a moment later and the avatar sailing through the air, Jason deduced that an upward swing from Gary had sent it flying.

"I'm beating it like steel on an anvil," Gary said, "but it comes back every time. It won't run."

"It will."

"It hasn't run from me and I'm a demigod right now, Jason. Your project up there is hardly subtle, but the avatar hasn't given it a second glance."

The avatar charged again. Gary and the avatar became a blur of motion and the avatar was knocked away once more.

"The avatar isn't smart enough to understand what I'm doing up there," Jason explained. "It's little more than power and instinct; it doesn't recognise the threat. It doesn't run from you because it knows you can't destroy it. Once it realises I can, that will change."

"If you say so. It's not like anything I'm doing works. But you know that I'm flooded with divine power right now?"

"You're enormous and covered in gold fire, Gary. As reminders go, it's a pretty good one."

"And your giant sky spider fortress is designed to destroy the avatar, which is a big lump of divine power."

"Yep."

"Should I be worried about standing under that thing?"

"Nah, you're good," Jason assured him. "Until I get my hands on a soul forge, I can't do much to Hero's power. You and I need to have a conversation about that later, but right now, I've only got the tools to mess this thing up. I couldn't put a dent in you if I tried."

"Why do you need a soul forge for me and not the avatar?"

"It doesn't have a soul. There's no one home to say no when I ask the power it's made of to change into something else."

"Jason, exactly how well do you understand what you're doing?"

"Well, no time to hang around here," Jason said. "You just make sure it stays put, yeah? I need you to keep it as directly underneath the cloud palace as you can."

Gary conjured a golden harpoon and threw it at the avatar. It moved in a golden streak. Until it stopped, impaled in the avatar, Jason didn't even see the golden chain attached to it. Gary was already hauling on it, pulling the avatar closer.

"You do what you have to do, Jason."

Jason pushed the hood of his cloak back to reveal his smiling face.

"Always reliable, Gary," he said, and then ascended into the air.

Essence-users had excellent control of their perception, able to isolate specific smells and sounds, or dampen their senses against horrifying stenches or blinding light. The adventurers observing from the ground deadened their hearing to avoid the alien howl coming from Jason's spider palace, but it didn't work. Miriam quickly realised there was a spiritual component, piercing through mundane senses to affect the magical ones.

Amos Pensinata was a step ahead of her, telling the group through voice chat to restrain their aura senses as much as possible. Miriam looked to their allies who didn't share the precision control of the senses that essence-users had. She could see that the brighthearts and Builder cultists were suffering, their hands clamped over their ears and their faces twisted in anguish, especially the silver-rankers.

Miriam next turned her gaze to the messengers in the distance. Most had landed on the ground, something they were loath to do. Sitting or resting on their knees, they were sweating as they all looked up at the palace. Miriam hadn't even known they could do that. Their expressions were not of pain but worry, anger and fear. Their auras, normally so controlled, barely masked their emotions.

Only the trio of gold-rankers remained floating in the air. They too looked like the desert air had finally gotten to them, their skin slick with sweat. Boris Ket Lundi turned to meet her gaze. He smirked to himself and cast his eyes back upward.

There was another inhuman shrieking, but this one was pure sound and easy enough to block out. It came from the avatar as it clawed at the rocky, sandy ground, trying to scramble free of the golden chains binding it. It ignored Gary as he brought his hammer down on one limb after another, rendering them useless for only a brief time before they snapped back into shape.

A column of faint light had come down from the palace maw to shine on the avatar and the demigod. This was what the avatar scrambled to escape, unable to get free of Gary and his chains. The light had been barely perceptible at first but grew stronger by the moment. Colours could be made out now, the signature gold, silver and blue of transcendent power.

The light eventually grew strong enough to affect the avatar. Black and purple flakes rose from it like ashes from a fire. It was slow at first, but more flakes broke loose of the avatar as the light grew brighter. With each passing moment, more of them drifted up toward the palace. They rose through the light, bursting into white flame as they neared the gaping maw of the palace, filled with dark smoke and flashing orange and blue light.

Miriam focused her attention on the flakes as they burned on approach to the palace. She had seen such fire before, ghost flames burning off the undead like dry scrub. The flames were weak when the flakes first combusted, like those of Jason's ghost fire. They grew brighter as they approached the maw, blazing like Death's miracle by the time they vanished into the smoke.

All of this was accompanied by an oppressive aura washing over the landscape from the cloud palace. It was Jason's aura at its most unyielding and merciless. His cloud palace and whatever strange magic his familiar wielded made it far stronger than anything Jason could accomplish alone. His aura brooked no challenge, but there was a benevolence to it as well, with the protectiveness and condescension of an adult to a child.

The aura seemed utterly unassailable, so Miriam was startled to sense it falter. It was only a brief moment; the silver-rankers were unlikely to have sensed it. But it told Miriam that whatever Jason was fighting, it was not the one-sided affair of Gary and the avatar.

Jason wasn't truly conscious inside the cloud palace. As his body reclined in a cloud chair, his soul was clashing with Undeath's power in a kaleidoscopic mindscape. It had no true form, playing against his senses as a maelstrom of colour and power. It was strange, but Jason knew what to do, pitting his will against the echo of the absent god.

It was a battlefield Jason had experienced before when the Builder had tried to force him into accepting a star seed. He had no true memories of the conflict, just echoes marked on his soul in scars like hieroglyphs on a tomb.

As Jason fought the amorphous will of the god in the mindscape, his body reflected the battle. It was a battle of the soul and Jason's body and soul were the same thing. Lying in the cloud chair, his body thrashed and flailed like someone caught in a night terror. His skin crawled and undulated as if Colin were trying to dig his way out. Light blasted from his eyes, sometimes blue and orange, other times the transcendent mix of silver, blue and gold. Occasionally, they would flash purple.

The dead remnant of Undeath was a paltry thing compared to the active will of the Builder he had fought in the past, but Jason lacked his singular advantage from that battle. Against the Builder, he had the shelter of his soul, an impregnable fortress that could only be breached if he opened it himself. This time, Jason's soul was already open. It was a necessary part of the process, something he had told no one. They would have tried to stop him.

Jason's cloud palace was also his spiritual domain. It was a physical expression of his power, like the sanctum of a god's temple. He had shaped the entire thing into a platform for Gordon's massive working of intrinsic-mandate magic, linking it to Jason. That was the first tool he needed to sanction the avatar's authority.

The other tool he needed was something that could work with the authority's affinity of undeath. A forge to reshape it into something he could claim for himself. Authority could only be altered so much, but death and undeath were essentially identical—pure or corrupted versions of the same power. Jason did not have any divine power, but he had something close.

The goddess of Death had shown Jason how to make fire in his soul, lacking in divinity but still shaped in the way that gods used power. And now some divinity had conveniently turned up. Jason was using the ghost fire to reforge the god's authority, turning the corrupt power of undeath into the clean power of death. Jason was then spending that authority to fuel his ghost fire, turning it from a pale echo to a divine weapon.

The shape came from Death and the power from Undeath, but the result belonged to Jason alone. It was no mortal weapon of sharpness and steel; it was a flame that would annihilate any undead power, second only to the goddess of Death herself.

Forging a divine weapon was no small undertaking, and Jason was not done. He was stealing from a god, and even the echo of it threatened to crush Jason before his work was complete. The danger was existential as he'd opened his soul to take in the authority. If he failed to eliminate the corruption of undeath, that corruption would claim him, undeath taking root in his soul. If his will fell short, Jason would become Undeath's new agent, as Gary was to Hero.

Jason's plan wouldn't have been possible if Undeath had even the meagrest sliver of active will in the fight. Jason could no more have taken the god's power than he could have swallowed a mountain, be it in the shape of his own head or not. Even just the leftover touch of the god, driving the avatar's simple instincts, threatened to crush Jason's will.

The battle of wills was something Jason had anticipated and believed himself ready for. His soul had his body scraped off it as it was cast through the depths of the astral. It had felt the touch of gods and the all-out assault of a great astral being. He had thought himself strong, ready to face the challenge. He had been naïve, once again failing to grasp the magnitude of the forces using him as a pawn in their games.

All he'd done, all he'd endured, was barely enough to get him into the arena alive. Without those experiences, just his first brush with the echo of the god's will would have annihilated his mind. In the wild mindscape, he was a tiny man with a knife, fighting a giant in a hurricane. Jason steeled himself and gathered his resolve; he was going to fuck that giant up.

The fight was imaginary; a clash in Jason's mind that played out on his body very differently. As he absorbed and reforged the power of undeath into death, the corruption flowed out of his body. Viscous liquid, like raw crude oil, ran from his eyes, nose and mouth. As more and more poured out, Jason's skin started to crack, more oil oozing out.

Inside Jason's body, Colin worked to keep Jason alive through the process, preventing his body from giving out before his will did. Countless dead leeches fell from Jason's flesh, coated in the purged filth of corruption.

Inside the mindscape, Jason fought on. The will of the god was absent, yet Jason was caught up in the aftermath of its presence. Like a man flailing in the wake of a ship that had already sailed on, he was constantly on the verge of drowning. He scrambled to keep his head above water, desperately swimming through the ocean of power trying to inundate him.

Jason took it all and remade it, turning it into power for himself. But he could not use it until he was done, unwilling to risk breaking the magic that Gordon had forged. The power of undeath kept coming, as indefatigable as the avatar he was stealing it from. It seemed limitless, while Jason himself was not. He fought on, the spirit willing as his resolve never wavered, but his body and mind were beginning to flag.

The observers watched as Jason's cloud palace started to break down. Sections fell away from the whole before dissolving into smoke. The ashes of Undeath's power grew closer and closer to the palace before burning up in white flame. Jason's aura faltered, pulsing like an unsteady heartbeat. The piercing noise was not gone but had been reduced to the point of background noise, to the relief of everyone.

Boris Ket Lundi flew away from his own people, the adventurers and their allies wary as he approached them alone. He went directly to Miriam who moved out to meet him. On arrival, he looked back up at the palace before he spoke.

"We need to be ready if Asano fails," he said. "If he does, he will become something like the lion demigod."

"Will he have the same power?"

"No. Asano has turned much of Undeath's power from undeath to death. Those two forces will be conflicting inside him. You must use your demigod to contain him until those powers destroy him."

"How do we save him?"

"You don't. Once he dies, the territories he and the avatar control will become unclaimed and we will have a lot of work ahead of us. Even more, for me, once we're out. Without Asano to save his world, I will have to do it myself. An ugly necessity that will have unpleasant consequences for the Earth."

Boris looked past Miriam as Jason's team and other companions approached.

"Jason won't fail," Humphrey said.

"Your confidence in your friend is admirable," he said, then turned his gaze on Sophie. "Hey, girl. Ever been with a winged man in a booth?"

"Really?" Miriam asked. "Now, and in this situation, you're acting like that?"

Boris grinned and turned to look at the cloud palace once more.

"I think," he said, "I might have some confidence in your friend as well."

"I hope you've got confidence in yourself," Sophie told him. "Once I get to gold rank, I'm going to kick you square in the balls."

He turned to look at her again.

"What happened to a good old slap to the face?"

Humphrey's hand slapped him in the face with a sound like thunder cracking. Boris rubbed his jaw while letting out a groan.

"I guess I had that one coming. Are you really silver rank? Might essence?"

"You'd best watch your mouth," Humphrey said, "or at gold rank, you'll find me standing in line behind the lady."

"You know messengers are some kind of fruit or something, right?" Belinda asked. "I'm not sure he has the equipment for either of you to kick."

"This is not the time," Miriam said in the incredulous voice of the only sane person in a world of madmen. "We need to be ready if Asano fails."

"He's not going to fail," Neil said, sounding bored. "He's going to almost kill himself and come back with some stupid new power and a freshly cooked batch of smugness. I always tell people and they never listen. Nothing's going to happen to Jason."

As Neil finished speaking, the cloud palace exploded.

"I'm sure it's fine," he said.

- Party leader [Jason Asano] has been compromised and is unable to maintain his abilities. Party has been disbanded and party interface has been revoked.

"Uh… that might not be great," Neil said.

INSTINCTIVELY PROTECTED

CLAN ASANO HAD TWO DOMAINS ON EARTH. ONE WAS IN SAINT-ETIENNE, France, covering most of the city. The other was close to Nitra, Slovakia, on formerly agricultural land. Both contained astral spaces rich in magic, producing far more magical manifestations than elsewhere on Earth. This meant essences, awakening stones and quintessence, although, far more than any of those, it meant monsters.

There were geographical restrictions on the manifestations that cities on Pallimustus would have waged wars to learn the secrets of. Within the city walls of Saint-Etienne, manifestations rarely happened, as infrequently or more so than on Earth. When they did, however, it was always treasure and never a monster. In the wild territory outside the walls, things were very different. The rich magic was given free rein, spawning hordes of teeming monsters.

Close to the walls, the magic was thick but not very strong. This produced the iron-rank monsters that the clan used to train their fledgling essence-users. The further one moved away from the walls, the stronger the magic became, affecting both the landscape and the monsters.

The clan's essence-users delved deeper into the wilds as they grew in strength, but it was still early days. The clan had raised an impressive contingent of bronze-rankers using the stockpile of magical items, training materials, essences and awakening stones left behind by Jason and Farrah.

Those stockpiles had diminished at first but were now being restocked from finds in the astral spaces.

The clan only had a few silver-rankers, mostly core-users taken in from the Network as it fractured into factions. They had reported seeing gold-rank monsters in the outer reaches of the territory where the astral spaces grew unstable. What little they knew of those zones came from very distant observation. Not only were the monsters too strong for their current forces, but the landscape itself was dangerous, shifting and changing.

Going that far out was strictly forbidden by the clan matriarch, Yumi Asano. She was Jason's paternal grandmother, although she looked a third of her actual age. Her flesh-shaping powers not only made her appear younger but offered true physical revitalisation. Wielders of body-morphing essence combinations were often looked at as creepy on Pallimustus, and they weren't known for their power. Neither fact hampered the popularity of such combinations when they offered a life-span lengthy even by essence-user standards.

Yumi stood at the window of a zeppelin flying over the Nitra astral space city. Within the high walls, the city could be mistaken for the life's work of a mad steampunk elf. Looming towers looked like skyscrapers built by industrial-age furnace makers, all rough, dark metal. The defensive walls looked much the same, only thicker and without windows.

The towers rose from a city that otherwise did not match them at all, full of pleasant cloud buildings and sweeping expanses of green. It was a sprawling metropolis in size, but not at all built for cars. Instead of street grids and freeways weaving like veins, it was a space built around walking and public transport.

Walkways passed through parks and tramways wove through gardens. Monorails ran along the ground or up and over trees. There were also zeppelins docked at the massive metal towers, or smaller towers made of cloud stuff. The central hub for the zeppelins was the centre of the city and its one truly unique building. A massive pagoda, taller than any of the metal towers, was topped by an ominous blue and orange eye, floating in the air. This was the administrative and travel hub for the city, including the portal aperture leading in and out of the astral space.

The city's transport infrastructure was all steampunk in design. Over-elaborate reflections of a period on Earth that never existed, they blended Victorian and modern technology with magic. The steam engines were driven by a mix of fire and water quintessence; there was no coal. There weren't a lot of accurate physics either, several scientists and engineers had assured Yumi.

It was not hard to get people interested in the chance to examine the city's infrastructure. There was an arms race going on, both in magic and the combination of magic and technology. Both of the astral space cities offered access to examples unlike anything on Earth, which had helped Yumi's recruitment efforts. Researchers were high on her list of recruitment priorities.

Magitech was the next arm's race, at least until more essence-users reached greater heights of power. There was also the matter of the Engineers of Ascension and their vault, left to Jason by the enigmatic Mr North. Jason had directed his grandmother to seek out ethical ways to continue EoA's terrible experiments.

From the zeppelin, Yumi could see people moving through the city below. The vast city was mostly empty, most of it a restricted zone. There wasn't any danger, just a lack of people to fully populate the vast city. Even the waves of refugees were unable to fill up all the space.

The residents were an eclectic group, fewer of them human than not. It had taken an amount of political wrangling, but almost every country affected by transformation zones had allowed those transformed into non-humans by the zones to emigrate to Asano territory. Getting the other nations to acknowledge clan land as sovereign was a whole other thing, but vampires holding most of mainland Europe had led to smoother relations. Desperate for friendly territory, Yumi had bled them for concessions before allowing their forces access to Asano territory.

The clan's territorial defences attacked those of ill intent, driving away many soldiers and even some of the refugees. This had been a major point of contention, but Yumi wouldn't have compromised the protective magic even if she could. She had enough to deal with already, without adding spies and vampire attacks to her slate.

Now there was a new problem. There had been incidents in the past she was certain led back to Jason—thunderstorms out of nowhere or the sky turning red. One day, without warning, the sky within Asano land turned to night while it remained day outside. Another time, the domain had been covered in a dome of bricks for several minutes, after which the landscape of the territories and astral spaces heavily reconfigured themselves.

This latest incident was worse than what had come before. It had the potential to bring everything down, and for the first time, Yumi was genuinely worried. There was sudden and rapid degradation in city infrastructure, most notably the walls. It had only been minutes, yet the city was on the way to looking post-apocalyptic. The growing state of alarm was visible even from this height. The people on the ground moved with swift agitation, like ants whose nest had just been kicked.

Yumi turned her gaze to the largest problem, which was the walls and the territory beyond it. The walls of the astral space city had built-in defences against the outside, made even stronger when the city had been reconstructed. In the Nitra city, this was automated Gatling gun turrets atop the walls, each emplacement the size of a delivery truck.

Normally, the defences were unnecessary. Monsters rarely took a run at the walls, the guns mostly dealing with the occasional flyer. But the degradation of the city was matched by a degradation in the monsters. The living monsters were turning undead. In the short time it had taken Yumi to enter the astral space and board a zeppelin, a horde of unliving monstrosities had come shambling to besiege the city walls. Worse, bronze-rank monsters that usually avoided the city were arriving.

If silver- and gold-rank monsters started arriving, things would get markedly worse. The wall turrets radiated gold-rank power, but even if they were enough, how long would that remain true? Like all the other city infrastructure, there were signs that the wall and its turrets were starting to break down.

The remains of Jason's cloud palace spread across the desert sky, streamers of dark cloud combusting explosively in the air, trailing fire as they burned up. On the ground, Jason's companions all watched in worry. Everyone but Gary. He was looking down at the avatar, now a shrivelled husk, motionless inside the gold chains binding it to the ground. He gave it an experimental kick and the body crumbled like charcoal, throwing up black dust as it fell apart. Shrinking down to normal size, still head and shoulders above everyone but the messengers, Gary moved next to the others in a blur.

"What's happening?" he asked as he joined the rest in looking up. "That system message about Jason didn't sound good, but the avatar is finally dead. Did we win?"

"No," Boris said. "Asano failed to refine all of the god's authority before it entered his soul. The battleground has shifted to inside Asano himself."

"Isn't that good?" Belinda asked. "He's all-powerful in his soul realm, right?"

"He has god-like power in there, it's true," Boris said. "But he allowed an actual god's power in there as well. By inviting that power in, he gave it a certain purchase within his spiritual realm."

"Why would inviting it in matter?" Sophie asked.

"Gods have their own rules," Clive said. "What is impossible to us is easy to them while the reverse is sometimes also true. Jason is fighting by their rules now."

"He's right," Boris said. "Like my kind, Asano exists on the border between the physical and the cosmic, between mortal and immortal. We messengers fall mostly on the physical side of that line, moving further towards the cosmic as we grow closer to becoming astral kings. Jason is growing ever closer to that line, and in this battle has one foot on each side. As this person said…"

He gestured at Clive.

"…sorry, I didn't catch your name. But as he said, Asano is fighting by their rules now."

Sophie glanced at Humphrey standing beside her, his face a storm of anger.

"We need practical solutions," Miriam said. "What do we do? Where even is he? In that exploding cloud?"

The cloud was still a maelstrom of darkness from which burning trails of smoke shot out like fireworks.

"We might be alright," Boris said. "I believe that Asano converted more of the power than got into his soul unchanged. Those forces will be at war within him right now, and he may win. If not, it will be obvious when he comes out of there as an undead monster."

"How do we help him?" Neil asked.

"Short of going into Asano's soul and joining the fight, I don't think we can," Boris said.

"That's as good an entrance line as I could asked for," Nik said. "Thanks, two-piece feed."

They all turned to see the rabbit-man and Shade standing in front of Jason's soul portal.

"Two-Piece Feed?" Boris asked. "Are you talking about me?"

"That's right, you chicken-wing motherfu—"

"Alacrity is our watchword, Master Nik," Shade pointed out.

"Right, yeah," Nik said, then jerked a thumb at the portal with one hand while pointing out Jason's team one by one with the other.

"You lot, you're plan B. Get in there."

"Only silver-rankers?" Miriam asked.

"Two-Piece Feed can come too," Nik said. "And the therapy lady."

"Mr Asano's soul realm is rather unstable right now," Shade explained. "Those he implicitly trusts and relies on will be instinctively protected, but others will be in danger. Messengers are able to endure exotic dimensional forces, so they can also bring aid."

"Then I will bring all my people," Boris said.

"Hold on, chicken wings," Nik said. "There's no way you nuggets of shi—"

"Please bring them all," Shade said. "And do so with—"

Colin staggered out of the portal in his blood clone state, but significantly worse for wear. Parts of him looked identical to Jason and others were glossy red. There were large wounds all over his body and dead, purple-stained leeches dropped from rotting flesh.

"Faster," Colin growled in Jason's voice, then staggered back through the portal.

Ketevan Arziani stood next to Yumi, likewise surveying the city. After factional conflict within the Network had broken up the branch Ketevan had been director of in Australia, Yumi had snapped her up. Her combination of administrative expertise and familiarity with magic had proven a boon to the Asano clan during their rapid initial expansion. More than anything, she had proven a loyal ally to the Asano clan.

"This seems worse than previous incidents you've described," Ketevan said.

"Yes," Yumi confirmed. "The combination of the walls being compromised and a wave of undead monsters attacking them is something I don't have a solution to. The cities in the astral spaces are our fallback position if anything happens with the territory on Earth. If the cities fall, we lose everything."

"Then, what do we do?"

"This is beyond us. Literally. This can only be something happening with Jason. All we can do is get people away from the walls and hope that whatever this is, Jason deals with it before we start losing people."

"What is happening to him that this is going on?" Ketevan asked. "If the undead overtake this place, it will turn into another Makassar."

"I don't know what's happening to him," Yumi said. "I'm not sure he told us everything he went through here, let alone in a world full of magic."

"So, we just wait?"

"No," Yumi said. "We wait and trust. If we'd done that a little more when he was here, he might not have left so angry."

Ketevan didn't respond, knowing it would do her no good. While she didn't strictly disagree with her new boss, she had her own views on how Jason had conducted himself. His anger and refusal to explain what he was doing in the wake of his brother's death was understandable, but also counterproductive.

Perhaps it was because Jason wasn't family to her, but Ketevan found herself struggling to have the faith in him that Yumi did. She looked at the massive metal wall rusting right in front of her and felt fear. Leaving her fate in the hands of someone else, unable to affect the outcome, was unsettling. He was so far out of reach, in circumstances she would likely never learn. It felt like being trapped in the hand of some capricious god.

The women's attention was drawn to the top of the wall. The turrets, even the ones that had been broken and stopped working, blazed with white-silver light. They spat out lines of light like tracer rounds, savaging the undead below.

"See?" Yumi said. "The boy is dealing with it."

Ketevan didn't say anything. One change did not mean the situation was resolved.

3 7

NO LIMIT

JASON'S SOUL REALM WAS BREAKING. TREES WERE ROTTING AND FALLING over. Buildings crumbled as whole sections fell away, leaving them unable to support their own weight. The ground was turning to purple-black sludge. Ghostly white flames resisted the encroachment, but it was a losing battle. The fire was driven by Jason's will and his will was spent.

Jason stood in the middle of a field, exhausted and barely standing. It had been a long time since pain had bothered him, after years of severed limbs, impalings and even decapitation at the hands of his foes. More than anything else, nothing had been the equal of his first encounter with the Builder. The great astral being had scoured his soul, scraping away at the exterior so Jason would let him in.

This was worse. The power of Undeath was devouring him from the inside out, stripping away his soul and claiming it for itself. It was still driven only by a mindless echo of an absent god, yet that echo struck Jason like thunder, battering him over and over. And once the power had claimed him completely, it would own his will, leaving Jason as nothing but a hollowed-out puppet.

He wanted to keep fighting. Keep resisting and claw back what had been taken. But there was no reprieve, as there had been with the Builder. No clock to run out if he just held on long enough. Jason wasn't rolling over, but there was no more fight left in him either. There was nothing left to fight with.

The soul realm was breaking down, not just physically but in its very nature. Everything was in flux, vulnerable to manipulation by anyone with the will to do so. His sense of the space was shaky at best; his former omniscience failed him. He'd focused enough to shore up certain areas. The space Sophie's mother lived in would hold out longer than most places, as would the underground caverns of the brighthearts. But nothing would last forever. When Jason fell, so would they.

Jason didn't even notice that he'd closed his eyes. Despite the pain, he felt an urge to lie down, as if gravity was growing stronger. He wanted to drop, to close his eyes and let go. He drew a sharp breath through clenched teeth, fighting back against his desire to give up.

Jason opened his eyes and looked at the god's avatar in the distance. It stood still, unmoving, towering over the trees like a kaiju. He knew the physical avatar was dead, but that had always been a shell. The true essence of it was the power of Undeath, and now it was inside of Jason's soul. Even this avatar didn't matter. It was just a representation in his mind, unconsciously created by Jason himself. The power was everywhere, as was the damage it dealt, chewing up the landscape.

Despair tainted Jason's mind, which in turn tainted the land around him. Colour leached from what remained uncorrupted while the corruption grew more vibrant, parts even showing a purple glow. Unable to hold himself upright, Jason dropped to his knees.

"Is this it?" Shade asked with scornful disappointment. "Is this all you amount to, Mr Asano?"

Jason looked up at Shade, pain and hurt written across his expression.

"Shade?"

"What are you doing, Mr Asano?"

"I thought… I thought I could…"

Jason bowed his head, tears pushed out of his eyes as he closed them tightly.

"I thought I was enough," he whispered in shame.

"And now you think you aren't?" Shade asked.

"I'm spent, Shade. I don't have anything left."

"You think will is like mana? That you can burn it off by throwing out a few powers? Use it all up in a fight? Who convinced you it was such a small thing?"

"I can't—"

"The brighthearts are here, Mr Asano. Everything that remains of their entire civilisation. What do you think they are going through right now as all this happens around them? How helpless are they? How fearful?"

"I want to fight, you know I do. I just don't think I can."

"If the spirit is willing, do you think it matters if the body is weak? In this place? You think that's air you're breathing?"

"I'm not breathing. Wait, did you just quote *The Matrix*?"

"I know you are in more pain than you have ever felt. I know that you are only clutching on to sanity because all the pain that came before has prepared you."

"It's not enough," Jason choked out.

"You think that you are at your limit, Mr Asano, but the will has no limit. The only way that your will can be exhausted is if you choose to quit. If you give up on yourself, on your friends, on all the people taking shelter here. You think you cannot fight, but you are fighting. Every moment you don't surrender, the battle goes on. You think you have exhausted your willpower, but it cannot be exhausted. Will has no limit so long as you have the resolve to keep fighting, keep standing."

"I don't know if I can."

"Mr Asano, I have known you for some time now. Do you know what makes you special? What has made you the focus of so many powerful forces, both ally and enemy? Why are people willing to risk everything for you?"

"Rakish charm?" Jason asked, the pained, half-sobbing delivery undercutting the attempt at humour.

"Resolve, Mr Asano. The resolve to help people for no more reason than they need it. To stand when no one else can or will. To make the insane choice because it has to be made, even if it kills you. Time and again you do this, and now you have to do it again. Stand because you have to. Because people need to. Stand, even if you don't think you can. I think you can. I know you can."

Jason looked up at Shade, realising that Gordon and Colin were beside him. Colin, more intimately connected to him than the others, barely stood, ravaged by undeath like the land around them.

"On your feet, Mr Asano. I know you think you've reached your limit, but there is no limit."

"It feels like there's a limit."

"The Builder once tried to convince you that was the case through pain. It was a lie because he knew that all you had to do was tell him no forever and he could do nothing."

"It didn't feel like nothing."

"No, but it was still a lie that you might surrender your soul. And now you are telling yourself that lie. Giving yourself an excuse to give up. To surrender to the pain. We need you to embrace that pain, Mr Asano. To accept it and the fight it represents. Do you have the resolve? Or will you surrender Colin to the god of Undeath? Will you give up on Miss Wexler's mother, on everything left of the brightheart people?"

Jason looked up at Shade as hope, fear and doubt warred across his face.

"I don't know if I can."

"You can, and I will tell you how. You have forgotten the most fundamental lesson about what this place is, or perhaps you never truly learned it."

"What?"

"You have not been human for a long time, Mr Asano, but it is what you still are in your mind. It's why you give yourself limits in a place where you have none. Perhaps you fear what happens when you truly let go of who you are, but that fear is a false one. That isn't who you are but who you were. You left that behind a long time ago, but refuse to admit it to yourself. You keep telling people you aren't human, as if saying it is a talisman that will let you keep hold of your humanity. I'm sorry, Mr Asano, but that slipped through your fingers long ago and you need to accept that if you're going to put up a fight. There is only so far you can push a human, Mr Asano, but you are not human. You've simply used the power of this place to turn yourself into one. When you let go of that idea, you let go of the limitations it imposes on you. It is not the spoon that bends; it is only yourself."

Jason took several sobbing breaths. He leaned forward, putting his fists on the ground to help him get unsteadily to his feet.

Jason's friends, Boris and his messenger army moved through an increasingly miserable landscape. Ethereal ghost fire and glowing purple corruption were all over, with everything else drained of colour and life. They were being led by Nik and one of Shade's bodies, heading for an obvious landmark: the towering avatar.

"I thought that thing died," Sophie said.

"No," Gary said. "The avatar I fought was just a vessel for Undeath's power. When the power moved in here, the vessel out there was left empty and inert."

"So, you can fight it again?"

"Unfortunately," Shade said, "the divine power infusing Mr Xandier will not avail him in this place. Not unless he uses it to try and take over Mr Asano's soul. Which I will thank him not to."

"Why won't it work?" Sophie asked.

"Because Jason's soul realm isn't a true physical space," Clive said. "We're basically roaming around in Jason's imagination."

"Really?" Neil asked.

"No," Clive said. "but it's as good an explanation as you'll get. The reality is nothing like that, but the full explanation is wildly complex and involves metaphysical theory that would take several years of study to grasp. I don't have the time to teach and you don't have time to learn."

"Or the inclination," Neil said.

"Or the ability, let's be honest," Sophie said. "There's no way I get through one lecture by Clive without falling asleep, let alone years of them."

"You don't know what you're missing," Belinda said. "A lot of people would jump at the chance to study under Clive."

"Thank you," he said.

"Mr Standish is correct in stating that Mr Asano's soul realm operates by different rules to a normal physical reality," Shade said. "That is more true now than ever. Because of the nature of this space, your essence abilities will be ineffective."

"Then how do we fight?" Humphrey asked.

"In this place, unless you start trying to take it over for yourselves, as Undeath's power is doing, the only thing that you can use is will. The intent to impose yourself upon the world around you."

"Using will as an active force is something only gold-rankers can do," Arabelle said. "Barring outliers like Jason."

"The nature of this place changes that," Shade explained. "As long as your intent is focused, you will find that enacting your will on the space around you is not just possible, but natural. It will even be a useful head start once they do reach gold rank."

"How do we use it?" Humphrey asked.

"As I stated," Shade explained, "the key is focus. Having a structure to use as the framework for that focus should be extremely helpful. I would recommend attempting to recreate your usual abilities, as not only will this give you a familiar framework but allow you to act in accordance with your own experiences."

"Wait," Sophie said. "You said that using our essence abilities would be ineffective, but now you're saying that the best thing to do is use them?"

"No," Shade said. "I am not telling you to use your essence abilities. I'm telling you to exert your will upon the world around you in a way that replicates the nature of your essence abilities."

"Which basically means using them while really, really wanting them to work," Sophie pointed out.

"That is... not entirely inaccurate," Shade reluctantly conceded. "But I would not call it genuinely representative of—"

"I can see why you're Jason's familiar," Sophie said. "You're awful at explaining things."

Jason stood with eyes closed, shutting out everything. He set aside his sense of the world around him, his own body. His emotions, his exhaustion. Reaching a state of empty mind, he was even able to set aside the pain. Each thing he set aside was left for him to examine in his state of meditative calm.

As always, Shade had turned out to be right. Standing apart from them, he could see how much of what he'd considered his core nature to be artificial. In his soul realm, even his mortality was a fiction he created for himself.

The things that were real were all external to himself, aliens to his personal realm. He could sense his friends, moving to his aid. The terrified masses of the brighthearts underground. There were also the messengers, both his prisoners and those who had arrived with his friends.

The last real thing was the pain. That was the power of Undeath, growing like a cancer to take over everything it could. It was the only thing that challenged Jason's absolute control, the only thing that could change the rules of his world. Jason could turn off death and keep his friends safe, but the enemy could revert that change and kill them. That was unacceptable. If there was going to be a fight over his soul, Jason was going to choose the battlefield. He would set up a fight where his friends would not be sacrificed.

He cast off almost every part of himself, cutting them away until there was nothing left but will, power and the resolve to fight. The pain he would have to keep, to let back into himself in order to fight it. He opened his eyes and found himself before the avatar. He moved forward to accept the pain.

3 8

THE HEGEMON

THE CONTINGENT MAKING THEIR WAY THROUGH JASON'S SOUL REALM HAD two groups. One was Jason's companions, led by Nik and one of Shade's bodies. The other was Boris and his group of messengers. At the advice of Shade and Nik, both groups moved swiftly but not at a breakneck pace. With the world crumbling around them, even flying through the air they could run into a sudden breakout of corruption. They moved quickly, staying close to the ground but not on it. The messengers could fly, while the adventurers who could not floated along in Onslow's shell.

Being in a half-formed astral kingdom in the process of being devoured by a god was the rarest of things for Boris: a completely new experience. For his messengers, it was unnerving in the extreme and he used his aura to keep them settled.

They made their way through gardens wilting with rot and forests where the trees were falling around them. The ground underneath them randomly turned into venomous bog. Tremors shook the ground and air alike, at least once with each passing minute. The cloudless sky occasionally shot lightning and shifted from day to night, swiftly and without warning.

Boris understood what was happening more than anyone in their contingent save for possibly Shade. The nascent reality of Asano's soul realm was unravelling, moving from a physical realm to a nebulous conceptual space. If it moved too far down that path, everyone inside it would be annihilated.

Their destination was the avatar, a looming monolith in the distance. It wasn't moving because it didn't need to. The real power was infesting the land around them. Boris understood it was just a conceptual representation of Undeath's power, but that didn't mean it wasn't useful. It was something for them to focus on in their attempts to aid Asano.

As they drew closer, the building-sized avatar seemed even taller. Belinda leaned out from one of the open sides of Onslow's shell to look up at it.

"What's it doing?" she wondered aloud.

"The avatar is just a representation of Undeath's power," Shade said. "Its attack is not against any specific thing but the realm itself. The corruption going on around us is the damage it is causing."

The group pulled up in a large forest clearing mostly occupied by the avatar's feet. The space around it was oddly clear of its corrupting influence.

"What do we do now?" Taika asked. "Hit it in the ankle?"

"Something like that," Nik said. "I'm going to mess this thing up."

"Is it safe for you to be here?" Humphrey asked. "You don't have essences."

"Were you not listening to Shade's terrible explanation?" Nik asked. "Essences don't mean a damn thing. It's no more or less dangerous for me than for you."

"And this is not truly the avatar," Shade said. "This is a creation of Mr Asano."

"Why would he make the avatar in here?" Taika asked.

"So we have something to hit," Sophie said. "Isn't that what you were talking about with frameworks and will and whatever? The evil power is all over, rotting this place from the inside out. Running around punching trees and dirt won't get us far, but this place is all imaginary. Jason imagined up something we can stick the boot into. If we can visualise something to hit, we can hit it."

Everyone turned to look at Sophie.

"What?" she asked.

"I think," Belinda said, "that they just realised that you find magic theory a lot more comprehensible when the end result is punching something."

"We're adventurers. If the end result isn't punching something, what's the point?"

"Miss Wexler is correct," Shade said.

"She is?" Neil asked.

"About Mr Asano's purpose, not about punching things."

"I'm completely correct about punching things."

"Mr Asano," Shade continued, ignoring her interruption, "created this representation for you all to focus on. There is a danger, however. The same factors that allow you to employ the representation of the avatar as a target allow the power of Undeath to embody the representation."

"Meaning what?" Humphrey asked.

"Meaning the avatar might decide to fight back," Boris said, moving to join the adventurers. "That would be a good thing, though. We're here to divert as much of this thing's attention as we can. If we can push it to inhabit this thing and fight us, that will be a major diversion."

"The suspicious man with the wings is correct," Shade said. "If you can prompt the power to inhabit the representation of the avatar, it will significantly reduce the challenge of Mr Asano's task."

"And standing around here having a nice chat will do nothing," Nik said. "I'm going to attack that thing."

"How?" Taika asked. "Are you going to throw a carrot at its knee?"

Nik started blowing air from his mouth with a sound like a wind passing through a gorge. He rapidly waved two fingers from one hand in front of his face, making a sharp swooshing sound. A small cloud appeared in the air and rushed down towards them.

"Bro, is that the Monkey Magic cloud?"

The cloud stopped in front of them and Nik climbed on. He then reached into the cloud at his feet, pulled out a massive flamethrower and slung it on. The cloud took off in the direction of the avatar, spewing white fire. Taika watched it all play out, jaw hanging down.

"What the hell was that?" Taika asked.

"The reality here is not reality at all," Shade explained. "This place is only a concept, and that concept is breaking down. It affords a unique opportunity for a will without vast power behind it to shape the world as a god might. Master Nik understands this better than most as he has an affinity for this place. But I would advise replicating your essence powers as the most effective—"

"Bugger that for a bag of chips," Taika said as a giant robot descended from the sky.

Nik immediately came flying back, shouting swear words.

"What are you doing?" the rabbit-man shouted.

"I summoned Voltron, obviously," Taika shouted back.

"You summoned *vehicle* Voltron!" Nik accused.

"It's the best Voltron!"

"I'm a month-old rabbit who's never left the pocket universe he was born in and I know that's the worst Voltron."

"How?" Taika asked.

"I don't know. I think knowing that vehicle Voltron sucks is a fundamental aspect of my species."

"Yeah, he was created by Jason alright," Farrah muttered. "Can we please stop talking about Voltron and go fight some evil?"

Farrah stepped forward, conjuring her massive obsidian sword. It was currently in its greatsword state, the blade made up of ragged stone protrusions like a crude saw.

"I'm going to use my essence powers as a framework," she said, "but if we're just making stuff happen..."

Music started blasting out of the sky and Farrah flew into the air, carried on wings of fire.

"Nutbush," Taika said. "Nice. Let's go, Voltron!"

"Pick a better Voltron!"

"Suck it, rabbit!"

Shade watched Taika get picked up by the giant robot, Nik flying alongside as they continued yelling at each other.

"I wonder if Anthony Hopkins needs a familiar?" he wondered.

"Who is Anthony Hopkins?" Clive asked.

"Was that out loud?" Shade asked. "Oh dear."

The adventurers all moved to the attack while the avatar remained still. It showed no signs of injury from any form of attack, which Shade assured them was normal. The goal was to threaten the power, spreading its focus and buying Jason time. The only path to victory was Jason converting what remained of the power from undeath to death energy.

The messengers also went on the attack. Under the direction of Boris, they all started shooting feathers from their wings. The feathers all changed from their original colour during flight, glowing with the silver, gold and blue of transcendent power.

Half of the adventurers followed Shade's suggestion and fought as they would outside the soul realm. Sophie, Humphrey, Rufus and Arabelle all fought as they normally would, expressing their will through confidence in their abilities. Gary fought like his mortal self, although he was still larger than normal with a mane of gold fire.

Stash did not follow Humphrey's example of fighting normally, as much as the shape-shifting dragon did anything normally. He turned into a massive version of Humphrey, as large as the avatar and Taika's robot. He had a bushy moustache and was naked other than for a sandwich board with VOLTRON written across the front and back.

"DID I GET IT RIGHT?" giant Stash bellowed.

"Still not the worst Voltron!"

"Shut up, rabbit!"

"STASH!" Humphrey roared. "Put on some pants!"

Neil, being a healer, ignored his essence abilities and joined Nik and Taika in taking a more imaginative approach. He was standing on the ground, sending a line of massively overweight Jason clones awkwardly waddling towards the avatar, many of them tripping and having trouble getting back to their feet. On reaching the avatar, each one tried to crawl up its leg, failed miserably and exploded.

Onslow floated into the air with Clive and Belinda inside his shell. Clive waved his hands like a conductor as lines of gold light filled the sky, drawing dozens of ritual circles. Not only did they surround the avatar but also stacked up like slices of sausage.

"It would be a waste not to experiment with some of my combat ritual plans for gold rank, given the opportunity," he said.

Ritual circles appeared over Onslow's shell, one in front of each of the runes on Onslow's back. Clive reached his hand out and the little humanoid tortoise that was Onslow reached up to grab it. Clive smiled down at him.

"Go ahead."

Elemental attacks blasted from the runes on Onslow's back; lightning and fire, scouring winds and razor-thin jets of water that could cut steel. They all hit the ritual circles in front of them and vanished. They reappeared, replicated many times over as they emerged from the circles surrounding the avatar. They passed through the layered stacks of circles, growing larger and more powerful with each one they passed through. Each attack became a storm of elemental power that crashed down on the avatar in a blinding cataclysm.

"I think we need some help," Belinda said over voice chat.

"How is the voice chat up?" Humphrey asked. "Is Jason doing it?"

"Nope," Belinda said. "It's just that we can do essentially anything. Made sense to use the weird magic thing to talk to each other at least. I blocked Taika and the rabbit from joining in, though."

"You said we need help," Humphrey said. "What kind of..."

The land shook with the thunder of footfalls as a fourth giant appeared alongside the avatar, the robot and Stash. It looked like Clive, except with the clothing, physique and hairstyle of a woman.

"Belinda," Clive said through clenched teeth.

"Yes, Clive?" she asked, innocent as a puppy.

"What is that?"

"I think you know who that is, Clive."

"That is not my wife!"

"Oh," Belinda said with an awkward wince. "Marital problems?"

Clive's response died in his throat as they all turned to stare at the avatar as it finally started to move.

Hegemon was empty. It had cast away almost every part of itself, from its mortality to its name. There was no space, no time. There was only will, power, resolve, and the pain. It needed to embrace the pain in order to destroy it, but it was unsure how. The pain was strong and hungry.

It was an external thing, something that did not belong. Then, there was something else. Something dancing around the pain like dry leaves floating on the hot air of a bonfire. If the fire flared, they would be burned up. Hegemon found that unacceptable but could not remember why. It just knew that they belonged while the pain did not. It would not allow the pain to burn them.

It knew what to do now. How to fight. Not like a man, as it was not a man. It was the hegemon, and it was time for the pain to understand that. It would not let the pain harm the things around it, even if Hegemon still didn't know what they were. It knew that they had to be protected, and protected they would be.

MIRACLES WORK ON A
DIFFERENT SCALE

THE AVATAR OF UNDEATH IN JASON'S SOUL REALM WASN'T THE MELTING, beleaguered mess the real thing had been when fighting Gary. It stood as tall as a fifteen-storey building, in the fullness of its might. Skinless, red-purple flesh. Wounds that showed not weakness but power, purple light shining from within.

Jason's companions had been attacking it by means ranging from the ordinary to the absurd, the messengers piling on as well. Through it all, there had been no sign of the avatar even noticing. From fire to explosions to transcendent energy, neither essence powers nor bizarre tools of the imagination showed any visible impact. Nothing they did could damage it, but they got what they wanted: a reaction from the avatar.

The looming undead behemoth turned to look around, purple light blazing from empty eye sockets. It took in the giant distaff Clive and the robot made from cheap toy plastic. It didn't blink at the humungous moustachioed Humphrey, naked but for a sandwich board, or the swarm of smaller combatants scattered around it like insects.

The aura of the god of Undeath crashed over everything like a tsunami. The raw potency of it washed away the expressions of will being used to attack the avatar. Essence powers faltered; Mrs Clive and vehicle Voltron vanished, along with Clive's ritual circles that had, moments earlier, filled the sky. Stash was returned to his natural form of an elephant-sized dragon with iridescent rainbow scales. The Tina Turner music stopped blaring and those flying suddenly found themselves falling.

The avatar reached out for the largest of its falling enemies, Stash, moving quickly for its massive size. It grasped only air as thunder went off like a bomb, rocking the avatar back while leaving everyone else untouched. The thunder sounded out a word that shook the air, rumbling but unmistakable.

NO.

The avatar recovered and grasped at Stash a second time. A cloud of sparkling light appeared around the avatar's hand, completely arresting its motion. Although the cloud seemed thin, just motes of blue and orange light, the hand would not shift. As the avatar tugged its arm helplessly, more clouds appeared to catch the falling people and deliver them gently to the ground.

The cloud holding the avatar's hand did not budge, no matter how much the avatar yanked at it. It finally pulled its arm free when the undead flesh tore apart, severing the arm at the wrist. Light sprayed from the stump in fits and starts, like spurting blood. The hand, still inside the cloud, was bleached to a sickly grey. Leached of colour, it burst into ethereal white flame.

On the ground, Jason's companions and their messenger allies were regrouping, recovering after being blasted by the avatar's aura. That aura had been pushed back hard from the moment the peal of thunder had echoed through the sky. Without it pressing on their minds, they could once again muster up the will to fight.

―――――――――

"Are we winning?" Neil asked as a trebuchet wheeled up next to him. "Getting a reaction is what we wanted, right? I'm assuming those clouds are Jason getting in on the fight."

"They are," Shade confirmed. "Mr Asano seems to have resumed converting the power of Undeath for his own ends. The question of whether he will succeed remains unanswered. My connection to him and my fellow familiars feels very odd right now and I am uncertain as to their conditions. I recommend continuing to distract the avatar."

"On it," Neil said. "This whole thing is bizarre."

"Yeah," Clive said, watching Neil pick up a van-sized bundle of Jason clones, squished together inside a net. "That's what's strange here."

Neil loaded the ball of Jasons into the trebuchet and pulled a lever. The trebuchet rocked as it flung the Jasons, who let out squeals of terror until they splattered against the avatar.

"I'm not going to lie," Neil said. "This day is going much better than I expected."

"Neil," Clive said. "People have died today."

"Yeah, but not many, given the circumstances. Can you honestly say you expected casualties to be this low?"

"No," Clive admitted.

"Then take the good news where you can," Neil said. "We haven't gotten a lot of it since we first crawled into that giant hole. I want this all over and done with so I can see some sunlight again."

"I think we're all ready for this to be over," Clive said, "and I think it soon will be, one way or another. I just hope we can endure the consequences."

"You're not wrong," Farrah said, placing a hand on Clive's shoulder as she joined them. "But don't get too caught up in how grim things can be. Jason can be a slow learner, so I hope you figure out faster than he did to take your fun where you can. And since this is the most Jason fight you'll ever have, you may as well go wild."

"Hey," Taika called out. "Does anyone know how to attach a chain gun to a pogo stick?"

The avatar did not dwell on its missing hand, instead turning its attention back to the people preparing to attack it. As it took a step towards them, a giant, nebulous eye appeared in the air in front of it. The avatar reached for the eye as it fired a beam of transcendent light. The beam was thick as it left the eye but narrowed to a pinpoint as it reached the avatar's remaining hand. It swiftly carved a sigil into the monstrosity's palm, the symbol shining with gold, silver and blue light. The moment the beam finished drawing it out, the sigil changed colour to blue and orange and the hand went limp, dangling from the avatar's wrist.

The beam immediately moved on, this time carving sigils into the avatar's forearm. More eyes manifested around the avatar, one after the other, each immediately drawing sigils across the avatar's body. The avatar started producing glowing purple ichor from its eyes, mouth and the missing sections of its body.

Glowing brightly, the viscous liquid crawled over the avatar's flesh. It erased any partially inscribed sigils but did not affect the completed ones. Those had already set in, paralysing parts of the avatar's body.

The avatar paid no more attention to Jason's allies as it concentrated on erasing the sigils. It was a losing fight; there was not enough of the liquid to cover its entire body. The progress was slow, but one sigil after another was completed, each one paralysing a body part. A foot, a forearm. An entire leg, although that was not enough to make the avatar topple. It floated in the air, the foot of one leg and the entirety of the other hanging limp.

On the ground, while the others renewed their attacks, Clive stood peering at the sigils being etched into the avatar's flesh.

"Those look like divine marks," he muttered to himself.

"What are divine marks?" Taika asked distractedly. Most of his attention was on the large round bomb he was manhandling into the sidecar of a motorcycle. He was rushing to get it done before the fuse finished burning down. After getting it in, he slapped Nik, who was sitting astride the motorcycle, on the back. The rabbit-man gunned the throttle and tore off in the direction of the avatar, tyres kicking up dirt and grass. Taika then moved next to Clive.

"What are divine marks?" he asked again. "Is there another god sticking their head in? Isn't it Jason doing that?"

"I have no idea," Clive said. "Divine marks show up when gods perform miracles. Churches record and study them, as you might expect. Mostly, they're hard to see, like soft etchings carved into the landscape around the area where the miracle took place."

Taika pointed at the sigils glowing brightly on the avatar.

"Those aren't hard to see, bro."

"Sometimes they're very easy to spot," Gary said, moving to join them. His conjured armour vanished, revealing glowing gold sigils carved all over his bare torso.

"These are Hero's divine marks," he said.

"They look different to the ones on that avatar," Taika said.

"Each god has their own," Arabelle said. She strolled over while streams of energy flew out from a jar floating over her head to attack the avatar. "I saw the site of one of Healer's miracles. Those markings were hard to find, mostly drawn into dust and dirt on the ground. We had to rush to record them before the wind blew them away."

"The symbols being drawn on the avatar belong to Jason," Boris said. "They are his, and his alone."

The others turned to look at Boris, still leading the messengers some distance away. The tan, muscular messenger's long blond hair whipped around him, the air kicked up by the storm of feathers constantly erupting from his wings. There were so many that they partially obscured him as they rushed forward in a deluge, transforming into transcendent energy as they went. The other messengers were attacking in the same way, but none with Boris' capability. Not only was he throwing more feathers than the others, but his formed a torrent that shifted back and forth like a slithering snake.

The group looked at each other and back at Boris, who didn't seem to be paying them any attention, yet his voice had appeared right amongst them.

"I'm manipulating sound with my aura to reproduce my voice," Boris explained, his voice once again coming from the air right next to them. "Technically, I'm employing an act of will to replicate my aura manipulating sound to reproduce my voice."

"What do you mean by those divine marks belonging to Jason?" Clive asked. "He's not a god."

"Divine marks is your term," Boris said. "I imagine you ended up calling them divine markings because gods are the only people on your world using that magic. The marks are the after-effects of using powerful intrinsic-mandate magic. When your gods do something to physical reality, they're using authority. If they want to project their image into a town square or send a message into the head of one of their worshippers, just having authority is enough for something like that. They don't need to expend any of it. Miracles work on a different scale. Authority isn't intended for use in physical reality, and when you use enough of it, it leaves a mark. For gods, that tends to be subtle because intrinsic-mandate magic is like breathing for them. Unless they use it to alter a person, it's a smooth process. Jason is still feeling his way through it, though. What he's doing is like carving his name in the laws of nature with a blunt knife."

"I didn't think Jason understood intrinsic-mandate magic enough to use it like this," Clive said.

"Oh, he's not," Boris said. "He's done something to himself to make this possible. I told you that gods have a natural understanding of it. I think Jason has used the fact that he's basically a god in here to make himself more like an actual god."

"I believe that my intervention was responsible for that choice," Shade said. "I convinced Mr Asano to take a characteristically drastic step. As I feel the bond with him grow more muted, however, I become increasingly fearful of where the course I have set him on leads."

They all looked up at the suffering avatar. There was little doubt that it was losing out as it hung in the air, mostly paralysed as it thrashed like a strung-up animal.

"What's happening to it?" Neil asked as he stuffed Jason into a cannon with a stick.

"Our efforts have given Jason the chance to play spider," Boris said. "While the power of Undeath was distracted, he snared it in a web. Now it's tangled up and he can slowly devour it. The good news is, we've won. We just have to wait for Asano to finish the job."

"What's the bad news?" Neil asked.

"The Reaper's shadow may have understated when he said Asano did something drastic," Boris explained. "Whatever Asano did to himself, I don't know how much of him will be able to come back from that."

"I think I know what he means," Farrah said. "My bond with Jason feels like what Shade described. Muted; blanked maybe. Like parts of him are gone."

"Bond with Jason?" Taika asked. "Have you secretly been his familiar this whole time? Is that how he brought you back from the dead?"

"No," Farrah said. "We do have a bond, and yes, it was formed when we came back from the dead together."

"You're totally his familiar."

"I am not his familiar!" Farrah snapped. "Once Jason started down this astral king path, that was when he realised the bond was there. We discussed it and decided to strengthen it, even though he had no idea what he was doing. We barely notice it, even now. Not unless one of us is really in distress, which is inevitably him, obviously."

"Get back to what Jason has done to himself," Clive said. "You said he's been blanked somehow? What did you mean by parts of him are missing?"

Boris answered in place of Farrah.

"There are conclusions we can draw based on what we've seen here and what the Reaper's child and the lovely Farrah have described."

"Might I suggest," Shade interrupted, "that you avoid harassing one of

Mr Asano's most precious friends while he is in the middle of a rampage using the same mechanisms as a god does when performing a miracle."

"That is an excellent point," Boris said. "Anyway, I believe that Asano has given over his mortal aspect to the part of himself that is becoming an astral king. But that astral king part is incomplete and his mortal aspect is too weak. He's in danger of losing himself."

"I know," Jason's voice said. "Scary, right?"

They turned to look at what looked like Jason standing behind them in his blood robes.

"Colin," Shade said. "You're his Voice of the Will; your connection to Mr Asano is stronger than anyone's. Do you know what is happening to him?"

"Yep," Colin said. "Dad basically put himself in a box so he could go full god mode."

He winced in pain and staggered as the front of his head turned into smooth, featureless skin. His blank face shifted as if something was crawling under it before returning to normal.

"That was rough," he said, his voice strained. "As I was saying, he put himself in a box so he could go back to normal when he was done playing god, and I'm the box. The problem is, while being so close to him meant he could copy himself onto me, he wasn't exactly precise about wiping himself away."

"Whatever he did to himself," Clive clarified, "it's spreading to you."

"Yeah," Colin said. "I'm going to need some help from someone else with a bond once he's done with his little project. As soon as he's done consuming the power, we need to turn him back to normal."

"What of Gordon?" Shade asked. "He's not a Voice of the Will, but he did bond with Mr Asano as an avatar. His connection is stronger than mine or Miss Farrah's."

Colin waved at the sky full of eyebeams.

"Dad roped him into making all that work. I don't think he'll be up to it."

"Well, then," Farrah said. "I guess you'd best tell us what we need to do."

4 0

RIGHT NOW

THE AVATAR WAS GONE. PIECES OF IT HAD BEEN WRENCHED AWAY, ONE BY one, and consumed by white fire. The final destruction of the avatar marked the final excision of the god of Undeath's power and Jason's soul realm immediately grew more stable. White flames kicked up into an inferno that was harmless to the living but swept across the landscape. Where it passed, damage was repaired and the marks of corruption were wiped away.

From the moment that process had begun, Shade, Farrah and Colin had been trying to contact Jason. They stood facing each other in silence, eyes closed, as everyone else looked on. They stayed that way for a long time, no one saying anything.

"So," Nik said. "This is exciting."

"Hush, you," Arabelle told him.

"You're not the boss of…"

Nik trailed off as he met Arabelle's gaze. As he bowed his head, Rufus gave him a brotherly pat on the shoulder.

Colin opened his eyes, followed by Farrah.

"This isn't working," she said.

"We're reaching him," Colin said. "He's not reaching back. I don't think there's enough of him left to understand who or what we are. If we can just get him to connect with me, it will all—"

He was cut off as his facial features were once again replaced with blank skin. It was happening for longer each time, and with each restoration, more of Jason's divine markings were being etched into Colin's body.

"We have to find a way to make him reach out for me," Colin said. "I don't know how much longer before I'm as blank as he is and we're both lost."

"We need something that resonates with Mr Asano," Shade said. "Something that links him to the parts of himself he left in Colin, but is still part of him as he is now."

"He purged all of that and put it into me," Colin said. "There's nothing left."

"Some things are left," Farrah said. "God Jason didn't just defend himself against Undeath's power; he protected us. He left enough of his normal self in there to know what was important. Part of him is still in there."

"That is what we need," Shade said. "Something from Mr Asano's very core. Something so intrinsic to who he is that it remains a part of him, no matter how much of himself he casts aside."

Farrah paced around, rubbing a hand over her tired face. She froze when her eyes fell on Nik.

"Something intrinsic," she said.

"That's right," Shade said. "To connect him with the aspects of his identity that he set aside, we need to find a fragment of his original identity that he retains even now. Something fundamental to who he is."

Farrah grinned.

―――――――

Hegemon was uncertain. It did not know the path forward. It had understood exactly what it needed to do: excise the antagonist, take the pain and consume it. That was done and now its purpose was gone. Its realm was clear. There were outside elements it did not understand, but they were not the antagonist. They were not the pain. They were from the outside, but they belonged.

Prisoners, friends, refugees. Hegemon knew the words, if not their meaning; taken from memories put aside because they kept it from being what it had needed to be. What it knew was that they'd needed protection, so protect them it did. Now, some of them were reaching out, but Hegemon did not understand. Strange connections reached out but they meant nothing. They spoke to parts of Hegemon that had been sent away that he might become what he was.

The connections stopped. It felt a loss but was unsure why. Then they came back, with one message, not the scattered meaningless garble of before. This was singular, speaking to a part of Hegemon that it did not realise remained. Something buried deep within itself, like the key to a lock. He heard a voice and thought of strawberry blond hair and a savage smile.

"Vehicle Voltron is the best Voltron."

Hegemon felt something surge up from within. A response, driven by a part of itself it did not know still existed.

Well, that is some bullsh—

"—it right there," Jason said, suddenly standing between Farrah, Colin and Shade. He blinked as if waking up to find he'd been sleepwalking. He was naked but for a pair of lion Voltron boxer shorts. Colin slammed into him, wrapping him in a hug.

"Oh, hey, buddy. You did good."

"I'm so glad you're back," Colin said.

"Me too."

"I want to eat people again like normal."

"He meant to say 'eat like normal people again,' right?" Neil asked.

"Sure," Jason said unconvincingly.

"All I've wanted to eat since this started is sandwiches," Colin complained. "It's been awful."

"I know, buddy," Jason said, patting him on the back.

"I haven't thought about marinating Neil's thighs this whole time."

"Wait, what did he just say?" Neil asked.

"Don't worry about it," Jason said.

"I'm extremely worried about it!"

"Neil, it's fine," Jason assured him. "Colin's a good boy and he's done very well. Which is why he deserves a treat, and since you're a healer…"

"Absolutely not! I want a soul portal out of here right now."

One popped up right next to him, and he immediately all but jumped through it. A moment later, he came back out with a glower on his face.

"Jason," he said through gritted teeth.

"Yes, Neil?" Jason asked as Colin finally let him go.

"That portal did not lead outside your soul realm but into a kitchen."

"Did it? The old powers must still be a bit wonky. I just fought a god, you know."

The messengers were shuffling through the portal to leave Jason's soul realm. The landscape was a blasted wasteland, ravaged by the recent battle. Boris stood beside Jason, watching his messengers leave.

"Not you," Jason said.

Tera Jun Casta was plucked out of the group as if by an invisible hand, loudly protesting as she was whisked away.

"Who is that?" Boris asked. "She's not one of mine."

"She's… it's complicated. She challenged me with a duelling power and I had to do something drastic to keep us both alive."

"You survived a duel power?"

"Yeah. But I had to break her to do it. Torment her soul until she opened it up and I could shut the power down. I purged her brand while I was at it, but I had no idea what I was doing. I still don't know how much damage I did. She's a true believer, and she hates me."

"That's good," Boris said.

"Really? Because everything I just said seems bad to me. She's in my soul, so I know everything she does. Everything she feels. The loss of purpose; the loss of faith. How she hates what I've made her as much as she hates me for doing it. Sometimes I wonder if it wouldn't have been kinder to kill her."

"The hate is good. She'll need to get past it, but it means she's fighting. There's passion there. The trauma of having your soul attacked until you capitulate and open it up is something few come back from. Most just shut down. Of course she's damaged, but she's alive and she's fighting. There's a path forward, however long and rocky it might be. That's good. And setting her free is good, even if she hates you for it. I have no time for that 'slavery is good because house elves like serving humans' crap."

"I don't know what to do with her. I have these other messengers who are keen to join the Unorthodoxy, but that also makes her angry. And they're a bit zealous. I don't think fanaticism from the other side of messenger politics is what Tera needs."

"You have messengers that want to join the Unorthodoxy?"

"I don't think they realise how many of you are out there," Jason said.

"Their leader seems to think it's a few isolated cells. Keeps talking about 'the seeds of revolution' and such. I don't think he'll know what to do with himself when he finds out the rest of you are out there. Can you take them off my hands?"

"I can do that. I'd like… could I prevail upon you to keep this conversation private?"

The air around them shimmered as a privacy screen was set in place.

"Thank you," Boris said. "As I was saying, I would like your aid in erasing my soul brand, and sooner rather than later. The astral king I used is an ally, but I don't like not being my own man."

"That's a lot of trust, letting me in your soul."

"I'm in yours right now."

"And what does being in mine tell you?"

Boris chuckled.

"That making you an enemy would be a very bad idea. I would like your trust, Asano. Jason. I know that's hard when I'm a messenger who knows so many answers you want. So much about you, and you aren't sure how or why."

"I know you have to have been on Earth, and not for a short time. I know that Earth went through a lot and I didn't see you coming out to help."

"We were there, and we did what we could from the shadows. Do you think a secret army of angels appearing would have calmed things down? When magic had just been revealed, the monster surges were happening and the religions were already in a frenzy?"

"I can see there would be complications."

"There was also the matter of an agreement made long ago. To hide ourselves from you until the time was right."

"An agreement with whom?"

"Noreth. You might know him as—"

"Mr North. The rune spider."

"We were wondering how much he revealed to you."

"I knew he had more secrets. Things he refused to tell me. For my own good, so he claims."

"For what it is worth, I believe he was right."

"Then you won't tell me what he was hiding? Other than your existence, obviously."

"I won't. I realise that will make it harder to gain your trust."

"Not as much as you'd think. Someone I already trust also warned me not to try and find out. That it would do more damage than it would prevent."

"You speak of Dawn?"

"You know her?"

"Only by reputation. And occasionally spotting her with you when there was footage of you on the news. Farrah is a somewhat known quantity to the people of Earth, but Dawn remains a mystery. The internet theories are—"

"I know what internet theories are like."

Boris laughed again.

"So, the issue of trust. It seems that if I want your trust, then giving you mine is a strong, perhaps even necessary first step. And since I need someone to go into my soul for some spring cleaning, that works out nicely."

"You've done this before, haven't you? Taken on a brand to infiltrate messenger operations?"

"Many times."

"You'd have to have a fairly well-developed soul space, then."

"I do. There's no budging a brand without an astral king's help, though. I can finish it myself, once the process has begun. I've done it enough times that I'm an old hand at it now, but I need someone to loosen the jar before I can get at the pickles."

Jason nodded.

"Once I step out of here, I'm going to get hit with the side effects of having claimed around a quarter of the whole transformation zone from the avatar. Once I get over that, I'll do it."

"What about side effects from your fight in here?"

"It's fine. I've rampaged through here a few times myself. Used my astral throne and astral gate more than I should."

"You're an incomplete astral king. You shouldn't be using them at all."

"I know, right? But I've battered things up in here enough that I'm pretty much inured to the level of damage Undeath's power did. It'll finish healing up before I'm done absorbing that massive chunk of transformation zone."

"You are a dangerous man, Jason Asano."

"I suspect, Boris, that you are more dangerous still."

"I've had a long time to work on it. You're younger than *Jurassic Park* and I'm older than the Jurassic period. By a considerable margin."

"How considerable?"

"Enough that I suspect I'll be dodging your friend Clive and his questions for some time."

"I might have a few questions of my own."

"As I said, there are some I won't answer. I suspect I have a lot of historical context to offer, but knowledge is power, and power does not come cheap."

"How about we start with why you're still gold rank if you're that old?"

"That is an important secret of the Unorthodoxy. Sharing it would be a greater act of trust than letting you in my soul. It imperils not just me but my entire people."

"You're telling me that the Unorthodoxy has some secret that no enemy astral king has dug out in the last however many squillion years?"

"That's not a real number."

"But that is a real deflection. You're trying to sell me a secret the other side probably found out before my planet existed."

Boris let out a villain's laugh.

"You can't blame a guy for trying. It is a secret, though, just not from the enemy astral kings. It's from the rank-and-file messengers."

"Because it's related to how their astral kings drain their potential for authority?"

"Exactly. What we've discovered is that we can learn to tap into our own potential. Stall ourselves out at a given rank in return for more power at that rank. We can't generate authority from it the way an astral king can, but it gives us what amounts to overcharged mana that we can use to enhance our abilities. I wasn't lying about its importance to the Unorthodoxy. It's one of our key weapons."

Jason looked around, despite it not being necessary to know anything happening in his realm. He had an odd sense that if he didn't take the time to act like a mortal, he might fall out of the habit.

"Your people are almost all out," he said, "and mine are getting suspicious about my secret talks with the enemy."

"I'm not your enemy."

"I'm not going to start putting everyone with wings into camps, Boris, but the messengers have a lot to answer for. Fair or not, it's going to take a lot to build goodwill with people. Including with me. At some stage, we need to talk about why you're here and what you want."

"We do. But, as you said, my people are all out and yours are looking at us funny. That's my cue to go."

Jason's companions followed the messengers out through the portal until Jason and Humphrey were watching the last of their friends depart.

"Not going?" Jason asked.

"Jason, you and I need to talk."

"It seems like my near future involves a lot of serious conversations. Is right now really the time to do this?"

"Yes, Jason. This is the time and the place."

41

LEADERSHIP ISN'T EASY

JASON WALKED ACROSS THE WIDE GRASSY MEADOW WHERE HIS companions had confronted the avatar. Humphrey followed as they headed for the forest surrounding the area, moving around holes left by giant feet. The sky darkened, day turning to night by the time they reached the trees ringing the space. Jason led them into the woods and they soon came across a much smaller clearing. A few logs were set up as makeshift benches around a campfire.

A glass-fronted refrigerator stood incongruously off to the side and Jason took out a couple of glass mugs full of beer. He handed one to Humphrey and they sat, looking at one another across the fire. Humphrey sipped at his beer and then peered into the mug, his expression startled.

"This tastes like... the feeling you get when a litter of adorable puppies jumps all over you."

"Yep."

"How is that even possible?"

"My house, my rules. Are you sure you don't want to do this somewhere we're on more even footing?"

"I'm not afraid of your power, Jason. Or of you reading my emotions. When we get out of here, you're going to be praised for doing yet another impossible thing. Deservedly so, but I need you to understand something before you get caught up in all that."

Jason nodded. "You're disappointed. And angry. Why?"

Humphrey looked down at his feet, not speaking for a long time. When he finally did, he asked a question in a quiet voice without raising his head.

"Do you still want to be a part of this team?"

Jason jumped to his feet.

"How can you even ask me that?"

Humphrey looked up, a sad smile on his face.

"Have you ever considered what it's like being on your team from the perspective of everyone else?" he asked. "Did you realise that since you and I formed this team, you've spent more time away from us than with us? Dead, or presumed so. Convalescing. On the other side of the world."

Jason opened his mouth to reply, but Humphrey raised a hand to forestall him.

"I know," Humphrey said. "There are always the best of reasons. But something being justified doesn't mean it didn't happen. It doesn't make the ramifications go away. We accept that you spend so much time apart from us, Jason, but that doesn't make it easy. We've spent a lot of time figuring out what our team is without you in it. We've had to."

"Humphrey…"

"Don't, Jason. Let me talk."

Jason looked unhappy but nodded and sat back down.

"I know how important trust is for you, Jason. It is for any team, but what you went through while you were away from us made you especially sensitive to it. So I know how much our trust means to you."

Humphrey let out a sigh.

"I also know that you're afraid, Jason. Afraid that what you are in this place will take you away from us. We're afraid of that too, and it almost happened today. The problem is, we didn't know what was happening or why. Not for far too long. There were dangers here we had no idea about because you didn't tell us."

Jason looked at the ground, unable to meet Humphrey's eyes.

"It had to be done."

"Yes," Humphrey agreed.

"I was afraid you'd try to stop me."

"Why?" Humphrey asked, loud and angry. "Why in the world would you think that? How many times have we been here, Jason? When did we ever not go along with one of your lunatic, self-sacrificial plans? When did we try to stop you? Was it when you overcharged your portal to get us out of that underwater complex, even when Clive said it would probably kill you? Which it very nearly did. Or when you got into a knife fight with the Builder, which actually did kill you. We went along with it all because that's what needed to be done, consequences be damned."

Humphrey got to his feet and stalked back and forth in front of the campfire in short, jerky steps.

"We supported you, Jason, even when we were sure we would lose you. You've always had our trust, always, but today, we didn't have yours. You didn't think we would trust you, so tell me when that idea crawled into your head. Tell me when we ever gave you a reason to doubt that we would do anything but stand by you."

"Never," Jason whispered, tears welling in his eyes.

"Never," Humphrey echoed. "You didn't tell us that you would have to open up your soul. What that would mean for us. You made a plan and only brought us in when you absolutely had to. Instead of giving us a chance to prepare, you had your minions tell us when there was no other choice. If we'd known, if we'd been ready, we could have done more. Done better. At the very least, we could have had some understanding of what we were walking into."

Humphrey stopped pacing, his voice growing louder as he talked.

"Instead of being warned by our teammate, we learned half of what we needed from a messenger and the rest we had to figure out ourselves. We had to figure it out when everything was already on the line because you wouldn't trust us to trust you. To support you. To be there for you the way we have been every time. Every single time."

Humphrey sat down hard enough to make the wood of the log creak. His shoulders slumped, and when he spoke again, his vitriol was gone. All that was left was a weary hollow voice.

"As your team leader," he said, "that is unacceptable. As your friend, you hurt me. We battled a god today, Jason, but the greatest wound I suffered came from you. You're so afraid of losing our trust that you're acting like you already have. We deserve better than that."

Jason nodded, too ashamed to meet his friend's gaze.

"You do. I'm sorry."

"I don't want your apologies, Jason. They don't matter. What matters is that you don't trust us the way we trust you."

"Humphrey, I—"

"Don't," Humphrey said. "We both know your mouth moves faster than your judgement. Instead of saying the wrong thing quickly, do the right thing slowly. Let the way you act going forward be your response.

We're not going anywhere, which is the whole point. We're always with you, Jason. You're the one who keeps leaving us behind."

Jason nodded again, his head bowed. Tears landed in the dirt.

"This isn't what you want to hear," he said, "but I'm going away again. After we get the soul forge. I don't know how long it's going to take, but becoming a full astral king won't be quick. Or simple."

Humphrey stood up, moved around the campfire and placed a hand on Jason's shoulder.

"We'll be waiting when you get back. We always are."

———

Jason stepped out of the portal and looked around. He waited for a moment and then smiled.

"I think it'll be okay," he said. "I don't feel anythiaaaARGH!"

He fell to the ground, twitching and groaning in the red desert sand. Humphrey leaned over him, looking down with concern.

"Jason?"

Jason let out a whimpering moan.

"I went to the toilet on myself."

———

In Jason's mountain lair, he was lying on the couch in his office with a bag of frozen peas on his face. Gordon, still recovering from being Jason's weapon in his hegemon state, was floating around the room unsteadily. The double doors swung open to admit Farrah. She leaned against the door frame in a relaxed pose.

"You should have knocked," Jason said with a groan.

"You've been dropping everyone who knocks through the floor trap in front of the door."

"I'm going to miss this place."

"Not if we don't get out of this transformation zone. Are you up for claiming some territories?"

"Territories plural?"

"You've been recuperating for almost two weeks. We may only be mostly using gold-rankers to clear them, but we've got a few set up for you to take. If you feel up for it."

Jason's response was a groan.

"Where did you even get frozen peas?"

"The supermarket. In the freezer section that you cleared all the ice cream out of."

"There was other stuff in there? Anyway, are you up for claiming some territories or not?"

"I'm still feeling pretty seedy. I'm not sure if claiming more territory before I've fully recovered from claiming the last one is a good idea. Ask Neil and Carlos to come check me out. If they give me the all-clear, I'll do it."

"Speaking of healers, Arabelle has been waiting to talk with you since the battle. She's worried about the impact of what you went through."

Jason groaned again.

"I'm definitely not doing that until my everything stops hurting."

"Is there something you don't want to talk about with her?"

"No."

"Nothing about Humphrey telling you off?"

"No, it's... it's like I'm waiting to not be okay after what happened. It feels like I should be more messed up than I am. I think I've been waiting for it to hit me harder before I talk to the person who can help me fix it."

"You think you're not messed up in the head enough? That's pretty messed up in the head."

"Go away."

Farrah stopped leaning against the door frame and moved further into the room.

"Jason you—"

She yelped as a trapdoor opened underneath her and she fell through. The trapdoor closed behind her, all but invisible set into the floor.

"I'm definitely going to miss this place."

———

"Since you finally claimed those cleared territories," Miriam told Jason, "I've completely excised all silver-rankers from the teams clearing territories, even under gold-rank supervision."

They were walking down the middle of a street that ran alongside the water. It led to the marina in the replica of Jason's hometown and the car park being used as a staging area.

"I thought you already cut out the silvers," he said.

"There were a few exceptions. People whose power and skill sets made them both useful and likely to survive. The territory that Boris handed over was an appreciable amount of land, even without the territories we cleared during your convalescence. Now that you've claimed them, the power of the anomalies has passed a risk threshold I'm willing to send any silvers into. I've even started consolidating the gold-rank groups."

"What about Boris and his messengers? You decided to use them in the end?"

"They're not any less trustworthy than the Builder cultists, and I'm using them. I'm only using the gold-rank messengers. They only have three, but Boris himself is a monster. You know they say that messengers are closest to matching an essence-user rank-for-rank?"

"Yeah, but I've never seen one close to an elite adventurer. Boris seemed strong from what little I saw on the battlefield, though. You think he stacks up?"

"More than stacks up. Other than our demigod, I don't think any of our gold-rankers could take him one-to-one. Maybe Lord Pensinata."

"Boris makes you uneasy."

"There's very little I've encountered since meeting you that doesn't make me uneasy, Operations Commander. If I'm being honest, you unsettle me more than he does."

"Really?"

Miriam pointed to the sky where a pair of messengers were flying overhead. Their hair and eyes were white and their skin was pale. Their wings were mostly white feathers, with a few scattered black, red and gold ones amongst them. Their wings were also wreathed in ethereal white flame.

"Boris Ket Lundi is strong," Miriam said, "but strength I understand. You've turned those corpse-looking messengers we captured into something else. Something that looks alive, and you did it with death energy, of all things. You're reshaping people. Reshaping reality."

She glanced up at the image of Jason's head carved out of a mountain.

"Your battles, your enemies," she continued. "They exist on a different scale to anything I understand. And I don't mean just further along the power scale; I mean on a different track entirely."

She stopped walking and turned to look out over the water.

"Jason, your conflicts are spiritual. Cosmic. I've taken reports from everyone who witnessed your final battle with Undeath's power, if you can even call it a battle. None of it makes any sense. You fight invisible wars where metaphors and imagination are deadly weapons. Where the prize is reality itself. You're a silver-ranker fighting gods, and that only works because there's a plane of existence I neither see nor understand. It doesn't align with the world in which I exist."

She gestured around with her arms.

"But now I'm here, in some liminal space where the laws of nature and magic are reduced to guidelines at best. I don't know what the rules are and I barely understand the stakes anymore. Death and destruction, spilling into the real world? What does that even look like now that we've dealt with the undead?"

"If we don't settle this transformation zone cleanly," Jason said, "what will result is a seeping wound in reality. How bad, I don't know, but it's enough that the god of Destruction was hoping for an outcome a lot like this. I chose to create this transformation zone; it was my plan. It's my responsibility to put an end to it, but I can't do it alone. Not even close."

They looked to the distant horizon and the tree jutting to the sky, impossibly tall.

"So," Miriam said. "You're saying it's a vaguely defined but extremely bad thing if we don't capture the big magic tree?"

"Yeah."

"Honestly," Miriam said, "you aren't the one I want to be talking to. You're *what* I want to talk about, not who I want to talk about it with. But I was trained better than to vent to my subordinates and you're the only one who doesn't answer to me."

"Leadership isn't easy. I highly recommend speaking with Arabelle Remore. She can help you, plus she understands me and my secrets better than almost anyone. I'll give her permission to talk about some of that if it will help you work with me. She's also oath-bound to the Healer to maintain privacy. An oath I can assure you she takes very seriously. You can speak with her without compromising the dignity of your position."

"Didn't I hear that she's been chasing you around to talk to her?"

"I have no idea what you're talking about."

4 2

A DECISION MADE POORLY AND IN HASTE

JASON AND BORIS WERE AT THE BEACH IN JASON'S REPLICA TOWN, SITTING in cheap folding chairs. Boris had put away his wings and shrunk himself down to human size, as he typically did around humans. His long blond hair was teased by the ocean wind, leaving it dancing around his square-jawed features. The sun shone from his tan, muscular chest.

"Could you please do your shirt all the way up?" Jason asked. "You look like the cover of a romance novel from the eighties, and don't even try and tell me it's not on purpose."

Boris laughed and left his shirt how it was.

"How are your messengers doing?"

"Not great," Boris admitted. "I railroaded them into all this and it doesn't sit well. Being around non-messengers without subjugating them goes against all their behavioural programming."

"They aren't ready for the Unorthodoxy?"

"They are not. On one hand, messenger indoctrination works. On the other, your aura is everywhere here. They can feel it in the territory you've claimed, even when you tamp it down. The incomplete but unmistakable feel of an astral king, but without the power. It's an undeniable refutation of everything they've been taught about who and what they are. The promises they've been made about their futures. The conflict between their indoctrination and the evidence of their senses is causing some dangerous cognitive dissonance."

"Some of them had to have at least had doubts. The gold-rankers?"

"One of my two gold-rankers was ready, thankfully. All she needed was to get away from her astral king and get a little nudge. She's been key in helping me keep a lid on all this. The other gold-ranker wasn't ready for this, but he's adapting. The silver-rankers are the issue. I've removed them from a life where they can only follow orders and don't have any choices, but I didn't give them a choice about it and I've been ordering them around ever since. This is not the way we like to do things."

"But circumstances didn't allow that."

"No," Boris confirmed. "No, they did not. We go slow and careful when bringing people in, like cult deprogramming. That's just not possible with everything going on. I was stuck choosing between killing them all or forcibly bringing them along."

"I'm glad you kept so many of the messengers alive that you claimed from the territories," Jason said.

"I'm glad that you've done the same," Boris said. "I'm sure many argued against it. How are *your* messengers doing?"

They looked up, spotting messengers on the wing. There were always a few to be seen in the sky over Jason's town. Disregarding living anomalies, and with the destruction of the undead army, the most populous group in the transformation zone were messengers. Only a fraction was under the command of Boris. Most had been sealed away in the territories of the transformation zone, then unsealed as territories were claimed.

These messengers were born with the power to speak every language and an understanding of the cosmos that some spent lifetimes striving and failing to achieve. Yet, they were children, amnesiacs without history or identity. Jason had freed all that he and his allies could safely steal away from the enemy, but many had been killed.

The survivors now lived within Jason's mountain fortress and could be seen flying around it and over the town. At first, they had been extremely hesitant to emerge from their dormitories. They clustered together like herd animals cornered by a predator. Slowly, they had grown more confident, and while they still kept to themselves, they claimed the sky as their domain. A place they belonged and could feel free.

"I'll admit that I'm at something of a loss," Jason said. "I have no more idea of what to do with them than they have of what to do with themselves."

"It's good that you freed them from outside control," Boris said.

"Even yours, which I appreciate. With enough patience—or ruthlessness —they represent a lot of power."

"Getting more power has never been difficult for me. It's holding on to my decency that's proven the hard part."

"Freeing them wasn't hard, was it? Freedom is part of the problem with my messengers. They're still branded by Vesta Carmis Zell and know that she'll kill them the moment they leave this place. Obviously, you removing their brands is the solution to that, but most of them aren't ready to take that leap. Letting you into their soul might be harder for them to accept than joining the Unorthodoxy. You had no such problems with the territory messengers, though."

"No. I didn't have to dig through their souls and find a mark to erase. It's like they were waiting for someone to give them a destiny."

"That is how young messengers are," Boris said. "Astral kings need to imprint something on them; it's a normal part of our reproductive cycle. In the beginning, the astral kings guided newborn messengers in forming their own marks, in their own souls. It laid a groundwork for them to forge their own destinies."

"Obviously not how it works anymore."

"Not outside of Unorthodoxy birthing planets."

"Are there a lot of those?"

"No. The orthodox messengers are diligent about hunting them down. If we have too many birthing planets, we get noticed. More resources are put into hunting us down. We hide because we lack the numbers to fight using different methods to mask our presence in each place. That way, losing one site doesn't expose all our methods."

"Is Earth one of your birthing worlds?"

"Not enough magic for the birthing trees. What would you do if I'd said yes?"

"Nothing," Jason said. "Even messengers deserve to live, and your people have been there a long time. Like the vampires. If I can tolerate vampires, I can tolerate messengers. How many of you are on Earth?"

"I don't know the exact number. Less than a million, I think."

"A million?"

"We live amongst the humans, leading mostly ordinary lives. We're citizens of Earth and have been since before the first civilisation. It's our home. A home many of us wanted to protect more actively as magic came into the open and the monster surges began. It was the most contention we've had amongst our people in centuries."

"But you didn't act."

"We did more than you think, and more still, after you left. We've become increasingly active in the Cabal, especially after the vampire schism."

"What is going on with the vampires on Earth?"

"It's war. Not open battle; more like skirmishes between elite forces, but a lot of them. Combat began in earnest shortly after you left, as if the vampires were waiting on your absence. I think you made an impression on the vampire leader, Elizabeth."

"What is the state of the war?"

"When I left, it had quieted into a stalemate. The vampires have most of Europe, although there are holdouts. The Cabal holds some of the UK and Scandinavia. The Network have set up in Greenland. Your domains are clear. The magic around them is too strong, making the sunlight dangerous for vampires. Your grandmother has been leveraging that, letting the human forces use your territories as staging areas."

"How unified are the vampires? I know at least some of them were fighting against the vampire lords."

"Most of the vampires chose not to follow the risen vampire lords. Like my people, they have been around longer than any of the short-lived humans. They only obeyed the vampire lords when they were forced to through bloodline magic or the threat of death. The priority of the Cabal has been freeing those vampires from the control of the risen lords."

"Weren't the Cabal vampires the ones who dug the old vampires up?"

"Yes, and there were eager collaborators even amongst those who weren't involved in bringing the lords back. But most of team Eat People to Death are new vampires, created by the lords themselves. The Cabal vampires escaped their influence as soon as they could. The whole mess caused a schism in the Cabal and cleaning house was ugly. We cast out any vampires that sided with the risen lords willingly."

"What happened to the vampires who went against the vampire lords? Humanity doesn't have a great track record of accepting people while at war with others of the same group, and that's when everyone is human."

Boris glowered.

"About what you'd expect," he said in an almost-growl. "The vampires siding with humanity should be one of their greatest assets, but the humans are as you've said. Most governments and magical factions are killing vampires on sight."

"Not even internment camps?"

"There were some attempts made, but camps mean logistics," Boris said.

"Ah," Jason said. "They're not going to set up a supply chain of human blood."

"No. Some did try holding vampires at the beginning. Very quietly. Smaller groups, containment facilities. The kind of experiments they'll be talking about fifty years from now in high school history classes."

"Only at the beginning? They stopped?"

"I imagine there are some still operating, but we liberated most of them. We think."

"We?"

"The Cabal. Some sympathetic members of the Network factions and even some within government groups. Humans can be crappy, but they can also surprise you at how far they can go to do what's right."

"I have a vampire friend. I hope he's alright."

"Craig Vermillion was alive and well the last time I saw him," Boris said. "Alive-ish, anyway. It's a grey area with vampires."

"You know him?"

"I didn't, but he's Cabal and we've been investigating you as best we can. Your friend is residing in secret with your clan. Vampires have long been good at hiding, and they have allies. Ultimately, a relatively small number were caught or killed."

"Relatively small is not the same as small."

"No," Boris agreed. "No, it isn't, and what the humans are doing is only turning would-be allies to side with the vampire lords. Fortunately, most of the refuges aren't secret, so a few vampires going over to the murdery side isn't hurting us."

"Refuges?"

"There are safe zones for vampires who aren't turning to the lords. Mostly in areas where the Cabal holds sway, where we've displaced the Network factions and openly joined or even completely ousted governments. Scandinavia, parts of Russia and Africa. Sulawesi and Papua."

"Sulawesi? Where Makassar is?"

"Yes. Indonesia is one of several countries where the rise of magic has turned old fractures into fresh breaks. Sulawesi and Papua have both declared independence with Cabal support. Military crackdowns failed miserably as the government's Network allies were too busy with their own factional conflicts to go up against the Cabal. The Cabal, on the other hand, has been getting stronger very quickly. So many of our members had stalled in power because of Earth's low magic. Now that magic has risen, it's like a drought has broken. Our people are growing stronger and stepping into the light."

"You think they can create havens for the vampires not going bad?"

"No. The same rise in magic making the Cabal stronger is making the vampires more aggressive. Not feral, but cold. It degrades their empathy even as it raises their hunger."

"A bad combination."

"Indeed."

"Will I even recognise Earth when I go back?"

"It will have changed," Boris said. "But will you have changed any less?"

"I suppose not."

They sat in silence for a time, looking out over the water.

"We are going to do this, right?" Boris asked. "Clear off my brand?"

"I still have doubts," Jason said. "When you first showed up, you said that Vesta Carmis Zell was your astral king and you needed to clear her brand."

"Technically, I implied it. Quite heavily, I'll admit. I was hoping you'd rush over and purge the brand if you thought it was hers."

"I was a little busy."

"It's months later and I'm still branded, so I figured that out."

"Lying to me didn't help your case."

"Oh, like you've never let someone make the wrong assumption for your own benefit."

"Sure I have. And I understand why they didn't trust me after."

"It was a decision made poorly and in haste, I'll admit. Far from the first, and doubtless far from the last. With age comes wisdom, but if you stop making mistakes, you've stopped living. New experiences are key to going through immortality without calcifying. All I can offer in my defence is the desire to stop being a slave. A chain is a chain, even when the one holding the other end is nice enough not to yank on it."

Jason sat quietly contemplating Boris' words.

"I've been inside the souls of messengers," Jason said. "I've seen the mark burned into their souls like cattle brands. I can see why you would want that gone. But what else do you want, Boris Ket Lundi? Why did you come looking for me? Why risk yourself to intervene? You said yourself that you and your people were meant to be hiding your presence from me."

"Things have been moving beyond the scope of our original agreement with Noreth. He certainly never predicted you becoming an astral king, and these linked planets are drawing a lot of attention. The great astral beings are moving their agents much more actively around Earth and Pallimustus."

"They are?"

"Your friend Dawn is not alone in taking an interest in these worlds, and you are a focal point of that activity. Did you know it was the prime vessel of the Keeper of the Sands who killed Mah Go Schaat to protect you?"

"No. Why would they do that?"

"I don't know. I imagine you will, soon enough."

"Why are they focused on me?"

"You're a catalyst. You became an outworlder through chance, at the exact right place and time. The World-Phoenix was the first to take advantage of that and nudge you onto a certain course, but that set into motion far more than she intended. You were close enough to a confluence of events that other powerful entities followed the World-Phoenix's course in nudging you this way and that. Knowledge. Dominion. The Reaper was quite open when he connected you with your shadow familiar, but what about the other two? A sanguine horror and an avatar of doom, both born right as you were calling for familiars? We've already talked about the rarity of a genuine avatar of doom, but do you know how hard it is to get something like a sanguine horror?"

Jason thought back to the Red Table cultists who attempted to sacrifice Jason and his friends to summon a sanguine horror. All the time, effort and expense they put into the endeavour, yet Jason had picked one up with an awakening stone and a half-learned ritual?

"It seems I have been quite the pawn."

Boris laughed.

"Aren't we all? But don't think of it in terms of someone picking up a piece and moving it as they desire. Great astral beings work on a macro scale. Their thoughts, if you can even call them that, don't encompass mere decades or a scope as small as a planet. That's why their vessels are more important than many realise. They don't just let great astral beings act on a mortal scale; they allow them to think on a mortal scale. It's why their vessels have such a large impact on their small-scale actions."

"And why ancient beings sometimes do things that are very stupid."

"Sometimes. As a relatively ancient being myself, I can tell you that we don't need help doing something stupid. But my point is that great astral beings don't play chess with pawns and kings; they play with the butterfly effect. They reach out and gently flick the cosmos and then wait for the ripples to shape events in ways they can use. That is when they deploy their vessels and agents to handle the finer details."

"And the World-Phoenix flicked me by giving me a token while my soul was passing through the astral."

"Right place, right time. But the ripple of her action sent you in the direction of that confluence of events I mentioned, prompting others to move. To use you as a catalyst."

"What confluence of events?"

"The Builder. The old Builder. The link between worlds. The Sundered Throne, if my guess is correct. Events on a scale beyond my power to influence. Trying to involve myself would be a good way to end a very long life."

"Isn't involving yourself exactly what you did here?"

"This? A transformation zone and an undead army? Some god of undeath doing what gods of undeath always do? No, this is my level. I'm comfortable with this level of stakes. Even if we mess it all up entirely, it wouldn't even destroy the planet."

"You're comfortable with this?"

"Yes. And you should be the same, given your history, but you're not and that's fascinating. You bet against a god with your soul as the ante, to save what? Ten thousand brighthearts and a city that's already destroyed? You saved the Earth. Billions, and you still need to do it again. Yet, here you are, putting it all on the line."

"Someone will save the Earth if I fall."

"Yes. Me, you idiot, and I won't do a great job. And that's compared to you, who has frankly been half-assing it this whole time."

"You?"

"Yes, me. Who else? You think dimension-hopping gestalt entities grow on trees?"

"Well… yes."

Boris looked at Jason, blinked a couple of times and both men burst out laughing.

"Okay," Boris acknowledged once they settled. "That may not have been the best-made point."

"Which has veered quite far from my original question. Why come looking for me?"

"Well, as I explained, events have become a lot more complicated than Noreth anticipated. Unsurprising, given that he never operated on a cosmic scale. We messengers do, and there was a growing number of reasons to be concerned. Not the least of which was Pallimustus suddenly becoming thick with messengers, one dimensional link away. That did not make those of us hiding from them on Earth very comfortable."

"Wouldn't coming here just draw their attention?"

"The greater concern was you becoming blindly antagonistic towards all messengers. The deal was to reveal ourselves when you returned to Earth under certain, specific circumstances. We realised that if you'd already been poisoned against all messengers, having a million of us appear out of nowhere and claim to be your allies wouldn't go well. Especially given how things went with the other allies you've had on Earth."

"You're right about my lack of trust for Earth allies. And I'll admit I have wondered if all messengers needed to be killed off."

"But you decided that wasn't the case. I'm assuming, based on all the messengers you've freed."

"They aren't that free. I keep boxing them all up in pocket universes."

"That's just a matter of logistics. I can help you unload them."

"Whether they want anything to do with you is their choice to make," Jason said.

"I appreciate your compassion for them. One of the reasons it was decided that I would come to Pallimustus and look into you was that you were not showing a lot of compassion by the time you left Earth. You were hurt. Angry. Reacting quickly and with definitive violence. The reasons were obvious enough. Loss. Emotional isolation from your support structure."

"That might have been a good time for an ally who understood to step in."

"There were those who argued we should."

"Were you one of them?"

"No. I argued that you would regard us as untrustworthy at best and refuse to work with us. At worst, you would see us as an enemy. One too powerful to fight, prompting you to do something extreme as you have done time and again. The very reason that Noreth, Dawn and now I refuse to tell you about certain things in your future."

"What did you do? Anything?"

"We came close to revealing ourselves not just to you but to the entire world. Trying to stop the race for reality cores. In the end, it was decided that the results would have been too unpredictable. We did put a stop to core chasing within the parts of the Cabal we controlled at the time. Unfortunately, that came at a point where the vampires had seized a lot of power within the Cabal. Their overt actions had diminished our quiet influence and it took time to properly re-establish that and excise the troublemakers."

"I understand that," Jason said. "I've made a lot of bold moves and watched others suffer the consequences. There's wisdom in moderation, but moderation never seems to be an option for me. Or maybe it is and I keep making the wrong choices."

"When facing extreme circumstances," Boris said, "there is often little choice but extreme actions. And extreme circumstances find you with some regularity. Or do you find them?"

"A bit of both. I imagine that you, of all people, are familiar with destiny magic."

"I had wondered if that was in play. It certainly explains a lot."

Boris let out a sigh.

"Asano, I will confess a hesitance in sharing the part my people and I played during events on Earth. In revealing our inaction. I feared it would anger you."

"I've learned to let go of my anger over that time. I hope. I don't think I'll know for certain until I go back to Earth."

Boris nodded.

"I am glad that you found your way to feeling compassion for my kind. When I arrived on Pallimustus and discovered that you'd started liberating messengers from Vesta Carmis Zell, that's when I decided to help you. I got a lot more than I bargained for in that deal, but I think it's worth it. You and I are going to know each other for a span of time you're too young to even comprehend."

"Then you *really* shouldn't have lied to me."

"It wasn't, strictly speaking, a…"

Boris noticed Jason looking at him from under raised eyebrows.

"No," he said. "I shouldn't have lied to you."

43

BINARIES

BORIS WAS HUMAN-SIZED AND WITHOUT HIS WINGS, BUT JASON COULDN'T help but notice the messenger was still a lot taller. They were still on the beach, Jason in a floral shirt and tan shorts. Boris was wearing what Jason could only describe as a blouse with only two buttons at the bottom done up. Like his hair, it was being gently tousled by a sea breeze that wasn't enough to cut through the scorching heat of the day. Jason looked down at Boris' legs.

"Are you wearing pantaloons?" Jason asked.

"I'm not going to take fashion criticism from someone dressed like a Japanese tourist in an American movie. From the eighties."

"Better that than the cover of some bargain-bin bodice-ripper. You look like you washed up from a pirate ship and have zero interest in consent."

"Are we going to do this or what?"

"Well, we were. The problem is that I'm starting to feel like the plantation owner's busty-yet-naïve daughter."

"I thought the problem was you suspected me of being a soul-engineered trap."

"What? Oh, yep. That's the problem. I didn't forget."

Boris shook his head and Jason raised a hand, one finger primed to flick.

"Really?" Boris asked. "You don't have a more mature way to—"

Jason flicked him on the forehead.

Jason and Boris stood facing each other, barefoot in the sand. Jason looked around Boris' soul space. It was a blank, unnaturally flat desert that stretched out to the horizon. There were no rocks, no dunes, no clouds in the azure sky. Just a flat expanse of sand and a sun with its merciless heat.

"This is quite a soul space you've got here," Jason said.

"An astral king first helped me form this space before your planet existed. I've had a lot of time to work on it."

"And this is the foyer. All your secrets, far off where no one can see them."

"We both know that you could find them with little effort. This is my space, but I don't have the tools you do."

"I'm not going to go rummaging," Jason said. "I only came in here because there's no other way to clear the brand off your soul. Taking advantage of that would be a violation of the highest order."

"I could show you around a little. That might help you trust me more."

"You just told me how long you've had to work on this place. Are you telling me that in all that time, you couldn't have sculpted up a reassuring and thoroughly deceitful playground to lead someone through? A theme park where the theme is you not being an evil scheming prick?"

Boris laughed.

"I could have done that, yes. In fact, I might get started on it as soon as we're done here."

"Put in a bouncy castle. Bouncy castles are awesome."

"If you aren't going to go poking around, I should lead you to the brand. It's located in the traditional throne room."

Jason lightly tapped his foot and sand rippled out from it like pond water after a rock was dropped into it. "That get it done?"

Boris tilted his head as if listening for something.

"Yes," he said, surprise in his voice. "I do believe that is enough that I can take it from here."

"Good. I'm leaving before any more of your sketchy pirate friends show up."

Jason and Arabelle stood in the middle of a residential street in Jason's replica town. There was no traffic, although there were parked cars. They were looking at a particular house.

"So, this is where you grew up," Arabelle said.

"Yeah. My sister and her family own it now. I think. Their living situation got a bit complicated there for a while, as did society as a whole. Looking back, I hit Earth a bit like a bomb."

"You blame yourself?"

"For what happened on Earth? Absolutely not. My arrival may have changed the exact outcomes, but things were going pear-shaped long before I turned up. With or without me, magic was going to go public sooner rather than later. The Builder's shonky door was waiting for an outworlder to claim it hundreds of years before I was born."

"I was more thinking on a personal level."

"If I hadn't returned, my family wouldn't have had a normal life because no one would have. Things would have played out a little differently, but the existence of magic was coming out. There was no stopping it and that was just the beginning. It could have turned out fine or gone full zombie movie, I don't know. Earth isn't made for regular people anymore, and my showing up or not couldn't change that. But I made my family not regular people anymore, and I left them as safe and well-off as I was able."

"But you have regrets?"

"I don't think there's such thing as a life without regrets. I wasn't equipped mentally for what Earth had waiting for me, but I did the best I could with what I had. There's no shame in doing your best, even when it doesn't work out."

Arabelle gave him a side glance and he chuckled.

"I know," he said. "Normally, after one of these crazy fights, I'm laid up for months and more than a little broody."

"This was more than a crazy fight, Jason. You risked not just your life but your soul and your very identity. I watched your soul being corrupted and broken down."

Jason nodded and started walking down the street, Arabelle following.

"It wasn't actual damage," he said. "Well, it was a bit, but not as much as you'd think. My soul is used to being knocked around from the inside and what you saw wasn't actually happening. It was a metaphor for control, a board game playing out as my will clashed with the echo of Undeath's."

"How does that even work? How does willpower have an echo?"

"Gods," Jason said and he clapped his hands together. "When I do that, it makes a sound. Something you and I can do because we're physical in nature. A god is spiritual in nature, and exhaustively powerful."

Jason clapped again, this time doing so with all of his silver-rank strength to cause a loud crack of noise.

"How loudly could a diamond-ranker clap?" he asked. "Could they knock over these houses with the sheer force of it? A god is far more powerful than even a diamond-ranker, so when they spiritually clap, it has power. Power enough to give the avatar something that mimics a will of its own. More power than I can handle as a mortal man. I have one foot in the spiritual realm, which is what allowed me to fight at all, but a god is a god."

"And in your soul realm, you are the closest thing there is to a god."

"Yes. But I had to let myself become more god-like in order to act like one. Once I did, the remnant of Undeath's will was a paltry thing, but I had to put both feet on the spiritual side to get there. Coming back wasn't easy."

"I find it hard to imagine going through that didn't leave some kind of trauma."

"I was surprised as well. I've been waiting for the backlash to come, but it's been just the opposite."

"Oh?"

"I'm changing. We've talked about my fear of what I end up becoming, but I just got a really good look."

"You're going to turn into some god-thing with no identity?"

"No, thankfully. That was me fumbling around with power I didn't understand. Again. But the experience gave me insight into the spiritual power that's been growing inside me. The aspects of myself that are shedding mortality."

He glanced at Arabelle walking beside him down the street of his hometown. The summer-like weather reminded him of his childhood.

"Most importantly," he continued, "the experience has helped me accept the parts of myself I've been holding at arm's length out of fear. I never explored the limits of my spiritual power because I was afraid of what I would become."

"But dealing with the avatar of Undeath forced your hand."

"Yes. A lack of understanding meant that my approach was more dangerous than it had to be because I was learning under the worst circumstances. The exact situation Humphrey told me off for forcing all of you into, as it happens."

"How do you feel about that?"

"Like I made the latest in a long series of stuff-ups. To be honest, I think Hump beat you to the punch in making me realise how I was sabotaging myself and the people that matter the most to me."

"What did you learn?"

"That I have to not just talk about trust but actually be trusting. The price of a mistake always seems so obvious in hindsight."

"I'm afraid that we've gone beyond the scope of my knowledge regarding mental health," Arabelle said. "What you're describing, what does it mean from a practical perspective? What's changed?"

"I've been exploring that over the last few weeks. As a gestalt being, my body has been both physical and spiritual for several years. Now, my mind is as well, and I've been delving into the spiritual parts of myself. If I'd been willing to do that when it was safer, I wouldn't have had to take such risks. If I had to fight that battle of wills again now, I wouldn't need to carve parts of myself away. I've stopped segregating my mind into the parts I accept and the parts I'm afraid of. I've stopped pretending it's a binary and accepted that I'm going to change."

They drew close to the beach and Jason led them off the road. He pushed the branches of a bush out of the way and took them onto a trail that ran alongside a small creek. It was Australian bushland; eucalyptus trees with their heavy scent and bushes sporting sharp prickles as often as leaves. Long grass crowded the trail on both sides and Arabelle felt some brush her leg. She stopped to inspect her pants and found a neat, straight slice in them.

"Cutting grass," Jason said as she stopped to examine her pants. "Likes to make unpleasant cuts. Paper cuts, basically. You're gold rank, so you don't have to worry."

"My pants do. What does this cutting grass look like?"

"The rest of the grass. Welcome to Australia. Well, fake Australia."

Arabelle watched as Jason crossed the creek by stepping on a sequence of unstable-looking rocks. Arabelle simply jumped across, a laughably easy task for her gold-rank physical prowess. Just as easy for Jason, but he'd chosen to hop across the rocks like a normal person. He did so with a confidence that came not from prowess but practise.

"Where are you taking us?" Arabelle asked. "Or is this just a tour of your childhood haunts?"

"This creek runs out of a duck pond," Jason said. "I wanted to see if the ducks were there."

"You already know the answer to that."

Jason nodded but kept walking. There were no ordinary animals in the transformation zone. They reached a clearing and the promised pond. There wasn't much to it but Arabelle could see why it would be a treasure to children. Hidden away in the bush, an escape from parents, even if that was an illusion. Those same parents would remember the way from their own childhoods, just as Jason had led them here now.

Arabelle watched Jason as he stood, staring at the small pond and the lack of ducks. She waited, giving him as much time to think as he wanted. He took a lot of it. There was an eerie quiet without animals or insects. A breeze occasionally rustled eucalyptus leaves.

"I remember it being bigger," he said, finally breaking the silence. "Nothing stays the way it was, does it? Even if a place doesn't change, it does to us because we change. Something that used to be so familiar feels the same, but also different enough to be uncanny. Like finding an old shirt that you loved growing up, one you wore until it had holes and then you kept wearing it anyway. But now it's too small, like it belongs to someone else. Someone you used to be but aren't anymore."

Arabelle stayed quiet. She recognised that he wasn't really talking to her.

"I'm going to change," he said, repeating his earlier words. "I'm going to trust myself that the changes will be for the better, and not cost me everything that I am. I didn't trust myself or my friends during the avatar fight. Not until I had to. If I'd had the courage to stop hiding from the inevitable, it wouldn't have been so dangerous."

He turned and smiled at Arabelle.

"Let's go," he said.

He led them to another path Arabelle had not noticed before Jason pushed aside a bush.

"I've been talking about my mistakes and my feelings," Jason continued. "We've covered that ground so often over the years that I already know how to move forward. There are other things that need my focus right now."

"Such as?"

"The transformation zone. I can feel it, stronger than ever now."

"Because you've claimed half of it?"

"That's part of it. I've gained a fairly good sense of it and it's different to the transformation zones I encountered on Earth."

"More powerful?"

"Yes, but that doesn't matter. It's more complex. On Earth, the zones were straightforward dimension patches, scabs grown over wounds in the universe. This transformation zone has been stuffed with extreme influences. Divine power, a warped natural array, a half-formed soul forge. Even me. I didn't have my astral gate and astral throne back on Earth, and they have definitely influenced this zone."

Arabelle turned to look, but the mountain shaped like Jason's head was obscured by the trees around them.

"We've noticed," she said dryly.

"All those factors are like infections trapped under the scab, making the healing process harder. It also means that claiming a quarter of the zone all at once hit me like a train. Not as bad as losing territories—nothing got ripped out of my soul—but that many territories all at once? It hit me harder than losing a much smaller territory did."

"Did you learn anything helpful from your connection to the transformation zone? Something we can use?"

"Yeah. I have a stronger sense of the territory than I did for the transformation zones on Earth, at least before I claimed them fully. I can feel the natural array. The soul forge. I think I've even figured out what the messengers kept getting wrong. Why their attempts to turn the natural array into a soul forge didn't work."

"Which is?"

"Better discussed with Clive and Farrah, frankly. The short version is that they kept looking at the natural array and its power as a single thing when they're actually two. Connected but not combined. The natural array and its power are binary, like the body and soul of a human."

"Body and soul," Arabelle said. "Not an accidental comparison, I take it."

"No," Jason said. "It's like the messengers were blinded by their gestalt nature. They thought of the soul forge as something belonging to astral kings and, by extension, messengers as a whole. It was theirs, not just *for* them but *of* them. That led them to applying messenger sensibilities and treating the two aspects of the array as a gestalt."

"Their gestalt nature is one of the cornerstones of the messenger sense of superiority," Arabelle said. "So, when they look at something they associate with themselves, they don't think in binaries. It's a blind spot for them."

"Exactly," Jason said. "What they needed was the power, but they kept corrupting it by trying to incorporate the physical array. I think the messengers gave us a device they thought would extract the soul forge, but they were wrong. It's a good thing we used it for something else."

"Does this mean you can take the soul forge if we manage to claim this entire zone?"

"I believe so. I have a better idea of what the soul forge is now. Only the very basics, but learning to use my astral throne and astral gate have helped. And there was Dawn saying I should leave them alone."

"You didn't listen to her at all, did you?"

"I did, but you know how it is. If you need a sword but the only one available has spikes on the handle, you still grab it. Saving a life is more important than a bloody hand."

"You and I have discussed your propensity for self-sacrifice, Jason. Be wary of overlooking alternatives and jumping directly into self-destructive behaviour."

"I know," Jason said in the tone of a child promising to make his bed.

"What other insights have you gleaned?"

"My improved understanding of my spiritual side and the soul forge have given me a better idea of what happens next. When I'm reforming the transformation zone and reintegrating it with normal reality, I'll separate the natural array and the soul forge that are corrupting one another, then claim the soul forge for myself. That will trigger my transfiguration into a full astral king. I'll begin the process of becoming a half-transcendent."

"A peak diamond-ranker?"

"No. That's the other half of half-transcendent. Transcending requires two things: transcending mortal power and transcending mortal nature. Peak diamond-rank is about becoming so powerful that mortality itself can barely hold on to you. That's the half that most people achieve first, often never managing the other half."

"But you just had to be different."

"I guess it's kind of my thing. I still have to get to peak diamond the long way. The part most people have trouble with is truly stepping over the line between mortal and immortal. To transcend mortality itself. That's not something you can do just by growing your power."

"And you'll do that by becoming an astral king."

"Astral king or nearest offer. I won't be the first to turn into an astral king the hard way, and those that do are all a bit odd, apparently. I guess regular folk don't end up at this stage. But becoming an astral king isn't the only way to shrug off mortality."

"Didn't Dawn go off to become a transcendent?"

"Yes, but I have no idea how."

"She didn't tell you?"

"I didn't ask. The fact that she was leaving always seemed more important than why."

Arabelle smiled to herself. Jason led them out of a bush and onto the side of a road. It was somewhere on the outskirts of the town with houses more spread out. She looked back and would have had trouble finding the path again.

They started walking down the middle of the road, which felt hot and soft. Arabelle's foot sank slightly into it at one point, a patch of road having melted underfoot. Jason turned to see why she had stopped and he broke into a broad smile.

"Cheap surfacing materials," he said happily. "Gets melty on hot summer days. I always loved that."

Arabelle shook her head and they kept going.

"What are the practical aspects of becoming an astral king?" she asked.

"It means consolidating my soul realm into an actual pocket universe. Something floating out in the astral that people could go and visit in a dimension ship. It will arguably become a dimension ship itself."

"That you can return to Earth in?"

"Yeah. Probably my cloud vessel too, given its connection to me. I can't steer it, though. Clive and I have been looking at dimensional navigation and we can't get our heads around it. Boris said he'll give me the magic I need to ride the link between worlds, no navigation necessary. Of course, Clive and I will check it as thoroughly as we can before ever using it."

"You're going to turn into an astral king. How long will that take?"

"Years."

"And you'll have to stay inside your soul realm the whole time?"

"More than that. I have to become my soul realm. A body-spirit gestalt is like a seed. Very close to literally, for messengers. When I become an astral king, that seed will germinate and become a universe."

"If your body becomes a universe, won't you be stuck floating through the astral?"

"Once the process is complete, I'll create an avatar. A prime avatar that embodies everything about me. They're normally peak diamond, with a goodly chunk of extra spirit power behind them, but mine will be stuck at my rank. You can only have one at a time, even when you're a full-strength astral king, but it lets astral kings operate in physical reality. They generate less authority than gods or great astral beings but, through their prime avatars, have a freedom to act in physical reality that other zenith astral entities can't match. Astral kings maintain that physical aspect that gods and great astral beings never had."

"Doesn't that mean that the astral kings could send their ludicrously powerful avatars here?"

"That's what I was wondering. Theoretically, yes. In practice, there's a lot of political wrangling with local gods. The disadvantage of maintaining a physical and spiritual existence is that you're subject to the rules and limitations of both. Gods won't let astral kings invading their world send powerful avatars, and astral kings don't ask. Replacing a prime avatar is, by all accounts, no small thing."

"That's a lot to take in."

"I know, right? I'm going to turn into a universe. And I'm going to be so obnoxious about it too. I'll talk about it more than if I became a vegan; I'll be completely intolerable."

Arabelle sighed.

"It's good that you know what is coming for you," she said. "Better that you seem at peace with it. But do any of these new insights help us with claiming the rest of the transformation zone?"

"Yeah, actually. Clive had a hypothesis that I can now confirm and we've been discussing how to make use of it. Right now, Gary is hard-carrying us in claiming territories, but we don't know what's waiting for us at the end. Clive, Farrah and I have been cooking up something to give us an extra bit of punch when…"

He trailed off and they both moved to the side of the road. They watched as a bright yellow car moved erratically down the street. Inside it was a messenger, shrunken down to human size but with white fire blazing in her eyes. They watched her unsteady progress, her expression of distracted determination not even glancing their way.

"Uh…" Jason said at an uncharacteristic loss for words. "Did I just see a messenger driving Mrs Berrigan's '73 Holden Torana?"

44

WHEN WE WORRY THE MOST

"I'm sorry," Jali Corrik Fen said as she walked alongside Jason in the mountain fortress. The corridors of black stone and red metal were high and wide enough to drive a freight truck through them. It was more than sufficient for the messenger to walk beside Jason without shrinking herself or dismissing her wings.

"What are you sorry for?" Jason asked.

"The messengers you've liberated aren't getting the indoctrination they normally would."

"I seriously hope you're not apologising for not brainwashing children."

"No," Jali said, her face flushing red. "It's just that we haven't replaced it with anything. The messengers are being left to their own devices and some of them are… going a bit odd."

Jason laughed. "There's nothing wrong with a bit odd."

"Um, alright. There's nothing wrong with a little structure, either. At some point, we have to find a place for them, and I don't think either of us want them in the hands of your Adventure Society."

Jason's mirth quickly shifted to a frown.

"That's a fair point," he said. "Do you have a suggestion?"

"The obvious choice is Boris Ket Lundi, but I don't think you want to just hand them off to the Unorthodoxy, either."

"While he's in dire need of a trip to HR, Boris seems a likeable sort.

But I don't want to push these messengers into a conflict they don't even know about. Their origins may be less than ideal, but at least they were born outside of your kind's civil war."

"A war most of us didn't realise was taking place," Jali said. "If the messengers as a whole learned how many Unorthodoxy are out there, it would fracture our society."

"It needs fracturing," Jason said.

"Not like this. If information that wildly contradicts the narrative we've been taught managed to spread, the astral kings would stage an unprecedented cull. They'd burn half our species to excise the rot. And the half that is left would be the ones that kept the faith. The ones like Tera Jun Casta who would fight any attempt to liberate them."

Jason nodded.

"There has to be a better way to shift messenger society than that," he said. "That isn't our fight, though; that's for Boris and the people behind him. You and I have to deal with these child messengers, and turning them into child soldiers isn't the way. That being said, I don't see how we have an alternative to sending them off with Boris. My soul realm is going to be closed for business soon."

"We will be in this transformation zone for some time yet. Enough to give them some manner of education about the worlds beyond this place."

"What kind of education are you thinking about?"

"My thoughts on this are inexpert and rather basic. But I have heard both Rufus Remore and his father Gabriel mention that their family runs a school."

Jason burst out laughing, to Jali's confusion.

"I don't see the humour."

"You don't need to. It's a good idea, provided you can get the messengers to accept tutelage from a pair of humans. And, despite my reservations, I think Boris should be in the mix. There are aspects of being a messenger that humans can't teach them. I want you to be part of that as well, but I want them to learn about being a free messenger. That's new to you as well."

"Some of the messengers will be more accepting than others. The ones freed directly by you and your closest companions never saw battle. They were never used as weapons. Many of the others were, by both your allies and your enemies. Those will be less open."

Jason nodded.

"All we can do is the best we can with what we've got. After the meeting clears out, I'll have Boris, Rufus and Gabriel stay behind. There's something critical you'll need to know before that, though."

"Which is?"

"Have you ever heard of drinking games?"

Clive stood at the head of the conference table. Jason's throne-like leather chair had been moved and the window looking onto the lava waterfall had been turned a smoky opaque. An illusionary map of the transformation zone floated in the air like a hologram. Sitting around the table were the leaders and important members of the alliance between adventurers, brighthearts, cultists and messengers.

"Scattered amongst the territories of the transformation zone," Clive said, "are those with environmental extremes that can be controlled. The control centres are well hidden and take time to learn to use, but it can be done. One of the key indicators separating the controllable environments from those that are ordinarily dangerous is an aspect of artificiality."

Clive waved his hand and the map was replaced with three images floating in place, as if seen through a trio of round windows. One showed lightning striking an iron tower. Another had lava passing through a series of sluice gates in what looked like a subterranean complex made of red brick. The third showed pipes rising out of a swamp to spray scalding water.

"I believe that most of us have encountered these territories, and most of them are now under our control."

"But do they do us any good?" Gabriel asked. "We've cleared out those territories in the process of claiming them."

"As they are, no," Clive said. "As you said, those territories have been cleared and claimed, so they're under our control now, but we can't just dig up their infrastructure and move it around. But ever since I learned that there were as many of them as there are, I started wondering about their purpose. I've developed a hypothesis and, if I'm right, they represent an asset that could be as useful to us as our resident demigod."

"How confident are you about this?" Arabelle asked.

"In the wake of his recent unusual and extreme experience, Jason believes my hypothesis to be accurate."

"You're going to have to narrow down 'unusual and extreme experience' for us," Neil called out. "For us, they're unusual. For him, they're something to spice up his week."

"I concur with the girthy elf," said Beaufort, leader of the Builder cultists. "There is no shortage of strange events centred on Asano, even in the short time I have known him."

"I am not girthy."

Clive continued, ignoring them both.

"While fighting the remnants of the avatar," he said, "Jason entered a spiritual state where he gained several insights. Most were personal in nature, but he also obtained a better understanding of the transformation zone. More than half of it is connected to him now, after all."

"What is this hypothesis you mentioned?" Boris asked. "Assuming that you are willing to share. And, while I mean no offence to Asano, have you tested this hypothesis beyond 'Jason thinks he figured it out while he was fighting a god?'"

"Exploring my hypothesis is the next step," Clive said. "It won't be a small undertaking, which is the reason for this meeting. When we needed everyone clearing territories and it was little more than postulation on my part, exploring this was logistically infeasible. Now there is a level of confirmation from Jason and our silver-rankers are sitting around with little to do. We also have the magic researchers who managed to survive the early days of the transformation zone. The Operations Commander has given me permission to use them."

"Use them how?" asked Lorenn, leader of the brighthearts. "And do you intend to use my people?"

"No," Jason said. "The adventurers and magic researchers should be sufficient to our needs. If it proves sufficiently safe and useful that bringing your people in makes sense, we'll make that request at that time. You won't be pushed into anything."

"The actual work involves setting up some laboriously large rituals around the control centres," Clive explained. "All in spaces that have been cleared, so I anticipate little danger. The idea is to have the silver-rankers working on that while the gold-rankers continue expanding our territory. We'll be taking precautions, obviously. Assuming there will be no threat is the best way to be blindsided by one. The only threats we anticipate are messengers or Undeath priests who either escaped the battle or haven't encountered anyone else yet. It's likely at least some people are still roaming around."

"You still haven't explained what you think these special territories are," Arabelle pointed out. "Or how you think we can use them."

"Jason affected this transformation zone from the beginning," Clive said. "You only have to look at where we are for that to be obvious. While his influence was unmistakable in his initial territory, I also believe that his influence extended throughout the zone. The effects here were more overt because this is where he arrived. Outside of that first territory, his influence was significantly lessened. That's why the rest of the transformation zone isn't as... personality-filled as this area."

"Shouldn't you have known that you'd influenced everything already?" Belinda asked. "How did you miss having rewritten a pocket universe larger than most countries?"

"I haven't rewritten whole sections of reality very often," Jason said. "It was only my third time. What I did manage was effectively unconscious expression. I wasn't actively trying to replicate my hometown or create a mountain in the shape of my head. It just worked out that way because I'm awesome."

"Jason subconsciously created a home base from which to expand his territory," Clive said. "While the results are... quite specific, it does meet our needs. It has the infrastructure and supplies to be a staging ground from which to take over the transformation zone. The space simply took a form that Jason subconsciously equates with doing that."

"You're saying that in Jason's mind," Gabriel said, "infrastructure and supplies means a mountain shaped like his head?"

"Our ultimate objective," Farrah said, "is to seize control of this transformation zone. We're in an isolated world that Jason knew he would need to take over. And I can promise you that, in Jason's mind, a volcano lair in the shape of your head is exactly how you start your plan to take over the world. The only thing missing is a..."

She trailed off as her eyes went wide. She turned to look at Clive.

"No," she said.

Clive let out the sigh of a man fresh from a losing battle.

"I'm afraid so," he told her.

Jason sat back in his chair with a grin so wide, it looked like he was propping his mouth open with raw smugness.

"I don't suppose you'd like to share with the group?" Arabelle suggested.

"To be clear," Clive said, his expression screaming reluctance, "what we're talking about is an integrated array on a geographic scope, with the power to manipulate the environment on a macro scale."

"Yeah," Sophie muttered. "That cleared it right up."

"He means a weather machine!" Jason said as he shook his fist in triumph.

"I do not mean a weather machine," Clive said. "Calling it that is not an accurate representation of the underlying—"

"WEATHER MACHINE!" Jason yelled joyously over him.

A fluffy white cat leapt into Jason's lap and he started petting it. The cat had a bushy moustache.

Clive sighed again.

"Let me explain where all of these environmental control territories came from," he said, eager to change the subject. "The transformation zone includes all the elements of the area in physical reality it overtook."

"That area being the home of my people," Lorenn said.

"Yes," Clive said. "We are anticipating a large part of the unclaimed areas of the transformation zone to be tainted by undeath energy, given how much of the brightheart city was affected. Many of our groups encountered such zones."

"We've scouted the territory Jason took from the avatar when it was finally destroyed," Miriam said. "Much of it was infested with undeath energy, and we're expecting to see more territories like that."

"I believe I can do something about that when I reintegrate the transformation zone with reality," Jason said. "I don't want to rebuild the brightheart home and leave a massive pit of undeath energy sitting in the middle."

"What will our home look like when all of this is done?" Lorenn asked.

"Come find me later today and we can discuss it more privately," Jason said. "While we have everyone together, we should focus on broader concerns."

"Thank you," Clive said. "Things brought in from the outside are changed by the zone, but their core nature remains. The corrupted soul forge tree, for example, is now the towering thing visible from all the other zones. I suspect we'll see a lot of elemental-messenger-shaped living anomalies when we confront it."

"You're suggesting that these territories where the environment can be controlled were brought in from the outside," Farrah said.

"Yes," Clive confirmed.

"You mean the natural array," Farrah said.

"Yes," Clive said with a nod. "We believe that the natural array was transformed into the scattered environmental control nodes we've been discussing."

"We also believe that they're connected," Jason said. "Just like the array from which they were derived. I learned to connect with things more spiritually while facing the avatar, and I could feel the ones in the territory I've claimed."

"Our current hypothesis," Clive said, "is that the segmentation of the transformation zone meant that the individual territories were cut off from one another. The links weren't entirely severed, however, which is what Jason was able to sense. But just uniting the territories they're in hadn't been re-establishing their link. That's what we're looking to do."

"The idea," Jason said, "is to pull all these environmental control nodes into one territory and repair the connections. That will turn the whole thing into a single, zone-spanning array. We have to claim all the zones anyway, so what we're proposing is that we unify the special ones we've already got. Then we add the rest as they get claimed. Even if we can't use the array until every node is integrated, having extra power for the final push on the tree will be of extreme tactical value."

"What that looks like from a practical perspective," Clive said, "is a lot of very large rituals being set up all across the transformation zone. We'll start by trying to link one pair to see if we've gotten this all completely wrong. If that's the case, we let it go and proceed as we have been. If we're right, or the results suggest there's value in further testing, we'll go from there. If we reach the point of full implementation, that's where our idle silver-rankers come in. We'll work on the control nodes we have access to now and cover the rest as we claim the zones they're in."

"Do we need all of them?" Neil asked.

"I don't know," Clive said. "It seems likely if they are based on the natural array."

"The avatar destroyed the control centre in the lightning field," Neil pointed out. "If we need every one of these areas to be connected, doesn't that mean we've failed before we begin?"

"That's something we'll need to figure out," Jason said. "I have considered that point, and I have a plan. You don't have to worry."

"I hate to break it to you, Jason," Belinda said, "but you having a plan is when we worry the most."

45

PARANOID

LIGHTNING STRUCK SO FAST THAT THE LAST PEAL OF THUNDER WAS STILL rumbling when the next one set the sky to shuddering. Adventurers took shelter under the forest of iron towers jutting from the blasted landscape. Most were silver-rankers, but a small number of golds worked to shield the others from the lightning as they worked. They were clearing rubble that had been a mesa until Undeath's avatar destroyed it.

The adventurers hauled away fragments of shattered rock while also extracting certain parts. The remains of the lightning catchment array that had once topped the mesa were being delivered to Jason, along with a small supply of the rubble. The catchment array was comprised mostly of magical iron, now broken and twisted apart.

Jason fed the remains of the array into his cloud flask, along with chunks of rubble. This involved poking the tiny mouth of the flask with large bits of metal and rock which were drawn inside. Dimensional compression visibly warped the chunks so they could be absorbed, looking like they were sucked in by a cartoon vacuum cleaner.

Miriam Vance watched this from under another giant lightning rod, her expression troubled. She was recovering her mana after a shift shielding silver-rankers, the lightning tough for even a gold-ranker to handle for long. Arabelle Remore moved next to her, likewise recovering her mana.

"Tactical Commander," she said by way of greeting.

"Mrs Remore."

Arabelle looked at Miriam's expression and then followed her gaze to Jason. She then activated a privacy screen that cut out the sound of thunder. They stood side by side, watching Jason work.

"Something about our Operations Commander has you troubled," Arabelle observed.

"I can't help but wonder what he's not telling me."

"As a keeper of most of Jason Asano's secrets, I can assure you that there are many things he's not telling you. I don't believe you need to be concerned about that, but I can see how you would feel differently as the one being kept in the dark. Jason has told me that I should share some things with you if I feel it is appropriate. If you can tell me what troubles you specifically, then perhaps I can alleviate your worries, if only a little."

"I still don't understand what happened with the avatar."

"I'm not sure that any of us do. Perhaps not even Jason himself, fully. That conflict took place in the realm of gods and we are but mortals. Even Jason, for now."

"For now?"

"You know the company he keeps, allies and enemies. You've heard the stories, even seen it for yourself, sometimes. Gods, great astral beings. The astral kings don't care about any of us as individuals, but his name they know. Their messengers hate him with a fervour I can only describe as religious."

"But it's more than that, isn't it? 'Mortal for now' isn't a phrase to be used lightly."

"No," Arabelle agreed. "It's not. Astral kings are not mortals. And if we succeed here, Jason will be one of them. While I believe that is meant to be a secret, Jason has proven unreliable at keeping them, at least those about himself."

"Jason's imminent ascension to the ranks of our most grave enemies does not ease my mind. I've been fighting messengers since they first arrived at Yaresh. Long before the Adventure Society staged an organised attack, I was standing beside the Holy Knowledge Army, who were ready and waiting. All anyone talks about is the adventurers fighting, but when the adventurers were fighting the monster surge, it was a scant few of us and some barely trained holy legions that held the messengers back. Kept them contained in their strongholds. Lady Allayeth, my team and barely a handful of other brave souls."

"You fought with Knowledge's forces?"

"You'd barely know they existed for all anyone speaks of them now. But they were the ones who held the line. They were the ones who took most of the losses. You know the goddess has been training them for more than a decade? There's no point sending any soldier less than silver-rank at a messenger. I can't even fathom how much money the church must have spent on monster cores. And these soldiers didn't even know what fight they were preparing for. And in the meanwhile, the god of War was pressuring them for overstepping their bounds."

"You hate the messengers."

"You've seen what they've left of my home. And now Asano is going to be one of their kings?"

"The astral kings are not as monolithic as we thought."

"So says the messenger our Operations Commander gets along with oh so well. And he's hardly the first, is he? It wasn't long before this expedition that he was hiding from the Adventure Society for stashing away messengers. Protecting enemy prisoners."

"You would have killed them."

"Not before extracting every scrap of information we could wring from their bodies."

"Which is why he protected them."

"I tried, Mrs Remore. Lady Allayeth told me that Asano could be trusted and I tried, I truly did. We get along, and we work together well. I've come to like him, rely on him even. But everything I see points to an agenda that's a mystery at best. At worst, it intersects with that of the enemy. We went underground to protect my city, but he came for the same things the messengers want. A soul forge, whatever that is. And with it, he'll become one of them."

"You have a lot more problems with our commander than just his fight with the avatar, I see."

"Maybe if I could understand. I've asked Asano about this several times and the more I try to get to the facts, the more he answers in riddles and metaphors."

"I believe that is all he has to give. I've discussed this with him at length now, and I have also had my fill of metaphors. Which he tells me, with a frustrating unhelpfulness, is the entire point. And I was there, so I believe him. I stood in a place where imagination and reality were one and the same. I witnessed that fight, as much as anyone can have been said to, but all I can tell you is what I already have done. We are mortals and it was a battle of gods. Jason almost lost himself to fight it."

"That may be the crux of what troubles me. That nonsense about coming back from some false god state by... I still don't understand. Something about a children's toy. How can such a monumental thing be so frivolous? So childish? So inconsequential?"

"I will accept frivolous and childish as valid, Tactical Commander, but not inconsequential. That was extremely important."

"How?"

"Jason Asano is not a stable man. By the time I met him, he had already been through several profoundly traumatic experiences. He'd acquitted himself well, but no one goes through such things undamaged. It's why they call in people like me, and this was a man who saved my son's life."

"That only suggests that you have a bias, not that he is in any way reliable."

"That's true. Often deliberately. But for all that he seems to walk with chaos, he always comes through. Always. I never saw Jason as he was at the very beginning. His world is safer than ours and he had to adapt quickly. He was thrown into events he didn't understand from the very first moment. No power, no training and he still managed to save my son. I will always owe him for that, so I will do anything in my power to help him."

"Even if he turns against us."

"This is why what happened with the avatar is not as inconsequential as you think. The adventuring life changes us all, and his experience was more exciting than most. I saw the early stages of his transformation from a fundamentally ridiculous young man into a very dangerous one. Not just to his enemies but to everyone; to himself most of all. You know that he left our world for a time and returned?"

"Yes."

"That was when he suffered the worst of it. When most of those he could rely on were out of reach, myself included. Those he should have been able to rely on were unable to accept what he'd been forced to become, to survive our world and to save his."

"He saved his world?"

"Yes. And as with the avatar, he almost lost himself to do so. When he came back, he was fractured. A maelstrom of rage, barely contained by the plastered-on façade of a man he used to be. None of us were sure he would ever be made whole, but I dedicated the last year to that goal. I've done other work over that period, but Jason has been my central project."

"You aren't painting a hopeful picture for me, Mrs Remore. You're describing someone not just unstable but so unstable that he shouldn't be in charge of a market stall, let alone this expedition."

"Is that what you've experienced working with him?"

"No," Miriam admitted. "He's been unconventional, but that has been what we needed. I don't think a conventional approach would have kept us alive this far. But he's led us beyond the edges of any map I've ever heard of."

"See?" Arabelle asked. "Sometimes a metaphor is the best explanation you have to give."

Miriam grunted her reluctant acceptance of the point.

"What happened with the avatar mattered," Arabelle continued. "The thing that pulled Jason back to himself, that spoke the very core of who he was, was just as you said: frivolous and childish. It made those of us who know and care about him ecstatic."

"Why?"

"Because it proved something that we've been hoping for ever since he came back to us. That he hadn't been entirely lost. That, at his core, he's still closer to the absurd man who arrived on our world the first time than the bloodthirsty maniac who arrived the second time. You asked what happens if he turns against us. We've been worried about that since he came back. He'll never be exactly who he was, but none of us are. Life changes us all, and the adventuring life more than most. Especially the adventuring life."

"That's true," Miriam said.

"What we saw took something that we believed and showed us absolute proof that we were right. That the man he is now is fundamentally still the man we knew. The man who infuriates almost everyone, yet draws heroes to him like flies. Who will take a good sandwich over a great treasure. A man who throws barbecues where diamond-rankers sit and eat with everyday people because he believes that they are worth the same. Believes it with such an unconscious conviction that, if only for a little while, they believe it too."

"That's nonsense."

"Yes! Utter nonsense! That's who he is: the man who does the nonsensical and makes the world accept it through sheer force of will. The man who helps people for no more reason than they need help. Even if they're messengers. Even if it kills him. And now we have proof of that."

"Proof for you. It still doesn't mean anything to me. I'm responsible for everyone in this expedition."

"So is he."

"But he didn't come here to do what this expedition was sent to do. We're here to protect what's left of my city, but he isn't. He's after that soul forge, just like the messengers. The messengers he brought into our base of operations."

"That's true," Arabelle said. "His primary goal was to keep the soul forge from the messengers. To take it for himself if he could. Sometimes, Jason won't be able to hold the same values as you or I. Not if he's going to keep working on a scale that includes gods and great astral beings. It's something that has worried him since he saw the path his life was taking."

"I don't care about that. Even assuming he won't betray us, that's not the same as being on our side. What happens if he has to choose between this soul forge and Yaresh? Between the soul forge and keeping the members of this expedition alive?"

"Those goals are aligned."

"And look at the madness we had to go through to get to that point. Madness that he led us into, every time."

Arabelle frowned.

"Tactical Commander, I think you need some sleep."

"Is that your professional opinion, healer?"

"Yes. Think about what you're saying. You're suggesting that Jason hatched a wildly elaborate plan that would have required not just the knowledge but the cooperation of the Builder cult, the messengers and an undead army. Not to mention multiple gods, two of whom have been antagonists for, as far as I can tell, as long as they've existed. If he could manage all of that, he wouldn't need to. He'd be in such control of the situation that he would get everything he wanted without any of us ever needing to come down here. He'd get it all and we'd never even know."

Miriam's cognitive dissonance was plain, as expressions of anger, fear and uncertainty warred on her face.

"That's not... I am tired."

"You need rest, Tactical Commander. Jason might be officially in charge, but you've been the one really running the expedition. You've scheduled the gold-rankers claiming territories for the next week already. Clive probably knows what he's doing here and there's nothing we can do about it if he's wrong. As the healer in charge of the expedition's mental health, I'm directing you to get a full week of rest. That way you might at least get a few days before you ignore me and go back to work. Do I have to go to Archbishop Shavar and have you formally removed from your position?"

"And if I say no?"

"Well, you could fight me on it, but I think we both know how that would go. What would your Lady Allayeth tell you to do?"

Miriam glowered, but finally gave a curt nod.

"She'd tell me to listen to the healer."

46

ACADEMICALLY UNSOUND

THUNDER AND LIGHTNING ASSAULTED THE GROUND LIKE AN ARMY OF angry angels. Rain hammered down, turning black dirt into sludge. The air was thick with the smell of ozone, mud and, for the silver-rankers clearing the rubble, tongue-coating stone dust. The amount of rubble was enormous, having once been a towering mesa. Much of it was scattered far enough away that it didn't need to be cleared, but thousands of tons of stone still needed to be removed.

It would have been impossible without the power of the silver-rankers. Their superhuman strength and vast magical power accomplished in a day what would have taken weeks or months on Earth. The scant few gold-rankers Miriam Vance had spared from claiming more territories shielded them from the lightning.

They were done in the late evening, although that made little difference to the light levels. The sky was filled with black clouds and pounding rain, the staccato lightning the only source of natural illumination. The lightning struck in such quick succession that the air was never entirely free of rumbling thunder.

The silver-rankers had finished their task and were sheltering under the massive lightning rods. They used various methods to stay dry, from magical umbrellas to force fields to heat zones that evaporated any rain that came close. Their conversations were loud to be heard over the constant noise, fresh claps of thunder frequently interrupting.

The space that had once occupied the mesa was now a broad disc of stone protruding from the ground. It was misshapen and jagged, ranging anywhere from barely clearing the ground to several metres high. With the rubble gone, the full result of the avatar's attack on the mesa was revealed.

"How powerful was that thing?" Clive wondered, looking it over as they waited for a gold-ranker to get in position. "The raw physical power to do this is astounding, even for a gold-ranker. I can't believe Gary went toe-to-toe with that."

"Yeah," Jason said grimly. "It took so much power that it's slowly killing him."

Most of the rubble had been piled up out of the way although certain parts had been dug out and handed over to Jason. The twisted scraps of metal that had been the lightning catchment array atop the mesa were most of it. There were also parts from the control centre it had hidden, drones that could be controlled from the mesa along with some of the mesa rock itself. Jason had fed it all into his cloud flask.

The gold-ranker finished her preparations. Ramona, a member of Miriam's team, Moon's Edge, projected a translucent dome into the air, spanning the entire space the mesa had once occupied. Lightning repeatedly struck the dome, scattering across it. Moving with Jason were Clive and Belinda, whose auras helped replenish Ramona's mana. Farrah, Taika and Nik joined them, the diminutive rabbit-man looking nervous. They hovered over the mud in a black skimmer that was more sleek and stylised than a cheap and colourful model.

"Are you sure this will work?" Nik asked loudly over the thunder.

"No," Jason said with a laugh. "No, I am not."

"What he *means* to say," Farrah corrected, "is that everything we know points to this working. Weeks of testing has confirmed that these control nodes are not just able but primed to be connected."

Farrah's specialisation was in magical arrays. Combined with the insight she gained into natural arrays from studying the grid on Earth, she had proven herself critical to the plan. Her expertise accelerated the testing of Clive's hypothesis and the linking of the environmental control nodes.

Farrah lacked Clive's broad grasp of magical theory, or even that of Belinda and her eclectic knowledge. Farrah had a traditional adventurer-first approach to magical study—she excelled in her specialty but only knew the fundamentals beyond it. Their project centred on her array magic specialty but dabbled in other fields. The gaps in her knowledge would have slowed them down if not for Clive.

On becoming an outworlder on Earth, Farrah gained the power to form bonds of trust, allowing her to copy knowledge from another person like a skill book. It had allowed her to rapidly learn about Earth from Jason, including a lot of information she wished she hadn't. However useful a qualitative comparison of different Voltrons might have recently proven, there were things in her memory now she never wanted and rarely admitted to possessing.

Sharing the bond with Clive was a more pleasant experience. His mind focused on magical theory with a single-mindedness that was almost scary, and she came to realise how staggering that mind was. She used Clive as a glorified skill book, shoring up gaps in magical knowledge as they worked. His mind moved so fast, though, and in such complex patterns that she struggled to absorb the knowledge. While taking breaks, she thought back to her original studies in magic. The combination of the bond and Clive would have been an egregious and very welcome cheat.

While working on the rituals that would link the environmental nodes, Clive, Farrah and Belinda demonstrated a formidable synergy. It had been the same when they were conducting the ritual that triggered the transformation zone in the first place, rushing to finish before they were overrun by the undead. The time constraints were less immediate this time, but no less real. The transformation zone was more stable than others Jason had been in, but it would eventually break down if not unified and reintegrated with reality.

"Devising the rituals to link these nodes may have taken us a few weeks," Clive told Nik, "but by magic research standards, it's been breathtakingly fast. We've already linked several nodes safely and successfully."

"This isn't a control node, though," Nik pointed out. "This is rubble."

"This is not rubble," Jason said. "We cleared off the rubble; this is a lump of rock."

"Which is somehow better?" Nik asked.

"Uh, no," Jason said. "Just more accurate."

"You know that all the information I was born with about this place went away when it was destroyed, right?" Nik asked.

"When the transformation zone was first forming," Clive said, "everything was in flux. Power became accessible in ways it wouldn't normally be and Jason used that, consciously and unconsciously. The conditions allowed him, in that moment, to do things that couldn't be done at any other time."

"I have a power that allows me to reshape reality when it is in a malleable state," Jason said. "It allowed me to tap into the physical material that formed the zone, and everything that was inside it. Including the soul forge and something the Healer gave me which is how you came into being."

Jason let out a groan as realisation crossed his face.

"Giving you the talk about where babies come from is going to be so complicated," he complained. "I might have to recruit a priest of Fertility. And one of Knowledge."

"Putting that *very* far aside," Clive said, "while Jason was changing things—and creating you—he also created a network of power. The territories like this one with hidden control centres are nodes in that network. We haven't confirmed that there is a central hub, a node that controls the network as a whole, but we think there is. We think it's here and—"

He was cut off by a fresh crack of thunder, close enough to drown out his words.

"Part of our developing hypothesis," he continued, "is that this site is the central node of the network. And that you are the key to making it all work."

"Except that this key is broken," Nik said and gestured at the rock they were floating over. "The lock is even more broken."

"We don't think that you've truly lost the knowledge you had about how to make this control node work," Clive explained. "As you said, the node is very broken. But we think the knowledge is still inside you, just dormant. The idea is that if we can replace the node, that dormant information will come back."

"I don't think that's how it works," Nik said. "You think this is the central node of some massive network, but I never got a sense of that at all. I knew how to control the lightning, more or less. The drones, the elevator, I guess, but that's all. There wasn't any sense of some inactive link or an unconnected network or whatever."

"Just like you don't have the memories of how to control the mesa now," Farrah said. "If we restore the mesa and that restores your connection to it, that's step one. Step two is linking other nodes to this one. If you gain the knowledge of how to control them as we do that, it means we were right."

"And if I don't?" Nik asked.

"Then we're not right yet," Clive said. "Research, experimentation and testing is an iterative process. We develop a hypothesis and look for where it's wrong. Then we refine and keep going until we can't find anything wrong."

Nik looked unconvinced.

"What you're saying," he said warily, "is that you want to get something wrong over and over again with me stuck in the middle of it the whole time."

"Exactly," Clive said happily.

"No!" Farrah said, shooting a scolding glare at Clive before turning back to Nik. "What he's saying is that we've already gone through the critical test stage. That's why we linked several other nodes before we came anywhere near this one. I am extremely confident this is going to work."

"Why?" Nik asked.

"Because you're here," Farrah told him. "You were literally made for this. Jason could have made some kind of control matrix, but he didn't. He made a person."

"So, I'm a glorified control panel?"

"No," Farrah said. "Jason is obsessed with doing what's right, even though he's wrong about what that is most of the time."

"Hey..."

Farrah was seated next to Nik in the skimmer. She shrugged down to bring her eyes closer to the level of the diminutive rabbit-man.

"You," she told him, "have what most people in the cosmos spend their entire lives looking for: a purpose. And it's not some small thing that a control panel can do. Your purpose is to keep us all alive. To prevent the destruction of a city full of people who have already suffered so much. To save the brightheart people, who will go extinct without you. You were born to be a hero, Nik. You're the most important person in this transformation zone."

"Really?" Nik asked.

"No, it's me," Jason said, earning a glare from Farrah. "You're definitely next, though, then probably Clive or Gary. Neil is near the bottom, between the magic researchers and the Builder cultists."

"You know the thunder doesn't muffle all the sound!" Neil yelled from his spot under a lightning rod. "Silver-rankers have very good hearing!"

"Quiet, you!" Jason yelled back. "This is why you ranked below that messenger who keeps stealing cars. If you…"

The air around Neil shimmered as a privacy screen snapped into place.

"Oh, no, he did not," an affronted Jason said.

"Operations Commander," Ramona said from somewhere below the skimmer.

Jason looked over the side.

"Sorry, Ramona," he said. "I forgot you were down there."

"Clearly. Not to complain, Operations Commander, but is there any chance you could get on with it? I can absorb some mana from the lightning to feed back into the shield, but I can't keep this up indefinitely."

"You should listen to the nice lady, bro," Taika said.

"Why are you here exactly?" Jason asked him.

"Rude," Taika said. "I wanted to see what it looks like from underneath when the lightning hits that shield."

They all looked up as a fresh lightning bolt struck the shield, electricity dancing across it in a brilliant display.

"Okay, that does look awesome," Nik said.

"I'm so glad about that," Ramona said. "CAN YOU PLEASE DO YOUR ACTUAL JOBS?"

"I like her," Taika said as Jason got to work. He plucked the shrunken cloud flask from his necklace and it returned to normal size. He set it on the dashboard in front of himself and Nik, sitting next to him, and removed the stopper. Wisps of cloud snaked out to form three small shapes: a mansion, a bus and a palace.

"Nik," Jason said. "Stick your hand in this one. The house."

Nik did as instructed and shoved his hand into the miniature cloud mansion. Jason did the same and the other two cloud models vanished. The image of the house started shifting, from the shape of a mansion to a replica of the mesa.

"Think about what you remember about the mesa," Jason told Nik. "Don't push it; just think about it and let the memories come."

"Those memories went away," Nik said.

"The ones on how to use the control centre, yes," Jason said. "But not your memories of the place itself. Of your time there with Dustin and Neil. What did it look like? What was the layout of the rooms? Where did you sleep? Did the elevating platform make a sound when it moved? Was the air dry or humid? What did it smell like? How did you launder the sheets?"

As Jason spoke, the cloud image became an increasingly accurate representation of the mesa. The array of lightning rods around the roof started to take shape.

"I think I'm feeling it," Nik said. "It's weird, like remembering something I forgot years ago."

"You're only a few months old, bro," Taika said, still looking up at the dome.

"Shut up," Clive told him in a sing-song voice, trying not to sound upset and interrupt Nik.

"Sorry, bro."

Once the cloud flask had formed a pattern based on the mesa, it started belching out cloud material. The skimmer backed off and Jason left the flask by the side of the mesa base, sitting in the mud. It continued spraying out cloud-stuff, ignoring the lightning. It was struck several times, the lightning appearing to be sucked inside.

"Should we have just used that to shelter us?" Taika wondered as they watched it.

While Ramona headed for Miriam and some much-needed rest, Jason and the others joined the rest of Team Biscuit under a lightning tower where Humphrey had set up an open-sided tent. He remained the best-equipped member of the team, having not just money but connections with adventuring supply specialists. The tent was pleasantly warm, magically repelling water and even had some basic cloud furniture.

"How much did this thing cost?" Jason asked.

"Not sure," Humphrey said. "Mother purchased it for me. Said I'd need it if I was still in Rimaros for the rainy season."

The main part of the work was done, not just for Jason's team and Ramona but all the silver- and gold-rankers. They all watched the cloud house mesa reach completion, the mass of cloud-substance taking on the precise look of the destroyed rock formation. Humphrey and Sophie were on a cloud couch, Belinda and Clive on another. The others stood around a table Jason had set up as a build-your-own-sandwich bar.

"That's exactly the way it was," Neil said as he handed a plate holding a salad sandwich to the rabbit-man, who could barely see over the table. "You did a fantastic job, Nik. How are you so much more competent than your dad?"

"Thanks, Uncle Neil."

"Nope," Jason said.

"Absolutely not," Neil agreed.

"We are not brothers," Jason insisted.

"Definitely not brothers."

"We're barely teammates. We're going to kick Neil out when we find a better healer. Or a thinner one."

"We would've kicked Jason out already, except he always figures it out and fakes his death before we have a chance. Or cripples himself and gets laid up for months. Or goes off alone and comes back brooding like a teenager."

"Will you two shut up?" Clive asked. "Nik, how did we do?"

"They're back," Nik said. "The memories of how to use the control centre. Nothing about other nodes, though."

"That's right within expectations," Clive said. "We need to get you inside and do some testing. Neil, you've been there before, right?"

"Yeah, the original version," Neil said and pointed at the base of the mesa. "The hidden entrance should be just down there."

"Then can you and Nik please lead us inside?"

"We're just about to eat," Neil said.

"We really should be acting with haste," Clive said.

"Oh, NOW we should be acting with haste?" Ramona called out from under another tower. She was reclining in a hammock that was hung on thin air.

"Can we please just go?" Clive asked.

"Okay," Nik said. "But we're taking our fu—"

A peal of thunder drowned him out.

"—ing sandwiches."

"Nik," Jason scolded. "Just because you can use those words doesn't mean that you should."

Shade bodies appeared and took the form of personal transport devices. They were floating discs that were normally round, but these black versions tapered to a sweeping point.

"You realise that round is more practical?" Clive asked as he moved out. His platform turned back into Shade and he landed in the black mud with a squelch.

"Apologies, Mr Standish. Please give me a moment to assume a more practical configuration."

"Ah, no thank you," Clive said wisely. "I'll just walk."

Jason used his aura to shield them all from the rain as he and Farrah brought up the rear. The mesa now shielded them from the lightning, the array of rods on top of the cloud version working like the original.

"I guess you were right," Jason said.

"Of course I was," Farrah said. "About what?"

"In being confident that this was going to work."

"Oh, that was a lie. Do have any idea how many academically unsound shortcuts we've taken over the course of this project? Half-tested hypotheses are the least of it. Half of the stuff I'm putting together I've taken from Clive using a questionable mind-reading power. These rituals we're using to link the control nodes are built as much on guesswork and hope as sound theory. The fact that we haven't made one of the Magic Society guys straight-up explode is a minor miracle."

"Uh, Farrah mate," Jason said.

"Yeah?"

"We don't have a privacy screen up."

Farrah looked around and saw everyone else looking back. Nik at the base of the mesa and the Magic Society researchers under a nearby lightning tower looked especially unhappy.

"Huh," Farrah said. "The thunder muffles sound less than you'd think, doesn't it?"

NOT ALL OF US ARE DEMIGODS

"THAT WAS HARD," GARY SAID. "NORMALLY, THE BOSS ANOMALIES ARE huge monstrosities, but this thing…"

He looked down at the odd, seemingly innocuous creature. It was round and purple with stubby arms and legs, like a child in a grape costume. It had a purple top hat and a face that was a couple of dots and a line, in the middle of its body, as if drawn on with a marker.

"What was that thing?" Miriam asked. "It's like it could remake reality."

"It came back from the dead more than Jason," Gary said.

In the end, it took Arabelle draining the creature's mana and using powers that impeded healing and even resurrection magic. That finally cut off its reality-warping powers and allowed them to kill it without it coming back to life.

They looked around the landscape that normally would have been pleasant, if rather odd. The territory was comprised of bold, simple colours, like a child's drawing. Hamlets comprising only a handful of little cottages were nestled amongst rolling hills. There was an unreality to it all, like an obviously false image somehow made real. The sky was too blue; the hills too green. The clouds too perfectly white and fluffy.

It was like standing in a child's dream, but one turned to nightmare by the living anomaly corpses scattered across the meadows and slumped against the yellow cottages. They were, like their surroundings, creatures that seemed more imaginary than real. Anthropomorphised shapes with stubby little arms and legs, their bodies shaped like circles, squares and triangles. They were all bright, bold colours. Red, blue or yellow; purple, pink or green. For most, their bodies and heads were the same thing, their faces drawn in simple dots and lines. Some had hats, others hair with pigtails or hairclips. One had bright red, high-heel shoes.

These were creatures of a child's fancy. It had felt wrong to cut them down, but their strange powers had made them dangerous. A purple triangle with a yellow hat and shoes moved so fast that gold-rankers had trouble keeping up. A square with a green hat hit Gary so hard, he was buried metres into a hillside. More dangerous were those whose powers were more esoteric.

A yellow circle man induced euphoria in anyone who went near him. Emir had stood lost in happiness as a pink heart-shaped creature almost squeezed him to death in a crushing hug. A blue circle with a flower in her hat told Gabriel to attack his wife, which did not end well for him. As she was healing him up after the fight, he was looking around at the strange landscape and its now dead inhabitants.

"Belle," he said, "do you know what I'm thinking about?"

"How you're going to make up for trying to stab your wife?" Arabelle asked.

"What? Oh, uh… yes? Yes. That's absolutely what I was thinki—"

He let out a yelp of pain.

"Is healing magic meant to hurt?" he asked.

"No," Arabelle said innocently. "Any pain you may be experiencing is likely a mental issue. Possibly brought on by guilt."

"Yes, dear. But, uh, the *other* thing I was thinking about was the Standish boy's explanation about Jason shaping this transformation zone. And a mountain shaped like his head."

"Mmm," Arabelle said as she rubbed her chin thoughtfully. "It would make sense for Jason to be responsible for… whatever is going on here. It does have his signature mix of whimsy and gruesome violence."

"It's creepy, right?" Gabriel asked.

"I think it might have been nice. Before we showed up and everything went berserk, anyway. Speaking of creepy, though…"

"Arabelle, you wound me," Boris said as he floated their way.

"Want me to wound you again?"

"Apologies, *Mrs Remore*. I can confirm that young Jason certainly had a hand in this place being as it is."

The three gold-rank messengers were too strong to not use in clearing territories but kept a wary distance. Like the Builder cultists, their alliance with the adventurers was uneasy. Only Boris Ket Lundi regularly approached the adventurers outside of combat.

"You know what these things are?" Gabriel asked the messenger.

"Indeed, I do, Lucky Husband."

"Stop calling me that."

"Oh, you don't think you were lucky in marriage? My dearest Mrs Remore, I'm afraid your husband's opinion of you is not as high as I'd hoped. If you and I—"

"I wonder how long messenger wings take to grow back," Arabelle casually mused.

"I'm just going to go over there," Boris said and floated away.

"That's right," Gabriel called out after him. "You keep walking. Or hovering or whatever."

"Gabriel?" Arabelle asked sweetly, her distracted spouse missing the warning sign.

"Yes, dear?"

"Do you really not feel like a lucky husband?"

Gabriel blinked, then blinked again, his face blank.

"I hate that guy so much."

Arabelle went to fetch Jason, who had portalled into a neighbouring territory he already controlled. The territory was a beautiful one filled with rolling hills and open plains filled with colourful wildflowers. The living anomalies belonging to it had been carnivorous plants and poison-spore fungi, and the place was much better for their absence. The sun shining from a blue sky made things just warm enough that the slight breeze was perfectly refreshing. The smell of flowers drifted on the air, pleasant without being pungent.

Arabelle had run to the rendezvous spot Jason had portalled to, gold-rank speed and stamina making a vehicle unnecessary. She found him standing next to what looked like an especially unnecessary vehicle: a fixed-wing glider trike with a large fan on the back for propulsion. It had two side-by-side seats and was entirely black.

"Wouldn't a skimmer be more efficient?" Arabelle asked as they looked at it sitting in the grass. "Or that aeroplane thing Shade often turns into? The one with a bar. I quite like that one."

"This is better," Jason said.

"I have my doubts. Until just now, I had been starting to believe that your world had universally superior vehicle design, despite the lack of magic."

"And there's the rub," Jason said, turning to point a finger at Arabelle. "A complete lack of magic, yet we still invented flying tricycles and you are somehow unimpressed."

She shook her head as she let out a chuckle.

"I shall concede the point. I am glad that you are thinking more positively about the world you came from."

"Yeah," Jason said. He reached up to rub his neck as his face took on a contemplative expression. "I'm even catching myself not dreading the idea of going back. I left a lot of unfinished business there. Emotional baggage. A vampire army. Do you ever stop and think that your life is weird?"

"Not since meeting you."

"Fair enough. Oh, and, I have to take back Taika and all those people from Earth that Humphrey's mum took in. I keep forgetting about them."

"You're silver rank," Arabelle pointed out. "With a silver-rank memory, you can't forget about them."

"Not with that attitude."

He grinned as she shook her head.

"Still," he said. "We have to deal with what's right in front of us before we look to the future. No reason we can't have a little fun while we're at it, though."

He claimed one of the seats in the trike glider and waved for her to join him.

The cartoonish landscape fascinated Jason. There were rolling green hills, roads that looked drawn in crayon and towns straight from a colouring book. Then he spotted the anomalies left dead from the rolling battle with the gold-rankers. Colourful shapes with little arms and legs. Some wore hats, others had hair the same colour as their bodies with clips or ties.

"I don't like this," Jason muttered. "This is just wrong."

"You know what these things are?" Arabelle asked as she fell into step with him.

"Yeah."

"The messenger said you would. This place is an echo of you, isn't it?"

"I wouldn't use the word echo."

Jason looked down at a thick shaft of frozen blood jutting diagonally from the ground. Dangling from it, impaled, was the body of a yellow circle creature with yellow hair and pigtails.

"Did she have some kind of light powers?" he asked, pointing.

"Yes," Arabelle said. "Searing beams of light. Not that dangerous alone, but she wasn't alone. This was the most dangerous territory we've cleared so far. Many of the anomalies had mental influence powers and tried to control us. Make us vulnerable to those with more conventional attacks. They had a lot of mental influence abilities, which is rare, and not often useful against gold-rankers."

"Because you can resist them with auras?"

"Yes. Vampires have strong mind-influencing powers and they still prefer targets two ranks lower than them. But the anomalies here have gotten so strong that only Gary, Boris the messenger and Lord Pensinata were able to fully resist them. My husband proved unfortunately susceptible."

"Is Gabriel alright?"

"The only thing my husband needs to be worried about is me."

Jason laughed, but lost his humour as he looked at the hanging body again.

"Her name was Sunshine," he said. "It's hard to deny that I influenced this territory, but I don't like the implication that this is somehow a reflection of me. Except, perhaps, my unconscious mind reflecting my habit of not properly thinking things through."

"How so?" Arabelle asked.

"The idea of a territory where these things are all just getting along on their own is nice. But they're still anomalies, so they turned bad once our people came here. It's necessary to claim the zone, so my nice idea turned into a horror show."

"What are these creatures?"

"For once, I'd rather not explain it. No fun in it. Should have been Care Bears."

"Care Bears?"

"Yeah. Those sinister little pricks have it coming."

The trike neared the ground where the adventurers and their allies were gathered. The final conflict with the boss anomaly and its minions had taken place on an open field that was too uniformly green to look natural. It had the largest collection of anomaly bodies, scattered across the ground.

The trike dissolved into a cloud of darkness rather than landing, dropping Jason and Arabelle to the ground. They landed, running before slowing to a walk. The shadowy cloud resolved into Shade, who moved alongside Jason. Boris moved quickly to join them.

"I have to say, Asano," Boris said, gesturing around them. "This is rather messed up."

"Agreed," Jason said.

They reached Gary, standing over the grape-like boss anomaly.

"Makes sense," Jason said looking at it. "His name was Impossible. I'm a little surprised you beat him."

"He kept coming back from the dead," Gary said. "He's worse for it than you."

"Can I have permission to loot all these bodies?" Jason asked.

"Please do," Gary said. "Something about seeing these things subjected to violence like this is unsettling. The sooner they're cleaned up, the better."

Jason nodded and Shade left, more Shade bodies pouring out of Jason's shadow to spread out and touch all the bodies so he could loot them. Jason reached down to touch the boss anomaly himself. Everyone stepped back and the body dissolved into rainbow smoke.

- [Stable Genesis Core] has been added to your inventory.
- [Greater Miracle Potion] has been added to your inventory.
- 10 [Gold Spirit Coins] have been added to your inventory.
- 100 [Silver Spirit Coins] have been added to your inventory.
- 1,000 [Bronze Spirit Coins] have been added to your inventory.
- 10,000 [Iron Spirit Coins] have been added to your inventory.

"Oh, hey," Jason said, pulling out the potion he just looted. It was a small vial filled with pale blue liquid and swirling silver sparks.

Item: [Greater Miracle Potion] (Gold rank, legendary)

Salvation in a bottle (consumable, potion).

- Effect: Fully restores health, mana and stamina. Negates all afflictions and effects of gold-rank or lower that prevent cleansing or are triggered by cleansing. This potion is only effective on gold rank and lower individuals. If administered to an individual of silver rank or below within moments of death, it will revive them. The magic of this potion lingers in the body longer than normal potions, meaning additional recovery health and recovery items will not be effective for a longer period.

"I haven't seen one of these in ages," Jason said. "The higher-rank ones are good."

"Miracle potion?" Gary asked.

"Yeah."

"I've heard the gold-rank ones are impossible to make. You get them accidentally, very, very rarely when brewing really high-end healing potions. And only while overdoing it with using exceptional materials or energy. Divine power and the like."

"You take it," Jason said, holding out the vial. "If something goes pear-shaped clearing these territories and a healer can't get to someone in time, you've got the best chance of not having been taken out. You could save someone, or maybe get a healer back on their feet."

Gary took the vial, pinching it with his thumb and forefinger. It looked tiny next in his massive hand. He slipped the vial into an empty loop on his potion belt.

"It's getting on time you and I had a serious talk," Jason said. "About what comes next."

Gary looked away.

"Have to get on to the next territory," he said.

"Not right now," Miriam told him as she approached. "Asano, claim this territory and we'll all head back to base. We've been going hard and this territory was the worst yet."

"I can keep going," Gary said.

"I'm sure you can," Miriam told him, "but not all of us are demigods. Gold-rankers have a lot of stamina, but the mind needs rest as well. I think that's true even for you. I'm not asking, Xandier."

"Yes, Tactical Commander," he murmured. It sounded like thunder with his rumbling lion voice, resonating with divine power. He strode off, his long legs quickly eating distance. Jason watched him go with a sigh.

Gary's booming laugh echoed through the massive hallway in the mountain fortress. With Rufus and Farrah at his side, he pushed open a set of massive double doors and stopped. The bar was empty aside from one person, the furniture pushed to the sides of the room. Only four chairs were left in the middle, set around the last remaining table. Of the chairs, three were normal wooden chairs while the last was a massive, throne-like affair. It was the only one that looked like it would hold Gary.

The chair opposite held the room's only occupant. Jason was pouring drinks into three glasses and one mug. The bottle held something bright red and, Gary guessed, sickly sweet. When he was done with the red liquor, he added a few drops of another liquid to each glass, and a splash to the mug. The red liquid started swirling with black, dancing inside each glass like living things.

Gary turned to leave, only to find Rufus and Farrah in his way.

"I can make you move," he growled.

"And I can make you stay," Jason said from behind him.

Gary turned to look at him. "You really believe that?"

"No," Jason said with a grin. "But it was a good line and I don't think you'll make me try."

Gary looked at Farrah and Rufus like they were traitors and stomped over to the large chair. He dropped himself into it, opposite Jason. The others joined them and the double doors closed on their own. The only light came from a glass wall and the lava waterfall beyond it, washing the room in red.

"What kind of madman has a lava waterfall as an indoor feature?" Gary rumbled. Jason just grinned. Gary took his mug and drained it.

"Not bad," he begrudgingly acknowledged.

Jason smiled. It was soft and warm compared to his usual amused smirking.

"It's time to stop dodging this conversation, Gary," he said.

"You had to get them involved?" Gary asked, inclining his head to indicate Farrah, then Rufus.

"You kind of made me, buddy."

Gary growled.

"Fine," he grumbled. "Let's talk about how I die."

4 8

THE PRICE

JASON LOOKED FROM GARY, ACROSS THE TABLE FROM HIM, TO FARRAH and Rufus on either side. He could feel the tremulation in their auras at being so close to the divine power coursing through Gary. The demigod couldn't contain the power as well as Jason could his own in his soul realm. The power didn't belong to him and his body was an imperfect vessel anyway. The power was slowly but surely eating him from the inside out.

Neither Rufus nor Farrah showed any discomfort on their faces. They would support their friend if it meant pretending they weren't on fire, let alone just being near a powerful aura. Given Jason and the company he kept, it was something they'd long gotten used to.

"Do you want them to stay?" Jason asked Gary.

"Yes," Gary said, after only a short hesitation.

"We'll need to explain some things, then," Jason said. "They'll have questions. We'll have to tell them why certain things won't work."

Gary nodded.

"Well," Jason said, "let's get the big things out of the way first. Yes, there is a way to potentially keep Gary alive. And yes, there are problems with it. Hero gave me something."

"Like Healer gave you something?" Rufus asked. "The thing that allowed you to create a new intelligent species?"

"The same sort of item, yes," Jason said. "They're like skill books for gods. Or made by gods for people like me, really. The gods already know what they're doing. But soul engineering is what they teach. Soul engineering isn't exclusive to gods, but they have a natural aptitude for it. Unlike astral kings, which is why Vesta Carmis Zell keeps buggering things up."

"Focus, Jason," Farrah said. "You don't get to ramble off on tangents. Not today."

"Sorry," he said. "The point is, the divine gifts Healer and Hero gave me show me how to do things and make sure I get it right the first time I try. That's how I managed to create Nik without him going horribly wrong, and why trying again probably would. It's also how I know that, if I try to save Gary's life, that won't go wrong either."

"What do you mean *if?*" Rufus asked, leaning forward in his chair. "There's no if here, Jason. If you can—"

"Rufus," Gary said, cutting his friend off.

"I know you're sad and worried," Jason said. "I know that anger makes you feel like you can do something about that, but we both know it's lying to you. Stop for a moment. Take a breath. Remember that every person in this room loves Gary. No one here wants him to die."

Rufus picked up his drink and leaned back in his chair.

"You sound like my mother," he grumbled.

"And you sound like Humphrey," Farrah teased, and they all laughed. For a moment they were just four friends sitting around a table, but the reason they were there settled over them again, dampening the mood.

"What Hero gave me isn't for creating life," Jason said. "It's about taking one source of external power within a soul and replacing it with another. Right now, Hero's power is inside of Gary. It can't reach for its god, but the moment we're out of this transformation zone, it will. Gary can hold on to it for maybe a few hours, but then it will be gone. And that power is the thing keeping him alive."

"What about your soul realm?" Rufus asked. "Hero can't get in there, right?"

"No, he can't," Jason said. "And if Gary was willing to stay there for the next few months, maybe as much as a year, then he could keep the power."

"A year?" Rufus asked.

"That's how long the power would take to kill me," Gary said. "My body was enhanced to endure the power, but not for a lifetime. The power keeping me alive right now will eventually and inevitably kill me."

"That's why Hero gave me the gift," Jason said. "When the transformation zone is reintegrated into reality, I'll be claiming it as a domain. Reshaping to my will. Not unconsciously, as when it first formed when my influence was scattered across the dividing territories. This will be deliberate. Unified. I've done it twice before and I didn't have anything like the tools I have now."

"And you believe that you can reshape Gary as well?" Farrah asked.

"If he lets me. If he trusts me."

"I do," Gary said.

Jason gave him a warm smile.

"I know. I'll have the soul forge then, and Hero's gift to guide me. If Gary wants me to, I can strip the divine power out of him and put something else in its place. Something with the power to keep him alive without being so powerful it also burns him out."

"Are you talking about your power?" Farrah asked. "Making him a Voice of the Will?"

"No," Jason said. "He'd need to mainline the power I draw straight from the astral. The infinite magic hose that allows me to control my soul realm like a god."

"It's god-level power?" Farrah asked.

"Yes," Jason said. "Transcendent power, like the divine power flowing through him right now."

"Meaning it would still kill me," Gary said.

"Yeah," Jason said.

"Then what?" Rufus asked. "The authority you took from Undeath?"

"I've already used that," Jason said. "I used it to reforge the ghost fire that Death showed me how to make."

"And it was also from a god," Farrah said. "I imagine the same problem about too much power applies."

"Why does it apply?" Rufus asked, his voice rising again. "Jason, why can you seemingly suck up any cosmic power floating around while the first taste of it is killing Gary?"

Jason sighed.

"Because I'm on the cusp of half-transcendent," he said. "I've been moving towards that, step by step, probably since my first soul scar. Some of it by happenstance and some through guidance and effort, but I've been moving towards a certain end. Even then, what was left of the avatar— less divine power than Gary has coursing through him—damn-near turned me inside out."

"I didn't take any of those steps," Gary said. "I wasn't prepared. I don't have a hardened soul and experience wielding vast cosmic power. I was grabbed and stuffed full of divine power that did its best to change me in a way that wouldn't make me explode on the spot. But I will explode, sooner or later, if the power stays inside me."

"Then what is it?" Farrah asked. "What power do you want to put into Gary?"

"It's not a matter of want," Jason said. "It's about having a chance, and an exceptionally rare one at that. Do you know how many people have survived drinking from Hero's cup?"

"None," Rufus said.

"No, there have been some," Jason said. "Hero told me as much. I think he doesn't tell people because he doesn't want them to hope."

"That's bleak," Farrah said.

"No," Gary said. "It's fair. If people drank from the cup thinking there was a way to survive, it's a choice built on deception. Even if it's self-deception."

"But some have survived," Jason said. "Very few, and only under extremely specific circumstances. And even then, I don't think they come out the other side the same way they went in."

"That's the price," Gary said. "That kind of power always comes with a price."

"Yeah," Jason said.

They sat in contemplative silence for a moment. Farrah was the first one to speak.

"Enough dodging the question, Jason. What's the power?"

"The natural array," Jason said.

"The natural array that corrupted everything and started all this mess?" Rufus asked. "The natural array that is so unstable that we went to prevent it blowing up, wiping out Yaresh and casting the whole region into perpetual darkness as the sky fills with ash?"

"Yes," Jason said. "Once this is over, I'll be remaking everything. Using my ghost fire to purge the taint of undeath energy. Extracting and repairing the soul forge. Re-establishing the natural array in a stable state. Rebuilding a home for the surviving brighthearts. Some other things, including swapping out the power inside Gary, if that's what he chooses."

"And you think this will work?" Rufus asked.

"Yes," Jason said. "The gods knew what was coming better than any of us mortals, which is why they made the choices they did. Undeath tried to seize control of events directly. Destruction cajoled and manipulated those depraved enough to work with him. Healer, Hero and Death understood that if Undeath and Destruction didn't get their way, it would not be a god that decides the ultimate outcome of events."

"They knew it would be you," Farrah realised.

"Yes," Jason said. "Healer wanted the home of the brighthearts healed and his gift set me on the path to participate. Death wanted the power of Undeath purged and showed me how. Hero wants one of his champions to live, and knew that I could do that if he gave me the right tool."

"Then what's wrong with doing it that way?" Rufus asked. "Our options here are Gary lives and Gary dies. Why are you acting like that isn't the easiest choice in the world? Why is using the natural array to keep him alive bad?"

"It's a specific and limited power," Jason said. "That's partly why it works. Like all of us, Gary shaped his soul with essences. Iron and fire. These match this natural array very well, making him compatible with it. But the divine power inside him changed those powers and I don't know how compatible the natural array will be with what's been done. Maybe he'd be almost as strong as he is now. Maybe he'd lose all his essence abilities. Maybe his iron and fire powers would change, becoming something new."

"I thought you said you were sure you could do this right," Rufus said. "This sounds more like you're going to butcher his soul."

Farrah put her hands on the table and leaned forward, about to retort to Rufus' accusatory tone. Jason quietly gestured for her to back off. She gave him a querying look from under raised eyebrows and he nodded confirmation. Her expression was sceptical, but she sat back in her chair, clearly unhappy.

"Rufus," Jason said. "You know the task ahead of us. We're talking about reshaping a section of reality that was ripped out of the universe, chopped into bits, and now we're putting those bits back together. Once we've done that, I have to blend the whole thing into sludge, take that sludge and make something new out of it. Something I can fit back into the hole we tore in the universe when we took it out in the first place. And somewhere in there, I have to take Gary, who drank from the cup of 'you're definitely going to die because the gods say so' and make him not die."

Jason rubbed his hands over his tired face.

"There's a reason I'm not skipping down the street in delight that I can keep Gary alive," he continued. "You're correct in that what I'm talking about doesn't sound like things going right. If Gary wants this, what I do to his soul will be ugly. He won't come out of it the way he was, or even the way he is now. 'Going right' means that any of this is possible at all. We need more than a miracle, Rufus. A miracle is what's killing him. We have to undo a miracle."

Jason slumped in his chair as if his words had taken all his energy with them. Rufus looked at him, unsure of what to say, so Farrah filled the gap.

"Do you remember what Jason said at the start of this conversation?" she asked Rufus. "That he'd need to tell us why some things wouldn't work. He was blunt in answering you, but do you think Gary doesn't know this? You think he doesn't feel what's happening inside him?"

Rufus turned to look at Gary who continued to sit impassively in his throne-like chair.

"He might not have known exactly what Jason was going to say," Farrah continued, "but he knew enough. He understands what's happening to him. He knows better than any of us that he made a sacrifice and there's no getting around that. Even if he doesn't die, there's a price he paid for the power we needed then and still need now. He knows it. He's accepted it. He's just been sitting there, barely speaking, because he's waiting for us to accept it too."

"Well, I don't!" Rufus yelled.

"Too bad," Gary said. "Jason had you bring me here so he could give me a choice, not you. All three of you are right. Farrah's right that I understood what I was doing the moment I chose to put that cup to my lips. Jason is right that this is something I have to face. And you, Rufus, are right that this is awful and unfair. But that doesn't make it go away."

Rufus chair fell over as he got up and threw his arms around the leonid. Gary was still taller, even sitting down. He put a big arm around a weeping Rufus.

"Your tears are making my fur wet," Gary teased.

"Shut up," Rufus said with a laughing sob.

The four friends sat around the table that had accumulated more empty bottles.

"Where did you get something that would make a demigod drunk?" Rufus asked.

"I am not drunk," Gary said. "Maybe a little tipsy."

"It's for diamond-rankers," Jason said. "There was some left after I made dinner for… it doesn't matter where it came from."

"I'm sorry, Jason," Rufus said as he absently rubbed his head with a cloth. "I never should have gone off on you like that."

No one at the table had managed to fully hold on to sobriety, but Rufus was more in his cups than the others and had a noticeable slur to his words.

"You don't have to be sorry to me," Jason said. "I know you don't expect me to do what I can't. The anger needs to go somewhere, and you should be angry. We all should. We just don't get to do anything about it."

"No," Rufus insisted. "It isn't fair."

"There is no fair here," Jason said. "I keep coming back, every time, but Gary gets caught up in one miracle and…"

He drew a ragged breath and let it out in sobs before draining his glass.

"Tell me what it'll be like," Gary said. "If I let you stick this natural array up my bum or whatever."

"It'll suck," Jason said. "I don't know what'll happen to your powers. Or your mind. I know you won't get any stronger. However strong you are is how strong you'll stay. You won't die, which is good. Like, ever. Not as long as the array is there. I can probably come back and move it when the planet dies. Shade, remind me to come back and move the natural array in five billion years or whatever."

"Of course, Mr Asano," Shade said from Jason's shadow. Jason failed to notice the headshake practically audible in his familiar's tone.

"The thing is," Jason continued, "you'll be completely reliant on the array. If anything happens to it, you die. And you can't leave it. You have to stay within its influence. You can live forever—terms and conditions apply—but you'll live your whole life in the brightheart city. So we should try to make sure that cultists and messengers and undead don't invade it again."

"I can't go anywhere?" Gary asked.

"Nope," Jason said. "Sorry. It's a pretty bad deal."

"You can't die, Gary," Rufus said.

"You don't have to choose now," Jason said.

"He doesn't?" Rufus asked. "Then why did you have us bring him here?"

"So he gets time to choose," Farrah said. "That's super obvious. I think your head wax is making your brain go runny."

"I don't wax my head," Rufus insisted.

"You're waxing your head right now," she told him.

Rufus looked confused and brought the hand holding the cloth he was rubbing his head with down in front of his face. He looked at it as if he'd never seen it before, despite it being monogrammed with his initials.

"How did that get there?"

49
GUARANTEED TO BECOME ENEMIES

JASON HAD A MEASURE OF CONNECTION TO HIS CLAIMED TERRITORY, although it was not as strong as that to his spirit domains. As the territory expanded to continental size, it took increasing amounts of concentration and effort to get a sense of what was happening in distant reaches. Standing in the control room of the lightning mesa, his eyes were closed as he extended his senses to a distant location. Neil, Nik and Belinda were observing and waiting.

"When we were being sold on the adventuring life," Belinda said, "no one mentioned the parts about standing around watching some guy concentrate quietly."

"I'd usually agree," Neil said, "but I think I've had quite enough living on the edge of life and death for a while. I'd be quite happy giving up excitement for a real sky, a reclining chair and a fruit platter."

"It doesn't have to be life and death," Belinda said. "Maybe just a nice heist where the worst case is having to beat up some rich prick's private guards as we make a break for it."

"You realise that we're all extremely rich ourselves, right?"

"We are?" Nik asked.

Neil looked at him, then back at Belinda.

"You realise that you and I are both extremely rich, right?" Neil amended.

"Oh," Nik said, hanging his head.

Jason opened his eyes.

"It should be any moment now," he said. "They're just about to complete the ritual linking the other node to this one."

They all looked at Nik expectantly.

"Okay," the rabbit-man said. "Now I'm getting performance anxiety."

"Don't worry," Jason assured him. "You shouldn't need to do anything; it'll just happen. It's like healing magic: it doesn't take any skill."

Neil turned his head to give Jason a look that was almost a special attack. Jason failed to keep a straight face, smothering a laugh.

"Nik," Neil said sweetly. "Do remind me to tell Rufus' mum what Jason just—"

"Hey hey hey!" Jason said urgently. "What happens in the lightning mesa stays in the lightning mesa."

"Yeah, sorry, Jason," Belinda said, "but that's not how blackmail works."

"I think it's happening," Nik said and all eyes turned to him. "Yeah, I can feel it. I can feel it. I feel… is that it? Wow, that's anticlimactic."

"But you're connected?" Jason asked.

"Yeah," Nik confirmed, "but it's like expecting a biscuit and only getting a crumb. We need to connect a lot more if you want this to be anything."

"I suspect," Belinda said, "that Clive won't be disappointed to hear that."

"How is it going?" Miriam asked Jason. They were catching up in his office in the mountain fortress. Jason was in his throne-like chair, the lava waterfall spilling down behind him.

"Over the last month, we've linked almost all the nodes we have access to. It's looking like we'll need to connect most, if not all before Nik can do anything effective with them. He can control the others remotely, but can't get the nodes to work together or function beyond their localised areas."

"But he will when the node network is complete?"

"He says yes. He compared it to trying to run a half-built machine. We need access to the rest of the nodes."

"Clearing the remaining territories is getting slower," Miriam said.

"I've started restricting even most of the gold-rankers. At this stage, Lord Pensinata, Mrs Remore and Boris Ket Lundi are the only ones I'm confident will return safely. If we didn't have Gareth, we'd have to take larger risks. But since we've got the power of a demigod on our side, we may as well play it safe. He works slower when almost alone, but he remains unstoppable."

"So long as we don't go so slow that the zone starts breaking down, I agree with your approach, Tactical Commander."

"Do you have any idea how long it will be until the zone destabilises?"

"No. I'm not seeing signs of it, so I think we still have a goodly amount of time. Even so, we shouldn't waste it on anything not worthwhile."

"I was hoping that we could try something that might accelerate the process," Miriam said. "Something that would require you to do more than just show up at the end to claim the cleared territory."

"Please," Jason said. "I've been feeling useless watching everyone else work. My magical knowledge is too specialised in astral magic to help set up the nodes and I'm too weak to clear territories. All I can do is swan in to claim them after everyone else does the work."

"I think you've made contributions enough, Operations Commander. You were the one to finally eliminate the avatar."

"Yeah, but that's weird cosmic power stuff. I haven't done much as an adventurer, or even as a commander. We both know that you're the one doing most of the work on that front. Which is not me trying to horn in, by the way. You're doing a great job."

"As an adventurer, Operations Commander, you're a silver-ranker. Do you think all the others without the expertise to help link the nodes feel any different?"

"I suppose not."

"Then, might I make a suggestion?"

"Please."

"Perhaps you should show some solidarity with those idle silver-rankers, and perhaps our brightheart allies. Build morale."

Jason slapped himself on the head.

"Of course," he said. "I can't believe I didn't think of that. What is wrong with me? I need to throw a barbecue."

"That's not exactly what I—"

"I have to go," Jason said, standing up.

"Operations Commander."

"There's a barbecue and outdoor supply shop in town I can raid for supplies."

"Operations Commander."

"I don't think the butcher will have anything edible left. I'll have to check the supplies we brought from the surface. No, that was all spirit coins and ritual materials. Maybe I can—"

"OPERATIONS COMMANDER!"

Jason was pulled out of his thoughts, looking at her distractedly.

"Hmm, what?"

"You may recall, Operations Commander, that this tangent began when I said there was something else I was hoping you could do."

"You didn't just mean the barbecue?"

"No."

"Because I have this whole barbecue to organise now."

"Mr Asano..."

"The barbecue was your idea in the first place, is what I'm saying. It seems odd that you'd be the one to—"

Miriam's aura rose angrily and Jason chuckled.

"You seem tense, Tactical Commander. We all are. We've all been in here for months. Breaking bread with our worst enemies. Facing power we can't match and fighting battles we don't understand. We need a tension breaker. A little bit of normalcy, as much as we can manage here."

"That... is not an invalid point. But there is something else I'd like you to do."

"You want me to see if the ghost fire I enhanced by eating the avatar can help clear undead territories."

It was a statement, not a question, but Miriam wasn't surprised. She knew that while Jason might seem hands-off, leaving everything to her, he was always watching. Often by means she didn't understand.

"None of this is easy," Jason said. "You and I have the greatest responsibility here and I'm the one with all the answers. All the secrets. The power to interact with the strange forces that govern this place. You're doing amazingly, Miriam, under extreme circumstances. When you want me to try with the undead, let me know. In the meantime, I have to try and find some viable meat."

Gary, Arabelle and Amos protected Jason as he delivered his afflictions. The ghost fire was applied alongside each other affliction in Jason's repertoire, although it did take time to be effective. The quality of the flames had massively improved since fuelling them with refined divine authority, but the source was still Jason and Jason was still silver rank.

As was the nature of afflictions, application plus time would inevitably reap results. While Gary disassembled individual undead at a pace that made Jason seem harmless, the territories poisoned by undeath energy teemed with unliving anomalies. The escalating power of Gordon's butterflies spreading Jason's afflictions could clear an undead territory faster than the demigod.

Many of the unclaimed territories were marked by undeath. It was a reflection of the zone being made from the subterranean realm of the brighthearts that was deeply tainted by undeath energy. One territory was like an Earth city that felt like a zombie movie. Another was a forest the size of a large nation, the trees leafless and dead as snow covered the ground. Ghoulish unliving elves stalked through the trees attacking in bursts of savage speed.

Territory after territory was claimed. They reached the boundary of the territory containing the massive tree, but it was impenetrable. Unlike the shadowy veils bordering normal territories, it was surrounded by impermeable darkness. They continued unifying the territories around it, adding any environmental nodes they uncovered to the growing network.

While territories were being claimed, the uneasy group of allies was increasingly idle. Some of the adventurers participated in linking the nodes, surrounding the control centres in massive ritual circles of carved stone or other resilient materials. But with the claiming of new territories slowing down, they soon caught up to all available nodes. After that, linking each new one as it was found became a leisurely affair.

Miriam and Jason's main task became preventing cabin fever. Their large and disparate alliance included former and potentially future foes, along with outright enemies. Even members of the same group could end up clashing if left with nothing to do. Adventurers, especially elite ones, were not known for their accommodating humility.

One of the ways they sought to keep the peace was by separating the groups. The largest group by far was the three factions of messengers. The smallest faction was Jason's prisoners, led by Marek Nior Vargas. They had quickly subordinated themselves to Boris, however, treating him like the Unorthodoxy messiah. They proved more enthusiastic than the people Boris had shanghaied into obedience.

Most of the messengers were those liberated from stasis as their territories were claimed. All were free now, courtesy of Jason, but discontent still simmered within many of them. No small number had been used as cannon fodder slaves, including by members of the alliance.

Given their numbers, the messenger groups were given the residential sections of Jason's town. The Builder cultists took over the nicer motels, of which there were many in the tourist town. The adventurers occupied the pleasure yachts at the marina or the mountain lair, whichever was their preference. The brighthearts all stayed in the mountain. The enclosed stone construction and lava waterfall were comforts to the subterranean people, as close as they could find to the home the transformation zone had annihilated.

The final group were the young messengers, released from stasis and with little idea of who or even what they were. Jali Corrik Fen took it upon herself to shield them from any influence or manipulation by the other groups. She was aided by Tera Jun Casta, the messenger Jason had forcibly freed. Jali was her only friend, and she was antagonistic to Marek and Boris both, loudly and repeatedly calling them traitors.

More than hatred, however, Tera felt a kinship with the young and unindoctrinated messengers. She shared their lack of purpose, not knowing what to do or even who they were. Some of these messengers grew experimental, exploring the town and trying to decipher the artefacts of Earth.

Jali had been unsure how to handle this but Jason told her to leave them to their curiosity. More than once, she found Jason amongst them showing off different bouncing devices. One was a springy pole that appeared to be a wildly inefficient vehicle. Another was an inflatable room that held no discernible purpose at all.

Jason held his barbecue. While the messengers were allowed to attend, few did. Boris and one of his gold-rankers showed up, the offsider getting along well with Jali Corrik Fen, who attended with some of the more curious young messengers. Marek Nior Vargas and his people didn't join in other than an adventurous woman named Mari Gah Rahnd. Boris found her name hilarious and she challenged him to a fight, despite his higher rank. She didn't seem to take the subsequent beating to heart.

Only the Builder cult was excluded, as the only ones guaranteed to become enemies again once the transformation zone had been escaped. They also didn't eat regular food, all being bizarre magical cyborgs.

The social gathering did help alleviate some of the tensions in the groups, but Jason and Miriam had no illusions of it being anything but a band-aid solution. They had been trapped for months in this strange place, facing lethal danger that claimed friends and allies. Now they were left idle, with little to do beyond think about what they had been through and what they had lost.

This was especially true of the brighthearts. They had been fighting longer and lost more than anyone else. Now they found themselves the safest they had been in a long time, which did not speak well of the previous circumstances. Most of their populace was dead and their home had been destroyed, yanked into a pocket dimension they didn't understand.

Jason found the brightheart resiliency inspiring. All they had lost, yet they were probably the most stable of the groups in the alliance. He had discussed this with Lorenn, their leader, hoping to find something that would help the others. She told him that before the arrival of the expedition from the surface, they'd been hiding with nowhere left to run, waiting for the last of their people to die. They had lost almost everything, but now they had hope. Although it was hard and strange, there was a path forward.

Jason wasn't sure if that was something he could use to keep the rest of the alliance from going full *Lord of the Flies*, but it certainly made him feel better.

Gary eventually became the only one clearing territories. Partly this was because of the danger, and partly because the last gold-rankers he had been working with were occupied. Jason also stopped, as Gary was uncertain of being able to protect him alone.

Boris became increasingly involved in managing the other messengers. Left alone, Marek Nior Vargas kept trying to recruit the new messengers. Boris knew that if that behaviour kept up, Jason would hold Boris responsible and it would hurt the burgeoning trust between the two men.

Arabelle had turned to her primary profession, tending to the mental health of the group as a whole. Miriam and Jason were grateful as their expertise stopped at discipline and barbecues respectively.

Amos Pensinata had become distracted, the famously stoic man uncharacteristically troubled. Jason one day noticed him in a metal dinghy, far out into the water. He flew out and joined him, sitting down but saying nothing. They sat there for hours before Amos started talking.

"I failed my nephew," he said finally. "I pushed him and his team into this. Now his friends are dead or broken. I don't know if any of them will be adventurers ever again."

Jason was unsure what to say. From his arrival on Pallimustus, he'd been startled about the cultural acceptance of throwing children into violence. It was a violent world and they had to learn to survive, but it still seemed brutal and savage.

The consequences had seemed obvious to Jason, but Amos seemed surprised. Jason wasn't sure how to respond, as Amos wasn't factually wrong. The now fallen team Storm Shredder had chosen their path, but it was Amos who had laid it out for them. Who wouldn't trust such a well-known hero's intentions for his own nephew? Jason himself had trusted the man as well.

Even if he'd been inclined to moralise, Jason knew he had no high ground to stand on. He'd thrown himself and his friends into everything team Storm Shredder had faced and worse. He wasn't Arabelle and didn't know the right thing to say without making things worse, so he didn't say anything. Instead, he took out a six-pack of beer stubbies and handed one to Amos.

"I didn't think you liked beer," Amos said.

"I don't, much," Jason said. "But I'm Australian, and one thing Australians know is that, for some things, only beer will do."

"That seems like an unhealthy attitude," Amos said.

"Oh, definitely," Jason said. "Our culture massively overlooks alcohol abuse."

50

ASSUMING WE WIN

JASON COULDN'T HEAR RUFUS, BUT THE ANGER IN HIS BODY LANGUAGE was easy to read. He watched Rufus and Gary from the observation room in his mountain fortress, set behind one of the eyes in the head-shaped edifice. His friends were in the town, standing in front of the ice cream store. If not for his silver-rank perception, he wouldn't be able to see them clearly from this distance.

Although he couldn't hear them, there was no doubt in Jason's mind about what Rufus was yelling. It was the same thing he had been for weeks. Gary refused to make a definitive decision while Rufus insisted there was no decision to be made. Farrah emerged from the ice cream shop looking disgruntled and once again went to work playing peacemaker.

Jason sighed. He understood Rufus, who had already lost Farrah and himself. By miracles of circumstance, he'd gotten them back, but he'd mourned them both. And they all knew that if Gary died, there would be no coming back. Jason feared that Rufus would end up regretting how he spent the last days with his best friend in the world, should Gary decide to let go.

Jason had spoken to both Farrah and Arabelle about what to do. Did he step up as a friend? Try to help Rufus see the precious time he was squandering? Or would that backfire and only fuel his anger? Arabelle had suggested giving her son space, so Jason had.

Arabelle had pointed out that Rufus might suggest Jason keep Gary alive, regardless of what the man chose. That wasn't how it worked, and even Rufus understood that, but he was far from thinking clearly. The danger wasn't that he would blame Jason for not doing it. The danger would come after, whatever Gary chose. Rufus and his inflated sense of responsibility would eat him alive over having asked that of Jason. Of trying to take away his friend's choice.

Accordingly, Jason had been avoiding Rufus, not that the man was seeking him out. His anger extended to Jason, despite knowing that neither he nor Gary deserved that anger. Rage cared little for logic.

Jason sighed, unhappy that the best he could offer his friend was his absence. There was no shortage of things to distract him, though, so he opened a shadow portal and stepped through. He arrived inside the control room of the lightning mesa.

Nik was standing on a floating platform, moving between control panels. Neil and Dustin Kettering were on the same side of a metal table fixed to the floor. They were playing a game that involved stacking colourful wooden poles and cardboard platforms to make a tower. None of them noticed Jason appearing.

"…because it's a weather machine, not a bloody satellite weapon," Nik said angrily.

"What's a satellite weapon?" Dustin asked.

"I don't know!"

"How do you not know?" Neil asked.

"Because I'm six months old. Most of what I know is random nonsense put in my head by a man *far* too invested in TV theme songs."

"What's a TV theme song?" Dustin asked.

"Yeah, that must be awful," Neil said. "Want a sandwich?"

"Yes, please," Nik said. "And some carrot juice—not because I'm a rabbit!"

"You're allowed to like what you like," Neil said with a chuckle. He got up and turned around, which was when he saw Jason, his body jerking in startlement.

"Why are you creeping around?" Neil asked, prompting the others to turn as well. "How long have you been there?"

"Long enough to realise that Nik doesn't properly appreciate a shadowy flight into the world of a man who does not exist."

"What does that mea—" Dustin started to ask before Neil cut him off with a hand gesture.

"No," Neil said in the firm tone of a dog trainer. "Do not ask."

"You're no fun," Jason said with a chuckle. "How goes the testing?"

"It's easy enough to control," Nik said. "I'm getting coverage across the entire unified territory, so that's all good. The issues are lead-in time before anything happens and imprecision when it does, because—"

"...it's a weather machine, not a satellite weapon," Jason finished. "That's where I came in."

"We've got the Magic Society guys doing direct observation in the areas we're testing it," Neil said. "Clive, Lindy and Ramona are running herd on them."

"Sounds like it's well in hand," Jason said. "When will you be ready to give Miriam a tactical feasibility report?"

"That's on Clive," Neil said. "You know what he's like, chasing down every little variable. With how rushed this whole thing has been, he's getting real fastidious now we've got it working."

"That will have to change," Jason said. "We've united all the territories but the tree, but we're running out of time."

"You're seeing signs of zone collapse?" Neil asked. "How long?"

"Not sure," Jason said. "That's my next stop. Tell Clive to finish up."

"Okay, but I don't know how quick he'll be about it."

"Tell him to come see me when he has a chance. Actually, leave out the bit about when he has a chance. In fact, don't tell him to come see me; tell him to report to the Operations Commander. No, forget all that. Where's Clive now?"

"You don't know?" Dustin asked. "I thought you could see everything going on in the territory."

"I can," Jason said. "If I look. This isn't my soul realm, so it takes a little more active attention to do things. It's possible I've been exaggerating my capabilities to keep a lid on internal discord."

Clive and Jason stepped out of a portal in one of the outlying areas of the territories. Clive was immediately taken aback by the border of the transformation zone, a hazy wall spanning up into the sky. It resembled the blurry image of a distant landscape viewed through a malfunctioning recording crystal. It was also throwing off a cloud of ultrafine dust.

"What is this?" he asked, moving forward.

"Don't get too close," Sophie warned him.

Clive dragged his attention from the wall to look around. They were atop a rise in a temperate climate, late spring or early autumn judging from the pleasant weather. He could see the land around them, including a river spilling out to sea. The wall crossed the land and over the body of water, extending to the horizon. Sophie and Miriam Vance had been waiting for their arrival.

"Come on," Sophie said and led them downslope, moving parallel to the wall. Reaching flat ground, a series of thin wooden poles had been laid out on the ground, end-to-end. They started at the wall and extended directly away from it. Clive noticed markings on the pole and saw they were units of measure.

"A measuring device," he said.

He examined the pole closest to the wall without getting too close. The pole was half-length, the ragged end looking like the wall had eaten the rest. As he looked at the numbers, it seemed like the measurements had started past the wall, but it had cut off around a pole and a half.

"You're measuring distance," he said. "The wall is moving in?"

"Welcome to the end of the universe," Jason said. "Unfortunately, the universe is getting smaller."

"I was assigned to watch the boundaries," Sophie told Clive. "Around the time you started working on the magic linky thing."

"The environmental control node network?"

"Sure," she said.

"Almost no one was informed of Miss Wexler's assignment," Miriam said. "Myself, the Operations Commander, Miss Wexler, Lord Geller and now you."

"Humphrey would have wondered why she kept running off instead of sticking around for sexy time," Jason said.

"*Commander*," Miriam scolded.

"No, he's right," Sophie said. "Have you not seen Humphrey? The man's a caramel biscuit."

"Biscuit?" asked a moustachioed mouse after poking its head out from a pouch at Sophie's waist.

"Not that kind of biscuit," she said with an amused smile.

The disgruntled mouse ducked back into his pouch.

"I found the zone breaking down at the edges," Sophie continued. "Didn't realise it was moving inward at first, but Jason told me to check, so I marked up these sticks as big rulers. And, sure enough, it was moving. Slow at first; just a centimetre the day I first measured. It's moving faster every day, though."

"We're standing in what was, pre-unification, a territory at the outer limit of the transformation zone," Miriam said. "What you're seeing here is happening in every outer territory. The zone is breaking down."

"How fast?" Clive asked.

"At the current rate of acceleration," Miriam said, "the outer territories will be gone in a week."

"The territorial consumption will only get faster," Jason said. "And the more of the zone that gets consumed, the worse things will go for us. The zone will destabilise and eventually collapse. Even if we finish before then, the worse things have gotten, the harder it will be to reintegrate the zone back into normal reality. Back on Earth, these zones left patches of janky reality sitting around in places they just don't fit. This, I have to imagine, will have more drastic results."

"You're saying that we have to move fast," Clive said.

"Yeah," Jason told him. "No more painstaking tests of the weather machine."

"The plan is to brief everyone this afternoon," Miriam said. "Tomorrow, we make final preparations and the day after, we go. The Operations Commander will expand his territorial influence over the last territory and we shall see what manner of fight awaits us."

Not knowing what form the final conflict would take, a simple and adaptable plan was put in place. What little information they had was built around guesswork, assumptions and Jason 'just having a feeling'—a standard of evidence that made Clive twitch every time he said it.

They were guessing that they would face elemental messengers. That was what the tree had produced in the brightheart realm and it was the closest to actual information they had to go on. The elemental messengers could be like the ones held in stasis in the other territories, living anomaly replicas or a mix of both. Or it could be something else entirely that they had no way to plan for at all. Every time that came up, Tactical Commander Miriam started twitching like Clive.

Beyond that limited information, they were largely relying on Jason's gut feelings. Being in control of everything but the final territory, Jason claimed a sense of what they would be dealing with. He openly admitted those feelings were vague and a rather sketchy basis for a battle plan.

Jason's feelings suggested that, at least initially, they would not be faced with the same level of power Gary had been while claiming the final territories. Jason believed that the battle would start at the same level as the transformation zone had before escalating over the fight. He had no clear sense of how or why, which Miriam did not care for.

As they had very little idea of what they would face, the plan was kept simple and mostly came down to facing whatever came out and hoping they could win. The nuance came down to whether or not Jason was right about power escalation, and they planned for both outcomes. The gold-rank forces would be the frontline, with the silver-rankers well back. If Jason was right, the silver-rankers could move in and join the battle. If not, they would evacuate.

Evacuation plans were put in place, with various transport powers and vehicles ready to go. Even if Jason was right and the silver-rankers joined the fight, the preparations were necessary. Once the power level of the enemy escalated, the silvers would need to make a swift withdrawal. Whatever the outcome, Jason was the only silver-ranker who would stay for the entire battle.

Along with final plans for the battle, individual plans were set in place. Death letters were written to next of kin, amongst other war movie death flags. Jason resisted the urge to institute an alliance-wide ban against showing people images of loved ones from home.

Allowing Marek Nior Vargas to mingle with Boris' messengers had brought an unexpected result. Boris' messengers were still under the mark of Vesta Carmis Zell, while Marek and the others had been freed. After weeks of interaction, Boris' people were ready to let Jason free them as well. As a result, Jason spent much of the final preparation day helping messengers form an inner realm and forge their own mark, purging that of their astral king.

In the free time he did have, Jason managed to catch Gary in a brief moment of solitude. It was on an open plain that had been a territory two over from the mountain fortress. Tall yellow grass spanned across the flat-lands, occasionally interrupted by patches of woodland.

"It reminds me of home," Gary said from the shade of a tree as Jason stepped out of a shadow behind him. "I'm never going to see it again."

Jason could hide his presence even from the gold-rankers now, but not from Gary's divine senses. He stepped up beside his friend, the top of Jason's head not clearing the leonid's shoulder. He bumped his head against Gary's arm but didn't say anything.

"I haven't—"

"You don't have to," Jason said. "Not yet. Assuming we win, I still have to initiate the process. I won't stall it for long because the place is falling apart, but there'll be time to make a final choice."

"Then what are you doing all the way out here?"

"Same as you, I imagine; taking the chance while Rufus is bailed up by his mum. Has he gotten any better?"

"He's still telling me there's only one choice. But he's starting to accept that things will change, whichever way I go. That the time we have now is important."

"I'm sorry I haven't had more time to give you these last few days. Bloody messengers. Should have left them to their fate."

"No, you shouldn't. But you already know that."

"I thought you hated all the messengers."

"In my situation, I don't see much point to hatred anymore."

Jason bumped his head against Gary's arm again.

"You really are the best of us. I'm sorry I couldn't wrangle better circumstances for you. You deserve better."

"Since when did deserve ever matter? I don't want to hear any self-recrimination, Jason. You don't get to take my sacrifice and turn it into your failure. If it weren't for you, I'd have died in a hole years ago and no one would have known. You gave me these years and they've been pretty damn good ones. However this ends up going, always remember that."

Jason wiped the moisture gathering in his eyes.

"I love you, you big hairy sod."

"Of course you do. I'm amazing."

Jason burst out laughing.

51

DON'T THROW OUR DEAD FRIEND'S STUFF OUT OF A TORTOISE

THE FINAL UNCLAIMED TERRITORY OF THE TRANSFORMATION ZONE WAS THE smallest of them all at roughly eight kilometres across. It was situated in the middle of the zone and was close to perfectly round. Unlike the permeable shadow boundaries of the other territories, the one containing the tree was pitch black and impenetrable, at least at ground level. At higher altitudes it became opaque and eventually entirely transparent, allowing the tree inside to be visible from across the zone.

The permeability of the barrier had been tested before. It remained impenetrable at all levels, even when completely invisible, with certain environmental exceptions. Clouds and wind could pass through normally, yet not when produced by magic or even the weather machine.

As the alliance prepared to make the final push and completely unify the transformation zone, the barrier was tested again. The tests were carried out from within Onslow's ever-useful flying shell. Jason, Taika, Belinda and Clive were there, along with Emir and Gabriel to see if any gold-rank powers could make a dent.

They had conducted a variety of tests, ranging from Belinda and Clive casting complex ritual magic to Belinda and Taika throwing random stuff at it. The invisible barrier was less invisible when coated in scorched ritual markings and smashed pumpkin oozing down the dome with fake paper money stuck to it.

"I can't believe you threw a board game at it," Jason said.

"Bro, Monopoly sucks," Taika said. "You know Monopoly sucks and you still have like five more versions of it. Are you really going to miss the Bass Fishing Edition?"

"No, Monopoly's terrible, but I inherited those from Greg."

"Why? He hated Monopoly more than any of us. He had what? Eight different t-shirts ragging on it?"

"You know what he was like with games. He just kept getting more and never got rid of the old ones, even if he didn't like them. I have about a thousand games of his and he died without playing at least a hundred of them."

"We can afford to lose a few then."

"I'm just saying that maybe we don't throw our dead friend's stuff out of a tortoise."

"Bro, I didn't know Greg as long as you, but I know one thing for certain: he would absolutely love to throw copies of Monopoly out of a magic flying tortoise."

"He would love that, wouldn't he?" Jason said with a laugh before his expression grew sad. "He'd love all of this."

Taika rested a hand on Jason's shoulder and changed the subject.

"This is a huge tree, bro. That trunk has to be a mile across."

"A mile?" Emir asked.

"Sorry," Taika said. "A bit over a kilometre and a half. It's weird that an alternate reality has the metric system and the Americans still can't figure it out."

"It's the link between worlds," Jason said. "It creates echoes. That's why even though Earth doesn't have elves, our folklore is full of them."

"We probably shouldn't tell the real elves about rule thirty-four," Taika said. "I'm pretty sure they feature heavily."

"You're pretty sure, are you?" Jason teased.

"I'm not ashamed," Taika said. "I'd say I like sexy elf cosplay as much as the next bloke, but the next bloke is Travis and that guy is anime-body-pillow lonely. Good thing he's still in Rimaros because he's bad enough around celestines. If he went to an elf city like Yaresh, I think he'd stroke out."

Jason looked at Taika from under raised eyebrows.

"Not like that," Taika said. "Okay, probably like that, but it's not what I meant."

They looked out at the tree, which towered over them even a half-dozen kilometres in the air. The trunk was around a kilometre and a half thick, as Taika said, and thinned little as it rose into the air. The tree topped out at roughly twelve kilometres high.

"Bro, this tree is a mountain. It's way bigger than the one in the shape of your head."

"Forget mine," Jason said. "This thing is taller than Everest."

"Probably a lot less poo, though. Not much of a tourist attraction when there's an impenetrable force field over it."

"Okay, I'm going to stop that conversation there," Belinda said. "I think we can safely say that no one is getting in until you make the attempt to claim it, Jason."

"How are the preparations going?" Gabriel asked.

"We've collected a lot of things from the zones that might help," Jason said. "Weapons like those you'd see in my world, but gold rank. Various magical tools. Some we know how to use, others we're figuring out."

"I saw the hover-tank, bro. It looked a bit rusty, though."

"Yeah, it was some post-apocalyptic sci-fi territory," Jason said.

"Too bad there wasn't a mech," Taika lamented.

"There was," Jason said sadly. "Unfortunately, Farrah hit it with her lava cannon when we were clearing that zone."

"That's a shame," Taika said. "Does anyone know how to drive the tank?"

"I do," Belinda said.

"She's the one we've got figuring all this stuff out," Jason said.

The adventurers and their allies massed on one side of the tree's territory rather than trying to surround it. They were spread out enough to avoid all but the largest of area attacks, but sufficiently close that they could focus their efforts and support one another as necessary. The front line consisted of gold-rankers with the adventurers, brighthearts, Builder cultists and messengers all represented. Behind them were the array of weapon emplacements and armed vehicles scavenged from the various territories.

Only a few of the scavenged assets were what Jason would categorise as 'sci-fi guns,' although many didn't fit the Pallimustus magical paradigm. There were steampunk belt-fed Gatling guns akin to weapons Jason had used in other transformation zones. There was what looked like a giant school-fair volcano project on the back of a wagon. It was able to conjure objects of sculpted light that looked and acted like gun drones armed with lasers. They contrasted starkly with the wooden wagon the device was mounted on.

Belinda was managing this section of the allied forces but was unable to operate the devices herself. The gold-rank requirements forced her to use proxies for each, taken from the brighthearts. The brightheart gold-rankers were mostly conscripted civilians, not trained warriors. The near-genocide of their people had been a harsh teacher, but they were still not the match of trained adventurers, brutal cultists and messengers born with the knowledge of war. This made them good candidates to operate the relatively simple weapons, even if it meant leaving a vehicle stationary and just using its guns.

Behind all of that were the silver-rankers, ready to charge or flee as circumstances dictated. They had resources for their evacuation ready to go, including some scavenged vehicles not built for war.

The sole exception to that ordering was Jason, stationed with the gold-rankers. This was not another territory where he could saunter up at the end and use a magic orb to claim it. He instinctively understood that this fight required him to participate. Miriam had assigned him a protection detail comprised of Rufus' parents, Emir and his wife, Constance.

Jason stood with Miriam at the rear of the gold-rankers. With them were the other factional leaders, Lorenn of the brighthearts, Beaufort of the cultists and Boris of the messengers. They stood behind Jason and Miriam, ready to issue orders to their people once the battle began.

Jason and Miriam shared a look before casting their gazes to the sky. The tree was tall enough that it poked through dark cloud cover thick enough to turn day into twilight. Silver-rankers had a good sense of time, but Jason took out a watch, wanting to be precise.

"We're on schedule," he said. "Is there anything else, Tactical Commander? Do I need to send a delay code to the network hub?"

"No, Operations Commander. There's nothing else."

"Then we go as scheduled. Four minutes."

The impenetrable barrier was not hard to remove. All it took was Jason wanting it gone.

It vanished like it had never existed and the transformation zone was unified. Jason felt it become one and immediately understood that the battle was for who would control it; him or an unstable, corrupted giant tree. He was confident the result would be bad if it was the tree.

There were three or four kilometres of open ground between the trunk and where the barrier had been. The land was nothing but rocky dirt and protruding roots. Floating in the air just off the ground, packed wing to wing, were elemental messengers. They immediately flooded out to attack.

There was a skyquake as twilight turned into blinding brightness and thousands of bolts of lightning struck down at once. With the barrier gone, the weather machine could do its work, turning the space around the tree into a realm of electricity. Lightning poured down in a constant onslaught, too imprecise to be used once the forces clashed, but devastating when striking the elemental messengers alone. The sound of it was like nothing Jason had ever heard—a cacophony of thunder that rattled the air.

The allies were untouched but the elemental messengers were all but annihilated. The lightning finally stopped, the brightness fading and the clouds breaking up as if they had no more to give. Everything had been poured out on the messengers. Daylight broke through the thinning coverage, illuminating what had been, moments ago, a massive army. Now, all but a scattered few lay dead on the ground. The earth was scorched, but the roots of the great tree were untouched, despite the cataclysm of gold-rank lightning that had rained down upon them.

"You were right," Miriam said. "Those were gold-rank auras but weak, like the anomalies when we first arrived."

"And I think I know how we escalate things," Jason said. "Boris, what do you make of that tree trunk now we can see it clearly?"

The leaders all cast their eyes at the tree, no longer obscured by the barrier. Set into the bark were hundreds, if not thousands, of crystals. Some were round like awakening stones, others square like essences. Most were rough and unshaped, like quintessence. Whatever form they took, however, they were all far too large to be the genuine version of what they appeared to be. All were in fiery or earthy colours.

"The lightning did nothing to those roots," Boris said. "I suspect the wood of the tree is extremely resistant, if not outright immune to attack. But those things set into it look as much like target points in a boss fight as you could ask for. The question is whether the raid has phases as we take them out."

"What does that mean?" Miriam asked sharply. "We don't have time to waste on explaining references to your world, Operations Commander."

"What he's saying," Jason said, "is that we need to destroy the crystals set into the tree. But the more we break, the more powerful the elemental messengers will become. He's also worried about thresholds at which the tree might display new abilities."

"The enemy messengers are destroyed," Lorenn said. "We should strike now."

"Yes, but with caution," Miriam said. "Destruction of the crystals may lead to further messengers being produced."

"Respawns," Jason said. "New and stronger enemies; it makes sense. That's the general pattern of transformation zones. Let's test the water and see what we learn."

Miriam directed her own team, Moon's Edge, to move up and destroy a crystal. They were not the strongest of the gold-rankers, but they were the fastest. When something inevitably went wrong, they had the best chance of pulling out safely. Miriam had them attack a round crystal, larger than the shards and smaller than the cubes. The hope was that this was important enough to provoke a reaction, but not an overwhelming one.

They got their reaction, the auras of the few remnant elemental messengers growing a little stronger. More messengers appeared as well, moving through the bark of the tree trunk like they were stepping through a waterfall. A waterfall with a clown car behind it, based on the numbers pouring out.

"Well, at least we know where we stand," Miriam said. "Let's just hope there aren't any more surprises."

"There are definitely more surprises," Jason said.

"I know," she told him. "I'm still going to hope there aren't."

52

BEWARE OF CHICKEN

THE FIRST WAVE OF ELEMENTAL MESSENGERS WAS WIPED OUT BY THE powerful but barely controlled lightning storm created by the weather machine. The clouds it had erupted from quickly dispersed, ending the artificial twilight as sunlight shone directly onto the battlefield. Fresh clouds converged on the tree in a massive spiral, but it would take time before the weather machine was ready to act again.

The crystals embedded in the tree proved resilient against attack, but team Moon's Edge were gold-rankers and it did not last long against their assault. Fresh messengers immediately emerged from the tree, passing through the bark as if it were a sheet of water.

The only member of the team not to deploy was the leader, Miriam, commanding the forces of the alliance. She did not send the rest of the gold-rankers to engage, instead calling for the silver-rankers to move up and for their scavenged assets to engage, testing their effectiveness against the enemy.

Belinda managed the slapped-together contingent from the hover-tank. She couldn't drive it without facing feedback from the higher-ranked item, but she could sit inside and yell at people through voice chat. The hyper-kinetic rounds fired from its magnetic rail cannon were fast enough to hit even gold-rankers.

The other eclectic weapons proved a mixed bag. The miniature drone-spitting volcano on a wagon seemed excellent at first, its hard-light constructs proving highly effective. They were short-lived, however, as was the volcano itself. Its detonation sent the brightheart manning it limping for the healers.

One that seemed innocuous was a thick iron pole, propped up at an angle by a smaller pole. At the end of the main shaft were eight small white balls, slowly orbiting the end of the pole. When activated, it fired eight spheres of electricity that moved slowly but sought out targets, blasting anyone who came near with arcs of lightning. After a few false starts where allies had to be shielded from the spheres, the brightheart using it learned to direct the spheres more or less at the enemy. Most of them ended up orbiting the tree, blasting at any messengers that emerged from it until the ball lightning's power was spent.

The elemental messengers kept emerging from the trunk of the tree, a full kilometre and a half in circumference. They streamed around it from all sides to attack the adventurers and their allies. While their numbers were vast, they were still weak and fell rapidly to area attacks, especially Gordon's butterflies. The gold-rank adventurers held back, letting the silvers do the work for now.

Miriam directed their forces to further attack the crystals embedded in the tree trunk. With each shattered crystal, the elemental messengers grew a little stronger. Their auras marked them as gold rank, but their level of power was still in the silver range, at least for the moment. Miriam called off the attacks on the crystals when the elemental messengers showed a strength close to the peak of silver rank.

"Our silver-rank forces won't be able to handle much more than this," she said. "These elemental messengers can't fight worth a damn, but power is power. The adventurers will still hold, but we need to start pulling back our allies. Adventurers too, once the enemy starts touching on gold-rank strength."

Jason had long since joined the fray, so he responded through the voice chat's command channel.

"It's good training for the adventurers," he said. "We've seen some real cracks in the silver-rank wall in the last few months, but we have other priorities today. Are you worried that something will change when the enemy messengers hit a gold-rank power level?"

"It's a consideration, but I'm more concerned about transitioning our forces out of the fighting without losing people. The adventurers can handle the current strength and numbers, but the silver-rank brighthearts, cultists and our messengers are struggling. We need to pull the non-adventurers back and bring the golds forward before escalating further. I'll get the gold-rankers organised and move in with my team. You're out there, so assess the silvers and signal them to start withdrawing, prioritising need and safety."

"I might have to stop slacking off and do some actual commanding," Jason said. "I'll organise— HOLY CRAP!"

"Jason?"

"This messenger just exploded into fire and ash, then the ash reformed back into a messenger. Did you see that?"

"This whole battlefield is magical explosions. Are you alright?"

"No worries; I'm super-good at fighting. That was crazy awesome, though. Is anyone recording this battle? Shade, grab a recording crystal and—"

"I believe you were saying something about being a responsible commander," she said pointedly, cutting him off.

"Responsible was your word. I never said that and you can't hold me to it. But yeah, I'll direct our adventurer forces to cover the withdrawal of the others. You want to crack some more of those crystals once we're done?"

"Once we've settled after the force transition, yes."

Clive's tortoise familiar had expanded to full size, akin to a large cottage. His shell was being used as a mobile recovery point while Clive stood atop it, acting as the gun to Onslow's tank. Rather than the usual open sides, Onslow had his shell more secure. The hole where his head would poke out was sealed over with only the holes for his legs serving as entrances.

The spaces were open as Onslow himself was in his adorable, child-sized humanoid form. Inside the shell, he was running around, making himself useful to the healers and resting or injured combatants. He delivered medical supplies like alchemically treated bandages and tins or healing unguent. He handed out oversized mana and stamina potions, the larger-than-normal bottles looking enormous in his tiny hands. He even gave out drinks of water and collected empty glasses.

While there were healers out in the field, there were also some inside Onslow's shell, led by Healer high priestess Hana Shavar. Farrah took swigs from a large mana potion as the high priestess reattached Rufus' arm, held in place with magic. They all occupied the simple wooden chairs Clive had set up inside the shell, along with a few tables and standing shelves to hold supplies. Simple rituals held the furniture in place against the occasional shake as powerful attacks struck the shell.

"You're lucky I could even find your arm," Farrah told Rufus. "It's getting hectic out there."

"I appreciate your efforts," the priestess said. "Having the arm to reaffix is much faster and less mana-intensive than growing a new one."

"I was, perhaps, a little reckless," Rufus admitted. "I'm not sure how much longer we can hold against the strength and numbers they have."

Taika came in through one of the corner doors and crashed into a seat next to Farrah. The fact that it didn't buckle under his massive frame as he carelessly threw himself onto it proved that the wood was magically reinforced.

"The gold-rankers have started moving in," he said, panting as he took a mana potion from Onslow and nodded his thanks. He removed the stopper and took a swig.

"These big mana potions are good," he said, holding up the large bottle. "They top me off pretty well without having to wait between drinks to avoid potion toxicity. That helps when this is my third time coming back to rest."

"Fourth for Farrah," Rufus said. "She's mana-hungry, even for a brawler."

"Has Humphrey come back in?" Taika asked. "He's a brawler too."

"Not once," Farrah said. "He uses a lot of mana recovery items."

"It's more than just items," Rufus said. "I'm not sure you understand how well-trained Humphrey is. And that's coming from someone whose family runs a school."

Farrah and Taika shared a look and Rufus glared at them.

"Don't even think about pulling out drinks in the middle of a battle," he said, pointing at them with the arm not held in place by Hana's magic. "My point is, it's easy to look at Humphrey swinging that big sword and think he falls short of Sophie in terms of skill. He doesn't."

He grunted and looked at the priestess.

"Stop shifting around," she told him.

"Sorry," he said, then turned back to the others.

"Using Humphrey's huge sword on a silver-rank battlefield is harder than you think. A lot of enemies are blindingly fast, but that's not his real skill. His real skill is judgement. You don't notice it unless you know to look, but Humphrey's management of his mana and cooldowns is perfect. Scarily perfect. That matters when you're a brawler, as you both demonstrate every time you go out there. Or come back here for a rest."

"Actually," Taika said, "what's going on with cooldowns? It's not a video game, bro, even if Jason can pull up your character sheet."

"It's about meridians," Farrah explained. "Your body moves away from lungs and heart and veins as you go up in rank. You develop a new system that channels your blood and mana."

"Meridians," Taika repeated.

"Yes," Farrah said. "In an essence-user, meridians develop in accordance with your abilities. Certain meridians become optimised for certain powers, allowing you to use more mana to greater effect. Your soul reshapes your body so you can use your powers better. It's more complicated than 'this is your lava cannon meridian,' but that's the basic idea."

"That's how ranking up works?" Taika asked.

"That's part of it," Farrah said. "When you use a power, it puts a strain on related meridians if it's strong enough. The actual mechanics are complicated, but it basically means you can't use the same meridians in the same way until they recover. If a power is minor, like Jason's special attacks, the cooldown is short or non-existent. Humphrey's Immortality power is on the other end of that spectrum, badly straining the related meridians."

"And that's how cooldowns work."

"Kind of. Clive would tell you that everything I said was an oversimplification and wrong, but I gave you the 'I didn't spend a decade studying magic theory' explanation. It's all about meridians. Powers that manipulate mana costs, lock out abilities or affect cooldowns all work by impacting meridians. Ones like Belinda's that can reduce or reset cooldowns are very specialised healing powers that help meridians recover faster."

"Learning to manage your cooldowns and mana costs effectively is crucial," Rufus said. "Especially for brawlers like you. You're tougher and more powerful than the average adventurer, but your mana costs and cooldowns are high, meaning you're out of the fight earlier."

"I bring more power to the table than most brawlers," Farrah said.

"Which is why we give her a treat if she stays in the fight a whole minute," Rufus said with a grin.

Farrah got up to slap his arm but was driven back by a look from Hana so sharp, it almost required healing.

"Humphrey's cooldown and mana management is perfect," Rufus said. "And I mean *perfect*. People always get better with experience, but he was better than most silvers at iron-rank. Now...? His mother built that boy up from the ground. I'd put money down on her planning the mana recovery gear he's wearing now before he learned to walk. Probably before the church of Fertility cracked him out of the vat. If you haven't seen thousands of adventurers at all ranks, and aren't looking for it, you'll probably never notice, but Humphrey Geller is the most skilled person on our team."

"Really?" Taika asked. "More than Sophie? More than *you*?"

"Yes," Rufus said. "Humphrey isn't just working around his own limitations and gear. He adapts in the moment to every tweak to his mana recovery and cooldown times. If he's in range of Clive and Belinda's auras. What buffs and debuffs are on him. How many potions he has, and how long until he can drink another."

"He's thinking about that the whole time?" Taika asked. "While also directing us in combat?"

"Yes," Rufus said. "And he keeps his cool so emotional decisions don't throw him off. It's how he stays in the fight while Miss Lava Cannon here stops to rest faster than you can say 'mana efficiency.'"

"I don't see Humphrey firing off a lava cannon," Farrah said huffily.

"No, he doesn't," Rufus agreed. "You might all be brawlers, but you have different roles. Taika is an initiator and you're a deleter. You make a problem go away. Humphrey is a stayer, which is rare for a brawler."

"Because of how hard it is to manage powers as well as he does."

"Exactly," Rufus says. "Brawlers are common because they're great, but they're also basic. Especially one that is more rounded than specialised, like you two. That specialisation is what keeps you effective at higher ranks."

"Which has people wondering why Danielle Geller pushed her son into one of the most commonplace, bread-and-butter roles in adventuring," Farrah said.

"Yes," Rufus agreed. "What they don't realise is that what she's done is take one of the most useful-but-basic roles in adventuring and create the greatest version of it that there is."

"Like how really good bread and really good butter is simple but also fantastic," Taika said.

"Exactly," Rufus said. "Like any brawler, Humphrey hits harder and survives more than most adventurers. The trade-off is endurance, which is why you two are back here resting, but Humphrey doesn't stop. He has less explosive power than either of you, certainly, but he's always out there, always putting on pressure. Farrah, you are the best there is at intervening in critical moments. He intervenes at *every* moment, not just the critical ones. Not as much as you, but he's always there; a perpetual influence. Next time you're outside, look at the impact he has. Not just on the fight he's in, but the whole battle. The way it moves around him like water shifting course around a rock."

"But isn't that kind of bad for typical adventuring?" Taika asked. "An adventuring contract is go out, kill maybe three things and go home. Farrah is way better for that."

"Yes," Rufus agreed. "It's almost like his mother wasn't training him for typical adventuring."

"Oh," Taika said, realisation in his voice.

"She was building him for some weird Jason stuff," Farrah said. "Long before Jason ever came along."

"Yes," Rufus agreed. "Danielle and I spoke about Jason days after he first arrived."

"And then she glued her son to the outworlder the moment he showed up," Farrah said. "That lady is kind of scary."

"Yes," Rufus agreed.

Farrah stood up, took a cleansing breath and stretched.

"Oh well. Time to get back to it."

"See you back in a minute," Rufus said.

"Hilarious," she said, then turned to Hana. "How long will this one be?"

"Another few minutes to make sure the arm reattached properly," Hana said.

"Out of curiosity, did you know his family runs a school?"

"He mentioned it," Hana said, drawing a snorting laugh from Taika.

Farrah grinned at Rufus' glare until her conjured armour covered her face in a helmet of black obsidian. She moved to the door and leapt out as wings of fire appeared at her back. Much of the battle was happening in the air as the elemental messengers could all fly, although not all chose to. Many had earth powers that were more useful while grounded.

Her eyes picked out Humphrey with ease. He was forming a defensive line with an army of condor-sized bird skeletons made of dragon bones. They were on fire and wearing armour that somehow didn't interfere with their flight. Humphrey's summoning power was most useful in pitched battles and his magic dice that altered them randomly had provided good results this time.

Humphrey and his forces were flying, enormous dragon wings spread out from his back. He and his summons were close to the ground as they covered the withdrawal of a silver-rank brightheart contingent. Silver-rankers were pulling back across the battlefield, but Farrah could see that none were doing so as efficiently as those shielded by Humphrey. He was effectively blunting the elemental messenger assault, aided by some of the team.

Sophie was everywhere and nowhere, almost impossible for anyone below gold rank to track. Any time Humphrey's line of summons showed vulnerability, she was suddenly there, stopping attackers dead until the line was reinforced. Jason was amongst the enemy, also hard to track as he flicked like a shadow. He was thinning them out as they approached, making sure they couldn't overwhelm Humphrey's summons with raw numbers. One of Belinda's familiars was present as well, the astral lantern helping with the group's mana recovery. It was behind the line with Neil who stood atop a giant bird, a moustache perched incongruously on its beak.

"WHY ARE YOU A GIANT CHICKEN?" Neil's voice rose over the sounds of battle.

"I'm a cockatrice!" Stash yelled proudly. "Look, I turned that guy to stone."

"That guy was already stone!" Neil yelled back. "He's a stone elemental messenger. YOU'RE A GOD-DAMNED CHICKEN!"

"Humphrey, Neil's being mean to me!"

"Both of you shut up," Humphrey told them.

Stash flapped forward, past Humphrey's dragon bone condors.

"What are you doing?" Neil yelled, gripping huge feathers to keep his balance. "You better not drop me in the middle of the enemy!"

Stash let out a rooster crow that sent shock waves blasting through the elemental messengers. Metal bodies warped and stone bodies cracked while other types bled from their eyes and ears, many dropping to the ground. Stash then curved his flight back behind the lines.

"See?" Stash said. "Not a chicken."

"You just yelled out 'COCK-A-DOODLE-DOO!'"

"And now you did too," Stash said. "At least I'm a chicken. You're the guy who yelled 'cock-a-doodle-doo' in the middle of a battle."

"I told you two to shut up," Humphrey scolded. "And, Neil, stop using chicken noises as a battle cry. You're making us look bad."

The giant chicken somehow managed to look extremely smug as Neil glared down at it.

"Oh, you little bast—"

The more vulnerable silver-rankers pulled back, the brighthearts along with most of the cultists and allied messengers. A few stayed, Beaufort and Boris judging which of their people were strong enough to stand with the adventurers. Once the withdrawing forces were safely en route to extraction points, Miriam ordered a fresh attack on the crystals.

As had happened previously, this prompted a fresh wave of elemental messengers coming from the tree, more powerful than those that came before. This time, they did not come alone, however. A hulking figure emerged from the tree that looked startlingly like the avatar of Undeath. Instead of skinless flesh, it was made of roots that looked like ropey muscle. The glow emitted from its eyes was molten-steel-orange instead of purple, but it shambled like the zombie had. Towering over the battlefield, only next to the tree did the fourteen-storey figure look anything but outrageous in scale.

"Gary," Jason said over voice chat. "I'm going to do you a favour and take all the little ones. That just leaves the one for you."

"Oh, thank you so much," Gary responded.

"You're very welcome."

Gary had been easy to spot already, wreathed in golden fire, but he became unmissable as his size grew to match the root avatar.

"Oh, come on!" yelled Rick Geller. He'd been standing beside Gary and had been half-buried in displaced dirt in the growth process.

"Sorry," giant Gary rumbled before moving forward in massive steps, careful to only tread on enemies.

Gary hefted his hammer, hoping this root avatar was easier to kill than its undead counterpart. The fire shrouding the hammer in his hand grew brighter and brighter until he finally threw it at the root monster. When the hammer landed, a massive blast of golden fire sent the root monster hurtling back. It struck the tree with enough force that even the vertical landscape shuddered, shaking loose leaves on branches kilometres above.

The explosion of flames outright disintegrated the messengers it washed over. The adventurers it touched were instead given a magical boon, enhancing their power and speed. The hammer, its flames diminished, flew back to Gary's hand as the root avatar pushed itself to its feet. Its root flesh was blackened and it had a rectangle indent in its torso, matching the shape of Gary's hammer. There were cracks on its body leaking orange light.

———

Miriam watched as the root monster struggled against the golden chains binding it as Gary hammered off parts of its body, chunk by chunk. She reflected that Gary's stalemate against the avatar of Undeath had made her forget how much power flowed through the leonid demigod.

"Looks like he's got us covered," Jason observed through the command channel.

"For now," Miriam said. "I just hope we handle whatever the tree has for us next as easily."

"Wow," Jason said. "A real bundle of sunshine, you."

53

A BETTER ADVENTURER

THE ROOT AVATAR HAD NOT GONE DOWN EASILY, BUT GARY KEPT IT largely contained. Once it was dead, the adventurers started destroying more crystals and the elemental messengers became even more dangerous. Clive was sent away when the expectations for another special enemy grew.

Clive and Onslow were amongst the last silver-rankers to evacuate, with only Jason staying longer. Clive had convinced Miriam to let them stay and continue to serve as a rest and recovery station. Miriam kept Onslow well behind the front line as, even when reinforced by Clive's rituals, the familiar's formidable shell was not indestructible. Once the elemental messengers were firmly into gold-rank power levels, Miriam ordered the less powerful gold-rankers to evacuate. Clive and Onslow withdrew with the first wave of them, carrying many to the evacuation point.

The evacuation sites were comprised of ritual circles in a line that headed directly away from the tree. Going over the circles in sequences granted a stacking movement buff that was equally applicable to individuals, vehicles and familiars like Onslow.

Onslow's shell drifted over the first in the sequence of ritual circles and immediately accelerated. Inside, Clive and Mini Onslow were seated on a heavily padded couch. The momentum increased with each circle until they were pushed deep into the cushions. Clive groaned as Onslow threw his little hands in the air, letting out a chirping laugh like a child on a rollercoaster.

Regrouping sites were set up at the points where the movement boosts ran out. They were sufficiently clear of the battle zone that even gold-rankers would take time to reach them. Onslow arrived in a pleasant grassy zone, one of the more common terrains amongst the territories. Several adventurers were portalling others back to the main base, but many had sat right down in the grass and started meditating.

The transformation zone had been a massive boon to the silver-rankers whose advancement had stalled following the monster surge. Most had taken between two to four years to go all the way through bronze rank to silver and found the subsequent slowdown frustrating. The early stages of silver hadn't been bad, especially when so many ranked up during the surge. The infamous wall at the fourth stage of silver rank was a stark change as advancement slowed to a crawl.

The transformation zone had proven a salve to frustrated silver-rankers. As the living anomalies had become more challenging, advancement picked up. It wasn't a match for pre-silver levels, but adventurers were finally reaching the fifth and sixth thresholds of their essence abilities. Coming less than a year after ranking up, those were impressive gains when a decade was considered a lightning-fast rise from silver to gold.

The adventurers came to a very adventurer-like conclusion: that for all its weirdness and danger, the transformation zone was a rare and precious opportunity. That had led to renewed frustration when Miriam benched them all after judging the anomalies as too dangerous. Now they had finally leapt back into the fight, many were eager to consolidate their gains, meditating as soon as they hit the safe zone.

It didn't take long for Clive's team to find him. Clive set up different décor inside of Onslow. The plain wooden tables and chairs used for the mobile clinic went into Clive's storage space. Only the couch was left out and it was soon joined by more soft and luxurious furniture. The team had developed a taste for large and plush furniture after living in a cloud house.

The team, minus Jason, climbed into Onslow's shell, once again set up with open sides. They started heading out overland, despite the portal and teleport powers they had access to. They weren't in a rush and didn't want those powers on cooldown; they wanted them available to move far and fast if needed. The team settled in before turning to Humphrey as he let out an unhappy sigh.

"It wasn't that long ago that I was lecturing Jason about leaving us out of things," he said. Sophie leaned into him, slipping her fingers between his and giving his hand a squeeze.

"Teamwork is good," she said. "But sometimes what you want has to give way to what's best. Jason needs to be there, but we can't help him now. If we were there, the only thing we could do would be give him another thing to worry about."

"She's right," Clive said. "Miriam was starting to move back the gold-rankers, let alone me. She wouldn't let you anywhere near the battle. Once whatever comes out of that thing next is dealt with, it will probably be Gary doing the fighting alone. Everyone else will either be sent back or hide with Jason in an invisibility ball."

"I just wish we could do more," Humphrey said.

"We can," Rufus told him. "We can get stronger."

Rufus left his armchair and took a meditative pose on the floor.

"And this is why I'm a better adventurer than you," Neil said, drawing all eyes.

"Really?" Belinda asked.

"Yes," Neil said. "I'm going to meditate too, but I'm staying in this comfy chair to do it."

Belinda looked from Neil to Rufus, then back to Neil before finally settling her gaze on Rufus.

"He's right," she said. "He is a better adventurer than you."

The root avatar had been hard to kill but ultimately not that much of a threat. With Gary onside, they had an invincible weapon against any individual combatant. The root avatar was powerful, but Gary had chained it down and beaten it to death. The largest problem it presented was tying up Gary, leaving him unable to aid the other adventurers. With the elemental messengers growing stronger with every smashed crystal, that was an increasing problem.

Once the root avatar was down, Miriam prepared for the next escalation. She didn't like having Jason stay, but he insisted his presence was necessary. She didn't think it was just stubbornness or bravado, so she arranged the best protection she could manage. She had Ramona, the shield specialist from her team, create an invisibility sphere in the air. It held her, Jason and the healers who weren't combat specialists, Hana Shavar and Carlos Quilido.

The weather machine had proven increasingly useful over the course of the battle. It took time to make changes to the weather and its targeting was not precise, but that became less of a concern as more and more allies evacuated the field. Fire tornados sucked in messengers as adventurers herded their enemies into range. When one wave of messengers had been almost entirely fire and magma types, gold-rank monsoon rain had severely dampened their powers.

Being babysat by gold-rankers, Jason had little to do but consider the potential threats ahead. It seemed obvious at this stage that there would be more singular threats like the root avatar and he considered the possibilities. The first major threat had been a copy of the now-dead avatar of Undeath. Would further copies replicate other powerful combatants that had appeared in the zone? Would the end fight be Gary vs Tree Gary?

Two other things were playing on Jason's mind. One was that Jason himself had undeniably imprinted on the transformation zone. He was too weak to be an end boss, but would the tree start producing versions of him instead of messengers? An army of affliction-wielding, life-draining root monsters? The area around the tree was already carpeted in the dead, with elemental messengers piled up on the ground.

The other concern Jason had related to the tree itself. Aside from the crystals set into it, the tree had proved impenetrable to any form of damage, even from Gary.

That level of imperviousness was rare and usually related to souls somehow. The tree was a corrupted soul forge, so that seemed possible according to Jason's admittedly limited knowledge. He intended to expand his understanding of soul engineering in the future, given how often it kept coming up.

He wondered if they were caught up in something like a messenger challenge power. When he had been in the past, that involved invulnerability to outside interference. That would make the key figuring out how to get past the invulnerability. The crystals embedded in the tree trunk were obviously part of it, but was there more to it than simply smashing all the crystals to expose the tree itself? With the transformation zone on the line, figuring out the rules was of critical importance.

Jason had managed to break the rules of a challenge power once before, but that had been against one silver-rank messenger. She was young, little more than a girl, and he had no illusions he could break whatever passed for a soul for the giant corrupted tree.

As they prepared to shatter more of the crystals, Miriam made sure that the other gold-rankers were ready to evacuate if necessary. The root avatar had appeared when a third of the crystals had been broken; they were about to reach the two-thirds mark.

She had already ordered some gold-rankers out of the fight. The healers were secure with Jason in case anyone needed drastic attention and others had already evacuated. She was ready to pull the rest at a moment's notice.

After the current wave of elemental messengers was cleared out, Miriam ordered Emir Bahadir to attack the crystals. His staff extended comically to strike them from a safe distance. The crystals were destroyed and, as anticipated, a fresh wave of enemies emerged.

Alongside the stronger elemental messengers, another towering figure stepped out of the tree, passing through the bark as if stepping through a waterfall. The giant was a replica of Gary, carved from dark wood. The head was carved into a fixed mask of Gary with blank-faced features. Instead of a mane, fire blazed yet did not scorch the wood.

The armour it wore and the hammer and shield it carried were an odd mix of iron, stone and packed earth. It was as if the material had been dug from the ground and pressed into the shape of Gary's armour. The same material comprised a replica of Gary's hammer and shield, both shrouded in orange flame.

Gary immediately clashed with his wooden doppelganger. The titanic clash between real and fake demigods filled the air with thunder as their strikes landed on one another. The adventurers were left to deal with the new messengers, once more having grown in strength. Miriam was in the fray as well, working with her team. She kept an eye on the larger battle as they fought, her team periodically shielding her so she could stay watchful. She assessed the enemy and her own forces, planning out the next move.

It became quickly evident that while the wooden replica could copy Gary's form, his divine power was harder to reproduce. It would be another hard clash, but Miriam had no doubt that Gary would be the victor. For the rest of the battle, her assessment was less optimistic.

The elemental messengers were approaching the power level of the adventurers. For now, the adventurers remained superior, their versatility and intelligence trumping the mindless surge tactics of the messengers. The problem was one of numbers. For every wave that was struck down, another came out stronger.

The adventurers, by contrast, were too few. That hadn't mattered when the elemental messengers were weaker, but that was no longer the case. With enough power, quantity became a quality that the adventurers were struggling to overcome. Superior abilities and tactics were still working for now, but it was becoming a losing battle. The gold-rankers were forming up, supporting each other as a rising tide of enemies washed around them. There was no battle line anymore, just an island in a sea of foes.

It was time to pull back while the adventurers held a thin advantage. If the messengers grew stronger, the withdrawal would get bloody in spite of gold-rank resilience. Miriam reached out to Jason through the command channel.

"I need a portal," she said.

"On it," came the succinct reply.

That added to Miriam's worries. If even Jason Asano wasn't taking the time to talk nonsense, things might be even worse than she thought.

A portal to Jason's soul realm appeared, a ring floating in the air. It was well back, near the closest evacuation point. Miriam knew that Jason was worried about opening it too close to the tree, fearing potential negative reactions between the two powers. With the transformation zone already starting to break down, Miriam had agreed that they should keep destabilising influences to a minimum.

The gold-rankers started pulling back, fighting their way through the army of messengers surrounding them. That was when Miriam was faced with another unwelcome surprise. The messengers and the giants summoned by the tree had shown no indication of intelligence. They had demonstrated only blind aggression; moving forward and lashing out was their only tactic. They had likewise not reacted to the tactics of the adventurers, getting caught out again and again.

Then something changed. For the first time, the messengers shifted their approach as if they'd sensed the intention to withdraw. They started using their numbers to not just surround and attack the adventurers but to dogpile, regardless of how quickly it got them killed. They pressed in, body to body from every side, from above and below. The living were pressed in with the dead, but it didn't matter. If a corpse fell out, there were countless more to take its place. The adventurers vanished into a rapidly growing mound of bodies, living and dead.

It was not a strategy that would have worked earlier. The messengers simply had not been strong enough to prevent the adventurers from tearing a hole through any barrier. Now, with enough numbers, the messengers were managing to contain them.

"Jason," Amos said through voice chat. "I need water. What we talked about."

"I'll see what I can do."

"Quickly, please."

Within the invisibility field, Jason opened another portal. This one wasn't to his soul realm, but a normal shadow portal to the control room of the weather machine. Nik's head poked through a moment later.

"What do you need?" he asked.

"Water ball."

"Can do," Nik said. "You know, my head's feeling funny being hundreds of kilometres from my body."

"Then go back," Jason said. "I need that ball *now*."

"Sorry," Nik said, and his head withdrew through the portal.

"Semi-portalling like that isn't good for you," Hana Shavar said. "I'm surprised he didn't throw up. I've seen people have seizures."

"He's good with dimensional forces," Jason said. "He gets it from me."

Nik's head popped back out.

"It should be starting now," he reported.

"Thanks," Jason told him. "Now, go back."

"Can't I stay and—"

"No," Jason said and pushed Nik's head back through, then closed the portal.

It was raining again, in as tightly concentrated an area as Nik could manage. The water was pooling into a giant ball as if collected in an invisible bowl, but that was beyond the scope of the weather machine's power. This was a power that belonged to Amos Pensinata. By the time the clouds emptied and the rain stopped, a massive sphere of water hung in the air. Underneath it was the mound of messengers with the gold-rankers somewhere inside.

From the water orb, a massive tentacle swept out, grabbing at messengers and dragging them into the orb, leaving a huge gouge in the mound. More tentacles sprouted from the orb until there were ten, digging at the mound like a monster from the deep, trapped behind a watery portal.

THE ONLY WAY IT CAN WIN

THE GOLD-RANKERS WERE TRAPPED INSIDE THE GROWING MOUND OF elemental messenger bodies. Whether the messengers were living or dead was irrelevant; so long as there were enough of them, the adventurers and their allies couldn't fight their way out. For all the power wielded by the adventurers, the messengers piled on faster than they could dig their way out.

The chance to escape came from Amos Pensinata and a well-timed use of the weather machine. The result was a Cthulhu Death Star hovering over the mound of messengers, a humungous orb of water from which numerous tentacles were thrashing about. The tentacles flailed wildly in all directions, but the ones jutting from the bottom of the orb were carving deep gouges in the mound.

Amongst the trapped gold-rankers, the two remaining non-adventurers were Boris and Beaufort, leaders of their respective factions. The head Builder cultist was the one that dug their way out, his body of metal blades carving a hole like a mining drill. They burst through into one of the deeper gouges and immediately fled before the messengers could rebury them.

The adventurers and their allies bolted through the sky, an army of messengers in pursuit. Their goal was an evacuation point where a portal to Jason's soul realm waited. If that somehow failed, the acceleration rituals would help them flee as the elemental messengers weren't attuned to them.

Not all of their members were exceptionally swift, some relying on personal transport devices. Those that could move faster held back so as not to split the group when the elemental messengers were nipping at their heels. They made a tactical withdrawal, balancing speed with the need to fight off any messengers who caught up.

One of the most effective delay tactics came from Boris, whose wings glowed yellow-orange hot. They trailed a wake of embers behind him that exploded when any messengers got near them. It was far from enough to take any out, but it slowed them down effectively. Boris's swooping path made an obstacle course the messengers had to slow down to avoid. If they failed and got hit, the damage was minimal, but they were slowed even more.

Boris looked at Beaufort, the largest of the gold-rankers. His body was a massive frame of narrow metal and sharp blades, like a man made of scaffolding. The flesh that normally hid his body was segmented and scattered around the framework like macabre decorations. He flew using bladed wing-scaffolds that weren't close to aerodynamically sound.

"I know we're allies," Boris pointed out, "but you are one of the most creepy-looking guys I've ever seen. And I've *seen* some stuff. It's like a bunch of robot praying mantises were in a plane crash."

"Shut up and fly," Beaufort snarled.

"Just so you know," Boris said, "the cyborg voice isn't helping your cause."

"If you have the time to run your mouth," Arabelle told him, "use the energy to flap your wings. They're still chasing us."

"Yeah, but that Pensinata guy is covering us, right?" Boris asked.

"What?"

"Yeah, he hid his aura and slinked off to that water orb while the rest of us did a runner. He's pretty good with aura for an adventurer."

The elemental messengers had split into two groups. Those closest to the fleeing gold-rankers and unencumbered enough to give chase did do. Others were too slow, too distant or part of the mound where living messengers disentangled themselves from the dead.

Those who had not been able to escape the range of the orb tentacles swiftly found themselves under attack. Amos Pensinata hadn't escaped with the others, instead heading straight for the water orb. Moments later, the thrashing tentacles had abruptly changed, going from wild thrashing to focused and efficient attacks. Instead of randomly crashing through the mass of elemental messengers, they acted with purpose, breaking the enemy lines and disrupting pursuit of the other gold-rankers.

The messengers unable to give chase to the fleeing gold-rankers instead turned their attention to the orb, plunging fearlessly into its watery depths.

Inside the invisibility sphere floating in the air, Miriam and Jason watched the gold-rankers fighting their way to escape.

"Pensinata didn't join them," Jason said. "He went into the orb."

Miriam turned her attention to the massive hovering sphere, noting the more organised behaviour of the tentacles. She opened a voice chat channel.

"Pensinata, what are you doing?"

"Tying up as many as I can," came the reply. "I'll see to it the others aren't overwhelmed before they get clear."

"They have an open run now," she told him. "You've done enough. Withdraw while you still can."

"This is the best way," Amos said.

"I wasn't asking, Pensinata," Miriam said. "Get out now. That is an—"

• [Amos Pensinata] has left voice chat.

"Oh, he did not," Miriam said, baring her teeth.

Jason sent several requests for a voice chat to Amos, all of which were ignored.

"Shade?"

The shadow familiar emerged from the void of Jason's cloak.

"What can I do for you, Mr Asano?"

"Do you have a body on Pensinata?"

"I'm sorry, but I do not. That water is dark, however, and I believe that I can get one there in short order."

"Do it."

Another Shade body appeared and immediately left the invisibility shield to shoot through the air. It was more open than how Shade normally operated and he was quickly spotted. Multiple messengers also heading for the orb diverted to go after him. Shade was far too weak to fight them but dashed into and out of the shadows on their bodies, confusing them long enough to escape. After a few such encounters, Shade vanished into the water, dark as the ocean deeps.

"Your shadow is capable," Miriam observed.

"Yeah, I'm holding him back when we fight together. My limits in power and skill become his. When it's all him, he knows his business."

"And what exactly do you have him doing?"

"I need a shadow-jump target."

Miriam turned to look at him as if he'd grown a second head.

"You intend to teleport into that sphere. The same sphere into which we are watching hundreds of elemental messengers enter."

"I need to go slap some sense into Lord Pensinata."

"You need to stay where you are."

"I know why he's doing this."

"I don't care. I don't want to lose Pensinata, but the hard truth is that we can. If we lose you while you're trying to bring him back, it's all over."

"And he knows that. It's why it has to be me."

"It's not an acceptable risk."

"That's for me to decide, Tactical Commander."

"If I believe your judgement is compromised—"

"You have the power and training to command this expedition, Miriam, and we both know you've been the leader in truth more than I have. Yet I'm the Operations Commander. The one with the last word. You think that would have happened if the Adventure Society didn't sign off on it? If your Lady Allayeth didn't?"

"Your relationship with the messengers—"

"Is a reason to put me here, not put me in charge. You get to gold rank with a little luck and a lot of caution. That means avoiding circumstances like the ones we're in right now. I go places that don't exist and do things that aren't possible. No one does that as much as I have without dying; not even me. That's why I get the last word, Miriam: I've been here before. I know when, where and how far I can push."

"The risk—"

"I can't promise I can get Pensinata back. But I promise you I'll get myself back, even if it means leaving him to die. I do understand what's at stake here."

For a long moment, Miriam stared into Jason's eyes, glowing inside the dark hood.

"Alright," she said finally. "I'm going to kick myself for not stopping you, but go. Bring him back."

Jason didn't reply, instead floating into Shade and vanishing.

At the centre of the watery orb was a pocket of air with ice for a floor. Amos stood in the middle, eyes closed as he took control of the water and the tentacles within it. The messengers were storming the sphere en masse, yet were killed almost as fast as they entered. It was the perfect environment to amplify Amos' powers, but he was not omnipotent.

The sheer weight of numbers would eventually overcome him and he would die, but it would cost the enemy the most precious resource of all: time. Time for the others to escape. Time for Xandier to put down his wooden doppelganger and face whatever came next. Even the tree's strongest minions could not match divine power. Unless the tree came up with an answer to that, victory for the adventurers was assured. Amos knew his life was worth setting that up.

Amos sensed the approach of Asano's familiar through the water. It was startlingly stealthy, but not to Amos' perception. Not here. He considered destroying it, but cutting off communication was one thing. Attacking an ally's familiar was another, even if it was quickly and easily replaced. Shade entered the pocket of air, standing on the icy floor. Amos opened his eyes to look at him.

"Why did Asano send you?" Amos asked. His eyes went wide when Asano himself stepped through his familiar.

Amos had his formidable senses spread across the battlefield, so he noticed the immediate reaction from the enemy at Asano's emergence from the invisibility field. Their aura locked onto him like sharks smelling blood in the water. The enemy knew what Asano was; they understood his importance.

The messengers pursuing the gold-rankers gave up the chase immediately. They turned around and started dashing back. The rest of the elemental messengers redoubled their rush to penetrate the orb, ignoring their deaths from tentacles and violent, churning water. Even the wooden giant exposed itself to attack in the attempt to get past Xandier and rush the orb with Jason inside it.

"They're coming for you," Amos said.

"Yes," Jason agreed. "Something's changed. The tree didn't focus on me earlier in the battle. On anything, really. It's different now, starting with that attempt to trap the gold-rankers. I'm curious why, but we don't have time for why. The fact is that the battle is coming to a head and our enemy is finally acting with a sense of the threat it faces."

"You need to go."

"You first."

"Don't be—"

"That's an order, Lord Pensinata."

Jason had not spoken in the voice Amos knew. This was the cold, hard voice his enemies heard, usually before an excruciating death. Amos had been tutoring Jason for months in aura use and had come to know him well. This was not a side of Asano he had seen pointed in his direction.

"Why did you come here?" Amos asked.

"Because I knew you wouldn't leave on your own."

"And I still won't. We don't have time for this."

"No, we don't."

"I can't fight our way out of here," Amos growled, his signature stoicism breaking. "Can't you sense how many of them are converging on us?"

"I can. You did a good job of helping me hone my aura senses."

"I can't hold them off. Not forever."

"Then we'd best leave."

"I can force a path to get you out, but not if I leave this place. I have more control here."

"Lord Pensinata, this isn't what you think it is."

"What are you talking about?"

When Jason spoke again, his voice was no longer the glacial tone used for enemies. It was soft and sympathetic.

"I've seen heroic sacrifice, Amos. Even done it myself a few times. I'd put money down that you've convinced yourself that's what you're doing, but you're wrong. I think you know that, deep down."

"Don't you—"

"You know how to die like a hero, Amos. It's something you've been ready for most of your life. It's a lot easier than standing in front of your nephew, ashamed and uncertain. You'd rather die like a coward than live to face the consequences of your decisions."

Amos may as well have teleported for all Jason saw. One moment, the gold-ranker was in the middle of the room. The next, then he was in front of Jason, fist arrested right before impact.

"We don't have the time for you to hide behind your anger, Lord Pensinata. I've done it plenty, but we don't have time for months of therapy."

A shadow portal opened close to them.

"Bottom line, Lord Pensinata: I'm not leaving until you do, and you know what that means."

"I can't go through a silver-rank portal."

Jason closed his eyes and held out a hand towards the portal, a sheet of void energy inside an obsidian arch. Streaks of gold, silver and blue flashed in the dark energy.

"Quickly, please," Jason said through gritted teeth. "This is quite strenuous."

Amos looked at the concentration on Jason's face and hurried through the portal. The energy holding it open was exhausted by his passage and the portal collapsed. Jason put his hands on his knees and took deep breaths as if he'd just run a marathon. He could feel the elemental messengers approaching faster without Amos and his active defences.

"Shade," he said and the familiar vanished into Jason's void cloak. Then Jason himself vanished into it. It floated to the floor, empty, dissolving into nothing as the first messengers broke into the air pocket.

———

Jason stepped out of the Shade body in the invisibility sphere. Amos was sitting on a personal flight cloud, rubbing his temples and groaning. Miriam was on Jason immediately, especially when he slipped a little, holding himself unstably with his aura.

"Are you alright?"

"Yeah," he groaned. "Tapping into my astral gate is a proper kick in the head, but I've gotten used to it."

Cloud-substance seeped out of the miniature flask on his necklace and formed a chair for him to collapse into.

"I just need to rest," he said. "I'll be fine by the time I need to fight."

"You are *not* doing any more fighting in this battle."

"He is," Amos said. "He has to. You must have felt how the tree reacted to him. It knows he's the one it needs to overcome, and that it can't beat the demigod, whatever it throws at him. It's going to challenge Asano the way a messenger would. It's the only way it can win."

55

WHEN VIOLENCE IS EASY AND WORDS ARE HARD

ONCE JASON HAD EXTRACTED AMOS PENSINATA FROM HIS ATTEMPTED suicide-by-messenger, the next stages of the battle were unsurprising. The gold-rankers escaped into Jason's soul realm safely. Jason, Miriam and a few others remained hidden in Ramona's invisibility shield.

Gary was the only one left in the open but was largely unassailable. Elemental messengers moved to intervene in the fight with Gary's wooden doppelganger but failed miserably. Some fired off powers that did nothing while others exploded in golden fire after getting too close.

Gary's wooden doppelganger could at least fight the demigod, but had no real chance at victory. Not only did it fail to match his divine power, but it also lacked the skill. Gary was an experienced warrior and simply outfought the wooden giant. It finally fell, toppling like a tree under a woodsman's axe.

The final question was what would happen when the last of the tree's crystals were destroyed? Gary didn't waste time trying to find out, going to work the moment his replica was felled. The messengers kept charging him, but he ignored them as if they were insects as he smashed the crystals. None of them were set too high on the trunk and Gary smashed them by throwing his hammer over and again, having it fly back to his hand each time.

From within the invisibility sphere, Jason and Miriam observed, tension evident in their body language. More so Miriam than the one in a recliner made of clouds.

"You still think that the tree will initiate some kind of duel power against you?"

"I'm not making any assumptions," Jason said, "but it's a solid hypothesis. The tree has started to demonstrate cunning, and it's demonstrated that it knows I'm the one it has to defeat. It also knows that isn't likely while I have Gary with me."

"It needs to isolate you from our demigod."

"I think so. It's demonstrated an aptitude for mimicry and it certainly utilises messengers, so it wouldn't be strange for it to mimic their challenge powers. It could do something else, certainly, but that's my best guess."

"I suppose we're about to find out," Miriam said.

Gary destroyed the final crystal. The remaining messengers dropped like puppets after the puppeteer was shot in the head. They fell to the ground, joining countless others of their kind in death.

One more figure emerged from the tree, this one unlike those that came before. It wasn't a giant like the root avatar or the Gary clone. It wasn't even as big as the elemental messengers. It had wooden flesh, like the Gary replica, but that was hard to see when it was almost entirely covered by robes and a hooded cloak made of rough, undyed cloth. From within the hood, its eyes stood out, glowing yellow and orange.

"That looks like you," Miriam said to Jason. "If your outfit was made from sackcloth."

"It's a strange choice," Jason said.

"Strange? That thing has clothes made of fabric while yours are made of apocalypse beast and what looks like a portal to space."

"Point taken."

The new enemy emitted an aura that was gold rank, yet revealed a lower strength than the enemies that had come before. The elemental messengers had been approaching peak gold rank in power. The aura of this foe suggested a power level closer to the peak of silver. The figure floated forward slowly, drifting towards the giant-sized Gary standing on the ground. Gary brought his hammer down squarely on its head. The hammer bounced off, not so much as slowing the figure down.

Jason sat on his cloud throne, reading through the lengthy system message floating in front of him.

- You have been affected by a challenge power. This challenge power is soul-based and cannot be overcome by external forces or withdrawn until a completion condition has been met or sufficient time passes for the challenge power to destabilise.
- While this power is in effect, you cannot be harmed by external forces other than those coming from [Voice of the Will] of the [Corrupted World Tree].
- While this power is in effect, [Corrupted World Tree] cannot harm you or be harmed by external forces, including you, until its [Voice of the Will] is eliminated.
- While this power is in effect, [Voice of the Will] of the [Corrupted World Tree] cannot be harmed by external forces other than those coming from you.
- Completion conditions for ending the challenge power are: Your death; destruction of the [Voice of the Will] of the [Corrupted World Tree]; you or the [Corrupted World Tree] surrendering to the other.
- If a completion condition is met, transformation zone territories held by the participants will be unified under the control of the victor. If sufficient time passes that the challenge power destabilises, all participants will be annihilated and destabilisation of the transformation zone will be massively accelerated.

Miriam turned to look at Jason, who was seemingly staring into space. "Operations Commander?"

Jason stood up, his chair turning to mist and getting sucked into the miniature flask amulet on his necklace. He held himself aloft with his aura, his void cloak vanishing. His expression was not determined but contemplative.

"Jason?" Miriam asked.

"Miriam, have you ever been in a situation where there were only bad options laid out in front of you? But there's a hole where a good option should be, if only you could see it?"

"I'm an adventurer, Operations Commander. I've felt like that far too many times."

Jason rubbed his hands over his tired face, then looked grimly towards the cloaked figure floating in front of Gary.

"Okay," he said. "Time to finish this, one way or the other. I'm sorry I don't have anything to offer as a contingency if I fail."

"Again, Operations Commander: I'm an adventurer. We all came down here as adventurers. I know you think you're the extra special boy who does god stuff, but we all walked into this with eyes open."

Jason turned to look at her, eyebrows raised, then burst out laughing. Miriam glared at him but couldn't quite smother a grin, the sides of her mouth curling up. Jason gave her a friendly slap on the bicep.

"You're good people, Miriam. I hope I'm not about to get you killed."

"So do I, Operations Commander. I look forward to complaining loudly about you when we're home safe."

Jason laughed again and floated out of the invisibility sphere. He moved slowly through the almost empty air, the messengers previously filling it now dead on the ground. His mirth vanished as he drifted over a sea of corpses. The roots of the tree were only sporadically visible now, despite extending kilometres around the tree trunk. They were covered in a blanket of the dead, once-living anomalies piled high on the ground. The bulk of the root avatar and now the wooden giant stood out amongst the casualties.

Hours of battle that had seen rain and sun belt down in equal measure had given rise to the horrid stench of war. The oppressive foulness of rotting flesh; the ozone tang of ambient mana, overtaxed by too much magic used too fast. Jason sadly reflected that it was not a smell new to him. Broken Hill. Makassar. Yaresh. All times he'd been praised, despite the casualties. Those he failed to save and those who had fallen by his hand.

No small part of the corpse field came from Jason and his afflictions. His powers were designed to exact a tormented demise, and that was what he'd delivered. By the thousand, and not for the first time. Be it monsters or living anomalies, they didn't ask to be what they were. To be put in a position where they needed to be put down for simply being what they were. They were soulless creations of magic, born to die, but their suffering was real.

Jason had grown used to killing en masse. On Earth, he'd cleared proto-spaces and beaten back monster waves. The wholesale slaughter had numbed him until he no longer felt a chill run down his spine at the sound of hundreds screaming in anguish. Screaming because of what he was doing to them.

There was a time, on Earth and after, when violence was the first solution he reached for. He thought he'd moved past that, but had he really? Was he doing as much as he could or simply taking the easy shots at benevolence and telling himself he was improving? Mercy was easy when you had all the power. He'd been offering it to messengers when his power over them was all but absolute. But was mercy the exclusive domain of the strong? Did he want it to be? Was there a way to give it to those who were a genuine threat and find a way to peace?

Jason floated down to where Gary and the figure were facing off, now on the ground. A rare patch of clear space was marked by scorched earth, Gary having blasted away the bodies. The roots of the tree were unaffected, even by the divine flames. Gary had shrunk down to his normal size but still towered over the Jason-sized figure in front of him. Jason alighted on a patch of scorched dirt, next to his friend.

"What is this?" Gary asked, nodding at the figure opposite. "Why can't I hurt it?"

The replica Jason neither moved nor reacted, as if giving them time to talk.

"It has to be me," Jason said softly. "You've carried us far enough, big guy. Further than we had any right to ask."

"You never had to ask."

"I know."

Gary looked down at the hammer in his hands.

"That was it, then. My last fight. Wasn't even hard, which I suppose is the point. It has to be power worth dying for or there's no point taking it."

"Go back," Jason said. "Find the others; this is your time now. You've earned your rest, however you ultimately choose to take it."

"I can stay."

"No. It has to be me, for better or worse. And I want to try something."

Even surrounded by death, with their fates on the line, Gary let out a chortle.

"Of course you do," he said. "I'll give you some space, but yell and I'll come running."

Gary walked away. A path opened up as he moved, corpses combusting into ash and golden fire as he drew near.

Jason turned his attention to the wooden copy of himself. He could see the wooden hands and the wooden face, the inside of the hood lit up by glowing eyes. They were yellow and orange instead of blue and orange, but otherwise a match for Jason's. The robes were a rough approximation of his in their cut but were made from what looked like coarse natural hemp. The cloak was nothing like Jason's, being fabric and not ephemeral darkness. Jason didn't have his cloak out.

"So," Replica Jason said in a voice like wood being carved. "This is the end."

Jason smiled. He'd hoped that the tree having a Voice of the Will meant that he could communicate with it in a meaningful way.

"Endings can also be beginnings," he said. "I imagine that a tree understands cycles better than most."

"This is just an end. For one or both of us."

"Do we have to fight?"

"You want to consume me. You need to consume me. So, yes; we must fight."

"What if there was another way?"

"There are only three potential outcomes: One of us wins, one of us surrenders or we are both annihilated."

"In one of those options, no one dies."

"If you win or we surrender, you will devour us. You want the soul forge."

"I do," Jason admitted. "I didn't know what that meant for a long time. I had a chance, recently, to explore the reaches of my soul I've been afraid to in the past. I've come to learn what I've been missing. What it means to become what I'm on the path to becoming. Part of that involved getting a better understanding of this place. Of you. Where you came from and what's happening to you. Did you know that the same forces that birthed you are twisting you?"

"Yes. It changes nothing. If you get sick, do you capitulate to death or fight all the harder?"

Jason snorted a laugh.

"Fight. Every time."

"Then you understand that your knowledge of what I am doesn't matter."

"I don't accept that. Knowledge changes everything. I come from a world where there was almost no magic, yet we've built a civilisation that rivals anything magic can do. Eclipses it, sometimes. Flying through the sky; speaking across the planet. Healing the sick. I have knowledge of you. Knowledge of me. Knowledge of what comes next. I think there's a path forward for both of us."

"Words are easy."

"Sometimes. Most times. But there are times when violence is easy and words are hard. This is one of them, but I'd like to try words anyway. If you'll let me. We can always fight after."

Jason's wooden doppelganger stared at him for a long time while Jason waited in silence. A thick root pushed its way from the ground behind Wood Jason and he sat. Jason called out his cloud chair and also sat.

"I have used the echo of you, imprinted on this realm, to create this body. To give myself a coherent mind. I understand that I am corrupted. A menace. I do not wish to be. I do not believe we can end this with anything but violence, but I am willing to listen. To see if you can bring me the hope I cannot find within myself."

56

A COCKTAIL OF IGNORANCE, ARROGANCE AND AMBITION

JASON WAS SITTING IN A CLOUD CHAIR ON A FIELD OF SCORCHED EARTH and giant roots. The air was filled with the stench of death, the rot of bodies and the worse smell of rainbow smoke. The battle had gone on long enough that the first to be killed were starting to break down. Jason looked across at his counterpart: a wooden clone of himself sitting on a wooden root.

"I want to be upfront," Jason said. "Much of what I'm going to be talking about is consolidating transformation zones into reality. It's something I've done a couple of times before, but each time is different. In this case, very different. Even if you refuse everything I'm going to suggest outright, a lot of what happens will involve figuring it out as I do it."

"Why are you telling me this?" the doppelganger asked in a voice that sounded like wood being planed.

"Because honesty is important. I don't want to be your enemy, so I'm not going to hide anything from you. And the reality is that all I can offer you are things that might work. The only promise I can give you is that I'll try my best. I can't promise results. It's only fair that you know that going in."

"Understood. What is your proposal?"

"Before I get into that, I'd like to go over the potential outcomes as things stand."

"Why?"

"Context. I believe that your prospects are sufficiently unpleasant that even an uncertain alternative is a superior option to those you currently have available to you."

"Go on."

"Let's start by assuming that we fight and you win. I suspect we both believe that you won't, but we can put that aside for the moment. If you win, you may or may not successfully reintegrate the transformation zone with reality. It's not an easy task, this zone will be harder to manage than others I've experienced. The whole place may break down, dumping everyone and everything in it into the astral. That will kill everyone but the messengers instantly. They'll die slowly."

Jason let out a sad sigh before continuing.

"Now, assuming you don't fail, you successfully consolidate the zone into normal reality. That puts you back where you started before any of these transformation zone shenanigans. Deep underground. Corrupted. Slowly spreading ruin while unstable forces build up within you. That's what brought us looking for you in the first place. Did you know about that? The destructive power accumulating inside you as the disparate aspects of your being clashed? This began long before my people entered the underground."

"I was aware of the danger."

"If you end up back out there, the only change will be scale. That power will go back to building up, but the end result will be more destructive than if we'd left you alone. Even if everything goes right for you, all that will happen is you'll corrupt everything around you until you finally destroy it and you."

"That is... in accordance with my assessment," the wooden Jason said. "But can you offer anything but faster annihilation?"

"I might argue that a faster annihilation would be better than what happens if you win. I think I can offer you a superior option, but not if we fight. We both know that if I win, I have to separate the elements that make you up. Do you understand what those elements are?"

"Does it matter? You are talking about taking me apart."

"It matters. You were born from an attempt by messengers to turn one thing, called a natural array, into something called a soul forge. They did not understand what they needed to do was separate out a part of the array and use that. Instead, they tried to force it all to stay together. The outcome was you. Not a natural array, not a soul forge."

"You know what I am? My nature?"

"I believe so."

"Can you explain it? I... do not know what I am."

"I can, although I will need to be a little roundabout in that explanation."

"Context?"

"Just so. I'll start with a soul forge. Exactly what that is doesn't matter; suffice to say that they are used by astral kings who are akin to gods to the messengers."

"Is that what you are trying to become in taking this soul forge?"

"Yes, although I'm not taking a conventional path. For most astral kings, they form a soul forge within themselves in the process of becoming what they are. They don't understand how an externally formed soul forge—like the one involved in your creation—works. That lack of understanding is how a cocktail of ignorance, arrogance and ambition set in motion the events that brought us here."

"What convinces you that you know better than they?"

"That I'm not also ignorant, arrogant and ambitious? Not as much as I'd like because I'm all three of those things."

"Why would you admit that?"

"I told you that honesty was important and I meant that. I want to try and help you, and this whole conversation is a rambling attempt to get what people where I'm from call informed consent. That basically means that before I do anything, I help you to understand, as best I can, what I intend and why."

"Claiming to be the same as those who failed does not incline me to accept any proposal from you."

"We are similar, but not the same. I am becoming an astral king, but not in the normal way. I need to find a soul forge externally, like the one attached to you. I have been slowly gaining an understanding of them because there is a hole inside me where one would perfectly fit."

"I still fail to grasp the relevance."

"An astral king becomes an astral king by creating a realm. A universe within themselves."

"Like this transformation zone."

"A lot more stable, but yes. When an astral king creates their universe, within it will be a birthing tree. A tree that creates messengers."

"Is that what I am?"

"I believe in part, yes. But like the soul forge, something has gone wrong. The attempt to create a soul forge went awry, somehow triggering the creation of a birthing tree. But the environment was wrong and the messengers trying to force the natural array turned it into a corrupting element. Then my allies and I created this place. It is, as you surmised, somewhat like an astral king's universe. It still wasn't right for a birthing tree, but it was a better environment. You remained incomplete and corrupted, but more thoroughly formed. The transformation zone, the forces making you up, and probably my influence turned you into what you are now."

"And what am I?"

"Unique. The sum of the elements that made you, bundled into a result that no one could predict. Which is not special, by the way; that's how all of us come about. Your process just happened to be a little more exciting than most."

"You are saying that you are a part of me?"

"An influence, at least. There is a being that I accidentally created while the transformation zone was forming. I think you ended up affected by that. It's how you wound up with a soul."

"I have a soul?"

"Yeah. At first, I thought the echoes of consciousness driving your actions were a soul-like construct created by the soul forge. What we call a motive spirit, which is what monsters have. But you..."

Jason gestured at the wooden replica sitting opposite.

"I can feel it through you," he continued. "There's a genuine soul in there. I mentioned creating a living being. His name is Nik. Even outside the transformation zone, I believe you had some level of primitive consciousness. You can tap into aspects of this transformation zone, and I think that's what you did. When I created Nik, you tapped into that same process and somehow created yourself. Or recreated. You exploited a highly unusual and wildly specific confluence of conditions and events to become an entity with a soul. You turned yourself into a person who also happens to be a twelve-kilometre-tall tree."

"That tells me what I am. Not what you intend to do with me."

"You began as a natural array and a soul forge, one born from the other and then mashed together to disastrous effect. As the soul forge came from the array, you were a product of both. One thing became two, then two became three. The problem is that you are all still intertwined. You are all corrupting one another, yet you all rely on one another as well."

"If you separate us, we are destroyed."

"Yes. If we fight and I win, I use the reformation of the transformation zone to separate the elements. Hopefully, functionally. I'm confident I can make one work. That will be the natural array, should my friend decide he needs it. The soul forge as well, hopefully. But those don't have souls. They're objects. Complex magical and spiritual objects, but things that can be manipulated."

"But I have a soul," the replica said, a hint of revelation in its flat voice.

"You have a soul," Jason agreed. "I can't do anything to it without your willing participation."

"So that is your offer," the replica said. "If I surrender the zone to you, you will attempt to extract the natural array and the soul forge without destroying me."

"Yes, although it's not quite that simple. The corrupting elements are a part of you, but not a part of your soul. If I extracted the natural array and the soul forge it would destroy you, but your soul would remain intact. I would need to create a new body when the reformation of the transformation zone allows me to, minus the corruption, and put your soul back in it."

"That is possible?"

"Possible? Yes. How likely it is to succeed, I cannot say. Even the attempt would require your active participation, and I can't promise it will work. I can't even be sure what you'll become if it does work. I can promise that I will try and that if it becomes a choice between saving you, the soul forge or the array, the choice will be you."

"You would give up the soul forge?"

"I'm going to live forever. I'll find another one eventually."

"You said your friend would need the array."

"He might."

"Why would I believe you and he would both give up the things you want?"

Jason leaned back in his chair and let out a frustrated sigh.

"That's the thing," he said. "That's where this all falls apart. There is a reason why we would do that, and it's a simple one. It's just not very convincing."

"What is it?"

Jason sat up in his chair to look around in the direction Gary had left. He had stationed himself some distance away, standing like a guard on duty.

"I think you should ask him," Jason said, then waved Gary over. With a blur of movement and a rush of air, the demigod was next to Jason's chair.

"What is it?" Gary asked.

"If I asked you to give up your choice for the chance to save a life, would—"

"Of course," Gary said. "I knew going into this that I wasn't coming out. You've offered me another option, but I never expected it. And we both know it's not as simple as going back to how things were."

The doppelganger turned its head to look up at Gary.

"I can see the power devouring you from within. You would give up the chance to escape that to help me?"

"Yes," Gary said.

"I am your enemy."

"Who told you that?" Gary asked. "We killed the enemy in this place. All that remains is getting as many people out as we can. If Jason thinks you're worth saving, then you are."

The doppelganger looked from Gary to Jason and back.

"Trust," it said.

"Yes," Jason and Gary said together.

"This one," the wooden Jason said to Gary, "told me to ask you why you would help me."

Gary looked at Jason, who shrugged, then turned back to the doppelganger.

"It's not a very convincing reason."

"That is what the other one said."

"He's right."

"I would still like to hear it."

"Alright," Gary said. "We'd help you because you need help."

"You didn't ask to be put in this position," Jason said. "This was done to you, at least partially by us. What if we don't have to fight? I told you our reason isn't convincing, but what do you have to lose by trying? Death from corruption and madness? I'm not sure I could do worse than what's waiting for you if you win."

"And that's saying something," Gary added. "He's extremely good at inflicting misery and suffering."

"Thank you, Gary," Jason said.

"Pain, torment. It's his whole thing."

"Gary, you can go back and—"

"Not just physical either. He's gotten really good at soul torture. There's a messenger girl who—"

"Not helping, Gary."

"Sorry."

Jason shook his head, then looked back at his doppelganger.

"You don't have a good reason to believe us. To believe me. And I'm asking for an amount of trust that's hard from a friend, let alone someone you spent the last few hours trying to kill. All I've got for you is that winning is worse than surrendering."

"If I understand what you are proposing," the wooden Jason said, "you wish for me to surrender the transformation zone, allow you to tear me into segments and then believe that you can and will attempt to recreate me, for which you will need my active participation in you manipulating my soul."

"Yes," Jason said.

"And you offer as assurance only the claim that you would help me on principle."

"Yes."

"With no more incentive than to do anything else would be worse."

"No, there is an incentive," Jason said. "Hope. You asked for it and this is as much as I can offer. If you want more than that, I'll have to start lying."

The tree's Jason-shaped avatar sat in silence for a long time. Gary went to speak several times but was waved to silence by Jason.

"Your hope," it said finally, "is a tiny thing."

"Yep," Jason acknowledged.

"It could easily be a lie."

"Yes," Jason agreed.

"I do not like being in this position."

"I doubt you've liked any position you've ever been in, for as long as you've existed."

"And you have offered the only chance at a better one I have ever known. I will grasp at it, even if it proves to be false. I will work with you, Jason Asano."

5 7

DIFFERENT ENOUGH

JASON FLOATED UP TO THE INVISIBILITY SPHERE AND DRIFTED INSIDE where Miriam and Ramona were waiting.

"It's done," he said.

"Just like that?" Miriam asked.

"Just like that."

"I couldn't hear what you talked about. You used your aura like a privacy screen."

"Yes."

"You didn't want me deciding that I didn't like how it was going and staging a sneak attack."

"I didn't think you would," Jason said, "but people can make bad decisions under extreme pressure. I'll admit that's projecting my issues onto you, as you've been nothing but graceful under pressure, but it gave me some peace of mind."

"How did you find us?" Ramona asked. "I moved us, yet you knew exactly where we were."

"This realm belongs to me now," Jason said. "I know where everything is."

Jason sighed as he looked across the table at the brightheart leader. Behind him, the lava spilled down on the other side of a glass wall.

"Lorenn…"

"No chance," she said firmly. "Not ever. That tree killed my people."

"The messengers killed your people. If someone drops a barrel of poison into the water upstream from your village, you don't blame the barrel for killing the villagers. You blame the person who put it there."

"And do you put up a massive statue of the poison that killed everyone?" Lorenn asked. "Because that's what you're asking, Asano. It's a giant tree. It will loom over us, every day."

She shook her head.

"Asano, out of every twenty of my people, nineteen were killed by that tree and its elemental messengers. If it stays in our home, even if you manage to shrink it down, we will burn it to the ground or die trying. That is my final word on that issue."

True to her statement, Lorenn marched toward the large double doors. Jason looked away, not really seeing the lava waterfall through the glass wall. He heard the doors open, then the voice that came from that direction. He looked up to see Lorenn paused in the doorway. She surveyed the otherwise empty conference room.

"Thank you for doing this with just us, Asano," she said, her tone having softened considerably. "You could have brought in everyone and tried to pressure me into accepting."

"Would it have worked?" Jason asked.

"No."

"Then you're welcome," Jason said, a smile teasing the edges of his lips. Lorenn left and the doors closed behind her.

The smile on Jason's face vanished. He took a long, calming breath before moving to a bookshelf. He tugged on a medical textbook about lupus and the bookcase slid aside, revealing a short secret tunnel to his office. He walked through, the bookcase sliding back into place behind him. He arrived in his office where another bookcase slid closed to hide the doorway he'd just used.

"How'd it go?" Neil asked from where he sat on a couch. There was a board game on the table in front of him that he was teaching Nik. A side table was next to the first, holding drinks and mini sandwiches where they wouldn't dirty the game components.

"Well," Jason said, "she didn't attack me."

Neil winced. "That bad, huh?"

"Yeah. Not that I was ever optimistic."

Jason crashed next to Neil before sitting up to grab a sandwich and a glass of juice.

"It's not like I don't sympathise," Jason said. "They lost their civilisation. Most of their species. I've been through some stuff, but I hope I never understand that kind of loss. It doesn't change the fact that this tree has to go somewhere, once I reintegrate this place into reality. I don't think repotting it will be viable, which means somewhere in my new domain. Which will be the new home of the brighthearts."

"You should put it somewhere else if you can find a way," Neil said. "It's unique, which means that lots of people will want to study it. Experiment on it. Take samples. And blaming it for all the death makes an easy excuse for treating it poorly."

"And there will be no appealing to local authorities to protect it," Jason said. "The brighthearts won't tolerate it. At all. Lorenn made that extremely clear."

"Well, just because you failed doesn't mean the objective has," Neil said. "You can let other people have a crack at Lorenn."

"No," Jason said. "There's no room to move there."

"You know there's another option, right?" Nik asked, not looking up from the game he was trying to comprehend.

"What do you mean?" Jason asked. "I have to change the tree through the transformation zone. That means I have to place it somewhere in the domain I create where the brightheart city was. It's not like I have a whole other…"

Jason trailed off as he realised what Nik was suggesting.

"No," he said, shaking his head. "I don't even know how many ways that could go wrong."

"What are you talking about?" Neil asked.

"Planting the tree in his soul realm," Nik said.

"Yeah," Neil said. "That sounds like a bad idea, even if it does work. Planting a tree with a soul inside *your* soul? I can't imagine that's wise."

"It's not," Jason said.

"That being said," Neil continued, "that may be the only safe place for it. People will want to use it. The brighthearts will want to destroy it. Is there safety you can offer anywhere other than your soul realm?"

"The new home I build for the brighthearts will be my domain," Jason said. "There's no getting around that. But if I protect the tree, that will put me at odds with the brighthearts and they've been through enough. Once more, I did something without fully thinking through the ramifications. I thought I was getting better about that, yet here I am again."

"The circumstances are both urgent and extreme," Neil pointed out.

"The circumstances are always urgent and extreme," Jason said. "That's just my life, and long past being an excuse."

"It's still a reason, though."

"Thanks," Jason said. "For being supportive."

"Well," Neil said. "As much as I love to kick you when you're down, it seemed like that wasn't what you needed right now."

"That is never what I need."

"But sometimes it's what *I* need."

Jason chuckled, got up and patted Neil on the shoulder.

"Thanks," Jason said. "I guess I have to go and give someone an uncomfortable choice between two crappy options. Again."

"Has Gary…?"

"Yeah," Jason said. "He has."

"No," Gary said.

He, Farrah and Rufus were in Gary's suite, an opulent but ominous series of chambers within the mountain lair. Gary had already told Farrah of his decision and recruited her for support when telling Rufus. She sat next to him on a couch while Rufus sat opposite, staring at Gary with unbelieving eyes.

"Gary, you—" Rufus started before Gary cut him off.

"I'm sorry, Rufus. Even if it wouldn't make things harder for Jason, I don't want to be a ghost, rattling around in a hole."

"That's not—"

"Don't tell me what it is and isn't," Gary growled.

"I know this has been preying on your mind," Farrah told Rufus. "But do you honestly think you've given these choices more thought than Gary? That he hasn't gone over *exactly* what those choices mean, over and over?"

"One of those choices means death!" Rufus shouted.

"Yes," Gary said, unhappy but calm and accepting. "The other means being stagnant forever, assuming I even come through the process still myself. It means being chained underground."

"For now," Rufus said. "Jason—"

"Will visit every few months. Like you. Then every few years. Every few decades. I'll watch you all grow stronger and stronger. Listen to stories of other worlds every century or so, when my diamond-rank friends come home. A little less recognisable each time while I'm forever the same. If I stay, you'll lose me anyway. Just not enough that you get to mourn me. I'd rather be a fond memory you get to revisit from time to time than an obligation that you have to."

While Rufus processed Gary's words in silence, Farrah put her hand on a massive, furry forearm, rubbing it gently. Gary spoke again, his voice a softer rumble.

"While you've been thinking about my death, Rufus, I've been thinking about my life. And your lives. We didn't realise it at the time, but we hitched our wagons to a comet when we met Jason in that basement. When we fought with him in that blood-soaked hole in the ground. Unless you end up like me, you two are going to be diamond-rankers sooner or later. There are too many powerful people and wild events around you for that to be anything but inevitable. I know it's strange to accept when people spend lifetimes trying and failing to reach diamond, but that's how it is."

"You're not done yet," Rufus said. "We can keep you alive now and figure out how to fix things later. We can get you back on track. Maybe we find that purity artefact and use it to purge whatever's killing you."

"That's not how it works, Roo. The thing that's killing me is the same thing keeping me alive. The fact that Jason has a way to even keep me half alive is a miracle. One that Hero slipped him on the quiet. But staying alive isn't the same thing as being saved. It's just… stopping. Gold-rankers live for a long time, but not forever. I'll have the lifespan of a diamond-ranker, but the life of a man that should, at some point, die. I'll never get stronger; never see what the limits of my craft could have been. I'll never see a real sky again."

He bowed his head.

"Once you think about it, Rufus—once you really think about it—I believe you'll understand why I made this choice."

Rufus shot to his feet.

"Why you chose to give up? To quit? No, Gary, I won't."

Rufus stormed out, the way he had a dozen times in the last week.

"It's not giving up," Gary said softly. "It's letting go of something that isn't going to work."

"I know," Farrah said, leaning into his furry wall of a body. "So does he. He just needs time to accept it."

She felt the huge man tremble.

"I don't have time," he whispered.

Jason flew through the air, standing in a black air skimmer that drove itself. His wooden replica was in one of the seats behind him.

"Why are we out here?" the doppelganger asked. Its wooden voice seemed like an uncaring monotone, but Jason could feel the tree's soul properly now. Like the messengers that had been unsealed, it was a young and confused child, despite how it looked. Like Gary, it was reliant on power that was slowly killing it.

In the tree's case, that power was also muddling its mind. The wooden avatar was able to think clearly in a way the tree's main body could not, but it was still troubled. It was so uncertain, so full of fear. The spark of hope inside it was a fragile thing, always on the verge of being snuffed out.

"I've consolidated transformation zones before," Jason said, "but this time is different. It was more instinct than anything else those other times. Now I have the tools to be more deliberate, and I have to be careful. I need to rebuild the home of an entire people. I have to help you achieve a sustainable state."

"And there is your friend."

"No. He's decided to… accept the fate he'd already chosen."

Jason didn't speak again for a while as he stared off at nothing. Then he brought himself back with a little headshake before continuing.

"I can perceive everything in the zone, now, but I want to understand it more directly. More intimately. I want to know exactly what I'm working with and go in with an idea of what I'm going to do instead of just figuring it out as I go."

"Why have you asked me to join you in this?"

"Because we need to have another talk. I made you a promise that I would do everything I can for you."

"Are you going back on that?"

"Not at all. In fact, it's looking like I need to go a little further, one way or another. Depending on what way you want to go. The issue isn't transitioning you back to reality; that remains no more or less challenging than it was before. The issue is what comes after."

"I know nothing of the outside world. When I came into being, I could not truly think. All I knew was the drive to consume and grow."

"And that's the issue," Jason said. "Your growth and consumption came at the cost of the people in whose land you will once again find yourself. I don't think they have it in them to forgive you. And there will be others, eventually. Greedy people who will see your uniqueness and strive to exploit it."

"That does not sound good."

"It does not. And I don't know if I'll be in a position to move you. You're a tree, and whatever changes you go through, I suspect you'll remain quite large."

"Your concern is that your help will be sending me to destruction?"

"Yes."

"You mentioned a decision?"

"I could send you to an alternative place. I have a realm of spirit, within my soul. We've discussed using a soul forge to stabilise it, but it's real and it exists right now. I have no idea what putting you in there would do to either of us, but I'm willing to try. If you are."

"Yes."

"That quick? You should take some time to think it through."

"Do we have time?"

"Not a lot, no."

"Then I have made my choice. All I have known, when I've had the mind to comprehend, is this small universe. Another one, with a man who offered hope, is preferable to something different that offers only avarice and vengeance."

"Different can be good."

"I imagine that what I encounter in your realm will be different enough."

Jason let out a chuckle.

"Yeah," he said. "You're probably right."

58

EVERYTHING I NEED

JASON WAS IN HIS OFFICE IN THE MOUNTAIN LAIR. HIS EYES WERE CLOSED, his elbows were propped on his desk and his chin rested on his hands. Scattered across the massive desk in front of him were copious notes he'd written, planning out the reintegration of the transformation zone. He felt Miriam's approach and heard the ostentatious double doors swing open.

"Well?" she asked from the doorway.

Jason let out a frustrated breath before raising his head and opening his eyes to look at her.

"This isn't easy, you know," he said. "The last couple of times I did this, I went by instinct. I wasn't so much making choices as desperately hoping I didn't mess anything up too bad."

"Did you?"

"Yes. I altered the magical landscape of the entire planet. Forever. I managed to prevent the planet from breaking up and drifting off into the astral, but I left it fragile."

"My understanding is that Pallimustus is more resilient than your world."

"Yeah. I'm not worried about punching a hole in the universe. This time, it's about the details. I have more control than before, which is good, but I only have one chance to get this right. I have to extricate the natural array, the soul forge and the tree. I have to be careful about what goes into my soul realm and what goes into reality. I have to build a new home for the brighthearts and keep everyone safe while I'm doing all that."

"Is keeping everyone safe a concern?" Miriam asked. "I thought we were moving everyone to keep them out of danger."

"We are," Jason said. "Each time I've done this, there's been a safe centre. I've just never done this with allies in place. Except for the ones I intended to betray and kill from the beginning."

Miriam raised her eyebrows.

"Don't look at me like that," Jason said. "Yeah, it felt crappy, but they were looking to betray and kill me as well."

"You just did it better?"

"There was one woman that played me and escaped. Vampire Lord. Call it a no-score draw. And I'm hardly going to betray anyone this time."

"Hardly?"

"What?"

"You're hardly going to betray anyone?"

"No idea what you're talking about. I'll thank you to not cast aspersions upon my character, Tactical Commander."

Miriam shook her head as she walked across the large room. She cast her eyes over the haphazard notes scattered across the desk.

"Are you ready for this?" she asked.

"I don't think ready is an option, but I'm as prepared as I'm going to get. How's the transfer going?"

"The mountain is almost empty. Just a few stragglers."

"I think I can sort that out."

Jason entered a code into a keypad next to a desk drawer and the drawer opened. Inside was a plastic container that he picked up and smashed on the desk. He picked up the two keys that came out of the container and stood up. He moved to a small table where there was a bronze bust of Beethoven. He tilted the head back, revealing that it was hinged and had a small red button underneath.

"What are you doing?" Miriam asked.

"Security procedure."

He pressed the button and a painting on the wall slid aside, revealing a safe door with two keyholes and a dial. He went over and slotted both keys but only turned one. This lit up the security dial that he turned left, then right, then left.

"Seriously, what are you doing?" Miriam asked.

"Some things are too dangerous to be easily accessible," Jason said.

After he finished entering the safe combination, there was a click. He then turned the second key and pulled open the safe. Inside was a small rubber mallet.

"A rubber hammer?" Miriam asked.

Jason took the mallet and went back to his desk, setting the mallet on top. He then opened an unlocked drawer, took out a glass case with a big red button inside and set it on the desk as well. He picked up the mallet and raised it to smash the glass.

"Is that special glass?" Miriam asked.

"No. Just regular glass."

"So, it's not something magical that can only be broken by that hammer?"

"No, it's a regular mallet."

He brought the mallet down and smashed the glass, exposing the big red button inside.

"You could have done that with your hand. Regular glass can't cut you."

Jason ignored her and held his hand over the button, quivering slightly as a serious expression crossed his face.

"You need to get on with whatever this is," Miriam said. "Don't make me go get Farrah."

Jason brought his hand down on the button. A monotone voice started echoing throughout the mountain lair, tinny as if speaking through a mediocre PA system.

"Self-destruct has been initiated. The mountain will be destroyed in fifteen minutes."

"What did you just do?" Miriam asked.

"That should get everyone out," Jason said.

"That button destroys the mountain?"

"You said you needed to get the stragglers moving."

"Why was that in an unlocked drawer while you kept a small hammer behind all that ridiculous security?"

Jason looked from the button to the open safe.

"You know, it occurs to me that I could have set that up more efficiently."

Miriam ran her hands over her face.

"You're doing this now? NOW?"

"Yep."

"THIS IS NOT AN APPROPRIATE TIME!"

"Self-destruct has been initiated," the monotone voice repeated. "The mountain will be destroyed in fourteen minutes and thirty seconds."

Jason laughed and hit a switch under his desk. A section of floor started lowering in segments to become a staircase.

"Come along," he said and headed for the stairs.

The gold-ranker moved in a blur to position herself between them and him.

"Is there an issue?" he asked lightly.

"This is an extremely serious moment, Operations Commander."

"Yes," he agreed.

"You need to stop playing around and get ready to transition the transformation zone."

He flashed her a tired smile.

"Tactical Commander, I started eleven hours ago."

Miriam suddenly found herself behind Jason as he walked down the stairs.

"How...?" she asked as she numbly followed him down the stairs.

"I'm manipulating the reality of the transformation zone."

"What about getting everyone to a safe zone first?"

"I told you that this time is different. Previously, the entire zone collapsed outside of the core safe zone. That was because I had almost no control. It was a dam and all I could do was open and close gates to control some of the water flow. This time, I'm sculpting clay. River clay, so it's rough, and I have to take care I don't get washed away, but I have my tools and some sense of what I'm doing."

"Isn't that reckless?"

"All I'm doing right now is trimming away the portions of the zone that are unsalvageable. The edges where the zone is breaking down. Plus tweaking a few things, like when people block my way."

"Trimming? Is that going to cost us?"

The stairs led down through a stone stairwell, illuminated in red by lights set into the ceiling. The stairwell turned into a spiral.

"It won't cost us much," Jason said, "and the loss is worth it. Better to lose a little than have corrupted elements incorporated into the whole. I'm amputating the rot."

"The transformation zone is so much larger than the normal reality space it's going to fill," Miriam said. "I suppose we can afford to lose quite a lot of territory."

"It's not that simple," Jason said. "The transformation zone is the same amount of reality as the space it occupies in the real world."

"Because it's made of that chunk of reality?"

"Exactly."

"Then why is it larger? Vastly larger."

"The reality is stretched thin. That's why it's become so malleable."

"And now you have to squash it back down? To fit back into the space it occupied in the first place?"

"Yes. Stretching out reality like this is barely sustainable when it's contained in the travel-size universe that is the transformation zone. Put it back into a full-size universe and it'll break down. I need to get it into a shape close enough to the space it originally occupied that it can graft back on."

"Like a healer repairing a severed limb before reattaching it?"

"Yeah, actually."

The stairs ended in a short tunnel that terminated in a large iron door. It swung open, giving them access to a catwalk set into the side of a massive natural cavern. A lake of magma making up the floor of the chamber washed everything in red light. Hanging from the ceiling were a bunch of cages at the end of chains, dangling over the magma.

"Who is that?" Miriam asked, looking at the solitary occupied cage. A man in a suit was attempting to cut the lock using a wrist laser.

"Don't worry about him," Jason said.

"Self-destruct has been initiated. The mountain will be destroyed in twelve minutes and thirty seconds."

"Was that really necessary?" Miriam asked.

"The self-destruct button? It's a volcano lair, Miriam. Of course it was."

Jason led her along the catwalk and into another stone tunnel with stairs heading down.

"Operations Commander, if you're actively reshaping the transformation zone, shouldn't you be somewhere you can concentrate?"

"No," Jason said. "I realise that I may seem calm, debonair and strikingly handsome..."

"Uh..."

"...but the reality is, I'm very nervous. So, I'm having a little fun to calm myself down."

"By remaking reality into forms that you find amusing."

"Remaking reality is kind of my thing, which is a weird thing to say. Did I ever tell you I used to sell bulk office supplies?"

"Self-destruct has been initiated. The mountain will be destroyed in twelve minutes."

"Operations Commander, I hope you realise that this isn't exactly inspiring confidence."

"It's inspiring my confidence."

"Oper... Jason. I understand that you are anxious about getting this right. I just don't think that this is the time for frivolity."

"It's practise, Miriam."

"Practise?"

"I've played around with reality before. A lot more than anyone should have or wanted to let me. This is the first time I've been able to do it with precision. Making a few innocuous changes here and there is giving me a feel for it. Once everyone is secure in the centre of the zone, I'll start breaking the whole thing down and rebuilding it to fit back into reality."

"The safe zone in the middle. The part that doesn't change. Where the tree is."

"Yes."

"The tree is going into your soul realm. Does that mean that you're taking a chunk of the transformation zone and putting it into your soul realm, instead of into normal reality?"

"It's complicated. The area where the transformation zone was is going to be my spirit domain. My soul realm and the space I'm recreating in normal reality will be physically distinct. Mostly. But the two spaces will spiritually overlap, and that will blur certain lines. You've felt what it's like in my cloud house. The way it doesn't just belong to me but is an extension of me. The altered space is going to be the same."

"Leaving the brighthearts living in what amounts to a city-sized temple to you."

"I wouldn't put it that way," Jason said. "Not where gods can hear, please and thank you. But yes."

"How do you think they'll feel about that?"

"What they do next is up to them. Whether they use the space I create or not, it's the best I can do."

They emerged into another large underground space. This was not a lava chamber but a submarine dock filled with water. Jason's cloud vessel was sitting in the water, its sweeping lines of red and black panels over cloud substance, tapering into points.

Jason's friends were waiting for him on the concrete dock. Rufus was talking to Gary, his voice low and his body language angry. He was punctuating his words with short, stabbing gestures while Farrah was trying to keep him calm. Taika was explaining Earth submarine design to Clive, Belinda, Neil and Nik. Belinda looked unimpressed and Neil was complaining loudly.

"What do you mean, no sandwich bar?"

"That's more of a yacht thing," Taika said. "Submarines are kind of tricky when you don't have magic."

Humphrey was looking around the space, glaring unhappily as another self-destruct announcement echoed through the chamber. Sophie was watching a moustachioed puppy splashing happily in the water.

"How are we going to get to the tree in a submarine?" Miriam asked as they walked along the dock towards the others. "And why not just portal?"

"Portals are a little wonky right now."

"Up until I came to see you, I was supervising portalling everyone to the tree with no issues whatsoever."

"That's weird. Anyway, it turns out that there's a network of massive underwater tunnels running beneath the entire transformation zone. It's definitely been there the whole time and wasn't created by me a couple of hours ago."

Miriam sighed.

"If you don't mind, Operations Commander, I'm going to go back up and finalise overseeing the departure to the centre of the zone."

"Sure," Jason said, then turned and pointed. "That elevator there will take you right up to my office in about twenty seconds."

"Self-destruct has been initiated. The mountain will be destroyed in nine minutes."

Miriam levelled a glare at Jason who met it with an impish grin. She sighed again.

"Is there anything else before I go, Operations Commander?"

Jason turned to look at his friends.

"No," he said. "I have everything I need."

59

THE WORK OF HIGHER BEINGS

THE TREE WAS QUARTER AGAIN THE HEIGHT OF EVEREST, CLOUDS HIDING most of it. The battle that had been waged around it was over, leaving little indication that it had even taken place. The roots of the tree, being impervious to damage, were untouched by the conflict. The earth they were buried in was a different story; countless destructive powers had churned it up and scorched it to black dust. At a glance, though, it looked like ordinary black dirt.

The thousands of messenger-shaped anomaly corpses had turned to rainbow smoke, mostly through the loot powers of various adventurers. That loot had been packed up and hauled away in dimensional bags and personal storage spaces. Although too many of the expedition would never make it home, those that did would bring treasure troves with them.

At the base of the tree, two cloud flasks were immeasurable specks in comparison to the massive trunk. Just as hard to see were the narrow streams of cloud-substance they were spraying into the air. The cloud material snaked up the trunk in two streams until they reached the lowest level of actual clouds, around a kilometre up.

The cloud material condensed into a pair of building complexes, highly distinct from one another. The larger of the pair was a single enormous building, an ostentatious sky palace. The other was smaller and hard to spot at a distance. A series of smaller structures, rather than a single massive one, they took on the shape, colour and texture of wood. The rustic complex was made up of modest treehouses, connected by rope bridges and crude counterweight elevators.

Emir and Jason were floating in the air, watching the buildings as they neared completion. Emir stood on a cloud that, being an essence ability, was superior to personal travel devices that looked similar. Jason held himself aloft with his aura. The icy wind that came with their altitude whipped his hair about.

"Really?" Emir asked as he cast his eyes over Jason's portion of the complex. "Treehouses and elevators that pull people up from the ground using rope? I appreciate the rustic appeal, but you could at least put in a proper elevating platform. There's something to be said for efficiency, you know."

"There's also something to be said for subtlety," Jason said, looking to the sunset blaze shining through the clouds of Emir's cloud palace.

"We're building cloud palaces on the side of a tree taller than most mountains," Emir pointed out. "If that's not a time for showmanship, when is? Also, of all the people who might lecture me about grandiosity, it shouldn't be the man who carved a mountain into the shape of his own head."

"There's a time and a place for everything," Jason said, his expression the picture of innocence.

Emir shook his head.

"Oh, look: mine's finished," he said. "I'm going to go in and poke around. How is it that mine is bigger, yet yours takes longer to finish?"

Jason nodded sagely.

"You did finish first," he acknowledged. "Constance said you like to do that. Poor woman."

"Wait, what did my wife say?"

"Oh, look," Jason said. "Mine just finished. I'm going to go inside and poke around."

Jason floated toward his cloud building, Emir following after.

"Hey! You have to tell me what my wife said!"

With everyone gathered up into the two cloud palaces, preparations for Jason to begin in earnest were complete. He had given everyone a choice between riding it out in his soul realm and remaining in the cloud palaces. Most had chosen the cloud palaces, whether out of curiosity or from reluctance to enter Jason's soul any more than necessary.

Jason had one last thing to do before engaging with the task of re-integrating the transformation zone with normal reality. Two people had made important decisions and he was going to give them one last chance to change their minds. He walked onto the balcony where they were waiting for him.

If not for the kilometre-high view, it would have looked like the porch of a log cabin. An invisible mist screen reduced the blasting icy wind to a warm breeze. Gary seemed at peace, his hands on the railing as he took in the vista. From their height, they could see the distinct boundaries of the once-separate territories. The sudden shifts in ecology and climate were clearly unnatural.

"It looks like one of your board games from up here," Gary observed. He was the only one who could always sense Jason's presence, even within Jason's spirit realm. Jason joined Gary at the rail, looking like a child next to the massive leonid. He didn't bother to say anything, simply happy to be in his friend's company. The other person on the balcony was standing by the wall, still and silent as a block of wood.

"Why did you put the cloud palaces all the way up here?" Gary asked.

"Because we could," Jason said. "It's an adventure, remember? There have to be joys and wonders to go with all the sacrifice and loss."

Gary smiled.

"Fair enough," he said. "You know, Rufus is going to be a problem for a while."

"Farrah has an idea about that."

"You talked with her?"

Jason shook his head.

"She's discussing it with some of the others now. I'm listening in."

Jason waved his hand at the air around them.

"Now that I control all of it," he said. "I can eavesdrop where and when I like."

"What's Farrah's idea?"

"I'll let her explain it. I don't know if Rufus will go for it, or how well it'll work if he does."

"You should ask his mother."

"I know. I'm sorry I won't be around to help with him. I'll be gone before you."

"We do what we can and accept what we can't," Gary said.

"If either of us was willing to accept that," Jason said, "neither of us would be here."

"And we've both paid the price," Gary pointed out.

Jason shook his head.

"No, you've paid the price. I always seem to come back stronger, but you've given up everything. It doesn't feel right."

"Don't," Gary said. "I get enough of that from Rufus."

"Sorry. This is your last chance to change your mind, though. If you want to stick around. I know you won't, but I still have to ask."

"What do you think I should do?"

"Whatever feels right."

Gary nodded.

"I thought you might say that. I was half-hoping you had a compelling reason for me to stay, but I know what's right for me. It's just easy to doubt, you know? Especially with Rufus telling me to cling on to life. Even if it's a ragged, broken scrap of one."

"It might not be that bad, and none of us want to lose you, Gary. But there's courage in letting go when holding on isn't right. Shade refuses to tell me what comes next, but he does think you're making the right choice."

"I am still not going to tell you why," Shade's voice came from Jason's shadow.

"Not even a hint?" Jason wheedled. "You know his situation."

Gary's chuckle came out as a deep, resonating growl.

"Leave him alone, Jason."

"I am not privy to what will happen to Mr Xandier," Shade said. "All I know are the possibilities—which I will not be sharing."

"Don't you let him push you around, Shade," Gary said.

"Of course, Mr Xandier. I wish you good fortune on the next step of your journey... Gareth."

"Thank you," Gary said. He pushed himself off the railing and looked over at the other person on the balcony. It was the tree's avatar, the wooden replica of Jason.

"At least I can do one last good deed, even if it is only stepping aside to make survival easier for someone else," Gary said. "I'll see you on the other side."

Gary left as Jason nodded, his eyes on his wooden doppelganger.

"You get the same chance," Jason told it. "Last opportunity to change your mind."

"Do you not still wish me to take root in your soul realm?"

"It's a risk for both of us," Jason said. "If we do this, we're saddled together for all eternity. I can't tell you how that will go, but I can tell you there's more risk to you than to me. At the end of the day, if we do this and we don't end up getting along, it's my soul realm. If push came to shove, I could probably strip the mind out of you and turn you into just another power for me to use. You're trusting me with your very existence with little time and less information to base that decision on. It's a terrible choice to have to make when you'll be living with the consequences forever."

"We have been over this," the replica said. "My mind is unchanged."

"Okay," Jason said. "I had to offer. All that's left is to get it done."

Jason stood alone on a wooden balcony. He let the invisible mist screen dissipate, allowing the chilling, high-altitude winds to wash over him. This wasn't his first time resolving a transformation zone, but this time, the training wheels were off. No instinctive, good-enough-will-do solutions would do; too many details mattered for him to be anything but exact. He couldn't afford close-enough when it came to the soul forge, the natural array, the tree or the new home for the brighthearts.

There was also the mass of undeath energy to deal with. Two hundred thousand dead brighthearts left to fester had created an energy that had permeated the old brightheart city. That power had been brought with them into the transformation zone, and while they dealt with the priests and the avatar, that power remained. If Jason didn't handle it properly, it could infest everything again, making the new would-be home of the brighthearts uninhabitable. If he let it infest the tree, he could create an adversary worse than the one they'd already fought.

For all these reasons, he couldn't just let instinct guide him. He needed to dig in and manage the details himself. Every mistake he made could lead to dire consequences.

"Well," he muttered to himself, "standing around brooding won't make it go faster."

"Oh, thank goodness."

"What was that, Shade?"

"Pardon, Mr Asano?" Shade's voice came from Jason's shadow.

"You just said something?"

"No, Mr Asano."

"You definitely said something."

"I have no idea what you're talking about, Mr Asano. It makes sense that you are distracted, however; there is a lot on your mind."

"Uh-huh."

Jason shook his head and chuckled. He took one last look at the panorama of the transformation zone and then, with a startling simple act of will, destroyed it. The landscape smeared like wet paint splashed with water. Reality beyond the reach of the tree twisted and warped until it was nothing but a blur of colour. The colour slowly faded as it swirled around until all that was left was black, deeper than any night sky.

What Jason perceived through the blackness was not something he would later be able to explain. It was not the stuff of the material world, but the space between potential and result; it was between what could be and what would be.

He was reminded of his time on Earth using the Builder's door, roaming in the space underneath reality. He'd been repairing the link between worlds and only now realised how crude and fumbling he had been. He'd gotten the job done, but he'd been trying to etch microchips with oven gloves, a blindfold and an axe. The result was just ugly, even if he did get the link more or less repaired.

Things were different now. Now he had the tools and experience to shape reality without making a complete ham of things. A large part was simply accepting that it was his work to do. This was the work of higher beings, and he had come to terms with the fact that he was on the path to standing amongst them. He was by no means an expert, but he wasn't the bumbling mortal he had been either.

Jason's first task was breaking down the transformation zone into a state he could work with. He was already working on that, with the zone at large no longer inhabitable. Only the safe zone of the tree and the buildings upon it remained intact. Even that space would get some changes, but it would remain a survivable area throughout the process. He could feel the occupants watching the zone break down from balconies and windows, although they would eventually be rendered unconscious.

In Jason's previous transformation zones, the safe spaces had been pagodas that became the heart of his spiritual domains. This time, Jason had decided to use the tree rather than create a new safe zone or use his head-shaped mountain. The tree was a sentient thing, and while he was going to change it, he didn't want to break it down and remake it from nothing, like the rest of the zone. He simply wanted to extract the natural array and the soul forge that were corrupting it.

Reshaping the zone required a precision and ability to multitask that was outside the scope of the mortal mind. Jason would not be able to carry out his task as he was. As he had when fighting the god's avatar, Jason had to become something else. The last time was dangerous, but he had learned much. He was confident he could come back to himself when the task was done.

He put his thoughts aside—not just his personal musings but everything. Mortal thinking would distract him from a task that required higher-order cognition. He let himself float off the balcony and join with the unformed space beyond. Once, this would have killed him. Now, it was what he needed to reshape himself, that he could reshape the zone in turn.

HEROES CHEAT ALL THE TIME

A MASSIVE SHAFT LED FROM THE SURFACE OF PALLIMUSTUS TO WHAT HAD once been the subterranean home of the brighthearts. The Adventure Society expedition had fought their way down through elemental messengers and monsters adapted to the extreme depths. Months after the transformation zone had been put in place, the dangers of the shaft had been tamed—a certain definition of tame. The messengers were gone and most of the monsters had learned to avoid the place. Those that remained, though, were not something a lone silver rank wanted to run into.

The elemental forces that had made the lower portions of the descent difficult were no longer a factor. With the natural array subsumed into the transformation zone, the ambient magic had returned to normal. The lessening of interference with personal and commercial flight devices granted access to people and infrastructure that previously wouldn't have survived the journey down the shaft. Even so, anyone short of a silver-ranker would find the environment hostile. Such subterranean depths were not hospitable to humans and their ilk.

Despite a few lingering threats, an outpost had been established at the bottom of the shaft where the impenetrable transformation zone cut it off. It had been carved from the walls of the shaft, with rooms and tunnels dug deep into the stone. It was almost a town, complete with ambitious merchants, shopkeepers and taverns. The deeper sections were where the less influential were relegated; Magic Society researchers and merchant delegations that inevitably cropped up when high-rankers gathered. The glass-fronted chambers abutting the shaft were the domains of the powerful.

The shaft-side chambers of the outpost all had huge windows of magically reinforced glass. From within, the most powerful of the outpost's occupants waited for the rainbow barrier of the transformation zone to drop. These were the people with real power, including gold and even a few diamond-rankers.

One of these rooms was a multi-storey tavern. Its exterior wall, spanning three levels, was a single pane of glass, the largest window in the outpost. It was spacious in a place where space was precious, and well-decorated for a chamber carved out of the rock. Every booth and table had a privacy screen, and the wood panelling could have been pried up and traded for a moderately sized airship. The window was further enchanted to keep out the rainbow light from the transformation zone below. Many observation rooms did not have this feature and were constantly painted in bright, shifting hues.

It was one of the most exclusive venues in Pallimustus, by location, patronage and cost. Not just any silver-ranker could spend time there; they needed the backing and reputation for at least some of the gold-rank patrons to recognise and accept them. They also needed to afford the food and drink on offer. The silver- and gold-rank libations being served had been brought down at exorbitant cost and cheapskate lingerers were not tolerated.

The clientele was impressive, and Jason would have recognised quite a few faces. The Sapphire Crown guild of Rimaros had been present since the early days of the outpost. Although Zara was only a former princess and had left the royal family for political reasons, the Storm King did not stop caring for his daughter. The royal guild had a full contingent in place, led by Trenchant Moore.

Danielle Geller had gotten used to being one of the most powerful people in any given room, but that was very much not the case in this room. Some of the auras she couldn't sense would belong to stealth specialists, but she had no doubt there were a few diamond-rankers on hand as well.

Danielle had sought out Allayeth on arriving in Yaresh, having heard she was close to Humphrey and his team. The diamond-ranker had expressed a desire to wait at the outpost, but she was far too busy. Not only was Yaresh still in dire need of rebuilding, but the messengers had renewed attacks after the transformation zone had appeared. None of them would even have known what a transformation zone was if not for the church of Knowledge.

There was one pair that Danielle was most wary of. She had seen them rebuff the social approach of another diamond-ranker, letting a brief glimpse of their auras show. These two were beyond the likes of Soramir Rimaros or Roland Remore. Danielle's money was on them being from beyond Pallimustus, contemporaries of Dawn. Her companion disagreed, betting them to be ancient diamond-rankers, perhaps unseen for millennia.

That same companion, Gwydion, now entered the privacy screen around Danielle's table. A priest of Hero, he had skin of dark chocolate and a thornbush of curly hair. He set a fresh drink in front of Danielle and put another down for himself before sprawling into the chair opposite her. After patting his pockets for a moment, he fished out a pack of cards and waved them questioningly. Danielle nodded and he started dealing.

"How are they?" Danielle asked.

"Well, they're bronze-rankers being kept in an underground chamber so far below the ground, they need the room enchanted just so they can breathe. They've been dragged across the world to wait for a son who will probably die right in front of them, so... not well."

Danielle looked out at the transformation zone barrier and frowned.

"This needs to end."

"It's not like you to be impatient."

"I knew strange days were coming," she said. "The movements of the church of Knowledge. The ever-extending time between monster surges. I raised my children to be ready for a world where being just an adventurer wasn't enough anymore."

"There you go," Gwydion said. "You prepared Humphrey for this."

"For *this*?" she said, gesturing at the window and the rainbow light shining through it from below.

"You think I'm not worried?" Gwydion asked. "My whole family is down there. Little Roo is going to be a mess over Gary. I'm just glad Mum is in there with him. Dad will probably be less help."

Danielle snorted a laugh. She looked at her cards and dismissively tossed them onto the table.

"A priest of Hero shouldn't cheat."

"Heroes cheat all the time. Tales are full of such deeds."

Danielle acknowledged the point with a nod as Gwydion dealt a fresh hand.

"I worry I made a mistake in pushing Humphrey and Jason together. I knew he would be caught up in things—that's the nature of outworlders—but I didn't expect…"

Her gaze wandered over to who she believed to be the most powerful pair in the room.

"…attention of quite this level."

"I'm looking forward to meeting this Asano," Gwydion said. "I'm not sure anything could live up to the rumours, now. My brother is very taken with him, according to Mum. They aren't…?"

"No," Danielle said. "Not as far as I know. My sources tell me that Jason's tastes drift towards women. Of the extremely powerful variety."

"Your sources being your son diligently calling his mother?"

"I would never use my son as a source."

"There are at least some lines you won't cross, then?"

"What? No, he'd just be a terrible source of information. Far too biased for me to take his word uncritically."

Gwydion chuckled and laid down his cards with a smirk that vanished when Danielle did the same. He stared at her cards disbelievingly.

"How did…?"

"Heroes cheat all the time," she told him. "I'm reliably informed that tales are full of such deeds."

He grumbled as he swept up the cards, only to stop and look at the window. Danielle did the same, both sensing the change before rainbow light flared up the shaft. It pushed past the magical treatment on the window to wash through the tavern before rapidly fading.

Danielle and Gwydion got to their feet and were not alone in doing so. Silver-, gold- and even diamond-rankers moved to crowd the window. Only one pair remained where they were, images blurred under their privacy screen. Danielle noted the two most dangerous people in the room not moving but then turned her attention to the window with everyone else. She watched the rainbow light recede down the shaft that was no longer blocked by the transformation zone barrier.

Jason woke up, face down, on a coarse wooden floor. His head was pounding and he could feel a sharp tug at his soul. He rolled into a sitting position and opened his eyes, but it was his supernatural senses that told him what he needed to know.

He was in his soul realm, in some kind of treehouse. Outside was not one mountain-sized tree but a sweeping forest, the trees as enormous as ancient redwoods. The treehouse felt like wood, but Jason knew it to be cloud-stuff mimicking it. He could sense the building and others like it spreading through the forest, reaching metropolitan proportions.

He reached out for the soul of the tree, permeating the entire forest. The response he got was a wave of confusion and grogginess that dwarfed his own but, also like him, felt healthy and intact. Jason detected no trace of the natural array, which had been pushed out of the soul realm entirely. The soul forge was elsewhere within Jason's realm and he would go see it soon. For now, it was enough to know that the tree—or forest, as it now was—was free of the influences that had corrupted it.

Jason tried to dig out his memory of reshaping the transformation zone, but it was little more than a blur. He had entered a very different state to make that possible, and the memories of that time were incompatible with his mind as it was now. He managed to tease out enough to be confident that everything had gone well and get a basic sense of what had happened.

Despite his fears, extracting the soul forge and the natural array from the tree had proven quite straightforward. Once their states were in flux, it was easy to guide them each to their true natures, which included being separate from one another. This allowed him to put each in its proper place and integrate the soul of the tree into his own soul realm.

Incorporating another soul into his own was, unsurprisingly, the trickiest and most intricate part of the entire process. It involved tapping into his new soul forge, healing the tree after it was separated from the forge and the natural array. After finding a state where the tree could exist free of their influence, Jason had to connect it to himself in a way that left them linked but still autonomous.

How well Jason had done with this remained to be seen. He imagined that time would reveal all, and there was nothing he could do in the meantime. As they were both rapidly recovering, things seemed to have gone well. There were already some interesting results that would have a major impact on his plans for the very near future.

With the tree successfully integrated, Jason had moved on to separating the rest of his soul from the transformation zone. There was no way to completely separate them and Jason would forever be connected, but he had successfully reforged the physical reality. His goal hadn't been to get everything perfectly right. The objective had been to avoid any critical mistakes in the details that truly mattered. Extracting the undeath energy, separating the soul forge and natural array from the tree. Building a viable home for the brighthearts. Those seemed to have gone well, so anything else he could live with.

The final touch was to repatriate the people in his soul realm and the transformation zone into normal reality. Some he retained in his soul realm while the rest were placed outside, into his new spirit domain. He hoped he had made a new home for the brighthearts that they would find acceptable. Jason's power infused throughout it was something they would have to live with unless they abandoned the area entirely.

Jason's friends and companions he retained in his soul realm and he could feel them scattered through the forest city. They were rousing just as he had, moments earlier. There were others in his soul realm as well— Sophie's mother and the growing collection of messengers.

The Builder cultists and remaining adventurers he placed in his spirit domain. This included not just the brightheart warriors who had fought alongside them but all the brightheart survivors. This area was outside of the transformation zone and outside of Jason's soul realm. It might have been infused with Jason's power, but they were back in their normal universe.

The bulk of the brightheart people had been carried inside Jason's soul throughout his time in the transformation zone. He hoped that the events his soul had gone through, including the battle with Undeath's avatar, hadn't traumatised them too much.

Jason finished casting his senses over his soul realm and pulled up the system window that had been blinking at the edge of his perception.

- You have established a new spirit domain.
- Exigent circumstances have allowed you to establish an additional domain despite existing domains exceeding the normal maximum territory.
- Due to low rank, links between spirit domains separated by dimensional boundaries are impeded.
- Your current spirit domain exceeds your maximum total domain size available by 1,743,621%. Increase your rank to increase available domain size.
- You have integrated another soul into your soul realm. Some effects that impact your soul realm will not affect the territory of the second soul.

- The avatar of this soul realm is now connected to you as a nascent Voice of the Will.

Jason nodded to himself as he closed the window. Everything seemed to have gone as well as he could have hoped, although how keeping the soul inside his own would go was an open question. His memory might have been patchy on the exact process of how it all took place, but he doubted he was forgetting anything important.

Yumi Asano snapped out orders, trying to stave off panic. The naked apparitions of her grandson wandering around like an oblivious tourist were gone, but now the central administrative buildings of the two domains had turned into trees. That had not been great for maintaining public order, especially after things had finally calmed down after the undead incident.

She resolved that Jason, once he finally made his way back, he was getting a *very* stern talking to.

The brightheart leader, Lorenn, wasn't sure when she lost consciousness. She'd been waiting in the cloud palace, attached to the abominable tree, for the transformation zone to be changed. She'd been dwelling on the hope of a new future for her people, and the dread of that hope being snatched away. Even now, with the danger ostensibly over, she didn't trust good fortune. It had been too long, and her people had lost too much.

She came to on a bed of moss. Pushing through a sopor that threatened to drag her back into slumber, she got to her feet and took in her surroundings. She was in what looked like a growth chamber from the old brightheart city. Only one had survived to be consumed by the transformation zone and this wasn't it.

It seemed like she was in a jungle of lush growth crowding in on her. The plants were a vibrant green, heavy with bright flowers and colourful fruit. Light filtered through from above, illuminating the space more than it should have, given the dense canopy. The air was thick, humid and heavy, with just enough breeze to brush against her skin and softly rustle the leaves. She could hear insects, birds, and small animals scurrying through the underbrush.

Overhead, she realised the canopy was partly artificial, with vines and plants dangling from stone walkways. She shook off the fog still clouding her mind and extended her magical senses.

She was in an underground chamber, hundreds of metres across and something like a kilometre high. It superficially resembled the growth chambers of the old brightheart city, but with some obvious differences. It was as if someone had tried to recreate one without brightheart sensibilities to draw on, which is exactly what had happened. It worked, but there was an unfamiliarity to it, an uncanny alienness.

"Asano," she whispered to herself.

He'd done it. Maybe. At least in part, he'd recreated their home. He hadn't gotten it right, because how could he? It wasn't his home and he wasn't one of them. But he'd promised to try and an excited part of Lorenn was ready to find out to what degree he'd succeeded.

She extended her senses again, pushing them harder. The aura of the chamber was vibrant with life, and she could feel the natural array. It was tamped down at the floor level, where she was, but felt much stronger up above. She suspected it was the source of the light that allowed her to see.

Lorenn grinned as she explored the natural array with her senses. This was not the warped and twisted thing that it had become, leading to the downfall of her city and her people. This was the power she had grown up with, warm and comforting.

The only part she found discomforting was a hidden undercurrent in the aura. She had to push hard to sense it, but once she latched onto it, she realised it was everywhere. Everything else existed within it, like islands in the sea.

It was the aura of Jason Asano.

She put that revelation aside for the moment, choosing to focus on the most important thing. In pushing her senses through the chamber, she had sensed some of her people scattered around it. There were perhaps a few hundred, their auras filled with tiredness and confusion. Looking around for a path through the thick foliage, Lorenn spotted some stone stairs hidden behind ferns and under moss. She set out to collect her people together.

YOU KNOW IT'S TROUBLE

TWO TUNNELS LINKED THE REALM OF THE BRIGHTHEARTS WITH THE surface of Pallimustus. Both had been cut off by the transformation zone, and both were now open again. One tunnel had been dug by the messengers for their first attempt to turn the natural array into a soul forge, triggering the subsequent disasters.

The messengers had been monitoring the tunnel, no longer impacted by the power of the natural array that had corrupted them into mindless berserkers. When the transformation zone vanished, they had poured down in search of answers, only to swiftly retreat.

What they found was a glassy smooth shaft of black crystal, shaped into a perfect cylinder hundreds of metres across. Blue and orange eyes had lit up the moment they entered, firing beams of blue disruptive force and orange resonating force. Worse were the afflictions that started infesting their body, turning pristine feathers and flesh into black rot. Added to the elemental forces of the natural array, easily felt in the shaft, and it was clear no messengers would find safe passage.

The second tunnel had a town where it met the surface, rapidly constructed through collaboration between the Adventure Society and Magic Society. At the bottom of the hole was an outpost occupied by a gathering of powerful adventurers and other interested parties. Various governments from the surface were represented, as were numerous organisations and associations, including many churches. There were also agents from opportunistic merchant cartels, curious noble houses and other parties of varying legitimacy.

When the rainbow barrier of the transformation zone vanished, it was not long before people were pouring down a shaft identical to the one savaging messengers at that very moment. Priests, adventurers and magical researchers moved alongside the agents of noble houses, criminal enterprises and merchants hoping to turn boldness into spirit coins.

There was a clear hierarchy in the descent through the shaft, aligning exactly along the lines of power. At the front were Raythe and Velius, the peak diamond-rankers from beyond Pallimustus. Then came the handful of other diamond-rankers, including Allayeth. She had not been waiting at the outpost, but word travelled fast and diamond-rankers travelled faster.

The gold-rankers came next, but that was where the jostling for primacy began. It was rare to see so many gold-rankers outside of a monster surge, and rarer to have them moving as one. Priests and officials of powerful and legitimate forces jockeyed for position. Gwydion Remore took his cue from Danielle Geller and let others go ahead, hanging back ahead of the silver-rankers.

The shaft was not as hostile to the group of essence-users as the other was to the messengers, but it was far from welcoming. Blue and orange nebulous eyes appeared on the walls like liquid behind glass. They followed the group as it descended through the shaft, imposing a growing sense of trespass on the people moving down.

That sense affected some more than others. Gwydion felt nothing at all while Danielle felt an aura that was familiar, but profoundly changed from the last time she had felt it. Most of the others showed different levels of unease, from discomfort to fear. Those driven by avarice, opportunism and malice felt as if the eyes of a god were watching them. Raythe and Velius showed no reaction to whatever they were feeling beyond sharing a quick glance.

For some, the feeling of unease and trespass grew stronger. Many amongst the silver-rankers turned back, shooting up the tunnel with a sense of having escaped some unseen danger. For those that persisted, the eyes on the walls grew more numerous and started tracking individuals.

When afflictions began affecting some of the people, most of them retreated up the shaft. Only a few of the silver-rankers attempted to tough it out, some trying healing or protection magic. It didn't take long for them to realise the futility and flee upwards as well. The eyes tracking them followed them up, pursuing them back to the outpost.

The impacted gold-rankers lasted longer, their protection and cleansing magic more effective. As the group continued downwards, however, it became clear they would not last. They shot back up the shaft, some growled threats at the air before departing.

Around a third of the initial group were forced into retreat, many already planning return attempts. Of those that remained, many were left unsettled by the aura but were, thus far, unharmed. They finally reached the bottom of the shaft.

The new forest city at the centre of Jason's soul realm had a soul of its own. Like Nik, Jason had unconsciously brought it into being with the transformation zone's inception. Unlike Nik, the results were not neat and clean. Nik had been spun from wholecloth as a humanoid rabbit, fresh and new as the Healer's gift erased any flaws.

The forest had not been a forest at first, but a single, mountainous tree. A living edifice, mad and hostile. Unlike Nik, it had predated the transformation zone as a corrupted and half-formed thing. The messengers had tried to produce a soul forge from the natural array and gotten it terribly wrong. The array had created an incomplete soul forge that, in turn, created an incomplete messenger birthing tree. The result was a warped whole in three parts, each reliant on—yet poisonous to—the others.

That mess had gone into the transformation zone, becoming the building blocks for the twisted antagonist at the centre of the zone. The tree, a living product of two unliving things, had developed a soul. Unlike Nik, the results were not divinely guided perfection. This was a second product, victimised by its corrupt origin and Jason's unknowing influence.

Jason's most laborious task in reintegrating the transformation zone had been untangling the mess that was the tree, the natural array and the soul forge. So far as he could tell, he had managed to bring each to a completed state, allowing them to exist separately and be extracted from one another. They had each become complete without the others and the tree changed most of all, from a single monstrous plant to a living forest city.

The array went back to the brightheart realm, where it came from in the first place and where it belonged. It was part of Jason's spirit domain, but also firmly rooted in a normal universe. The soul forge and the tree were both in Jason's soul realm, which was a reality in and of itself, but a much less stable one.

The results of Jason claiming the soul forge were simple and predictable enough. His soul realm was in the process of breaking down, the astral throne, astral gate and soul forge setting him on the path to becoming an astral king. As for the tree merging with his soul realm, the ramifications would take time to be fully revealed.

The tree's form was the most obvious difference. Instead of a single, mountainous tree, now it was a forest spanning from horizon to horizon. Spiritually, the change was far less, with the tree's soul retaining its integrity. While the rest of Jason's soul realm was slowly breaking down, the forest city remained fully intact.

Jason was holding off the process of becoming an astral king, staving off the breakdown of his soul realm outside of the forest city. He needed to make preparations and wanted to say his farewells. He didn't how long it would be before he saw his friends again, and there was one he never would.

Only one portion of the wider soul realm was not in the process of slowly collapsing. High above the forest city was a mountain resting on an island of clouds. At an altitude too high to be seen from the ground, the exterior was frozen and wind-blasted with air too thin in oxygen to breathe. The mountain had been carved into the shape of Jason's head.

Inside, the mountain had been dug out into a complex of giant hall-ways and cavernous rooms. The construction was dark stone, carved from the mountain, and crude industrial metal. The air was hot, wet and heavy. The lighting came from thick glass pipes that moved in and out of the walls and ceilings or were set into the floor. Glowing magma pumped through the pipes, painting everything in shifting, ominous red.

The magma came from the central feature of the mountain interior: a massive shaft running from above the highest level to under the lowest. A waterfall of magma spilled down through the shaft, not touching the walls. The walls were covered in a mix of small waterfalls that quickly turned to steam, windows into the surrounding rooms and tropical plants growing right out of the stone.

Jason arrived at the lowest level of the complex. It was akin to a grotto or a cenote, but with magma pooling below instead of water. A metal catwalk was bolted to the coarse stone walls, and five heavy iron doors were spaced evenly around the walls. One held an elevating platform that led up to Jason's office. Three of the others led to the astral throne, astral gate and soul forge.

The last door, even Jason was unsure where it led. What he did know was that it was the reason the mountain wasn't breaking down like the rest of his soul realm. He also suspected who was responsible for it. He made a casual gesture and the metal door slid slowly aside with a loud, mechanical grinding.

Behind the door was a vast and starry void. Off in the distance, he could see nebulas of blazing colour. The closest was the familiar eye-shape of blue and orange, matching both Jason's eyes and his most alien familiar. Those more distant were of other shapes and colours, only one of which he recognised. He spotted the mountain-shaped nebula belonging to Carmen, an avatar of doom like Gordon.

"This is you, isn't it?" he asked.

Gordon manifested next to him, the orbs around him glowing blue in confirmation.

"Is this the next bit of trouble coming our way?" Jason asked.

Half of the orbs turned orange.

"You don't know if it's trouble?"

The orbs all turned orange.

"Oh," Jason said. "You know it's trouble; you just don't know if it's next."

The orbs turned blue.

"That's what I thought."

Jason tilted his head, as if listening to something, and sighed.

"Just what I did not need: house guests."

The large group reached the bottom of the shaft in darkness. The glowing eyes on the walls were no longer present, having chased the now-departed members of the group back up the shaft. Danielle guessed that it was feelings of hostility or exploitative desires that triggered the defences, and was curious as to how accurate that detection was. If it could accurately sense such feelings in the auras of the diamond-rankers, that was impressive, and likely to make said diamond-rankers angry. Most were centuries past anyone being able to peek at their feelings.

Seeing in the dark was not an issue for this group. They had all known they were heading underground, so those without appropriate powers had picked up magic items instead. Seeing through non-magical darkness was not expensive to overcome by adventurer standards.

The bottom of the shaft was smooth and glossy, like the walls. Being a mother, Danielle smirked as she idly imagined how easily it would pick up grubby little fingerprints. Neither Humphrey nor Henrietta had been shy about playing in the dark, rich dirt of the Greenstone delta.

There were two doors set into the wall, both dark metal and both closed. One was the size of normal double doors while the other was freight-warehouse sized. The larger door slid open, revealing a long hall-way, wide and tall. It curved off into the distance, beyond which some light source offered at least a little illumination.

Some of the group moved forward, but the moment they did, an odd figure manifested in the doorway. It looked like a floating cloak, blacker than midnight, empty save for a single oversized eye in the hood. The eye was blue, orange and nebulous, like those that had chased off some of their group with bleak afflictions.

The figure made no sound, but its presence arrested those who had been moving forward. There was silence, as no one knew quite what to do, until it was broken by footsteps echoing down the tunnel. The group watched as a single man rounded the curve of the tunnel, making his way towards them in unhurried fashion. Wandering through the tunnel as if strolling through a market, he wore a garish floral shirt, tan shorts and sandals. He held a glass of fruit juice in one hand and was munching on a sandwich held in the other.

6 2

STEVE, LORD OF UNDEATH

JASON HAD GONE THROUGH A CHANGE SINCE DANIELLE HAD LAST SEEN him in Greenstone, yet many of the hallmarks were the same. He was noticeably taller, although still short by adventurer standards. His features had the usual smoothing out that came with rank, although his chin was still prominent under the neatly cropped beard. The wavy hair was still the same, black and glossy to the point of reflecting the dim light shining from the tunnel.

The big difference was in his eyes. They were the same glowing nebulas that had chased part of her group back up the shaft, and the single eye of the guardian creature floating by the door. It left no question as to whom the power guarding this place belonged.

That power tied into the supernatural changes Danielle saw in Jason, far more drastic than the physical ones. His aura was more powerful than anything Danielle had ever sensed in a silver-ranker; it was probably as strong as her own. More arresting than the raw power of it was the way it blended into the ambient magic of their surroundings.

Admittedly, the whole area was permeated with what she now recog- nised as Jason's aura, but it was hard to tell where he ended and his surroundings began. Danielle had seen that before, from the Mirror King. Jason's technique was definitely lesser but, to Danielle's knowledge, the Mirror King was the most skilled aura master in the world. Being on the same scale as him would be a triumph for a gold-ranker. Doing so at silver was simply monstrous.

The group watched in silence as Jason made his slow passage down the long hallway. Occasionally, someone would stir, as would the guardian creature floating in the doorway. Danielle cast the occasional glance at the diamond-rankers up the front, but they seemed content to wait.

"That's him?" Gwydion asked in a whisper.

"That's him," Danielle confirmed.

"I think he might like to make an entrance more than my dad."

As Jason was about to reach the shaft, Danielle was suddenly aware of a new presence nearby. The entire group felt the sudden rise in power, divine in strength and heinously corrupt in nature. The group scattered to the walls of the shaft, even the diamond-rankers, leaving the god Undeath alone.

Danielle looked the god over. He was tall and corpse-pale, with dead eyes and limp, grey hair. There was a faint glow of purple in his milky corpse eyes, only visible in the darkness of the shaft. Jason wandered right up to the god, who was half again Jason's height, and continued eating his sandwich.

"You devoured my avatar," Undeath accused Jason. The god's voice had the grinding quality of stone closing over a tomb.

Jason held up one finger in a pausing gesture as he chewed his food.

"Do not try denying it," Undeath warned Jason. "I can feel what you turned my power into."

"You're the one who left it sitting around," Jason said after swallowing. "Things would have gone smoother if you hadn't chucked a bunch of your power in there with us. A lot was going on in there and having to clean up after you did not simplify things."

"You have made powerful enemies here, Asano," the god said. Just the sound of his voice made Danielle feel like she was being buried alive, but Jason showed no sign of being intimidated by the figure looming over him.

"Maybe you and the god of Destruction should take a step back," Jason suggested. "Reassess things. Take a look at who won and who lost here, and start worrying about the enemy *you've* made."

With one hand occupied by a glass of fruit juice, Jason gripped his half-eaten sandwich in his teeth to free up the other. He wiped his hand on his shirt and plucked a glowing purple marble from his pocket. Danielle felt a hideous power from it, an echo of that coming from the god. Jason tossed the marble up and the god caught it.

"You think tribute will spare you from my ire?" the god asked.

Jason took the sandwich out of his mouth.

"I just didn't want it sitting around," he said. "You know what renovating is like. You find a bunch of nasty stuff lying around and you get a guy in to chuck it all out. So, now that you've collected the garbage, your invitation to this domain is rescinded. Get out of my house, Steve."

The god lingered for a moment, glaring at Jason, then was gone as if he'd never been.

"That guy sucks," Jason announced to the room as he cast his gaze over the people gathered around the edge of the shaft.

"Okay," he called out. "My friend Shade will start approaching people. If he offers to take you inside, follow him. If he doesn't, go away. I think you all know what not going away means, but let's not make things any more unpleasant than necessary."

Shadows started moving and Danielle realised that Jason's shadowy familiar had been there the whole time. Far more numerous than before, and now able to hide from her senses, despite her own rank-up since last seeing the familiar. The shadows were barely perceptible in the dim light coming from the tunnel until they started partly glowing white. This made them more visible, as well as reflecting a design she found familiar.

Back in Greenstone, Jason had proven something of a social butterfly, particularly at the symphony. In typical Jason style, he'd foregone local formalwear fashion, although she could not blame him when she'd seen Greenstone fashion for herself. She recalled that he'd had one of the Bertinelli brothers make something based on designs from Jason's home world. Her excellent gold-rank memory threw out the word 'tuxedo.'

"Did he just call the god of Undeath 'Steve?'" Gwydion whispered.

"Yes," Danielle said.

"Why?"

"You'll come to learn that, with Jason, it pays to let the incongruities pass."

Danielle was not surprised that the first people Shade approached were the two most powerful diamond-rankers. She was a little surprised that they were old acquaintances.

"Lord Velius; Lady Raythe. If you would follow me, please."

"Shade," Velius said. "It's been some time."

"Indeed, Lord Velius. I was rather caught up in something your master had taken from the Builder and had been left long-abandoned."

"I heard you'd been betrayed by your summoner. An unbecoming affair. You know it was Umber who—"

"I am quite aware, Lord Velius. Perhaps we shall talk as I show you around Mr Asano's newest spirit domain. Lady Raythe?"

"Thank you, Shade," she acknowledged and followed the familiar as he led them towards the tunnel.

Other Shade bodies approached others and likewise led them in that direction. After the god of Undeath left when told to, no one else was stupid enough to think they knew better. Those that remained were mostly Adventure Society and Magic Society representatives, along with adventurers connected to those who went on the expedition with Jason.

Jason himself shadow-jumped in the gloom, appearing in front of Danielle and Gwydion. He ignored the people watching them as he flashed Danielle a smile before turning to Gwydion.

"We haven't met," Jason said.

"That was the god of Undeath, right?" Gwydion asked.

"Yep," Jason confirmed.

"Why did you call him Steve?"

"I was concerned he would turn himself into a sexy version of himself called Stefan."

"Funny you should say that. I was spying on some Undeath priests once when their god appeared before them," Gwydion said. "He was a lot less growly and corpsy with his own people. Had kind of a handsome dad feel to him."

"The god didn't notice you spying?" Jason asked.

"Oh, he noticed," Gwydion said with a laugh. "I was chased very far."

Jason laughed with him as Danielle shook her head.

"You remind me of someone," Jason said to Gwydion. "You're more relaxed than the person I'm thinking of, but you have the same obnoxious level of handsomeness. Where did you get your training?"

"My family runs a school," Gwydion said, his expression turning confused at Jason's triumphant grin.

Jason shoved his drink and sandwich into his storage space and replaced them with a filled shot glass in each hand instead. He held one out for Danielle and kept the other for himself, looking at her expectantly. She held it in her fingers, rolling her eyes after reading the words printed on it. She gave Jason a look dripping with reluctant motherly indulgence, but still joined him as they drained their glasses in a gulp. Her face immediately took on a pinched expression.

"Oh, that is sickly sweet," she complained. "I see there are ways you still haven't changed, Jason."

"Can someone please explain what's going on?" Gwydion asked.

Danielle held out her now-empty glass so he could see the words 'my family runs a school' printed on the side.

"That," Gwydion said, "leaves me with more questions, not fewer."

"Allow me to introduce Jason Asano," was Danielle's only explanation. "Jason, you've clearly noted the family resemblance, but allow me to introduce Gwydion Remore."

Jason chuckled as he took the empty glass from Danielle and stowed it with his own, back into his inventory. Now with his hands free, he held out one for Gwydion to shake.

"G'day, mate."

"A delight to meet you," Gwydion said. "I must say, I wasn't sure what to expect after all the rumours, but—"

"Excuse me," a man cut into their conversation. He was gold rank, but plainly through monster core use from his aura. Danielle and Gwydion shared a look of surprise while Jason just looked annoyed. Seemingly oblivious to their reaction, the man continued.

"You're obviously ignorant of my identity as your servant has approached several people before me, but I can assure you that—"

He made a gurgled sound as his aura was crushed, not by Jason but by the ambient magic as it became significantly less placid. The man then shot up the shaft as if fired from a cannon.

"I think it's me," Jason said. "I think I attract them. Did that guy not see me tell an actual god to sod off? And have him actually do it?"

He shook his head, the good mood gone from his expression. He gestured absently and a soul realm portal arch rose from the floor.

"I'm on a bit of a clock and have to go see some people out here, but I'll send you into my soul realm to see your families."

Danielle and Gwydion looked over the portal.

"This isn't a normal portal," observed Danielle, whose dimension essence made her extremely familiar with dimensional forces. "Where does it go?"

"My soul."

Her eyebrows raised in surprise.

"Really?"

"It's a bit more complicated than that. I do have to go, though."

She shrugged and stepped through. Gwydion only hesitated a moment before following. The portal closed and a normal shadow portal appeared in its place. Jason stepped through, leaving people either standing around or being led through the large door by Shade.

One of the men standing around looked at his friend. "Reks, I don't think we're getting in."

"No kidding."

"Do you think the god of Undeath's name is really Steve?"

"No, Daniel. The god of Undeath's name is Undeath."

"What if that's more like a title?"

"You think his name is secretly Steve, Lord of Undeath?"

"It would explain why he just uses the title. You think that's worse than Undeath, the god of Undeath?"

"I'll concede that's not great, but yes, I do think it's worse. You're positing that all of the gods secretly have different names but are embarrassed about them?"

"I always imagined the goddess of Wind as a Susan."

"Susan?"

"It's got that wooshing sound. SOO-san. Like the wind."

"This conversation is going to get us both killed. Probably by the god of Idiocy."

"What do you think of Steve as a name for the god of Idiocy?"

"I thought the idea was that Undeath's real name was Steve."

"There can be more than one Steve."

Lorenn had been roaming through the new brightheart home, gathering her people together. It consisted of three main areas, one being the growth chambers in which she had awoken. A network of interconnected chambers, they were part hanging gardens, part water source and part orchard. The edible vegetables, fruit and fungus they produced would exceed the needs of the diminished brightheart population.

There were animals, mostly birds and insects, as there had been before. She was pleasantly surprised they had made the transition from city to transformation zone and back. The growth chambers, especially these new ones, would have felt alien without their presence.

The second part of their new home was made up of chambers taking full advantage of the natural array. Where the growth chambers used the array for light and temperature regulation, these functional chambers employed it for more practical purposes. This included forges, hot springs, ceramic workshops and even quarries where high-quality stone was not just available but grew back like plants.

The final and most central part of the new subterranean realm was the main city. Lorenn had finally wandered into it while exploring their new realm, finding it the only place not teeming with life. It was made up of mostly stone in many varieties, from granite and sandstone to marble and quartz. The other main material was metal, also in various iterations.

There were some signs of life she found as she walked through the empty streets. She wasn't entirely alone, with scattered members of her people also exploring the space. Some were gathering into groups while others remained solitary. Lorenn greeted everyone she met, sometimes moving with people until they formed groups of their own, but mostly, she moved alone.

She wandered through parks with ponds and plant life far more spread out than in the growth chambers. Little animals rustled through the bushes and skipped over the grass. She encountered an entire canal district where she could see fish swimming through the clear waters.

Unlike the growth chambers, there was no illusion of not being underground. Light came not dappling through jungle canopy but from two orbs of white fire, moving slowly across a ceiling two kilometres up.

The other thing dominating the skyline was a massive spherical building, suspended in the air. A single column held it up from below while a second affixed it to the ceiling above. The round building was reminiscent of the citadel, one of the most important buildings in the old brightheart city. It was not a recreation, however, the original building being a centuries-old mess. This was clean, new, and organised, with fresh stone and neat design. The exterior was covered with windows, balconies and landing platforms, with what looked like high-capacity air skimmers parked on them.

The city was not what the brightheart home had been, but this was no surprise. Aside from the citadel and one growth chamber, Jason Asano had only seen it in ruins, overrun by undead. It was no surprise that he'd not recreated the brightheart home but his own idea of it. Lorenn was grateful for what he'd done, but this was not the home she'd lost. She hoped that it would become home in time.

Her wanderings brought her to the base of the column leading up to the new citadel. It was made of white marble, streaked with grey. Archways were set into the column at even points, each containing a large elevating platform.

"I know the old citadel was in a separate chamber," Jason said, startling her.

She found him standing beside her.

"Thank you," she said. "This is more than we could have asked for."

"But not what you lost," Jason told her. "I can't replace what was taken from you."

"What about all the undeath energy?" she asked. "I know you dealt with the god's avatar, but what about the energy from…"

She paused with a grimace.

"…from the city full of dead people. Before the transformation zone, almost everything was tainted. Many zones stayed that way, even after the priests and their avatar were dealt with."

"I got rid of it," Jason said. "It's not coming back."

"How?"

"I gave it back to the god of Undeath."

Lorenn took several steps back from Jason, glaring at him with anger.

"You gave that power to him? After what he and his people did to us?"

"That power needed to go. Giving it to him was the only way to excise it cleanly. I could have destroyed it, but that would have left a mark. A taint on this place that is meant to be a new start for your people."

"And a taint on this new territory of yours. Because that's what this place is, isn't it? Under everything, it belongs to you."

"Yes."

They stared at each other, Jason's expression neutral. Lorenn's was a mix of anger, hope and fear.

"I'd like to take you up into the citadel and show you around," Jason said, "but I lack the time. There are a couple of things we need to talk about, like the people from the surface coming here. I've done my best to protect this place, but people far stronger than me will take an interest in you now. You will need to decide how your people are going to handle diplomatic relations."

"I don't think we're ready for that."

"It's been my experience that the world doesn't care if you're ready. There is one thing I must show you, though, even if I can't offer the full tour. We should go directly since I don't have time to take the elevating platforms."

He opened up a shadow portal and stepped through.

63

TIME TRAVEL IS THE WORST

JASON AND LORENN TOOK A SHADOW PORTAL INTO A MASSIVE DOMED room. Panes of crystal levitated around in the air, each showing different images of the city outside. In the middle of the room was what looked like a padded marble armchair on a circular platform.

"It'll take some trial and error," Jason said, "but that chair will let you control the city."

"Control how?" Lorenn asked.

"The growth chambers and the more functional ones, those are as they seem. You can make adjustments to the heat, light and water. The main city is not as it seems. While it looks like it is made of stone and metal, with a little ceramic and wood, it is none of those things. The plants, the soil and the water are real, but everything else is a facsimile."

"The city is fake?"

"It's made of clouds, like the buildings you've seen Emir and I make with our flasks. It just looks like stone and steel. And from that chair, you can control it all. You can remake the whole city, flattening and constructing buildings in minutes. It's going to make maintenance very cheap. You can take what I've built here and make it into something entirely different. You can make it into your image of your people's home."

He panned his eyes over the monitors showing various parts of the city.

"The outer chambers will have to stay as they are," he said, "but other than this room, everything else can be changed. By you, or anyone you allow. As it stands, only you can use that chair, but you have the power to give others permission."

"You can't use the chair?"

"I am the chair."

Jason turned from the monitors to give her a sad smile.

"My hope," he said, "is that, over time, you'll evolve the city to accommodate a growing population. I mentioned that people will be coming here. I highly recommend you prioritise meeting with the church of Fertility, but that's for you to figure out."

"I don't have any experience with diplomacy, outside of our bargain with the Builder cult. Where are they, by the way?"

"I've got them contained inside the city."

Jason gestured at one of the screens and it switched from a park to a group of people inside a stone building. She saw no doors or windows, although there was some kind of light source overhead, out of the screen's perspective.

"I have some friends who can perhaps help you with diplomacy. Danielle Geller and Constance Bahadir are the ones you want to talk to, although Danielle is reuniting with her son right this instant."

Jason opened a portal to his soul realm, from which Emir and Constance emerged.

"Jason?" Emir asked.

"There are people already coming in from the surface," Jason explained. "Shade can fill you in on the details and I'd like you, Constance, to help guide Lorenn through the diplomatic relations. That's something I'm famously bad at and I need to go make sure Boris doesn't convince Clive to attempt time travel."

"What?" Emir asked, but Jason was already through the portal and gone.

In the new forest city in Jason's soul realm, the material from his library had been shifted into a new building, high in the trees. In a room full of tables covered in scrawled notes and open books, one small, round table had a ritual circle floating over it like a hologram. The illusion formed a rough sphere, made up of dense lines and intricate sigils.

The lines of the diagram glowed gold and the sigils blue, washing the room in colour. Boris and Clive stood beside the table, observing the diagram. Clive jabbed a finger at one of the sigils.

"This variable," he said, frustration painting his voice. "Until I understand what this variable represents, I can't move forward with dimensional navigation. I know it's a keystone aspect, but I can't figure out what it represents. The only clue I have is that Jason doesn't understand it either, but he was able to feel his way through when travelling between this world and the one he's from."

Clive ran a hand through his already dishevelled hair.

"'Feel it through,'" he repeated. "I understand that he has a sense for dimension forces, but feelings are not an appropriate methodology by which to conduct complex magical workings!"

Boris smiled as he walked around the table, tilting his head as he looked over the intricacies of the diagram.

"Where did you get this model?" Boris asked.

"What?" Clive asked distractedly. "Oh, I threw it together while I was figuring out astral geography. Or trying to, anyway."

Boris stood up straight from where he'd been leaning over to examine the lower sections of the diagram. He turned to Clive and looked at him from under raised eyebrows.

"You just threw it together?"

"Yeah," Clive said and turned to look at Boris. "Is there something wrong with it?"

"Weren't you trained on the astral magic of this world? You know there's been an active effort to keep the astral magic theory here stunted, right? To keep the link between worlds hidden?"

"I didn't know that, but it makes sense. Astral magic hadn't made any real advancements in centuries until around fifteen years ago. Which turned out to be when the Cult of the Builder started actively using it here. That's when they started getting sloppy."

"But in that environment, you got to the point of being able to do this," Boris said, gesturing at the diagram.

"That's hardly a feat," Clive said. "I've had access to outside astral magic for years now."

"How many years?" Boris asked.

"Well, I've had access to my mentor's notes going back almost twenty years. He spent his life piecing together fragments of astral magic from off-world sources, although it was all very patchy. I always wondered how Landemere Vane always seemed to be ahead of me, but it turns out he was a Builder cultist the whole time. Given what he must have had access to, he was actually kind of bad, now that I think about it."

"How long have you had full access to off-world astral theory?"

"Five years. Plus a few weeks with the library of a diamond-rank messenger. He had some more advanced stuff, but I've barely touched that particular trove. It's hard to get away from saving the day from cataclysmic events when Jason is around."

"Oh, I know. If he doesn't fix the link between worlds, I have to."

"You?"

"I did tell you I knew some astral magic myself."

"And the World-Phoenix tapped you as Jason's backup?"

"Nothing so direct," Boris said. "The World-Phoenix doesn't just grab someone and tell them to go fix a thing."

"It told Jason."

"*Dawn* told Jason. You'll find that the great astral beings and their prime vessels don't always see eye to eye. Especially a vessel preparing to hand over the role to someone new. Prime vessels last wildly varying amounts of time in their roles, and I've suspected for a while that it's more than being burned out by raw power. I suspect that the real problem is ideological incongruity developing over time as the vessel develops an independent identity."

Clive looked thoughtful for a moment as he contemplated the idea.

"You're suggesting that because a vessel needs to fully embody a great astral being, independent thought that diverges from their master's objectives creates a dissonance that results in an escalating incompatibility? Resulting in the need to pass the position on, ideally to someone indoctrinated into service?"

"Exactly," Boris said. "It's a balance, though. Sometimes you need some independent thinking in the top role. Dawn didn't come into the World-Phoenix's service by being raised in the cult. Same for a lot of the current prime vessels, actually. I suspect they needed people with more flexibility as the fallout of the Sundered Throne gets worse."

"Sundered Throne?"

"You don't need to worry about that. It's the reason the Builder is running rampant and the World-Phoenix is gambling with worlds instead of forcibly stepping in to save them. Get me drunk some time and I'll tell you all about it."

"You could tell me now. Wait, no; we're getting distracted. You were saying about the World-Phoenix picking you to fix the link?" Clive said.

"Well, she didn't pick me. She engineered a circumstance where someone with the expertise to fix the link also happened to be invested in seeing it fixed. But if I do it, there'll be problems. It would take an unusual and specific set of circumstances to produce a person who could fix it perfectly. I was always a backup option she set up millennia ago, in case nothing better came along."

"And then Jason came along."

"With a few nudges from the World-Phoenix, yeah. She spotted his soul rocketing through the astral along that link and it was right place, right time. She slipped him something that would get him hopping between worlds, and even managed to land him where the closest city had you in it."

"Me?"

"Someone needed to start teaching him astral magic."

Boris looked over at the glowing diagram again.

"The fact that someone like you even exists on this planet is bizarre luck," Boris told Clive. "When I say the World-Phoenix picked Jason at the right place and time, I don't just mean a person flying through the astral at that given moment. I mean him, who he is, how he thinks, that idiot trying to summon a clockwork king in the middle of a magic barren. You, me, the god planning to…"

Boris let out a sigh.

"The World-Phoenix," he continued, "works with variables more numerous and scattered than you or I could ever comprehend. That's just how great astral beings perceive the cosmos: ripples of coincidence clashing, over millions, even billions of years. Events so numerous that we don't have names for numbers that high, interplaying in a framework so complex that no mortal mind can fathom it. We can't comprehend it any more than they can understand things on our level. That is why they have vessels and mortal agents. They need people to think like us for them."

"You're saying this is all a game they play, with us the pieces?"

"None of us were chosen, Clive. It goes much deeper than that. Events were set in motion countless times over countless years, with incomprehensible complexity. All to make each of us, or someone close enough to fill a given role, arise when and where we were needed. The World-Phoenix found Jason's soul flying through the astral along the link between worlds. If not him, it would have been someone else. The link has been there a long time and conditions were ripe for outworlders. On the World-Phoenix's time scale, it's barely a wait. Sometimes their machinations work and sometimes they don't, but there are contingencies on contingencies. And sometimes, they'll cut their losses and move on, even if it means letting a world burn. They can live with that. We're talking about vast, alien minds. They don't think or care in the same ways we do."

"Landemere Vane," Clive said.

"Who?" Boris asked.

"The man you mentioned trying to summon a clockwork king. He was the only person I've met with the inclination and intelligence to push the boundaries of astral magic, given the state it was in. And he just happens to also be in some low-magic backwater? You said if it wasn't us, it would be someone like us. Are you suggesting that my hometown exists because some cosmic entity decided millions of years ago that there needs to be someone like me?"

"It's a lot more nuanced, complicated and intricate than that," Boris said. "But broadly, yes."

"Then I have one question," Clive said.

"And what's that?" Boris asked.

Clive stormed over to the diagram and jabbed his finger again at the offending variable.

"WHAT IS THIS?" he yelled. "You clearly understand this magic. You probably understood it before any civilisation I've heard of existed! What is it?"

Boris burst out laughing.

"It's time," he said.

"Time?" Clive said. "That doesn't make sense."

He started pacing as he continued thinking out loud.

"The deep astral doesn't have time or space. Any perception of time or space is a subjective one from those travelling in a pocket of reality like a dimension ship. Unless…"

He turned to look at Boris, growing excited as he continued.

"Each reality, each universe, has its own space and time. They serve as waypoints for astral geography, and travelling between them requires adjustment for relative time. Jason managed to skip out on that because Earth and Pallimustus are linked, synchronising their time-space… something. There really should be a word for it."

"Continuum," Jason said, having arrived without either of them noticing. "The word is continuum."

"I thought you were horribly busy," Clive said.

"I am, but I had to drop in on this. Boris, are you trying to convince Clive that time travel is possible and that he should do it?"

"It might be possible," Clive postulated. "I suppose astral travel could be used to transgress relative temporal alignment by hopping between the right universes."

"I would avoid that," Boris said. "For several reasons. The first is that it will kill you. To interact with another universe, you have to travel through the astral. That means bringing some reality with you because the astral doesn't have any. Usually, that's a dimension vessel, but gestalt entities, like messengers, are something akin to nascent dimensional vessels."

He gestured at the space around them, which belonged to Jason's soul realm.

"Some more developed than others," he continued. "That reality, though, is synchronised with the space-time continuum of whatever actual reality the dimension ship or gestalt being was last in."

"Okay," Clive said. "I think I'm starting to get my head around this time variable. Part of astral navigation is synchronising the time of the universe you came from with the time of where you're going. That's why, despite each universe having its own time, they are subjectively passing through time together. If you didn't align the relative time, there would be dissonance."

"Dissonance?" Jason asked.

"You'd exist in multiple times at once," Boris said.

"That doesn't sound like something people can do," Jason said.

"It's not," Boris confirmed. "You'd stop existing in any time, maybe even stop having ever existed. That's where you start getting into paradoxes and reality ruptures. That's why the Keeper of Moments doesn't let it get that far. I'm a little surprised the link between Pallimustus and Earth has been left alone this long."

"Because they're synchronised in time," Clive realised. "That's why travelling between them is easier."

"Yes," Boris said. "But that also exposes them to manipulation through that link. If someone had greater than normal access to that link…"

He looked pointedly at Jason.

"…they could, in theory—"

"Attempt time travel," Clive finished. "Jason, you asked if Boris is trying to get me to time travel, but I think he's trying to get you to not."

"He's right," Boris said. "Even making the attempt is highly policed. The Keeper of Moments comes down hard on anyone who comes close to trying it. In terms of bad ideas, even on a cosmic scale, time travel is the worst. Probably. It's a big cosmos, but it's way up there. You do not want to get on the bad side of Raythe, the Keeper's prime vessel. She's so powerful, she could trip over and transcend by accident. I don't know of anyone who has held a prime vessel position as long as her. Someone like your friend Dawn is an infant by comparison, although I believe the two are friends. They were friendly last I heard, anyway. Which was around the time people on Earth started experimenting with agriculture, so who knows?"

"Raythe?" Jason asked. "She's here. Shade is showing her around the brightheart city right now."

"She showed herself, then? I wasn't going to say because I don't want to interfere with her business. I did hear she was poking around the link, finally. I doubt that the Builder synchronising the timelines of two universes made the Keeper of Moments very happy. It's a little odd they left things this long. The original Builder made an absolute mess of things when he created these worlds."

"I'm sure I'll find out why she's here soon enough," Jason said. "Speaking with her is on the list, but I've got a handful of hours to deal with it at most. I'm struggling to hold off the process of turning into an astral king, and I have a lot to organise before I do."

Jason gestured at the diagram floating over the table.

"One of those things is setting in motion final repairs to the link. What do you think, Clive?"

"Now that I have a way to quantify that errant variable," Clive said, "I can start looking into how to repair the link properly. You'll have to do the actual repairs, but I can do the research in your absence. Actual research, rather than the slipshod, rush-job nonsense I've been forced into during this whole blighted sojourn. I'm talking about assistants, laboratories, archives, retesting. Time, gods help me. Actual time to study and test without a civilisation dying if I don't get it right in the next half-hour."

"Time you'll have," Jason said. "And resources. I have no doubt you'll have your own setup on the surface."

"I am so looking forward to seeing sunlight again," Clive said.

"I'll have something for you here in the tree city as well," Jason said.

"You can work with one of my avatars and tap into what my soul realm can do. That way, I can absorb everything the avatar learns while I'm off making my astral kingdom."

"That won't work," Boris said. "Your soul realm will be in flux during the process of becoming an astral king. You can't leave anyone in here."

"It's fine," Jason said. "I've got a workaround. The trick will be getting the avatars right. They can't replicate me in full, so I have to have specific ones set up. One to work with Clive, another to work with Carlos Quilido, who can finally get back to his big project. I'm setting up a work-space for him too, so you'll be neighbours, Clive. A space for Sophie's mum too. Can't have her leaving and turning evil again. Carlos can hope-fully help her, in time."

"That's not how it works," Boris said.

"That's why it's called a workaround," Jason said. "Don't worry, I have a plan."

"It had better be an impressive plan," Boris said.

"It is," Jason assured him.

As Jason was giving his confident assurances, Boris' eyes were on Clive, who stood behind Jason, shaking his head.

UNIQUE IN THE ENTIRE COSMOS

JASON'S TRINITY OF ASTRAL THRONE, ASTRAL GATE AND SOUL FORGE WAS now complete. From the moment the soul forge had settled into place, the process of becoming an astral king had begun. The first step, it turned out, was the annihilation of his now-vestigial body. He was holding off the process with willpower, but that would only work for so long. Before his body collapsed entirely, there were arrangements and farewells to be made.

Even though his body worsened with each passing moment, Jason took a much-needed break. The arboreal metropolis of the tree city was enormous and empty, spread across a massive forest and multiple levels, from the ground to the high branches.

The entire place was alive, not just the trees but the buildings and walkways. It was connected to Jason, irrevocably now, but also separate. He hadn't just consumed the tree's young soul but formed a symbiosis with it. The tree's avatar was still present and still a wooden replica of Jason. He could feel it, sitting with the rabbit-man, Nik. They had both come into being through Jason's unconscious intervention when the transformation zone formed. The zone was now gone and both had to find their places in a wider world.

Jason lay back in a recliner, attempting to meditate through the growing pain of his body attempting to trigger the astral king transformation. He groaned as Shade emerged from his shadow.

"I do apologise, Mr Asano, but our two most powerful visitors have shown a remarkable level of patience, given who they are. It would be best to attend them sooner rather than later."

"Is that lady really the queen of time?"

"While your description is wholly inaccurate, Mr Asano, I believe the meaning behind it is not. Lady Raythe is, indeed, the prime vessel of the Keeper of Moments. And Lord Velius is the prime vessel of my progenitor."

"And I'm guessing it takes a lot more than a transformation zone and a soon-to-be astral king to get them working together."

"Indeed, Mr Asano. My impression is that they have been waiting for some time. That suggests the import of their purpose is not small, even for such as they."

"Great," Jason lied and rubbed his hands over his weary face. "You know I can feel my body trying to pull itself apart?"

"I can sense it doing so, Mr Asano."

Jason groaned, stood up and opened a portal out of his soul realm. He stepped through to a cloud building within the new home of the bright-hearts. It was another balcony, although very different from the one he'd just left. Rather than wood and the smell of earth and pine, it was cloud-stuff masquerading as stone. The two diamond-rankers were sitting in a pair of cloud chairs. A third rose from the floor for Jason to fall into.

The prime vessels shared a glance as Jason casually plopped into his chair. He splayed out as if he'd just gotten home after a long day and was lounging about with his friends.

"Oh, I feel like crap," he complained. "Sorry about the lack of amenities. Rewriting reality kind of takes it out of you, and I have a lot to do before I come apart at the seams. No time to shop for home décor."

"We are aware of the constraints on your time," Raythe said. "We share your urgency as we need you to make a decision before you step onto the path that lies before you."

"Meaning you need something before I go full astral king. Well, I don't have time to faff about, so what do you want?"

"What do you know of the Sundered Throne?" Raythe asked.

Jason let out another groan.

"This sounds like faffing about, but you're serious people, so I'll play along for now."

He took a laboured breath as he rubbed his sore head.

"Sundered Throne," he muttered. "Some busted cosmic magic thing. I have some connection to it through one of my familiars. Gets used as a prison for people like you two."

"Succinct enough," Velius said. "Once upon a time, the throne wasn't sundered. It was the power that regulated cosmic forces, keeping the great astral beings adherent to their respective purposes. You think of authority as power, but it is not. Transcendent entities have what, on any practical scale, amounts to infinite power."

"To mortals like us," Raythe said, "authority is indistinguishable from power. In truth, it is, as the name suggests, authority. The right for a transcendent being to employ their infinite power in a specific way. Authority is what keeps the cosmos in balance when it is filled with entities of infinite power. The Cosmic Throne was what regulated that balance. The ultimate authority, if you will."

"Let me guess," Jason said. "The great astral beings didn't like being told no by a space chair and busted the thing up."

"A colourful, but not inaccurate guess," Velius said. "But they weren't foolish enough to leave each other completely without boundaries. The great astral beings agreed to a system of pacts between them. Agreements and concessions that would give them the freedom they sought while providing a framework to prevent infinite anarchy."

Jason erupted into laughter, rocking in his chair.

"A bunch of supreme beings…" he said, forcing out the words between peals of laughter. "…decided that what the fundamental operation of the cosmos needed was…"

He continued trying to tamp down his mirth, trying to keep his mouth shut as a fist hammered on the arm of his chair.

"…industry self-regulation," he managed to finish, laughter once again running away with him. Only the encompassing nature of the cloud chair stopped him from falling onto the floor.

Velius looked on in disbelief before making a silent appeal to Raythe.

"He's your friend's pet," Velius said.

The moment he said that, the laughter stopped dead. He turned to look at Jason, who was now sitting up and staring directly at Raythe.

"So," Jason said. "You and Dawn are still friends."

"We are," Raythe said.

"How is she?"

"Busy doing something not so removed from what you're about to: Going through the part of transcendence that isn't just accumulating power."

"But she's good?"

"She is," Raythe said. "She didn't think you would come across a soul forge so quickly. You've pushed back the timeline she warned you about. The expectation was that you would complete the dimensional bridge first."

"You know what I've got coming? The thing she warned me about, but refuses to explain?"

"I do know it, yes. I'm even going to tell you about it, but not today. You and I will have dealings, but not until you're an astral king, or whatever you end up turning into. Right now, there is another affair at hand. But Dawn knew I would be around and asked me to look in on you."

Jason narrowed his eyes.

"Mah Go Schaat," he said. "The diamond-rank messenger. You're what happened to him."

"Yes. Your death would be inconvenient and having you owe me a favour will be useful to me. In the fullness of time."

"You aren't as restricted in how you act here as Dawn was, are you?"

"No," Raythe said. "The messengers deploying a diamond-ranker against you was all the pretence I needed to intervene. I talked about the pacts between great astral beings. My great astral being was never party to them. The Keeper of the Sands opposed the sundering from the beginning and refused to participate in any of it. As the Keeper's first representative, I similarly have freedoms that others do not."

"And the other great astral beings let that slide?"

"Those that stood aside were special," Velius said. "They have ever stood apart from the rest, even before the sundering. The Keeper, the All-Devouring Eye, the Word in the Silence."

"If all the cool kids thought it was a bad idea," Jason said, "maybe your boss should have taken that as a sign."

Velius closed his eyes, and when they opened, they were black orbs. When he spoke, his voice had turned cold and bleak.

"Our perspective is not that of mortals," the Reaper said. "That is why we have vessels. What might seem obvious to a limited mind is overlooked by one that spans infinity."

"Which is a sanctimonious way of admitting you knobbed-up because your cosmic mind can see infinity while missing the blindingly obvious."

The Reaper stared at Jason through black eyes. Jason stared back, grinning at the great astral being.

"It's nice to meet you, finally. When I'm more than a disembodied soul, anyway. Thanks for being cool about me resurrecting so many times, by the way. More than that, thanks for sending Shade my way. Having him as a friend and companion means more to me than I can say. I know being facetiously insincere is kind of my thing, but I'm genuinely grateful for that."

"Are you willing to repay the kindness?" the Reaper asked.

"If I can. As long as it's nothing too outrageous."

"They want you to repair the Sundered Throne and re-institute regulation on the great astral beings," Raythe said.

Jason turned and gave her a flat look.

"Were you not listening to what I just told that guy?" he asked, pointing at the Reaper. Then he let out a sigh. "I guess that's on me for leaving myself open with a line like that. Should have known better. Fine, I'll fix the cosmos or whatever."

Even the Reaper looked mildly surprised.

"Just like that?" Raythe asked.

"You think I haven't been paying attention?" Jason asked. "I'm willing to bet that all the big-ticket craziness I've been through traces back to you great astral idiots chucking a tanty and telling your mum that she's not the boss of you. I'm going to go out on a limb and guess that the original Builder playing silly buggers with a couple of worlds was early in the process of realising it was a real bad idea. You sorted him out, but the replacement wasn't much better. Probably got shoe-horned into those pacts you mentioned, but he wasn't there from the start, was he? Is that why the new Builder gets to run as rampant as he does? He's an addendum to whatever you all agreed on in the first place?"

"There are mechanisms in place to control him," the Reaper said.

"That's what Shako was trying to tell me, isn't it? About the handle you've got on his boss. But it's some cludged-together solution that isn't working out for you, isn't it?"

"Many of us who participated in the sundering have come to the conclusion that revisiting that decision would be prudent," the Reaper said.

"Meaning you've finally admitted to yourselves that you cocked-up. The question is, what do you need me for?"

"When the throne was sundered," Raythe said, "specific requirements were put in place to restore it."

Jason looked at the Reaper.

"You didn't want one of your own to fix it, did you? So you made sure none of you could."

"A methodology was put in place, should restoration of the throne prove appropriate," the Reaper said. It closed its eyes, and when it opened them, Velius was back in control, unsteady in his seat.

"You happen to meet the requirements the great astral beings established," Raythe explained to Jason as Velius recovered from the possession.

"What requirements?" Jason asked.

"The idea is to connect to the Sundered Throne during a transcendence process and restore the throne as a part of that. You will be undertaking such a process very soon."

"It won't be full transcendence, only half."

"It is sufficient."

Velius let out a groan, holding his head between his hands.

"I really wish it would just tell me things," he complained. "He saves up everything he wants me to know and then dumps it all on me the next time he's possessing me."

"Like a cosmic skill-book situation?" Jason asked.

"Something like that."

"Regular skill books are bad enough," Jason said. He got up, pulled a sandwich and a drink from his inventory and set them of a side table made of clouds that rose up from the floor. Velius looked at them blearily, nodded thanks and immediately winced as he moved his head.

"I can't be the only one who has met your requirements," Jason said as he returned to his seat. "I know I'm out of the ordinary, but unique in the entire cosmos? Even I'm not arrogant enough to think that. Dawn is transcending, right? Why not her, or some other transcending minion?"

"No servant of the great astral beings can be used," Raythe explained. "The pacts prevent it."

"Still, there must be a bunch of people like me when you take the whole damn cosmos into account. And the great astral beings didn't decide this yesterday, either. I'm guessing that this choice was made long ago."

"It was," Raythe confirmed. "I won't go into the factors that narrowed the available pool of people; suffice to say that it involves the complexities of interrelated time-streams across different universes. The point is that the great astral beings have been waiting for the right person in the right place at the right time. They believe it is you, here and now."

"What are these requirements exactly?"

"Someone going through one of a short subset of transcendental methodologies. Even if only to the point of half-transcendence."

"That subset including becoming what the messengers call an original," Jason surmised.

"Yes," Raythe confirmed. "Such instances are common enough, on a cosmic scale. The more difficult requirement is a pre-existing connection to the Sundered Throne."

"Which I have through my familiar."

"Yes. The All-Devouring Eye is not one for communicating, even with other great astral beings. But we believe it created the being you named Gordon specifically for this potential outcome."

"It's done it before, though, hasn't it?" Jason asked. "I'm not the first guy to get an avatar of doom familiar."

"You are not," Raythe confirmed. "And yes, we believe that was the All-Devouring Eye setting things into motion. Perhaps the others did not play out as intended, or they were steps leading to this outcome. There is little point asking questions of the All-Devouring Eye."

"So why me?" Jason asked. "What makes me different?"

"It's the power," Velius said, still woozy but looking better for the food. "If you do this, if you turn the Sundered Throne back into the Cosmic Throne, then you'll be sitting on it."

65

A POWER THAT NO ONE AND
NOTHING SHOULD HAVE

"RAYTHE CALLED THE COSMIC THRONE THE ULTIMATE AUTHORITY,"
Velius said, "and with good reason. It's a power that no one and nothing
should have. The potential for damage is like no threat the cosmos could
ever face."

"Reaching transcendence requires ambition," Raythe said. "That
ambition comes in many forms and, whether selfish or altruistic, it takes a
powerful drive to surpass mortality. Those with both the ambition to seek
such a thing and the capability to achieve it are rarely willing to give up
power. Even if they want to use it for good ends, they want to use it."

"That's what you want from me?" Jason asked. "To repair the
Sundered Throne and then never use it? To claim the vastest of cosmic
power, only to give it up without so much as making melted cheese
healthy?"

"Yes," Raythe said. "We've been waiting for someone we believe
would be willing to claim the ultimate authority, then give it up without
ever exercising it. You obsess over the power you already hold and the
potential for abusing it. The belief is that you, of all the candidates that
have come and gone, are most likely to respect the damage you could do.
Whether for yourself or in service of your ideals, you understand the
danger in combining power and ignorance."

"Not just never use it, then," Jason said. "You said 'give up the
power.' Who do you expect me to give it up to?"

"To no one," Velius said. "The throne must be left empty. A neutral arbiter without will, only purpose."

"As it was before the sundering," Raythe said. "When the cosmos was in balance."

Jason swallowed a pithy reply and made himself stop and think. He frowned, absently scratching the back of his head.

"So, you don't want me for all the weird magic crap I've got going on. I mean, you do, but you have other options in that regard. You want me for *who* I am, not *what* I am."

"Yes," Raythe said.

"That's actually really flattering," Jason said. "Thank you."

"You agreed to do this already," Velius said, "but you should not have answered so hastily. It warrants proper consideration."

"No kidding, but we all know I only have time for hastily. I've barely got time for this conversation, and we all know I'll agree in the end. Someone's obviously been paying enough attention to have a good handle on me. I do have questions, though."

"Such as?" Velius asked.

"When he was talking about changing his mind about the sundering, your boss said 'many of us.' Many. Not all. Who am I going to make cranky by doing this?"

"There are risks inherent to this process," Raythe said. "And you will be opposed."

"What risks?"

"Connecting to the Sundered Throne during your transcendence process will expose your soul to intrusion."

"Like a star seed sticking out of the side of someone's soul?"

"Yes," Velius said.

"And someone is going to take that chance to intrude," Jason said. "The opposition you mentioned. What will they be trying to do?"

"Stop you," Raythe said. "By crushing your will."

"Awesome. What does my will getting crushed look like, exactly?"

"If your will gets burned out," Velius said, "the process of becoming an astral king will continue. With no sentience guiding it, though, you'll be a small pocket universe, drifting through the astral. Eventually, you will recover; give it a couple of million years and you'll be up and about again. Probably won't remember anything before you woke up, but you'll be functional. A blank slate."

"Yay. How does this fight play out?"

"In the process of reaching transcendence, your soul will become a liminal space. Not the soul realm you're familiar with, not an astral space or a pocket reality. Something in between, shaped by you, but within certain limits. While you are connected to the throne, others can access that liminal space, if they have the power."

"Great astral beings."

"Yes."

"How much control will I have?"

"It will become a battleground, but it will still be your soul. The nature of the battle, the ground it is fought on and the rules all must follow are for you to decide."

"Okay. And who is it that I'm up against? Who wants to stop me?"

"The World-Phoenix prefers the current state of affairs," Velius said. "The pact system introduced politics to the great astral beings and the World-Phoenix has navigated them to its advantage more than most. It will be your antagonist."

"The World-Phoenix still needs me to fix the link between worlds."

"If the throne is restored, the World-Phoenix will have less flexibility in choosing how such issues are handled in the future. It considers the throne staying sundered a significantly higher priority than keeping your worlds intact and is willing to allow contingencies to play out. Less perfect solutions, but solutions nonetheless."

"Okay, but I'm not ready to go toe-to-toe with the World-Phoenix. Not even close, home-court advantage or no."

"It is rare for transcendent beings to clash directly," Raythe said. "It's only possible when unusual circumstances create some form of battlefield, such as the one that will form in your soul. A great astral being cannot enter your soul, even with an opening, but it can invade with an expression of its will."

"Like an avatar?" Jason asked.

"Not exactly," Velius said, "but close enough for practical purposes. The thing is, you get to shape those expressions of will. There are limits to what you can do with them, but you shape the battlefield, along with those who choose to enter it."

"I think you might be overestimating me here," Jason said. "By really quite a lot. Firstly, I'm not a transcendent being. I'm working on getting halfway there, which, by definition, means I'm not there now. And even if I were, it's not the power-oriented half I'm working on. And a clash of wills? I know how that works. I just came from clashing with a dreg of a dreg of a god's avatar. The god wasn't around, I was in control of the battlefield and it still nearly kicked my arse from the inside out."

"You fought a god's avatar?" Velius asked.

"The local god of undeath," Raythe said. "He allowed an avatar to be drawn into the transformation zone to aid his priests. It would appear that it fought Asano and lost."

"No," Jason said. "That thing fought a demigod of Hero until it was running on fumes. I didn't fight an avatar; I fought the rotting skin flake some god left behind and it still all but wiped me out of existence. And now you're setting me up to face the World-Phoenix?"

"You will not be alone," Velius said. "Others can access your soul to defend it, buying time for the throne to be restored."

"You will stand with great astral beings who were against the sundering in the first place," Raythe said. "Along with those who supported the sundering but have come to see it as a mistake. Not all of them will join, however. Some are not committed enough to a side to fight for it. Others are best kept out of such conflict."

"You do not want the Keeper of the Sands and the All-Devouring Eye waging war in your soul," Velius said. "Even if they are on your side."

"So, to summarise," Jason said, "you want to turn my soul into a cosmic war zone for entities that could wipe me out of existence with no more effort than wanting to."

"We are asking for a battle, yes," Raythe said. "But you underestimate what you are becoming. What you already are. Even now, you have moved beyond the stage where any entity has the power to destroy you. That body is dying because it is no longer your true body. You're already immortal."

Jason leaned back in his chair and let out a slow breath.

"You're sure?"

"We cannot promise victory," Raythe said. "Only that the fact that we were sent means there is a genuine fight to be had."

Jason rubbed his temples. Time was passing and his headache wasn't getting any better.

"Who are the sides?" he asked. "If it was just the World-Phoenix versus the cosmic all-stars, it would be bit of a drubbing, wouldn't it?"

"As best we can tell," Raythe told him, "only the nameless will stand with the World-Phoenix against you."

"The nameless?"

"Great astral beings are entities that govern the functions of the cosmos," Velius explained. "Life, death, time, matter. The great astral beings at the pinnacle of cosmic authority have names, but the vast majority do not. They are the functionaries of all that is, unseen yet utterly necessary."

"They have been very happy with the removal of the Cosmic Throne's oversight," Raythe explained. "They remain unseen as ever, yet are unbound from the strictures of their duties."

"They were also an oversight on the part of the named great astral beings," Velius said. "The original pacts governing great astral being behaviour after the sundering did not include the nameless. The others saw them as nobility sees servants: furniture without will and ambition of their own."

"The results of this mistake were not immediately apparent," Raythe explained. "Just as the nameless were invisible in conduct of their duties, so were they invisible in their misconduct."

"The problems arising from the sundering became evident," Velis said, again taking up the narrative. "The old Builder was sanctioned and the new one brought into the pacts, along with the nameless. But this addendum to the original pacts was not an effective curb on the behaviour of these late additions. The new Builder and the nameless have both proven flexible in their level of adherence."

"The mistake in overlooking the nameless may be the one with the gravest consequence," Raythe added. "The trouble caused by the old Builder was greater than any individual problem the nameless are responsible for. But his trouble was both visible and singular. The nameless cause lesser problems, but those problems are many. They also fester in the dark, accumulating and growing worse. The original Builder highlighted that there was a problem, but it was containable. The nameless represent countless problems, cascading towards infinite anarchy."

"The Builder and his one problem have been plenty for me," Jason said. "What does infinite anarchy look like?"

"Imagine the very mechanisms of the cosmos falling apart," Raythe said. "A cavalcade of issues as the fundamental rules of reality and beyond come apart at the seams. The Builder brought this issue into relief, but the nameless are the ultimate threat. The danger they present is what convinced many who had supported the sundering to alter their perspective."

"And the best idea a cosmos full of super gods came up with is to have *me* fix it? People say my plans are bad, but I'm amateur hour compared to this."

"There are contingencies," Velius said. "That is the way of great astral beings, but the contingencies are ugly. They also involve things that cannot be spoken of."

"Suffice it to say," Raythe added, "that your success would be the superior option by far."

"But the World-Phoenix doesn't agree?"

"It may believe that it can handle the nameless, or that it can thrive in what remains after they are dealt with otherwise," Velius said.

"What remains?" Jason asked.

"Of the cosmos. Which is as much as you'll get from us on what will happen should you refuse or fail."

"No pressure, then."

"Velius speaks of the final contingency," Raythe said. "If you do not accomplish the task, it will be asked of others like you. You are not the final line of defence for cosmic integrity. You are simply the best option we have right now."

"I'm starting to feel extremely expendable, here. If we've got the World-Phoenix and the nameless on one side, who's joining me on team It's Okay If Jason Dies, We'll Find Someone Else?"

"The Celestial Book and the Seeker of Songs were both against the sundering from the start," Raythe said. "Those who have come around and will fight are the Reaper, Legion and the Whisper in Corners. Others remain neutral or are poor choices for such a fight."

"And they are enough to handle all of these nameless?"

"It's not about numbers," Raythe said. "It's about will. This isn't a fight in the conventional sense."

"That much I understand," Jason told her. "I learned that fighting that avatar. It was my soul, my battleground, just like this will be. Once I learned to be the god of my own universe, the avatar wasn't so hard to deal with anymore. The only trick was not losing myself while in god mode."

"The key is to anchor your identity in something," Raythe said.

"Oh, I figured that out. It was a bit touch-and-go my first go at it, but I'll know what I'm doing next time. But that doesn't mean I'm ready to face the World-Phoenix, though, even if it is in my house. Having allies is all well and good, but it will be me they're coming for, won't it? In the end, it will be my fight to win or lose."

"Yes," Raythe said. "In the end, it will be your fight."

"Then what makes you think I can win? There's a chance, sure, but that's not very reassuring. All they lose if this doesn't work is me. They can try again with the next person, and the one after that and so on. Then they've got that contingency you mentioned, even if it does suck a lot. I'm pretty sure my spending a few million years brain dead is a lot more acceptable to them than it is to me."

"Then say no," Velius said. "There will be someone else eventually."

Jason sighed, already knowing he wouldn't. He turned to Raythe.

"What does Dawn have to say about her boss trying to burn the sapience out of me?" he asked her.

Raythe's mouth turned up in amused smile.

"She told the World-Phoenix not to do it," she said. "Not for your sake, or because she wants the throne restored. She told the World-Phoenix it was going to lose."

As a huge grin split Jason's face, Velius turned to look at Raythe.

"Really?" Velius asked.

"Yes," Raythe said. "I was in the World-Spark Crucible with Helsveth and witnessed the entire exchange. Dawn has a lot of faith in you, Asano. I'm not sure where it comes from, given that you've known each other all of three minutes, but you clearly made an impression."

"Young people," Velius muttered, shaking his head.

"Asano," Raythe said, "you still fall within the World-Phoenix's plans. It only pivoted to acting against you because the Sundered Throne matters more to it than the welfare of a couple of worlds."

"Yeah, I've met the back-up plan," Jason said. "Look, I get this is important and all, but I still have other things to take care of. Is there anything else I need to know before all this kicks off? How do I do the linking to the Sundered Throne bit?"

His thoughts drifted to a strange void that had appeared in his soul space.

"Never mind," he said. "I think I know that part."

"Trust your familiar; he will guide you," Raythe said. "As for other things you should know, there is one."

Jason looked at Raythe, the ancient being showing reluctance in her expression. She'd told him with a straight face that the World-Phoenix, arguably his most powerful ally, was going to crawl into his soul and try to scoop out his insides. After that, what would she be reluctant to tell him?

"What is it?" he asked warily.

"I left one name out when I was talking about who was going to fight alongside you," Raythe said.

"Who?" Jason asked.

"The Builder."

"Oh, what the fu—"

66

PARTY TO BETRAYAL

THE BUILDER CULTISTS WERE IN A BUILDING IN THE BRIGHTHEART CITY. IT was a single-room construction with neither doors nor windows. It looked to be made of large stone bricks, with a few crystals in the ceiling shedding warm light. The cultists were variably looking lost, confused, despairing and angry. A few looked oddly hopeful. Some were lying on the floor looking ill, and all looked human. There was no sign of the body-horror metalwork that was the signature of the cult.

What metal could be found was in the corner, piled in a heap. It was made up of tiny orbs, mostly silver but a few of gold. From each orb ran a rat's nest of threads, like spider webs, now all tangled in the pile.

When a door-shaped section of wall turned from stone to cloud-stuff, all heads not groaning on the floor turned. The leader, Beaufort, leapt up from where he'd been hunched against the wall. Jason Asano walked through the cloud material that turned back into bricks behind him.

Beaufort marched up to loom over the smaller man.

"We had a deal, Asano," he snarled.

"Yes," Jason said. "That I'd let you go alive. Release you to the Adventure Society. Which is exactly what I'm going to do."

Beaufort flung an angry gesture at the pile of metal.

"You didn't say anything about that."

"No, I didn't," Jason agreed. "I was pretty sure it would work, but I couldn't be certain. You're welcome."

"You expect me to thank you? You took away who we are!"

"Were," Jason corrected. "I took away who you were. And who you were sucked, so again, you're welcome."

Beaufort angrily searched Jason's expression.

"You don't feel any remorse for this, do you?"

"How many people have you killed for the Builder, Beaufort? Do you even know? By rights, you should have burned up any compassion I could feel for you long before we met. But I still did this for you."

"*For* us?" Beaufort asked, shouting his incredulity. "You did this *to* us, Asano. I don't even understand how."

"Surely the Builder warned you about me. Star seeds are a really bad thing to have inside you. They poke a hole in the side of your soul. Gives people like me an access point. A handle they can grab on to and rip. Normally, that's a crude and extremely final process, but it just so happens that I was rewriting some reality recently. It gave me the chance to slip them out, nice and smooth. That's all I did, by the way; I didn't go rummaging in anyone's soul. Could have, though. Those star seeds are trouble."

Jason looked over at the pile of extracted star seeds and sighed.

"I just got asked to do a job with the Builder. If I remember, I'll tell him you guys are out of his little club. I'm pretty sure he knows, though."

"We'll get new star seeds the first chance we get."

"That's your business. If you get that chance, though, you can thank me for it. If I hand a bunch of Builder cultists over to the Adventure Society, I'm guessing they'll torture you for any information you have and then dissect you to see what they can learn. A bunch of former cultists with their star seeds removed, though... you're practically victims. Everyone knows that isn't true, but play it up enough and you might make it out the other side alive."

"You betrayed us, Asano."

"Are you sure everyone here feels the same way, Beaufort? I don't know what kind of state you're in after the extraction, but my aura senses are feeling some hope in this room. A chance to be something more than a puppet on the strings of a mad god. I know he's not an actual god, but he's close enough, and you have to admit that was a great line."

"Take this seriously!" Beaufort snarled.

Jason used his aura to crush that of the cultist, pick him up and slam him against the wall. The gold-ranker fought back with his own but got nowhere. He was weak after the extraction of his star seed and Asano's aura seemed to come from everywhere.

Jason's feet lifted off the floor and he floated over to look the taller man in the eyes. His expression was serious, just as Beaufort had demanded.

"Is serious really what you want?" Jason asked, his voice a whisper. "Because I can do that, Beaufort. I can start taking a real interest in how you spent your life before you and I met. I have a strong feeling that just asking the brighthearts how they feel about you would lead to me cutting you into tiny pieces, scraping your soul with each slice. How about it, cultist? Do you want me to take this seriously? Or would you rather I forget you ever existed and let the Adventure Society deal with you?"

Still pinned to the wall by Jason's aura, Beaufort choked out a reply.

"Adventure Society."

Without another word, Jason floated around Beaufort and through the wall that again briefly turned to clouds. The cultist slumped to the floor against the wall, almost exactly where he'd been before Jason came in.

***

Leaving the cultists behind, Jason walked through the empty streets of the cloud city. He could feel buildings shift as Lorenn experimented. He could feel the brighthearts in scattered clusters, far too few for the city he had made them.

He took pride in the growing hope he felt in their auras. The brighthearts were finally out of his soul realm and, more importantly, out of danger. They had spent so long in despair, watching their civilisation be chewed up and then spat back out as horrors that tried to destroy what remained. The hope they had was just a spark for now, after so long without it. But it was there, in the thousands of brighthearts who had managed to survive.

As for the expedition members, Jason could sense their reunions as more people descended from the surface. He could sense Allayeth with Miriam and her team, as well as the messengers awkwardly avoiding everyone else. Carlos was angry at someone and the High Priestess of the Healer was meeting with a contingent from her church.

Jason considered popping in to speak with Allayeth briefly, but he'd let himself be delayed enough. His body was attempting to unravel itself and begin the process of forming a true astral kingdom, and he could only hold it off for so long. He opened a portal back into his soul realm and stepped through. He had his own reunions to hold.

Jason appeared on a platform fastened to the trunk of a massive tree. He looked around the wide-open deck at his friends, companions, and Boris. He didn't want to trust the messenger, yet found himself doing so in increments. Maybe he was trustworthy and maybe he was an unfathomably ancient being that could run rings around Jason's ability to read him. The best Jason could hope for was it being probably both.

Humphrey, looking chastised, was standing at a buffet table with his mother and Sophie. The Remore family and Gary were having a heated discussion, with most of the heat coming from Rufus. Farrah, Belinda and Clive stood around a table, looking fascinated by something Boris was drawing. Taika was also there, looking confused, but the discussion was muted by a privacy screen. Neil was napping in a lounger made of clouds with a half-eaten sandwich resting on his chest. A moustachioed dog, despite the table full of food, was sneaking up on Neil's sandwich.

Gary spotted his arrival and left the Remores to walk over.

"Jason, you look hung over. Badly hung over."

"Yeah, well, you're not the only one who knows what your body trying to explode feels like. How are you holding up?"

"In your soul realm, there's no tug for Hero's power to go back to the god. It's in there, though, burning away like a furnace. If I stay here I can hold on for a few months, but my understanding is that here will be going away when you do your astral king business."

"No," Jason said. "The tree—the tree city now, I guess—will stay intact. A secure heart while the rest of me gets broken down for parts. You can stay here until it's too much."

Gary looked over at Rufus.

"I'm not so sure that's a good idea. I think a clean break might be better in the long run."

Jason clapped Gary's huge, furry forearm.

"Still looking to others, even now."

"How long can you keep it together?"

"Not as long as I'd like. Long enough for farewells. I'm not going to be seeing anyone for a while."

"What's that going to be like for you?" Gary asked. "Kind of like meditating as you turn yourself into a small universe?"

"I think that was the idea."

"Was?" Farrah asked, patting Gary on the arm as she joined them.

"Turns out I have to... not save the cosmos. Take a first crack at saving it? Make it a little less crappy, maybe."

"The whole cosmos?" Farrah asked.

"I'm not sure. At this point, we're talking about a scale way bigger than I can comprehend. The more I learn about the wider cosmos, the more I realise how ignorant I am."

"Then should you be messing with things on that scale?" she asked.

"No," Jason said with a laugh. "No, I should not."

Gary and Farrah both shook their heads.

"I guess it's nice to know some things won't change when I'm gone," Gary said. "You'll still be off doing Jason things when you really shouldn't."

"There's something we need to talk about," Farrah said. "Before we make our farewells."

"I know," Jason said. "And it's a good idea. Going to be a hard sell, though."

"You know?" Farrah asked. "Right, I forgot that, in here, you're the god-emperor of fancy pants and can listen to all our conversations."

"I don't wear fancy pants."

"Well, I'm not the god-emperor of fancy pants," Gary said. "You could tell me."

"Yeah," Jason told Gary. "You're just a demigod of heroism."

"I miss Erika," Farrah said wistfully. "I need more regular friends."

They moved to where Clive, Belinda, Taika and Boris were standing around a table. They entered the group's privacy screen and were suddenly able to hear the discussion within.

"...would need the knowledge of astral magic theory to actively manage the shell," Clive was saying. "That means one person. Maybe two, if they *really* knew what they were doing."

"I do really know what I'm doing," Boris said. "It's not a question of capability but of..."

He paused as he turned to look at Jason.

"...trust."

"I don't suppose someone could catch me up?" Gary asked.

"They want to send me into space in a magic coconut," Taika said.

Clive winced, rubbing his temples.

"I should not have used that analogy," he muttered as Belinda consolingly patted him on the back.

"It's more like a big brown egg," Boris said.

"The idea," Belinda told Gary, "is that someone with a gestalt body/soul combination like a messenger or Jason—or you, I suppose—can create a kind of bubble with their aura when they move through the astral. They basically turn their aura into a dimension ship for one passenger."

"Two, if they're good enough," Boris corrected. "It requires constant adjustment of the aura to dimensional forces experienced during travel."

"The point is," Farrah cut in, "that Boris can take two people with him when he goes back to Earth."

"It won't be a pleasant trip, as I've been warning Taika, here," Boris said. "My kind developed the technique to drag around mortals we needed for whatever reason. In-flight comfort options weren't a primary concern. It's spiritual travel that really does hold up the Spirit Airlines tradition."

Boris grinned expectantly as Belinda, Clive and Gary looked confused while Jason and Farrah rolled their eyes.

"That was sad, bro," Taika said, shaking his head. "I knew you were from Earth, but I didn't know you were a stand-up comedian from 1998."

That got Jason and Farrah laughing and left an offended look on Boris' face.

"Don't give me that look," Taika told Boris. "A domestic airline from the USA? That's a little too specific a reference when most of this group have never been to Earth."

"Too specific?" Boris asked. "Aren't you the *Team Knight Rider* guy?"

"Knight Rider?" Taika asked, looking confused. "Not ringing any bells. Jason?"

"Never heard of it," Jason said.

"You both suck," Boris said with a pout.

"I'm still not entirely clear on what's going on," Gary pointed out.

"Boris," Belinda said, "has an unpleasant but harmless means to take someone with him to Earth. Two people. One will be Taika."

"As for the other," Farrah said, "I left an apprentice back on Earth with only the beginnings of training. I thought we could send someone with the right skill set to finish the job. Someone whose family runs a school."

Gary turned to look over at Rufus, catching his eye. Despite being caught up in discussion with his family, Rufus' gaze never strayed from Gary for too long. The leonid turned to look thoughtfully at Jason and Farrah.

"When he thought you two were dead," Gary said, "Rufus took a lot of comfort in putting adventuring aside and becoming a teacher. I can see what you were thinking on this, but you're talking about a much bigger change than the Greenstone branch of the Remore Academy."

"Change might be just what he needs," Farrah said. "For now. We need to talk to Arabelle about this."

"You need to decide quickly," Boris said. "I have no intention of staying around once Jason's transformation has begun. The Adventure Society will be far too interested in making the acquaintance of me and my messengers. Which leads to the question of whether I'm taking your messengers with me, Jason."

"Yes," Jason said. "I think Marek Nior Vargas and his would-be Unorthodoxy will be happy to follow you, but the others aren't mine and they aren't yours, Boris. They do as they like, and if they want to join your cause eventually, that's their choice. But they are taking refuge in my domains on Earth while they figure themselves out. If I get to Earth and find you've crossed me on this…"

"You don't have to worry yourself on that front, Asano," Boris said. "I was fighting for messenger autonomy before your universe existed."

"So you've said. But now I need to trust you with one, possibly two of the people most important to me in the world."

"I understand how you feel," Boris told him. "Living as long as I have, I've been betrayed more times than the number of days you've been alive. And I won't deny that I've been party to betrayal, just as you have. But we're out of time, playing for stakes that don't give us the chance to make incremental steps toward trust. I'm all too familiar with that as well. You have to decide now, Asano, to trust me or not."

"Yeah," Jason agreed grimly. "I know."

67

FAREWELLS

EVERYTHING OUTSIDE OF THE TREE CITY THAT WAS NOW THE HEART OF Jason's soul realm was off-limits. Beyond the point where final trees stood was a sharp edge where reality came to an end. Beyond that was border, nothing could be seen but gold, silver and blue haze. There was a private mountain fortress hidden within in the haze, but only Jason himself could reach it or survive there.

The realm's remaining occupants had moved into the tree city. Jason was busy making use of his limited time, so his avatars were making arrangements. Accommodation and facilities were set in place for those who would be visiting the intact portion of Jason's realm while he reshaped the rest of it.

Before the arrival of the sentient forest, Jason's realm only had one permanent occupant: Melody Jain, Sophie's mother. She had been moved to a palatial estate comprised of multiple treehouses, linked by rope bridges. Close by was the research centre that would hopefully allow her to one day leave the soul realm without her mind being taken over by divine brainwashing.

The research centre was set up for Carlos Quilido. The priest of the Healer had joined the underground expedition, putting his research on pause as Jason was critical to its next stage. The avatar Jason had left for Carlos would help his research by using the soul realm to help people survive their experimental treatments. The avatar would otherwise function as one of Carlos' assistants so Jason could absorb the knowledge on his return.

Clive also had a research centre being set up, although he was not as reliant on the soul realm itself. Clive would use the space as he needed it, but would mostly be out and about with the team.

The other occupants of the soul realm were messengers, but they would soon be departing for Earth. Part of that group were the messengers Boris had shanghaied in the transformation zone. They were now free of their astral king's influence, thanks to Jason helping them replace Vesta Carmis Zell's brand with marks representing their own identities and autonomy. They had been forced into their current situation but were largely coming around.

More enthusiastic about following Boris were the messengers Jason had held as prisoners since the Battle of Yaresh. Marek Nior Vargas and his people had surrendered to Jason in hope of escaping astral king control and joining the Unorthodoxy. Boris represented their hope of joining a grand cosmic rebellion.

The largest group of messengers in Jason's soul realm were those liberated in the transformation zone. Many of them were variants of normal messengers as a result of how they came into being. Orthodox messengers would never accept them, and Jason wouldn't let the astral kings have them anyway. On top of everything else, they were only a few months old.

Two messengers stood apart from the other groups. Jali Corrik Fen had become aware of her slavery but thought that she would never escape it, even inside her own mind. Jason had rescued her from that when she'd expected him to kill her, transforming her future and winning her loyalty.

Tera Jun Casta had been a zealous follower of the messenger orthodoxy before her forced liberation at Jason's hands. When she forced him into a death match, inflicting soul torture on her was the only way he could keep them both alive. He had freed her from astral king bondage at the same time, yet she was anything but grateful.

Jali and Tera had been friends, once. Jali's growing doubts and Tera's growing zeal had ended that relationship, but their shared experiences with Jason brought them back together. During the months they spent in his soul realm, they once again found themselves sharing each other's company.

Their reunion had not been easy. Their differences in the past were reflected in their relationships with their shared liberator. To Tera, Jason was the man who tore her away from everything she knew. To Jali, he was the man who saved her from it. Jason was a hard topic to avoid when they were inside his soul, and always led to contention.

It was the group of young messengers that had brought them into alignment. Whatever their views on Jason, they both wanted the best for the young, impressionable messengers. Neither wanted them to have bad influences—Jason for Tera and Boris for both of them. Unfortunately, there were no perfect options.

One possibility was to have them stay in Jason's soul realm. Letting them out onto Pallimustus was not an option, as either the astral kings or the Adventure Society would quickly snatch them up. The other option was for them to go to Earth with Boris. Ultimately, Jason had left the choice up to the young messengers themselves, and they had chosen Earth.

Jason had made clear that he would not tolerate Boris turning them into child soldiers, which Boris at least claimed to completely agree with. Neither Jali nor Tera trusted the man's word and insisted they travel to Earth with the others.

As for what fate awaited them, that was a tricky proposition. There were, apparently, large and extremely secret Unorthodoxy enclaves on Earth. As an alternative, Jason had given Jali messages to pass on to his family about offering the refugees shelter. As for what haven the messengers chose when they arrived on Earth, that was up to them.

There was a gathering in the tree city, on the balcony of one of the larger treehouses. Boris left as Emir, Constance and Nik joined, completing Jason's core group of friends. This was how Jason wanted to use his limited remaining time. Not making plans or setting things in motion, just being together with the people that mattered most. He put aside the separations soon to come as, for the moment, they simply enjoyed one another's company.

They ate and chatted. Jason and Neil were even vaguely nice to each other. The closest to an outsider was Gwydion, but Rufus' older brother was quickly fitting in. The priest of Hero was lying back in a cloud chair almost prone, between his father and brother. He picked at the food piled high on a plate resting on his chest, sauce stains marking his fingers and his priest robes.

While the group could pretend they had all the time in the world, Jason's ticking clock became hard to ignore when streams of golden energy started rising off him as his body entered the early stages of breaking down.

"Bro," Taika said. "I think you're regenerating."

Jason let out a sigh.

"Looks like my time is coming to an end," he said. "Sadly, there is more to be done, so I have to go."

Danielle Geller got to her feet.

"I know that there are some impending departures," she said. "Most, only for a time, but Gary for the last time."

She looked at him with sad warmth.

"I can offer little consolation for those we won't see again. It's a loss we can never get back, but we should take joy in the chance to say goodbye to Gary. Too often, people are taken from us suddenly and unexpectedly. With Gary, his sacrifice was anything but unexpected. There's so much hero in him that making the choice he did seemed almost inevitable, in hindsight. If anything, Hero doesn't deserve him. No offence, Gwydion."

"You're fine," the priest of Hero said. "He can't hear you in here."

"What I can hopefully help you with," Danielle continued, "are the partings that, while long, are not forever. You will all learn, in time, that temporary parting is a natural and healthy aspect of relationships that run into the decades and centuries. My husband and I are together and apart as we need. It does not diminish our love for one another. We adventured together. Raised our children together. When our children made their own ways in the world, so did we. Having spent time apart since then, we've just recently been enjoying time together again."

She gestured around the group.

"Friendship is the key. Passion and ardour can get you far and fast, but they won't keep you together as one year becomes ten and ten becomes a hundred. My husband is my best friend in the world, and that is why we will always find one another again, however long we might part."

Humphrey and Sophie shared a look, nervous but hopeful, as Danielle continued talking.

"I have not been a gold-ranker for long," she said, "but I am older than I look."

"You're older than fifty?" Jason called out.

"*Jason!*" Humphrey hissed. Danielle glared at Jason, but the grin she failed to smother undercut any sternness.

"I am older than I look," Danielle resumed, "and I've come to terms with parting ways for years at a time. Today, it's time for many of you to start doing the same. Friends will part, today, but the road is longer than you can understand from the short time you've been together. Your friendships are still in their infancies. That you have forged such strong bonds in only a few years impresses me greatly. I have no doubt that you will be part of one another's lives for longer than any of us can imagine right now."

She turned to Gary again.

"Which makes permanent loss all the harder. I'm sorry to speak of the many years we'll all have together, Gary, when you will not get the chance to journey through them with us."

"No," Gary said. "I made the choice that brought me here. And I like to think that making it is the reason you will all be together for so long, instead of dying in a hole. I can't ask for more than that."

"Are we *sure* we can't swap Jason out for Gary?" Neil asked. "He'd probably come right back to life; you know what he's like."

"Yes, Neil," Humphrey said. "For the eighth time, we're sure."

"What about my backup plan?"

"How is pouring sticky syrup over Jason's head a backup plan?" Humphrey asked.

"I don't know," Neil said. "I just don't think we should dismiss any options until we've tested them thoroughly."

"Are your friends always like this?" Gwydion asked his brother.

"Yes," Rufus said, staring at Gary as he had been the whole time.

"They're a fun bunch," Gwydion said.

"It's not the time for fun."

"They seem to disagree."

"Are you here for Gary?" Rufus asked.

"Someone was going to be here for him. It just made sense to send me. Are you going to make your and his last moments together this maudlin thing? Don't you want to send him off with some joy?"

Rufus frowned, looking at his big brother with a troubled expression. Gwydion's expression grew serious.

"As you said, I was sent here. It's not all family reunions and new friends. I do have an important question in need of an answer."

"What's that?"

"Sophie and Humphrey; how open do you think they'd be to a less-conventional relationship?"

Gwydion's father reached out to flick his son on the ear.

"Ow! What was that for?"

"So your mother doesn't have to get involved. Behave yourself."

Gwydion lifted his plate and sat up looking over at his mother. Arabelle was looking at him from under raised eyebrows with an expression that held no amusement.

"Thanks, Dad," Gwydion whispered.

———

Jason quietly made farewells with his friends, one by one. He met them in a room just off the balcony where they had all gathered.

"I know you still wonder about your place in the team," he told Belinda. "I don't. You have a perspective that only Sophie shares, and she's so determined to look forward. You're the only one who looks back, into the dark corners the rest of us don't understand. There are threats that only you will see coming, and I see you watching for them."

"Where is all this sincerity coming from?" she asked as she gave him a hug.

"Maybe I'm growing more mature."

She let him go and gave him a flat look.

"It could happen," he said unconvincingly.

———

"...be able to effectively map out astral geometry once I've run sufficient testing to accurately designate variable values for non-synchronous time streams across—"

"Clive," Jason said, cutting him off.

"What?" Clive asked, distracted. "Sorry, what did you say?"

"I said that this is the last time we'll see each other for at least a few years."

"Oh, right. Becoming an astral king."

"Yes."

"Just make sure and take a lot of notes. In fact, let me get out some instrumentation that will measure dimensional interactions far better than subjective observations while—"

"I'm not taking a bunch of tools, Clive."

"It's not like you'll be busy," Clive complained. "It'll basically be like meditation, right?"

"Clive, I'll be fighting the World-Phoenix."

"I'm sorry, what?"

"Remember how I mentioned that I have to kind of fix the cosmos a bit?"

"I probably wasn't listening. You're always doing stuff like that, *and you never take proper notes.*"

"I'll see what I can do."

"What you could do is take some basic dimensional analysis tools."

"No. Maybe you could find an actual wife while I'm away. You're not still hung up on Farrah, are you?"

"When was I ever 'hung up' on Farrah?"

"Back in Greenstone, when we first met."

"I think all those resurrections have affected your memory."

"They definitely have not."

"In any case, while Farrah is appealingly intelligent, she's also rather socially aggressive."

"You two didn't…?"

"No. As much as I like the idea of shutting you all up, that's a bad reason to select a spouse."

"I wasn't suggesting she was going to marry you. I was wondering if she dragged you into a closet for a tumble at some point."

"Definitely not. And if I was going to go to the trouble of developing a relationship, it would be more efficient than that. Long-term relationships have a superior effort-to-result ratio than casual encounters."

"That sounds like someone who hasn't had a lot of long-term relationships. Or casual encounters, for that matter."

"The point is, I'm not going to rush into something frivolous, and it's not easy finding the right person for extended companionship."

"I can't argue with that."

"In terms of a prospective spouse," Clive said, "I don't want to call people dim, but it's hard to find someone who can… keep up. I'll be interested when you show me someone as smart as Belinda, but is the opposite of a risk-taking burglar whose idea of experimentation is to throw fake babies off a cliff with bombs strapped to them."

"That's a highly specific example. What were you testing?"

"Safety features on a pram."

"A pram? As in, something to wheel babies around in? I don't remember you making those."

"It was while you were on Earth and we thought you were dead. Belinda and I tried a few money-making projects, including a pram that you can link to another personal transport vehicle, like a flying cloud."

"Did they ever work out?"

"Yes, actually. Danielle Geller helped us set up a business. We're operating out of Vitesse and Cyrion, for now, but we're looking to expand into other major centres. It turns out that adventurer parents really like explosion-resistant prams."

"I can see that," Jason said. "Life can go in unexpected ways."

"The point is that it's a great source of funding for research. And for special projects."

"Like you and Belinda raiding a Magic Society Archive Vault?"

"I have no idea what you're talking about."

68

COMPASSIONATE STRANGERS

"You really are starting to look rough," Humphrey told Jason.

"Yeah," Sophie agreed, wrinkling her nose in distaste. "That pretty gold light coming off you is turning into rainbow smoke—including the smell."

"It's only going to get worse," Jason said. "That's why Neil is last."

Humphrey and Sophie had come together for Jason's round of individual farewells, in a room just off the deck where the others were gathered.

Sophie laughed while Humphrey gave a disapproving head shake.

"There's something we need to talk about," Jason said. "You told me to not keep things from the team, so I should let you know about something that happened. The great astral beings want me to do something while I'm sorting out my astral king business."

"Which astral beings?" Humphrey asked.

"Most of them, I think? Most of the ones with names, anyway. The ones without names are all on the other team."

"There's another team?" Humphrey asked, his expression darkening. "And that team has great astral beings on it?"

"Yeah," Jason said. "Look, Humphrey, the details don't matter. What matters is that it's important and I'm doing it. I would love if we could all do this together, but that's just not how this works. It isn't something the team can help me with, but I didn't want to go into it without telling you."

Humphrey let out a low grumble as he ran his hands through his hair in frustration. Sophie placed a hand on his massive bicep.

"When did you find all this out?" she asked Jason.

"Less than an hour ago."

"You couldn't have at least talked it through with us?"

"I made my decision fast," Jason said. "I wasn't going to change it and time is short enough as it is."

Humphrey let out a long, growling sigh.

"You need to get a lot better at including us, Jason."

"He's working on it," Sophie consoled. "He's still terrible at it, but he's trying. Like a three-legged puppy trying to climb stairs."

"Thank you?" Jason said. "Look, the good news is, I have a plan."

Humphrey and Sophie shared a worried look.

"Don't look like that," Jason complained. "It's a good plan. Plus, it will help me keep up with you lot while you're out there fighting monsters to rank up."

"What kind of plan?" Humphrey asked.

"Well," Jason said, "how much do you know about people from Earth punching each other for money?"

"I know you and I have that link," Farrah said, "but I have no interest in becoming your Voice of the Will. I don't mean to put down Colin or whoever else you rope in, but there's an obedient-messenger-slave aspect I want no part of."

"That's fair," Jason said.

They were lounging comfortably across from one another in cloud furniture.

"How risky is this Sundered Throne business you've got going on?"

"Humphrey didn't waste any time, then."

"He did not."

"Did he tell you about the plan?"

"He said it was completely incomprehensible. You are still terrible at explaining things."

"That's not my fault; they changed the name of the country."

"And that was a relevant detail?"

"Humphrey and Sophie haven't been to Earth. They needed context."

"And that context included something about a king with big hair?"

"It did, as it happens."

Farrah let out a long-suffering sigh.

"How big a risk are you taking here?"

"By my standards? Very little. If my plan works the way it should, I've got this in the bag."

"*If* your plan works the way it should."

"I have some unusual advantages."

"Such as?"

"Such as great astral beings not knowing what happened in the transformation zone."

"Information gaps aren't something they would be used to," Farrah said.

"No," Jason said. "I don't think they would be."

"Just come back alive, yeah?"

"I'd say yes, but it's kind of complicated."

"Complicated how?"

"Technically, I'm not going anywhere. I'm leaving a portal open for people to come and go."

"How does that work exactly? Boris seems convinced that your soul realm and anyone in it will break down entirely."

"That's what gave me the idea for my plan."

Rufus entered the room, empty save for himself and Jason. He looked rougher than Jason felt, eyes bloodshot and baggy in a way no silver-ranker should be.

"You want to sit?" Jason asked.

"No," Rufus said.

They stared at each other in silence until Rufus finally broke it.

"There's nothing you can do? Really?"

"I did do something, Rufus. I let him choose his own fate."

"You couldn't have sold not dying a little harder? It shouldn't be hard to convince someone to live."

"I gave him an honest choice."

"Then you should have given him a dishonest one!"

Jason sighed, not rising to the outburst.

"You don't believe that," he said.

Rufus slumped down and a cloud chair rose from the floor to catch him.

"No," he said, his voice barely a whisper. "No, I don't."

The chair grew wider, turning into a couch, and Jason sat next to his friend. Not knowing what to say, he leaned into him a little and stayed silent.

"Farrah thinks I should go off to your world," Rufus said. "Teach your niece to be an adventurer."

"I think you should go too," Jason told him. "As for what you should teach her to be, that's for her to decide. The last I saw her, she wanted to be anything but an adventurer."

"You think distraction is what I need?"

"Not distraction. Purpose. I don't think you want to be an adventurer right now, but maybe you want to be a teacher."

"But is it my purpose just because my family runs a school?"

"It's your purpose because you love doing it and you're good at it. Because it's building the future instead of holding on to a past that will slip through our fingers, whatever we might do to stop it. You once told me that helping people learn from your mistakes was more fulfilling than the fear of making the next one."

"I didn't make a mistake, Jason. Sometimes you do everything right and it still goes wrong."

"Yeah," Jason agreed. "But I think we both know you're a sackful of bad decisions waiting to happen. I think a completely new context would be good for you. Force you to come at things with a clean slate instead of with all the baggage you have now."

"You aren't pulling punches."

"You've got your mum to take the sensitive approach. Sometimes being a friend means telling someone what they need to hear, not what they want to hear. More than once, I've spent months and years stewing in my own juices when life kicked me in the beans. I'm not saying that you have to perk up and be happy. Our friend is going to die. But this isn't about you. It's about Gary, and you owe him a goodbye that lets him know you're going to be alright, even if it's not today. I'm not saying that means going off to Earth, but it does mean showing him there's a future for you beyond lying around being sad. You know, the way he was after losing Farrah and me until you came along and kicked him in the pants."

"So, this is my kick in the pants?"

"Yep. You don't have to get better now, but you do have to get better. If that means going back to teaching in Greenstone, then do that. If it means spending time with a mental healer like your mum, then do that. If it means a clean break in a world where you don't even know the language, you can do that too."

"Why would you want me anywhere near your niece in this state?"

"Because I trust you. And I trust my family. They weren't equipped to support me through all the weird cosmic crap I was dealing with, but losing someone you love? That they understand, but they'll also have the objectivity of not knowing you and all your baggage. Take it from someone who already jumped worlds: sometimes compassionate strangers can be exactly what you need."

"Bro, you're not regenerating anymore," Taika pointed out. "You're leaking rainbow smoke like a dead monster."

"Yeah," Jason said. "I don't have a lot of time left."

"I won't take too much of it, then. Thanks for keeping your promise and finding me a way home."

"That was Boris, not me. But I'm glad you'll see your family again. Keep an eye on mine until I get back there myself, yeah?"

"No worries, bro."

"Wow, this rooms smells bad," Neil said. "Oh, wait; it's you."

"Neil."

"Yeah?"

"I would never say this in front of the team, but you are arguably the most important member in it. I am exceptionally glad that you will be keeping them safe in my absence, just as you do when I'm here. You're an important friend and you mean the world to me."

Neil blinked in surprise.

"Thank you for saying that, Jason. It means a lot. It would mean more if you said it in front of everyone else."

"I know," Jason said, nodding his head sagely. "I know."

Neil left the room and reached into the pocket where he'd placed the recording crystal in case Jason said anything heart-warming. The crystal was missing and his fingers found something else instead. He pulled it out to find a picture of himself at the Standish family farm, in a tub full of eels, wearing only a hat 'with rub-a-dub-dub' stencilled onto it.

"You have the power to see and change everything here, don't you?"

"Yes," Jason said as he emerged from the room to rest a hand on Neil's shoulder. "Yes, I do."

Jason had one last person, not for a farewell, but for a goodbye.

"You don't have long," Gary told him.

"How can you tell?" Jason asked.

He was alone with Jason, who now had energy pouring off him like a steamed bun. The golden light had turned to rainbow smoke, complete with the extremely unpleasant smell.

"Give me your sword," Gary said.

Without questions, Jason plucked the sword Gary had forged for him from his inventory. He held it out for Gary to take.

Gary gestured at the air and a golden blaze appeared. He took the sword, scabbard and all, and shoved it into the flames. He held it there for around a minute as Jason looked on with curiosity. He was connected to the sword through a soul link and he could feel something about it changing. Finally, Gary pulled it back out and the flames vanished.

- Items [Hegemon's Will] and [Hegemon's Dominion] have been reforged.
- Items have changed from (silver rank [growth] legendary) to (silver rank [growth] relic).

- Relics require transcendent power. Most of their abilities are sealed until their owner, Jason Asano, gains access to transcendent power.
- The owner of a relic always knows its location, regardless of magical or non-magical obfuscation.
- Relics cannot be used without permission of the owner.
- Relics can be summoned to avatars of the owner or designated servants of the owner.

- Relics cannot be destroyed by most forces. A destroyed relic can be manifested again by the owner using transcendent power.

Gary held out the sword in its scabbard for Jason to take back.

"Sorry," Gary told him, "but you won't be able to use them properly until you're an astral king. It smells like you're about to get onto that, though."

Jason laughed as he took the weapon and put it away.

"It's not much of an upgrade on the surface," Gary explained, "but you'll never lose it and you don't need resources and rituals to rank it up now. It'll match its power to yours."

"Thank you," Jason said. "It's been six years since you first gave it to me. It feels like forever and no time at all."

Jason stepped up and hugged Gary tightly, his head only coming up to the huge leonid's chest.

"You smell so bad," Gary choked out and Jason laughed through the tears spilling from his eyes.

Jason pulled away from the big man.

"How do we do this?" he asked. "How do we say goodbye? How can it ever be enough?"

Gary put a comforting hand on Jason's shoulder.

"Jason, you're going to live a long time. Probably forever. And in that time, you're going to do a lot of amazing things."

Gary gestured at Jason, leaking rainbow smoke.

"Starting in about three minutes, from the looks of it," Gary continued. "We both know you can lose your way at times. You have Shade and all of our friends, but maybe you can do something for me. When you find yourself uncertain of a choice, or wondering if you're doing the right thing, maybe think back on your old leonid friend, and see if you can't find a way to choose compassion."

Jason stared at Gary as tears poured from his eyes. He lunged forward and caught Gary in another hug.

Jason stayed with Gary as long as he could. His last sight of the big man was of a wide smile and a casual wave as Jason vanished. He reappeared in a hidden chamber, in the mountain fortress of his otherwise collapsed soul realm.

He hadn't been able to hold back his tears in front of Gary, but now he fell to his knees, wracking sobs shaking his body. He would never see his friend ever again.

Two gentle hands found his shoulders. Shade and Colin were both standing over him while Gordon floated nearby, somehow managing to convey concern in his alien body language.

"I'm sorry, Mr Asano," Shade said, "but you have left things too long already."

Jason nodded and started slowly pulling himself together. He got to his feet and looked around. He was on a catwalk around a magma water-fall, with multiple doors leading out. One led upstairs and three led to his astral throne, astral gate and soul forge, respectively. The fifth and last opened onto a void dotted with colourful nebulas, blazing in the dark.

"Goodbye, Gary," Jason whispered, then stepped out.

PART II

69

WHAT I'M SCARED OF ON THE OTHER SIDE OF THIS PORTAL

WHEN JASON ENDED THE TRANSFORMATION ZONE, BRINGING IT BACK INTO reality, he claimed the soul forge for himself. Having done so, he had all the tools to become an astral king: the forge, the gate and the throne. With the full set completed, the clock on his mortality had started ticking.

The moment Jason had the power to become an astral king, his soul began the process of doing so. His spiritual realm was his true self now, and had been from the moment he acquired the soul forge. His mortal body was now nothing but a vestigial appendage. Like an unplucked apple, it would fall away and rot. Only willpower allowed Jason to hold it together long enough to settle his affairs.

Jason's willpower was strong. He had forged it in fires of tribulation few mortals could equal, clashing with gods and monsters and the fundamental forces of the cosmos. But it was not infinite and Jason's time was up. Barely able to keep his mortal shell standing, he stepped into the void of nebulas.

That was the end.

His body dissolved into rainbow smoke, like the countless monsters he had put down. It would not resurrect, as it had before, as this was not death. It was the shedding of skin, like a snake, leaving his old self behind him. He could no longer have a mortal body because his time as a mortal was done.

Rufus looked at himself in the bathroom mirror. His eyes were bloodshot and there were heavy bags under them. It looked like he hadn't slept in a week and he felt like it too.

"What are you doing?" he asked his reflection.

He was aware that Gary's sacrifice had not brought out his best behaviour. His every instinct drove him to the worst choices, despite his best intentions. He felt trapped inside his own body, screaming at himself to be better, even as he kept getting worse. He mistreated the people around him, most of all Gary, who deserved nothing but his unswerving support.

Gary was Rufus' best friend in the world. He had made an incredible sacrifice for the best of reasons, yet all Rufus could do was ruin the precious time they had left. Echoes of past loss were poisoning his mind. Jason and Farrah had come back, but he'd believed them dead for years. That grief had been real, and there was no coming back for Gary.

It was time to stop. Stop giving in to his worst instincts. To stop trapping his better nature in his head and start letting it drive his actions. To be the man—the friend—that he knew he should be.

He closed his eyes and concentrated on his body. He'd been trained better than the sloppy body control he'd been showing. When he opened his eyes, his sclerae were clear and the bags were gone. He looked fresh and ready, like an adventurer should.

He ran a hand over his head, feeling the stubble that had grown as he stopped taking care of himself. He reached for his bag and the depilatory cream inside, but stopped himself. Maybe it was time for a change. He wasn't going to grow the wild mess his brother lugged around on his head, but something different would be good. Change, inside and out.

He grabbed his bag, slung it over his shoulder and walked out.

There was a battleground in Jason's soul. A liminal space, neither real nor unreal. Jason chose what it became. What it was, and what one had to be to exist within it. There were limits, mostly on what he could do with those who invaded his soul, but ultimately, their form was his to choose. He made the rules, and any who entered would have to obey them.

The shape Jason chose for the space was a massive flagstone road the width of a freeway with two-dozen lanes. Straight as an arrow, the road stretched out to the horizon in each direction. Spreading out from either side was dense jungle, the road cutting through it like a perfect sword stroke. The sun blasted heat from a clear sky and the humid air felt thick enough to be cut into slices.

Only Jason knew how long the road truly was, but, at the very midpoint, there was a building on each side of the road. Constructed from the same grey stone as the road itself, one side had a small building, the size of a garden shed. The other side was much larger, the size of a massive warehouse with a giant sliding door to match.

Painted across the road, in rough but massive letters, were four words in bright yellow. It was crude work, the letters rough and surrounded in paint spatter.

The door to the small building opened for seven people to exit. They were humanoid, but would only pass for human by the vaguest of descriptions. The first out was a corpse-pale man with dark hair, dark clothes and solid black orbs in place of eyes. The next had golden skin and fire blazing on her head in place of hair. Her loose clothes rippled in shades of orange and yellow.

The third person was extremely tall. His long hair and a long beard were both a mossy green tangle. He was draped in hide cloth and had deer antlers rising from his head. Of the group, he had the most trouble leaving the building. It took him almost a full minute, awkwardly turning and crouching to get his horns and massive frame through the doorway.

Four people were stuck inside waiting until he finally cleared the way. The first to follow him out was a woman with plain features and simple clothes. Where the others boasted imposing, alien beauty, she had a dumpy physique and plain looks. Her clothes were cheap and ill-fitting; if not for the blue light shining from her eyes, she would not look out of place in a thrift shop.

Next came a tall woman dressed head to toe in black. Her face was hidden behind a veil and her willowy body was draped in black lace. Following her was what looked like a wizard, but less Gandalf and more cosplay. His beard was scraggly and short from an unfortunate attempt to grow it out. His robes, pointy hat and staff looked like he'd ordered them online, only for them to arrive looking cheaper than the pictures and a size too small.

The final person to leave the building would have been recognised by members of Greenstone high society as Thadwick Mercer.

The six stood on the grass around the building, the only area other than the road not heavily encroached by tropical growth. They looked themselves and each other over.

"He's given us mortal forms," said the fire-haired lady in the tone of someone who found a bag of poop on her doorstep.

"Of course he has," said the wizard. "I rather like it."

This was the Celestial Book, responding to the World-Phoenix's complaint. The woman with blue eyes was the Seeker of Songs and the woman in lace was the Whisper in Corners. The man with the antlers was Legion and the pale man was the Reaper.

"I don't like it," said the Builder in Thadwick's whining voice. "This is the body of the worst vessel I ever possessed."

"You shouldn't be possessing vessels like that at all," Legion said in a deep, rumbling voice. "There are rules."

"I'm not the one who replaced the Cosmic Throne with a bunch of loophole-riddled agreements," the Builder replied. "I'm the one here to fix your mistake."

"You'll fix nothing," the World-Phoenix said. "You're a foolish child."

The Builder's face twisted with rage.

"You're the ones who—"

"Enough."

The Reaper's voice was little more than a raspy whisper yet it cut across the others, arresting attention like a body falling into a grave.

"None of us are well-suited to mortality," the Celestial Book said. "These bodies have minds, which is not a limit we are used to. We normally have our vessels and can use their minds, but we're stuck with whatever Asano has given us. We'll probably find ourselves susceptible to emotions and odd behaviour. Such as engaging in petty squabbles."

"Obviously part of the fool's plan," the World-Phoenix said. "If we cannot think properly, we cannot react properly. Cannot see through whatever he has plotted."

"Given that everyone but you is on Asano's side," the Seeker of Songs said, "the rest of us can simply ask him."

"Where are the nameless?" the World-Phoenix asked.

They all looked around and spotted the huge building on the far side of the road. In doing so, they spotted the writing on the road.

"Rumble in the Jungle?" the Builder asked. "What does that mean?"

"We're in a jungle to have a fight," the Celestial Book pointed out. "It's not exactly complicated. I think Asano may have given you a defective brain. Oh, I was right! This is a petty squabble. It's kind of fun."

"It is a song from Asano's world," the Seeker of Songs said. "'Rumble in the Jungle' by Fugees, featuring A Tribe Called Quest, Busta Rhymes and John Forté."

"Is it any good?" the Book asked. "And how can you tell? Why do I know what songs are? I'm troubled that this brain came with information already in it."

"You should be troubled by a lot more than that," Jason said.

Everyone turned to look at him, not having noticed his belated exit from the small building. Being surprised was not something these entities were used to, and it showed in their expressions. Most showed shock and displeasure, although the Celestial Book looked delighted. Legion seemed impassive, although most expressions would look that way from behind the beard.

"You're here," Legion said to Jason.

"Ooh, stating the obvious," Jason said. "You're getting the hang of mortality nice and quick. I'm guessing you're all just starting to realise how much you were reliant on your vessels while possessing them. You never needed to learn how to school your expression because they already knew. I put a few things in your mortal brains, but not as much as your vessels have. You've got language; motor functions; what songs are. The conflict between innocent fun and racist iconography in *The Dukes of Hazzard*."

"This is not a game," the Builder said.

"Yes, it is," Jason countered, turning to look at him. "This is my game. You all decided to make a battleground out of my soul, but that puts you in my house. I set the tone and I set the rules."

Jason looked the Builder up and down and frowned.

"I was a little petty with you. Go back into the Building."

"Why?" the Builder asked, narrowing his eyes in suspicion.

"Don't, then," Jason said. "If you like being Thadwick, that's fine. Stay where you are."

The Builder rushed back through the door and it closed behind him. It opened a moment later and he returned looking very different. He had the form of a tall human, thick with the muscle of work rather than body-building. He was dressed like an archaic stonemason, with simple clothes, a leather apron and tools in his belt. He was ruggedly handsome, with a short-cropped beard.

"Better?" Jason asked.

"Yes," the Builder said. His new voice was deep and solid. "Whatever issues we might have, I am deserving of respect."

"Mate, what you deserve is to be kicked in the plums so hard, you bounce off the moon. Let's not get into what we deserve because none of us come out of that discussion clean."

Gary was standing nervously in front of the portal leading out of Jason's soul realm. He was so distracted that he didn't notice someone approaching from behind until Rufus slapped his friend lightly on the back. Gary looked down in surprise as Rufus moved to stand next to him. He looked better, and it wasn't just that his eyes weren't bloodshot. They no longer held the anger that had been simmering behind them since Gary made his decision.

"I'm sorry," Rufus said. "You need a friend more than ever right now, and I've been making things harder for you."

"It's not—"

"Don't," Rufus cut him off. "Don't try to make me feel better. I'm sorry it took me so long to be the friend you always are."

"Rufus…"

"What has you hesitating?" Rufus asked, forcibly changing the subject. "What's waiting for you on the other side? You're worried about Hero's power trying to leave your body?"

Gary shook his head.

"I won't be out that long. I can hold the power inside until I come back into the soul realm, and I need to face the god. Jason said he gave Hero permission to come into the brightheart city."

"I don't know what's worse," Rufus said. "That gods can be kept out or that it's Jason they need permission from."

Gary laughed.

"He certainly doesn't need an ego boost. Gods show up and he's annoyed they're bothering him. You're going to have to keep him grounded after he turns into a messenger god or whatever it is."

"I think I'll be leaving that to the others. I might take Farrah's idea and go to Earth."

"Really? I didn't think you would."

"I want to stay here. Stay with you for however long you have left.

But I haven't been handling this well, and I think making a change is better than falling into old habits."

"I'm glad," Gary said. "I'd like the last time we see each other to be when we're at our best. I don't want you to watch me slowly degrade until I can't take it anymore and give back the power. That's what I'm scared of on the other side of this portal. Your brother brought my parents here, and they will stay with me. No matter what I tell them, I know they'll stay and watch my body break down. Watch me get sick and weak. Watch me die. I'm halfway inclined to give back the power now and spare them."

"But you can't do that to them either."

"No, I can't."

Rufus reached way up to put a hand on Gary's shoulder.

"Well," he said. "You may only have me for a day or so, but I'll stand next to you, brother."

"I know," Gary said. "You always have."

70

WE SET OUT TO HAVE
ADVENTURES

On a wide road in an otherworldly jungle, Jason and the World-Phoenix stared at each other.

"I had this whole speech planned out," Jason said. "About how you used me, only to throw me away when something more important came up. It had this great running metaphor about how people respect their tools. But that would be for me, not for you. I may have taken the extension of your will you poked into my soul and stuck it in a person-shaped box, but that's just my impression of you. It's not what you are. So, we might as well go ahead and get started."

He turned to walk off, then froze when the World-Phoenix spoke.

"Thank you for Dawn," she said.

Jason turned to look at her, eyes narrowing with curiosity.

"Same," he said after a long moment. "Thank you for sending her my way."

He marched into the middle of the flagstone highway and the great astral beings followed.

"The game," he announced, "is simple enough. In that large building over there are all the nameless GABs that will be fighting alongside the World-Phoenix."

He pointed down the road behind him.

"They will be attempting to fight their way down this road. The rest of us…"

He pointed in the other direction.

"…will be trying to fight our way to that end of the road. If we get there, you all get kicked out and I can repair the Sundered Throne in peace. Either way, the game ends when I complete my astral king transition. Once that's over, so is everything else, whether the throne is fixed or not."

"And if I reach the other end of the road?" the World-Phoenix asked.

"Every time I'm forced back down that road," Jason said, "it damages my will. If you can eradicate my will entirely, then my consciousness goes away. Stops fighting back. I'll come back to my senses eventually, so I'm told, but not for a very long time. And I'll come back funny in the head."

"You'll be more than funny in the head," the Celestial Book said. "Your mind will effectively be destroyed. You'll only be lucky enough to generate a new one because you're in the process of becoming an astral king. You'll be a new person, with no memory of the old one. And by the time you come to, everyone you know will be immortal or very long dead."

"Then I'd appreciate you making sure we don't lose," Jason told him.

"This is foolish," Legion said. "You make the rules here. You can only bend things so far with our wills influencing events, but you could have given us far more advantages. You have to know this, so why would you arrange it like this?"

"Because of what we took from him," a voice whispered, seemingly coming from all around them.

The group turned to looked at the laced and veiled Whisper in Corners. It was not a great astral being Jason had heard of prior to his meeting with Raythe and Velius.

"He will be forever," Whisper continued. "But for now, he is young. His friends will grow stronger and his family older in the time he is with us. He will not be there to see or share in those experiences. If not for the fight we have imposed upon him, that time would be far shorter. We have taken time from him, and he chose this path to gain a measure of it back."

"This won't accelerate the process," Legion said.

"No," the Reaper said, "but it will help him become stronger. His astral king ascension will only take him to a half-transcendent state. Until he completes the path of mortal power and transcends in full, he will have access to the infinite power of the cosmos yet be unable to tap into it. His purpose in setting the board as he has is to accelerate his progress to gold rank. Rather than design it to his advantage, he has designed it to give himself constant challenge, with stakes for failure. He has put in place the conditions to push himself to his limits, and made of us a whetstone upon which to hone his power."

The Celestial Book burst out laughing.

"You're saying," the Seeker of Songs said, "that this man is hosting the largest gathering of great astral beings since the sundering, and he's using us as a training tool?"

"We have used, and are used in turn," Whisper said. "My approval is not required for this arrangement, but you have it, Jason Asano."

"We are great astral beings," Legion said. "We do not get 'used in turn.'"

"Petty pride," Jason said. "I did a good job with these mortal brains."

"Approve or not," the Reaper said, "the course before us is set. Our options are to participate or to leave. All that remains is to make that choice and begin."

Jason's clothes were replaced with conjured blood robes and his void cloak appeared, draped around him. He took his sword belt from his inventory and strapped it around his waist.

"Yes," he said. "Let's begin."

In the distance, by the side of the road opposite where they'd come from, was a large building. The massive warehouse door on the front exploded outwards. It was reduced to splinters that rained down on the monsters pouring through the massive and now-open doorway.

It was a fight that Jason was familiar with. The nameless great astral beings had taken the form of a horde of monsters; wild, savage and multitudinous in form. The World-Phoenix served as horde leader, somehow commanding what looked like an army of anarchy and madness. More monsters poured from the building than ever should have been able to fit, even with its considerable size. Some were large enough to require dimensional distension to emerge, squeezing out of the door like a cartoon character. These were cyclopian giants, hydras with talons in place of heads and other humungous monstrosities that towered over the horde.

Jason hadn't been as attentive with the countless monster forms as he had with those of the great astral beings. The monsters came in myriad shapes with no unifying theme. Some were comical and others horrifying. There were tiny swarms and some bordering on kaiju proportions.

Their forms weren't the monsters Jason had personally encountered. He glimpsed a xenomorph in the horde, or something looking very like one. The most horrible thing he saw within the horde chilled his blood: a street gang from eighties television. They were all white guys with no tattoos but wore leather jackets and bandanas around their foreheads.

"Come on, guys!" one of them yelled. "Let's show them what the Downtown Beat Boys can do!"

"Oh, this is going to get weird," Jason muttered to himself.

On Jason's side were all the great astral beings other than the World-Phoenix. He had chosen the form of their bodies, but not that of their powers. What he did set was their limitations, with all the combatants restricted to silver rank. The great astral beings were further restricted to essence-user rules, their powers amounting to self-designed sets of essence abilities.

The results of this were formidable. Jason had seen some of the most capable adventurers in the world, and considered himself able to hold his own amongst them. Amongst the great astral beings, even limited to silver rank, he quickly discovered that he was at the bottom of the bunch. By a wide margin.

It didn't come as a surprise. There were many limits on them, limits matched not to Jason's ability but to his potential. The great astral beings had found and reached those limits instantly. It was now on Jason to find it within himself to catch up to the examples set out before him.

It did not start well.

The named great astral beings were far more powerful than the name-less ones making up the monster horde. Only the World-Phoenix could hold her own one-to-one, but there were no duels taking place. Monsters moved forward like the tide as the great astral beings slaughtered them. Every one that was killed respawned some time later, further back down the road. The same was true of any great astral being taken down. That usually meant the World-Phoenix had swept in on someone almost overrun by monsters, or was ambushed herself by multiple of her peers.

The weak link was unquestionably Jason. He had set the balance such that it was only winnable if he did his part. He was not doing his part. Time and again he failed. Swarmed by monsters or struck down by the World-Phoenix. He wasn't slower or weaker. He just wasn't as good.

The monsters had a panoply of powers, and were not unskilled them-selves. Jason was used to numbers, but not numbers this fast or this capa-ble. While some managed to resist his powers with their own, most didn't.

The simple fact was that he couldn't output his afflictions as fast as the monsters kept coming.

The monsters didn't make it easy for him, forcing him to work for every spell or sword strike he landed. He quickly found that his familiars needed to be used with care and precision as well. The trick of spreading afflictions with butterflies was a non-starter, the monsters eliminating each other as necessary to stop their spread. They were intelligent and didn't need the guidance of the World-Phoenix leading them for that.

Colin, normally a weapon of mass destruction for Jason, worked wonders at first. It became clear that the monsters knew exactly how he operated, however, sacrificing their numbers until the leech monster overextended, and then they swooped in. Colin could not reproduce his biomass as fast as it could be destroyed by those with the power, precision and intent to do so, and that was exactly what the monsters did.

Gordon did well enough, ignoring his butterfly powers, which had proved ineffective. He stayed in the backline, adding more direct impact to the battle than Jason's afflictions, although he was not a definitive presence.

Shade was the familiar who proved most capable, faring better than Jason himself. Elusive and careful, he aided Jason by scouting and using his bodies as shadow-jump points. Even so, he could do little more than facilitate Jason, and Jason was falling short. Time and again, he was cut down, overrun, torn apart or simply trampled to death.

The other great astral beings on his side were not happy. Even the previously cheery Celestial Book gave Jason accusatory looks.

"It is too late to change what you have done," Legion told Jason as they fought side by side. "You are throwing away a chance we have waited eons for."

The tall man with green hair and antlers was fighting in a style Jason could only think of as druid from *Dungeons & Dragons*. He was summoning wild beasts and turning into them himself to savage the monsters. He cast spells that unleashed poisonous spore clouds or had grasping, thorny vines erupt through the flagstones of the road.

"You're still getting used to mortal sensibilities," Jason told him. "Who and what you are doesn't change. For us, being good at something always means starting bad. After that, it's about opportunity and persistence. This is a long road we're on, literally and figuratively. You just wait and see how I change."

Jason had faced powerful monsters, skilled monsters, cunning monsters and overwhelming hordes of monsters. Never before had he encountered monsters that were all of those things at once. For the first time since his early days as an adventurer, Jason was failing to cover for the drawbacks of his abilities.

Every power set had strengths and weaknesses. Some were more balanced, with fewer flaws but no great strengths. Jason's powers were the opposite extreme, capable of incredible things but with some glaring vulnerabilities as well. The most prevalent was the lack of immediate, impactful damage.

The current situation punished every weakness in Jason's power set, and not by accident. The battleground had taken shape not just by Jason's conscious choices but also by instinct. And what he had wanted was a situation that would hammer at every flaw and vulnerability in his fighting style.

From early in his adventuring career, Jason had learned to cover his weakness. Using stealth to buy time. Having familiars or allies to cover shortfalls or distract while he set himself up. Exploiting the environment or the stupidity of monsters that would fall for obvious traps.

None of that was in play now. There was no good luck to be had; nowhere to hide. No environment to exploit or twist of fate to save him. The enemies had the wits and knowledge to punish lazy tactics that had served him well against unintelligent monsters.

His familiars were being punished, Jason quickly realising that he had fallen profoundly short on developing tactics for them. He had always used them, and if they didn't work for a situation, pulled them back. That wasn't going to work here. He couldn't afford to leave any advantage on the table, so he would need to learn how to work with them more effectively than he had in the past.

He also had no allies to assist him; the astral beings were not covering for him. Not only were they busy fending off the nameless horde, but they had an instinctive disinclination to help him. Jason had put the conditions in place, right down to the instincts within their new mortal bodies. Those instincts drove them to leave Jason to reap what he'd sowed on the battlefield he had established.

Jason had everything set up to leave himself no options and no excuses. He had his powers, he had his enemies, and all he could do was get better or fail.

One of the major changes Jason had made from the original brightheart city was how to access it. The shaft leading down from the surface no longer terminated in the ceiling of the massive city cavern. Instead, it led to an extremely defensible tunnel through which the city could be accessed.

At the end of that tunnel was an area Jason had set up for Lorenn and her people to use as a diplomatic ward. Emir, Constance, Danielle and Lorenn were dealing with the people who had arrived from the surface. It would take a long time to organise relations with the surface world and, for now, they were in diplomatic triage.

It wasn't just the brighthearts being shielded from the surface. Boris and the messengers had no interest in meeting the Adventure Society. They were in one of the city's many quiet areas, making final preparations to leave Pallimustus and ride the link between worlds to Earth.

It was a city square that wouldn't have been wildly out of place in areas of Europe. Two flat, lacquered wooden platforms were laid out on the ground. Boris, Clive and Belinda were drawing ritual diagrams onto them, preparing to transport Rufus and Taika.

"I know it's a rough workaround," Belinda said. "If this needed to last a couple of weeks, that might be an issue, but this magic will take seconds to activate and then be done."

"It's a crude solution," Boris said, "but as the adorable Miss Callahan suggests, it will save us an amount of complication. Practicality suggests we tailor our efforts to the task at hand rather than some other task out of principle."

"Call me adorable again and you'll find yourself dealing with the practical application of a war hammer," Belinda said.

"I can assure you I meant it only in admiration and ardour," Boris said.

"You keep your sleazy hands to yourself, bird man," Belinda told him. "You couldn't handle what I've got going on anyway. If you got anywhere near me, I'd break it off."

"Break what off?" Clive asked.

Belinda and Boris turned to look at him.

"Is he serious?" Boris asked.

"He's an innocent flower," Belinda said.

"I feel better now," Boris said. "He didn't respond at all when I hit on him."

"Wait, what?" Clive asked.

Humphrey, Sophie and Neil were saying their goodbyes to Taika.

"You'll be missed," Humphrey said. "Your contribution to the team—oof!"

He grunted as Sophie elbowed him in the ribs.

"…is nothing compared to what we lose in a good friend," he finished.

"Smooth, bro," Taika said with a grin.

"We are sorry you're leaving," Neil said, "but we understand. My family is only on the other side of the planet and I miss them. I can visit them when I like, and think it will be past time when we're done with all this. I don't envy you having been stuck, not knowing when or even if you'll see yours again. We hate to see you go, but I'm glad that you get the chance."

Taika, the size Gary had been before his demigod growth, wrapped a surprised Neil up in a massive hug.

"See?" Sophie asked Humphrey. "That's how you do it. Did your mother not teach you to talk to people outside of high society functions, diplomatic meetings and battlefields?"

"I think she wanted me to learn on my own," he said defensively.

"Yes, because she's famous for leaving things up to chance when it comes to your upbringing. I think she and I need to have a talk."

Taika burst out laughing at the hunted look on Humphrey's face. He moved forward to collect them into a group hug, Neil unwillingly caught up as Taika dragged him into it.

Gary, Farrah and Rufus stood together, off to the side. Gary's parents, after a tearful reunion, were settling their possessions into their accommodations in Jason's tree city. Gary was making his final goodbyes with his best friends.

Farrah, Rufus and Gary's team had officially been disbanded years ago. Gary and Rufus had turned away from adventuring after Farrah's death, and they had never reformed after her resurrection. The friendship had been far more than just a registry with the Adventure Society, however.

"You know," Gary said, "the first time we met was in a town that was burning to the ground and full of zombies. The last time we met was in a magic city deep underground, next to a crowd of rebellious angels. It's only been about ten years, but we can't say it wasn't exciting."

"We set out to have adventures," Rufus said. "No one can say we didn't succeed."

Farrah didn't say anything, grabbing Gary's much larger frame in a hug, looking like a child grabbing a parent. Her tears wetted the fur on his arm.

STARING OUT AT THE DARK

RUFUS AND TAIKA WERE HANDED DIMENSIONAL BAGS FILLED WITH ITEMS, including recordings from Jason and Farrah. They each moved to the middle of a ritual platform and were slowly sealed inside egg-shaped conjured dimensional vessels. The brown ovoids spread from the platform up, and Rufus locked eyes with Gary until their line of sight was blocked.

Boris conducted a large-scale ritual, at the culmination of which the messengers and the two vessels all vanished. The onlookers departed, almost everyone having more than enough to do in the wake of the expedition's return. Farrah and Gary didn't rush off, instead taking an aimless stroll through the empty streets.

"Are we heading somewhere in particular?" she asked.

"Anywhere quiet."

"Everywhere is quiet here," she said. "What are…"

She trailed off as a divine aura announced the arrival of a god. Hero looked not unlike Gary's demigod form—a leonid too large for even Gary's hulking species.

"Thank you for waiting," Gary said.

"If not the ancient and immortal," Hero asked, "then from whom can you expect patience? In any case, Asano's invitation to this place was contingent on letting you make your goodbyes first."

"Excuse me, your godness," Farrah said, "but I didn't think deities could enter Jason's spirit domains at all."

"His control over his power grows," the god said, "and will only continue to do so. I had hoped he would use it to vouchsafe your life, Gareth Xandier."

"He gave me a choice," Gary said. "I chose."

Hero nodded.

"I know that you intend to hold my power a little longer. Please continue with my blessing, for as long as you can tolerate it."

"It's your blessing that got us here in the first place," Farrah muttered.

"*Farrah!*" Gary admonished.

Hero held out a restraining hand.

"She is not wrong," the god said, sadness tinging his voice. "I am sorry that this is all I had to offer you."

"Yeah, well, maybe come up with a less lethal miracle," Farrah said.

"*Farrah!*"

"I would like that," Hero said. "But change is hard for my kind, and often comes with consequences we neither foresee nor welcome. We only have to look to Purity for that."

"I am sorry for her disrespect," Gary said. "*And so is she.*"

"It's alright," Hero said. "I would not act this way with every god, Farrah Hurin, but I am the god of heroes. I, of all, understand that actions, not power, are what makes one worthy of respect. And all I do is kill heroes."

The sadness emanating from the god's aura was on a divine level and Farrah felt caught up in it, as if struck by a tidal wave. Tears spilled from her eyes. She felt the god's despair at his role, undeniable and sincere.

"I'm sorry," she said.

The god placed a large hand on her shoulder as she bent her head. His voice became warm and paternal.

"Feel no shame in standing for a friend, child. Instead, take pride in doing so, especially in the face of a god."

"With respect," Gary said, "I'm not sure you should be encouraging that behaviour."

The god let out a laugh, startling the mortal and the demigod.

"You are fine heroes, both of you. And being a hero is more than just weapons and battlefields. I know of your project, Farrah Hurin. Working to connect the world. More good will come from that than any 'glorious war.'"

Hero said the last two words as if they left a bad taste in his mouth.

"To be honest, I'm mostly doing it for the money," Farrah said, and the god laughed again.

"To be honest? You should not lie to gods, Farrah Hurin."

Gary looked up as Gwydion Remore approached them, wandering down an empty street. The priest bowed before his god.

"Lord Hero."

The god nodded his acknowledgement, then turned back to Gary. When he spoke, his paternal tone had once more become divine and imposing.

"I have permitted you to keep my power for so long as you can hold it, Gareth Xandier, but there is one order of business to be settled now."

The god stepped back and Gwydion moved to stand before Gary. There was none of Gwydion's normal amusement in his expression as he bowed before Gary, as deeply as he had for his god.

"Gareth Xandier," he intoned. "You are a hero, to be sung through the ages. Your battle is done and your well-earned time of rest draws near. I ask that you bestow your relic upon my church, in testament to your deeds."

Gary looked at Gwydion for a long time, the priest still bent over in mid-bow. Then he held out his hand, into which an enormous hammer appeared with a burst of golden fire. He looked at the words 'Gary's Last Hammer' engraved into it and shook his head. The word 'Last' started glowing like molten metal, then reshaped itself so the hammer read 'Gary's Medium Hammer.' He held it out and Gwydion stood up. Despite his serious expression, Gwydion couldn't keep the mirth from his eyes as he read the inscription.

"Thank you, hero. I wish you nothing but joy in the time that is left to you."

"I didn't do it to be remembered," Gary said. "But there's not much point holding on to the thing. We both know that when you say my battle is done, I don't have anything useful left to do for anyone."

"Gary—"

"Don't, Gwydion. I gave you my hammer. At least have the decency to not pay for it with a nice lie. I never wanted to be a hero."

Gwydion looked at Gary in silence, his expression conflicted. He turned and left, carrying the hammer reverently, if somewhat unsteadily, away. Although the priest's gold-rank strength was enough to lift it, it still weighed many times more than he did. It was also large enough that he looked like a child making off with his father's weapon.

When Gary and Farrah turned to look back at the god, they realised he was gone, only his divine aura lingering.

"That's it, then," Gary said. "No more obligations. Not until the end."

Farrah gripped Gary's much larger hand and gave it a squeeze.

The aftermath of the expedition to the underground was a mess. The Adventure Society and the Magic Society both wanted answers. The emergence of a new polity, deep underground, was a complication to their closest neighbour, and Yaresh had enough problems already.

The appearance of the transformation zone had led the messengers to realise that the soul forge their astral king had put so much effort into was almost certainly lost to them. The truce with Yaresh came to a violent end as fighting resumed for the first time since the messengers invaded.

Yaresh itself was not the centre of the fighting, with its magical defences being the one thing left largely intact. Instead, skirmishes took place in the smaller population centres in the region. Not long recovered from the monster surge, the towns and villages left alone for their lack of strategic importance were suddenly subjected to raids for no better reason than to slake an astral king's anger.

Yaresh and her adventurers struck back hard, repeatedly raiding the remaining messenger strongholds. With so many resources dedicated to rebuilding the city, they could not afford to besiege fortifications reinforced by advanced messenger magic. Even so, they forcefully struck back against the messengers.

Rather than dedicating the forces required to breach the strongholds, Yaresh and the Adventure Society deployed powerful champions to periodically hammer the enemy defences. Attacking with elites only saved on valuable manpower and avoided unaffordable casualties. Rather than successfully penetrate the defences, they bled the messengers of the resources required to repair their defences after each attack.

The messenger strongholds boasted magnificent protective magic, beyond anything found in Pallimustus. Diamond-rankers were the ultimate trump card, however, and while Yaresh had two, the only one on the messenger side had died invading the city. Not only did Charist and Allayeth punish the messenger defences but also pushed them to the limit. The messengers had to fully restore them after each attack if they wanted to withstand the next.

The skirmish wars lasted for months, defined by logistical shortcomings. The messengers weren't allowed to withdraw, yet were no longer being reinforced or resupplied. Their astral king drove them to spend their lives on petty, inconsequential revenge.

Yaresh and the Adventure Society wanted to crush their enemy, but were unwilling to divert the requisite people and resources. With messenger attacks in the region ongoing and the city under reconstruction, the decision was made to let attrition end the messengers. If their astral king wanted to sacrifice them in dribs and drabs for nothing, her enemies were happy to let her.

The main casualties on both sides came from the messenger attacks on towns and villages. Despite the increasingly dire situation the messengers were in, they continued their pointless attacks against now mostly evacuated towns and villages. The adventurers became increasingly adept at predicting and countering their unevolving patterns of attack. By the time the transformation zone opened up, it was less a defensive patrol program than an exercise in messenger hunting.

It was clear that the messengers were done in the region. Their numbers fell too far and their resources dwindled too much to effectively defend their last stronghold. They were beyond the point where they would have needed to spring a trap that revealed their poor tactics to be grand strategy.

In the end, the diamond-rankers all but strolled in to eliminate the final defenders. The messengers fought to almost the very last, with only a few notable leaders absent when the fortress finally fell. That was a little more than a month after the transformation zone ended and the expedition finally returned to the surface. What was left of Jason's team even participated in the final raids.

The messenger war had ended for Yaresh, at least until another astral king found some reason to return. The celebration was enthusiastic but modest, as the aftermath was bitter. The astral king's ambitions had been destructive enough, but her spite in failure was worse for the pointlessness of it. She had let her own people die for no more reason than to scorch as much earth as they could. The reconstruction would be more daunting than the wake of any monster surge.

One bright light had been the growth chambers of the underground city. They had the capacity to sustain hundreds of thousands, yet had only ten thousand to feed. The ability to solve the region's food problem instantly was a massive boon for the brighthearts, who were now faced with diplomatic relations for the first time in centuries.

Jason's team, like the rest of the expedition, faced weeks of debriefing meetings with the Adventure Society. Their insistence that they would not answer to any Magic Society representatives caused contention but was ultimately accepted. Danielle Geller did not have the reputation on this side of the world she did in her homeland... at first. That changed in direct proportion to the bureaucratic pressure applied to her son.

Danielle also teleported Farrah's parents in from Rimaros. Despite her desire to return to her personal project, Farrah and her parents joined Gary and his in what remained of Jason's soul realm. While the rest of their friends were dealing with one debrief after another, Farrah quickly fled to the tree city and didn't come back out.

Others had migrated into the tree city as well. Mostly this consisted of Carlos Quilido and a new research team he'd assembled. His previous assistants had returned to Rimaros while Carlos was underground, although many returned. The funding was not a problem due to the father of Gibson Amouz, the young nobleman in the care of Carlos.

Gibson had been trapped in a customised stasis chamber for around a year, rescued halfway through a conversion process meant to turn him into a zealot slave. Undoing the horrors visited upon him was the focus of Carlos' work. The Healer priest hoped that success would lead to saving others thought lost forever to vampirism and related conditions.

Jason had set up a research centre in the tree city, the hope being that his power to manipulate reality there would help advance the research while keeping the subjects alive. One of those subjects was Sophie's mother, Melody Jain. The zealots of the Order of Redeeming Light she had once led were the rest of the subjects. Some accepted being led into the tree city and some did not. Those who refused were confined in the brightheart city with the permission of Lorenn.

Also staying were former teammates, Arabelle Remore and Callum Morse. Arabelle was a part of Carlos' research project, trying to keep the subjects sane while he kept them alive. Those subjects who had entered the soul realm had the influence controlling them turned off by Jason's power, like Sophie's mother. Arabelle's role would be to help them through their trauma.

As for Callum Morse, Arabelle wanted to help him as well. She blamed herself for failing to notice the deteriorating mental health of her friend. He had spent years searching for Melody with what became an unhealthy obsession. With Melody wanting to reconnect with Callum, Arabelle intended to do her best to help both.

———

Jason's team was down several members following the underground expedition. Jason himself had been a critical source of damage, but the absence of Rufus and Taika was also felt. They had been temporary members from the start, but how temporary had always been an open question. With how well they had fit in, bringing welcome power and versatility, their departure left a hole.

After weeks of unceasing questions, the team was extremely ready to move on. Especially when more and more answers began with "I don't know."

"I don't know, it was a weird Jason thing."

"I don't know why it was shaped like his head."

"I don't know. It looked like a bunch of magic carriages all stuck together to make a giant golem."

After a final visit to Farrah, Gary, and Melody in the tree city, Team Biscuit prepared to leave. The destination was the city of Vitesse, in the nation of Estercost. When they left, it was with another temporary team member, to try and patch over the hole in their ranks.

———

Team Storm Shredder was over. The surviving members were Rosa, the team scout, Amos Pensinata's nephew Orin, and Zara Nareen. Amos took Orin back to Rimaros and Rosa went with them. The scout had been shaken to the core, and Zara knew that she would not return to adventuring soon, if ever. The silent Orin was as hard to read as ever and she had no idea how the trauma had affected him.

Despite being a latecomer, Zara had built a strong camaraderie during her brief but exciting time with the team. In the aftermath of its destruction, she was left shaken, alone and fragile. When she had been at her most lost, the team was the place she found. Her intentions had been foolish at first, but as her sense of belonging had grown, that belonging had become her purpose. Now, there was nothing left to belong to.

She had no place left. Her father had sent people to bring her home, and she had followed, but the messes she had left back home had not gone away. The political fiction of being cast out was still a necessity and it was not long before she returned to Yaresh. In the last days of the messenger war, she threw herself into the fight against the messengers. It was good work for good people, but it wasn't a purpose.

When the last messenger stronghold fell, Zara was once more at a loss. On the night of the victory celebration, she stood alone on the city wall, looking out into the dark.

"There's that look again."

Zara turned to find Sophie standing next to her. She hadn't snuck up so much as been moving faster than Zara's aura senses could detect.

"How do you move that fast without kicking up the wind?" Zara asked.

"The wind is kind enough to get out of the way," Sophie told her. "What's in your way, Princess? I saw you out there, fighting the messengers. You went hard. Harder than a lot of people like you I've robbed. But here you are, with the same look that was on your face when we came out of the hole."

Sophie's expression softened. She moved to the stone balustrade next to Zara and stared into the night.

"It's not easy losing people," she said. "I know that, and I've never lost anyone who meant anything to me other than my dad. But I have people that matter now. Lindy, Humphrey... all of them. I don't know what kind of kick in the teeth that would be. I spent so long keeping people out. Now that I've finally let them in, I think losing them might break me."

"I'm not broken," Zara said, hesitant as she looked for the words. "The team mattered to me, but we weren't so close that..."

She closed her eyes, squeezing out tears.

"It hurts, but I'm not broken. I'm lost. I was starting to belong; to have a purpose. Being part of something; building it together."

"And you threw yourself into tearing up the messengers to push all that aside, if only for a little bit. I get that."

"It was doing good for good people. But that's not a purpose."

"It's purpose enough for me. But I'm just a thief, not a princess."

"I'm not a princess anymore. And you're not a thief."

"But you can be a princess again. If you want it. Maybe not the Hurricane Princess, but there are worse things to be than ordinary, everyday royalty. I understand there are fewer decapitations if you don't stand out."

"You know nothing about how royalty works, do you?"

"No, and I don't care. And as for thieving, I haven't entirely left that behind. Adventuring calls for it more often than I expected."

"Do you think I'm playing at adventurer? Waiting to go back to my palace?"

"Nope. I've seen you bleed, Princess. Seen your team members drag you out of the fight for refusing to leave people behind. Even if you had to prove anything to me, which you don't, you'd have proven yourself just fine."

"Then what are you saying?"

"I don't know. I'm just talking. It's not for me to tell you how to live your life. I guess, if I'm saying anything, it's that good work for good people isn't so bad. While you're waiting for purpose to come along, you can spend your life staring out at the dark, or you can spend it doing some good."

"The messengers are all dead."

Sophie let out a chuckle.

"There's plenty more where they came from. And if you're tired of dealing with messengers, there's always good work to be done somewhere. I even know some good people, if you're looking."

72

VACATION DAYS

In a section of central Australia, the landscape was flat and dry, the red dirt occasionally marked by scraggly yellow grass. There had been a town there once; a pit stop between nowhere and nowhere else. The last few residents had been evacuated when the monster surges hit and no one had bothered coming back.

Jason and Farrah had chosen the town because there was nothing worth coming back for. The buildings were falling apart, leaning like old men under the punishing sun. There had been an old footy oval that hadn't seen a game in forty years. Grass had long given way to dirt and gravel, only the old bar seeing use in the town's last days. They built a circle of standing stones, like a rune-carved Stonehenge, on the flat ground of the oval. Not long after, they vanished into it and no one on Earth had seen them since.

The pair had left a mysterious artefact behind in a world ramping into a magical arms race. The magical factions, governments and even corporations rushing to get in on the new world of magic all rushed to investigate. The Australian government made the most of it, extracting favours and contracts from every interested party in return for access. What was left of the old town was knocked down, the buildings not worth using. In their place, caravans, motor homes and prefab constructions popped up overnight.

That first investigation was wiped out by a wave of magic that gushed out from the circle. What little remained of the town was wiped away, along with everything that replaced it, barring Jason and Farrah's stone circle. Even many of the people had vanished, presumed dead. All that remained was a ring of standing stones in a circle of red earth, scoured flat.

In the wake of that event, efforts to study the stone megaliths were both better funded and more cautious. A ring of buildings was constructed around the standing stones. These were proper facilities, not a hurried research camp. The Australian government's presence was obvious, along with the magical factions, the UN, the US, and China. A few corporations had paid through the nose to secure a position, looking to exploit the new reality of a magical Earth. There was little cooperation, only sharing resources as was strictly necessary.

In the middle of the night, two low-level workers were in a monitoring station belonging to the Australian government. Each screen was fed by an extremely expensive camera, zoomed in on the stone circle, including a satellite shot and several covering light spectrums outside of the normal human range. The camera feeds were live, but the shift between day and night was the only change they had ever shown since their installation. Even the weather stayed the same. The only season was the dry, endless summer.

Lenora Coleman had been excited to join the program right out of university, but a year in that room siphoned any of that excitement out of her. Even in the middle of the night, sweat dripped off her as a standing fan ineffectually pushed around the hot air. She had her feet up on a desk as she read yet another book about pregnant werewolf men. Her supervisor, Barry, was far from criticising her inattention as he played a game on his tablet.

Lenora got up and grabbed a can of soft drink from the fridge.

"Want one, Boss?" she asked, holding it up for Barry to see.

"Any sugar-free ones left?" he asked, looking up from his game.

Lenora bent over and peered into the fridge, digging one out from the back.

"You're in luck," she said and wandered over to hand him the drink. She looked down at the game on his tablet.

"*Vampire Survivors*? Isn't that in bad taste when there's an actual vampire war going on?"

"It's a video game, Nora. That doesn't have any vampires in it, by the way."

"It's got 'vampire' in the name."

"Maybe they already survived the vampires, I don't know. I didn't make the—"

Both snapped their heads to stare at the monitors as multiple alarms rang out. Alarms they hadn't heard since their initial training for the monitoring station. An alert for motion on the cameras was paired with one from the system that monitored the magical grid, restricted to local events. In the year they had been there, no monster, essence, or awakening stone had manifested in the area, despite the high regional magic.

Lenora and Barry both stared at the monitors. There was a huge, vaguely sphere-shaped zone of rainbow energy floating over the stone circle. It lit up the night with kaleidoscopic brightness, strong enough to shine rainbow light through their window, kilometres away from the site.

"It's throwing off a lot of heat," Lenora said, glancing at the thermal monitor. "Around eighty degrees Celsius. I don't suppose this is just a normal magic manifestation?"

Barry tore his eyes from the monitor bank and moved to the systems panel for the grid monitor.

"The grid is registering this as an anomalous category-four incursion," he said.

"Gold rank," Lenora corrected. "We call it gold rank now."

"Tell that to whoever updates the software; this says category four."

"Whatever it's called, how boned are we?" Lenora asked.

"It just says anomalous."

"You used to monitor the grid for the Network, right?"

"Yeah, but the grid isn't equipped for much more than pointing at magical stuff. My job was to make a phone call when it did, and that's as far as it went. Speaking of which, check that the messages were sent."

Lenora moved to a systems panel and looked it over.

"The automated notifications have all gone out correctly," she said. "We shouldn't have to do anything, right? This is all above our head."

"It might be worth making a call," Barry said. "If the minister doesn't hear about this promptly, I don't want us to be the people everyone between us and him takes his displeasure out on."

"Good idea," Lenora said.

Barry moved to the landline on the wall and hit one of the speed dial buttons.

"Put me through to the office of the Minister for Supernatural Affairs," he said. "Me? This is Barry Sinise at the monitoring station for the Asano Circle. No, *Barry* Sinise. No, there isn't any bloody relation. Just put me through!"

"Uh, Boss?"

Something in Lenora's uncertain tone grabbed Barry's attention. He turned to look at her, noting that rainbow light was no longer coming through the windows. He looked at the monitor bank where she was pointing.

"Am I imagining things," Lenora asked, "or is that a host of angels?"

No one needed to sleep during the battle in Jason's soul, but the rules included three mandatory breaks per day. No violence was possible during these breaks, but there was always a food cart waiting by the side of the road, along with enchanted training weights tailored to a silver-ranker. These went ignored by most of the great astral beings. The exception was the Celestial Book, who merrily plundered each new food cart.

None of the great astral beings had proven interested in speaking with Jason during the breaks, which suited him just fine. He used the time to meditate or work out his body, creating an optimal balance for advancement. While he did, the cosmic entities stood around awkwardly, including the World-Phoenix and her monster army.

It was more than a month before any of them broke the unofficial embargo on speaking with Jason. He was floating just over the ground, meditating cross-legged when he opened his eyes to look at the Builder standing in front of him.

"You have provided me with a better vessel than I have chosen for myself in our previous encounters," the Builder said.

"That wasn't hard. You were scraping the bottom of the barrel with Thadwick."

"I thought that we should talk, now that the others cannot stop us."

"And how would they stop us?"

"When the other great astral beings ascended me to their ranks, they took precautions to control me. When they bestowed upon me the sanctioned authority of original Builder, they set conditions on that authority."

"What kind of conditions?"

"They have the power to revert my mind to the state it was in during my last moments as a messenger. I keep my memories, but my personality reverts."

"Weren't you sixteen years old then?"

"Yes. Brash, impetuous, foolish. Arrogant to an unrivalled degree. I was a prodigy on a level previously unseen amongst my kind. Given the nature of messengers, you can imagine what this did to my judgement. You do not have to, I suppose."

"I do not."

"I have, over time, learned to maintain the wisdom of years instead of needing to rebuild it each time. Even so, they can still revert my mind for a time."

"Can great astral beings even have personalities when they aren't inhabiting a normal vessel?"

"Not as such. To have one imposed is a highly unnatural state."

"That explains a lot of the behaviour I've seen from you. Why would they do that?"

"I know now that their intention was always to restore my predecessor at some stage, shifting the authority given to me back to him. They never truly considered me one of them. That is why I am building my own universe. Not from a seed but something different, belonging to only me."

"By pillaging worlds. Stealing astral spaces."

"Yes. It is so that when the others finally move against me, I am left with an option beyond a fight I cannot win. The universe I am building will be my astral kingdom."

"You're saying that you've been pillaging worlds for billions of years so you can become an astral king?"

"The greatest of astral kings, with a kingdom unrivalled in the cosmos."

"Unrivalled in the cosmos, huh? Couldn't you just become a regular astral king? The kind that doesn't need to kill who knows how many people in the process? Billions at this stage? Trillions?"

"A necessary price. How could you expect being a normal astral king to be enough when I have forged universes? Such a thing is beneath me."

"Well, congratulations," Jason said. "I've officially met a worse person than Thadwick Mercer, so it makes sense that you and he were the same person for a while. Why are you here, fighting to restore the throne? What's in it for you?"

"The great astral beings could only do what they have done to me because they have become unbound from their core purposes. If the throne is restored, they will be more restricted in their actions against me."

"Yeah, that figures. I'll say this for you: you've definitely restored my faith in your being an evil, selfish piece of crap. I'm going to go get a hot dog."

———

Boris did not like the way he was returning to Earth. Leaving had been easy enough. Earth magic and technology had been easily circumvented when he was on the Earth side and leaving alone. Returning, though, he had no access to the surveillance infrastructure watching the circle. Even if he did, there was no hiding the magical signature of messengers arriving by the hundreds. The only way he could arrive was in spectacular fashion.

Most of the hundreds of messengers were only months old, liberated from the transformation zone. They appeared in the air over the stone circle, along with two giant brown eggs. Those eggs dissolved almost immediately, dropping their contents to the ground. Rufus Remore recovered quickly and used his aura to float to the ground. It was a pale echo of what a messenger aura could do, but as a silver-ranker, he could levitate himself slowly. It was enough to at least not fall on his face. Taika Williams fell on his face, hitting the ground like a boulder.

"That legit sucked, bro," he mumbled into the dirt.

Boris didn't bother to watch Remore moving to check on his friend. Instead, he extended his senses over the gathered human monitoring stations. There were some familiar auras in the Cabal section, currently being very surprised.

———

"No, Minister, the monitors are accurate," Barry said into the phone. "There is what appears to be an army of angels out there. As of yet, no one has—"

The door slammed open as a portly man in a moderately well-fitting suit burst into the room.

"Give me that phone!" He marched over to snatch it from Barry. "Minister," he said into the phone. "This is Gordon Truffett. I'm onsite and taking command of operations."

Barry shrugged and moved to where Lenora was working at a computer.

"Anyone muster up the balls to go over there yet?" he asked.

"Not yet, although I'm seeing a lot of activity on the Cabal side. That makes sense with what facial recognition turned up."

"We got hits?"

"Two," Lenora said. "Each promising to be its own special can of worms. One is Boris Ketland. Our database lists him as a Cabal executive, but a human, not a ten-foot-tall angel."

"It's not that shocking. Since when has any human member of the Cabal turned out to be an actual human?"

"Never. The next hit is on one of the two humans. Or the two that look human, anyway."

"The ones that fell out of those egg things?"

"Yeah. The system pegs the big Māori as Taika Williams. Member of Clan Asano—the Australian Clan Asano—and known associate of Jason Asano. Also, one of the people killed when the circle sent out that magic surge that got us all stationed here."

"He survived the magic wave?"

"Looks like it. Assuming that's actually him, he'll be the first survivor, right?"

"Yeah," Barry said as he turned to watch Truffett talking rapidly into the phone. "I'm glad this isn't my job to sort out. I wonder if they'll let me take my vacation days."

73

I WOULD LIKE TO BUY A MEAT PIE

THE TWO-KILOMETRE STRETCH BETWEEN THE RING OF STANDING STONES and the surrounding facilities was a flat expanse of magic-blasted ground. There was no trace of the town that had once occupied the space, only red, barren dirt.

The standing stones had been inert since the blast that had wiped out the town a year earlier, until the arrival of Rufus, Taika and an army of messengers. The facilities were abuzz with activity as the various groups watching the circle were deciding on a course of action. The Cabal was the first to act, sending out one man in a four-wheel-drive. The vehicle was caked in red dust and looked forty years old, but solid, like it would still be running in another forty.

Boris and the messengers had been floating in the air since their arrival. Rufus and Taika had dropped to the ground with varying levels of grace. The pair wandered out of the standing stones to meet the vehicle while Boris floated down to join them.

"This could be complicated, bro," Taika said to Boris. "I think us showing up will be a big deal."

"I am unfortunately inclined to agree," Boris said. "I know the man approaching. I will attempt to simplify our situation in the short term, although we'll all have to face the ramifications in time."

"Simplify how?" Rufus asked.

"Our first move needs to be reaching Jason's territory. The major complication with that is his territory is on the other side of the planet."

"I thought you said we were arriving in Jason's homeland," Rufus said.

"This is Jason's homeland," Boris said. "But, in his absence, politics have left it a less than welcoming place for him. Or, by association, us."

"Will they know we're related to him?" Rufus asked.

"Magic is new to this world," Boris said. "When major magical events happen, Jason Asano's involvement will always be in the top three guesses. You and I, Mr Remore, just emerged from Jason's big magic circle with Jason's big brown friend. There is little point trying to hide the connection."

"I'm not sure I can be called big around a bunch of nine-foot angels," Taika said.

The car pulled up and the driver got out. He was silver rank and looked human, but his aura was not that of an essence-user. He was large, not just tall but muscular, with a loose tan shirt, khaki shorts and brown work boots. He had a wide-brimmed hat and a leathery tan that suggested a lot of time in the sun.

"Boris Ketland, you sneaky bugger," he called in a thick Australian accent. "I don't know if anyone won the pool on you. A bloody angel? Who'd guess that, you skirt-chasing sleazebag?"

Boris chuckled, holding out his hand for the man to shake.

"It's good to see you, Bruce. I'm hoping your presence here can smooth things out."

"I wouldn't go pinning your hopes on smooth, mate. You've right kicked the hornet's nest. Showing up with these two blokes and a divine host at your back? Some bloody powerful people just got woken up."

Boris nodded.

"I guessed as much. Anyway, Bruce Montgomery, allow me to introduce Taika Williams and Rufus Remore. Taika, I'm sure you know of already. Rufus has yet to learn any Earth languages."

"Yeah, facial recognition pegged Taika the moment he brushed the dirt off his face. Had bit of a rough landing, mate?"

"The trip was a bit rough," Taika said as he shook Bruce's hand. "What was that about a pool?"

Bruce laughed.

"In the Cabal," he said, "none of the human members ever turn out to be human. There's always a pool on anyone who hasn't shown their true colours."

"It's generally not polite to ask," Boris said, "but Bruce here is an ogre. Or so he says."

"Oh, don't you bloody start," Bruce said.

"I think he rigged the pool," Boris said. "I think he's not an ogre but three humans in a big coat."

"Where would I even get a twelve-foot coat?" Bruce asked. "And you've seen me in my real form. You bought me those stretchy purple pants, you cheeky sod."

Boris let out a chuckle.

"Can you get us to Europe, Bruce?" he asked. "Or keep everyone off us until we get there?"

"Europe's tricky, mate. All you'll find there are vampires and Asanos, and I assume you're not looking for vampires. People want to ask you all some fairly pointed questions, and I don't know they'll let you hit Asano territory before answering them."

"Given the power at my command," Boris said, "they'll have to throw a lot at us if they want to force the issue. My gold-rankers can each handle any two of the ones they have here. And I can handle a lot more than two."

"And you'll fight if it comes to that?" Bruce asked.

"We are entirely capable of fighting our way across the planet," Boris said. "It would, however, be something of a pain. That being said, I think my non-winged companions have had enough of uncomfortable rides. I imagine they would prefer an aeroplane over being carried halfway around the Earth like a mouse in an eagle's claws."

"Well," Bruce said, "you're at least five steps above me in the Cabal hierarchy, so if you say we're telling everyone else to back off, I guess that's what we're doing. I don't think they'll push, but if you had some kind of bone we could throw the other factions, that would go a long way."

"Promise them spirit coin farming techniques. That will be valuable now the magic levels on Earth are rising."

Bruce let out a low whistle.

"Yeah, that'll do it. Everyone's been trying it, but only the Yanks have had any success."

"Meaning that everyone but the US is going to be happy with us, and the Americans will hate us."

"Yep. You've never done things by halves, have you, Boris? Even before you showed up with an army of angels."

"We're not actually angels," Boris explained. "We're called messengers."

"Doesn't 'angel' mean messenger in Greek or Latin or some such?"

"Close enough, but we're definitely not the messengers of God, Bruce."

"Who are you the messengers of, then?"

"The will of the cosmos," Boris said. "It's a load of crap. Religion mixed up with racial supremacy."

"So... pretty much angels, then."

Boris let out a groan.

"It's definitely what they're going to call us, isn't it?"

"Yep," Bruce said. "Magic has made things wonky enough when it comes to religion. You lot turning up might start a holy war or three."

Boris let out a weary sigh, then set his shoulders with determination.

"That's tomorrow's problem," he said. "Right now, the priority is getting our travelling companions to safety. I don't want any of the silver-rankers getting caught up if some golds decide to attack us. Jason Asano will not be happy if anything happens to them, and he is not a man to cross, regardless of how much power you have."

"Is he showing up too?" Bruce asked.

"Not anytime soon," Boris said.

"He and the grim reaper are fighting a giant space bird," Taika said. "It's going to take a while."

"What?" Bruce asked.

"I'll tell you later," Boris said. "Right now, we need to get to somewhere secure. One of Jason Asano's domains will do for a start and I'd appreciate it if we got moving before the other factions try something foolish."

"Yeah, fair enough," Bruce said. "It'll take me a bit to sort out the plane, but I think we can fit you all in the Cabal cafeteria."

"That's a big cafeteria, bro. Let's go; I haven't had a dagwood dog in a year."

"You actually eat those things?" Boris asked.

"Yeah, bro. You've got to have a daggy every now and again. Wouldn't mind a couple of dim sims either."

The Cabal managed—more or less legitimately—to secure two massive passenger jets. While doing so, they also negotiated to have the other factions to leave the group alone, at least for the moment. The negotiations went smoothly for the most part, aside from one small incident.

A gold-ranker from the United States arrived via portal and was arrogant for exactly as long as it took him to sense Boris' aura. Seeing a gold-ranker scamper away with his tail between his legs successfully quieted the others, although Boris knew it would lead to problems down the line. If he and his people were seen as a threat, the world powers would eventually attempt to eliminate them.

For now, however, they were allowed to go on their way. The silver-rank messengers shrank down to fit human-sized plane seats while Boris and the other gold-rankers flew alongside as escorts. The planes landed at a joint operations military base outside of Nitra, Slovakia.

The region was one of the few footholds of non-vampire power in Europe, due to the presence of Jason's domain. As with the domain in France, the one in Slovakia was the centre of a zone high in magic. This affected the sunlight, making it more dangerous to vampires.

The military base featured actual cooperation between the various magical factions and government allies. In most places, that was political fiction, but the people fighting the war understood that the vampires were the real enemy. The base abutted Jason's domain, even partly existing within it. The boundary was marked by numerous warning signs and an actual black and yellow line painted onto the concrete.

Rufus and Taika disembarked the planes first, joined by Boris and the other gold-rankers hovering just over the ground. They were met at the painted boundary line by two people. One was a bronze-rank woman with Eastern European features and a prim business suit. The other was a middle-aged Japanese man with dark green fatigues and a sword at his hip. He was silver rank and, like the woman, had an aura marked by monster core use.

"Keti," Taika greeted. "What are you doing here?"

"My Network branch in Australia was broken up," Ketevan Arziani said. "I was offered a position assisting the Asano clan matriarch."

"Yumi hired you?" Taika asked. "She always was smart."

"Let's go see her, then," Ketevan said. "She's waiting for you."

Taika shook hands with the Japanese man before they set out.

"Good to see you, Shiro."

"And you," Shiro Asano said. "You got strong."

Taika grinned.

"Bro, you have no idea."

Boris, Rufus and Taika sat across from Yumi Asano, Jason's paternal grandmother. She had come to magic late in life, but her flesh-warping powers had restored her youth, giving her the same mid-twenties appearance as the people sitting across from her. She was flanked on one side by her son, Hiro, who looked twice as old as his mother. On the other side was Ketevan. Yumi turned her gaze to Rufus.

"I recognise you from my grandson's recordings, Mr Remore. Before we begin, let me thank you for being a teacher and a friend to him when he was in desperate need of both. I'm told that you can understand me, even without speaking my language."

"I am use translation magic," Rufus said. "It is wobble when not soul."

"Translation magic that's externally applied instead of an inherent power isn't excellent, I'm afraid," Boris said. "He'll grasp the basics, but it would be best to keep our speech simple so he can follow effectively."

"I am thank nice for your mouth noise," Rufus said.

"He'll pick up the languages here very quickly," Boris assured Yumi.

"I have no doubt," Yumi said. "Our silver-rankers have excellent memories, so I've had them all learning multiple languages. It's been very useful. Now, tell me about my grandson."

"He gave me a recording," Taika said. "A bunch of them, actually, but this one is for you."

He took a recording crystal from the dimensional pouch at his waist.

"Do you have a projector?" he asked.

Yumi nodded at Ketevan, who got up and went to a panel on the conference room's wall. Cloud stuff rose from the table and formed a small recording crystal projector.

"This is cloud palace?" Rufus asked.

"Jason's domains have inherited many properties from his cloud palace," Boris said. "A welcome side effect of binding the palace more closely to his soul until it became a palace itself."

"You seem to know a lot about Jason," Taika said, giving Boris a suspicious look.

"I'm part of a magical faction on Earth," Boris told him. "Finding out about Jason Asano is at the top of all our to-do lists. I just happen to be better at it than everyone else."

Taika's narrowed eyes lingered on Boris for a moment before he turned back to the task at hand. He placed the crystal in the projector and a recording of a haggard Jason shimmered into being above the table. He was on the balcony of a tree house in a cloud chair, a forest panorama spanning out behind him.

"Hello, Grandmother," he said. "I know you won't let anyone do anything until you've wrung answers to all your questions out of them, so let me tell you what I've been up to since we last met."

In a luxurious guest suite, Rufus listened to an oddly non-magical recording device.

"Hello," a woman's voice came from the device. "I would like to buy a meat pie."

"Hello," Rufus repeated. "I would like to buy a meat pie."

As the recording repeated the sentence, Rufus plucked a lolly from a huge bag of them and popped it into his mouth. He was sitting on the floor in front of a coffee table scattered with language-learning materials and a five-kilo sack of mixed lollies.

"I would like to buy a meat pie," he mumbled while chewing on the sugary goodness.

There was a knock on the door and Rufus pressed on the tablet to make it stop. Deciding he'd probably got it right, he went to the door and opened it. On the other side was a bronze-rank woman and Rufus saw a resemblance with Jason.

"Hello, Mr Remore. I recognise you from my brother's recordings. I'm Erika Asano."

"Hello," the recording behind him said. "I would like to buy a meat pie."

Erika raised her eyebrows as Rufus turned to scowl at the tablet.

"Help?" he asked her.

He moved out of the doorway and she stepped through. She walked over to the coffee table and tapped the tablet to pause the language program.

"Thank you," Rufus said and waved her into an armchair while he took another.

Like all the buildings in Jason's domain, this one was comprised of cloud material masquerading as other things. The furniture didn't hide it very well, having the familiar impossible plushness.

"How is my brother, Mr Remore?"

"Call me Rufus."

"Alright, Rufus. How is my brother?"

"Good," Rufus said. "Was bad. Very bad. Got help."

"I understand your mother is his therapist?"

Rufus creased his brow, not understanding. "There-a-pissed?"

Erika thought it over a moment.

"Mind healer," she said.

Realisation dawned on Rufus' face. He nodded.

"Jason is fragile," he said, tapping his temple. "Up here. Comes back stronger, though. Different, but stronger."

"Yes, he does," Erika said. "But he's alright now? I'm told he's off fighting some war with the Grim Reaper?"

"With the Reaper, yes. Strange things. Jason things. We all would like to help, but sometimes Jason things. Not easy to accept."

"No," Erika agreed. "Not easy to accept. I'm also told that you are here to what? Train my daughter?"

"Yes," Rufus said. "Learn language first."

"You've come a long way for someone who didn't speak any English two weeks ago."

"Thank you."

"That doesn't mean I'm going to let you take over my daughter's education. Why should I even consider doing that?"

"My family runs a school."

"A school for warriors. I don't want my daughter to be a warrior."

"Not warriors. Teach to fight, yes, but also teach to not fight. Your child will have power. Those with power can choose peace, but peace not always choose them. Will not train warrior, but will teach. Will make ready."

"Ready for what?"

"For everything."

Jason's domain in France covered most of what had once been the city of Saint-Etienne. Each of the two domains contained an astral space, and each astral space contained a wondrous magical city. Like the new bright-heart city, these had far more space than population to fill them.

After using the portal linking the Slovakian domain to the French, Rufus and Taika took a second portal into the French astral space. In the populated part of the city, Rufus felt oddly at ease. Most of the population were refugees from around the world who had been affected by transformation spaces. No longer human, they were a multiplicity of other species that reminded Rufus of home.

They took a small dirigible from the massive docking tower the portal left them in, the airship flying itself into the city. It landed atop the arena-sized main training facility for the Asano clan.

"I'm a little nervous," Rufus admitted. "I'm not sure my English is good enough."

"Bro, let me take you to a pub back in Australia. Then you'll see your English is just fine."

Taika led them into the building and down several sets of stairs. They went into a gymnasium-sized room with all manner of exercise equipment set out. It ranged from mundane gymnastic setups like parallel bars to obviously magical devices with floating components.

There was one occupant in the room who dismounted from the uneven bars at their entry, making a smooth landing. She was in her early teens, wearing tracksuit pants and a faded Airwolf t-shirt. She jogged up to them and hugged Taika.

"This is him?" Emi asked, looking Rufus over.

"This is him," Taika said.

Emi continued to look Rufus up and down, finally nodding as she made some kind of internal decision.

"I think you looked better bald," she told him.

74

AN EMPTY CHAIR

THE ASANO CLAN HELD TWO ASTRAL SPACES, CONSISTING OF CITIES CUT off from the surrounding wilderness by massive defensive walls. The cities were mostly empty, as they could hold far more people than the population living there. To avoid them feeling like ghost towns, specific sections were regulated by the Asano clan, with shops, residences and other facilities all assigned to the occupants and proprietors, free of cost.

That was especially important when the residents were all transplanted from elsewhere. The Asano clan was mostly Jason's extended family, brought over from Australia. Their association with him not only disrupted their lives but put them in danger from those who would exploit them. Most of the residents were refugees from transformation zones around the world. Magically removed from the human race, they had to deal with not just a new place, but new selves.

There were a few residents who didn't fit into those groups, with a few other families brought into the Asano clan. Like Jason's family, their connection to him made them targets for exploitation and harm. This included the families of those who had fallen into Jason's orbit, such as Greg and Asya. His dead friend and lover were both examples of the dangers that came with being involved with Jason.

There was also Chloe Baudrillard, the epidemiologist Jason befriended, along with her family. As they were French, they had been displaced by the vampire occupation. Most of the European civilians had been evacuated to other continents, but some had been taken in by the Asano clan, mostly people close to the two spirit domains in Nitra and Saint-Étienne.

Jason had a habit of triggering internal strife in ancient Japanese families; ousted leadership and their loyalists had joined the clan. This included members of the Japanese Asano clan and the Tiwari clan. The old leaders of both had helped Jason, and both had paid for it by being forced out of their own families. Yumi Asano had been sure to repay that aid as best she could, offering homes and safety.

One of the advantages of only opening parts of the city was that space was not at a premium. There was no need for dense housing and they had chosen open, highly walkable parts of the city. The least congested residential section was the Park District, which was a combination of low-density housing and botanical garden. Within that district was a secluded grove, ringed by flowering hedges and bisected by a stream running through it.

In that grove was a very small cottage belonging to a very large woman. Raina Williams was far from her native New Zealand. Five months after Rufus arrived on Earth, he was one of several people seated at the picnic table outside of Raina's house.

"You eat up now," Raina said as she spooned another heap of tartiflette onto Rufus' plate.

"Mrs Williams, I couldn't," Rufus said.

"That's what your mouth says," she told him. "The way you're eyeing that plate says something different."

"Maybe just a little more," he said.

"Boy, don't come here telling me 'a little.' I do not know what they're feeding you in that other universe, but my Taika got skinny as a rake over there and you're even worse."

"Skinny?" Hiro Asano said. "I know magic turned a lot of fat into muscle, but he's still as wide and brown as a station wagon from the eighties."

Hiro reached for the dish of garlic bread and got a rap on the knuckles for his trouble.

"Garlic bread is for polite young men," Mrs Williams scolded.

"I'm fifty-eight," Hiro complained. "I *can't* be a young man."

"Then you're old enough to know better," Mrs Williams said, earning a helpless look from Hiro that made Emi giggle.

"You shouldn't talk back, Boss," Taika warned Hiro. "Not if you want to keep eating."

It had been several years since Taika had worked for Hiro in their criminal days, but some things just stuck.

"I really should go," Rufus said, but made no move to do so as he continued demolishing the food on his plate.

"You've done really good work with the refugees, Rufus," Hiro said. "We were having a lot of trouble with all these traumatised people who suddenly found themselves not human anymore. As someone who grew up in and around people who weren't human, you've been a settling presence."

"I haven't done anything special," Rufus said. "It's just joining in group therapy sessions and telling people about home."

"Well, it's very nice," Raina said. "It's starting to feel like a real community around here. I scooter into the community centre a few times a week."

"You have a mobility scooter?" Hiro asked. "Does it do alright without a sealed road?"

"Mobility scooter nothing," Taika said. "She has a stand-up scooter. Some carbon-fibre monstrosity that reaches highway speeds. It isn't safe."

"Oh, you know I don't run it that fast," Raina said. "I just need something with the power to transport a full-figured lady. And I always wear my safety gear."

"We're inside a magic realm," Taika said, "in a continent occupied by vampires. Where did you even find motorcycle pants in your size?"

"Good news, everyone," Raina said. "It looks like there's extra dessert to go around because my son doesn't want any."

"What? Mum, no…"

———

Hiro took Emi home after lunch while Rufus and Taika headed for the sprawling community centre complex. It included the medical and food distribution centres along with other key facilities. The heart of the place was a large recreational lounge that served as a gathering place and central hub for the rest of the complex. It offered easy access to everything from the medical centre to child-friendly play areas and a large bar.

There was a cheerful mood when Rufus and Taika arrived in the central lounge. A gathering of people was celebrating the first child conceived amongst the transformed. Rufus smiled and laughed alongside everyone else until he heard the happy couple mention the name of their doctor. Not being the centre of attention, it was easy enough for Rufus to slip away.

Moments later, he was storming through the nearby medical centre. He found the office door marked 'Dr Velius' and barged in without knocking. The doctor looked up from the laptop on his desk.

"Something I can help you with, Mr Remore?"

"It is you," Rufus said. "Why are you here? *How* are you here?"

"I'm the prime vessel of the Reaper, Mr Remore; I'm very well-resourced."

Velius brought out what looked like a car fob and pressed the button on it. The office door swung closed and a brief shimmer indicated a privacy screen settling around them.

"What are your intentions?" Rufus asked.

"Benign, I can assure you," Velius said. "While I could fend off the defences of Jason Asano's territory if I were hostile, doing so long-term would be quite the chore. Especially in this astral space where his power is stronger."

"What are you doing here?" Rufus demanded.

"Helping, Mr Remore."

"Why?"

"You are aware that what has befallen this world stems from how the original Builder created this world and yours?"

"I am."

"I won't go into the full context, but that was an unfortunate consequence of a decision the great astral beings made long ago. One that your friend Jason is currently fighting to undo. As for you and me, we find ourselves surrounded by people who've had their lives, and even their very bodies, transformed into something they no longer recognise."

"Why do you care?"

"That, Mr Remore, is rather offensive. I may be immortal and my position rather lofty, but I'm still a person. The concept of compassion is not alien to me."

Rufus frowned. He took a deep breath and slowly let it out. His body lost its tenseness, the anger in his expression falling away.

"You're right," he said. "That was offensive and I apologise. Let me ask the question I should have: Why would the Reaper have someone as important as you here, doing this?"

"Normally, a disaster like this is where the local gods start earning all that prayer and devotion, working to rectify things. Unfortunately, it will be centuries before this world has enough magic for gods to start manifesting."

Velius smiled.

"You presumably dashed in here after recognising my name," he said. "Presumably, Asano told you about my recruiting him to his current task."

"Yes. And one look at that aura told me I was right. You tailored your aura mask so the locals wouldn't see through it, but someone like me would."

"Yes. There are things that need to be done here, but the people of this world aren't ready for some of the higher truths behind them. Like the first servant of the grim reaper being their obstetrician. So, hopefully, you and I are going to quietly help certain things along."

"You still haven't told me why. You might be at the very boundary of mortality, but you're still one of us. I can understand you wanting to act out of sympathy for these people. Why is the Reaper letting you?"

"You're aware, obviously, that I recruited Jason Asano for his current task. Do you know what he asked for in return?"

"That's why you're here? Jason asked you to help these people?"

"No," Velius said. "Your friend didn't ask for anything at all. It never even occurred to him. Once he understood that it needed to be done, he just decided to do it. In light of this, it was decided that a reward was warranted, asked for or not. The great astral beings decided to step in where the gods normally would."

"And they sent you? To do what?"

"Not just me. We're here to discreetly help things along. I know from personal experience that if you fail to effectively set things in place in your home world, things can get messy. Being forced into extreme choices early can have severe repercussions in just a few centuries, let alone millennia. We're here to smooth out the process of Asano's family establishing themselves as a power on this world."

"By being a fertility healer?"

"By bending a few rules before your friend stops that from being possible anymore. That's what he's doing, ultimately: putting the old rules back in place that stops the great astral beings from getting creative in their roles."

"What kind of rules are you looking to bend?"

"Nothing overt. Not unless you know what you're looking at, anyway.

But the people here will find a lot of luck coming their way for a few years."

"Alright," Rufus said. "Assuming I believe all that, why you? What can the Reaper do for these people?"

"As you've noted, I've taken on the role of a fertility doctor," Velius said. "The Asano clan matriarch went to some lengths to recruit an expert medical team. The changes people go through as they rank up are one thing, but the bulk of the population here has non-human physiology. I arranged credentials for my assumed identity so that I would be accepted."

"How are made-up credentials going to help anyone? And what does that have to do with the Reaper?"

"Through the Reaper, Mr Remore, I have access to the medical expertise of everyone who has ever died in any universe. Ever. My credentials are so profoundly understated that I'll probably advance this planet's medical knowledge a century or more by accident."

"That's why you're here? Because you have that knowledge?"

"That's part of it. The more specific reason is that the first generation born to the transformed people here will have an incredible impact on them and this planet as a whole. They and their children will face profound challenges if they ever seek to be anything more than a strange little collective, hiding in an astral space. If they are going to do anything other than die out within a few generations, they need to be remarkable."

"And you intend to make them remarkable?"

"I'm rather hoping you will, Mr Remore. My part is to give them the potential you will help them live up to."

"And how are you going to give them this potential?"

"By providing something that this new generation could desperately use: old souls."

When Gary became a demigod, he was a vision of physical might, wreathed in divine power. Almost a year later, the divine power was wrapped around a haggard, skeletal figure that hobbled about when not carried in a floating cloud chair. The golden light of Hero's power danced around and through him, his body barely able to contain it.

"It's time," he told his parents, his once-booming voice a thin echo.

His parents nodded, accepting. They had watched their son wither away, knowing that although he said it was time, it was well past time. Jason had set his realm such that neither pain nor death could affect Gary's body. But there was no stopping pain that went soul deep. It had gotten too hard for him to hide some time ago, but he had held on. Only when his parents were eager to see him released from it, rather than continue their time with him, did he finally make the choice to let go.

Gary had made the rest of his goodbyes long ago, and several times over. His friends had come by time and again, chain-portalling across the world to see him. One such visit had come from Gwydion Remore, bringing bittersweet news.

"Hero has decided to sanction himself," Gwydion told Gary. "It's something that he has been considering for longer than any of us have been alive, but he's finally going to do it."

"Isn't sanctioning dangerous?" Gary asked.

"Yeah," Gwydion said. "But he's not going to be as drastic as Purity. He wants to give himself another miracle option. Something less powerful than the Cup of Heroes, with less of a price. For millennia, our church has been collecting the relics of heroes who have drunk from the cup. The relics can only be used by the demigods to whom they belonged and they are all dead. That makes the relics nothing but a remembrance, despite their power. But Hero wants to make them usable again, if only for a short time. To let the stories of heroes past live on in heroes of the future."

"That's a nice sentiment," Gary said. "It would have been nice if he'd come up with that a year ago."

"You inspired him, in part. It's not a decision made for any one reason, but you are one of them. He tried to give you a path to survival but, right or wrong, you chose not to take it. And the cup will still be there when needed. It would have taken more than a relic for you to accomplish what had to be done."

Gary thought of that visit and every other he'd had over the last several months. He smiled through the now constant and severe pain—all worth it for the memories. With his parents beside him, he floated in his chair along the walkways and rope bridges of the tree city. It had been a fine place to spend his final days, but now those days were over. It was time to give the god back his power and find out what came next.

The portal leading out of the soul realm was in a central area at ground level, close to the research facilities being used by Carlos and Clive. Clive was off somewhere with the team, and Gary didn't disturb Carlos. He was an acquaintance and an ally, but not a friend. He did call in on Sophie's mother and Callum Morse. He was a friend and she had become one, albeit with a 'cool aunt' feel to the relationship. They both understood what Gary was about at a glance and did not keep him long.

Finally, Gary descended on an elevating platform made of wood and rope. At the bottom was a wide-open area, a grassy space between distant trees. The portal leading out of Jason's realm stood in the middle of it.

One of Jason's avatars waited where the rope elevator reached the ground. Most of the soul realm's avatars looked like Jason but were blank-faced automatons. They spoke in a monotone and had only the knowledge, skills and influence over the realm required for their assigned tasks. The avatar waiting for Gary was the only exception.

This avatar was the one with almost no knowledge or skills, to the point of being a little clumsy. What it did have was a subdued but recognisable facsimile of Jason's personality. It was still a little uncanny valley, but only unnerving instead of outright creepy. This made it much easier for the residents and visitors of the tree city to interact with. As this was its primary task, it had taken to calling itself 'the Concierge.'

"Is it time?" the Concierge asked.

"It is," Gary said.

At Gary's words, mist started rising from the ground. The space between them and the portal was soon engulfed in fog, obscuring their view.

"I thought you couldn't change things like this," Gary said to the Concierge.

"Yep," the Concierge said. "The boss set this up to trigger on the day you... he set it up for today."

The fog created a long, wide tunnel of cloud substance. It ended at a wall, around where Gary judged the portal to be, but it wasn't in sight. The walls became smooth, shifting from blank white to a swirl of colours. The colours swiftly resolved into moving images, each one a different scene featuring Gary.

"My true self can do many things in this place," the Concierge said. "Even some that are normally impossible, such as reading a mind. But if others let him, he can do that here. This hall is comprised entirely of memories from your friends and your family."

"Mum?" Gary asked. "Dad? You knew about this?"

"We didn't spend a lot of time with your friend Jason," Gary's mother said, "but he seemed like a sweet young man. We liked this idea very much."

"I'm not the person I look like," the Concierge said, "so I will not offer you an empty farewell in his stead. The best I can do is leave you be. This place belongs to you, for as long as you want to stay."

The Concierge stepped through the wall, briefly disturbing the image of Gary as a child, watching his father make soup. Gary looked around from his chair, his parents beside him. He saw himself hammering on steel, the orange glow of the forge casting his grin in a sinister light. There were dozens of little moments scattered across the walls of the long hallway.

He started telling the stories of each memory to his parents, or talking about memories they shared. The closest images mostly came from his parents, featuring Gary as a young and often difficult child.

As they slowly made their way forward, it moved on to Gary becoming an adventurer. Meeting Farrah and Rufus in the wild panic of a burning zombie town. The three of them running across a field as a flour silo exploded behind them. Making his way through a cultist blood chamber with a skinny, wild-eyed man.

"Gods," Gary said with a laugh. "I forgot how big his chin was back then."

All the way to the end, there were no images of Gary as a demigod or battling Undeath's avatar. Only a handful of the scenes showed combat or action at all. The hall was dominated by moments of friendship and camaraderie. Handing Jason the sword he had made for him. Grilling meat while surrounded by friends. Stealing food as a cub. He noticed, looking around, that a lot of them seemed to involve food.

The tunnel formed a rough timeline, but not a strict one, and the occasional memory would pop up way out of sequence. Gary and his parents watched little boy Gary's ill-fated attempt to pilfer his uncle's hammer, the tool larger than Gary at the time.

"Such a rascal," his mother said, almost managing to not have her voice break.

They made an extremely slow passage down the hall, barely moving forward before stopping again. They didn't count the hours as they watched memory after memory play out. Gary told the stories of friends made and good times shared. His parents pointed out that his recollections of childhood were never quite the way he remembered them.

By the time they finally reached the end, it felt like they had laughed and cried so much that there was no more of either left inside them. On the wall at the end of a hall was an image of Gary, Rufus and Farrah, lazing in the shade of a tree. There was no telling what they were chatting about from the silent image. Gary couldn't place the memory; it could have been any of a thousand days and he realised that was the point. There were too many good times to remember them all.

Gary sat and stared at the image for a long time. He watched himself and his friends talking, neither knowing nor caring what they were saying in the silent projection. What mattered was the happiness. The laughter. Just being together.

"I'm ready," he said.

"Good," Farrah's voice came through the wall. "I had to use ritual magic to keep all this warm without it going bad."

The image vanished and the cloud wall it was on dispersed, revealing Farrah waiting by a table full of food.

"Your timing is awful, by the way," she said. "I had an important test scheduled today, but instead, I had to come here and cook a last meal for…"

Farrah's voice broke, unable to maintain the jovial fiction. She rushed around the table and hugged Gary in his chair.

"I love you so much, you big, hairy bastard."

―――――

Gary emerged from the portal in his cloud seat, Farrah and his parents right behind. His parents each took one of his hands as the golden light around him drifted up and away. Rainbow smoke drifted up with it, leaving three people standing around an empty chair.

75

SUSPICIONS

"FORMATION INTERACTIVITY IS A FASCINATING MAGICAL SPECIALTY," THE projection of Clive said. "I very nearly pursued it myself, but there was very little material on the field where I was trained, and a surprising plethora on astral magic. Which may not be as much of a coincidence as I thought, I realised after talking to Boris. You may have met Boris by now, in which case you should try and get him to reveal some of his knowledge because—"

"Clive..." Farrah's voice came from out of shot.

"Sorry," Clive said. "Where were we? Right, formation interactivity. If you're looking to specialise in it, which I highly recommend, there are a variety of essence combinations that are appropriate, depending on what else you'll be getting up to. If you want to mix in some adventuring, you'll want something with some combat options, while—"

Emi shut off the projection as there was a knock on the door. She got up from her bedroom floor, picked up the projector and set it on her desk. When she opened the door, her father was outside.

"Rufus will be here in about half an hour," he said. "Make sure you're ready to go."

"I was ready an hour ago, Dad."

"Okay, Emi. What are you watching in there?"

"The magic instruction recordings Farrah sent me."

"Not the recording your uncle sent you?"

"No, Dad," she said with a scowl. "Now that I've finally picked my essences, I have so much to learn."

"You've made the final decision on your essences?"

"Yes."

"Again?"

"Shut up, Dad!"

He laughed, the grin slowly morphing to a look of concern.

"Your mother made me ask about the recording," he said. "But she's not wrong, sweetie. Watching it over and over won't make him come home any faster."

"I said I wasn't watching it!"

"Okay, okay," he said, holding up his hand in surrender. "Taika is taking you for training today. I'll call you down when he gets here."

Emi went back into her room, grabbed the projector and plonked onto the floor, setting the device in front of her. She reached to resume the playback, but her hand stopped halfway. After hesitating a moment, she took out the recording crystal and returned it to the carousel of them on her desk. She then took out the very first crystal, slotted it into the projector and tapped it to start. Jason's haggard face shimmered into being, with a forest panorama behind him.

"Hey, Moppet," he said wearily. "I'm sorry I'm not there to give you this in person, but the grim reaper has recruited me to fight a giant space bird. Like the spaceship in *Battle of the Planets,* kind of, but I'm going to turn it into a person. It's going to get real cranky when it figures out why."

The projection of Jason let out an evil chuckle that turned into a tired wheeze.

"I know I'm not looking my best right now, but I promise you I'm fine. It's just been a rough few months, and this body is…"

Jason shook his head.

"All you need to know is that I'm becoming immortal. Proper immortal, so literally nothing can take me out. The bad news is that this means I won't be coming back to see you as soon as I'd like. The good news is that I'm definitely coming back. No power in the universe can stop me, and I've basically checked at this point. Before that, though, I have to go through a whole transformation sequence. Not a magical girl one, although I can't rule out inappropriate nudity. I'm going to be kind of a god for that angel-type folk you've probably seen by now."

He groaned and rubbed his temples.

"I don't have a lot of time right now. But since we won't be seeing each other for a while, I'd like to spend some of it telling you all the crazy stuff that's happened since I last saw you. So, settle in and let me tell you what I did on my holidays."

As he rode in the zeppelin over the city, Rufus watched a handful of messengers flying about in the distance. It was night and their wings seemed especially good at catching the moonlight. Not good for stealth, he mused, but certainly pretty.

Almost all of the young messengers from the transformation zone had chosen to stay in Asano clan territory. They had been living with Jason's aura infusing the very land around them for most of their lives, and his spirit domains gave them a sense of continuity when faced with extreme change.

The locals had also taken some time to adapt. They had been through some profound changes in recent years, from monster surges to astral spaces to their home being surrounded by hostile vampires. Even so, having hundreds of angels as new neighbours was one of the more surprising quirks of Asano clan living.

Rufus moved to run his hands over his scalp—an old habit that was no longer possible. His once bald head now sported a neatly trimmed afro and he ran his hands along the side of it instead. It was nothing like the ridiculous hair his brother had been sporting the last time they met. That mess looked like a topiary jester's cap.

His mind dwelled on an upcoming meeting with Velius. Rufus hadn't spoken to the man in most of a year, since he informed Rufus of Gary's death. He had quietly investigated the man, though. In his identity as a fertility doctor, Velius was one of a slew of experts recruited by the clan to help the transformation zone refugees.

The experts were mostly experts in medicine and, as much as was possible on Earth, magic. Jason's spirit domain had filtered out those with ulterior motives, no few groups having attempted to slip in spies. Rufus' concerns about Velius were not that, the Reaper's servant far above such petty concerns. His fear was that Velius had an agenda beyond what he claimed.

From everything Rufus could find, Velius was earnest and diligent in his work. He was in a role normally carried out by the church of Fertility and he seemed to know all of their magic that didn't require divine influence. Rufus had been surprised that the prime vessel of a great astral being could spend so much time on Earth, the main source of his concerns about some greater motive. His worries had been allayed by, of all people, Jason's precocious niece.

Emi knew more about Jason's activities on Earth than anyone bar Jason himself. While Jason had omitted the more gruesome details, she had eagerly devoured knowledge about his adventures and especially the magic involved. This extended to Farrah and, while she was with them, Dawn.

The result of this was that Emi's overeager and meticulous interrogations had given her a better understanding of avatars than most. She knew tell-tale physiological differences between an avatar, an essence-user and a normal person. Anything from how often they blinked to how their skin reacted to sudden temperature changes could be an indicator.

Her assessments had all the precision of a polygraph machine—none whatsoever and any accuracy was basically luck. Nonetheless, as the princess of the Asano clan, she found herself ignored off to the side in rooms with many of the clan's most important people. When she found someone who kind of creeped her out and she couldn't pinpoint why, she knew what to look for.

At first, she quietly freaked out. She was fifteen years old, knew magic was real but not what the limits were, and had a list of people she suspected were secretly puppet people for some unknown force. In the absence of her uncle or Farrah, she was uncertain of who to take her suspicions to. At that stage, she had been unsure about Rufus, yet to build the connection she'd had with Farrah.

As for her family, she wasn't sure they would believe her. In the last few years, magic had turned out to be real, there had been a monster apocalypse and now they were living in a city made of clouds in France. Despite all that, her family were all too often stuck in what she thought of as 'Earth sensibilities.'

Earth sensibilities were what she considered thinking predicated on a pre-magical world. Things were changed now, forever, and old people were utterly failing to realise that. It was like they hit thirty and were incapable of accepting new ideas. Emi was aware that every teenager ever had considered their parents wildly wrong and out of touch, but she was the one that was right. If only they could just see it.

In the end, she had gone to Taika. He, in turn, immediately dragged her to the modest cottage Rufus had chosen for himself. When she started talking, Rufus didn't dismiss her as a teenager. He didn't talk over the nervous and rambling explanation that didn't sound convincing even to her own ears as it tumbled out of her mouth. He sat and listened, his unnervingly direct gaze never flinching from her face. She wanted to look away but couldn't turn from his dark, compelling eyes.

When she was done, she felt like a defendant awaiting the judgement of a court. Rufus sat without response, finally breaking eye contact as he considered her words in silence. Taika, a calming presence beside her, gave her shoulder a comforting squeeze. Finally, Rufus spoke.

"That makes a lot of sense," he said.

"It does?" Emi had asked, as if she hadn't been the one to bring the whole thing up.

Rufus laughed, his eyes seeming to see right through her. "Yes."

He then explained about great astral beings, in a way that was less colourful but made more sense than anything her uncle had told her. His explanations were easy and clear, like a good teacher. He told her about their relationship with Jason and the linked worlds, all knowledge she had touched on but never really known. Then he told her about what the great astral beings were doing with the clan, helping the transformed people.

"It makes sense that they are using avatars," he said. "I had been worried about such important people spending so long here on Earth, doing this."

"Because it would suggest they're here for more than what that doctor said to you?" Emi asked.

"Exactly," Rufus said. "But if these are just avatars doing a side job while their real selves are out doing whatever it is they do, it means this isn't some Jason-style cosmic nonsense about to start up."

He let out a long breath and gave her a warm smile. Suddenly, he wasn't so intimidating.

"I haven't told anyone this," he told her. "Taika knew some of it, but your family isn't ready to deal with things on this level. They don't understand what level it's on, and I fear they would try to do something about it. Which they cannot. So, I've been keeping the activities of these avatars quiet. If they're benevolent, it's all for the good. If they're not, only Jason could do anything about it, and he's busy."

"I understand," Emi said solemnly. "Earth sensibilities."

"Earth sensibilities?" Taika asked.

Rufus laughed again.

"She's right. The people here are still too caught up in how their world used to work. The problem with having older people in charge is that they are slow to adapt."

"Exactly," Emi said.

"And the reason they're in charge anyway," Rufus said pointedly, "is that young people lack the wisdom that comes with experience."

"And part of that wisdom is knowing when to keep a secret," Taika told her. "What we're talking about here is proper adventurer stuff. Hidden knowledge of the universe. Rufus is trusting you with this, and that's trust your uncle earned for you. Now, you have to prove you deserve it all on your own."

Emi couldn't stop grinning as she walked away from Rufus' cottage.

"You seem happy," Taika said.

"He didn't treat me like a kid. No one but Farrah and Uncle Jason do that."

"What about me?"

"Yeah, people treat you like a kid too."

"Hey!" Taika exclaimed in fake outrage as Emi laughed maniacally. She stopped when they reached his car.

"Can't we fly?" she wheedled.

"Why would I fly you home when I then have to come back to drive my car?"

"Aren't you strong enough to carry the car? I'll get in and you fly back holding it."

Taika tried saying no to the innocent puppy eyes he knew hid the face of an evil genius. Instead, he let out a defeated groan.

"Your mum is going to poison my food for this."

76

NOT ALL OF THEM HAVE A PLAN

MUCH OF EMI'S NERVOUSNESS ABOUT HER SOON-TO-BE-CLAIMED ESSENCES had faded away. She only realised after the fact that a lot of that had been thanks to the daunting but capable mentor who would be conducting the ritual. His lessons were excellent, but she found him intimidating, not connecting with him the way she had with Farrah.

After Jason and Farrah left Earth, the whole family had grown strangely protective. While they were still on Earth, Emi had been trusted. Important, even, as Farrah set her to essential magical tasks. She may not have had her essences, but she was a wizard, with greater command of ritual magic than most people on Earth. Once Jason and Farrah left, she had suddenly gone from wizard back to teenager, like Cinderella after midnight.

Things changed after Taika forced her to go see Rufus and explain her concerns. Not with her family, but once again, there was someone who treated her with respect instead of protectiveness. Once that happened, she went from nervous to excited about finally getting her essences.

Once the anxiety had gone, another troubling emotion reared its head: guilt. She knew she was a special case. All the clan members had access to magic and training superior to that of the magical factions. Even the secretive US and Chinese Network training programs were not a match for Asano clan resources, especially following the arrival of Rufus. And within the clan, no one was inundated with as much support as Emi.

Only Boris and his people had the off-world experience of Taika and Rufus, but the messengers weren't essence-users. While the two adventurers trained all the young clan members, only Emi received regular, one-on-one attention.

Because she was Jason's treasured niece, she had unfettered access to essences and awakening stones. The rest of the clan had to claim those resources through a contribution system. Contribution points could be accumulated starting at age sixteen, with an initial allotment based on school grades, training achievements and other actions beneficial to the clan. They could also be traded, and with food and lodging being provided by the clan, contribution points were a valuable commodity.

Points could be spent on essences and awakening stones. As the clan was in its early days, this mostly centred around parents looking for the best opportunities they could give their children. They settled for cheap essences for themselves, or forewent essences altogether as they saved for more desirable essences for their children.

Emi's great-grandmother was the clan matriarch, the now young-seeming Yumi Asano. The only authority above her was Jason, who had made it clear that she was in charge. Even if he hadn't been absent, he had neither the interest nor the skill set to manage the clan. He had left certain directives, though, both before his departure and in the messages he sent with Rufus and Taika.

Before he left, he made it clear that no expense was to be spared in the development of Emi's magic. In the recordings, he stated that Rufus was to be in charge of directing that development. Erika had not welcomed her brother trying to control parts of her daughter's upbringing by fiat, but had found Rufus much more respectful.

Rufus had proven highly accommodating to the wishes and limits of Erika and her husband in his approach to Emi's training. That did not always endear him to his trainee, who had her own ideas about what was appropriate. This tension had been the beginning of Emi's now-resolved uncertainty about him.

It had never been easy making friends for Emi. She'd always gotten along better with adults than children, being heavily indulged when she was younger. But with each passing year, her more adult intelligence seemed less remarkable. Now she was a teenager, she oddly found herself treated more like a child. It was easy to dismiss the opinions of a teenager.

Her first real friend had been made only after the full-time move to Saint-Étienne. It had been a time when her uncle had been at his most dangerous, like a live wire dangling over water. What little remained of his old persona felt like a tattered mask over a volatile and menacing creature that no one wanted to provoke. He was killing people, not just monsters, and she still remembered his nightmare that had invaded her mind. She didn't remember the specifics, but the sense of inescapable dread still haunted her.

Moving to Saint-Étienne after they stopped travelling with her uncle, Emi had found herself around people her own age for the first time in a long time. Lina Karadeniz was a cousin of Jason's girlfriend, the one who had died along with Emi's Uncle Kaito. Lina had been hostile at first, with her family only joining the Asano clan out of necessity. The Karadeniz family had been wealthy people living good lives in the days before magic. They laid the blame for losing that as well as the death of Asya at Jason's feet.

Time had changed things, at least for Emi and Lina. Two whip-smart girls who couldn't seem to get along with anyone else, they kept finding themselves together—especially in the face of increasingly interested boys. Many of the young boys in the clan were relatives, but there were still plenty that weren't, and the pair drew attention. Against her better judgement, and often to her annoyance, Emi found herself with a social life.

After her nervousness passed about her soon-to-be essences, she became excited and started talking about them more. That was when she realised things were getting awkward. Her new friends had always understood who her uncle was, and that her great-grandmother ran the clan. But when she started talking about choosing her essences and being shown into the essence vault, they all started to realise the difference between them.

Emi's new closeness with Lina became tense as wider family issues began to intrude. The Karadeniz family saw Emi and the privileges her uncle had mandated as an indication that the Asano family were turning themselves into oligarchs within the clan.

As Emi was treated more like a tool of politics than a person, it poisoned her new friendships and she was soon isolating herself all over again. She was torn not just by the people trying to use her but also by the fear that they were not entirely wrong. She enjoyed advantages that her friends did not. Opportunities she was freely given were things their parents struggled and strived for. She knew it wasn't fair but, at the same time, did not want to give them up. She had large ambitions, and the advantages her uncle had given her were the launching pad for them.

Her father found her sitting on the balcony of their townhouse, legs dangling through the wrought-iron railing. He looked out at the sun just dipping below the skyline, turning the sky orange. He sat beside his daughter and slipped his legs through the bars as well.

"You seemed happy there for a little bit," he said. "I know it's not cool to talk to your dad, but I think we both know you were never cool, so how about you give it a try?"

Emi gave him a withering look but couldn't hold it, cracking up in spite of herself.

"It's not fair," she said. "The things I get, just because of Uncle Jason and Nana Yumi."

"Don't let her hear you call her that," he said in a warning that was mostly a joke.

"Dad, if you aren't going to take this seriously—"

"I'm sorry," he said. "I'm sorry, sweetie. You know, it's very mature of you to think about what you have that others don't."

"Dad, I'm not a child."

"I know. I know, I really do. But I'm going to be honest with you, Emi: You've always been hard to parent. You thought you were smarter than me by age seven, and by age nine, you were right. And I'm not an idiot."

"You're kind of an idiot."

He scoffed, putting a hand to his chest in mock offence.

"I'm considered quite intelligent, I'll have you know," he told her. "I'm a doctor."

"So you tell people," she muttered.

He gave her a scathing look, her feigned disregard lasting only seconds before a laugh escaped her lips.

"Now who's not taking this seriously?" he asked. "But really, Emi, I didn't know what to do with you. You were a child, yet so like an adult in a lot of ways. I didn't know how to handle that. I'm not sure I ever figured it out. And now you're a teenager. Not a child anymore, but not an adult either. And you're so accomplished, with all your magic studies."

He leaned over, briefly reaching out to give her a side hug.

"But for all that you're special," he continued, "you're also a normal teenager. You're going through the amazing and terrible process of figuring out who you are, but I'm going to let you in on a secret: I am too.

Still, at my age. There's this illusion that adults have figured it out and gotten their lives together. And I have done that in a lot of ways. I became a doctor and married a woman far too good for me. But there's always something fresh and confounding to deal with. Going from husband to parent. From doctor to magical healer. Life always has new things to throw at you. You figure out one thing and along comes the next. You don't have to live in a magic town in France for that."

"Is this meant to be encouraging? It doesn't sound encouraging."

He let out a long sigh that turned into a laugh.

"It doesn't, does it? What I'm trying to say is that it's okay to feel overwhelmed. You don't have to figure it all out today. I know that your mother and I aren't always doing the things you want us to. Sometimes we're going to get it wrong, and I'm sorry for that. But sometimes we're going to get it right, and you aren't always going to like it."

He leaned his head against the railing, enjoying the sensation of cool metal against his forehead.

"Emi, our first job as parents is to prepare you for the world you're stepping into. But the world is changing, maybe faster and more drastically than it ever has before. Magic is like the Renaissance and the Industrial Revolution happening at the same time, in fast forward. We don't know how to equip you for that, and it terrifies us. Because we love you more than anything in the world."

"I love you too, Dad. But I'm going to be honest; you telling me you have no idea what you're doing doesn't fill me with confidence."

He laughed as he wiped a tear from his eye.

"Well, you're a teenager now, sweetie. You're on the path to becoming an adult, and the first lesson is that none of us know what we're doing. We're just better at faking it than kids are."

"So, you can't help me, then."

"Well, I didn't say that. Adults do figure some stuff out before moving on to the next anxiety attack, so there's experience to draw on here. You said you were worried that you're getting better treatment than your friends, right?"

"Yeah."

"Well, how about this: We turn down the free stuff your uncle said to give you."

"I kind of don't want to, though."

He let out a belly laugh.

"I can see why you wouldn't. But you don't have to lose out on the essences you want. Your mother and I are pretty high up in this whole organisation, you know? We've accumulated a lot of contribution points, so we can get you the essences you want. It'll come out of our points, the same way everyone else does it."

"You realise that I've chosen some expensive essences, right?"

"I know, sweetie. You change your mind every few days, but you always seem to go for the expensive stuff. But, believe it or not, your mother and I have a lot of clan contributions. We can afford it. You might have to wait a little longer on the exact awakening stones, if you keep going for the rare stuff. And you'd better believe that we'll be dipping into your points when you start racking them up, Miss Master Wizard."

"Is that okay?" Emi asked nervously. "Doing it this way? Do you think that's fair?"

"Fair is a hard thing, Emi. I don't think any system can be completely equitable. All we can do is our best with what we've got, and try to make it a little better for whoever inherits it from us."

"Well, no one's inheriting anything from me," Emi said. "I'm going to live forever."

"See, I knew there was an age-appropriate thought somewhere in that head. All teenagers think they're going to live forever."

"Yes, but not all of them have a plan. I'm going to reach diamond rank."

"That's higher than silver rank, right?"

Emi gave her father a flat look.

"Did you not read all the documentation on ranks and advancement?"

"I'm only bronze rank, Emi. That high-rank stuff doesn't apply to me. And it's a lot of material. All those binders."

"You know there's a digital copy, right? I can't believe you skipped the reading. Were you like this in medical school?"

"No!"

"I feel sorry for the people who come to you, thinking you're a doctor."

"I am a doctor!"

———

Emi, Ian and Erika entered the gymnasium, the nervous girl walking between her parents. She looked around at all the people in the stands, their low chatter an unsettling susurrus. They stood at the doorway and looked around.

"Where's Taika?" Ian asked.

"He's just getting something for me," Emi said, a little too innocently.

"Did you change your mind on your essence combination *again*?" Ian asked.

"No," she lied.

"Emi…"

"Yes," she sullenly admitted.

"You can call it off," Rufus said as he approached them. "There's no rule that says you have to do it the moment your body will accept essences. We can put it off until you're absolutely certain."

"No!" Emi half shouted, drawing more attention from a crowd already watching them.

Her face crinkled up in a blushing wince.

"No," she insisted quietly. "I'm doing it today. Who came up with this idea of doing these rituals in public?"

"I don't know, but it's a good idea," Rufus said. "Becoming an essence-user in this world is no small thing. It means being a notable figure, and they need to adjust to that. Starting here, surrounded by friends and family, is a good way to ease people into it."

"As an alternative suggestion," Emi said, "how about we do it with no one around?"

"You'd tell all these people to just go home because nothing's happening?" Ian asked.

"Or you could do it," Emi said.

"No," her mother said. "If you want to not have your ritual in front of all these people, you have to tell them. You also have to tell your great-grandmother."

They all turned to look at Yumi. She was sitting with Emi's paternal grandmother, Nana Evans, in the front row of the stands. They had a prime position, right in front of the ritual circle Rufus had set up.

"I guess we can do it like this," Emi said.

"Good choice," Rufus told her. "But again, you can wait until you're certain about your essence selection."

"I am certain."

"As you have been about every combination you've been picking out twice a week for the last year," her father pointed out. "There's no shame in patience."

"We're doing it now," Emi insisted. "Even if it does have to be in front of all these people."

"Very well," Rufus said. "As soon as Taika gets back from the vault."

"While we're waiting," Erika said, "have you given any thought to what you want to do for your sixteenth birthday?"

"Fight a monster," Emi said immediately.

"Nope," her father said.

"No," Rufus told her.

"Absolutely not," Erika said. "You can fight a monster when you're old enough to make that decision for yourself."

"I just did make that decision for myself."

"Oh, Daughter," Erika said. "You are a very clever young woman who is right about a lot of things. But when you are wrong, you are so very wrong. You take after your uncle in that way. You are not going to fight a monster for your birthday. Better yet, you could fight no monsters ever. You can use monster cores, like your father and I have. Once you turn sixteen, you'll be allowed to earn your own contribution points to buy them. All that ritual magic you know will be very useful for that."

"I am not using monster cores. You can't get to diamond rank like that. I'm going to fight monsters."

"Not at sixteen, you're not," her father said.

"How old, then?" Emi asked.

"Forty-eight," Ian told her.

"Dad…"

"She's right, Ian," Erika said. "Don't be absurd. Sixteen is out of the question, but this is important to her, so let's be sensible."

"Thanks, Mum."

"She can decide for herself when she's twenty-one."

"Mum! Five years? Rufus was really late fighting his first monster, and he still did it by nineteen. In the other world, lots of people my age are fighting monsters."

"And lots of people your age die," Rufus said. "Mine is a brutal world. You saw what it did to your uncle. Be grateful that your civilisation isn't watered with the blood of the young."

"Thank you, Rufus," Erika said. "For your reasonable—if horrifyingly grim—support."

"You are very welcome, Mrs Asano. I know you have concerns about your daughter's safety," he continued. "My priority will always be to keep her safe. Her birthday is very near, but the day I am satisfied she's ready to face a monster is not. It will be far longer than she wants before I am satisfied she is ready to face a carefully chosen monster under carefully arranged conditions. Only then will we even start to properly discuss the possibility. If nothing else, I won't let her just jump in when she's chosen a combination not built for combat."

He looked at her with suspicion.

"Taika is bringing back a non-combat combination, right?" he asked.

"Yes," Emi said. "Not that it matters. You told me yourself that every combination can fight. Look at Mum and her knife powers."

"What combination did you choose?" Erika asked her daughter. "If you picked three legendary essences, I'm not sure even we have the contribution points for that."

"Of course I didn't." Emi failed to meet her mother's eyes. "It's two legendaries and an epic," she mumbled.

"Uh, we can afford that, right?" Ian asked.

"Yes," Erika said, her voice not that much higher in pitch than normal. "You're the medical director and I'm the food logistics director for the whole clan. We can afford it. Probably. What essences specifically did you pick out, my sweet girl?"

"Vast, Myriad and Harmonic," Emi said. "It produces the Unity confluence."

Rufus nodded.

"One of the combinations Farrah suggested," he said. "Good choice. You'll want to be careful with your awakening stone choices, though. We can save those discussions for later, though."

"Okay, that's not too bad," Erika said. "High rarity, but none of the truly exotic ones. It could be worse."

"You could still give them to her for free," Rufus said. "The way Jason intended."

"It's too late for that," Erika said. "Grandmother has already started sharing the fact that we're using contribution points like everyone else. She wants to forestall any tension between us and the other families. It's inevitable that they'll think the people who share a name with the clan will get special treatment, and she wants to head that off."

"Uncle Jason would have wanted it like this anyway," Emi said.

"He's the one who said you should get it all for free in the first place," Ian said.

"Yes, but he'd prefer it be fairer once he thought about it. Sometimes he can be slow on the uptake."

"Sometimes?" Rufus muttered under his breath, earning a grin from Emi.

Yumi Asano made a ceremony of the whole affair, taking the chance to do a little politicking. She made a speech about the future of the clan, fair treatment and the unprecedented challenges that the upcoming generation would face. Other members of the clan's ruling council did the same; Yumi was the only one to speak from the Asano family.

In the end, the rite Rufus conducted to grant Emi her essences was almost an afterthought. It was the simplest of ritual magic and he had her absorb all three essences at once. She absorbed her confluence and then bolted for the bathroom, her face turning a sickly yellow.

The onlookers laughed sympathetically. Many had gone through the same experience or watched friends and relatives do so. They were all familiar with the violent body purge that came with reaching iron rank. When Emi emerged from the bathroom, looking rather wrung out, she was met by thunderous cheers. Her parents and Rufus hurried up to her, huge grins on their faces. Her parents hugged her and Rufus solemnly shook her hand.

"Welcome," he told her. "You've joined a larger world than you can possibly imagine. It's only the beginning, but you're walking the same path as me, Farrah and your uncle. You're one of us now."

77

THE RESPONSIBILITY OF MAKING
IT POSSIBLE

THE PRESENCE OF AVATARS MADE SENSE IMMEDIATELY TO RUFUS. Someone as powerful as Velius was a danger to Earth's fragile dimensional boundary, just as Dawn had been. Avatars allowed him and the others like him to operate on Earth not just with less power but while leaving their true selves free to be elsewhere.

Knowing that their real bodies were off doing more important work put Rufus' mind at ease. Important cosmic figures spending this much time on Earth suggested an agenda beyond what Velius had told Rufus. Avatars treating Earth as a side gig meant it was less likely that some Jason-style cosmic nonsense was about to break out.

That did not stop Rufus from being anxious when a request arrived from Velius for a meeting. Especially when the meeting was in the maternity ward of the clan medical centre in the middle of the night. His arrival left the medical centre receptionist, a typically attractive elf woman, suspicious of him. A call to Velius had her let Rufus through, but she had a man from security escort him.

Dennis the security guard was visibly uneasy as he escorted Rufus; he knew who he was. Rufus had taken on the role of not just teaching Emi but instituting a top-to-bottom revision of the Asano clan's essence-user training. Farrah and Jason had done a decent enough job during their time on Earth, but they were ultimately amateurs. Rufus' family ran a school.

"I'm sorry about this, Mr Remore," Dennis said. "I'm well aware that if you wanted to get in here, there's nothing I could do to stop you."

"Don't apologise for being diligent in your work," Rufus assured him. "For all you know, I could be a shape-changer."

"Are you?" he asked nervously and Rufus just laughed.

"Thank you, Dennis," Velius said. "You can leave us now."

"Of course, Dr Velius," Dennis said, already retreating down the hall.

That left Rufus and Velius standing together in front of a large window. On the other side of the glass were newborn babies, although fewer cribs were occupied than left empty. Velius turned to look through the window as the air shimmered around them.

"A privacy screen?" Rufus asked.

"An aura manipulation technique, not a magical device. Hard to learn when you can't physically manipulate sound waves. I do envy the messengers and your friend Jason having that."

"And why do we need privacy?"

"You just passed the nurse station. This is not a conversation I can allow to be overheard. Even discussing this with you is probably a mistake."

"Discussing what?"

"Your friend Gareth was an admirable man."

Rufus scowled.

"I know that far better than you," he said, almost growling the words.

"I suppose you do. But I admire the way he chose to end things. He could have clung to his last gasp of life, getting by on borrowed power that weighed him down like an anchor. Instead, he chose to face his fate and accept death, not knowing what it would mean for him."

"Why are you telling me things I already know?"

"Because I'm also going to tell you something that you don't. That you probably shouldn't. When we met, I told you that rules would be bent. Now it's time to show you."

"Show me what?"

Velius nodded at the window.

"What do you think of these children?"

"They're newborns; there's not much to think about. I'm glad they're healthy."

"You see the leonid one? The one that looks like a kitten."

"I know what a leonid baby looks like."

"Did you know his parents rather unfortunately named him Gary?"

Rufus turned to Velius. "Why would they choose that name?"

"Really?" Velius said. "The man who won't stop telling people stories about his friend the heroic leonid can't figure it out? There aren't a lot of leonid role models on Earth, Mr Remore. They've been hearing all about the one you know for months, so is it all that surprising?"

"You said it was an unfortunate name," Rufus said. "Why?"

"Look at the child's aura."

Rufus stared at the baby as he extended his perception.

"That aura," Rufus said. "It almost feels like Gary. Not the same, but it does feel like him."

"Of course it doesn't feel the same. You can't just shove a soul into a child without taking it through a renewal process. Especially when the soul itself needs to be reformed after dying as a gestalt entity."

"You're talking about reincarnation? Are you saying... are you saying that child really is Gary?"

"If you mean your friend Gary, then no. I am very emphatically saying this child is not your friend. He is a different person who happens to have inherited your friend's soul, which is part of what makes the name so unfortunate."

"How can he have Gary's soul and not be him?"

Velius let out a groan.

"Conversations like this are why we don't normally let this happen. Yes, that boy has the reincarnated soul of your friend. But reincarnation is not the resurrection or rebirth of the person who came before. It is the arrival of someone new who just happens to have an old soul. They are shaped by that soul, but they are not the people they were in their past lives. Not anymore. This Gary will be his own man, not the one you knew."

"Then why? What's the point of reincarnation if the person doesn't come back?"

"If you want the why of what happens after death, you'll have to ask the Reaper. The most he ever gives me is the what, and that's more than most mortals get. I can tell you that reincarnation is only one path of many. When it does happen, the soul is normally reincarnated far off in the cosmos. Somewhere so removed from the origin point that most transcendents couldn't find it, and no small few of them have tried. But that's not a rule, strictly speaking. It's something the Reaper does to avoid problems. Problems like you."

"How am I a problem?"

"This boy is not the friend you lost, Mr Remore. He never will be. He will never have a memory of you, or of anything from any of his past lives. He will not have the same personality or follow the same life path. You will see echoes of the man he was because yes, that was your friend's soul. Now it is this boy's soul. He will grow up to be his own person. To make his own choices and his own mistakes. This boy is not your friend but your friend's legacy. He is the gift that your friend has left to the cosmos. Gareth Xandier is gone, and he's never coming back."

Velius bowed his head.

"I'm sorry to be so blunt about your loss," he said. "But it's critical that you understand what I am trying to tell you. As I said, there is a reason that reincarnated souls are sent where no one they knew will ever find them."

"How did this happen? Becoming a demigod made him like Jason and the messengers. He wasn't meant to be able to come back."

"He hasn't come back. This is a new person. That's what I'm repeating over and over, and will keep doing so until this sinks in."

"But his soul wasn't able to enter a new body."

"Reincarnation is not simply a matter of grabbing a soul and shoving it in the first available meat sack. The soul absorbs the changes that come from a lifetime of experiences and undergoes a metamorphosis. A renewal. Only then it is ready to be the genesis of a new person."

"His soul was altered?"

"No. His soul changed by itself; that's what reincarnation is. It was not altered by an external force. Not even the Reaper can do that. Change is a natural part of the reincarnation process. Your friend changed himself. I said this boy was your friend's legacy and I meant it literally. Your friend prepared his soul to gift a new life to the cosmos."

"He did seem accepting," Rufus said. "So, that's what happens to people when they die?"

"Some people. There are other possibilities, but we're definitely not talking about that. It's one thing to speculate on the afterlife and another to get confirmation. You've already learned more than a living person should."

"You want me to keep quiet, then."

"I want far more from you than that. Or, perhaps, less. You will teach these children as they grow. Even if you leave this world before they're of an age for you to do so directly, what you leave behind will guide a generation. You can be a mentor to this boy, if that's how it plays out, but if you cross the line, there will be repercussions."

"What line?"

"There is a reason I have been so emphatic that this boy is not your friend. That they share a name will be an unfortunate and constant reminder, making it harder to stay objective. The line is that you must always treat the boy as who he is, not who he was. And if I ever catch you trying to turn him into your lost friend, then no one can save you from me. I am the first guide of the dead in the cosmos. If you make it necessary, I *will* start guiding you earlier than expected."

"Then why tell me at all? Why not just leave me ignorant?"

"Because you would start to suspect, over time. An expression you recognise. A look in his eyes. His aura will not be the same, but the root is the same soul. It's close enough to recognise."

"And the damage I could do in my ignorance would be worse than if I know what's happening."

"Yes. This is why souls are not normally sent to places where they might be recognised. We are showing you considerable trust in this, Mr Remore. Watching the man who was your friend grow up will require discipline. The temptation to introduce aspects of his past life will be great. It is easy to convince yourself that you see an aptitude he once held and push him in that direction."

"It sounds like you speak from experience."

"I was not always as I am now. Once, I was just a man. A man convinced that he found the soul of a lost love in the body of another."

"Were you right?"

"I was. And the damage I did ruined us both. That was how I first came into the Reaper's service. To make amends."

"If there are so many risks, why do this? Why reincarnate him here?"

"Because for all that he is a new person, the man he was is still inside him. And he was an exceptional man indeed."

"Yes, he was."

"That legacy I talked about? This is where it plays out. That's what the Reaper is gifting this planet. They say, on this world, that all people are born equal. Even if you disregard reincarnation, that's laughable. This boy has a hero's soul and what I imagine will be a highly motivated mentor. He's born for greatness, in a place where greatness will be sorely needed."

"And if he doesn't live up to that greatness?"

"Then guide him to happiness. I suggest that be the priority, in fact, and fit in greatness if you can. A life doesn't have to be exceptional to be worthwhile."

"But isn't the whole point of sending him here is for him to be great?"

"Well, sure, but no one asked you about it, so who said you have to follow the plan? The great astral beings are the ones who set in motion the events that sent this world off-kilter. They're helping things along on Earth out of a sense of responsibility. That's what great astral beings are, in the end. Responsibility on a cosmic scale. They tried to change that and messed it up to the point of relying on Jason Asano to fix it. That's bad. This world, and to a lesser extent, yours, have gone wrong because of what they did. That cosmic consequence is what they care about, not the people. To them, the people are just a means to an end."

"But you care."

"Yes. That's literally my job, in fact. I'm still mortal enough to care about something as tiny as a person. Did you know that's why the World-Phoenix sent Dawn here? Her perspective was getting too cosmic to be of use to the World-Phoenix and she needed someone to ground her in mortality. I think it underestimated just how grounded Jason Asano is, and Dawn's replacement had to be called up early anyway. That man is a disruptive presence."

"He is that," Rufus agreed with a chuckle.

"Look, Mr Remore. I've worked for a great astral being for longer than most who end up in my position. Something I've learned in that time is that as long as I fulfil the Reaper's directives to its satisfaction, I get to manage the details however I like. And the Reaper does not care about the living. Happy or sad; great or insignificant. It doesn't care what they are and it doesn't care what they do. Not until someone like your friend Jason starts resurrecting over and over, anyway."

"So, the great astral beings won't intervene if I end up guiding these people to just live fulfilling lives? No path to greatness?"

"I can't speak for the others sent here like me, but I can tell you what I was told to do. I was sent here to accelerate the development of non-human medical knowledge and make sure a few reincarnations went smoothly. That's as far as my orders go."

He gestured to the window and the newborns on the other side.

"If you want to turn these kids into a gaggle of blissfully content, perfectly ordinary people, Mr Remore, then I am more than happy to help."

"Is ordinary even possible, given what they're being born into?"

"I guess the responsibility of making it possible falls to people like you and me."

78

THINGS MORE INTIMATE

IN THE WAKE OF JASON'S DEPARTURE, TEAM BISCUIT HAD TAKEN A BREAK in Vitesse before going on an intense contract-taking spree, pushing themselves through silver-rank as fast as they could. After the monster surge and the subterranean expedition, taking ordinary contracts like normal adventurers was almost a vacation in itself.

The Messenger War was over in Yaresh, at least until some other astral king decided the region was of interest. Around the world, however, the messenger invasion continued unabated. Where Yaresh had seen one rogue astral king seeking out a soul forge for their own ends, the other astral kings moved with singular purpose. They were determined to search every nook and cranny of Pallimustus until they found the artefact left behind by the god of Purity.

Team Biscuit fought messengers on and off, but were not focused on the interdimensional interlopers. Monsters didn't stop spawning just because of the messengers, and the invasion made it easy for regular monster hunting work to fall through the cracks. The team found a niche in clearing out the contracts that otherwise fell by the wayside.

After two years, though, it was time for a break. Clive had more projects than time to do them, and the others split up for personal pursuits. For Neil, it was a return to Greenstone where the team would eventually reunite. It was a chance to visit family and check in on Nik, who was training at the Geller estate.

Being normal rank when even silvers and golds were helpless in the face of gods and demigods had left Nik feeling vulnerable and weak. His only ability to act was with the borrowed power of the elemental spires that placed a network of magical systems at his command.

When Nik chose his essences, it was that feeling of being at the centre of something powerful he was trying to recapture. He did not want borrowed strength, however, the way it had been in the transformation zone. He was determined that the power at his command would be his own, something no one could take away or deny from him.

Nik's essence combination was actually one from Earth, using an essence brought back by Jason. Jason had left the bulk of his essence stores with his family, but had brought a few with him. This included the technology essence, knowing it would fascinate Clive. Nik had used that essence, along with the myriad and vast essences to create the network confluence. He had no idea that he had chosen such a similar combination to an adoptive cousin he had never met.

Unlike Emi in the other world, Nik had no mother telling him not to fight monsters. On the contrary, an introduction from Danielle Geller had seen his entry to the Geller family's most elite training program, in Greenstone. Nik was developing a support power set that involved being the central hub of a team, coordinating each member and helping them form powerful synergies.

Now that he was bronze rank, it was time for Nik to leave Greenstone behind. His problem was that he had no idea what was next. He'd been working with a lot of different teams training with the Gellers, and even a few local ones that weren't. The Geller instructors had told him that learning to work with different people would make him stronger and, as usual, they had been proven right.

With his training over and no permanent team to be a part of, Nik had no clear path forward. He was hoping that the soon-to-be-reunited Team Biscuit would have some advice. For the moment, he had Neil, who was not always focused.

"How many sandwiches do you need?" Nik asked.

The Island was a very nice haven for the wealthy and powerful of Greenstone. Nik and Neil had been having regular picnics in the park district since Neil's arrival in the city. They were currently sitting on a huge blanket with a dazzling array of sandwiches set out in front of them.

"You're going to be eating some as well," Neil pointed out.

"I have a decent sense of how many sandwiches I want, and it is significantly fewer than this."

"It's not that many sandwiches."

"The bakery made and packed the whole picnic basket, right?"

"Yeah."

"What did they call this particular bundle?"

"I have no idea."

"I think you do."

"I don't remember."

"I really think you do."

"Fine," Neil grumbled. "It was their picnic for six bundle."

"There aren't six of us."

"I can count, Nik."

"Then why didn't you count in the bakery?"

"It was an elven bakery. They always make small portion sizes."

"Well, I'm smaller than an elf, so I'm one portion size at most. Are you five times larger than an elf, Neil?"

"I am an elf!"

"Then you are eating five portions."

"Just shut up and eat your sandwiches. You'll miss them when you're adventuring on the road. Are you still figuring out how that's going to work?"

"Yeah. It feels daunting, you know? I'm very young, and there's always been a path laid out for me. I made decisions for myself, but there was always someone giving me a manageable number of options. Now I have the whole world opened up to me and it's overwhelming. Too many options feels oddly like no options at all. Maybe just some guidance, you know? Point a guy in a direction."

"Are you actually asking for advice or just venting?"

"I'm asking, if you have any advice to give."

"I don't have any great insight, but I can tell you the approach a lot of adventurers take when leaving Greenstone. If you don't have a permanent team, you want to avoid the famous adventuring cities. Places like Vitesse and Cyrion are for the adventurers who already know what they're about. People who have teams or are in with a guild."

"You're in a guild, right?"

"I am. The Burning Violet Guild, operating out of Vitesse. All of our team are members except for Jason and Taika. If that's the way you want to go, graduating from the Geller training grounds will put you in good stead. Especially with the new Remore Academy training annex. You could do well in Vitesse, although I don't know I'd advise that. You'd have a lot of eyes on you, and you'd be caught up in guild politics. There's some tension in the guild right now, and you'd inherit that."

"What kind of tension?"

"A lot of people in the guild think the Remore Academy has too much influence over guild affairs."

"Do they?"

"Probably. Not a lot of Greenstone adventurers can jump right into the deep water like that, and I'd advise following their example and steering clear of that mess. What they tend to do instead is look for a big city in one of the moderate-strength magic zones. It's a natural step up from Greenstone. The monsters aren't so dangerous that you need a high-rank escort, just in case. You get more adventurers assembling teams for individual jobs, the way they do here. You can get a lot of group contracts without the need for a permanent teams. Did you get any team offers from the Gellers?"

"I did. Nothing felt quite like the right fit, though."

"Yeah. It feels off, not having the right team. Especially for support roles like ours who need a team around us. But that's not such a bad place to be when you're starting out. I know it can feel directionless, but sometimes it's good to see what the world has for you. Finding out what doesn't fit is a step towards finding what does."

"It would be nice to have at least some direction. A goal to strive for."

"Goals are all well and good, but getting everything you ever wanted might not work out the way you thought. By the time you do, you might find you're a different person to the one who wanted those things in the first place."

"Is that why Cassie isn't here with us?" Nik asked. "Was she meant to eat some of these sandwiches?"

"Stop talking about sandwiches."

"Well, maybe you should start eating them."

"I'm self-conscious about it now."

"Then tell me what's going on with Cassandra."

Neil shoved half a sandwich in his mouth.

"Very mature, Uncle Neil. Is something going on with Cassandra?"

Neil mumbled through a mouthful of sandwich. Nik gave him a judgemental look, saying nothing until Neil finished his oversized bite.

"Back when I was training to be an adventurer," Neil said, "I had dreams of travelling the world. Of being on a team with incredible companions and doing things that really mattered. Helping people, you know? I didn't join the Healer's church by accident. But I was stuck on a team built around a self-serving coward while nursing a crush on his sister."

"And now you're on a famous team with good people. And you and the sister are—"

"Yeah."

"So, you got everything you ever wanted, but you don't look or sound ecstatically happy. What's the issue?"

"Well," Neil said, "it isn't the team. Everything is great, there. Rufus, Taika and Jason left a hole, but they also left a proclivity for getting involved in mad cosmic events. It's been nice, just being adventurers for a while."

"Yeah, you're giving off a real 'lady trouble' energy."

"Should I even be talking to you about this? Aren't you less than three years old?"

"Uncle Neil, I was born with the memory of *Wild Orchid II: Two Shades of Blue*. I can handle you and your girlfriend and your feelings. But yes, keep any bedroom stuff to yourself, please and thank you."

"Gods, you really are his kid, aren't you?"

An adorably happy smile lit up Nik's leporine face.

"Really?"

"Yes. You're happy about that?"

"No," Nik said, forcing a scowl onto his face. "What's going on with you and Cassandra? Is it that you're eating too many sandwiches?"

"I am not eating too many sandwiches!"

"You have to tell her that a lot, don't you?"

"I don't… look, Nik, you want to talk about hearing something a lot? What does she ask you about every time you see her? *Who* does she ask you about?"

"Ah," Nik said with a sympathetic wince. "That. It's not hard to see where she's coming from, though. You have to expect it to play on her mind, Neil. Put yourself in her place. Your ex-boyfriend dies. Okay, sad, but not a huge deal. Then you hear he's come back to life, and the stories just keep rolling in. He had a secret affair with a princess. He's spending time with diamond-rankers. Including a literally scorching hot redhead who blows up cities and turns out to be a space princess. Gods are paying him a lot of attention. He tells the great astral being who is invading the planet to leave and he actually does."

"What's a space princess?"

"It's like a regular princess. But in space."

"I didn't know that, so I'm fairly certain Cassie doesn't know that."

"Not the thing to focus on, Uncle Neil. The point is, Cassandra dumped a guy, not because she wanted to, but because her family decided he wasn't going to amount to anything. Now he's a living myth and she's quite naturally wondering what could have been. That's something that's going to play on her mind until she meets Jason again and gets some closure. Hopefully."

Neil groaned and sullenly bit into his sandwich again. Nik shrugged and grabbed one for himself. They ate in thoughtful silence.

"I see what you're saying," Neil said when he was done. "It makes sense. It's understandable that Jason would be on her thoughts like that. But it doesn't make it any easier to hear her talk about him every day. Ask about him every day. I could tell her to stop, but that just means she's not doing it out loud."

"Yeah," Nik said. "Like I said, she needs closure. Maybe suggest she sees a mind healer like Arabelle. That's just a good idea for any adventurer. But your best shot at her letting it go is having her meet with Jason and get it all out of her system. I'm not saying that it'll solve all your problems. There's no guarantees when it comes to what's going on in someone's mind. But if she's fixated on the image of him that's stuck in her head, she probably needs to see the reality to at least start moving past it."

Neil picked up another sandwich, looking at it forlornly.

"How bad is it?" Nik asked.

"It's become clear that Cassandra and I won't work until she gets past this."

"Are you sure?" Nik asked. "Because Jason's not coming back any time soon."

Neil let out a resigned sigh.

"Yeah," Neil said. "Thanks, Nik. I think I already knew what I have to do. I was just, I don't know. Scared, I guess. It was all just mixed up enough that I've been talking myself out of doing what I have to."

"You know you're going to stuff it up, right?"

"Yeah," Neil said with a sigh. "I know."

"Why?" Cassandra asked.

She was watching Neil pack his clothes into a dimensional duffel bag resting on his childhood bed.

"Because you're not with me," Neil told her. "You're with the closest person you can find to a man you dumped eight years ago."

"This is about Jason?"

"Yes, it's about Jason. Do you even realise that's the third question about him you've asked me today?"

"I haven't seen him in years."

"Which is probably the issue. He's on your mind and that makes sense. If I didn't know him, it wouldn't be a problem. But I do, and that makes me a source to assuage your curiosity. It's planted between us like a thorny hedge. If we try to force our way through it, we'll just get torn up. Until you see him and get some closure, it's always going to be there. The timing's just wrong for you and me right now."

"What's closure?"

Neil flashed a sad smile.

"I've been seeing a mind healer regularly. I think all adventurers should. It's helped me with how I look at the world."

"What? Why are you talking about mind healers?"

"Closure," he said. "Confronting an aspect of your past and tossing out all of the baggage that comes with it. You need to sit down with Jason and sort through your feelings."

"You think I want him instead of you?"

"No. I know it's not like that. It's a complicated bundle of feelings and you need to untangle it before you and I can have anything together."

"Neil, this is crazy. You're being jealous and insecure about a man I haven't seen in years."

"I'm not jealous, Cass. Well, I am a little, knowing that he's the one on your mind. It makes sense, though. You weren't with him for that long, and you've known everything about me since we were teenagers. I don't have any mysteries left for you, and there are always questions about Jason."

"You think I'm a cat chasing after the most interesting thing that tumbles into view?"

"You don't have to ask what I think about you, Cass. What I feel. You've known since I was a kid smitten with his friend's big sister. Since a boy's infatuation became a man's love. But there are things you need to settle within yourself before you and I can be anything more than a casual fling. And a fling isn't enough. Not with you. It has to be all or nothing; I won't accept the middle ground. And since it can't be 'all' until Jason Asano stops living in your head, it has to be 'nothing.' At least for now."

"You're not worried that if you let me go now, something might happen when I see him again?"

"No. I know Jason, Cassandra. Better than you ever did. He's a long way from the person you knew, and he's my friend."

"He and I were a lot more than friends, Neil."

"Who says a lover is more than a friend, Cassandra? There are things more intimate than sharing a bed."

He went back to shoving his clothes into a dimensional bag.

"So, that's it?" Cassandra asked. "You're accusing me of being hung up on Jason and you're just leaving?"

He paused packing his clothes and took a slow, calming breath. Without taking his eyes from the bag, he spoke with the careful enunciation of someone straining to hold in an outburst.

"Do you remember what you asked when I got back from having lunch with Nik? About Jason making a person, and what Jason's fight with the astral beings was like. It's like this every day, Cass. I'm not going to be your consolation prize."

"You're not a second choice, Neil."

He turned on her with wild eyes.

"Then don't treat me like I am! Cassandra, it was always you for me. Long before Jason came along. Why do you think I was so pissy when the two of you were together? It wasn't on Thadwick's behalf, I can tell you that much."

"Maybe instead of walking out the door with no warning, you can sit down with me and talk about this?"

"What's there to talk about, Cass? Having you stop asking about him every single day? Even if he's not on your lips, he'll be in your head. Nothing I can do can fix this. All I can do is make it worse, and that's why you and I aren't going to work right now."

"Is that what you think of me? That I'm just using you as a surrogate for him?"

"No. I don't think you're faking the good times we have together. I don't think you want to trade me out for him. But I'm here for this relationship, Cassandra, and that's all I'm here for. It feels like you're here for something else as well, and this is only going to work if it's you and me, not you, me and him."

"I'm not looking to resume my relationship with Jason Asano."

"I know. But it doesn't have to be romantic for him to be a palpable presence between us. The man in your head and the one in the stories are so different that you can't let it go, and I understand that. I can tell you all day that the man you remember hasn't existed for years, but you need to see it for yourself. And that isn't possible right now."

"So we wait. That doesn't mean you have to leave. You don't have to punish me for it!"

Neil's eyes went wide and he dashed forward, wrapping her in a comforting hug.

"I'm not trying to punish you," he said. "None of this is your fault. Or my fault. It's just timing and circumstance. Your feelings aren't wrong. Not the ones about him, or the ones you have for me. If I didn't know Jason, I wouldn't be this constant reminder in your life. But I am. The way things stand, my presence is only making things worse for you. I hate doing this. I'm so scared of destroying everything."

Tears streamed down both of their faces as they continued to hold each other.

"If you hate doing this," she said, "then don't."

"I have to, Cass. Some things don't work out, no matter how much you want them to. And right now, we don't."

79

NO QUESTION OVER WHO IT WAS

GREENSTONE WAS DIVIDED INTO TWO SECTIONS. THE SMALLER PORTION OF the city, although still large, was an artificial island. It was the domain of the nobility, adventurers, and those with the wealth and influence to keep such company. In a stunning failure of imagination, the artificial island had been named 'The Island.'

The larger and older part of the city showed creativity in being named 'Old City.' It hugged the coast where the magically fed Mistrun River created a sprawling delta. Old City was raised up on thick foundations and secured behind a massive wall. Numerous inlets fed the city with the magic-infused water on which much of its infrastructure relied.

Old City had been run by a trio of crime families since the wealthy and powerful had all moved to the Island. So long as the trade kept moving and the money kept flowing, the noble houses and merchant barons were satisfied to let them. The situation had gone unchanged for more than a century until the last few years saw sudden upheaval.

Two of the big three crime families had been eliminated. The leader of the third had been legitimised and installed in the newly formed office of mayor of Old City, answering directly to the Duke of Greenstone. It was part of a wave of change, following a number of events centred on the Adventure Society.

In the Old City, crime obviously hadn't been eliminated. But with the legitimisation of the last crime family standing, much of what had been shady business was brought into the light. The darkest corners of the city were cleared out; the worst depravities quietly eliminated before they could embarrass the new mayor.

The famously corrupt city militia were disbanded as protection rackets became security services. They still took the money but offered actual protection, and no longer clashed over territory. Gambling houses and brothels were no longer subject to conflicting crime families and corrupt militiamen, but now they had to pay taxes.

The most recognisable landmark in Old City was the Fortress. A holdover from Greenstone's early days as a colony, it had long been the place where old money and Old City sleaze came together. Even as the city changed, the Fortress did not, remaining the place where the reputable of Greenstone could slake their less reputable appetites.

Former Magic Society director Lucian Lamprey had been shameless enough to maintain a large and highly visible office amongst the stands for the Fortress' fighting arena. Such brazenness had led to his downfall, however, and his successor was not so careless.

Pochard Finn had been Lucian Lamprey's long-time deputy. He had done the actual work during Lamprey's famously corrupt tenure. Pochard was a man who understood the value of discretion and the consequences of failing to maintain it. He did maintain an office in the Fortress, like his predecessor, from which to conduct his less savoury business and occasional indulgences. Rather than being used for garish displays of power, however, it was hidden away from prying eyes.

It was also well guarded, relative to the city it was in. The essence-users of Greenstone were famously weak, and good thugs were getting harder to come by. The once atrociously corrupt Adventure Society was getting cleaned up alongside Old City, and there were fewer dropouts with every passing year. Those that did were quickly snapped up by the noble houses or the mayor of Old City for relatively honest work.

Pochard had a few of the scarce bronze-rank criminals as guards, although it was more to secure his affairs in his absence than through any need for protection. Pochard's silver rank, though gained through cores, made him one of the most powerful people in the city.

That held true right up until some adventurer came waltzing into town, usually a Geller. Fortunately, the Gellers mostly kept to their compound in the delta and stayed out of local politics. When they didn't, things could change drastically, however, as the last few years had shown. The city was still settling into its new normal after the last time adventurers had thrown their weight around.

Pochard realised they were throwing it again, specifically in the form of one of his guards. The door to his office in the Fortress exploded as his guard flew through it, sending splinters of wood raining down. The guard didn't slow down until he sailed across the office and crunched into the wall.

The man didn't move from where he fell in a heap, although a whimpering moan indicated he was still alive. That kind of force only came from a silver-ranker, and one with proper aura training, if Pochard hadn't sensed them.

When a large man stepped through the now-smashed doorway, it was inevitably a Geller. It could have been worse, Pochard reflected. It could have been Danielle Geller, rather than her son. What trouble he would be was yet to be seen, but there was no way he could be as much trouble as his mother. That woman had walked into the heart of the Magic Society campus and thrashed the director half to death in his own office.

Pochard remembered the Geller son from various high society events. Polite, forthright and a little lacking in confidence, given his background. He had always been a large boy, but seemed smaller, almost shrunken in his hesitance. Years had clearly hardened him up as he strode through the doorway like the chiselled image of a god, needing to turn a little to fit his broad shoulders through the passage.

Pochard got up from behind his desk, ignoring the moaning guard as he stepped around him to greet Humphrey Geller.

"Lord Geller," Pochard said. "It's been some time. I didn't realise you were back in the city."

"I'm not, officially," Humphrey said. "That's why I'm here in the Fortress. It's the place for illicit affairs. It's my first visit, actually, although my fiancée is more familiar with it."

"Your fiancée?"

"Surely you remember, Mr Finn? You're the one who brokered the deal to have her handed over to your old boss. To be used in service of his depraved appetites."

"I have no idea what—"

"Don't lie to him," a female voice cut him off. Pochard turned to see a woman standing behind him. There was only one doorway to the office and he hadn't seen her use it. He recalled that her powers were focused on speed, not stealth, which was rather disturbing. She'd gotten inside too fast for him to see, without kicking up so much as a breeze.

The celestine was still the most beautiful woman he had ever encountered. The chocolate skin, contrasted by silver hair and eyes, was as striking as ever. She looked little different, despite ranking up, as there had been little to improve upon. The changes were subtle, the sheen of her hair and the lustre of her skin.

"Sophie Wexler," he said, realising he'd stared a little too long. "Are you here seeking recompense for your treatment at the hands of my predecessor?"

"Are you going to claim you had nothing to do with it?" she asked.

"That would be an obvious lie," he said. "It was no secret that Lucien Lamprey would have accomplished very little on his own. A dire lack of discipline. So, I will admit that certain arrangements were facilitated by me."

"I grew up around people like you," she told him. "Slime clinging to the walls. I don't blame you for your part in my unpleasant days here. You were doing your best to slink towards the light, and I understand that. But Humphrey is a good man who never waded into the muck like you and I have. He has ideals, and those ideals take a certain view on people like you. So don't lie to him, Finn. And don't try to keep from us what we're here to take. Otherwise, you might find out just how intolerant he can be of your kind. Especially ones who have done things to me."

"He's not going to cross the line," Pochard said. "He's an adventurer, and quite the upstanding example of one. I remember his mother making very sure of that. He's not going to sully the Geller name."

"Yes," Sophie said. "He is a Geller. Old Greenstone nobility. And here in the Fortress, Greenstone aristocrats do the things that they don't talk about after they leave. Like putting their hands on either side of your head and slowly squeezing them together."

"Sophie, I'm not doing that," Humphrey said.

A look of annoyance crossed Sophie's face.

"Humphrey, I'm intimidating here. Just stand there looking large and handsome."

"I'm not going to slowly and painfully kill anyone," Humphrey insisted. "I'll do it quick and clean. It's easier to get rid of the body that way."

"Oh, like you know how to get rid of bodies," Sophie said.

"I've spent a decent number of airship rides sitting next to Belinda,"

Humphrey said. "She told me all about the best ways to discreetly eliminate corpses in Greenstone. No matter how many times I asked her not to.
I don't think she's really killed as many people as her stories implied,
though."

"She hasn't," Sophie said. "She used to do cleanup for the Silva
family when they killed people. You remember the Silva family, don't
you, Finn? Your boss teamed up with them to go after our friend and, as a
direct result, that family and your boss are both gone."

"What do you want?" Pochard asked.

"We want your archive code sequence sheet," Sophie said.

Pochard's eyebrows shot up. "You're after the archive vault?"

He looked from Sophie to Humphrey and back.

"You're a thief," he told her, "so that makes sense. But him? Does
your mother know what you're up to, Geller?"

"Talk about my mother some more and see what happens," Humphrey
said. "Where is the archive code sequence sheet?"

"There's a safe in my office on the Magic Society campus. It's secured
in there."

Humphrey stepped forward but stopped at a gesture from Sophie.

"That's the last time I stop him when you lie, Finn," she warned.

"It wouldn't matter, even if you got it," Finn said. "There are
numerous failsafes on the archive vault and that code is just one of them.
If I give you my code sequence, it would still take two more sequences
from directors in other branches to open the vault in my branch. The code
is constantly changing, so they need to be communicated simultaneously.
Might I remind you that the water link system is managed by the Magic
Society, and has alarms set up if it's used to transmit vault code sequences
outside of scheduled times."

"Yes," Sophie said. "Assuming that we had friends dealing with other
branches, we would need an alternative to the world's only long-range
mass-communication system. So, there's nothing to lose in handing your
code sheet over, and a head to lose if you don't."

"You know that if you do this, the Magic Society won't let it go,"
Pochard said. "Even if you fail. Even if they can't prove it was you, they
can't be seen to have let you walk over them. They'll come after you."

He turned to look as a new person entered the room. Unlike Sophie,
ranking up had made generous changes to Clive Standish. The awkward,
gangly researcher Pochard had known was now lean and handsome. His
old perpetual nervousness was nowhere to be seen. If Standish was

involved, Pochard had no doubt the vault would be successfully breached. The man had always been frustratingly thorough.

"Has he handed it over yet?" Clive asked.

"Not yet," Sophie said. "The relay towers for communication?"

"In place and tested," Clive said. "All we need is the last sequence fragment. Strip him and scrape him down. He always liked to hide things on his body with false skin."

Pochard failed to hide his surprise, drawing a smile from Clive.

"Yes, Deputy Director," Clive said. "I've always known about your inept little tricks. Did you really think no one would see through them at the Magic Society of all places? It makes sense, I suppose. The society is all politicians now. If it wasn't, I wouldn't have to do something this drastic."

"It's Director now, Standish," Pochard said, mustering what he could of his dignity. "I haven't been deputy director for several years."

"Really?" Clive asked. "You're in this situation and you're being fastidious about a title? This is a reflection of a much larger problem. But you don't have to worry, Director; I don't think they'll let you keep the position. Not after your part in publicly releasing the archive vault research. Centuries of hoarded secrets, open and available to all. Aside from the restricted content, obviously. If we're going to make an enemy of the Magic Society, best not make one of the Adventure Society as well."

"They'll never let you go for this, Standish."

"Then I suppose you'll feel vindicated when they string me up. Hand over the sequence sheet, Director."

Scowling, Pochard lifted up his shirt and peeled the false skin off his abdomen and placed it on his desk. On the opposite side of the fake skin side was a sheet with a row of coloured splotches, as if dabbed on with paint.

"That's it?" Humphrey asked.

As they all watched it, the colours all changed. Clive took a crystal from his pocket and waved it over the sheet. The colours glowed for a brief moment and Clive put the crystal away.

"That's it," he said. "I was worried he'd have a dummy sheet, but this is the real thing. I guess he's not as smart as I thought."

"No, he's smart," Sophie said. "It's trying to fob a fake off on us that would be stupid."

"True enough," Clive agreed.

He opened his dimensional space, a small portal ringed with floating runes. From it, he pulled out a hand mirror. He tapped the face of the mirror and a three by three grid of symbols appeared. He tapped on the symbols in sequence and they vanished, replaced with a pulsing light. A humming sound rose and fell in time with the pulses. After a few moments, the light and sound stopped. In their place, an image of Belinda appeared in the mirror. She looked to be holding one similar, and a large steel door was behind her.

"You've got it?" she asked without preamble.

"We've got it," Clive told her.

"Okay. Before you tell me the sequence, wait for the next sequence shift to give us the most time. These sequences change every minute."

They waited for the colours on the sheet to change again and Clive read off the colour sequence.

"Blue. Red. Indigo—"

"What in a god's wet crevice is indigo?" Belinda asked.

"It's a darker purple than violet," Clive said.

"Then just say purple."

"What if there's another shade of purple later?"

"You've got the sheet. Is there another shade of purple?"

"Not right now," Clive admitted, "but the colours change."

"Then just say purple!"

"There's nothing wrong with being precise."

"There isn't going to be another shade of purple, Clive."

"How can you know that?"

"Because no sane person wants a conversation like this! Look, we've wasted too much time. Wait for the next sequence."

"Fine," Clive grumbled.

Humphrey, who had moved next to Sophie, leaned in to whisper.

"How confident are you in this burglary plan?"

"It's called a heist, honey."

"How confident are you in this heist plan?"

"Just trust in Lindy," she told him, a smile teasing at her lips.

"Look, can I go now?" Pochard asked. "I think my part in this is done."

"Head for that door and it will be," Sophie warned.

The colours on the paper shifted again.

"Go, Clive," Belinda said. "And don't you dare say chartreuse or I will come over there and smack the ability to see colour out of you."

Clive rolled his eyes but read off the new sequence.

"Okay, we're in," Belinda said. "You can pack it up and get out."

She vanished from the tablet as she cut communication.

"That's it," Clive said. "we should go."

"You're going to kill me, aren't you?" Pochard asked. "So I don't tell them it was you."

"We don't need to kill you," Clive said. "Frankly, I take no small delight in what you will face from the Magic Society after this. And as for knowing it was us…"

Clive let out a chuckle filled with uncharacteristic malevolence.

"…with what I have planned, there will be no question about who it was."

Clive strode out, putting Pochard behind him, and Humphrey followed. Sophie kicked Pochard square in the crotch and he fell, hands clutched over his groin as he let out a whimpering moan. She bent down to speak amiably into his ear.

"This is why adventurers say training is important," she told him. "A silver-ranker should be able to manipulate their body so no part of it is as vulnerable as that."

Clive returned to the doorway.

"What are you doing?" he asked. "We need to go."

"I owe this guy one," Sophie said.

She kicked Pochard hard in the stomach.

"And that's for sleeping with Clive's wife," she added.

"Wha…?" Pochard asked as Clive rolled his eyes.

"Really?" Clive asked. Sophie flashed him a grin and then was past him in a blur of movement. Clive shook his head and followed.

TIME, RESOURCES AND
DEDICATION

JASON'S MARTIAL ART, THE WAY OF THE REAPER, WAS UNLIKE ANYTHING from Earth. Anything realistic, at least; there were plenty of sketchy ninja movies from the eighties with a similar feel. More than just a martial art, though, it was a full training system for a magical assassin. It incorporated combat skills, acrobatics, stealth, and traversal techniques from climbing to parkour.

The training system had methods for incorporating essence abilities. These were focused around assassination-friendly powers of deception, mobility, and afflictions like poison. It all suited Jason very well. There were also an escalating array of techniques for higher ranks, where super-human prowess turned the impossible into the merely outlandish.

It was all too much for normal humans. Too much to learn. Too much to keep in practice without skill degradation. It was designed from the outset to use skill books. To be learned by those with the enhanced mental and muscle memory of an essence-user. Someone who could live for decades at peak physical fitness and beyond. Who could use a skill they mastered a dozen years ago as if they'd kept in practice the whole time.

Most of all, it took time. More time than a normal human had. Even essence-users couldn't properly approach it without skill books. A combat savant like Sophie could take parts and create her own variant style, disre-garding the rest. Jason lacked her talent and had to learn it all the normal way.

Even with skill books and years of experience, there were massive parts of the martial art that Jason had never explored. Some he never would, being for inhuman body shapes or employing magic powers he didn't have. Others he had taken to as he ranked up, gaining the superhuman strength and speed they required.

As time passed in the otherworldly combat zone, Jason faced defeat after defeat. However much he improved, however much he grew, he was inexorably pushed deeper and deeper into his own soul.

Although he'd made the rules of the battle, he had also been forced to maintain balance with his opponents. He'd given them forms, but he wasn't free to just make them all weak. He was able to balance them out against himself, but there had to be give and take.

Knowing that he would need opponents that would push him, he made sure that they would always outdo him in combat potential. As his long-stalled essence powers finally started to grow, so too did his enemies grow more powerful. Whether his advancements were in his skill or his finally advancing essence abilities, the great astral beings stayed ahead of him. If the trade-off for always being stronger was being maybe a little oblivious in areas unrelated to battle, that was part of the balance too.

As Jason grew stronger, he started adapting the way he fought. He'd stopped using his own arms to wield his sword, instead giving it to a conjured shadow arm. These arms were more flexible, less vulnerable and could shift around his body instead of being attached at the shoulder.

Freed from the limitations of a purely human form, Jason could use the flexibility to expand his combat repertoire. He could draw on techniques previously unavailable, which were especially useful when fighting in the open. When shrouded by his cloak, fighting him was more like facing a cloud of darkness than a person. Flexibility in where his sword was made the position of his body and the source of his attacks even harder to predict.

The cloak itself was part shield and part weapon. Able to become tangible or intangible, in full or in part, it never restricted Jason. The same was not true for his enemies who were faced with a versatile constriction tool. In trying to strike at Jason's hidden form, limbs could be tangled and attacks yanked off course.

The cloak was easy enough to pull free of, but fragments of seconds mattered. Jason had long understood that a battle between wielders of powerful magic was a war of stolen moments. That only become more true as rank and power escalated.

Slowly but surely, Jason progressed in his mastery of the Way of the Reaper. He shored up his ability to stand his ground in a fight, albeit in his own elusive way. He better learned to use his powers in open battle and not just skulking hit-and-run attacks.

The most misused powers at his command were those of his familiars. To varying degrees for each, he had been using his companions as separate entities and not integrated aspects of his own power set. The more he rectified this, the more he realised how foolish and wasteful he had been.

Shade had always been the familiar Jason had worked with the closest. The shadow companion was Jason's best teacher and would never have allowed him to completely waste the potential of their synergies. The more Jason improved, the better able he was to work with Shade. As he increasingly focused on working with Shade, the more Jason realised his familiar had been waiting for him to catch up. Once Jason found the humility to truly listen and learn, he found that Shade had much to teach.

The practical results of this was that Shade was much harder to pin down. Jason had often used him for shadow-jumping targets, but that had left Shade in the open as a forest of shadows. As they were no longer low-rank, there was no shortage of enemies with magic who could cut down Shade's ethereal bodies. Under Shade's tutelage, Jason worked on communication and anticipation between himself and his familiar. He learned to aim for Shade when he was still in hiding, in the shadows of the battlefield or even the shadows of the enemy.

The result was Jason becoming less predictable and Shade less vulnerable. This allowed the familiar to become more active in his own right. He could actively set up shadow-jump sneak attacks, knowing Jason would seize opportunities he would have missed in the past. Shade could also make good distractions with sudden and unexpected mana draining.

Shade was the easiest familiar to work with. He was ancient, experienced, and had the strongest natural synergies with Jason. Improving his teamwork with the other familiars was harder. They were both young, being no older than Jason's adventuring career. Their powers were also less directly convergent with Jason's own, especially Gordon's.

Colin was, at least, a powerful source of afflictions. Jason had been wasteful of his potential, however, mostly dumping huge piles of leeches and hoping it worked out. Now that Colin had a variety of forms, he and Jason strove to make the most of each, turning the familiar into a force multiplier instead of an unreliable trump card.

Colin's original form was simply a mass of leeches. Instead of hosing enemies with massive swarms, Jason learned to distribute them in targeted clusters. Not only was this a more efficient use of Colin's biomass, but it prevented one well-placed area attack from wiping most of it out.

If the leeches proved effective and weren't being efficiently countered, Colin's second form became a solid option. The worm-that-walks form was a bundle of leeches, bound into a vaguely humanoid shape by a mass of bloody rags. This form wasn't fast, but the rags could shoot out, grab opponents and drag them to the leeches for devouring.

In instances when Jason's own abilities were proving most effective, Colin's blood clone form could mimic him. Colin inherited many of Jason's skills and abilities in this state, and while the clone didn't double Jason's power, it certainly provided a serious additional threat.

Finally, Colin's last form was for the times Jason still needed to use him as a powerful trump card. Colin's blood abomination form was energy-intensive, needing to constantly feed to simply maintain its existence. That was exactly what Jason wanted it for, however, the ever-shifting and always ravenous monstrosity always having an impact on the battlefield.

Gordon was the familiar Jason had the hardest time working with. Jason usually kept him at a remove in combat due to what he had considered a power incompatibility. Shade's shadowy nature and Colin's afflictions aligned with Jason's powers to greater and lesser degrees, making what was already strong even stronger. Gordon's beams and shields were useful but didn't seem like a good fit with Jason's stealth and afflictions.

When Jason had first initiated the epic training battle against the great astral beings, his core intent had been to strip away his crutches. To take away every external advantage he'd relied on to cover his weaknesses. While two years of fighting had helped him better understand those weaknesses, it hadn't made them go away.

The revelation had come when Jason learned to stop thinking of Gordon as an external force, separate from himself. Over the span of Gordon's short life, he had shown Jason time and again that they were connected, intrinsically and forever. When he finally learned to see Gordon and himself as parts of each other, he felt like a bad friend. He finally came to understand that he had been wasting Gordon by sending him off to fight alone. That the very reason the pair were different was that the very nature of their powers was to cover for each other's shortcomings.

Where Jason had to evade, Gordon could shield. When heavy armour or a magical barrier prevented afflictions from being applied, Gordon could crack them. As for the familiar, his beams excelled at penetrating defences, but dealt limited damage once through them. For that, he needed Jason. Gordon could expose a heavy defender in the front of a formation, or shielded healer in the back, and then Jason could go to work.

Jason was startled at how effective working more closely with his familiars made all four of them. He felt like a fool for having wasted so much potential, underutilising them so drastically over the years. Of all the things he had failed to make effective use of, one stood out when he started employing it more.

Gordon's most underused ability was the power to detonate his orbs. So different from Jason's mindset of sneaking and whittling enemies down with afflictions, Jason had rarely called on it. As he forced himself to try different combat strategies, Jason came to appreciate a simple truth that his narrow approach had been hiding from him: sometimes you just need to blow stuff up.

As he worked with his familiars and mastering his martial art, there was one other aspect of combat Jason had been focusing on as he battled the great astral beings. The combat trance was a semi-meditative state that, while not an essence ability, could only be achieved with a magically enhanced mind. As it was a skill and not an innate power, it was easily missed by improperly trained essence-users. Like aura mastery, it was a key indicator of an elite adventurer.

At low ranks, everyone's combat trance was the same. Primarily useful to melee combatants, it 'turned off' certain aspects of the mind in order to reach a state of heightened focus. Something akin to the early stage could even be achieved by some exceptional normal-rankers. Jason had first achieved it at bronze rank.

As rank and mastery of the technique increased, essence-users tailored their own combat trances to their own needs. What they did, when they were used and for how long varied from person to person. For some, it was a near-perpetual state of empty mind, hyper-focused on every moment.

This was common to sword masters, and Sophie took a similar approach. She spent most of her fights in a combat trance that allowed her to better control her blinding speed. For Humphrey, it was about fighting by the most efficient means, from how he moved to how he spent his mana. Others, like Clive and Neil, focused on broader battlefield awareness, taking most of the combat out of their combat trances. Their trances operated in short bursts, letting them parse complex battlefields in a moment.

Jason had been attempting to shift his combat trance to be closer to that of Clive and Neil. He wanted important bonuses in critical moments rather than an extended enhancement to his swordplay. The basic form of a combat trance worked best with orthodox fighting styles anyway, which was not the way Jason was going. Rather than enhance a fighting style he was moving away from, he was looking to the challenges of the future.

Many essence-users had enhanced speed. Essences like swift and lightning were common while exotic choices like the time confluence could be outright terrifying. Even something like the sun essence gave Rufus flashes of brilliant speed. It was too strong a weapon to have no answer to.

It was more than just other essence-users. Smaller, lighter monsters were usually faster, and even the larger ones could have powers that accelerated them in bursts. That would only become a greater problem with gold-rank monsters whose powers were more exotic and more numerous.

What Jason needed against such opponents was time. Time to react. Time to strategise. Time to adapt to an ever-changing battlefield. Time to see an enemy moving at Sophie's pace before it was too late. She was already borderline gold rank with her speed, to the point that Jason could barely track her. It would only get worse at gold rank.

Jason did have one way to compete. He could speed himself up by draining the remnant life force of slain enemies. Not everyone would be kind enough to throw mooks at him as if they were bosses in a video game, though. In any case, competing was the wrong approach.

Trying to match up to someone like Sophie was pointless. She didn't have just one ability to enhance her speed, but an entire power set built around it. Sword masters were the same, known for being better against other essence-users than monsters. As for monsters themselves, one essence ability could not keep up with a creature whose entire physiology was built for magically enhanced speed.

Jason didn't think that a combat trance could compensate for all that. Other essence-users had their own combat trances, and he would never beat them at their own game. But he didn't need to be as fast as the other guy. He just needed to think fast enough to see the other guy coming.

What Jason wanted was to accelerate his perceptual speed. It was beyond the scope of a trance to actually speed him up, at least at silver rank. There was no telling what diamond-rankers were capable of, but that was a question for the future. All Jason wanted for now was to think faster. To give him the mental moment to plan, or react to someone whose speed wildly outclassed him.

The process of altering Jason's combat trance started by giving up its strengths. The extreme focus that aided his swordplay was diminished, and he could not hold the trance state for as long. The monsters he was endlessly fighting helped. Like him, they returned after every death, and were reacting to his needs. They slowly but surely became faster, forcing him to adapt.

It took time for him to notice the gradual improvement. The less time his combat trance lasted, the slower the world seemed to get, but he barely realised it was happening at first. As days passed into months and months into years, the trance got shorter and his mind got faster. Two years into his otherworldly battle, entering his combat trance felt like stepping into treacle, his body barely moving. He knew he had further to push, but he also knew he shouldn't take it too far.

He could feel the strain as he pushed his silver-rank mind to its limitations. It lasted only moments and no longer placed him in a zen-like state of unfettered hyperawareness. Pushing the ability to a more exotic variant meant that it would require more to master, and his silver-rank mind was already nearing its limitations. He would keep working on it, but knew that he would be gold rank before he considered it a completed technique. But for now, he was satisfied.

Mastering the Way of the Reaper in less than a century was unrealistic. To do so would require years of endless, gruelling combat. A ceaseless war against opponents with the skill, power and numbers to make survival impossible.

And then surviving anyway.

Jason let out a groan as he came back to life. Years of endless, gruelling combat left an inescapable echo of exhaustion, even when he respawned in a fresh and energetic body. They'd entered a break period while he was respawning, one of the precious and too-short reprieves from combat. The food carts for the current break were supplying soft pretzels, so Jason grabbed one in each hand.

He looked over at the Reaper in his pale human incarnation. He was staring off into space, the way he did during every rest break. Jason walked over to stand beside him, looking off into the jungle that lined the wide road.

"The Order of the Reaper," Jason said. "An offshoot of your cult on Pallimustus, yes?"

"Yes," the Reaper said. "They paid only lip service to my principles while using my name in the pursuit of secular power."

"That's what I've heard. It's left me wondering about the martial art I got from them, the Way of the Reaper. Is that something they developed when they turned into political assassins, or a holdover from when they were proper cultists? Basically, did you have any input, or is the name just a branding exercise?"

The Reaper finally moved, turning his head to look at Jason with curiosity.

"Searing a mark in flesh with a heated iron?" he asked.

"Uh, no," Jason said. "Branding, in this case, means using a name to add implied value in lieu of adding actual value. In short, is this a style you had a hand in, or did they just slap your name on it?"

"The techniques you practise were developed by my cult. They are traditionally restricted to individuals raised within the cult and selected to train for decades, in preparation of the most difficult missions. You should understand, now, that the study of these methods is not to be undertaken lightly. Without time, resources and dedication, one can only display the shallow results you did when this battle began two years ago. Only now are you beginning to show actual results."

"Huh. So, I'm starting to get it right?"

"'Starting' being the operative word."

"You don't have to be a dick about it."

"I have to do something with my time here."

Jason peered at the Reaper with narrowed his eyes.

"Was that... a joke? That was a joke, wasn't it?"

Jason turned and waved his arms, dripping cheese and mustard from his pretzels as he shouted to the scattered great astral beings.

"Hey everyone! The Reaper just made a joke!"

"Really?" the Celestial Book mumbled through a mouthful of pretzel. "Was it any good?"

Jason stopped to think about it.

"You know, for a first attempt, it wasn't bad. Very deadpan, but what do you expect?"

81

NOT ENOUGH FOR FOREVER

"...CAN'T BELIEVE YOU DIDN'T TELL ME," ZARA CONTINUED, AS SHE HAD been doing since Greenstone.

"You would have insisted on participating," Sophie said. "We couldn't allow that."

"I may only be a temporary member of this team," Zara said, "but—"

"It's been two years," Belinda said. "You can stop telling people you're a temporary member every single time."

"And part of being in the team is adhering to your role," Neil said, looking off to the side with an innocent expression. "Even if we only tell you what your role was afterwards."

The four were in a sidewalk café in Pranay, a portal stopover point on the way to Estercost. Pranay was the last of the isolated city-states they would visit for a while, with Estercost being a large and densely populated kingdom. It was the homeland of many of their friends, and the land from which Greenstone was colonised centuries earlier.

While the rest of the team were shopping at a nearby market, the four were sipping iced tea in the welcome shade of the café's awning.

"You excluded me from the robbery because of my family, didn't you?" Zara asked.

"Heist," Sophie corrected.

"What?" Zara asked.

"It wasn't a robbery," Sophie said. "It was a heist."

"Isn't a heist a kind of robbery?" Zara asked.

Sophie and Belinda shared a long-suffering look before shaking their heads and giving up.

"Fine," Zara said. "The reason you kept me out of the *heist* was because of my family, wasn't it?"

"Of course that's why," Neil said. "The political ramifications of raiding the archive vault—"

"Allegedly," Belinda qualified.

"Of *allegedly* raiding the archive vault," Neil corrected, "will be bad enough as it is. They'll know it was us, regardless of what they can prove."

He looked over at Belinda.

"They won't be able to prove it, right?"

"No," she said, her voice full of affront. "And I'd appreciate it if people would stop asking that."

"She doesn't like it when people doubt her heist credentials," Sophie said with a smile.

"Just your association with us will complicate things," Neil told Zara. "If people start to think you actually participated, it will be much worse. That's why my job was making sure you had a nice, visible alibi. In a place where they'd checked for illusion magic and shape-shifting, as well, so no one can claim it wasn't you."

"It wasn't easy convincing the venue to ramp up security so they'd check for that either," Belinda said. "I had to threaten to—"

"Probably best you don't tell them what you threatened," Sophie said.

"It's not a problem," Belinda said. "I made sure all the alchemical bombs were easy to find."

"Wait, there were actual bombs?" Sophie asked.

"What was I meant to do?" Belinda asked. "Bluff?"

"YES!" Sophie and Neil exclaimed together.

"Well, I know that now," Belinda said. "You don't have to yell. Look, the others are back."

They watched as Humphrey, Clive and Estella Warnock approached along the crowded market-day street. The pink-haired celestine spy snagged a chair from a neighbouring table and slid in next to Belinda.

Estella had been working more directly with the team since their return from the subterranean expedition. The lack of a luxurious cloud vehicle to hang back in required her to move and live more closely with the group. Having her close at hand had proven useful as an effective urban scout had become increasingly valuable.

Adventuring work traditionally involved a lot of trudging through the wilderness to hunt monsters. Danger in isolated regions was nothing new, but now the cities were suffering greater threats as well. In the wake of the monster surge, the Builder invasion and now the messenger invasion, messenger spies, leftover cultists and intelligent monsters were all lurking dangers.

Even without external threats, simple overpopulation was causing problems. The extended monster surge had been bad enough, but many people either couldn't go home or had no home left to go to. That led to housing and resource shortages, with more food required and less coming in from abandoned farmlands. City infrastructure was overtaxed and mundane criminal enterprises flourished as people focused on magical threats.

Estella's skills might be little use once the fighting started but, in a city, finding the fight was often most of the job. Her ability to navigate the physical and cultural geography of a city's darker corners had proven useful time and again, and an excellent complement to Sophie and especially Belinda's own skills.

"What were you two yelling about?" Estella asked Neil as she, Humphrey and Clive joined the group.

"Neil was complaining about getting dumped again," Belinda told her.

"I was not…"

Neil closed his eyes and took in a long breath and let it out slowly.

"Nope," he said. "Not going to bite."

"We should get moving anyway," Humphrey said. "Especially if we're going to detour to Kazlahk."

Belinda and Estella shared an awkward look.

"Yeah," Belinda said, her voice slightly strained. "Let's get going."

Kazlahk was a city of sandstone, palm trees and money. A coastal city situated on the eastern border of Estercost, it was surrounded by desert. As with Greenstone, the empty desert was a premium site for spirit coin farms, although the higher magic made for more valuable denominations.

Kazlahk's spirit coins and prime location for sea trade made for a lot of wealth. Massive houses belonging to coin barons and major adventuring families lined the gorgeous beaches. The pristine water was a welcome balm from the region's famously scalding climate.

There were a few sites abutting the beach that weren't private homes, including a luxury resort for visiting merchants, adventurers and nobility. The most notable was the Kazlahk University of Medicine. Most schools and research centres dedicated to healing focused on essence and ritual magic, with alchemy lagging in distant third.

The main reason for that focus was funding. While the church of the Healer contributed, the bulk of the money came to such institutions from the Magic Society and the Adventure Society. As a result, their studies and research focused on what was of most use to their benefactors.

KazMed was a prominent exception, focused on the advancement and practical application of alchemical medicine. While part of their funding still originated with the church of the Healer, most came from a large alliance of trade associations. Such groups were the largest employers of essence-users outside of the Adventure Society, but most of the healers became adventurers.

While not adventurers, the essence-users hired to escort trade convoys through the wilds faced genuine danger. From sea monsters to sky pirates, the most active ones faced as many monsters and bandits as some adventurers. A lack of healers amongst them, however, made cost-effective healing options essential. This had been the impetus for founding a school where graduates wouldn't be snatched away by the Adventure Society.

KazMed had recently completed construction of a new research centre, the School of Alchemical Efficiency. While the university had found success in producing alchemists focused on healing, it had fallen short on some of its core intentions. The research centre was designed to rectify that by advancing cost-efficient alchemy. The new school would do this through the twin approach of well-funded research in the field and a new wave of alchemists who would focus on it.

Belinda made her way nervously through the campus alone. The buildings were widely spaced, with flagstone pathways and gardens of palms and hardy desert plants. The sounds of the nearby shore were carried on a breeze with the scent of the sea, not as dry as the air deeper into the city.

She reached an administration building for the School of Alchemical Efficiency and asked for the location of the dean. She was given directions to a large building that looked a little different to the others. There were no windows, and the sandstone walls were covered in reinforcing metal bands, engraved with sigils. The roof was covered with chimneys, like a metal garden.

Belinda found herself compelled to examine the sigils set into the reinforcing metal of the walls. It was intricate and complex work, and she was certain they would have needed a formation interactivity specialist in the design. Such specialists were rare and their services expensive.

She shook her head.

"You're stalling," she muttered to herself. "Time to face the music, Callahan."

She headed for the large doors leading into the building, a sign above them denoting the building as housing the student labs. She asked the receptionist inside where she could find the dean.

"He's in one of the labs with first years right now. You should probably wait."

"I've put this off longer than I should," Belinda said. "I'm done waiting."

"Alright, just hang on a moment."

The receptionist took a sheet of paper from under his desk and started reading in a monotone voice.

"The Kazlahk University of Medicine and the School of Alchemical Efficiency accepts no responsibility for burns, poisonings, flayings, melted body parts—"

"Flayings?"

"There's a device used to mix large containers of liquid in a specific way," the receptionist explained. "It's a metal orb with numerous thin wires extruding from it. There was an incident involving someone's frenzy spider familiar."

Belinda was forced to listen to the whole thing before the receptionist sent her looking for laboratory six, but soon enough, she was standing outside a pair of metal doors. They were reinforced with further metal, heavy bands etched with strengthening sigils. Some of the reinforcement on one door appeared newer than the rest while the other looked to have been recently replaced in its entirety.

There were no handles to open them. Touch plates beside the doors would only unlock them for those of silver rank and above. The receptionist had told her that anyone likely to die in an explosion was only allowed access under supervision. Belinda only hesitated a moment before pressing her hand to the panel.

The doors slid aside with a hiss, letting out a sickly yellow haze.

Inside was a large room in an amphitheatre style, with tiers rising up from a stage at the front. Instead of seating, however, individual alchemy stations were set up.

The yellow haze lingered heavier around the high ceiling. It was being actively extracted through vents while more vents near the floor pumped clean air in, setting the haze into a swirl. There was a group of students all gathered on the stage where the air was clearest. In front of them, Jory was speaking in the 'not angry but disappointed' voice normally reserved for mothers.

"...come to my attention, Trent, that your repeated concoction of noxious gas is not as accidental as it would appear."

"I don't know what you're talking about, Professor."

"No?" Jory asked, his tone offering the boy enough rope.

"No, Professor."

"It's just a coincidence, then, that each of your premature eruptions are perfectly timed so that the evacuation lets you bump into Miss Katarina Anwan of the Body Reinforcement Department as she leaves her Skeletal Transfiguration lecture? Not to mention giving you a handy topic of conversation."

"Professor Tillman—"

"I am going to explain the situation in which you find yourself, young man. Know that while I do so, there is no noise your mouth is capable of producing that will do anything but make that situation worse. Take my advice then, and keep that mouth closed."

Jory waited for the student to make a bad choice, but realisation was dawning on the young man's face. After a long, awkward moment, Jory continued.

"You lack the courage required to talk to a girl without concocting an elaborate scheme, yet easily muster the courage to sabotage my classes. That, Trent, tells me everything I need to know about what you value amongst the opportunities this institution offers. You are a transparent little boy."

Trent's good judgement in staying silent didn't last. Rather than being cowed, his expression grew angry as Jory berated him.

"My parents—"

"No doubt paid considerable money to get you here," Jory interrupted. "As I have had the misfortune of grading your work, I'm certain you didn't arrive in my class on the basis of academic merit. I was halfway inclined to allow you to continue, should you show any contrition after being confronted on your behaviour. What you have instead demonstrated is an attitude that is beyond the scope of my ability to correct. So, collect your things, leave this room and do not darken my door again without the signed testimonial of multiple staff that you have changed your entire personality."

Trent looked like he was about to haul off on Jory when another student put his hand on Trent's shoulder. He wheeled on the other student, but his anger vanished on seeing who it was. The other student shook his head and Trent stomped away in a huff.

Trent stomped up the stairs and cleared off his alchemy station. He shoved his possessions into a dimensional bag before storming back down, past Belinda and out of the lab.

Everyone in the room watched in silence until the sliding doors closed behind him. Jory, whose back had been to the door, finally noticed Belinda's presence. His eyes went wide for a moment before he turned back to his students. When he spoke, his voice was softer, the anger and disappointment replaced with tiredness.

"I am aware," he said, "that Trent lacked the expertise to so precisely spoil his practical work time after time. I know that he had help in this, but I have no interest in throwing good students out with the bad. I will simply express my hope that whoever it may have been…"

His gaze settled on one very nervous-looking young man.

"…they are more considered in how they attempt to advance their social standing in the future. Your time at this institution is one of transition. You are here to learn more than just how to brew potions and heal the sick. This is your opportunity to go from children playing games to serious adults learning serious things for serious reasons. But it is up to you to claim that opportunity. Over the next few years, you have a choice to make, and you will make it through your actions. When you are done here, will you be as children, nestled under the protective wings of your families? Or will you step into the world as adults deserving of respect, ready to stand on your own and make your marks on the world?"

His expression softened and his voice lightened as he continued.

"That's not to say you can't have fun, or that mistakes will not be forgiven. You should have fun, and this is the best chance you will ever have to make mistakes and learn from them."

He glanced up at Trent's empty work station.

"For those not paying attention, 'learn from them' was the important part of that sentence. Because that's what you're here for: to learn. We don't expect you to walk in here knowing everything about how the world works. I can promise that if you think you did, you were wrong."

He glanced back at Belinda before returning his gaze to his students.

"You don't know it all," he told them. "You never will. I don't. The woman behind me doesn't, and she's the smartest person in this room and almost every room she's ever been in. She's walked with diamond-rankers and watched mortals battle gods, yet she's only just figured out that she should have broken up with me years ago. We all have more to learn, and in your time here, the most valuable thing you can learn is how to learn more."

He let out a long, cleansing breath.

"That, however, is the broad perspective. In specific, there will also be a lot of making potions, and Trent's little experiment has mostly vented out. So, I want all of you to take what remains of our time and show me a workable potion base by the end of the session."

He stood looking at them as they stared blankly back.

"That means go do it now," he told them, not hiding his exasperation. The students started scrambling for their alchemy stations. Jory turned and looked at Belinda with a grin on his face. He walked over, reached into his pocket and a privacy screen shimmered into place, muffling the sound and blurring them to those outside it.

"I can't leave them in here alone," he said. "You'll have to do this with a gaggle of teenagers watching us."

"You know why I'm here," she said.

"I've known this day was coming since the start. It was always me more than you, Lindy. I know you care for me, but not enough for forever. And we've lived different lives for a long time now. How many times a year do we see each other? I'm the settling down type, but Greenstone was always a trap for you."

"You're not in Greenstone either," Belinda pointed out.

"No, but I'm always looking for a place to settle in. You always have an eye on the door. You need someone who can travel the world with you. Get in trouble, have adventures. We both know that's not me. I hope the new person you've found can be that for you."

"What makes you think—"

"You're a better person than you think, Lindy. You're loyal, and you're kind, whatever you might want the world to think. That's why this conversation hasn't happened earlier, and why it's happening now. You've found someone, but you don't want to start with them until you've ended things cleanly with me."

He reached out and gently wiped a tear from her face.

"Don't be sad," he said. "There are no surprises here. What we had was good, but it was never going to last."

"Then why didn't you end it?"

He looked at her as if she had missed something blindingly obvious.

"Because you're amazing," he said. "I was never going to give you up for as long as you would have me. I know we haven't seen each other a lot in the last few years, but I don't regret a single one of those precious moments."

Belinda looked like she'd been slapped.

"Then why not try and change my mind?" she asked.

"Because loving you means wanting what's best for you. And that isn't me, however much I might want it to be."

She let out a crying laugh.

"Well, now I just feel crappy," she said. "Why do you have to be so… decent?"

"It's just how I am. And we both know that decent isn't what you're looking for, Lindy. It's just what you told yourself you should. But you're not Sophie. You don't want someone to be better with. You want someone to be clever and devious with. Frankly, sometimes, I felt more like your father than your lover. Which did make me feel a little creepy from time to time."

"Is that why you freaked out that time I called you—"

"Yes," Jory said. "You remember that we're in a room full of students, right?"

"They can't hear us."

"Even so, I feel a professional responsibility to not discuss bedroom matters in front of them."

She smiled at him, eyes still wet with tears.

"I should go," she said.

"Yes," he said. "I should check on my charges before one of them accidentally makes a bomb. Again."

They shared a last, long look in silence. Belinda brushed a hand lightly against Jory's chest, then moved to walk out of the privacy screen.

"Belinda," he said.

She stopped and turned around.

"He's a lucky man," Jory said. "Don't ever let him think otherwise."

Looking guilty, Belinda left. She opened the sliding doors and when they closed behind her, Jory finally let his expression break. Tears ran down his face and he let them flow for a minute as he stood in place, head bowed. Then he took out a handkerchief, wiped them away and put it back in his pocket. He took an eyedropper from his jacket, putting a drop in each eye to eliminate how bloodshot he knew they would be. After schooling his expression, he dropped the privacy screen and went to check on his students.

———

Belinda found Estella waiting outside the main campus gate, looking nervous.

"How did it—"

Belinda cut her off by rushing forward and wrapping her arms around her. It wasn't amorous, just a need for comfort.

"I feel so crappy," she mumbled into Estella's shoulder.

"Did he make it hard?"

"No. He made it easy, but he's never been good at aura control. I could feel his emotions crumbling the whole time."

"You had to do it."

"I know. He knew. But I hurt him."

"It was never going to be easy. But it's done now."

Estella stepped back, put her hands on Belinda's shoulders and looked her square in the eye.

"It's done now," she said again. "Which means I can finally do this."

She grabbed Belinda and pulled her in for a lingering, passionate kiss. When they finally separated, Belinda started laughing.

"Oh, you found that funny, did you?" Estella asked.

"No, it's just... I was told to tell you you're a lucky man."

STARTING TO UNRAVEL

THE WAR WAS NOT GOING WELL FOR THE VAMPIRES. ON THE GROUND, they were dangerous and powerful, overwhelming any conventional forces not fielded by the magic factions. Their leadership, however, had been sleeping for centuries, if not millennia. These gold-rank vampire lords were personally powerful, but lacked any understanding of the contemporary world. With only a handful of exceptions, they had also proven slow to learn.

Earth had seen the integration of magic and technology accelerate in the last few years. It no longer needed to be hidden and magic levels were on the rise. While a vampire could handle someone with an enchanted gun, they were unprepared for a magical drone strike, and weapons were only the beginning.

A vampire lord from 1487 was not prepared for the advantages of real-time communication across a battlefield, let alone a continent. Satellite images, spy planes and even motorised vehicles were alien to them. Most found themselves at a loss, both mentally and militarily. By the time Rufus started hunting vampires, they had been excised in real numbers from most of the world.

There were younger vampires amongst their ranks who were not so oblivious, but this was of limited value. The mentality of older vampires didn't let them accept that anyone younger and less powerful had anything to offer, even in the face of overwhelming evidence. Dominance was in their nature, while humility and adaptability were not. The ability to over-come that nature was proving the key survival trait for the risen vampire lords.

The inability to listen to advice was not the only aspect of vampire nature holding them back. The vampire lords were independent, territorial and resistant to change. They were convinced they could resume the old ways, acting alone and dividing the world into territories between them.

Those unable to let those ideas go paid a heavy price. Their minds still thought of vampire hunters as grim, grizzled men, sneaking into a gothic fortress. They were not prepared for bunker-busting missiles modified to explode with magically intensified sunlight.

The Americas saw the heaviest fighting, with both continents scoured of vampiric presence. In North America, the vampire threat provided unity to a USA on the brink of civil war. With an external danger to point at, power could be quietly consolidated while the nation was distracted with war on their home grounds. It was a one-sided affair, the US military adapting quickly to a magically enhanced arsenal.

In South and Central America, as well as Africa and Russia, the Cabal rose to the fore. Although the vampires were originally members of their ranks, the rest of Cabal turned on them savagely. Hidden beings of myth and fairy tale came out in the open, the world's rising magic enhancing long-stalled power.

The vampire lords who failed to adapt to a world very new to them were hunted down and slaughtered. Some strongholds remained in Africa, Russia and South America, but North America and China were scoured clean by the highly aggressive Network factions. Any remnant vampires were running and hiding, not maintaining territories.

As for the vampire lords that did manage to change with the times, Europe became their stronghold. They realised that old traditions must give way to new ideas, working together and adopting the technology of the humans. While territoriality was in their blood, making alliances frac-tious, they came together in an uneasy union.

Their leader was known only as Elizabeth. She was a gold-ranker, and extremely tired of people asking if she was Elizabeth Báthory. Those around her learned to stop asking once she started immediately eating anyone who did.

Under Elizabeth, the vampires had managed to establish something of a détente with the rest of the world. Despite the global purge, every major city in the world had vampires still hidden away. Bombings of major vampire strongholds in Europe had been met by assassinations of high-ranking political officials in Beijing, Washington, Moscow and London.

Humanity attempted to eliminate Elizabeth with a nuclear missile modified to flood a region with magically enhanced sunlight. It was a design based on a nuclear device Travis Noble had once modified for Jason. The device had detonated in Rome, inflicting minimal structural damage but sending energy washing through the city. The energy moved like living fire, seeking out the dark places and flooding them with artificial sunlight.

While it had eliminated most of the vampires and their blood servants in Rome, most of the high-ranking vampires had either been sufficiently sheltered or elsewhere entirely. Elizabeth retaliated with a conventional nuclear device, taken from Russia but used in Guangzhou, China. This brought about the first formal agreement between humans and vampires: an official declaration of war from both sides that defined the terms of the conflict.

From that point on, it became much more of a skirmish war. Staging out of bases in the UK, Ireland, Northern Africa and Asano territory, humanity waged a combination of logistical attacks and rescue operations. In both cases, the goal was the same: extract the humans being used as food. Getting the people out was not only a humanitarian objective, but it also put pressure on the vampires as their food supply dwindled. Most Western European nations were defunct as vampires overran them. Millions had died while millions more were evacuated by human forces or rounded up into blood farms as cattle.

The rising magic on Earth was both good and bad for the vampires. It made it easier for them to grow strong, most having been bronze rank for decades. Many were now silver rank and a dangerous number had even reached gold. Of all the gold-rankers on Earth, more of them were vampires than anything else.

Essence-users were also seeing an uptick in gold-rankers, but far less quickly than the vampires. The Cabal was enjoying similar growth, but were secretive about the numbers. It was doubted they had the numerical strength to match the vampires, but rumours abounded that they were poised to claim their own territories.

Cabal fear-stoking was in the realm of conspiracy theories, however; the magical factions were not concerned. The simple reason for that was the Cabal had already quietly spread their influence over much of the world, to the point that greater ambition would only hurt them for little gain. Much of Asia, Russia and Africa was heavily under their influence, along with Central and South America. In the Pacific states especially, the Cabal was often the de facto—or even actual—government.

Cabal territories had initially been a safer place for vampires than those controlled by the Network. While the Cabal had unambiguously split from the vampire lords and those who followed them, most of the world's vampires did not. On Rufus' world, vampires were ruthless and amoral, without decency or mercy. On Earth, they had lived peacefully amongst humanity for centuries.

The rise of magic changed all that. Sunlight had affected vampires weakly, especially the younger ones, only diminishing their strength. As the magic rose, so did the effects of sunlight upon them. In the regions with the highest magic, sunlight could even burn them, like movie vampires.

More dangerous were the long-term effects. Vampires found their need for blood increasing, and their minds being affected. They were becoming more like the vampire lords: domineering, amoral and violent. At first, it was little more than mood swings, but the vampires slowly turned into cold, unfeeling predators.

When the vampire lords first arose, the bulk of the vampire population opposed them. Siding with the humans, they strove to eliminate the lords. That situation grew worse over time for multiple reasons. One was just that humans didn't do much to differentiate good and bad vampires.

Humans being humans, they lumped all vampires in together. Certain sections within media and politics stoked hatred for their own goals, especially in nations where the rise of magic had caused massive political fractures. An external enemy they could point at was exactly what they needed. Nuance and compassion were not.

As the magic continued to rise, the vampires became more dangerous. When some nations started forcing them to register or even rounded them up for public safety, little incentive remained for any vampire to side with humanity.

Some joined the lords, letting themselves become full-blown predators. Others sought advocacy in political circles, fighting to remain a part of the societies in which they had long been secret participants. They fought their growing predatory natures, although the increased need for blood was making that difficult.

In the end, humans and vampires became incompatible. Political reconciliation became impossible as vampires were caged or even executed. Many nations passed laws saying they were not human and had no rights, causing tension with countries where the Cabal held sway.

Most of the remaining vampires escaped to Europe. Many nations unwilling to put them in camps or kill them with death squads deported them, washing their hands of the problem. Others had to escape increasingly oppressive conditions to leave their home countries.

In Europe, there were two camps willing to take the vampires in. One was the nation of vampire lords led by Elizabeth, in need of reinforcements for the war with humanity. Vampires who had initially been against them were swayed by their treatment at the hands of the humans. The changes they were going through as magic rose only made it easier. The alternative was the Asano clan. It meant braving the dangers of a high-magic zone, but the payoff was worth it.

Many, if not most, of the fleeing vampires wanted to reclaim what they had lost. Lives where they weren't monsters, enslaved by their base nature and constant thirst for blood. The Asano clan alone offered this. The clan's most prominent vampire, Craig Vermillion, had put out an open call, claiming to have a safe haven. Many didn't believe it, yet were desperate enough to come anyway. Better a thin thread of hope to cling to than being adrift entirely.

The spirit domain in France, both the outside and its astral space, was vampire free. The population was made up of humans from the Asano clan, transformation zone victims of many species, and the messengers. The angelic strangers from another world were victims of transformation zones in their own way.

The domain in Slovakia was smaller and most of the humans there were refugees of the vampire war. Most of those lived outside of the astral space there, while the vampires lived within it. Outside, the high levels of magic caused the daylight to savage any vampires caught in it. Inside the astral space, the rules were different. This was a place that obeyed not the magic of Earth but the intentions of its master, Jason Asano.

The magic in the astral space was even stronger than that of the outside, yet was not harmful to the vampires. Even the sunlight barely weakened them, and the days grew shorter as the astral space shifted slowly to accommodate them. The longer they spent there, the more the changes wrought by Earth's magic began to abate. The hunger lessened, the predatory rage dimmed and their empathy returned.

In the years since Rufus arrived on Earth, the Slovakian astral space had become the only community of human-friendly vampires left on

Earth. The rest had turned ruthless and bloodthirsty, any compassion they once had long gone. Some had held out longer than others, but all eventually either found their way to the Asano clan or lost their way entirely.

The camps amongst the nations of the world were shut down and their occupants executed. The vampires still hiding within human societies were serial killers, hunting for blood. Many were operating as agents for the vampire lords, while others were just uncaring and hungry.

Rufus had come to fill many important roles in the Asano clan. Along with teaching the Asano clan princess, he also finished what Farrah had started and established a comprehensive training regime for the Asano clan. Fortunately, the domains and especially the astral spaces seemed to change to meet the needs of the people living there.

Part of what Rufus needed was already in place and in use on his arrival. Outside of the astral space cities, magical manifestations were extremely common. The further out one went, the stronger the monsters to be found. Along with being a perfect training ground, it was also a treasure trove of magical materials. Rocks and plants were infused with magic, while essences, awakening stones and quintessence spawned right along with the monsters.

An additional task that Rufus took to with enthusiasm was joining the vampire war. The most powerful combatant below gold rank on the planet, he quickly developed a reputation as someone worth fighting beside. He ignored factional politics and joined whoever was operating out of the military bases the Asano clan allowed on and near their domains. So long as they were fighting vampires and rescuing people from the hideous blood farms, Rufus was an enthusiastic participant.

One group he fought with repeatedly was the messengers. These were not the young messengers who had arrived with Boris and lived in clan territory. These were the Cabal messengers, many of them centuries or even millennia old. They were the most powerful force within the Cabal, and now they were no longer hiding.

Fighting the vampires was both a show of force and a demonstration of the Cabal's good intentions. Rufus had never found them to be joining vampire hunts from cold, political intentions, however, at least not entirely. The messengers he met seemed fully motivated to deal with the vampires as a moral good. While they had a definite streak of arrogance about them, they seemed nothing like the messengers invading Pallimustus. They weren't much worse than Jason on one of his smug days.

Their gold-rankers were especially welcome on these raids into vampire territory, with Boris himself often participating. Gold-rank vampires were a constant threat on such expeditions, and without gold-rankers of their own, things could easily end in tragedy.

Although the Network factions provided most of the key forces for anti-vampire operations, they were reluctant to deploy their gold-rankers. This was less a matter of risk than of politics. Knowing who had how many was a game that Network factions had been playing with one another since the original Network fractured.

Boris had been happy to fill in the gap. He and his messengers, especially the gold-rank ones, frequently made themselves available for anti-vampire operations. This didn't endear him to the upper echelons of the Network factions, but made him very popular with the rank and file. They, even more than Rufus, became very welcome outsiders.

Rufus did not at all envy Boris. While Rufus had made a name for himself amongst those fighting the vampire war, Boris had become one of the most well-known figures on the planet. He was the most prominent figure amongst what the media was still calling angels, and the new face of the Cabal.

The Cabal remained the most enigmatic of the factions. They had the most secrets and their members seemed to have stepped straight out of folklore and fairy tales. This tied them into the belief systems of myriad cultures, complicating their presence on the world stage. Boris and his messengers were constantly needing to deal with people who believed them to be angels of the Lord, despite Boris' constant denials. The larger religions continued to avoid definitive statements, despite mounting pressure.

Rufus had little ability to make sense of Earth religion and even less inclination. Where Boris had been unwillingly thrust into the position of a major religious figure, Rufus wanted none of it. He'd seen some things about a group who had strange ideas about Jason and definitely didn't want to be caught up in that. If they found out half of what Jason got up to, they would only get worse.

Rufus was already more famous than he wanted to be. War correspondents embedded with anti-vampire forces seemed obsessed with him. Emi kept showing him articles about the mysterious warrior from another world, fighting for the reclusive Asano clan. He took solace from Boris having it much worse, from addressing the UN to meeting the Pope.

Another task Boris had taken to was establishing spirit coin farms. Farrah had left information on how to do so, but had little more than inexpert general knowledge from Pallimustus. She was no spirit coin farmer, and the people of Earth hadn't done well at the task. Boris rectified this, helping to establish farms across the planet. It was another thing that kept the messenger so busy, which left Rufus suspicious about one thing: why did Boris visit Clan Asano so frequently?

Rufus had the chance to ask on their return from a joint vampire hunt. They had successfully eliminated a blood farm, liberating the victims trapped there. While the victims were devastated physically and mentally, at least they were alive. Not for the first time, he ruminated that they could use someone like his mother. The local mind healers were adequate, but still new to magic and what it could do to people.

The victims had been evacuated to England, while Rufus and the squad he was working with returned to the base in Slovakia. They disembarked a transport helicopter just outside the demarcation line for the spirit domain, and the helicopter vanished. It had been conjured by a vehicle essence-user, allowing for relatively secure transportation.

Rufus was heading for the carpool where he could get a ride back to the central tower of the domain. The domain in Slovakia occupied what had originally been rural land, and didn't mimic the original space the way the domain in Saint-Étienne did. Here, the cloud buildings didn't hide their nature, creating a small but overtly magical city.

Boris landed nearby, having made his own way back. The messenger didn't need a helicopter when his wings could push him through the air faster than the speed of sound. As for safety in numbers, he was probably the most powerful being on Earth. He noticed Rufus glancing in his direction and strolled over, shrinking to human proportions as his wings vanished.

"Something on your mind, adventurer?"

"I was wondering why you spend so much time here. I'd think it was you trying to lure away the messengers, but they're all in France while you keep coming to Slovakia."

"I don't like lying to people," Boris said. "It's inelegant when a few judiciously placed and entirely true facts can get them lying to themselves. I don't want to do that to you either, so I will simply say that there is a secret that is not mine to share."

"Very well," Rufus said, and they started walking together.

"Is your primary charge still refusing to use monster cores?" Boris asked him.

"You heard about that?"

"By all accounts, it's hard to avoid hearing about it, given her screaming matches with her mother."

"Her grandmother has decided that eighteen is the age where people can choose to participate in monster hunts for themselves. As her birthday grows closer, the tension between them has grown worse."

"What about you?" Boris asked. "As the girl's teacher, have you found yourself caught in the middle?"

"Erika is worried, but she's no fool. She understands that there's no stopping her daughter and that I'm the one who will be keeping her safe."

"Does the girl really want to fight monsters? Or has she simply railed against her mother's restrictions for so long that she'll do it on principle?"

"That is definitely a factor, but she does wants to fully master her abilities. I'm afraid my biases against monster core use have had an impact there."

"You're that set against them?"

"I used to be. Not as much anymore, but I find myself denigrating them out of habit."

"Ah, old habits. They can so easily come back to bite us. For example, if young Emi was willing to use monster cores, it wouldn't have soured her relationship with her mother. It sounds like this whole situation might be your fault."

"It isn't."

"I didn't say it was."

"Good, because it's not."

"I just said that it sounds like it is."

"Well, it's not."

"Technically, I didn't say it sounds like it is. I said it sounds like it might be."

"Will you please stop? This is like talking to Jason."

"You miss your friend?"

"Not right this second, I don't."

Boris chuckled to himself.

"You know, I heard some odd rumours about her confluence."

Rufus stopped walking and gave him a sharp look, then reached into his pocket and activated a privacy screen. He glanced around, noting that no one seemed to be listening. It was late and the people around the base were all busy.

"I know you hear a lot of things that maybe you shouldn't, Boris, but some things you should keep to yourself."

"Oh, come on, Remore. You think you can keep something like that a secret? It's a fundamental shift in the nature of the cosmos. You know this has to be a result of what Jason is up to."

"You don't know that."

"Don't I? The girl got the wrong confluence, Rufus. Vast, myriad and harmonic are meant to produce the unity essence. But they didn't, did they? What did she get?"

Rufus stared at Boris for a long time before answering.

"You don't know?"

"Do you have any idea how hard it is getting information out of the Asano clan? Any malicious intent and your flesh starts rotting off. I learned what I have out of curiosity and good intentions."

"Is that so?"

"Yes. Is it that hard to believe? What have I ever done other than help you and the people you cared about?"

"Spent billions of years learning the patience and skill to manipulate me and the people I care about."

Boris blinked in surprise, then burst out laughing.

"I can't argue with that. I like you, Remore. But you might as well tell me her confluence. It's going to get out sooner rather than later."

"Resonant. She got the resonant confluence."

Boris nodded.

"Makes sense. Seems like it would be on the list for that combination."

"What list?"

"Well, you shared a secret with me. One that I'm kind of amazed has held this long, and definitely won't once she starts fighting monsters with a team. But I'll still share one with you, in turn. You might even call them different parts of the same secret."

"What are you talking about?"

"Do you even understand what Jason is doing? The ramifications of that? You know that essence combinations have only one potential confluence. It's been that way for longer than this universe has existed, which seems like forever to someone barely three decades old. But, before the Cosmic Throne was sundered, things were different. More flexible. In a lot of ways, but how essences combined was one of them. Once upon a time, an essence combination could produce different confluences, from person to person. Some had more options than others, but it was never locked into one. Not until the throne was sundered."

"And that changed how magic worked?"

"In a way. The Cosmic Throne was a regulatory measure on the function of the cosmos. After they broke the throne, the great astral beings had to take steps to maintain cosmic order in its absence. Because they couldn't do what the throne did, the way the throne did it, they needed to enact restrictions. Some went unseen by the denizens of the cosmos. Others were sweeping changes to how things functioned."

"Like essence combinations being restricted to a single confluence?"

"And giraffes existing. I've never seen a planet with complex life where some kind of giraffe didn't evolve. I saw one that's amphibious. Their heads pop out of the water like the telescope on a quadrupedal submarine."

"I feel like we've drifted very far off topic here," Rufus said.

"Right, yes. So, after the sundering, the Celestial Book locked off essence combinations. I have no idea how that helped, before you ask. The operation of the cosmos is a machinery more complex than anyone who isn't a great astral being can understand. But, if Jason repairs the throne, all those restrictions will be undone. If I'm not mistaken, he's already working on it, and those restrictions are already starting to unravel."

"Then why aren't we seeing more of it?" Rufus asked.

"If I'm right, we will. Isolated incidents, to start with. Probably connected to Jason, if your little apprentice is any indication. The great astral beings should have noticed already."

"What does that mean for Jason?"

"I have no idea."

83

THE PROMISE OF GOLD

RUFUS, ERIKA AND HER HUSBAND IAN WERE WALKING TOGETHER towards the administration centre of the Asano clan's French domain. Incongruous amongst the buildings of Saint-Étienne, the towering pagoda was too tall and too Asian to do anything but stand out. It was still off in the distance, the trio having decided to walk in the pleasant summer evening.

"I'm just saying that we need to loosen the reins before she throws them off," Ian said. "She's nineteen years old, Eri. An adult."

"Not in America. There, she wouldn't be allowed to drink, let alone fight monsters."

"Except she would be old enough to join the army and kill people," Ian pointed out.

"Also," Rufus added, "the US training programs allow their essence-users to fight monsters at sixteen."

"I'm her mother and I don't like her going out and risking her life," Erika said. "Is that so hard to understand? People treat me like I'm being unreasonable when all I want is for my daughter to not be ripped apart by the claws of some monster."

"Of course that isn't unreasonable," Rufus said. "But the reality is, facing monsters is something she needs to do right now. When it comes to essence-users, if you won't use monster cores, risk is a necessary part of the equation."

"Exactly," Erika said. "She doesn't have combat-oriented powers and there's another option on the table."

"An option that won't get her what she wants," Ian pointed out as if they hadn't had this conversation a dozen times. "You know our daughter, Eri. She won't accept compromise in her ambition and she's old enough to make her own choices, now. Our job—all three of us—is to guide her as safely through those choices as we can. I'm sorry, Eri, but relitigating choices that have already been made only makes things harder."

"We do what we can," Rufus said. "Not just for her, but for all the trainees. But I will say again that risk is a part of the process. Managed risk, but it has to be real, at least to them."

"And if you keep harping on her, she's going to pack up and go," Ian pointed out. "She's old enough to claim her own place from the clan, and she certainly has the contribution points. She's basically a professor of ritual magic, not to mention a magic researcher. And then there are the problems it's giving you at work. You answer directly to your grand-mother, which is hard to do if you refuse to speak with her."

"She doesn't get to decide how we raise our daughter."

"But she does get to determine what adults can choose to do for them-selves," Ian said. "At this point, Eri, I'm not sure if our daughter is going out there because she wants to or because you don't want her to. She's just as capable of acting out of stubbornness and spite as you—"

Erika's eyes impaled her husband.

"…know her uncle can be," he added hastily.

Rufus kept an awkward distance. He didn't want to side against Emi's mother, but he was responsible both for Emi's growth and safety now she was fighting monsters. He knew that Ian was, if anything, understating the stubbornness of his daughter. Erika's ongoing resistance was muddling Emi's motivations, causing her to focus on monster fighting more than she should. Emi was, after all, a student of magic first; confronting monsters was meant to be a means to an end.

The Asano clan's training regime was well established. Emi was spending much of her time with the materials Clive and Farrah had sent, with which Rufus was no help. Rufus had more time to himself, and he was using it more and more for fighting. The old drive was coming back and he was pushing himself, looking ahead to the promise of gold.

He spent more time hunting vampires, working with any government or faction staging operations out of Asano clan territory. He also spent time out on the borders of the Asano clan astral spaces where the monsters were most dangerous. He'd avoided many gold-rank monsters and even killed two of them alone when the conditions were just right.

Rufus was forced to admit that his activities were not helping with Emi. Drawing as much satisfaction as he did from facing vampires and monsters in combat did little to dissuade her from following his lead. But Rufus was not going to stop in hope of setting a different example. Not only were his excursions valuable but he had a more personal drive as well.

Gary had been gone for years now. More and more, the sadness was replaced with fond recollection, remembering the good times instead of the end. It was not lost on him that this was what Gary had wanted in encouraging Rufus to leave. More and more, Rufus thought of their adventuring days, especially from the beginning.

In the early days, Gary, Farrah and Rufus had dreamed of what their adventuring life would be. In many ways, Rufus was now living the dream they'd envisioned. Growing stronger; helping people along the way. Back then, they had chafed under their silver-rank chaperones, the way Emi did against her mother.

It was not lost to him, however, that when he and his friends got their freedom, they learned the hard way what being on their own truly meant. Being captured by the blood cult had been a hard lesson, and one that almost cost them everything. Only the arrival of Jason had been their unlikely saving grace, changing their lives forever.

Gary had been the first to understand that adventuring wasn't everything. Looking back, Rufus realised his friend had always known. Gary had always been a craftsman at heart, not an adventurer. But he'd also been a hero, so it was as an adventurer that he had died.

Rufus was determined that Emi would not suffer the same fate. She showed flashes of her uncle's boldness, but she didn't take to the life the way he had. Jason had taken to adventuring so fast that he had lost himself in many ways, needing years to find himself again. Emi also had drive, but magic was her uncharted country to explore.

Clive and Farrah were the role models Rufus wanted for Emi. Fortunately, they had both left a trove of recordings to drive Emi on. The problem was that Erika was threatening to put Emi on a course that chased after Jason, and that would only lead to disaster. Not everyone could keep coming back from the dead.

Rufus didn't blame Erika. Every good parent charted a course for their children, consciously or not. And they all struggled with when and how to let their children deviate from that course. Knowing how and when to let their children find their own way forward wasn't easy.

Having seen two worlds now, Rufus felt that Pallimustus was too reckless with its children. Earth was still finding its way, but he worried it leaned too far towards caution. That was especially true in nations used to wealth and safety. They deluded themselves that the world of a decade ago would carry on with only a few changes from the rise of magic. Those that had seen the vampire blood farms had no such illusions.

"Rufus?"

He stirred from his thoughts at Erika's address.

"I'm sorry," he said. "Did you ask me something? My mind was elsewhere."

Even he wasn't immune to complacency. The safety of clan territory was making him soft. He would never have been that unalert in the open back on Pallimustus.

"We were wondering about Emi building a more permanent team," Ian said. "Erika might be more comfortable if Emi had reliable companions around her."

"Good companions are, indeed, the most valuable thing an adventurer can have," Rufus said. "But Emi isn't an adventurer. She shouldn't have a fixed team because that would only incline her to go out more. What we need, right now, is for her to find the right balance. Gradual improvement over time. And I'm sorry, Erika, but Ian is right that the more you push in one direction, the more your daughter will pull in the other. But your concerns are valid too, Erika. Emi is not an adventurer. She doesn't have the power set or the mentality to make monster hunting what she does full-time. She's not her uncle, she never will be, and those are both good things. The problem is, she's acting like him."

"Then what do we do?"

"You're both right here," Rufus said. "Emi is far too focused on going out and fighting monsters, to the point of disrupting studies more central to what she wants even for herself. And a lot of that is because she's running from you, Erika. From your natural and completely understandable desire to keep your daughter safe. But completely understandable doesn't always include teenagers when it comes to people telling them what they can and can't do. That's natural too. It's the age where they can and should be pushing the limits of who they are and what they can do."

"This isn't about being peer pressured into smoking cigarettes," Erika said. "This is about life and death."

"Yes," Rufus agreed. "The role of the adults in her life has always been to guide her, not just into being safe but in knowing how to keep herself safe. That hasn't changed from the days before this world had magic. We're just running with tighter margins now. The challenges are the same, but the consequences are greater. That change is hard to accept, but refusing to do so will only cause greater harm in the long run."

"So, I let her run off and fight whatever monstrosity comes shambling along? At a time when the domain is growing increasingly unstable?"

"No," Rufus said. "I've been hands off in this regard, and perhaps it's time to change that. Emi doesn't need to be told what she can't do; she needs to understand the boundaries of what she can. And we need to accept that those boundaries are going to expand. Sometimes into places we might not like."

"What are you suggesting?" Ian asked. "From a practical perspective?"

"First," Rufus said, "the three of us should sit down and discuss what we feel Emi's boundaries should be. You are not going to enjoy that conversation, Erika. Then, we have the same discussion with your daughter. She's not going to enjoy that conversation either. But somewhere in there, we'll find a balance."

"And if she wants to just keep constantly fighting monsters, to the exclusion of everything else?" Erika asked.

"She's too smart to keep that up for long," Rufus said. "You both know that. I suspect much of your frustration is waiting for her to make a choice you know she inevitably will. To help that along, I suggest we start exploring other forms of education. Things that she should be doing anyway, and will entice her away from endless monster hunting."

"Such as?" Ian asked.

"Travel," Rufus said. "She hasn't left this domain since Jason did. It's time to let her see the world."

"That might scare me more than monsters," Ian said. "When she sees the world, the world will see her, and a lot of it isn't friendly to us. Not to our clan and not our family."

"Just look at what the Australian government did with Asano Village," Erika said.

"Even the outside forces who ostensibly support us will be a problem," Ian said. "The UN is constantly prodding us to share resources and knowledge, and they won't be above exploiting pressure points."

"And those are the sensible ones," Erika said. "What are those lunatic

Jason worshippers going to do when they know his niece is running around without the domain's protection?"

"You can't shelter her forever," Rufus said. "This is about exposing her to managed risk as well. This is the world your daughter will have to deal with. Are you going to wait decades until she's gold rank before you let her out of this city?"

"I like that plan," Ian said. "Who we should send away are all the boys her age. Or close to her age. Especially the good-looking ones. Honey, why are you looking at me like that?"

"Is this what I've been sounding like?" Erika asked Rufus, gesturing at her husband.

"No," Rufus said. "You're a lot scarier. Otherwise, kind of, yes."

Erika drew a deep breath and let it out in a half growl.

"You haven't been wrong," Rufus said. "All of your concerns have been valid. You've just taken the right feelings and the right ideas a little far."

"Until they were wrong," Ian clarified. Erika and Rufus both stopped to stare at him.

"I said a bad thing again, didn't I?" he asked.

"How did this man convince you to marry him?" Rufus asked.

"I honestly don't remember."

"It was a sexy nurse outfit," Ian said.

"He got you to wear a sexy nurse outfit?" Rufus asked Erika.

"Oh, I wasn't the one wearing it," Erika said.

"I think we just hit the part of the conversation I do not want to be involved in," Rufus said and set out again for the towering pagoda.

Jason respawned in the middle of the road, naked as a Terminator. As per the rules, the endless horde of monsters broke past the defending great astral beings and surged forward. Jason paid no attention, dropping to his knees and clutching his head. Having his willpower shaved away, slice by slice, was more excruciating than he had imagined. It had been fine in the beginning, but that had been years ago. Now it rivalled the assault on his soul by the Builder.

"This might not have been the best plan," he croaked to himself.

He let out a snarl as he forced himself to his feet. He plucked a pair of boxer shorts out of thin air and pulled them on before his robes and cloak manifested around him. Only then did he look up at the approaching wave of monster vessels, each one holding a nameless great astral being.

He held his hand out and his sword flew from where he had fallen, arriving gore-coated from where it passed through monsters to reach him. It slapped into his hand and he walked forward, unhurried, towards the wall of angry flesh bearing down on him. He watched them approach as the sun dipped below the horizon, washing the world in gold.

8 4

DIFFERENT RULES

THE ASTRAL SPACES BELONGING TO THE ASANO CLAN WERE ATTACHED TO Earth while also being separate, like an artificial limb. They operated by their own rules, especially regarding magic. Inside the cities that were the heart of each astral space, both physics and magic were stable, balanced and reliable. Beyond the towering walls, stability and reliability were harder to come by. The further one went from the walls, the stronger and less predictable things became.

Biomes could shift across very short distances, with muggy jungles giving way to bone-dry desert. The terrain could also diverge from Earth norms altogether, with bizarre and seemingly impossible conditions. Frozen labyrinths of ice wound through lakes that steamed with heat. Sky fields where gravity held no sway had clouds that shot out gusts of wind to ride from one cloud to the next.

Emi and a team of fellow clan members had just made their way through one of the most used training grounds for the clan's bronze-rankers. Before the arrival of Rufus, bronze-rankers hadn't been considered trainees, but now only silver rank was considered graduation from the training program. The clan had an increasing number of people reach that stage, but was yet to have any gold-rankers.

The training ground was a broad valley with ever-shifting landscape. It was constantly windswept, and every few hours, that wind brought in a fog that blanketed the valley. When the fog passed, the terrain had undergone massive change. Winter might have shifted to summer, snow and barren trees turning to thick growth. It may have rendered the landscape alien altogether, with looming fungus instead of trees, or floating islands with waterfalls spilling from them.

The fog also left a fresh swathe of monsters with every passing. Bronze ranked and adapted to the terrain, their variety and regular replenishment made for ideal training. The trainees had started calling it the gauntlet valley, as they were expected to make their way from one end to the other.

At the far side of the valley was the sweet reward of a pleasant and relatively safe zone to rest in. It was a region of rolling hills, flowering meadows and pleasant breezes. The monsters were sparse and mostly iron-rank, with the occasional bronze-ranker amongst them.

Emi's group made their way out of the valley looking and feeling bedraggled. They had thought they'd been home-free hours earlier, only to get caught in a late rush of fog. What it had left behind was a valley full of plant monsters; no living thing could be trusted. The trees shot out hungry vines and even the grass underfoot would shoot razor blades without warning.

Bloody, dirty and tired, the group of bronze-rank trainees picked a hill with a good vantage and trudged up it. The leader, Lauren, assigned one member to keep watch while Emi set up an array of warning rituals. The rest collapsed happily into the soft, thick grass.

The group was a semi-random assemblage. Rufus was broadly against trainees forming permanent teams until they were silver rank. He felt that the different training conditions and real combat experience warranted a different approach from Pallimustus. The Asano clan lacked the numbers to let their trainees experience as wide an array of styles before settling into teams. There was the potential option of joint training exercises with other factions, but that remained politically tricky.

Emi walked around the hilltop, drawing magic diagrams that lingered in the air. She traced them out with a finger that left trails of pale blue light behind every swish and swirl of her hand. The boy assigned to be on watch followed her around. He was almost two years younger, his parents having let him face monsters from a younger age than Emi's had.

"Will, you're meant to be watching our surroundings, not me," Emi pointed out. She didn't pause or turn from her work as she chided him. Her words did not deter his attentions.

"So, uh, hey," he said.

Emi paused just long enough to roll her eyes and sigh before resuming her work.

"You have a job, Will."

"Your magic spells will catch anything sneaking up on us."

"My 'magic spells' aren't finished."

"I'm sure it's fine."

"You shouldn't be."

Will let out an awkward laugh before trying a different tack.

"Are you still working on that Rubik's cube thing?"

"It's not a Rubik's cube, Will. I've explained that before."

"It looks like a Rubik's cube."

"And you look like you could muster up a basic level of competence. And yet, when put on watch, the only thing you watch is me. If you want to get my attention, Will, what I find attractive is intelligence and competence. Since one of those is clearly off the table, I suggest you work very hard on competence. You have a long way to go."

Will's expression turned to a scowl at the young woman who refused to even look at him.

"You don't have to be such a—"

"That's enough," barked Lauren, who crankily rose to her feet. She marched over to Will, giving him a scowl much fiercer than his own.

"Will, if you want to see what bitchy looks like, keep hitting on people instead of doing your damn job. You do realise we can all hear your inept attempts to sleaze on the princess, right?"

Will looked around, seeing the rest of the group looking at him from where they were lying out on the grass. He suddenly remembered that he was the only guy in the group.

"Yeah," Lauren said, reading his expression. "You're not going to get a lot of sympathy here. We all heard you bragging to your friends about 'building a harem' after the groups were assigned."

"That was just a joke."

"And we all found it hilarious. Now, try looking in a direction monsters might actually come from."

Lauren moved to stand next to Emi as she worked, moving around the hill slowly as more circles were drawn out.

"Not worried that this is overkill?" Lauren asked.

"Better to have it than not," Emi said, then lowered her voice. "Thank you."

"It's something you'll have to get used to. Especially if that's how you're going to react. You'll scare off the nice ones and only leave the creepers who want to crack the ice princess."

"I don't like being called that."

"Well, tough. When your uncle comes back, the Princess of Earth is exactly what you'll be."

"Uncle Jason isn't going to conquer the Earth."

"You think that matters? Look at Instructor Remore. He makes every silver-ranker we have look laughable. What about when he's gold rank? Now, think about what happens when he ranks up and your uncle arrives with a dozen more just like him."

Combat rituals were unusual on Pallimustus, and unheard of on Earth. Specialised essence abilities were required to make combat rituals viable at all, and they were famously unwieldy. Emi was literally the one person on Earth able to use them, courtesy of her extensive training recordings. Farrah had predicted Emi would get the right powers and made sure Clive provided plenty of support. As one of the rare combat ritual users, he was able to provide hours of useful instruction footage and piles of material to read.

Emi's ritual circle shields were the most perfect expression of her efforts to use combat magic effectively. They were moderately strong on their own and she could move them around to shield herself or her team as needed. She used multiple ritual shields at once, each slightly different from the others.

The shields operated in the core principle to Emi's entire power set: synergy. When put together in certain sequences, they gained additional effects. They might become stronger against specific attack forms or inflict different forms of retaliatory damage. The strongest configuration was also the simplest: putting the shields in a stack.

By stacking the shields, not only did an attack need to pass through them all, but each shield magnified the strength of the others. This mattered when unexpectedly faced with a silver-rank monster when Emi and her team were all still bronze. The manticore was a silver-rank beast with a lion's body and a scorpion's tail.

With a sweeping gesture of her arms, Emi sent all her ritual shields to interpose themselves between Lauren and the monster. They slid into place scant moments before the monster fired a spine from its tail.

Emi didn't see the projectile. She only heard the gunshot crack as it broke the speed of sound. The stack of shields shattered like glass and Lauren was flung back, as if snatched by an invisible giant. She was hurled on a near flat trajectory before finally hitting the ground, skipping across it like a stone.

Emi only let herself stare for a moment before tearing her eyes away. The manticore was already moving, launching itself at Will. He used his strongest defensive ability, Bunker, and was shrouded in metal-reinforced stone. None of the group had been able to so much as scratch it in training, but the lion-like manticore was tearing through it like a dog digging up the backyard.

Emi was already using another ability. Consolidate Mana was a spell that collected unstable elements in the ambient mana, such as from a collection of broken rituals, and made it the power source for follow-up magic. Pulling in the power of her broken shields, she drew out the most powerful attack magic she could muster. It wasn't fast, but she wasn't being attacked and nothing else she had would even dent a silver-rank monster.

She drew one circle after another, all tightly packed together. Normally, this would make them interfere with one another and see them all collapse. Instead, they worked in harmony, resonating with one another to amplify the magic she fed into them. She kept going, past any level she had tried in the past. She created more ritual circles and fed them more power, generating a matrix that thrummed with magical energy.

As she continued to work, her skin started to burn from the power the matrix was throwing off. The ritual circles started to tremble, pushed to their limits and beyond. Only then did she finally release the power. Her Matrix Beam spell unleashed a torrent of magic wider than she was and too blindingly bright to look at.

When the light faded, Emi saw that the beam had an impact on the manticore. Much of its fur was gone and there were burnt patches of skin. The bunker next to it had also been partially melted, finally impacted by a bronze-rank ability. Despite being marred by the beam, the monster didn't look substantially damaged. What it did look was angry as it turned on the source of its fresh injuries. It turned away from the bunker, accelerating in a few strides before springing at Emi.

She barely had time to react when she saw the manticore lunge at her. Her dodge was too slow and her shields were broken, even if she hadn't sent them away. As the monster reached her in a blur of motion, she closed her eyes to wait for the end. Several lumps of flesh hit her at speed and she stumbled, falling to the ground.

She opened her eyes as more lumps of flesh fell into the grass around her. They were chunks of manticore, roughly cubed, with the sides seared like barbecued meat. The smell of the burnt flesh was acrid, invading her nostrils. This was not meat fit for consumption.

She stood up and looked around for Rufus. He was kneeling over Lauren in the distance, tipping a potion into the unconscious girl's mouth. She rushed over to join them, seeing Lauren's body glowing from within with red light. Rufus was slowly pulling out a savagely barbed spine from where it was lodged in her gut, her body healing around it.

"Rufus…"

"Instructor Remore," he snarled with a savagery she'd never heard from him. "Today, Trainee Evans-Asano, you call me Instructor Remore."

Riding back to the city in a conjured helicopter, Emi again glanced up at Lauren, sitting opposite. The girl was fully healed now, Rufus having used a potion he brought with him from the other world. It was not just high rank but high quality, beyond anything Earth alchemy had even come close to.

Lauren stared in Emi's direction, but clearly not seeing her, caught up in shell shock. Emi couldn't see her own face, but guessed that she was just as pale. She was still trembling after a rollercoaster of emotions as the adrenaline wore off. She still had adrenaline, as she wasn't high enough rank to transmute her body into a more magical one. Even with diligent training, there was only so far she could go without advancing her rank or getting a head start, like being an outworlder.

After the team landed, they were sent off with their parents. Each had insisted they were adults at one time or another, but today, they were children again, in need of the comfort of home. Emi's parents were no different, waiting anxiously at the helipad. Emi was half expecting an 'I told you so' from her mother. But all she saw was fear, and all she got was the fiercest, warmest hug of her life.

That night, Rufus stood over Emi as she sat on the couch in her lounge room. He loomed over her in a way he'd never done before.

"I know that Lauren was in charge," he told her. "But we both know that you aren't like the other trainees. That there are different rules for you. Not just who your family is, but who you are. You've got talent for days, with better training and more resources to hone it than anyone on this planet has ever enjoyed. Ever. Anything short of exceptional from you is inadequate, and you've lived up to that at every turn."

He paced across the room and back, agitated. She knew he didn't drink coffee, but he looked as jittery as someone who had just chugged two pots.

"You aren't like the others," he said again. "Like it or not, fair or not, you are different. Your uncle had to learn the responsibility that comes with that, and now you do as well."

"Rufus—"

"This isn't a conversation," Rufus said. "We'll have a lot of those, and I'll be sympathetic to you then, but right now, I am too damn angry. How many times have we warned you? You've heard about the dangers more than anyone. I don't care whose idea it was to go further out than you were told. You are who you are. If you said no, and stuck to that, they would have listened, regardless of who had been assigned team leader. You know it and I know it. Whether it was your idea in the first place or you just let it happen, it was in your power to stop."

He ran his hands along the side of his head.

"You aren't the only one who will be getting this talk," he continued. "I will be visiting every house of every member of that team, and I will be explaining to every single one of them what colossal imbeciles they have been. What is the one rule I have hammered into you, more than any other? The first priority?"

"Stay safe," Emi said hesitantly.

"STAY SAFE!" Rufus roared. "That is the thing I have never been able to cram into your uncle's head. He always makes the sacrifice play, always goes for the victory. But he's different too. Like you, the rules for him are different. The universe seems to bend over backwards to keep him alive, then brings him back when it doesn't. Maybe you're like him. Maybe you'll always get out at the last minute, or find some way to come back from the dead. He always does. But it doesn't work that way for the rest of us. We fight beside Jason, but when we get caught up in fights between gods, when we sacrifice…"

He wiped tears from his eyes and turned away. Emi sat in awkward, scared silence, unsure of what to do. Finally, Rufus moved to an armchair and sat, bent over with his head in his hands. When he spoke, his voice was soft and quiet.

"I once told your uncle, right after we met, that he had the chance to remake himself into the person he wanted to be. You're a lot like him. Generous. Loyal. Self-centred, arrogant. Blind to how the thing that makes you special hurts the people around you who aren't. He's smart and you're a lot smarter, but you're both stupid in the same ways. So now I'll tell you what I told him: now is the time for you to decide who you are going to be. You're not going to be him, despite the similarities. I think you learned that today. Or remembered it, maybe."

"Rufus, I—"

"Don't. He moves before he thinks. If nothing else, be different from him in that. Stop. Consider. Things will be changing for you from now on. You'll get a say in some of it, and some not. I'm banning all trainee excursions beyond the wall for now, so you'll have time to think. To pursue other things."

He let out a long sigh, finally looking right at her.

"Being special means that you have responsibilities, Emi. Like it or not, that's just something you have to live with, and I know it's not easy. Your uncle and I have both been damaged by it, and you've seen that."

"With him. Not with you."

Rufus nodded.

"I hold a position in my family a lot like you do in yours. I've never talked about that with you, and maybe that was a mistake. I know what it's like to feel pressure. To watch my friends get hurt and realise I could have stopped it if I'd made better choices. When you get special treatment, everyone expects you to live up to that. To be the best. I've put that same pressure on you myself. But it's okay to lose sometimes, even when you are the best. It's okay to fall short sometimes. Even the best can always get better. I said you were arrogant, but you have nothing on me when I was your age."

He stood up and gave her a weary smile.

"Some other time, ask me about my friend Kenneth and his duck essence. For now, spend some time with your family. You're going to sleep like the dead tonight, trust me."

He moved to the door and stopped, glancing back.

"There will be no monster hunting for a while," he said, "but other opportunities are coming up. For you and some of the other trainees. We'll talk about that soon."

"Rufus?"

"Yes?"

"How is Lauren?"

"Physically, she's fine. As for the rest, it's too early to tell. She suffered a brutal attack that she could do nothing to stop. She could use a good friend who understands what happened to her."

Emi nodded.

"You realise that you probably saved her life, right?" Rufus asked. "Your shields couldn't stop a silver-rank attack that powerful, but you mostly likely turned it from deadly to very nearly deadly. Good job, trainee."

He slipped out the door and her parents came in from where they'd been shamelessly eavesdropping. They joined her on the couch, taking a side each and wrapping her in a collective hug.

"Your mother had to stop me from coming in," Ian said. "I didn't like the way he was talking to you."

"That wasn't a teacher-student talk," Emi said. "That was a commanding-officer talk."

"That's why I didn't like it."

85

HOPE ONLY NEEDS A CHANCE

JASON STEPPED OUT OF A MONSTER'S SHADOW, HIS BLADE ALREADY flickering through the air. All around him, a sea of monsters was slowing down and dying under the effects of his afflictions. It didn't put much of a dent in their overall numbers as, like Jason, they would just respawn. He was satisfied, though, to be forcing those respawns instead of struggling just to stay alive.

That feeling of power came to an end when the World-Phoenix arrived. Her superhero landing sent out a ring of fire that expanded in a flash, incinerating everything in its path. It reduced a large circle of her own forces to ash that drifted on wind kicked up by the heat.

Jason was caught in it as well. His amulet had built up a powerful stack of shields, one for each infliction delivered to the monster army. Even so, the fire burned through them all, along with Jason's blood robe, to scorch his flesh black. All the shield stacks were converted to healing as they were consumed, and added to Jason's already considerable regeneration. His flesh and skin grew back, as did his robe.

The World-Phoenix hadn't moved from where she landed, massive wings of fire rising from her back. The monsters hadn't swarmed back in to fill the empty space either. They weren't mindless brutes but vessels for nameless great astral beings, and not stupid enough to re-enter the blast zone. That left Jason and the World-Phoenix staring at each other in a makeshift arena, surrounded by monsters.

The World-Phoenix looked like the hero to Jason's villain. She was draped in loose white clothing, tinted with orange and yellow. With her massive wings of fire, she had the fierce beauty of an avenging angel. The heat from her blazing wings stirred up the air, causing her long red hair to dance around her head.

Jason was a sinister figure with his void cloak and robes the colour of dried blood. His nebulous eyes looked out from the dark hood that shrouded his features, and the stench of charred flesh hung around him. They stood, unmoving, while the battle raged around them, yet did not close in. In a storm of violence, they stood in the eerily calm eye.

"Why do you struggle?" the World-Phoenix asked. A trick of aura allowed her voice to carry over the sounds of unbridled magical warfare.

"Isn't struggling the whole point?" Jason asked, copying the voice projection technique.

"Give up while you still have willpower to keep your mind and personality intact. I have no need to rip them apart unless you make me."

"Make you? Lady, you're the one who invaded my soul; I didn't ask you to come here. Why are you even doing this? You know the price of leaving the throne as it is. What do you get out of this fight?"

"You think the sundering is such an ancient event, predating the universe that spat you out. On a cosmic scale, you, your universe and this new Builder are nothing. The astral has no time of its own. We mark the passage of events using the life and death of universes like the ticking of a clock. A clock more complex than your mind will ever comprehend, even when you are an astral king. The astral kings are children, with minds still stuck in mortal ways of thinking. With time, they will, perhaps, learn to comprehend eternity. For now, even the oldest of them are too young for that to have happened yet."

"Well, that was a cracker of a monologue," Jason said. "I didn't love my cosmic insignificance being the central theme, but I can appreciate the effort. Was that off the cuff, or have you been rehearsing it in your head while you fight me and your friends? I've got to say, though, your central thesis is a little undermined by your having sought me out. More than once, at this stage. I mean the first time, sure. You gave me a token and let me go on my way. One more pawn on your very big and complicated board. But this time, you came to me. You're playing on my board. Telling me how insignificant I am when you all came into my house rings hollow. Also, you're not the only one who can monologue. I may not be able to match you in a fight, but if you want a melodrama battle, that's a whole other story."

"That your soul is the location of this conflict matters not at all," the World-Phoenix said. "We, the great astral beings, are the ones that matter. When we walk on the dirt, the dirt is not hallowed by our passage."

"I'm pretty sure a lot of religions disagree, but I'll accept it as a valid counterpoint."

"You lack the ability to conceive all that has passed in the vast span of the cosmos. The sundering is the oldest event you know of, yet it is to us as recent as last week is to you. I cannot explain how limited you are because you're too limited to understand. You are so simple that you think time and space are different things."

"Yeah, I never did get around to that Stephen Hawking book my nan got me for my birthday. But your point is made. There's only so many ways you can explain that you are very big and I am very small before the motif becomes repetitive. It sounds like you're trying to get me to do that scene from Monty Python where they keep telling God how huge he is, and I'm not going to do it. Okay, I'll do it. Oooh Lord, you are so very big. We're all really impressed down here, I... You know, I'm getting this wrong. I haven't seen it in a while. You remember the scene, right?"

"Yes," the World-Phoenix said, drawing the word out like a threat. "You have filled this ridiculous body with worthless knowledge."

"Ridiculous? I modelled that after Dawn, who was your prime vessel. I even gave it bigger... fiery wings."

The World Phoenix glared at Jason and conjured a whip of dancing fire into her hand.

"I'm not going to enjoy this, am I?" Jason asked.

"No."

"Just so you know, I've changed my safe word. The new one is 'coquettish.'"

The World-Phoenix launched herself forward, blazing wings leaving a trail of sparks behind her. Jason fought with a greater command of skill and strategy than he ever had before. He fought hard, he fought fast and he fought smart. He also fought briefly, and was soon respawning further down the road.

While Jason had certainly improved against the horde of monsters possessed by the nameless great astral beings, things were very different against the World-Phoenix. She had the advantage in power, speed and strength. Where he had worked hard to adapt his abilities for open combat, hers had been ideal from the beginning. After years of fighting, his skills had grown considerably, but she had seen him perfecting all his tricks. For all that Jason had advanced, he remained staggeringly far behind.

When the war in Jason's soul first began, the rest breaks were short and the battles were long. Years later, the breaks were extending. Jason's abilities had pushed into the higher reaches of silver and the old ways of advancement were becoming less effective. As he had been warned, the path forward was shifting from external pressures to inner enlightenment.

In this, Jason found himself well prepared. Ever since leaving Earth, coming to grips with who and what he was had been a consuming preoccupation. He had spent years in introspection, on his own and with the help and guidance of others. Arabelle Remore especially had been readying him for this stage. Alongside that, Jason had been pushed to the limit over and over.

Hard choices had forced Jason to confront who he was and who he was willing to become. To decide what he was willing to accept and when to be defiant, whatever the cost. As a result, Jason's transition to a more contemplative form of advancement went very smoothly, his abilities not slowing in their growth.

Jason could feel his approach to gold rank, seeing an open path with no obstructions in his way. The only issue was the willpower being cut away in battle, but that wouldn't get in his way. He had more than enough remaining to reach his advancement first.

Progress centred on his essences. His soul was the power, but they were the shape. They found parts of himself and drew them to the fore. Advancement required Jason to understand that process, pushing it forward and smoothing it out. He'd been warned that doing so improperly could have detrimental effects on one's personality.

This was part of the reason why those who advanced to gold through monster cores could suffer personality deviations. It was rarely a large problem, with petty, arrogant and selfish behaviour being the most common result. Given that monster core-users at that level were usually aristocratic scions who were handed their positions, it was hard to tell whether the cores actually did anything or if that was just their personality.

There were instances of more extreme behaviour, however, with people becoming depraved, twisted and outright malevolent. There were certain essences known to present a higher danger of this, including the dark and blood essences possessed by Jason.

He wasn't a core-user, though, so he wasn't worried his essences would negatively affect him. He was going to be fine; there was nothing to worry about. Any concerning behaviour he demonstrated in the past was just run-of-the-mill psychological trauma, not the start of a magical descent into depravity and madness.

His meditation having gone rather off track, Jason opened his eyes and saw the World-Phoenix eating a bagel. He got to his feet and went to the bagel cart. It was manned by one of his one-eyed avatars who assembled his meal telekinetically. Ingredients floated through the air and jalapeño cream cheese spread itself across the bagel. Jason took his food and walked over to stand beside the World-Phoenix. She stood alone, looking out at the jungle.

"How are you doing it?" she asked, before he could say anything.

"Doing what? Getting my butt kicked for years in a row? That just kind of happens."

"Things are changing. Restrictions we put in place after the sundering are beginning to unravel. You're repairing the throne already."

"Am I?"

"How are you doing it?"

"With rakish good looks?"

"There are rules."

"My rules. There are restrictions on what I can do with them, but this is my house. I know that any level of ignorance or any need to make concessions is foreign to you. But you're the one that came in here, knowing that it was my game you'd be stuck playing. And I still don't understand why you did. What are you so loath to let go of, that you'd let the cosmos fall into chaos? I understand that the Cosmic Throne is an authority you don't want to be under. The irony of an antiauthoritarian like me trying to reinstate a system displaced by rebellion isn't lost on me."

She turned to look at him before returning her gaze to the jungle.

"I told you that what you see as ancient is recent for my kind."

"Yep."

"The Builder is not the first great astral being to change. Long before the sundering, there was no World-Phoenix. There was a great astral being called the Boundary. But it wanted to be more than it was. More than its role."

"It sanctioned itself."

"Yes. The Boundary was gone and the World-Phoenix came into being. The Cosmic Throne did not accede easily to changes in the grand order. It resisted my decision to become something other than what the cosmos decided I should be. It was a constant fight to not be turned back into what I was. The sundering freed me from that pressure."

"And now I am trying to restore the source of that pressure."

"Yes."

"I'd like to tell you that I can change it. That I can restore the throne in such a way that you can be what you choose. But I can't offer you that. There's no easy solution."

"I am aware. The passive effects of the throne's restoration will be disruptive enough. If you try to make active use of the power, the ripples of that choice are incalculable."

"On Earth, we call it the butterfly effect."

"It frustrates me that they chose you. Although I resist oversight in my role, I still fulfil my purpose as a great astral being. Restoring the integrity of your universe matters, and you were my solution to resolve that danger. Fighting you here works against that purpose, and doing so costs me more than you understand."

"I'm sorry. I really am. But I'm fighting for the integrity of the cosmos."

"This was not your fight. They brought you into this."

"The way you brought me in to saving the Earth. That argument gets you nowhere."

"I suppose not. It is hard to think, in this body. Even as it gets closer to gold rank, it is still so limited. We use vessels at the peak of mortal power for a reason."

"I'm not imagining it, then," Jason said. "You are getting stronger. I was kind of hoping I could rank up and turn this whole thing around."

"You actually thought that would happen?"

"No, but hope only needs a chance; it doesn't have to be a good one."

"That is a very mortal way of thinking."

"Sometimes you need a mortal way of thinking. You have to defy the odds if you want to make miracles."

She turned to look at Jason again. This time, her gaze lingered.

"I am glad that I sent Dawn to you."

"Really? I thought you'd be cranky at how you and her aren't on the same page as much as you were."

"I don't need her to be like me. That defeats the purpose. I need vessels that will see things in ways I will not on my own. Choosing those who do not align perfectly with my ideals shortens the time they can be my vessels. Other great astral beings choose vessels more aligned with themselves, so they last longer. I consider this short-sighted. My hierophants, those who were once my vessels, still serve me. They are more independent than they were, but that makes them more valuable in many ways."

"You don't hold disagreement with you against them?"

"On the contrary, that is their role. Dawn does not want me to win this fight. She believes that I won't. I had thought her naïve until I felt the changes begin and realised that the throne is already being restored. How are you doing that?"

"I'm still not telling."

"It was worth a try."

Jason grinned.

"Despite your complaints," he said, "I have an inkling that you and the others are beginning to enjoy being stuck in mortal bodies. In spite of yourselves."

"We do not occupy our own vessels for anywhere near so long as we have these ones you have provided. It is a novel experience, and our kind do not get those often."

Jason nodded.

"I'm not going to say that I hope you win," he said. "But I hope that, when all this is done, things go well for you."

"Even though we are enemies?"

"I don't think we're enemies. We just want different things. The Builder is an enemy, even if he's on my side for now. I don't like what you all did to him, though. It doesn't excuse what he's done, but given what you've just told me, I'm surprised you went along with treating him that way."

"It seemed easy to justify when I was thinking more broadly. A mortal mind has a different view of moral dilemmas. A great astral being has no empathy. That is why we have vessels, and why those vessels need to stay grounded. I did not want Dawn to lose that when she was so close to transcending. It would be harder to get it back once she left mortality behind."

"I worry about that for myself," Jason said. "I'm in my thirties and I've gone through so many changes. What is eternity going to do to me?"

"When you are immortal, every tribulation has its time and everything passes. Even the Builder, with what we have done to him, understands that. Whatever you go through, whatever is done to you, eternity gives you the time to make of yourself what you will. We are each responsible for who we become. No excuses."

86

WHAT WILL GET YOU TO GOLD RANK

ON THE PODIUM OF A REMORE ACADEMY LECTURE HALL, BELINDA pointed at the floating hologram of a partially complete ritual diagram.

"Unless you are lost or getting expelled at the end of the semester," she said in a magically amplified voice, "you will all recognise this. The Hagstrom Cycle is one of the most common bases for bronze- and silver-tier rituals. It is reliable, it is efficient, and—if enacted properly—will keep a ritual running for years given proper maintenance. Knowing the Hagstrom Cycle backwards and forwards is a fundamental skill for anyone serious about the study of magic, regardless of specialty."

She made a casual gesture and the podium's magic sent the image to hover by the wall behind her.

"I learned the Hagstrom Cycle when I was a street rat in a magical backwater learning from the scant few books I could steal. There is no excuse for all you little rich pricks."

There was laughter through the lecture hall. Over the course of scholastic year, the students had become accustomed of the peculiarities of their professor. That was known to be part and parcel of studying at Remore Academy, famous for recruiting adventurers, especially those close to or just having reached gold rank. It was a time when adventurers tended to slow down and pursue more contemplative approaches to advancement.

"I fully acknowledge," Belinda continued, "the eminent usefulness and undeniable value of the Hagstrom Cycle. Can anyone explain, then, why I personally detest it?"

A sea of hands shot up. Belinda panned her eyes across the room and spotted a particular student not seated in his normal position with his friends. Even more unusual was the fact that his hand was one of those in the air.

"Young Master Burkis," she said. "I am positively quivering with anticipation of the rare treat of hearing an answer from you."

"Setting up the Hagstrom Cycle is an intricate process," Burkis said. "It takes time, care and precision to implement, which isn't easy when a furnace drake is spewing flames everywhere and the thing you're hiding behind is on fire. It's better to use something that you can establish quickly and has a more generous margin for error. It doesn't matter that it only lasts twenty minutes if you only need it for five."

"An exquisite answer, Master Burkis. Given that this is the introductory unit of Practical Use of Ritual Magic in the Field, one might even call it a perfect answer. One I would expect from someone who had spent years around an adventuring team with multiple ritualists. Like my team, for example, that includes not only myself but the Archchancellor of the Magical Research Association. It is such a good answer that it warrants a trip to the biscuit table..."

Burkis was halfway out of his seat, eyeing the table off to the side of the podium stage. He froze as Belinda continued.

"...assuming you are, in fact, Mr Burkis. And not a shape-shifting dragon taking students' lectures for them in return for payment."

The whole room turned to look at Burkis in an excruciatingly long moment of still silence. He then turned into a mouse and scurried off between the seats.

"Attention here, please," Belinda announced.

The students stopped looking under their chairs for the fleeing rodent and looked back to the podium.

"Yes," Belinda said. "The handful of you suddenly very worried have extremely good reason to be. Now, I'm all for cheating—"

A loud throat-clearing sound came from the back of the lecture hall.

"Oh, hello, Dean Remore. Anyway, as I was saying, if you're going to cheat, you have to be aware of who you're trying to cheat."

"Professor Callahan..."

"We can chat when I'm done, Dean. Keep your pants on. What was I saying? Right, if you're going to cheat, be aware of the consequences of getting caught. If you aren't willing to accept those consequences, then I strongly advise against trying. And as cheating is an expulsion offence, trying it here is a very bad idea. Do you think the faculty of the Remore Academy have never dealt with this kind of issue before? This school is staffed by some of the most capable, experienced and cunning people in the world. If you had the ability to put one over on them, you would be teachers here and not students. And for those of you who listened to me say that and still think you can put one over them, you might as well pack your things today. That is not an attitude that will get you to graduation here, so you might as well save us the time and bother."

The playful tone permeating the lecture hall was now a deathly stillness. Belinda sighed.

"I don't think we're likely to get much more productive work done today, and you now all have rumours to go spread. So, lecture over; off you go."

Students started scrambling, avoiding Dean Remore as he made his way down to the podium. Belinda had sat down on the edge of the stage by the time he arrived.

"Good morning, Dean. Is it weird being Dean of the Ritual Magic School when your actual name is Dean? Dean Remore is your full name and your title. I'd have thought that, of all families, one that runs a school would know better."

Dean sighed but otherwise ignored Belinda's question.

"You know, Professor Callahan," he said, "you are fitting in here all too well. I do wish Roland would recruit some vaguely sensible people for once."

"I thought it was a good speech," Belinda said. "Practical advice with a set-them-up-and-knock-them-down structure. By the time word spreads, which will take all of six minutes, everyone who has been employing this little shape-shifting ring to skip classes will be wondering what we know and how long we've known it."

"Indeed. We have this issue once or twice a decade. There will be a slew of expulsions and contrite second chances. Each instance has its own quirks, though. This time, it's a member of the Geller family letting his familiar run amok. Not a minor member of the family either."

"Oh, I would advise just telling Humphrey. He's so upright that he'll do your work for you."

"That's not for me to decide. Thankfully. Something similar happened when I was a student here and they expelled a member of the royal family. A minor one, but still. I would not like to be the person dealing with that."

"Is that a big deal?"

"It's the royal family of Estercost. One of the most prominent kingdoms in the world."

"Was that a yes or a no?"

"You think royalty is some small matter?"

"You know a member of my team used to be the Storm Kingdom's Hurricane Princess, right?"

"What?"

"Do you not know what my adventuring team is?"

"I wasn't told. Wait, do you know Humphrey Geller because—"

"He's my team leader, yes."

"Oh. Oh dear. I really wish people would tell me these things."

Belinda gave him a sympathetic smile.

"Would you like a biscuit before I pack them up? Maybe a pastry?"

"No, th—"

His eyes fell on the table.

"Maybe just one."

A few minutes later, Dean finished a biscuit the size of a teacup saucer.

"I am forced to concede that you handled the release of that information to the student body well," he told Belinda. "There will be a staff meeting at the start of next week about next steps."

The dean left as Belinda was putting her baked goods into containers and then her storage space. She was around halfway done when she felt a slight breeze behind her and smiled.

"I have trouble understanding how this is what will get you to gold rank," Sophie said.

"You and I both know that I'm the worst fit out of anyone in the team," Belinda said as she turned to face her friend. "In my head, I'm still a thief, more than an adventurer. My power set reflects that. Deception, entrapment and thievery."

She tapped her forehead.

"Up here, I know my skills and powers are useful to the team. That I am an adventurer. But there are still doubts I can't shake. Insecurities about who I am and what I have to offer."

She tapped over where her heart would have been.

"In here, it's harder to convince myself that I'm an adventurer and not still a criminal."

"You realise that you don't have a brain or a heart anymore, right?"

"And you know metaphors exist, right?"

Sophie laughed.

"I shouldn't try to outsmart you, should I?"

"No."

Belinda turned to take in the lecture hall.

"This place," she said. "This is where adventurers come from. If I can matter here…"

Sophie gathered her friend up in a hug.

"You are amazing," Sophie told her. "Don't let anyone tell you different."

"Should I be jealous?" Estella's voice came from the back of the hall.

"Are you kidding?" Belinda said, extricating herself from Sophie. "She's got Captain Good Boy waiting for her at home. I can't compete with that."

Sophie gave her a teasing slap on the arm, then spotted a small figure moving along the side of the room. The mouse froze as Sophie pointed and Belinda turned to look. It turned into a trembling puppy staring up at them. Sophie rolled her eyes.

"Okay, one," Belinda said.

The puppy turned into a young man in the Remore Academy uniform. He looked like Humphrey when Belinda and Sophie first met him, but with silver eyes and hair. He snatched two biscuits from the table and made a break for the exit.

"Hey, I said one!" Belinda called after him.

"You shouldn't reward bad behaviour, Lindy," Sophie scolded.

"Making him behave is your job," Belinda said. "I'm the fun aunt."

"I'm not his mother, Lindy."

"Sure you're not. Speaking of which, have you told Hump you're leaving yet?"

Sophie steeled herself with a long, slow breath.

"That's a no," Belinda said.

"I wanted to say goodbye to you first. Once I tell him, I'm gone."

"Well, go do it," Belinda said, grabbing Sophie in another hug. "The sooner you go, the sooner you come back."

"No," Sophie said. "I'm not coming back until he comes to find me. Goodbye, Lindy."

They pulled the hug in tighter.

"Bye, Soph."

Sophie was suddenly gone, as if she'd teleported. Belinda went back to the table to finish packing things away.

"Get the job done?" she asked Estella, who'd been waiting by the table, eating a bun.

"Yeah. Whole thing was a grift, like I thought. Turns out it was his grandson. That was how they were going to get him to sign over the airships."

"His own grandson?"

"Yeah. Paid me a nice bonus to keep quiet too. I love working for noble families. Lots of money and lots of secrets means lots of paydays for me."

"It sounds like you're buying lunch, then."

As they walked out of the lecture hall side by side, Estella slipped her fingers between Belinda's.

"Are you okay?" she asked.

"Yeah. I'm fine, Stel."

"Are you, though? I know you and Sophie don't spend a lot of time apart."

"We've done it before."

"And she went and fell in love with the person least like you I've ever met."

Belinda gave her a sharp look.

"Oh, please," Estella said. "You think I don't see it? We've all carried a torch for someone who wasn't on our vibe, Lindy. I see that pain in you, and I see that it's old. You've moved on, which can't have been easy. And I don't hate the idea of it just being you and me for a while."

Belinda squeezed her hand.

"I don't hate that either," she said.

"We can talk about it."

"You don't want to talk about that."

"No. But I think that maybe you need to. And maybe I need you to. She's always going to be around, Lindy, a few excursions like right now aside. Best get it out in the open, at least between you and me. Otherwise, it'll always be there."

Belinda sighed.

"This lunch is going to be a lot less fun than I hoped."

SOMETHING THAT'S INSIDE YOU ALREADY

THE FAMOUS TOWERS OF VITESSE LOOKED LIKE LIVING SKYSCRAPERS. With flowering vines covering the walls and plants dangling from the balconies, they were the reason Vitesse was called the City of Flowers. Not only were they beautiful, but the magical flowers filled the air with sweet aromas.

On a high balcony of a tower belonging to the Geller family, Sophie was leaning into Humphrey as they sat together of a couch.

"You're leaving?" he asked.

"It's not just like that, Humphrey. We've talked about this."

"You never set a date."

"And now I have," Sophie said.

"When exactly?"

"When this conversation ends."

He wrapped his arm around her a little tighter.

"You need a shock, Humphrey. You're human. Your natural advantage should have you advancing faster than everyone but Clive."

"I am advancing. My essence abilities are—"

"What about your dragon essence?"

He slumped.

"I'm not a dragon," he said quietly. "I'm a lot of things, but I'm not that."

"I'd ask if you even listen to your mother, but we both know the answer to that. It's not about you being a dragon. It's about the dragon essence bringing out something that's inside you already."

"And if I don't have anything it wants? Most people never get to gold rank."

"This is why I'm leaving. I like that you can be soft around me, but it's not what you need right now. You're never going to find the dragon inside when you insist on being the little spoon."

Humphrey cast a worried glance at the door.

"It makes me feel safe," he whispered.

"I know. But what you need isn't to feel safe. It's for everyone else to feel in danger. Power. Dominance. These are what make a dragon. You're kind and compassionate, and I love you for that. But you're also right-eous. Maybe that is the path to finding the strength you need, I don't know. What I do know is that my presence isn't helping. And I have my path to follow as well. You're not the only one who needs to indulge their essences if they want to reach gold. The wind needs freedom. I have to go where I will, unfettered by anything that might tie me down. At least for a time."

"Is that what I'm doing? Tying you down?"

Sophie shifted from her place next to Humphrey, sliding into his lap where she could grab his face in both hands and kiss him.

"Of course you're tying me down," she told him. "I want us to be bound to one another, which is why I agreed to marry you. But we will live very long lives, Humphrey Geller, and there will be times to be together and times to be apart. We just aren't used to it yet because we're young."

"You've been talking with my mother."

She flashed a mischievous grin.

"Does that scare you?"

"Extremely," he told her, and pulled her in for another kiss. "Do you have to go right now?"

"Jason has started hitting gold rank with his abilities."

"How do you know that?"

"The light in his soul realm. It's turned gold a few times now."

"Your mother told you?"

"Yeah. Farrah and Travis set me up with one of their communication devices that you can carry around and still connect to the network. That way, I can still talk to her while I'm on the move."

"And to me. We have a communication node here in the tower."

She stood up.

"No, Humphrey. Not until you've found your way with your dragon essence. I don't want to give the communication tablet back to Farrah, but if you reach out to me, I will."

He grimaced, but nodded.

"Alright," he conceded. "Go, then. But go knowing that I love you, and if you stay away too long, I am going to come find you."

She smiled and leaned down for a kiss.

"There's my dragon."

Then she was gone, a breeze stirring up the scent of flowers. Humphrey sat for a long time, looking out at the other flowering towers. It was a typically gorgeous day, with only a few fluffy white clouds marking the vibrant blue of the sky.

A weight plopped down on the couch beside him. It was Stash, unusually in his natural dragon form. It wasn't his natural size, which was close to that of a winged elephant. He was more graceful than those lumbering beasts; sinuous and lithe, with iridescent scales that made him shimmer like a rainbow. His full scale was not convenient for sitting on a couch, however, so he was currently the size of a medium dog.

"Everyone is like that," Stash said.

"Like what?"

"Everyone has their own stories about dragons. Some people think we're unseen guardians, endorsing their claim to the throne. To others, we're little more than intelligent monsters. Terrorising the countryside and sleeping on a hoard of treasure. Demanding the occasional princess."

"You're saying that's not what you do with your time?"

Stash poked out a forked tongue at Humphrey, who laughed.

"The point is," Stash said, "that dragons aren't what people tell them they are. Dragons are what they want to be. And yes, if what they want is princesses and piles of gold, then you damn well better send them a wagon full of cash and tied-up royalty. Sitting here and letting Sophie tell you what to do isn't how a dragon would do things."

"But letting her go is what I want."

"You don't sound convincing."

"I don't like it. But what I want is for her to be happy. I will do everything in my power to see she gets everything she wants and needs. And if letting her go is what she needs right now, then I can do that. She's been talking about going off and following the wind for a while now. We all have to find our own ways to gold rank. I just wasn't expecting it to be so sudden when she did. I don't know why she did that."

"It's because you're a slow burn," Stash told him. "You don't make emotionally manipulative arguments like Jason does. You wear people down by being decent at them. If she gave you time, you'd probably convince her to stay."

"When did you become so insightful?"

"I've been watching you people for most of my life. Did you think I wasn't paying attention?"

"Well… yes."

"That's hurtful."

"Sorry."

"You being shamelessly callous doesn't matter."

"Shamelessly callous?"

"Shut up and listen. What's important now is what you do next, and you have to do it like a dragon. You have to decide what you want to be, and what you want to do. Then you do it, and don't let anyone stop you. Look at Jason. Gods don't stop him. Death doesn't stop him. If he thinks something needs doing, then it gets done."

"Then he should have had the dragon essence."

"He's not the one who needs it! You think your mother picked your essence combination on a whim? Everything she does for you and your sister is to give you what you need. And what *you* need is some dragon. Stop being what you think you should be, or what other people want you to be. Don't even be what you think you *need* to be. Dragons don't do what they need; they do what they want."

"What if they don't know what they want?"

"They do. They always do. Maybe they aren't ready to admit it to themselves. Maybe they can't explain what it is, exactly. But they know. They feel it."

"What if I don't feel it?"

"Don't give me that crap. Even I know what you want."

"You do?"

"Think about when you're standing at the front of the team. When you're the last barrier between some god-awful monstrosity and a village full of people who'll die without you. Tell me you don't feel like you're exactly where you're meant to be in those moments."

"That's just being an adventurer."

"Yeah," Stash said in the tone of someone explaining something obvious to an idiot. "Yeah, it is."

"That's it? You're saying it's that simple?"

"Yes, it's that simple. Because I hate to break it to you, but you're kind of simple. Not stupid, but simple. You're not like Jason, always conflicted over whatever nonsense he's got in his head that day. You want to know what's right and to do what's right. That's all you've ever wanted."

"Okay," Humphrey said thoughtfully. "Let's just say, for the sake of argument, that what you're saying was resonating with me. What do I do with that?"

"You live your life. You do what you want, and gods help anyone who gets in your way."

"That sounds like dangerous thinking."

"Dragons *are* dangerous!"

"I don't want to be dangerous."

"Yes you do! You just want to be dangerous to the right things. Monsters. Villains. People who make unsweetened shortbread."

"What?"

"I know, right? You wouldn't even think that was something people did. I mean, you have to mess with the recipe until it isn't even really shortbread anymore."

"I think you may have wandered off topic."

"Huh? Oh, sorry. But you see where I'm going, right? When you're with Sophie, you want to be soft, like a jelly cake. But with your enemies, you want to be hard. Like a tray of biscuits some damn fool left in the oven too long, even when you specifically told them to—"

"Stash."

"Sorry. The point is, you don't need to overthink this. You're not that complicated. We both know that what you want is to do the right thing in any given situation. When you know what that is, don't let anyone stop you. Anyone. Don't let Jason make you doubt yourself, or your mother convince you she knows better. You've seen her make mistakes."

"And if I make mistakes?"

"Of course you're going to make mistakes. When you do, you do your best to fix them. This is not hard to figure out."

Humphrey ran a hand through his hair.

"I need to think about this."

Stash let out a groan.

"Why do people who aren't dragons always overcomplicate things? If you aren't talking yourselves into what you were going to do anyway, you're talking yourselves out of what you were never going to do anyway. You should just decide what you want to do and do it. Like me."

"If all dragons did that, you'd have a cave somewhere with a massive hoard of biscuits."

Stash's eyes darted left and right.

"I definitely don't have one of those," he said.

"I know. If you did, then you wouldn't need to make money helping students with more money than sense skip their classes."

"You, uh... you heard about that?"

"I did. And we are going to have a talk about you *not* doing whatever you want."

"Look, you have a lot to think about, so I'm going to go."

In a blink, the little dragon was gone, vanishing over the edge of the balcony.

"Your first ability hit gold?" Farrah asked as she looked up at the night sky.

"It did," Clive said. "My perception ability, of course."

"Congratulations. The others will follow soon enough."

They were on the roof of the main administrative building of the Magical Research Association, Vitesse branch. It was a modest campus, especially compared to that of the older and more established Magic Society. There were still a few signs of vandalism, although that had mostly stopped. The courts had been quite punitive after the Magic Society were proven to be behind most of it.

"Travis' idea of using satellites has solved the problem of monsters attacking the relay towers," Farrah said. "I can see why they stuck with the water link system for so long. Monsters don't block off rivers all that often. There are a few monsters that fly that far out from the planet, but space is big and we can afford to lose a few. Rather than monsters bringing them down, we've lost more to the Magic Society."

"I have some more information on that. Estella confirmed they are making progress on replicating your satellites."

"They want to set up their own network?"

"Yes. The Magic Society has had control of long-distance communication for centuries with the water link. They don't want to give it up."

"I was discussing the idea of them making their own network with Travis. He said that even if they successfully replicate the technology components, which is far from a given, they have no understanding of orbital mechanics."

"What are orbital mechanics?"

"It's the theory related to non-magical aspects of how the satellites stay up. The non-magical stuff is his area, not mine. He's been talking about getting me into something else, though. A new project, now the communication network is out of the research stage and into rollout."

"What kind of project?"

"One that he said might help me get to gold rank. If I can get my head around the non-magical theory behind it. You know, that kid's a lot like you, Clive, just with his science instead of magic. He has his area of expertise, but I suspect he's also better than most in a lot of different areas."

"Having the enhanced memory that comes with magic helps," Clive said. "It would be a considerable advantage on Earth. If they got their essences early enough, were dedicated to their studies and were fairly smart in the first place, I imagine they could be quite impressive."

"He's a little more than fairly smart. When it comes to research, anyway."

"What else is there?" Clive asked, and Farrah shook her head.

"That priestess has him wrapped around her finger," she said.

"Gabrielle? Humphrey's former lover?"

"Yeah. In fairness, her intentions seem honest enough. It's not a surprise to see a priestess of Knowledge interested in someone merging the knowledge of two worlds. She's just a little too religious for my liking."

"She's a priestess, Farrah. Being religious is the entire point."

"I suppose. And the church was a big help on this project. They were very keen on a new way to disseminate knowledge."

"What was that you were saying about helping you get to gold rank?"

"Right, yeah. It might surprise you to learn that spending all my time researching a magical communication device hasn't done wonders for advancing my volcano essence."

"I'm startled."

"But now Travis is talking about something called geothermal energy," she said with a sigh.

"You don't sound excited."

"Yeah, well, it sounds promising enough that I might have to actually learn more science theory. It's like learning magic theory all over again. I thought I was done with learning."

"We're never done with learning," Clive said. "Learning is the best thing there is."

"I'm starting to see why your wife gets around so much."

———

Vitesse had many shopping districts. In one of the canal districts there was a patisserie called 'The Pastry Stash.' A bird flew in through an opening in the roof, turning into a person when he was inside. He went into the front where the manager, Janice, was working with the counter staff to handle a gaggle of customers. She saw him gesturing and headed into the back of the shop.

"What is it, Boss?" she asked.

"We need to hide the tunnel better. Good enough that gold-rankers can't find it."

"Boss, I'm going to ask why. Again. The illusions and warding magic we have on there now cost more than six months' profit. And we're doing really well; we make a lot of profit. I'll remind you that Miss Farrah said that scaling up any more than what we have already would be multiple times more expensive. Is it really worth it when there's nothing down there but baked goods and food stasis enchantments?"

"Yes!"

88

A POWER YOU CAN'T
OVERWHELM

IN A LUXURY VAN MOVING THROUGH THE STREETS OF MANHATTAN, RUFUS sat up front, next to the driver, while five Asano clan scions were in the back. These weren't the strongest or most promising essence-users but the ones most suited to future leadership. They were seen to have the most potential for the increasing amounts of administrative and diplomatic work the clan was faced with.

Emi's inclusion had surprised no one, but three of the five being from outside the Asano family had been a clear message from the matriarch. This was no token gesture either, as this diplomatic expedition was not a minor outing. The driver of the van was no less than the Under-Secretary-General of the United Nations Office of Supernatural Affairs, Annabeth Tilden.

Rufus turned to look back into the van. Sitting with the young people was Shiro Asano, Emi's great-uncle and the matriarch's son. Shiro had taken the wealth into which he was born and made more wealth as a high-end property developer. That made him the most appropriate diplomatic agent of the clan, compared to his brothers. Hiro was well known as a former organised crime figure while Ken was a landscape architect.

"How many essence-users can you sense observing us right now?" Rufus asked the young clan members.

"I didn't think that this was about our essence abilities," said Lina Karadeniz. She was Emi's best friend but did not share her friend's former enthusiasm for monster hunting. She was ambitious, like her cousin Asya had been, and had set her sights on clan leadership from an early age.

"Your essence abilities are about a lot more than fighting," Rufus said. "When you're advancing using monster cores, your abilities grow stronger on their own, but your mastery of them does not. That means you have to be diligent about learning to use them. The ones that are most important to whatever path you choose for yourself, at the very least. I'm sure that Under-Secretary-General Tilden can confirm that perception is key in diplomatic circles."

"Indeed, I can," Anna said. "If nothing else, it will help you notice when a lunatic sneaks into your kitchen in the middle of the night, makes a sandwich and then complains that you don't have quality sandwich ingredients."

"Jason did that?" Shiro asked. "Was he concerned about you and your people using his family as leverage?"

"Yes," Anna said.

"Should he have been?" Emi asked.

"I want to say no," Anna said. "But I wasn't in charge, and the people who were saw him as an exploitable resource. If I'm honest with myself, I played a large part in keeping him working with people who didn't act in good faith. There's a reason that I left the Network, and why it fractured into four different factions."

"How well did you know my uncle?" Emi asked.

"Well enough to trust him," Anna said. "And well enough to be scared of him."

———

By the time the pain faded, the World-Phoenix was already standing over Jason's freshly spawned body. He let out a racking cough as he dragged himself to his hands and knees.

"Is that all you've got, George?" he croaked.

"Your will is in tatters," the World-Phoenix said. Her voice wasn't gloating or triumphant; it was matter of fact.

"Yep," Jason croaked as he pushed himself unsteadily to his feet. "Honestly, I was hoping that hitting gold rank would let me fight back a little better. I knew you would get the same power bump, but I didn't realise you would adapt that much faster than I would. It seems obvious, in hindsight."

"You are mastering your new abilities well, but you made these vessels too strong."

"I might have made the one I'm using a bit weak. It was hilarious when I hit gold rank and it just exploded. It's all about balance, managing these vessels. With great astral beings, even a strand of your willpower is extremely hard to contain. It was just easier to make you all powerful. And I needed you stronger than I am to help me grow, so it worked out."

"You have grown stronger, Asano. You have reached gold rank in impressive time and learned to make good use of your abilities. You have an astral kingdom to complete, friends and family to return to. If you keep fighting until you lose yourself, they will be eons dead before you even remember they existed. If you stop this pointless fight now, you can retain your mind. Take the considerable gains you've already made here and cut your losses. Give up."

Jason had conjured fresh clothes and started doing some stretches while she talked.

"Coming back from the dead is kind of my thing," he said. "So is being rude to people in positions of institutional power. Blasphemy. Overly sweet beverages. Mid-to-heavyweight Euro games. I have a lot of things, is my point, but giving up isn't one of them. When death and failure are certain, I don't just close my eyes and wait for the end. You'll never do anything impossible that way."

"We all have a point at which we must bend, Asano, lest we break."

"Which is why most people bend, even your fellow great astral beings. It's the reason we're here, after all; they did a thing and they couldn't hack the consequences. Now they're trying to undo it. But some people don't bend, do they? You and I are alike in that way. We take it until the world breaks us or the world bends. The whole reason you're fighting is that the cosmos wants you to bend and you just won't. They picked me because I'm the same. That's why, for all the great astral beings fighting here, it really just comes down to you and me."

"I suppose it does. But you must have realised by now that between the two of us, it is you that will break, not I."

"The writing does seem to be on the wall. Except there aren't any walls here, are there? I had to put the writing on the road, back where we started."

"You put a lot of foolish information in these vessels. Why didn't you give us the information to interpret the meaning of those words?"

Jason drew his sword.

"I just told you: with these vessels, it's all about balance. And now, it's past time we got back to the fight."

"Mr Ambassador," Rufus said, "you and I were both trained in diplomacy. Our training took place in extremely different cultures, however, where power was seated very differently. In your world, power has always been collective. Any one person with the power to level a city can't act without a nation behind them. A president might control a nuclear arsenal, but they don't control it alone. Checks and balances is the term, is it not? Complex structures of political and military might before that power can be unleashed."

Rufus looked around the conference table at the assembled UN ambassadors. Shiro Asano was at his side, and the young clan members were seated behind him, against the wall. The various aides to the ambassadors were likewise positioned, and Anna was seated at the end of the table. Sitting directly across from Rufus were the UN ambassadors from China and the United States. Rufus continued addressing the Chinese ambassador.

"In my world, the power is within the individual. Groups do have power, but that power is ultimately determined by the most powerful people in that group. It's not a fair system, but at least it doesn't pretend to be. Your system isn't fair either, but you do a much better job of hiding it, distracting from it or convincing people it doesn't matter. It's impressive, in a hideous kind of way. The power hierarchy in my world doesn't need to hide itself because it's not mandated by controlling the masses. You don't have to fear an army when you can kill it by yourself."

Rufus put a hand down on the file in front of him.

"Your world started becoming like mine centuries ago. This proposal tells me that either you don't understand what is changing or you think I don't. From the moment your people learned how to claim magic and not just be born with it, the nature of power in this world began to shift. Your society has always used money and influence to centralise authority and control, but you always needed to control the populace. Magic takes every metaphor you have for power and makes it literal. Nuclear weapons are no longer the ultimate strategic force on this planet; gold-rankers are. They walk the world, wielding powers like the men from your holy books. Wiping out plagues. Striking down kingdoms. You already see what gold-rankers can do, and you've never even seen a real one."

"Clan Asano has no gold-rankers," the Chinese ambassador pointed out.

"No," Rufus said and slid the file contemptuously across the table. "No, we don't, or you wouldn't present such an insulting proposal. It's only a matter of time before our resources and training programs produce gold-rankers that make yours look like children playing in the sand. You want to dig your tendrils into the clan before we're properly established."

"We?" the ambassador asked. "Our? You talk like a member of Clan Asano, Mr Remore, when my understanding is that you are not."

"Mr Remore has been chosen by the clan to represent our interests here," Shiro said. "At the current time, he best represents the will of the patriarch."

"Jason Asano," the ambassador said. "The *absent* patriarch."

"Yes," Rufus said. "And, as you are aware, he reached gold rank some time ago. Your observers noted the day of golden light in the clan territories, and subsequent increase of magic levels."

"My country makes no admission to employing any such observers," the ambassador said. "But our sources have confirmed that the magic of the Asano clan territory has become increasingly erratic. The magic that shields those domains had started to periodically weaken and even shrink. Temporarily, but with increasing frequency."

"Yes," Rufus admitted. "That is the case."

"You have claimed that Jason Asano is engaged in some form of conflict," the ambassador said, and slid the folder back at Rufus. "It would seem that the patriarch is not doing well. You would be well advised to accept these terms before he dies and the foundation of your clan dies with him."

Rufus burst out laughing.

"Whatever world you are in, Mr Ambassador, making assumptions about something of which you are ignorant is a good way to get in trouble. As Jason has discovered to his cost, but that is beside the point. Yes, it does seem like he is having trouble. I've seen Jason in trouble, so I know that makes it a very bad time to be his enemy. The Asano clan asked me to represent them because I understand Jason better than they do. I know who he is and how he does things. You know Jason Asano only from his time here on Earth. If you had even an inkling of what he's gone through and the battle he's fighting, you would understand that he will be a very different man when he comes back. And you definitely wouldn't insult his family with a proposal like this."

"*If* he comes back," the ambassador said.

Rufus smiled.

"The first thing I learned about Jason Asano is that he's a fool. The second thing is that he's a hero. The third is that when his enemies are far too powerful and victory is impossible, that is when you see who he truly is. I'm not sure how powerful Jason is going to be when he comes back, but assuming he's not some kind of god entity, he'll be gold rank."

"Is him coming back as a god likely?" Shiro asked.

"You can never be certain, with Jason, but probably not. Not entirely, anyway. He'll be a gold-ranker and so will his friends, myself included. He may have hit gold rank obnoxiously fast, but he's not the only one getting stronger. And these will be proper gold-rankers, not the sorry excuses you have on this planet. And I know that this is what you all really fear: a power you can't overwhelm."

Rufus panned his gaze slowly around the room. A few people went to speak up, only to stop after looking in his eyes. There were silver-rankers amongst them, but they were core-users all. Other than Rufus and the Asano scions, only the security personnel for the US ambassador had no taint of monster core in their auras. Rufus could sense them outside the room, their own senses focused sharply on him.

"You fear Jason's return, and you should," Rufus told the ambassadors. "His arrival will change this world forever. You've never had a single ruler before."

"Will he return with the intent to conquer?" the US ambassador asked.

"No. But whatever he chooses to do, only two things can potentially stop him. You and your nations aren't either of them."

"Then what can stop him?" Anna asked.

"I said *potentially* stop him," Rufus said. "One is his friends asking him not to. As for the other, I have seen Boris Ketland at war. He is the most powerful gold-ranker I have ever seen, and that is a more exceptional statement than any of you realise. I don't know how many more like him the messengers have hidden away, but that is the only power that could stop Jason and his allies."

Rufus tapped the folder now back in front of him.

"We know that you have been interfering with our attempts to recruit people, especially magitech experts. You need to understand that the way you treat Jason's people, here and now, will define how he treats you when he gets back."

"That is your approach?" the Japanese ambassador asked. "Gunboat diplomacy? You have the power, so participate or suffer?"

"You say that as if it isn't the way this world has always worked." Rufus said. "Decency is the luxury of those with the power to afford it. What I can tell you, Mr Ambassador, is that he won't be looking for trouble. But the last time he was here, he was forced to tolerate the powers of this world. This time, he will not."

"So," the Japanese ambassador said. "If he decides that we're doing something he doesn't like, he will intervene? Even if it has nothing to do with his family?"

"I honestly don't know, Mr Ambassador. I know he's not coming here to rule, so your nation would have to do something both heinous and immediate to get him to act."

He picked up the folder and stood. The other Asano representatives did the same.

"My ultimate suggestion," Rufus said, "is to not mess with his family. I don't know whose idea this proposal was, and who amongst you were the ones who pushed it forward. I would strongly recommend that anyone not in that group give those who were a wide berth. They are going to get you in trouble."

He tossed the folder on the table and walked out, the Asano clan members following. Anna Tilden hurried to do the same.

"Is that how they do diplomacy on your world?" she asked as she caught up to Rufus.

"I'll admit that I channelled Jason a little bit there. But yes, that was fairly tame by my world's standards. I know a man who once opened a meeting by putting an axe through someone's head."

"And it didn't devolve into a fight?"

"They were gold rank. It was more an annoyance than anything. He just wanted to make a point before they started talking."

"Your world sounds rather terrifying."

"For you, politics is about trying to deal with hunger or disease. On my world, it's about dealing with armies of people like Boris Ketland."

"You know that they will all be scrambling to make an alliance with Ketland now. If he's as powerful as you say."

"He is."

"Then why let them know that?"

"So they at least have a chance of grasping the futility of trying to ally with him. And maybe to mess with Boris a little. He crossed universes and revealed his people, all to get on Jason Asano's good side. What no one in that room understands is that on the level Jason and Boris are at, they don't care about something as insignificant as nations."

The World-Phoenix looked at an empty road where Jason failed to respawn.

"That's it, then," she said. "He's done."

At the airport, the Asano group were heading for a private plane, driving across the tarmac in their luxury van. Emi's phone rang, and after a brief discussion, she held the phone out for Rufus.

"You need to get your own phone," she told him.

"But then people might call me on it," he said.

"It's Great-Grandmother," she said.

He took the phone.

"Matriarch," Rufus said. "What can I do for you?"

"Get back to France now. Jason's aura just vanished from both territories."

"What about the astral spaces?"

"Still stable. We're evacuating everyone into them now. I know there's the risk of the apertures closing, but there's a continent full of vampires about to realise that nothing is keeping them out anymore."

89
BECOMING WHO YOU WANT TO BE

THE GREAT ASTRAL BEINGS STOOD IN THE MIDDLE OF THE MASSIVE ROAD while the nameless ones formed an army of monsters around them.

"It is over," the Reaper said. "Asano chose the scenario poorly. He prioritised mortal growth over completing the greater objective and failed. It is time to leave his soul and these vessels behind."

"No," the World-Phoenix said. "Asano somehow started to restore the throne even while fighting here. There is more to this."

"The battle is done and he lost," the Celestial Book said. "There is nothing left to be done."

"We are inside his soul," the World-Phoenix said. "He cannot keep us out and his willpower is destroyed. I can use this vessel like a star seed and seize control. Use his connection to the throne to make sure it can never be restored."

"We will oppose you in this, obviously," the Whisper in Corners said. Her mouth did not move, her voice instead a susurrus of whispers all around them. "Beyond the issue of the throne, there are lines that even we should not cross. Will you become like the Builder, World-Phoenix? Forcing your way into unwilling souls."

"He has already let us in," the World-Phoenix said.

"He has done no such thing," Legion said. "He agreed to help us and the process of doing so made him vulnerable. We exploited that to come here, which is far from an invitation."

"Asano chose to accept responsibility for the Sundered Throne," the World-Phoenix said. "That is invitation enough to determine its fate, now that we are here, even if the process is unsavoury."

"Unsavoury?" the Seeker of Songs said. "You're talking about hijacking his soul while his willpower is too diminished to stop you. That is not unsavoury, World-Phoenix. It is unconscionable."

"You are letting your mortal vessel affect your judgement, Seeker. We are outside morality. Our rules are beyond something as petty as mortal ethics."

"I believe that all of our judgements are compromised," the Celestial Book said. "As is our ability to achieve insight into the circumstances in which we find ourselves. Asano made us weak in that area, giving us strength and power instead."

"Precisely," the World Phoenix said. "He set something in motion so that he could win, even in defeat. He is running a larger game, and this is not the first time he's made a sacrifice play. But I will take a page from his own book and flip the board. I will follow this road to the core of his soul and seize control of it. Then I will use his link to the throne to see it is never restored."

"Then we will continue to fight against you," the Reaper said.

They all looked around as all two hundred and eleven Shade bodies emerged from the shadows between the monster horde.

"Progenitor," Shade said. "The battle is done. The rules do not allow for anyone to continue it beyond the point where Mr Asano has fallen."

"He can't stop it like that," the World-Phoenix said. "He makes the rules, but he must maintain a level of balance. He can't just make us stop here. There has to be an allowance for us to continue."

"Yes," Shade said. "Against my advice, Mr Asano has designated that only those who wish to move forward in order to control his soul from the inside may advance."

"Why would he do something so self-destructive?" Legion asked.

"Mr Asano has already tried the path of attempting to be worse than his enemies and it very nearly destroyed who he was. More than once, I was required to draw him back from the brink of the abyss. His hope was that I could do the same for you. If you go forward, it can only be with the intent to enslave his soul. He is appealing to your better natures."

"And that is what these vessels are for," the World-Phoenix realised. "He is trying to infect us with mortal morality."

"We have our own standards," the Celestial Book said. "We do not need mortal bodies to know that this is not a thing we should do."

"Too bad," the World-Phoenix said. "All this does it make it easier. Any of you who want to stop me now can only do so by seizing Asano's soul for yourselves to force the restoration of the throne."

The great astral beings looked around at one another. The World-Phoenix's gaze fell on the Builder.

"What of you?" she asked him. "You tried to claim Asano's soul once before. Now the opportunity stands before you, and will get you what you want in the bargain."

"Phoenix," the Whisper in Corners whispered. "Why would you entice others to stand against you?"

"Because she is not as immune to ethical pangs as she would claim," Legion said. "It is easier to make an immoral choice when you are not doing so alone. To be the only one, observed by those who took the higher road, is no easy thing. For a mortal, in any case. Asano's choice to put us in these vessels was not without cunning."

The World-Phoenix ignored them, keeping her gaze on the Builder.

"What will you choose?" she asked. "Moving forward costs you nothing, morally. You have already tried forcing your way in here."

The others all turned to look at the Builder, awaiting his response. He panned his gaze over them with an expression of contempt.

"I know what you all think of me. The things you have done to me made that clear from the beginning, so my words and actions here will likely mean little to you. But, before all of this, only I had faced Asano as an enemy. Not as a game, albeit one with high stakes, but as a true foe. Yes, I could move forward and once more fight to claim his soul. What I will do is leave. What you take from that is up to you."

The Builder stalked off, the crowd of Shade bodies and nameless great astral beings parting to let him through. A small building had appeared unnoticed at the side of the road and the Builder walked to it and went inside. No one said anything as he left, watching him make the long walk across the absurdly wide road. Once he was gone, Shade was the one to break the silence.

"Now, the rest of you must choose. Mr Asano's ideals are naïve, it is true, but he has come to see value in naïveté. He has long held that the first step to making the impossible possible is being willing to try. To make an innocent hope a reality, we must first accept it as a possibility, even when others call it foolish. I recognise that this means little to you all; these vessels are not who you are. But I also understand you in ways that Mr Asano does not. You have your own standards. Your own rules. You broke them to sunder the Cosmic Throne, but you are here for restitution. To move forward is to violate the very thing you came here to enact."

"It's not what I came here for," the World-Phoenix said.

"No," Shade acknowledged. "But how far are you willing to take this?"

"All the way. I told Asano as much, and he told me the same. I have discovered, during this time, that he and I are alike in certain ways. I hold no contempt for him."

"Yet, you would corrupt his very core while he is at his most vulnerable. Someone you hold no malice for. Are you willing to move forward and do this alone?"

"She will not be alone," the Reaper said. "Asano made bad choices and he failed. If the price of rectifying his mistake is that I must take over his soul to make certain the throne is restored, that is a price I am willing to pay. My conscience will only last so long as this vessel does."

All the Shades vanished, except for one. He moved to stand in front of the Reaper.

"Don't do this, Progenitor."

"You would do well not to ask that of me, Progeny."

"I am not asking."

The other great astral beings took an instinctive step back.

"You are my shadow," the Reaper said. "Mine. Our connection transcends some paltry familiar bond. He is the latest of how many summoners? And far from the first to reach immortality. How many are still out there, unthought of in eons? You left each of them behind while you and I are forever. I know you refused a deeper connection to Asano, and rightly so. Even he understands that."

There was a heavy silence in the wake of the Reaper's words. The pale-faced man and the shadowy figure in front of them each stared, as if daring the other to speak first.

"You are right, Progenitor. Father. I am your shadow. And I have been vouchsafing for myself the freedom to leave Jason Asano behind."

"Wise," the Reaper said. "For now, he will become a puppet, to the World-Phoenix or myself."

"No," Shade said. "I have been a guide and a teacher to each of my summoners, but they have all had something to teach me, in turn. Time and again, they have shown me that change is the mandate of the young. That friends are better than servants or allies. That even the impossible can be accomplished if you have the will to try. These are far from unique lessons, it's true. I have seen them time and again, from many summoners."

"Those are the convictions of the young and foolish," the Reaper said.

"Yes," Shade agreed. "But, perhaps I am at a stage in my journey where I am more open to the convictions of fools. One thing Mr Asano has shown me especially resonates in this moment. Sometimes, being who you are, or becoming who you want to be, means making the foolish choice. To fully commit, even when failure seems certain. Anything less is to save the body but lose the soul."

Shade's form started to flicker, like an image on an old television. More bodies started to emerge from the one already present, rising up to hover in the air. They too flickered, their shadowy forms going blurry and then snapping back into shape. Sometimes they flashed, turning into bright white light for fleeting moments before returning to a void-deep darkness.

The air crackled with power as Shade made use of authority accumulated over tens of thousands of years. Wind flared, roaring through the jungle and yanking at the great astral beings. Rain poured from a sky suddenly darkened by a great spiralling cloud. Lightning crashed and electricity pricked their skin, rattling their teeth and setting their hair on end.

"You're sanctioning yourself?" the Reaper asked loudly, over the din of wind and rain. "You would use everything you've built up for this? For him?"

Shade didn't answer as bodies continued to spill into the air. Only when all two hundred and eleven were present, hovering like a dark cloud, did the flickering stop. Two hundred and ten bodies then returned to the one on the ground, merging into one. A display window appeared in front of each named great astral being.

- Shadow of the Reaper [Shade] has sanctioned himself.
- Shadow of the Reaper [Shade] has become a Shadow of the Hegemon.
- Shadow of the Hegemon is no longer compatible with familiar essence ability [Shadow of the Reaper].
- Familiar contractor [Jason Asano] is in a state of self-sanction.

- Familiar contractor [Jason Asano] has accepted external sanction.
- Essence ability [Shadow of the Reaper] has become [Shadow of the Hegemon].
- Ability [Shadow of the Hegemon] has been set to the minimum level for the current rank.
- Ability [Shadow of the Hegemon] is set to Gold 0 (0%).
- Shadow of the Hegemon [Shade] has accepted avatar status from familiar contractor [Jason Asano].
- Familiar contract through [Shadow of the Hegemon] ability is now permanent.

Suddenly, everything was still.

"That was a foolish act," the Reaper said. "Are you alright? Sanctioning can so easily go wrong."

"I am well," Shade said. "And yes, it was foolish. But sometimes fools can be catalysts for great and important change. Look at what Jason Asano has done in his short scrap of life. What will he do with a thousand years? A million?"

"Nothing," the Reaper said. "His will is annihilated and will be subject to myself or the World-Phoenix soon enough."

"Perhaps," Shade said. "But a good measure of a man is to judge him by his enemies. Mr Asano's greatest enemy had the perfect chance for revenge and chose to run. I would advise you to judge Mr Asano on that."

"You have ever been unruly," the Reaper said, "but clearly, I should have reined you in before you lost your way."

"That is not for you to do anymore, Father."

"Stop calling me that."

"But it is what you are now. I am not your shadow; I am your offspring. Independent. I know that you have shielded me many times, and I thank you for that. But now, my mistakes are mine to make, and their consequences mine to deal with."

"Alone."

"Not alone, Father."

"No, I suppose you are not. You claim to be independent, but all you have done is shackle yourself to a new master."

"That is the misconception of a great astral being. There does not always have to be a hierarchy. You can walk beside someone without serving or ruling them. Jason Asano will continue to grow in influence, and if all he ever becomes is an astral king, I will be the power behind the throne. A guiding hand, for he needs a lot of guidance. But he also helps me walk a path I have been hesitant to for so very long."

"He has no potential left to fulfil, Progeny. He has ruined himself, as have you in joining him."

"We shall see. I'll will leave you now to your choice, Father. I hope you and the World-Phoenix change your minds."

"What has Asano done?" the Reaper demanded before Shade could move. "How is he restoring the throne?"

Shade tilted his head like a curious dog.

"Odd," he said. "I imagine not being subject to your commands will take getting used to for both of us."

Shade stepped into the shadow of a monster and was gone.

"You're angry," the Celestial Book said to the Reaper. "That is the vessel. Don't make haste and let the emotions rule you."

"Silence!" the Reaper roared.

"I am not yours to command, any more than Shade now is," the Book said. "And while he was ever the oddity amongst your progeny, he has never been a fool. For all his claims of being one now, you and the World-Phoenix should consider that he knows something we do not."

"I said be quiet!" the Reaper snarled and shoved his way through the monsters that scrambled to escape his path. The World-Phoenix moved to join him.

90
REGRETS

THE WORLD-PHOENIX AND THE REAPER HAD BEEN WALKING DOWN AN empty road for two years. No fights, no obstacles. No objective to fight over. The pair walked in silence along the unchanging and seemingly endless road. Two years almost without pause, except for one moment where the World-Phoenix stopped.

"What is it?" the Reaper asked, also stopping.

"I miss food."

"That is because of your vessel."

"Knowing the reason does not obviate the circumstance."

"Agreed."

They continued on.

In Venice, in the vault of what had once been a bank, Elizabeth opened her eyes. She could feel it was night in the relaxing absence of the sun's magic. The sunlight couldn't harm her underground, but she could still feel it during the day. It niggled at the edge of her perception like an itch that couldn't be scratched.

She left the vault, then showered and dressed before going upstairs. She would have liked to head for the roof and luxuriate with a book under the cool light of the moon. Books were such a pleasure, and so easy to obtain in this modern age. She suspected that was not to be, based on the vampire she could sense waiting in her office.

The very concept of an office left Elizabeth shaking her head. Once upon a time, she had a throne room. A study was one thing, all antique wood and leatherbound books, but that was not enough for contemporary needs. Managing a modern vampire nation required such dark artifice as spreadsheets and—she shuddered at the thought—PowerPoint presentations.

The bank was a fortress. After some magical enhancement, it would now withstand another attempt by the humans to go nuclear. It was also well-prepared for more conventional forms of attack, be it by essence-users or vampires. Doing all of that without compromise made it a utilitarian space, not a pleasant one in which to live or work.

For a more pleasant place in which to enjoy her nights, Elizabeth maintained a nearby palazzo. A short walk away, along the canal, it was close enough to reach in less than a second if she put on her full speed. That was not necessary this evening, and she meandered under a clear night sky.

The moonlight pleasantly lit up the clear water of the canal, untainted by the long-gone human population. Before Elizabeth took over the city, it had been an apocalyptic nightmare. The vampire lords ruling it had conducted wholesale slaughter with their unsanitary blood farms. The exsanguination centres had been set up in quick and nasty fashion to infuse human blood with magic as quickly as they could obtain reality cores.

Elizabeth had changed all of that. The transformation zones stopped appearing, cutting off the reality core supply. Most of the city's population was gone, either dead, fled, or transformed into monstrous ghouls. Some few were also blood servants—humans made more powerful by drinking the blood of greater vampires.

After taking over, she had instituted a new regime. The superhuman strength and speed of blood servants and lower-rank vampires made short work of construction. Humans with the knowledge to guide them were given reprieves from serving as blood stock.

The humans who had failed to escape the city were kept to be farmed for blood, but in more humane fashion than elsewhere. Instead of being caged like factory farm chickens, they were given more freedom within the largely empty city. Many were let out onto farms, producing the food to feed them. Acceptance over resistance came with privileges and better treatment.

Those who hid instead of reporting to be fed on were soon sniffed out. Those who fled Venice found that beyond the city limits, things were significantly worse. Europe was now completely under vampire control, aside from the British Isles. The Asano clan had retreated into their astral spaces when their domain magic failed and had not been heard from in two years.

Elizabeth's edicts regarding the humans had not gone down well with the other vampire lords, but she was not doing it out of compassion. Treating the humans better had critical upsides, starting with sustainability. Weak and sickly humans produced less blood of lower quality, while dead humans produced none at all. The herd was not easy to grow, so she kept it healthy and strong.

The other major advantage was optics. Key to Elizabeth's leadership was her adaptation to the modern world and human civilisation. She knew the humans drummed up a lot of anti-vampire sentiment with footage of the blood farms. If the vampires were to ever hold their territory peacefully, they would need to be accepted, if only as a rogue nation.

Acceptance meant at least appearing to be something other than a land of horrors. The vampire threat was largely eliminated from human-controlled territories, and humans were so quick to forget when the bad things were only happening to someone else. Only during election years, or when distraction from a scandal was required, would the vampire threat suddenly be on the rise again.

The largest barrier to making a vampire nation palatable was the vampire population itself. Too many of the lords still failed to grasp the existential threat the humans posed. They blamed those who had fallen for being stupid or weak, asserting their own power and cunning that no human could bring low. For some, that was braggadocio and they were careful to remain under Elizabeth's unified banner. The trouble came from the ones who genuinely believed themselves invincible.

The Asano clan retreated into their astral spaces as the magic shielding them faded and ultimately vanished. Without the protection of the domains, the joint military bases in France and Slovenia had been abandoned, and the vampires had overrun the territories. Elizabeth had counselled caution, but her hold over the more wild vampire lords was tenuous at best.

Taking over the luxurious magical cloud homes of the Asano clan had emboldened those who questioned Elizabeth. For many of the vampire lords, it was a return to the old ways of ruling in opulence. Every month that passed with Elizabeth's warnings coming to nought yet again served to undermine her authority further.

Elizabeth reached the door of her palazzo and it was opened by her blood slave, Gerling. He looked much as he had in life, but with blood-red sclera and swarthier skin. It amused her to see his body so obedient and feel the soul, trapped within, thrashing in agony for release.

She made her way to her office where a gold-rank vampire was waiting. He was one of a pair of lords who had overcome their hedonistic instincts exceptionally well. This allowed them not only to adapt to modernity better than most but also to work with Elizabeth, rather than vying for control. They also shared her wariness of Jason Asano and the threat he would pose on his return to Earth.

"Mademoiselle Elizabeth."

"What do you have for me, Élie?"

"Barnabus Cope continues to establish himself as a central figure amongst the vampire lords in the former Asano territories. I would predict a covert attempt to remove you in the coming weeks. Should that fail, expect open hostilities by the end of the year."

"Hardly news, Élie," Elizabeth said. She took a seat behind her desk and gestured to the one opposite. Élie sat primly in his seat.

"Barnabus has obtained some of the human magic specialists," Élie reported. "Turned them, to assure loyalty, and flout your restrictions on new vampires."

"He's trying to break into the sealed astral space apertures again?"

"He is."

"How is that going?"

"He deployed his new experts to try and breach the apertures. They exploded."

"The apertures or the experts?"

"The experts. The apertures remain as impenetrable as ever."

"Have their attempts had any impact on the magic levels?"

"No, mademoiselle. The magic levels remain lower than when the Asano domains were in place, consistent with the surrounding regions."

Elizabeth leaned back in her chair, absently tapping her lips with a finger as she thought.

"What do you think of the fact than Asano's aura is gone, but the magical cities he created remain?"

"If I were a suspicious man, I would think it reeks of a trap."

"Are you a suspicious man, Élie?"

"Yes, mademoiselle. I am."

Amusement teased at Elizabeth's expression for a moment, before it turned grim and contemplative.

"Here or not, Asano is a problem," she said. "If he dies on some other world and his magic here diminishes, it emboldens those who would undermine us. If he stays away and things remain as they are, the result is similar but not as deleterious to our position. That may be the outcome with the least negative impact for us."

"And if he returns?"

"What do you think?"

"I once ran from Asano when he was silver rank. If he comes back stronger…"

Elizabeth nodded.

"His clan believed that Asano reached gold rank well before they withdrew into their astral spaces. We have to assume that, if he returns, it will be at gold rank. If he brings enough gold-rank allies with him, then it will be more than just us worried about our longevity. The balance of power in this world will change."

"Asano is known to have antagonism towards most major authorities. Perhaps there is room to exploit that?"

"Our concern should focus on the vampires in the former Asano clan domains. If Asano returns, we could easily be swept up in his response to their occupancy."

"You speak of appeasement."

"I speak of survival."

"I don't disagree, but distancing ourselves from the excesses of our kind is tricky. It will be abdicating control of the vampires already uneasy about you. Barnabus Cope will sweep them up, and if Asano does not return—or even return soon enough—we will pay the price for that."

"A price that can be endured, while the full ire of Jason Asano cannot. We prepare for the thing that will kill us, not the one that will merely hurt us. I managed to escape Asano once. He will be more diligent should he try to kill me again. My best chance is to convince him not to."

"Do you think he will tolerate our continued existence?"

"No. Not as things stand. The best we can do is prepare and hope to find an opportunity for survival in whatever circumstances come about.

Start with finding ways to distance us from Cope in the eyes of the humans."

After two years, the World-Phoenix and the Reaper finally encountered something other than flat, straight road. It began with the appearance of mountains in the distance, rising out of the jungle. The road diverted from its previously unshifting course, narrowing as it drew closer to the mountains.

The pair continued to walk as the road wound up into the mountains. The trees lining the road changed as the air grew cooler with altitude. Many sections had no growth at all, only barren patches of dirt filled with obsidian slate. The road itself changed, the wide flat stones now black obsidian; a worked and polished version of the slate by the side of the road.

High in the mountains, snow covered everything but the road. The obsidian flagstones were heated from underneath, melting any ice that fell upon them. The melted snow left them smooth and slick, but the great astral beings with their preternatural balance did not slip or fall.

"This whole region is volcanic," the World-Phoenix said. "I can feel the fire beneath the ground. The echo of it in the stone."

Finally, there was a crest, giving them a panoramic view as the road descended. They stopped to look over a massive caldera spread out before them. Running through the mountain range, it formed a long, wide, high-altitude valley. Within the caldera were lakes giving off steam amongst a forest wholly unlike the jungle at the feet of the mountains. Towering trees reached as high as a hundred metres or more.

The forest was far from empty. It was an expansive woodland city, partially constructed and partially grown. Treehouses were built on multiple levels of each trunk, relying on their width and strength. The keen eyes of the great astral beings picked out furnished hollows grown into the trees. There were rope bridges and elevators using crude rope mechanisms. Despite the vastness of the tree city, it looked uninhabited.

"That forest," the World-Phoenix said. "Is it…?

"A nested soul," the Reaper confirmed. "This forest is a single, living thing, with its own soul."

"How did we not sense this? Nesting a soul leaves traces we would have seen, even in these limited vessels."

"I do not think he used soul engineering. Not in the usual conscious and controlled way. These souls were connected willingly and through abnormal means. The transformation zone hid this from us, and Asano used the reintegration of the zone to implement it instinctively."

"Who showed him that this was even possible? The gods of Pallimustus?"

"Their doing so would not have escaped our attention. Asano may have discovered this process on his own. He has been given many tools for manipulating reality, with precious little instruction. Largely by you, World-Phoenix."

"Once again, I have set him on a path he has followed further than I ever intended. We have been labouring under a misconception. We believed that our presence in his soul would alert us to any manipulations to this game he has staged. But there is no telling what he had hidden from us in that nested soul."

"All that is left to us is to find out," the Reaper said. "Let us move forward."

"Wait a moment," the World-Phoenix said.

"Why?"

She nodded at the panorama before them.

"Because it's beautiful."

The Reaper turned his head to look at her.

"You should indulge in your mortal vessel," she said, keeping her gaze on the vista. "In our normal state, experiencing pleasure or appreciating beauty is beyond us."

"We are not here to enjoy ourselves."

"That doesn't mean we shouldn't. I think we both realise that Asano has played us, Reaper. That I don't get what I want. And that you do, without having to get your hands dirty."

"We are not mortals. I suppose it is futile to try and make you accept that what we are is important. Your very purpose here is to maintain what you made of yourself."

"Don't talk to me as if you hold the moral high ground, Reaper. You agreed to sunder the throne. You came here to enslave Asano's soul. I've lost that chance, and you know what? I'm relieved."

"Mortal weakness."

"Yes. I wouldn't have regrets if I wasn't in this vessel. But I am."

"You were always too fond of your prime vessels. You go through them so fast because you raise them like pets instead of using them like tools."

"Says the man who got sad because his boy left home."

"I FELT NOTHING!" he roared, earning a raised eyebrow from the World-Phoenix.

The Reaper said nothing, levelling a glare at her as he tugged adjustments to the drape of his suit. Without another word, he marched away. The World-Phoenix watched him go, then turned to take in the panorama one last time. She looked down the road where the Reaper was striding downhill. With a sigh, she started walking.

91

THE ONE YOU FEED

THE WORLD-PHOENIX AND THE REAPER WALKED DOWN THE ROAD leading into the caldera valley. The whole mountain range was a melange of geographical quirks that, individually, would be highly irregular. While not as high as the peaks framing it, it was odd to have a valley so far above sea level. An expansive caldera valley was also unusual, but far from unheard of. Jason had family on his mother's side who lived in such an area.

Along with the valley having its own temperate microclimate, the air was not as thin as it should have been for the altitude. Then there were the hot springs scattered through the forest, steam visibly rising from them. Taken all together, the features of the region showed off its otherworldly nature. That, or Jason's deficit of knowledge regarding geography, geology and climate science.

The icy winds of the high mountains gave way to mild, pleasant breezes as the great astral beings moved downslope. At the point where the barren mountainside met the tree line, they knew their journey was over. The road continued on, but not for them. They had reached the soul of the tree city and it would not admit them.

After being accompanied only by the sound of the wind, a new noise reached their ears from within the forest. The source was revealed when Jason Asano meandered into view along a woodland trail, watching a video on the phone in his hand. His other hand held a half-eaten sandwich.

The unsealed trail joined with the road that continued into the forest. Only when Jason reached the road did he look up at the great astral beings standing at the tree line. He looked at them contemplatively as he took a bite from him sandwich and chewed on it.

"How?" the World-Phoenix asked.

"Right on time," he said as he sauntered towards them. "It's almost like this was all part of an elaborate and well-orchestrated plan that was pulled off in spite of people being generally derogatory regarding my ability to plot and execute a scheme."

He arrived in front of the pair and paused the video.

"Sorry about that," he said. "I'm watching an old boxing match. I'm not normally a sports guy, which is not very Australian of me, I know. Especially when I was named after a footy player. This boxing match, though, it's an interesting story. They called it the Rumble in the Jungle."

Emi sat cross-legged on a rooftop in the astral space city. Nine cubes floated around her in an orbit. The cubes were forged from a shimmering dark metal only found in the outermost reaches of the astral space. Each face of each cube was divided into nine sections, each bearing a different glowing rune. The cubes could rotate each row and column to change the configuration of the runes.

"Hey, Asano. How do you solve it if the colours keep changing?"

At silver rank, Emi was past the need to breathe. Even so, she took a long, slow breath to contain her temper.

"I've told you so many times, Vincent. They are not Rubik's cubes."

"Yeah, they've got those glowing bits instead of the flat colours. Do you want me to get you some stickers to put on them? A print shop opened up a couple of months ago that could probably do them."

Emi turned to look at the young man standing in the doorway to the stairwell. His face was blank and his aura control was solid. As usual, she couldn't tell if he was teasing her or genuinely dense.

"What are you doing up here?" she asked.

"Your mother has just pulled a tray of savoury scones from the oven."

"Well, you should have started with that. I'll be down in a minute."

He grinned before turning to head back down the stairs. The cubes flew towards Emi and stowed themselves in her satchel. She was organising them a little better in her bag when she felt herself being watched and froze. After years of having aura senses, it was unnerving to feel nothing from them while still instinctively recognising a presence. She slowly stood and turned to see her uncle sitting on the short brick wall at the edge of the roof.

"You and I look almost the same age now," he said, his voice tinged with sadness.

After staring wide-eyed for a moment, she flung herself forward to wrap him in a hug.

"Why do you feel like you're made out of rubber?" she asked.

"This is just an avatar, Moppet. It's going to be a little bit longer before I can see you in person. I'll tell you all about it when I get there for real."

She drew back, looking him up and down.

"Your eyes aren't strange."

"Neither are yours."

"You look even more like Uncle Kaito."

"Gold rank. It spruces you up."

"The domains—"

"I'm not here talk about any of that. I'm here to see you. I know I wasn't in the best place, the last time we saw each other. I know I've been gone a long time, and missed one of the most important parts of your life. Time when you could have really used the terrible advice of a shady uncle."

They both laughed. They both had wet eyes.

"There's no making up for not having been there," he said. "But I'll be there soon."

"Have you seen Great-Grandmother yet?"

"No. This is my first chance to reach out and I wanted to look in on you properly. I wasn't able to project like this before, but I'm very close to done and I don't have to hide anymore."

"Hide from what?"

"I've been running a rope-a-dope on some entities that watch the whole cosmos, so information control had to be the priority."

Emi looked at him with suspicion.

"What's a rope-a-dope?" she asked. "Is that a sex thing?"

"No! It's not a sex thing."

"It sounds like a sex thing."

"It's a very famous thing that isn't related to sex at all. Does it involve very fit, topless, sweaty men in shorts? Yes, it does. But that doesn't make it a sex thing."

"Topless, sweaty men, you say?" Emi asked, sounding intrigued.

"Oh, no," Jason said, waggling a finger at her. "I do not approve of this whole 'adult' thing you've got going on. Where's my precious little niece?"

Emi's expression went cold and Jason winced, knowing he'd made a mistake.

"She spent half her life waiting for her uncle to come back," Emi said.

Jason nodded and bowed his head.

"I didn't want to stay away for so long," he said, his voice almost a whisper.

Emi's expression softened and she moved to hug him again.

"I know," she said. "Some of it, anyway. What Rufus told me. Doesn't mean I have to like it."

"No. No, it doesn't."

He tousled her hair and she shoved herself off of him.

"You know I always hated that. And now I'm an adult, Uncle Jason."

"Which I still don't approve of."

He tilted his head, as if trying to hear a distant sound.

"What is it?" Emi asked.

"This is my first time holding simultaneous conversations in different universes. I'm talking to the grim reaper and a cosmic phoenix right now."

"About what?"

"Boxing."

"Boxing?"

"You asked. Look, I'll be there for real when I can be. No promises, but not too long now. I'll grab my friends in the other universe and bring them for a visit. Some things are going to happen before I get there, though. Tell your grandmother that once the domains are back in place, she doesn't have to worry about them fading anymore."

"She's going to have a lot of questions."

"Yep. Sorry about that. But I'm not here for her. I want you to know that even though I couldn't be here, I have been watching."

"You have?"

"I have."

She narrowed her eyes.

"How closely?"

Jason chuckled and looked at the empty doorway to the stairs. The one Vincent had left through, right before Jason's arrival. Emi followed his gaze and then looked back at him.

"What?" she asked.

"He's cute."

"No, he's not! I mean, who? I mean... shut up!"

Jason let out a belly laugh as his niece turned red.

"You should get to those savoury scones, Moppet. Paying attention to things in different universes is something I'm still getting used to, and I need to concentrate on the other thing. I just wanted to check in, now that I finally had the chance. I love you, and I'll see you soon."

Then he was gone and she was alone on a roof that suddenly felt very empty.

———

"A boxing match is like a duel," Jason explained. "And the Rumble in the Jungle was one of the most famous ones ever. There was this one guy. He had a mouth on him; problems with authority. The other guy had power. He was the one everyone thought was going to win."

"There is no point to this," the Reaper interrupted. "You need to—"

"You need to shut your damn mouth!" Jason snarled, his affable demeanour replaced with spitting savagery in an instant. "You two are new to mortality, so you don't understand what it cost me to be dragged into your little game. Well, the game is over and I won. So, you are going to stand there and listen to my Bond villain speech, Reaper, or I will use the Cosmic Throne to give everyone in the universe ten free resurrections, do you hear me?"

The Reaper stared at him for a long time before giving a curt nod. As soon as he did, Jason was all smiles again, as if his spittle-tossing rage had never happened.

"Now," Jason said. "Where was I? Right, the guy with the power and the guy with the mouth. You see, everyone thought the guy with the power was going to win. That the guy with the mouth couldn't take the beating he was going to get. Except that he did. He took it and he took it, and the whole time, he was setting the other guy up to lose. Hard. Which he did, and he wasn't happy about it. It took him a long time to accept that he just got beat. By the greatest there ever was."

"You think you're the greatest there ever was?" the World-Phoenix asked.

"No," Jason said. "I'm not Muhammad Ali, so I had to cheat. I don't have to tell you that splitting your willpower is a basic skill of a transcendent. You're doing it with those vessels you're in right now. I've been doing sort of a 'baby's first willpower segmentation' with my avatars for a while now. I've never tried to fully seat my consciousness in multiple places before, though. Not until this. And doing it slice by slice was a *huge* regret. I haven't felt pain like that since the Builder tried to make me cough up my soul. Kind of necessary for the ruse, sadly."

"When you were losing willpower," the World-Phoenix said, "you were never really losing it. You were siphoning it off into this nested soul where we couldn't sense it. Using it to work on restoring the throne while the rest of you was fighting us."

"That's pretty much it," Jason said. "Embezzling my own soul. As you said, the game was rigged from the start. You lost the moment you agreed to participate. Making that happen is why I set everything up the way I did. "

"You fooled us," the Reaper said. "Even your own allies."

"I don't like allies," Jason said. "They are using you, inherently. If they think it's worth it, they'll turn on you in a second. Some are even depraved enough to betray you so completely they would enslave your soul to get what they want."

"I will not apologise," the Reaper said.

"I wouldn't expect you to," Jason said. "That's kind of my whole point. So, yes. I played you all, enemies and allies both. But I couldn't do everything the way I wanted. There's only so much influence I can have on great astral beings, even if it's just fragments of their willpower I'm dealing with. Even in my own soul. But I also had some cards up my sleeve. I knew that you wouldn't know about the soul inside my soul. And I knew how much you rely on your prime vessels when thinking on a mortal scale."

"You gave us mortal shells with the strengths and weaknesses you needed us to have," the World-Phoenix said. "To make us easier to deceive."

"Exactly. If you were using your actual prime vessels, with their years of experience, they would have realised that I was pulling a shifty. They wouldn't have just gone along with the program, and I needed you to play the game on my terms. I put you into mortal vessels that were young, dumb and full of power. All that strength was to balance key deficits in your reasoning and judgement. Not so naïve as to make it obvious, but just enough to exploit the natural arrogance of beings unused to having any limits at all."

"If you are explaining this now," the Reaper said, "it means that you are done. You are ready to take the final step, completing your passage to astral king and the restoration of the Cosmic Throne."

"Yeah," Jason said.

"Why bother telling us all this?" the World-Phoenix asked. "What does revealing your plans now get you? The chance to gloat? To give one of the little speeches that you love?"

"I won't deny the appeal of explaining my evil scheme," Jason said. "And it's a little hurtful that everyone makes fun of my plans, so I wanted people to see how well this one went. If either of you runs into my team, please tell them about this."

"I'm not going to do that," the World-Phoenix said.

"I will see them when they die," the Reaper pointed out.

Jason shook his head.

"The real reason we're talking here," he said, "is that I gave you both a choice. For you, Phoenix, to accept the loss, and the Reaper to accept the win. Instead, you both chose to come in here, looking to strip mine the joint. But you only got into my soul in the first place because the gate was jammed open while I repaired the throne. And now, I'm done. I can swing the gate shut before you can withdraw your strands of willpower from those vessels. And without a star seed to let you slip through the soul barrier, any willpower that's in here will stay here. Cut off from the rest of you. That will leave me free to refine it down into authority that I will very much be in need of as a newly minted astral king. Not a quick or easy process, but I have a long, long time."

"You baited us here to consume us," the Reaper said.

"I baited nothing. I tried to get you to stay away. Your own son—"

"Don't you talk about him! You took him from me."

"You didn't lose me," Shade said, emerging from Jason's shadow. "Every child must make their own way in the world, sooner or later. It does not stop the father from being the father or the son from being the son."

"Your drama doesn't matter," the World-Phoenix told the Reaper. "These vessels and their emotions won't matter when Asano drags the willpower out of them and refines it. There aren't a lot of way to genuinely hurt our kind, Asano. I have to congratulate you on finding one of the few."

"Yeah," Jason said. He looked to Shade and then the Reaper.

"Alright, you two," he told the great astral beings. "Sod off."

"You're letting us go?" the Reaper asked.

"Yeah."

"Why?" the World-Phoenix asked. "We came here to enslave your soul."

"It's not about you. My father once told me that when I'm in situations like this, the real choice is whether I want to be the person who was ruthless or the person who showed mercy. So, you two came here to do something truly heinous. And I chose to forgive you."

"We are not yours to judge," the Reaper said.

"I explained this once already, Reaper; it's not about you. Now, go and wait until I restore the throne. I assume you'll want to be there."

"Yes," the World-Phoenix said. "For what it's worth, Asano, I find myself glad that I failed to enslave your soul, even as I hate that failure means you will restore the throne."

Jason nodded.

"We all make mistakes," he said. "Sometimes terrible ones. You were lucky, this time, in that no damage was done."

He pointed behind them and they saw a small building that hadn't been there before. The two great astral beings walked over and went inside. Immediately after the door closed behind them, the world outside of the forest city started to warp like running paint. Jason and Shade watched it from inside the forest, which remained unaffected.

"Thank you, Mr Asano. For not hurting my father."

"I hope he can be a father to you, Shade. I've got a pretty good one, and I'm looking forward to seeing him again."

EVERYTHING IS GOING TO BE FINE

THE RESIDENTS OF JASON'S SOUL REALM WERE SITTING ON THE LONG DECK of a treehouse. Furniture was set out in a long row for them to watch the swirling kaleidoscope of unmade reality beyond the tree city's boundary.

"Once this is done, I can finally move to the next stage," Carlos said.

"We're sitting here, watching a universe take shape," Melody told him. "Maybe you should just let yourself indulge in this extremely rare experience and let go of your other concerns for a little bit."

"Tell that to Gibson Amouz. The poor boy has been in a magically induced coma for a decade. Or to those idiots."

They both turned to look at another pair of Carlos' test subjects. Like Melody, they had the influence of the Order of Redeeming Light suppressed while in Jason's soul realm. Unlike Melody, they had been making plans to open an amphora shop.

"I'm telling you, Jaime, the time is now."

"Rhett, why would the time be now? There's what? A dozen people in this whole place?"

"We'll be getting the jump on the market!"

"With what? We don't have any amphorae."

"We can start a workshop. Dig up some clay, make a kiln."

"You want to make amphorae out of some guy's soul? Actually, that could be a real way to stand out, now that I say it."

A hand clapped down on each of their shoulders.

"You might want to wait until all this is done with, lads."

Gabriel Remore had been trapped inside Jason's soul since the portals to the outside had closed. He had been visiting his wife, who had spent considerable time with Melody and the other Order of Redeeming Light victims. This had happened several years ago, when Jason began the process of reshaping his soul realm into a full astral kingdom. In that time, Gabriel had not complained about having to give up all the tasks he'd been browbeaten into by his father to be trapped in carefree luxury with his loving wife. After chiding the pair, he joined Arabelle on a cloud couch.

"Are we sure it's going to end today?" Carlos asked. "I know Jason said it would, but didn't he say it would be quick when it started?"

"It will be today," came a wooden version of Jason's voice. "I can feel it. It has already begun."

The others turned to look at the avatar of the tree city, standing behind them with one of Shade's bodies. The avatar had been almost entirely absent while the soul realm reshaped itself. Before that, it had been somewhat like a curious child, constantly asking questions of the city's few residents.

"I would also like to take this chance to announce something," the avatar said. "After long consideration, I have selected a name."

"Finally," Gabriel said. "Did you end up going with Tim?"

"Are you certain?" Arabelle asked. "I know you thought you had the right one several times before."

"After talking this through with Shade," the avatar said, "I have made my final decision."

The group collectively turned a worried look on Shade, then back to the avatar.

"Well, let's hear it, then," Melody said.

"My name," the avatar said, "is Arbour."

"I like it," Gabriel said. "I would have liked Tim as well, but that's good."

"Arbour," Arabelle said. "That's a word from Jason's world, isn't it?"

"Yes," Arbour said. "In his language, it refers to natural growth over an artificial framework to create a sheltering space. It is also derived from an older language where it means tree."

Melody got up and wrapped the wooden avatar in a hug.

"We've both been messed with pretty badly by people, haven't we?"

she whispered. The avatar hesitantly moved his arms to return the embrace.

———————

Jali Corrik Fen had a rather lonely existence within the Asano clan. As unofficial leader of the messengers in clan territory, she stood apart from the people of Earth. The only friend she had was Tera Jun Casta. The firebrand messenger was living with Boris Ket Lundi and his Unorthodoxy messengers, which had been an interesting choice given her views on them. Tera would occasionally join some of Boris' many visits to the Asano clan, prior to the clan's retreat into their astral spaces.

Although she had many messengers around her, Jali was not truly one of them either. Her origins were different, as she had come from the orthodox messenger population and its indoctrination programs. She was older than them all, and far less sheltered. She had to be guide, teacher and, in some ways, parent, and desperately feared making mistakes.

The young messengers had been born into enslavement, albeit a different one from hers. They had been brought into being by a corrupted birthing tree, then mind-wiped and sealed away in a transformation zone. They were subsequently altered by the power of those who awakened them, and the wielder of that power had complete control of them. Some had treated them decently, keeping them out of the fighting. Others had used them ruthlessly. Ultimately, the survivors were all freed by Jason Asano.

One group within the messengers stood out from the others. They had not been awakened into enslavement because it was Jason himself who woke them up. He had outright rejected their subjugation and had the power to undo it. As they had awakened, he had guided their half-slumbering minds to mark their own souls, instead of being branded by others.

Jali had come to realise, however, that their link to Jason was not entirely eliminated. Even on Earth, they had a vague sense of him. One day, several years ago, that connection had grown stronger. They had come to her and informed her that Jason was in the final stages of becoming an astral king. They even sensed the presence of his avatar in the astral space.

Now, they had come to Jali again, telling her the process was almost complete. Jali immediately headed to inform the Asano clan matriarch that things were about to change.

The tree city, now named Arbour like its avatar, was not the only stable place in the unformed reality of Jason's soul realm. The other was a fortress in the shape of Jason's head, floating on a cloud. In the deepest part of the fortress was a round room with catwalks set into the walls around a magma pit. Jason stood on the catwalk, leaning against the metal railing.

"This is taking way longer than I thought it would," Jason complained. "The transformation zones took hours at most. This has been years."

"A transformation zone is a small addendum to reality, being reattached to the place it always belonged," Shade said. "You are taking a soul and using it to build an entire universe, Mr Asano."

"You could have said something."

"I did not know. This is my first time experiencing the ascension of an astral king, and you are outside the norm of even that. There is some question as to whether you will become an astral king at all. You already have the power to claim domains like a god, and then there is your connection to the Cosmic Throne. Even the great astral beings cannot say what the impact of that will be."

"They aren't worried about the throne's impact on me," Jason said. "They're worried about my impact on the throne. I'll admit that I'm a little concerned myself."

Jason stood up straight and walked to one of the doors set into the stone sides of the shaft. Aside from the way back up, doors led to the astral throne, the astral gate, and soul forge. The final door led somewhere else entirely, and that was the one Jason went to. Like the catwalk, the door was heavy industrial metal that looked decades old. It slid aside with a groan as Jason approached.

Beyond the doorway was a cosmically large void. Originally, it had held vast and distant nebulas, and nothing else. Now there was a path of blue and orange light, leading to a gothic castle floating in the dark.

The castle was marked by a single, dominant feature: it was split down the middle, as if struck with a giant axe. That massive gap was now filled with same blue and orange light as the pathway.

"I don't suppose there's access to five robot lions through that," Jason said.

"It was made by you, Mr Asano. Even if the details were determined unconsciously, the possibility is dismayingly high."

With a surge of Jason's aura, Gordon manifested into being. Bloody mist rose from Jason's body and coagulated into a bloody clone of his body. The blood dried and took on more colours, becoming a perfect copy of Jason except for his eyes. Colin's were crimson orbs where Jason's were orange, blue and nebulous.

A shadow portal archway rose from the catwalk and a wooden replica of Jason emerged.

"Arbour," Jason said. "I like the name choice. You weren't worried it was a little on the nose?"

"I was, but Shade said it was fine."

Jason looked over at his shadow familiar.

"Why are you looking at me like that?" Shade asked.

"It's kind of like Jason deciding to name himself 'Smug,'" Colin said.

"Ah, I see your point," Shade said.

"You see *his* point?"

"Even so, I believe the name works," Shade said.

"It does," Jason agreed. "It's a good name, Arbour. Will you be joining us?"

"I am a part of this now," Arbour said. "Forever."

"Yes," Jason said with a huge smile. "Yes, you are."

Colin slapped Jason on the back and started walking along the glowing path.

"Come on, Smug. Let's get a move on."

"My name isn't Smug!" Jason called after him as the others followed, leaving Jason behind.

"Smarmy?" Colin called back.

"That's worse!" Jason and set off after them. "I liked you better when you just made gloop noises and ate people."

The five followed the long path into the void, slowly making their way towards the castle. The glowing road brought them to an open drawbridge. The massive split in the castle was so deep that even the top of the archway had been sundered.

They went inside, following a hall that looked to have once been glorious, but long left to ruin. Once opulent red carpet was now threadbare. Sculptures, tapestries and other display pieces were tarnished, chipped and torn. The hall was washed in blue and orange light that swirled above in place of a ceiling.

"I like it," Jason said. "There's an appropriate otherworldliness, rather than those regular ruined castles you always see."

"Mr Asano, when exactly do you see so many ruined castles?"

"All the time. You're not always watching."

"Yes, Mr Asano. I am."

"Not going lie, Shade; that creeped me out a little."

The hallway led to a throne room that also had swirling light for a ceiling. It was a cathedral-like space, large and high, leading to a dais at the end on which rested a throne. While the rest of the room shared the hallway's dilapidation, the throne itself was gleaming. With large gemstones and rich purple cushioning set onto an ornate framework of polished gold, the throne had the look of an oversized crown. It was marred, however, by a split identical to that of the castle, as if cleaved by a massive axe. Also like the castle, the gap was filled with blue and orange light.

"Not my style," Jason said, looking at it. "Except for the glowy bits."

The orbs floating around Gordon shone brighter and voices sang from them like a celestial chorus. The words, unfortunately, spoiled the effect.

"I like the glowy bits too."

Doors opened at either side of the throne room and great astral beings entered, once more in mortal bodies. This time, they were using their own prime vessels, not the ones Jason had provided. From one side came most of those who had fought in Jason's rigged battle, joined by a few others. This included Raythe, vessel of the many-named great astral being of time. Another vessel was of a species Jason didn't recognise. It was an orb of leathery flesh, larger than a person and draped in a dark green cloak. The front of the orb was an open mouth, ringed with long needle teeth. From inside the gaping maw, a single huge eye peered out.

Only one figure came from the other door. It was Dawn's replacement as prime vessel of the World-Phoenix. Jason hadn't met her before, but knew from Dawn that her name was Helsveth. At that moment, however, she was the embodiment of the World-Phoenix.

Another figure stood out to Jason even more than Helsveth or the All-Devouring eye's strange vessel. The Builder's vessel was a messenger, heavily modified with artificial parts, but Jason could feel the soul inside. His flesh had been replaced with pristine alabaster and his wings with silver. His eyes were amber orbs and he had no hair at all. His outfit was a toga of interlaced metal shards that shimmered in the blue and orange light.

"So," Jason said as he looked around at the gathering. "Is there a ceremony or something or do we just get to it?"

"Ceremonies are pointless mortal practices," said the Reaper through his vessel, Velius.

"I rather like them," the Seeker of Songs said.

"It's fine," Jason said, then marched up to the throne and looked down at it.

"It's not like I'm going to make a fundamental change to the entire cosmos, right?"

He sat down.

Very few events happened on a truly cosmic scale. Of those, even fewer were noticed by mortals. All across the cosmos were people whose worlds had magic enough to manifest essences. On all of those worlds, in all of those universes, at that moment, the same thing happened to every person who either had essences or had the potential to get them.

An intangible screen popped up in front of them. To some, it looked like an illusion, and to others, a hologram. Many had never seen anything like it. Every screen had the same words, more or less. For those that didn't communicate through words, they didn't use words at all. They made sounds, released aromas, pulsed with aura or employed whatever other means the species in question used to communicate.

The meaning, however, was always the same.

Don't Panic.
Everything is going to be fine.
Welcome to the System.

The story will continue in He Who Fights with Monsters 12!

THANK YOU FOR READING HE WHO FIGHTS WITH MONSTERS, BOOK ELEVEN

We hope you enjoyed it as much as we enjoyed bringing it to you. We just wanted to take a moment to encourage you to review the book. Follow this link: He Who Fights With Monsters 11 to be directed to the book's Amazon product page to leave your review.

Every review helps further the author's reach and, ultimately, helps them continue writing fantastic books for us all to enjoy.

Want to connect with Shirtaloon?

Discuss He Who Fights With Monsters and more, join Shirtaloon's Discord!

Follow him on www.HeWhoFightsWithMonsters.com where you can find great HWFWM merch and other great content.

Also in series:

HE WHO FIGHTS WITH MONSTERS
BOOK ONE
BOOK TWO

Check out the entire series! (tap or scan)

Want to discuss our books with other readers and even the authors? Join our Discord server today and be a part of the Aethon community.

Facebook | Instagram | Twitter | Website

You can also join our non-spam mailing list by visiting www. subscribepage.com/AethonReadersGroup and never miss out on future releases. You'll also receive three full books completely Free as our thanks to you.

Looking for more great LitRPG?

Check out our new releases!

KOS PLAY

START MENU
► NEW GAME
CONTINUE Y/N
QUIT GAME

Order Now!

(Tap or Scan)

---

he Gods are dead. The Seven Evils reign. Only Hope stands between humanity and extinction... When Sorin's parent's mysteriously die, he is starved for truth and thirsty for revenge. He begs the Eighth Evil, *Hope*, for assistance, and his prayers are answered... ...Though not in the way he ever expected. He is made a Poison Cultivator, a rare class who are shunned by high society. Unable to continue his medical practice, Sorin turns to adventuring to make ends meet. Though he's only able to afford to team with a ragtag crew of outcasts as companions—An armored polar bear, a stern archer, a sleep-deprived pyromancer, and a peeping-tom rogue. Oh, and a rebellious rat familiar who won't stop eating the party's loot when no one is watching. Things are looking up, until Sorin discovers his ancestor's hidden research notes about forbidden medical research. What dark deeds was his family up to? Only he can find out... if he and his party can survive the coming Demon Tide. **Don't miss this new Cultivation Progression Fantasy series from Patrick Laplante, bestselling author of *Painting the Mists*. Featuring loads of power progression, demon slaying, dungeons, loot, crafting, and even a rebellious pet rat, it's got something for everyone!**

Get Pandora Unchained Now!

Order Now!

(Tap or Scan)

A wizard's first quest. An unlikely companion. Grand adventure awaits! Wanda and Wumble are a small pair with vast ambitions. One an aspiring alchemist, and the other her faithful hound, the pair bond as wizard and familiar to begin their pursuit of magic. As a newly made wizard without any training, resources, or even a home to return to, Wanda will have to forge her own way on a path where constant dangers lurk. Even the simple act of furthering her alchemy education swiftly becomes a harrowing ordeal. Luckily for Wanda, Wumble is no ordinary hound. Contained within her one-eyed companion is a power many factions of the world are actively hunting for. A seed with unfathomable potential waiting to sprout. And anyone who trifles with Wumble's wizard is in for a ruff time. **Experience a brand new universe from Drew Hayes, the bestselling author of *Super Powereds* and *NPCs*. Featuring a lovable pair of heroes out on their first adventure, learning about both magic and life in a progression fantasy suitable for all ages!**

Get Roverpowered Now!

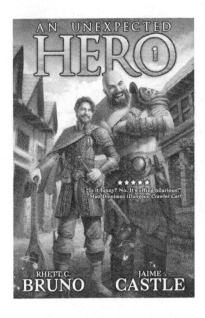

A magical new world. An ancient power. A chance to be a Hero.
Danny Kendrick was a down-on-his luck performer who always
struggled to find his place. He certainly never wanted to be a hero. He
just hoped to earn a living doing what he loved. That all changes when
he pisses off the wrong guy and gets transported to another world.
Stuck in a fantasy realm straight out of a Renaissance Fair, Danny
quickly discovers that there's more to life. Like magic, axe-wielding
brutes, super hot elf assassins, and a talking screen that won't leave
him alone. He'll need to adapt fast, turn on the charm, and get stronger
if he hopes to survive this dangerous new world. But he has a knack
for trouble. Gifted what seems like an innocent ancient lute after
making a questionable deal with a Hag, Danny becomes the target of
mysterious factions who seek to claim its power. It's up to him,
Screenie, and his new barbaric friend, Curr, to uncover the truth and
become the heroes nobody knew they needed. And maybe, just
maybe, Danny will finally find a place where he belongs. **Don't miss
the start of this isekai LitRPG Adventure filled with epic fantasy
action, unforgettable characters, loveable companions, unlikely
heroes, a detailed System, power progression, and plenty of
laughs.** From the minds of USA Today bestselling and Award-winning
duo Rhett C Bruno & Jaime Castle, *An Expected Hero* is perfect for
fans of *Dungeon Crawler Carl, Kings of the Wyld,* and *This Trilogy is
Broken!*

Get An Unexpected Hero now!

For all our LitRPG books, visit our website.

ABOUT THE AUTHOR

Shirtaloon was working on a very boring academic paper when he realised that writing about an inter-dimensional kung fu wizard would be way more fun.

To discuss He Who Fights With Monsters and more, join Shirtaloon's Discord!

Made in the USA
Coppell, TX
25 July 2024

35115602R00444